The Valin Chronicles

MW01113764

Born of Air

Born of Stone

Born of Embers

Born of Blood

By R.A. Lewis

Also by R.A. Lewis

Duchess of Spies
Secrets & Swords

The Valdir Chronicles
Born of Air, The Valdir Chronicles Book 1
Born of Embers, The Valdir Chronicles Book 2
Born of Blood, The Valdir Chronicles Book 3
Born of Stone, The Valdir Chronicles Novella
The Valdir Chronicles Full Series

The Elemental Kingdoms Series
The Stolen Element, The Elemental Kingdoms Series
Prequel
Kingdom of Wind & Fire, The Elemental Kingdoms
Series Book 1
Kingdom of Spirit & Sorrow, The Elemental Kingdoms
Series Book 2
Kingdom of Dust & Bone, The Elemental Kingdoms
Series Book 3
Kingdom of Mist & Chaos, The Elemental Kingdoms
Series Book 4

The Crowe Trials
Crystalline Raven, A Crowe Trials Novella

Other
Wicked Wishes: A Fiction Atlas Press Anthology, Date With
a Demon
Burning Skies

Contents

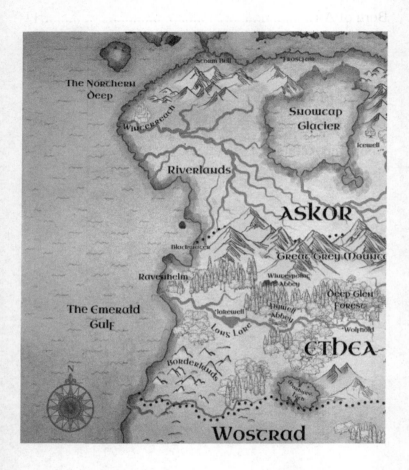

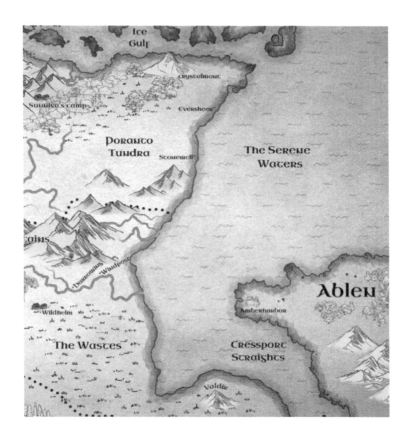

RA Lewis

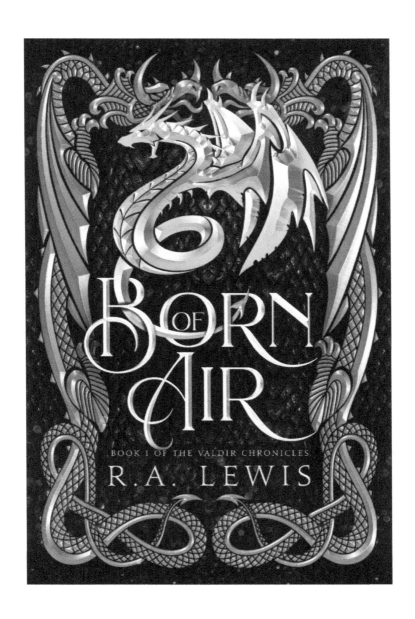

BORN OF AIR

BOOK 1 OF THE VALDIR CHRONICLES

R. A. LEWIS

RA Lewis

Born of Air

Book One
Valdir Chronicles

By R. A. Lewis

Dedication

For the real Kalina. And for lost little girls who just want to belong.

Dedication

Chapter 1

DARKNESS WRAPPED AROUND HER, the dense trees blocking out any trickle of moonlight. It was nearly impossible to see anything, even her own hand waving in front of her bright blue eyes. Kalina stood still, listening to the faint rustlings of small nocturnal animals snuffling for food around her. There was panting from an enormous creature coming from her right. Her heart began to race both from excitement and fear.

She had ventured into the forest for a reason, but now in the darkness, that reason seemed small and silly. Mari was a village girl who had had it out for her since they were small. Every day, that girl had made life a living hell since Kalina was small, and the final straw that broke her back was when Mari had called her a coward.

Kalina was anything but, and she refused to let Mari and the other girls believe it. Just because she was an orphan didn't mean she was less than any of them. Mari may have the opportunity to be courted by village boys and marry above her station, so why couldn't Kalina have the same chance?

Kalina's heart sank slightly at the thought. Mari already had plenty of suitors. Kalina hadn't managed to turn the head of even one boy, even at sixteen.

She hoisted her pack on her back and shuffled forward, one hand outstretched feeling for trees or rocks in her path. She turned towards the noise, waiting until she was right upon the creature to light the torch she had strapped to her pack. These beasts had to be taken by surprise, and like any self-respecting creature, it slept at night, so Kalina had set out at sunset to make her way into the forest.

Her outstretched hand bumped into the cold surface of the rock outcropping. She had been to this place many times during the day to look for signs of the beast, but at night she was disoriented, the creature's deep snores the only things guiding her steps. The sound was now immediately to her left. There was a small cavern in the rock, just big enough to fit one of the Abbey's largest oxen, and inside was the prize she sought.

Kalina inhaled deeply and slid to her left. When the warm

whoosh of its' breath ruffled the wisps of hair at her temples, she pulled out the flint and striker from her pocket and struck it once. The resulting spark lit the cave and surrounding forest like a lightning bolt, throwing everything into bright relief. Kalina bit back a muffled gasp at the sight of the coiled green scales, leathery hide, and glinting sharp talons. She quickly pulled her pack off, her fingers feeling for the pitch wrapped torch. The breathing hadn't changed as the torch dropped softly to the ground. Either the creature was unconcerned by small thumps or it was a deep sleeper.

She struck her flint again, letting the sparks fall on the torch, the embers coming to life. When the small torch finally caught, it lit up the cavern as bright as daylight. The beast finally stirred, blinking enormous yellow cat-like eyes. Its' scaled head raised, a forked tongue slithering out to test the air, tasting the tang of the burning torch.

"Who are you?" It asked, in a melodic, deep voice.

"I am Kalina, daughter of none. And I've come here to conquer you, Dragon." Kalina's voice rang out without a tremble of fear into the quiet of the nighttime forest.

"But I am no Dragon, Littling," the creature said. "I am a Wyvern, a smaller cousin of Dragons. How do you seek to conquer me?" The Wyvern was puzzled but pleasant. Kalina, surprised, squinted, holding her torch up high. Sure enough, this beast had no proper forelegs, only wings that had talons on the end for gripping and climbing, not for tearing and fighting.

"So you are." Kalina sighed unhappily. Mari would call her an idiot as well as a coward. She began to lower her torch, disappointment rising in her chest. She was prepared to walk away, her quest unfulfilled, when an idea struck her. Maybe, there was a way she could still show them she was no coward. She turned back to the Wyvern.

"What is your name?" The giant lizard swiveled its head back towards her.

"I am Savath of the Deep Glen, Kalina, Daughter of None." The Wyvern moved closer to her, the torchlight bouncing off its scales, creating a rainbow pattern on the walls of the little cave. "What has happened to your face, Littling? Has someone hurt you?"

Kalina's hand flew to her eye, lightly fingering the slowly

healing bruise. It had turned a nasty shade of green just that morning. She dropped her hand and straightened up. She refused to let the shame of having been beat up by a girl only a year older show on her face.

"It was nothing." She looked up at the Wyvern through her muddy brown hair that fell in front of her face. Her hair should have been a bright, shining silver, but ever since she could remember, Gwen had helped her dye it every fortnight.

"Don't let the silver show, Kalina." Gwen would always say. "You know the High Father doesn't like the color." One time when her silver roots had shown when Gwen was too sick to dye it, Mari had dubbed her the Old Crone and made fun of her for a week. The girl had never let her forget it and still called her the name on occasion.

Kalina set her jaw. She needed something, anything that could make her stand out and give her a fighting chance.

"Do you think-" she paused, excitement and hope roaring in her chest at the thought of what this Wyvern could do for her. "Do you think you could help me?" The Wyvern blinked its lamp-like eyes slowly, considering.

"Are you pure?" Its voice was calm, like it was the most normal question in the world.

"Pure?" Heat crept up her neck in embarrassment and confusion. She'd heard stories about dragons seeking only virgins, she was definitely "pure" in that sense. But perhaps it meant something different. There were rumors that Wyverns had peculiar habits or desires. Some only wanted shiny things, some were obsessed with virgins, some refused to sleep on rocks.

"Are your intentions pure? Do you seek knowledge or to better yourself? Or do you seek revenge, to hurt someone?" The Wyvern hissed out the last question like a snake. Kalina paused, she realized a part of her did want help for selfish reasons, but ultimately she wanted to put a bully in her place.

"I think so. I want you to help me prove I am not a coward." She straightened her neck and jutted out her chin. "You can judge for yourself if my motives are pure." The Wyvern nodded sleepily.

"Very well then, Kalina, Daughter of None, I will help you; but in the morning. I think better on a full night's sleep." It gestured with a flick of its tail. "You may sleep in that corner there." The giant lizard then curled back up, its tail gently lying over its nose like a kitten.

Kalina chuckled slightly. She was going to spend the night alone in a cave with a Wyvern. If Mari only knew, that alone would prove she wasn't a coward. She settled the torch into a v-shaped niche in the wall and then lay down on the sandy ground. Yawning, her adrenaline began to fade. Lacing her fingers behind her head she propped her head on her pack, admiring the great sleeping beast beside her. Her mind wandered, watching Savath in the dwindling torchlight until she fell asleep.

She dreamed that night of flying through the clouds, the whole world stretched out below her, crowds screaming her name in a triumphant swell of noise.

Chapter 2

KALINA WOKE TO THE SUN STREAMING through the trees into the cave, glinting off the silver roots of her hair, that had begun to show and lighting her warm tan skin. She blinked and stretched, having slept the best she had in months. She had learned to sleep with one eye open which meant she rarely got an entire night's sleep. The other orphans were mostly nice enough, but Mari's cronies ranged far and wide, and some of the older girls in the orphan's dormitory were all too happy to do Mari's bidding. She woke up at least once a week soaked in some sort of liquid.

She looked to where the Wyvern had been the night before and jolted upright. The lizard was gone! Kalina hurried out of the cave, scanning the dense trees surrounding her for any sign of the creature, but found none. She turned slowly, disappointment and shame at having been tricked building in her chest and throat, threatening to spill over in her eyes, when a voice rang out.

"I've been contemplating your situation, Littling, and I think I have an idea." Kalina's head snapped up to the rocky crags above the cave. On the rock's grey surface close to the edge, the green Wyvern lay sprawled, sunning itself. The rock stretched out behind the creature into the distance, too far for Kalina to see the other edge. A huge smile spread across her face at the sight of the creature, relief blooming in her chest.

"What is your solution, Savath?" She sat down on a rock just outside the cave mouth and followed the flick of the Wyvern's tail as it swished back and forth.

"You want to prove you are brave? A force to be reckoned with?" Kalina nodded. "Then I think riding into town on my back would serve that purpose." Kalina was stunned. It was more than she had hoped for.

"Are you sure? I get to fly?" She began to shake in excitement, her stomach doing flip-flops. She'd get to fly like the dragon riders she'd read about once in the library.

"Yes, Littling." The Wyvern did a lengthy stretch, arching its body like a giant cat, extending its talons, each as large as Kalina's hand, and raking them across the rock, scoring deep gouges. It shook itself, wings snapping out, sun glinting off their jewel-like tones.

19

Kalina shivered in anticipation, picking up her pack and hoisting it onto her back once again. Savath jumped onto the ground before the cave, its large bulk shaking the ground slightly with its impact.

"Climb on just behind my wing joints. Grip me with your legs and you may hang on to my shoulders as I fly. Trust that I won't drop you or let you slide off." Kalina made a slight croaking noise as she climbed up, using Savath's hind leg as a step. Nerves were getting the best of her voice. Once she was settled, she searched for a place to grab, the Wyvern's shoulders sloping and moving beneath her uncertain grip. She didn't feel secure at all, and she realized that riding a Wyvern would take all her courage.

"Hold on." Savath rumbled, and suddenly the world dropped away from Kalina's feet, her stomach going with it, and she was very grateful that she hadn't eaten the bread and cheese in her pack. Soon they were soaring above the trees and Kalina's stomach caught up with her and remained fluttery as the great wide world spread out before her. Her knuckles had turned white as she'd griped Savath's scales, but she gently loosened them as they steadied and she became more comfortable. Kalina looked around them in awe.

Stretching below them and off into the distance was the great green expanse of the Glen Forest and off to their right, the rising peaks of the Great Grey Mountains, their tops snow-capped year-round. Kalina had only seen these places in maps within the Abbey's library, her personal domain consisted of a small portion of the Glen forest. She had been abandoned at the Abbey as a baby, as orphans and unwanted children often were, and there she had stayed. Flying with Savath gave Kalina a feeling of freedom she had never known, and as Savath began to descend towards the small town that surrounded her Abbey in the depths of the forest, circling around, Kalina strained to see farther, to take in every detail before her world once again shrunk to the few miles of forest she called home. She knew this was possibly the most adventure she'd ever have in her lifetime and she wanted to cherish every moment. Flying felt like she had put on a second skin, one that fit her perfectly, and her heart sank as they did, not wanting to give up the joy of flying.

The screams echoed up to her as the Wyvern circled lower, great wings outstretched to better display the sheer size of the beast that Kalina rode. She grinned in delight at the thought of what they saw: a brave girl riding a dangerous beast.

Savath landed with a thump that shook the ground, a great cloud of dust rising around them. The gathering crowd gave out a final gasp as the dust settled. Kalina dismounted from Savath's back, positive she didn't miss Mari's blonde curls bouncing in the crowd. She turned to the Wyvern to thank her.

"Thank you, Savath of the Deep Glen. I owe you a favor, should you ever need one." Savath eyed her with those yellow orbs and huffed. Then the great bulk of the Wyvern was propelled into the sky with one mighty sweep of its wings and Kalina was forced to shut her eyes against the dust that swirled as Savath flew away, back into the forest.

A brunette, slightly plump girl around Kalina's age with round, red cheeks, came sprinting breathlessly up to Kalina, a look of awe on her face.

"Are you kidding me?" Delisa blurted out. "What were you thinking, Kalina? You could have been killed!" Delisa was always the more cautious of the two of them. Kalina smiled in confident triumph as townsfolk and Mari alike looked at her with newfound trepidation and perhaps a little respect and fear. Mari stared open-mouthed at Kalina until she noticed Kalina and Delisa grinning at her.

"Be careful, Mari, or you might start catching flies," Kalina's voice cut across the crowd, and Mari's mouth snapped shut, her eyes practically molten with rage. She seemed to be about to march over and teach Kalina a lesson when suddenly she stopped, looking behind Kalina, and smirked. She turned and walked away into the crowd, as if Kalina hadn't just ridden in on a Wyvern. Kalina's heart fell. Maybe it hadn't made the impression she was hoping for. Mari had seemed more eager than ever to come to blows with Kalina.

There was the sound of a throat clearing behind her and Delisa as the town around them began to return to its normal morning rhythm. Kalina winced as she turned to find Father Martin behind her, flanked by Father Nic and Father Lane. Father Martin did not look pleased in the slightest.

The High Father cleared his throat again, clearly waiting for Kalina to give an explanation. Kalina's mind raced to find a lie, as she had so often done to get out of trouble with him, but there was none. He was the man in charge, and he dictated the lives of all the abandoned children of the Abbey. Kalina had a penchant for getting into trouble, and she had encountered this dark-eyed look from him many times before. Behind him, Father Nic was obviously trying to hide a smile. Kalina looked down at her dusty, worn boots, and decided on the truth.

"Well Father Martin, you see, Mari called me a coward for not punching her back, so I thought I could prove that I'm no coward…" she trailed off, her explanation dying on her lips and the look in his eyes only darkening. Her mouth clamped shut.

"You thought?" Father Martin's tone was calm, but his look was all thunder. Kalina winced at his words. "What did you think, Kalina? That you'd ride in here on a giant lizard and everyone would hail you as a hero?" When he put it like that, Kalina began to feel small and ashamed. "You have disrupted this abbey and this town, terrorized the people, and made a mess of the main square, all just before St. Martin's Day!" His voice went up at the end, his outrage at her possibly ruining his namesake holiday coming out. Kalina looked around sheepishly, noticing that the multicolored decorations covering the buildings surrounding the square were windblown, some torn down, all of it covered in a layer of dust. The townsfolk were slowly putting the square to rights again, casting annoyed looks her way.

"I'm sorry, High Father." Her voice was very small, as he looked down on her. Delisa was still beside her, hands clasped behind her back, head down.

"You are never to go looking for that beast again. Ever. You are sixteen, Kalina. Too old for this nonsense. You should be learning a trade, or finding a husband, not gallivanting about on a lizard! You will begin to make up for your impulsiveness by helping Father Nic clean up the square." He glared sternly down at them. "Both of you." Delisa's head came up in protest but Father Martin lifted a finger. "Both of you," he repeated, shutting down any argument. With that, he turned on his heel, Father Lane following in his wake, shaking his head sadly.

Kalina looked up at Father Nic, who had turned to watch the High Father stride away. When he turned back to Kalina and Delisa, he had a grin on his face. Father Nic was a jolly man, with laughing green eyes and smile creases next to his eyes and mouth that never seemed to go away. His balding head always gleamed in the morning sun and Kalina had often wondered as a child if she would see her reflection in it if she looked down on it. Father Nic tapped the side of his nose knowingly and gestured for her and Delisa to follow him.

They spent the rest of the morning cleaning up the square with the townsfolk, sweeping up dust that had covered the pretty carpets that had been laid out for dancing, and shaking the dust off the fallen banners. Soon the square was full of bright colors again. Father Nic turned to them both.

"I know what Father Martin said, but I think you girls have done a fine job of making the square look lovely again." He beamed down at them both and Kalina felt some of her shame slip away. Delisa grinned at her. "Now, run along to your chores, girls. We want the abbey spic and span for St. Martin's day!" Father Nic smiled benevolently down at them, winking at Kalina. She finally grinned back, grabbed Delisa's hand and ran across the square, back down the dirt road towards the abbey proper. They spent the afternoon cleaning the High Father's chambers and scrubbing the floors after grabbing a quick bite to eat with Gwen in the kitchen.

The Abbey was laid out like a hexagon, many wings stemming off the main foyer. Kalina and Delisa slept in the east wing in a small dormitory for girls, farthest away from the High Father's chambers in the west wing. Across the hall was the boy's dormitory. The boys had the chance to grow up and become monks, or even Fathers as Father Nic had. But the girls only got the chance to be chambermaids or cooks, or were married off to men in the town.

Kalina often was distracted from her chores with daydreaming of adventures she would have, leaving their little town, and finding her way in the great wide world. A world she had only seen in books; a world she knew nothing about. Father Martin often told her that she would never leave the abbey, that he intended for her to take over Gwen's position in the kitchen when the time came. She always felt defeated after those conversations with the High Father, as though he purposely crushed her dreams in order to keep her here forever. Other girls were allowed to leave, why not her?

Chapter 3

TWO DAYS LATER, KALINA AND Delisa were cleaning the hall outside the High Father's chambers when they heard a clatter. Kalina's hand froze halfway to the bucket of soapy water before her, the brush still clutched in her hand as her ears strained to catch the sound again. Delisa froze beside her, as voices rose from inside the High Father's chambers. Kalina put her finger to her mouth, motioning to Delisa to be quiet a she stood and tiptoed to the door, pressing her ear against it, listening to the voices beyond. That morning a stranger had ridden into town and presented himself at the abbey. Kalina hadn't caught a good look at him but any time a stranger arrived it often meant changes within the abbey.

"I received a letter saying Sir Gregan and his men will be attending the St. Martin's celebrations tomorrow." The voice was that of Father Martin. Her curiosity peaked, Kalina pressed her ear harder. She held her breath when a chair creaked as someone shifted inside. A second voice rang out, one she didn't recognize but was somehow familiar.

"Will you tell the girl?" The voice was deep and rough.

"Kalina?" She jumped at the sound of her own name. "No. She doesn't need to know. The less she knows, the better." The High Father's voice sounded sad, almost tired, and Kalina was more confused and intrigued than ever. Why would she care if a knight was in town? She had to fight back the urge to burst into the room and demand answers. Instead, she motioned for Delisa to keep cleaning as if all was normal. A chair creaked again, and Kalina took a breath, waiting. "I'm trying to keep her safe." Safe from what?

"The girl deserves to know who she is. Why it's so important she not be discovered." The stranger seemed to know things about her that she had never heard. Who was she that they talked about her so? Questions swirled in her mind.

"She deserves a normal life, gods willing." Father's Martin's voice was weary. "She deserves to grow up free from expectation, from responsibility, from danger. The entire reason her father sent her with you into my care as a baby was to save her from the prince's wrath."

"But if knowing could help her to fight him, to run..." The stranger's voice rose with passion.

"No." Father Martin's voice was sharp and cut through the room beyond the door like a knife. "No. If she knew she was a Valdir, she would run right into their trap. I will see to it she continues to have a normal life." There was a clank and a clatter of teacups being put down. "Now, would you like a little supper? I will fetch us some from the kitchens." Kalina didn't wait for the High Father to get up from his chair, or for the stranger to respond. She bounced back from the door with alacrity and grabbed her bucket and brush from where she'd left them. She ran down the hall to the end and began scrubbing the floors as if her life depended on it, which it did if she was caught eavesdropping. Delisa looked at her, terrified, frozen right outside the High Father's door as it opened and Father Martin stepped out into the hall. The tall, dark stranger wearing a hooded cloak stood beside him.

"Delisa!" Father Martin exclaimed, and his head swiveled to take in Kalina scrubbing vigorously at a spot on the floor a few paces away down the hall. "Kalina." His voice sounded brittle and the look on his face was strained. He rubbed his worn face with his hand, as if trying to scrub the weariness from it. Kalina paused, wiping her brow with the back of her soapy hand, leaving a wet spot that a few stray wisps of her silver hair stuck to. She felt like her insides were shaking, either from excitement at what she'd heard or adrenaline for almost getting caught, she wasn't sure. She took a deep breath before responding, trying to steady herself.

"Yes, Father?" she said as nonchalantly as she could. He stared at her with such intensity for a moment that she almost looked away.

"Fetch two trays of supper from the kitchens, please. Delisa can help you carry them." He paused, eyeing them for some sign of disobedience. "Quickly now." Kalina stood swiftly, wiping her hands on her dirty apron and motioning for Delisa to follow her. Together they raced off towards the kitchens as the High Father looked after them.

Kalina and Delisa practically fell over each other to get inside the kitchen, both giggling nervously from their close encounter with the High Father. The cook, Gwen, always knew everything and Kalina was sure she'd know at least something of what the High

Father had been talking about. Gwen was busy kneading dough for the next morning's bread when the two girls flew in.

"Well aren't you two in a right hurry," she groused at them. Gwen had a tongue that Kalina never escaped, but she was still kind to the two girls and sometimes gave them extra sweets when there were leftovers. And every few weeks she dyed Kalina's hair, to hide the silver. She knew that time was coming since her roots were shining silver once again.

"The High Father ordered two trays of supper," Delisa said, still giving Kalina sideways looks. Kalina shook her head slightly, telling her friend they'd speak later. Gwen nodded.

"You know where to find everything." She motioned to the kitchen behind her and Kalina and Delisa began gathering the things they needed.

"Gwen, do you remember anything about the night I arrived at the Abbey?" Kalina's voice was breathless, her heart racing in anticipation and leftover adrenaline. Her mind tumbled over itself trying to make sense of the High Father's words. Gwen wiped her flour-covered hands on her apron and came to help the girls cut some fresh bread for the trays.

"Well, I remember well the day you showed up here. It was the longest night of the year, dark as can be, a chill wind blowin' straight down from the Great Grey Mountains." Kalina listened raptly, forgetting the tasks before her as Gwen spoke. Gwen had never told this story before. "A lone rider with a strange insignia on his cloak knocked on the gate, a small baby with silver hair in his arms. I had to fetch the High Father from his bed! He came runnin' and him and this stranger spent an hour in a secret conference as I rocked you to sleep by the fire." Gwen paused, her hands stilling over the loaf of bread, part way through a slice. Kalina began busying herself once again, hoping she would continue. "When Father Martin came into the kitchen after, he stared down at you for a long while." Her voice was wistful now. Kalina wondered not for the first time why she had been forced to hide her hair. Gwen went back to slicing. "Then he told me to raise you up like any other orphan dropped on our doorstep, and to dye your hair." She looked over at the two wide-eyed girls. "Now you girls get these trays to the High Father, quick as you can. Don't want to keep him waiting!" She placed the slices of bread on the trays next to the two bowls of steaming stew that Kalina had scooped out and the butter and jam Delisa had prepared. Gwen shooed them out with both hands and they quickly shuffled out, their arms laden with the trays.

Kalina knocked quietly on the High Father's door. He opened it immediately, as if he'd been standing on the other side, waiting. He directed them to place the trays on his desk. The dark stranger's eyes followed Kalina as she crossed the room, her silver roots shining behind her. Kalina shivered at his stare.

"You may leave us now girls. Thank you. Please take the rest of the night off before the work of tomorrow morning and the festivities in the afternoon." Kalina looked at him in shock. They had only cleaned half the west wing, and Father Martin rarely gave them time off when there was still work to be done.

But she nodded and gave a little curtsey, Delisa following suit beside her.

"Thank you, Father." They both murmured and turned to leave. Father Martin followed them out and caught Kalina's arm. She turned.

"I think you'd better dye your hair and wear your headscarf the next few days, Kalina." She looked into his cool grey eyes and saw the seriousness there. She longed to ask why, to have him explain who the Valdir were, who she was, and why she was in danger. But she couldn't, so she only nodded." He let her go and watched her join Delisa as they collected their buckets and brushes and went to the kitchens to put them away. Gwen looked at them sternly when they entered, hands on her ample hips.

"You girls haven't finished cleaning that hall yet!"

"Father Martin told us to take the rest of the night off," Delisa said, looking sideways at Kalina, who was lost in thought. Delisa elbowed her in the ribs and Kalina finally looked up. Gwen looked shocked, and she looked them both up and down with a suspicious eye.

"Night off you say? Well, I guess I better trust you. Enough work to get done in the morning before the festivities begin at sundown." She reached into her pocket and withdrew two silver pennies and a few coppers. She picked out the two pennies and handed one each to the girls who took them excitedly. "Here. Go buy yourselves something hot in town and enjoy yourselves. It's not every day you get an evening off!" Delisa squealed in delight and Kalina grinned. The thought of a warm beef and onion pie, followed by an orange tarte lifting her spirits considerably. She may not have all the answers, but at least she would have a night off to think about it and maybe even investigate. Before they left, Kalina turned to Gwen.

"Father Martin asked if you could dye my hair." Gwen sighed and looked up at Kalina's hair.

"I don't have time between now and the festival." She sounded exasperated. She pursed her lips thinking. "Better wear your headscarf for a few days until I can get the dye." Kalina nodded and went to fetch her pale blue headscarf. She quickly tied her hair into braids before donning the scarf, covering her roots. Delisa smiled at her.

"Blue is such a lovely color on you. Matches your eyes." Kalina smiled at her friend, grateful for the compliment and attempt to make her feel less strange, less like an outsider.

"Let's go."

Together the two girls left through the kitchen door and walked arm in arm down the dusty track that lead to the town where evening food sellers and vendors were hawking their wares.

Chapter 4

AS THE WARM PIE AND SWEET orange tarte settled in Kalina's stomach, her mind began to wander back over the conversation she had overheard. She and Delisa sat on the edge of the fountain that adorned the center of the main square, the early evening breeze playing around them, the banners and garish decorations for St. Martin's day flapping in the wind. Delisa was soaking her bare feet in the fountain beside Kalina, chattering away about the next day's festivities and the village boys she wanted to kiss, but Kalina was barely listening. She desperately wanted to know more about her past and who she was, a need she had rarely thought of before today, but she was also concerned about what danger Father Martin seemed to think she was in.

Who were Sir Gregan and the prince? And what threat did they pose her? Who were the Valdir and how could she be related to them? Questions swirled in her head as she stared off into the distance.

"Have you been listening, Kalina?" Delisa's question finally broke through Kalina's thoughts. She looked over at Delisa's round, kind face, now full of frustration.

"I'm sorry, Delisa." Her friend eyed her.

"What did you overhear?" Kalina looked at her. "In the High Father's chambers. What did you hear?" Kalina sighed and began explaining everything she had overheard, and together they began speculating what it might mean. "What if you are some high lady of the court? Or a lost princess?" Delisa always knew how to make Kalina laugh. She smiled at the images it conjured. Her, a princess? It was absurd!

"I doubt it. More likely my parents did something to offend the crown, and I was sent here so that I could be kept safe." Or as some kind of punishment. She knew very little about life beyond her abbey. The fathers and monks had taught her the basics about life in their little kingdom, and about the basics of reading and writing and doing sums, but she never learned any history, anything beyond religion and learning a trade. She knew what she needed to do. She needed to learn more about the outside world; it might give her a clue as to who her parents were, and why the prince might be after her. "I'm going to the library; would you like to come?" Delisa wiped her wet feet off on her dress and grinned.

"Of course!" Kalina followed suit, and soon the two of them were walking back to the abbey's north wing and the library.

As they approached the massive wooden doors, Kalina brushed the hair back from her face and tried to calm her racing heart. It was pounding both from exertion and from excitement. The father who ran the library was Father Ben and he guarded his books with zeal but he was very willing to give out information when asked. Kalina had often spent hours in the library asking him question after question, but never about history, usually about dragons or Wyverns.

Father Ben sat at the large wooden desk just inside the heavy wooden doors. Father Ben looked up expectantly as they filed in.

"Ahh, Kalina, Delisa. How can I help you two this evening?" Kalina swallowed nervously and came to sit in one of the two chairs before his large desk. She wondered if her past could be found in a book, or if only Father Martin knew about it. She had to try.

"We have questions, Father Ben. About history, and about our kingdom. Can you help us?" She hesitated from asking about the Valdir directly, worried it would somehow get back to Father Martin.

"Of course, my child. I can even get you some reference books if you'd like." Kalina smiled and nodded.

"Yes, please." They waited in silence for him to return.

"Why are you ladies so interested in our history all of a sudden?" He asked as he returned with a small stack of books.

"Someone in the village mentioned something about St. Martin's and we wanted to learn about it!" Delisa pitched in, looking sideways at Kalina who smiled back gratefully.

The library had always been Kalina's favorite place. Books were stacked on every surface and along huge bookshelves that lined each wall. Kalina had always loved this room, and she often came here to read the stories Father Ben found for her on adventure, dragons, and maidens fair being saved by brave knights. She didn't want to be a maiden though like most little girls. She had wanted to be a knight who went on adventures and fought dragons! Although now, it seemed a little silly. And a part of her wanted to ride on dragons, not slay them. Her heart soared at the thought, her mind wandering to the great green expanse of the forest stretching below her, and the great wide world opening up before her, ripe with possibilities and adventure.

"I was able to find you some recent histories of our kingdom, but they are a bit dry and you might not find them that interesting. I also found a few reference books on our nobility and one that references the various clans on a map that might give you a better idea of how our kingdom is divided up. Now, is there anything more you need, girls?" Kalina shook her head and reached for the books.

"Thank you, Father Ben." She said politely.

They made their way to a large window in the far corner of the library that looked out over the Abbey grounds towards the chicken coops and the kitchens. They plopped down into two comfy chairs with worn cushions and began to look at the books and scrolls.

Kalina pulled a recent history book towards her, while Delisa grabbed an old one judging from the state of the pages. They read for hours, each showing the other any possibly relevant information. They learned about Tiberius the Great, a king from a hundred years ago who supposedly married a woman who rode into the capitol on a sea dragon. Or about how knights of old would hunt down dragons and Wyverns for their teeth or wing membranes. Kalina read a dry text about the grain trading routes between her country, Ethea and their neighboring country to the north, Askor. Askor was a barren country, full of ice and snow almost year-round. Only their southern plains were hospitable all year round. She remembered what Father Martin had taught her years ago, that there had been a war that lasted fifty years between Askor and Ethea over mining rights within the Great Grey Mountains that separated their two kingdoms. Askor had few resources and felt they were entitled to mine the mountains, while Ethea felt they also had a right to mine. Kalina didn't remember much else but had heard the war had stopped the year she was born because the princess of Ethea was wed to the younger son of the king of Askor and peace was brokered. It was all very interesting, but it had little to do with her.

The sun had gone down behind the trees, and Father Ben had come by to light some lamps, and Kalina still hadn't found anything interesting. She closed the book before her in disgust and put her head down on the table, her eyes burning from so much reading.

"Have you found any interesting history, Delisa?" She asked, her words muffled by the book and her hair around her face planted on the table.

"Just a somewhat recent history of our kingdom. The last 100 years or so during the war, but nothing since. But it does list who our current King and Queen are." She pointed to the newer book she held, the binding still crisp, the golden letters on the front still shining in the lantern light. Kalina reached out a hand for the book. Delisa closed it and handed it over. At that moment Father Ben walked over. "But nothing about a missing princess, sorry." She grinned at Kalina, and Kalina grinned back. No, she wasn't anyone special. But that still begged the question, why was the prince after her?

"It's time to close the library and say your evening prayers, ladies." He began gathering the books on the table.

"Father Ben, may I take this one to read tonight as I fall asleep?" Kalina gestured to the recent history she held. Father Ben cocked his head to read the title and then nodded.

"Yes, you may, but please, don't read it while eating anything that can stain the pages, like jam." He looked pointedly at her as she had once ruined a page in her favorite adventure book from some jam slipping off her scone and onto the page. She smiled sheepishly at him and nodded. "Then run along and get some supper and go to bed. Tomorrow is going to be a long enough day for all of us." Kalina and Delisa left the library, heading for the kitchens.

"What are we going to do now?" Delisa asked, the noises from the other orphan children echoing in the hall. The orphans ranged in age from toddlers to teens and were already eating dinner within, which meant Kalina and Delisa would likely not get seconds. Kalina didn't mind. As one of the oldest, she got to work in the kitchens, which meant she got the food fresh and warm from the ovens.

"I don't know. I think I need a bigger library, one with more books or at least more recent ones. Perhaps the one in the capital!" Delisa shrugged at her words. Kalina sighed. "Let's get in there before Jon steals all the apple pie." She pushed past Delisa and into the noise and light of the busy kitchen. Delisa followed after and soon they were lost in conversation with Gwen and the other children who sat around a large wooden table eating dinner.

Chapter 5

KALINA AND DELISA WORKED HARD in the kitchen all morning, baking the loaves of bread, pastries, and pies for that evening's festivities. They fetched water from the well and firewood for the ovens, and Kalina pumped the bellows to heat the ovens many times throughout the day. As the sun began to set, they loaded the abbey's cart with food and helped Gwen wheel it to the town center where other vendors were setting up their carts with food, ale, wine and little trinkets for the celebrations. Once they had helped her set up her pies and pastries for sale, Gwen handed them each two silver pennies and sent them on their way. They wouldn't have to work again for two days and the thought lightened Kalina's steps. As Delisa pushed her way into the gathering crowd, the lamps were being lit and a large bonfire was being stacked and lit, flickering in the deepening gloom.

Kalina followed more slowly. She was scanning the crowd, searching for someone who looked malicious, like perhaps they were coming to get her. Suddenly she bumped into something solid and was knocked to the ground.

"Ouch!" she exclaimed, grabbing her head where it had connected with someone else's and heard an answering groan of pain before her. She looked up, stunned to see a boy around her age lying prone on the ground. He sat up slowly, clutching his head, and when his eyes fell on her they went wide, and then he smiled. Kalina had never seen him in the village before, and he wore livery that was strange.

"Sorry about that." He stood and offered her a hand up. Kalina took it, hesitating for a moment before placing her hand in his. His hand was warm as he hauled her to her feet. She tried to dust herself off.

"That's alright. I should have been looking where I was going." She had been so preoccupied looking for an adult, she didn't notice the teenager. Strangers often came through town, but none wore livery in green and gold, and certainly, none had an insignia of two crossed swords on their left breast.

He placed a hand on his chest. "I'm Talon, squire for Sir Dyelan of his Majesty's court. Who are you?" Kalina eyed him. Most of the local boys never gave her even a moment's notice. Many of them were also subjects of Mari's bullying, or if they weren't, they were in love with her blonde hair and blue eyes. Kalina had always been overlooked, so it was a strange sensation that a boy was paying her attention.

"I'm Kalina, Daughter of None." She smiled a bit at the alias she had given herself. It seemed fitting and gave her a sense of mystery that she quite enjoyed. Talon's eyebrows rose at her title, but he smiled.

"Well Kalina, Daughter of None, would you care to join me for an ale and a meat pie? I could use the company." He offered her his arm and gestured into the crowd. Kalina hesitated. He had said he served a knight master, not Sir Gregan, but perhaps a knight in the man's retinue. It struck her suddenly that he might know who she was, or who the Valdir were, so she nodded and took his arm.

"Alright, I know a place." She led him to the best meat pies in town, a little stall by the fountain, run by a grizzled old woman named Jeanie who had been making the pies since she was a little girl and her own mother had taught her. Kalina asked for four lamb and beef pies. Jeanie pulled out four pies, placed them onto a large cloth and tied it up. Talon dug in his pocket and paid for their pies. Kalina thanked him graciously. Once they had their food, she led him to the nearby tavern, whose doors had been thrown open, light, music, and sound pouring onto the cobblestones out front.

"The best ale in town is in here." She gestured with the pies towards the noise and bustle. Talon smiled and nodded.

"Why don't you wait out here and I'll go get us some drinks." He pushed his way through the crowd. Kalina stood there, her hands full of pies, questioning her own sanity at spending time with a boy so close to those who were trying to find her. But tonight was all about drinking and eating, and tomorrow the real fun started. There were games played in the town square for all ages, foot races run, art displayed, and theater performances. In the afternoon there was a horse race that anyone could enter, that circled the town and Abbey twice. And in the evening was storytelling around the bonfire and dancing. She decided there wasn't any harm in enjoying herself. Besides, her silver roots were covered, and no one from outside the abbey knew her or what she looked like. Plus, Talon was handsome, and she enjoyed having his attention, even if it was only for the night.

Talon returned, holding two tankards filled to the brim with a light brown ale. He grinned at her and she rolled her eyes. She motioned for him to follow her and she led him through the crowd to a low wall that bordered a small garden on the side of the tavern. There they sat and exchanged pies for ale. They ate in awkward silence, Kalina giving Talon sideways glances between bites and watching the crowd. Talon smiled happily and watched her as she ate. She smiled slightly at him and he beamed back at her smile.

"So, Kalina, tell me about yourself?" Kalina scrambled for words. Nobody had ever asked her that question, and as she thought about what she could say, she realized the things she'd overheard from Father Martin, and the fact that she had ridden on a Wyvern were the most interesting things about her, and they were things she couldn't reveal. She sighed and looked up at him.

"Well, I am an orphan of the abbey. I wash dishes and do chores for the High Father." She felt incredibly pathetic having said it out loud. Talon's eyes lit up.

"An orphan? No kidding! What is it like growing up in the abbey? Is the High Father really as formidable as they say he is? What do you do when you aren't working?" His questions came rapid fire, and Kalina was momentarily overwhelmed by his attention. She decided to redirect.

"Yes, the High Father is. What about you? What's life like being a squire for Sir Dyelan? What's the capital city like?" She hoped he wouldn't notice she hadn't answered most of his questions.

"Well, Sir Dyelan is an alright man. He treats me fine, doesn't beat me when I make mistakes." Kalina's eyebrows rose at this, but Talon waved it off. "I get to travel the kingdom a lot and I get to fight in battles sometimes and in tournaments, oh the tournaments, Kalina! The pageantry and the excitement! It makes your little St. Martin's celebration look like a dull birthday party." Kalina's face flushed a bit and she looked down at her hands. Of course, she was ignorant of the outside world. A worm of jealousy squirmed in her stomach that this boy, because he was a boy, could travel the world at a knight's side. "And Sir Gregan has us traipsing all over the country in search of something for the Prince." Kalina stiffened, excitement and fear thrilling through her. "It must be pretty important. We've been at it since I joined Sir Dyelan." He looked at her and took a sip of ale, his eyebrows raised.

"What do you think he's searching for?" Talon shrugged.

"We're searching for a girl with silver hair. Or at least that's what they all talk about." Kalina resisted the urge to double check her head scarf, instead twisting her hands in her lap as he spoke.

"And you just travel the country, searching for one girl? Why?" Talon shrugged again.

"Not sure. Sir Dyelan says she's important to the Prince somehow. But from the way Sir Gregan searches, you'd think this girl was a danger."

"What do you mean?"

"Well, Sir Dyelan usually searches each house or abbey, asking to see all girls around your age. I would bet that after the celebrations here he'll do the same thing." Kalina's blood ran cold. She had to find a way to dye her hair on her own if Gwen wouldn't do it. Or she needed to disappear. It frustrated her that she still didn't know why the prince wanted her, but from the way Father Martin spoke about it, she knew in her bones it wasn't so he could throw her a party. She decided to change the subject.

"Talon, do you know anything about the Valdir?" It was a gamble, but since she hadn't found a single mention of them in the library, perhaps a boy who was raised in the capital knew of such things.

"Aren't those the dragon riders that disappeared at the end of the war?" Kalina's heart leapt into her throat. Dragon riders. Could it be?

"I don't know, that's why I'm asking you. I only just heard of them but our library is sadly lacking." Talon nodded, drinking off the rest of his ale before answering.

"Well, I don't know much. There isn't any mention of them within the last century except that they helped in the war on the side of Ethea, and then once peace was declared, they just disappeared. Nothing has been said of them since." He nudged her with his elbow gently. "I'm only telling you what I remember from my schooling, mind you. I haven't read up on them in years."

Kalina felt like her insides were shaking. She was a dragon rider. She had no idea how to process that information. Everything she knew about herself was a lie, kept from her by Father Martin. Did the prince hate the Valdir? Was that why she was being hidden from him? So many questions swirled in her head. Talon sat across from her watching, and she was sure she wasn't able to keep the emotions from playing across her face. She ducked her head in embarrassment and even some fear. Could he read how much the news of her people affected her?

"Are you alright?" He asked, reaching out to touch her arm. Kalina blushed furiously and she stood up.

"Yes, I'm fine. Thank you for a lovely meal, Talon." She turned on her heel and quickly walked away through the crowd. She didn't turn back when Talon called her name and she kept walking until the high walls of the abbey cast her in deep shadow. The sun had set while they'd sat talking, and the deepening gloom around her hid the flush on her cheeks. She wasn't used to being watched or cared about, or even as Talon had touched her. And from the way he made it sound, her own people had abandoned her here at the abbey before disappearing. She felt more alone than ever.

Chapter 6

WHAT HAD THE STRANGER SAID? "The girl deserves to know who she is." Kalina had lain awake all night, contemplating what the stranger and Father Martin had said, and what Talon had told her. Who was she? She felt like a storm had risen inside her, threatening to swallow her whole.

Delisa had woken her early, eager to go into town and join in the day's festivities. Kalina dragged her feet, tired from the night before. But once they made it into town, her own trepidation lifted slighting at the funny antics of the acrobats from the traveling trope that had come for the celebrations.

They spent the afternoon with Delisa, dancing around the maypole, eating fried pork fat, and licking the sticky jam of pies from their fingers in the hot afternoon sun. It was still Spring, however, and evening came on quickly with cooling temperatures. As the sun drew down the sky, heading west towards the horizon, Talon found them sitting in the shade of the tavern, enjoying the cool breeze. He seemed out of breath and had a worried look on his face.

"Kalina." She sat up straight at his words, her awkwardness from the night before starting to creep in. "I need to talk to you." Talon slid his eyes to Delisa and back.

"Talon, this is my best friend Delisa. Delisa, this is Talon." Talon nodded to Delisa, and Delisa gave him a flirty smile.

"Where are you from?" She asked, patting the low wall they sat on, encouraging him to sit. Talon hesitated, eyeing the spot between the two girls. Kalina rolled her eyes at her friend. Delisa was a sweet girl who'd always been there for Kalina, but she was also a shameless flirt, especially within the last year. Delisa was determined not to stay in the kitchens like Kalina. She wanted to move out into the town, someplace where she could have lots of babies and raise a family. Kalina didn't blame her, but sometimes it made her insufferable around the boys.

"Never mind her," Kalina said, playfully waving Delisa off. Delisa grinned. "What's wrong?" Talon again looked between the girls, clearly unsure if he should speak.

"I just came from my knight master's tent. I overheard them

talking about you." Her blood went cold.

"What do you mean." Talon finally sat between them.

"A villager told Sir Dyelan last night that you flew in on a Wyvern and almost destroyed the town square. Sir Dyelan told Sir Gregan this morning and now he's convinced you are the girl he's looking for." His eyes flickered up to Kalina's head scarf. "I knew I had to come and warn you." Kalina's heart was racing by the time she finished speaking, and Delisa's face was white with horror.

"We have to get you out of here!" Delisa whispered fervently.

"I know," Kalina murmured. She looked around the square as if Sir Gregan, whom she'd never seen, would pop out of nowhere.

"The good news is, he doesn't know what you look like yet. He said he's going to kill that Wyvern too, just for fun." Talon's own face showed the disgust he felt at that.

"Why are you helping me?" Kalina asked suddenly. She had no idea why a boy she'd met briefly the night before would be willing to help her. Talon brushed his brown hair from his eyes and smiled at her.

"Because I like you, Kalina. And I can't stand to see someone like Sir Gregan destroy a creature like the Wyvern. Is it true you flew on it?" She nodded, her mind only partially there.

"Then we need to find a way to warn the Wyvern, and dye your hair." Delisa chimed in. She grabbed Kalina's hand across Talon. "Go tonight and warn the Wyvern. And when you get back, I'll have gotten the dye from Gwen, and will be ready to dye your hair. We'll get it done before he can come for you."

"Did he mention when?" Kalina's bright blue eyes searched Talon's green ones.

"He did say it could wait until after the celebrations." Talon shrugged.

"Then we go tonight."

"I'm coming with you," Talon said. She didn't protest.

Kalina and Delisa ran back to their dorm. She collected her cloak and her small pack she had stocked with a flint and steel, and a jar of pitch for torches from her last outing into the woods to find the Wyvern. She paused at her shabby little bed, wondering if she should take anything else with her, just in case. She grabbed the book from the library and her small pouch of money she'd been saving for a rainy day, and made her way out through the kitchens. The kitchens were oddly deserted and she grabbed a loaf of stale bread off the counter. It had been baked the day before, stuffed full of nuts and dried fruit.

Delisa hugged her at the edge of the village, squeezing her tight. Kalina's eyes filled with unexpected tears.

"Thank you for helping me." She whispered to her friend. Delisa squeezed her tighter in response.

"It's what friends do. Now hurry. And when you get back, I'll be ready for you." Kalina nodded. Talon was waiting at the tree line and she hurried to catch up with him.

The sun had gone and the only light came from the bonfire in the center of town, bouncing off some low hanging clouds that had moved in over the last hour or so as Kalina waited.

"Thanks for your help, Talon." He smiled softly at her.

"I couldn't just let them hurt you. Or the Wyvern. They are an endangered species, only a few hundred left in existence that we know of. Neither of you deserves the Prince's wrath." The prince's wrath. That was the second time she'd heard him described that way. This prince must be a pretty awful person to get so bent out of shape about a missing dragon rider child. Kalina shrugged.

"Let's go find Savath."

"Who's Savath?" She gestured for him to follow and she made her way into the dark wood, only pausing to make a torch and smear it with the pitch and even then she waited until it was too dark to move before lighting it.

"That's the Wyvern's name." Talon nodded and followed her deeper into the forest.

The darkness around them seemed to breathe, and Kalina felt like the forest itself was waiting in anticipation as they made their way closer and closer to the cave. The large rock outcropping loomed in the darkness before them. Kalina paused, and called out, hoping not to startle the beast.

"Savath?" She craned her neck for movement within the cave and the telltale breathing of the beast. There was nothing. They moved forward cautiously, Kalina holding the torch high, trying to illuminate as much as possible. The cave seemed empty, only the faint markings of claws on the dusty floor and the little bed of springy boughs Kalina had slept on in the corner. She walked into the cave, Talon following behind. She placed the torch in the v-shape in the rock like she had the last time and then stood with her hands on her hips, looking around.

"What now?" Talon's voice echoed in the cave. Kalina looked up at the ceiling and sighed.

"We wait. I can't risk them killing the Wyvern. Plus, I do owe it a debt." She sat down on the bed of boughs left from her previous visit and began digging in her pack, pulling out her book. Talon came to sit beside her.

"What debt?" He wrapped his cloak around him as a chill wind rushed through the cave.

"I told it I owed it a debt for helping me." Kalina began, laying the book in her lap and looking sideways at him. He sat close enough that their shoulders touched. Despite the fear that felt like it was about to consume her, she felt a thrill go through her at his nearness. Talon looked sideways at her.

"Makes sense." She was grateful for his quick acceptance of everything and she impulsively leaned over and kissed his cheek. He went bright red, and a hand flew to cover the spot her lips had touched.

"What was that for."

"For everything."

They sat side by side, staring out into the night for a while until they both grew sleepy. She began to read the book in her lap as they waited, and soon the torch was burning low, and she was beginning to drift off. Talon beside her had already begun to snore lightly, his head falling onto her shoulder. She wondered sleepily how long they had been waiting for Savath when her head fell to her chest and she was asleep.

Chapter 7

THE CLOUDS WERE RED ALL AROUND her as she flew through the sky, the gigantic wing beats of the enormous dragon rising and falling below her. She could hear the sounds of screams echoing all around her as she flew. She looked around in confusion, where were the screams coming from? She looked up and the giant maw of a dragon opened before her and she flew right in. It snapped shut around her, spelling certain death…

Kalina woke suddenly, looking around her in confusion. The early morning sun was beating down on her through a break in the trees to the east, and Talon was nowhere to be seen. That's when she heard the yelling.

"Kalina!" Talon's voice rang out through the forest and she jumped up, the book falling from her lap. Talon broke from the nearby trees, his hair streaming away from him, his face bone white as he hurtled towards her.

"What? What's wrong?" she asked as he practically ran into her, her outstretched arms catching him before he stumbled and fell.

"They are coming!" he gasped between deep breaths, his hand clutching his side as he heaved for air. "The knights, they're coming. We overslept! They will be here soon. We have to go!" He reached for her pack that lay on the floor of the cave. Kalina looked around confused. There was still no sign of Savath.

"But where's Savath?" she breathed. She walked out of the cave as he began shoving her book into her pack. She looked up and saw a glint of green atop the rock face above her. Could that be the Wyvern laying in the sun on top? Suddenly, she knew in her bones it was the Wyvern. "We need to climb!" She reached and took her pack from him, slinging it on. Talon looked at her like she had three heads.

"Are you kidding me? We need to run! If they catch you, you'll be dragged back to the Prince! I can't be caught here!" His voice was tight with fear. Kalina ignored him and began to climb. The rock was larger than she expected but it was pitted and grooved so climbing was relatively easy once she got going. Soon she was cresting the steep side and she could walk upright up the angled rock face to the top where the shining patch of green was stirring. She could hear Talon behind her scrabbling on the rock. She kept walking determinedly, never breaking stride or eye contact with the green thing. Soon she could make out the shape and knew with a flip-flop of her heart that it was Savath. Savath lay curled up in a ball atop the rock, soaking in the morning rays of the sun. Kalina marched up to the Wyvern and put her hands on her hips.

"Savath! It's Kalina, wake up!" The Wyvern sleepily opened one eye to stare at the slip of a girl in front of it.

"I know who it is, Kalina. What do you and your friend want from me?" The Wyvern lifted its massive head and peered past Kalina to the stumbling Talon who now came running up the rock face to them.

"This is Talon. We waited all night to find you. There are knights in the woods and they are coming to kill you! You must leave!" Kalina said desperately. Savath looked her in the eyes.

"I knew you were here. When I returned late last night, I saw you and young Talon asleep in my cave. I chose to let you sleep rather than wake you up." Talon stood panting next to Kalina from the exertion of the climb, his hands on his knees. Savath sniffed at him in curiosity. Kalina wished with all her heart that the beast had woken them.

"Did you hear me, Savath? You must flee!" Kalina was becoming more desperate by the moment, her panic rising. Savath swung its head towards Kalina.

"From those that are just now climbing my rock?" It looked beyond their shoulders. Kalina and Talon whipped around, and sure enough, a group of knights armed to the teeth were climbing over the edge of the rock. They spotted Kalina, Talon, and the Wyvern and began to yell. She couldn't make out what they were yelling yet but she knew in her bones she had to leave with the Wyvern. There was no way she could go back to the abbey now that Sir Gregan knew who and where she was. She looked at Talon, his green eyes matching the creature beside them. She took his hand.

"I can't go back." Talon nodded sadly in agreement. "I'm going to run with Savath."

"What will I tell Sir Gregan? He can see me now." He gestured to the men coming closer by the second.

"Say you were trying to stop me. That you were following me to see where the Wyvern was and that you tried to talk me out of it, of turning myself in."

"Will I ever see you again?" Kalina looked at him and smiled a soft smile.

"Maybe." And with that, she turned to the Wyvern. "May I ride with you Savath?" The giant lizard nodded its head and lowered its body to the ground. Talon grabbed her arm and pulled her into a tight hug. Kalina hugged him back, and then quickly climbed on to Savath's back. Talon stepped back as Savath beat her wings in a giant sweep, launching them into the sky just as the knights caught up to Talon.

Kalina looked down at the retreating figures of Talon and the knights as she flew higher and higher on Savath. She looked out into the forest and could see the steeple of the Abbey in the distance, getting smaller and smaller as Savath flew towards the Great Grey Mountains. She thought wistfully of her own bed, warm meals, Delisa, and the certainty of her life, but when she saw those snow-capped peaks before her, her heart swelled with excitement, adventure and the unknown.

They flew for hours straight north into the Great Grey Mountains, until the sun was beginning to set in the west. Savath touched down on a rocky outcropping high up on one of the mountains. Kalina slid from her back, her body stiff and sore from clutching the Wyvern's shoulders for so long and the cold of the wind that had seeped into her bones. She shivered and her teeth chattered loudly as she clutched her torso with her hands, trying to keep in what little body heat she had. She'd had her cloak on when they took off, and it wasn't doing nearly enough to combat the cold of the mountain. She looked out over the world, the ledge she was standing on jutting out from the snow-covered, rocky side of the mountain, the wind howling across the surface, a small cave behind her echoing the high keening of the wind.

Savath crouched on the ledge beside her, looking out over the world for a moment, enjoying the setting sun they could see to the west. Despite the cold, Kalina was in awe of the beauty of the world that lay before her. The setting sun threw colors of orange, pink, purple, and blue in a riot across the sky. The deep green of the forest below, the blue, white, and greys of the mountains around her, and in the distance, more greys and deeper blues of large bodies of water to the west. She stood there admiring it all, drinking it in, as Savath beside her turned and lumbered into the cave. Finally, Kalina couldn't handle the cold any longer, her fingers were turning blue, and she could no longer feel her face. She followed the Wyvern inside and soon the chill wind was blocked and the lizard's large bulk began to warm the enclosed space.

"Lie down, Littling, and sleep." Savath's deep voice echoed around the cave. "We will make a plan in the morning." Kalina nodded and yawned, the warmth beginning to lull her to sleep. She laid down beside the Wyvern and a giant wing enclosed her, further keeping in the warmth, and soon she was drifting into an exhausted sleep.

Kalina woke to the sound of the wind. It seemed wind was the only constant this high up on the mountains. She sat up, her body still stiff and sore from the ride, and now from sleeping on the solid rock floor of the cave. Savath crouched at the mouth of the cave, looking out on the world. She approached, wrapping her cloak around herself and munching on the loaf of bread from her pack. She was now very grateful she had packed that loaf of bread. It was stale but her rumbling stomach accepted the food with a grateful gurgle. Savath looked her over with one enormous eye.

"What is your plan, Littling?" Kalina looked out onto the still cold world, down at the green expanse and out into the distance.

"Savath, do you know where there are dragons?" She asked musingly. She had no real plan, other than that she couldn't go back. But she also knew she couldn't stay here. She needed to find her people.

"No, I do not know where the dragons are. I thought they might be here, in the Great Grey Mountains as they have been before, but we are here, and I have not seen any. Only Wyverns live here, and in the forests." Kalina nodded in understanding, chewing on her lip as she thought.

"Then I need to find out where the dragons are. I need to learn, and to find others who might know who I am or why the Prince is so concerned about finding me." Savath looked at her.

"What do you mean, Littling?" Kalina sighed and pulled the crumpled piece of paper out of her pocket.

"I overheard my High Father talking to someone about me. I am

Valdir, one of the dragon riders. And the Prince of Ethea is after me for some reason. He sent those men after me." She paused for a moment, looking out into the distance. "I can't just sit here, not knowing, Savath." Inspiration struck. "I need to go to the capitol, and I need to find people who can help. Maybe a college or huge library." She paused, thinking. "Can you fly me close to the capitol, Ravenhelm and I will walk from there?" Savath nodded its huge head.

"Yes, of course, Kalina." Savath's voice rumbled through her, making her shiver slightly. She was scared of what the future might hold. She had no idea what awaited her in Ravenhelm, and she had no idea who to contact who might know more, but she knew that in order to find her people, she needed to find the dragons.

Chapter 8

THAT NIGHT THEY TOUCHED DOWN in a remote clearing in the forest, and Kalina was grateful for the warm spring breezes that played along the soft grasses growing there. She cut springy spruce boughs and made herself a comfortable bed to sleep on and slept much better than she had the night before, the boughs' spicy scent filling her nostrils. The next morning dawned foggy and dew dripped from every blade of grass in the clearing. Kalina wrapped herself in her cloak before getting up to speak with Savath. She had no more bread left, having finished it the night before for dinner and her empty stomach protested loudly.

"How far from Ravenhelm are we now, Savath?" Savath stretched like a cat, the green scales shaking off the dew that had collected there.

"We are not far. No more than a few hours flight. I will drop you at the edge of the forest." Kalina nodded and gathered her things before they continued their journey. She savored every moment atop Savath's back. She might never fly again if she didn't find her people and the dragons, and despite the cold of the air this high up, she was in love with the feeling of freedom and the views she got to see of a country she never thought she'd ever explore.

She got down off of Savath's back rather reluctantly when they landed. The sun was setting, casting the trees around them in a golden glow. She patted Savath's neck in gratitude.

"Thank you, Savath. I couldn't have done it without you." Savath rumbled deep in its throat, and it sounded to her much like a cat's purr. She impulsively hugged Savath around the neck.

"I will always help you, Littling," Savath said. Savath bent down and blew softly on a small green pebble on the ground. The rock began to glow. Kalina gasped and stepped back.

"This is part of the deep magic. All magical creatures possess it. If you should ever need my help, hold this rock against your chest and call my name. I will come.

"What is the deep magic?" She eyed the rock dubiously.

"Millennia ago, when the world was created, magical creatures like Wyverns and dragons of all kinds sprang from the heart of the sun. We were created with the deep magic, unlike humans who came from the mud of the world itself. We can use it to create small magics, like this." Kalina still didn't understand. Clearly, the Wyverns had their own lore about the way the world was born. Father Martin had taught her about each of the gods, and how Freyre, the Mother, in her benevolence had created one man and one woman from the mud of the world. But there was no magic in his stories.

She bent hesitantly and scooped up the rock, admiring its likeness to the Wyvern's own scales before placing it in her dress pocket. Her eyes brimmed with unshed tears at the kindness. She hugged Savath once again, and before she could change her mind, began walking away towards the city, wiping her eyes on her sleeve. Behind her, she heard the thumping of Savath's huge wings as the giant lizard launched into the sky.

Kalina paused inside the tree line and watched the Wyvern fly away until she could no longer distinguish Savath from the clouds that swallowed it. A melancholy settled into her chest and she felt like some part of her had flown away with the Wyvern. She turned back towards the forest awaiting her and began moving back towards Ravenhelm and whatever adventures awaited her there.

The road leading to Ravenhelm was a bustle of activity: oxen pulling carts laden with goods for the market, horses carrying people to and from the capitol, and travelers on foot. More people passed Kalina on this road than she had ever seen in her entire life at Hywell Abbey. She trudged along the side of the road, away from the carts that churned up the spring mud and flung it onto passersby. A few people gave her curious glances, but she had pulled up the hood of her cloak to cover her face. If she had to remain hidden in the abbey, then her identity must be at risk; she didn't want anyone recognizing her. She realized belatedly that she was putting herself further into danger by entering the capital. The prince lived in the castle within the city walls. But maybe he wouldn't suspect her to be just under his nose.

As dusk began to fall, she finally approached the outside of the sprawling city. Before her rose high walls; inside she could only see rooftops, and high on a hill, a large and imposing castle loomed. Outside the walls, a prospering town had risen, full of those hardy enough to survive without the walls' protection, or those too poor to live inside the walls. To the west of the town ran the Greenfall River, and she knew from maps she'd seen in the abbey's libraries that on the far side, the Ravenhelm Bay stretched into the Emerald Gulf beyond. She had never seen the sea, but as she approached the city, she hoped she could make it through to the other side and stand on the edge of the ocean.

The road became cobbled and less muddy, now crowded with people and wagons, stalls for selling food and trinkets, and buildings. Kalina looked around her in awe, her head whipping back and forth, trying to take in all the sights as well as trying to watch out for danger. Life in the city was more overwhelming than she realized and she urgently wished for a quiet forest glen to sleep in for the night. She had to fight the urge to run from the city as anxiety began to build in her chest at the press of bodies around her.

Torch lighters were out igniting the large torches that lined the streets leading inside the city. As Kalina approached the wall, she noticed the gigantic wooden doors were closed and guards stood outside, not allowing anyone to enter. She milled about, listening to the chatter and gossip around her, wondering what in the world she was going to do now. She had no plan.

"We won't open until sunrise, how many times must I tell you, Nell?" A guard's rough voice cut across the general din of the city. Her heart sank at those words. She was trapped outside the city for the night.

"But my wife'll kill me if I'm late for supper again!" A man's nasally voice called out in desperation.

"Then you should have thought of that before you went off to find yourself a bed to lie in!" The guard retorted, and Kalina caught sight of the pair between passersby just as the guard shoved the older man backward. The man stumbled and tripped, falling hard onto the cobblestones, letting out a grunt of pain as he struck. Kalina rushed over to him, and she levered him up with an arm under his shoulder. Once the man was back on his feet, he looked down at Kalina and smirked.

"What's a pretty little thing like you doing outside the walls so late at night?" His words were slurred and he stank of stale ale. Kalina let go of his arm in a hurry and backed away a few steps, but his hand snaked out and grabbed her upper arm, his grip instantly causing pain. He was strong and fast despite the ale he had been drinking. "Where are you going? Don't you want to keep a man's bed warm for a penny?" Kalina began to panic, her eyes going wide at the thought of what this man might do to her and she tried to shove him off. Suddenly, the man was thrown back once again, and Kalina was dumped onto her bottom in the street.

"Leave her alone, Nell. She doesn't want to sleep with an old codger like you!" The guard who had originally thrown Nell down offered a hand to Kalina, which she eyed warily. "I won't hurt you," he reassured. "Just help you up." Kalina hesitantly put her hand in his much larger one. He hauled her to her feet and she dusted off her skirts before thanking him.

She looked into his face more carefully. He had kind green eyes, and a shock of brown hair that stood at unruly attention atop his head, reminding her vaguely of Talon. He could not have been more than a few years older than she, perhaps in his mid-twenties. His livery fit him very well and he had a nice smile.

"Why were you helping him?" He asked, his smile slightly crooked.

"Because he had fallen." Her answer seemed silly now, but she hadn't known he was drunk or that he was a disgusting pig.

"Well, next time, steer clear of drunkards at night." The man eyed her. "Are you new here? I've not seen you before." She nodded, wondering if he was someone she could trust.

"Do you know somewhere I can sleep for the night?"

"Do you have any money?" She shook her head. She didn't want him knowing about the small stash of coins in her pack. The man rubbed his chin. "I suppose you could sleep on our kitchen floor. Won't be much but it will be clean and dry and safe. Perhaps my wife will even let you help her with the washing for a coin or two. What do you say?" Kalina was hesitant to accept but this was the first person not to yell at her to get out of the way, shove her, or curse at her. But this man had kind eyes, and his offer was more than she could have hoped for.

"Thank you. I would really appreciate the help." She made a small curtsey. The man laughed and shook his head.

"No need to curtsey to me, girl. I'm just a lowly guard. Save those for the nobility or the King." He stuck out a hand to her. "I'm

Anders. Who are you?" Kalina took his hand.

"I'm Kalina."

"Well Kalina, welcome to Ravenhelm!" He gestured behind himself at the great stone wall. "I promise it's more interesting in the daylight." He looked over at his fellow door guard. "Hey, Clary, can you watch for a few moments while I walk Miss Kalina here to my home?" The other guard nodded. "It's just through here." He opened a postern gate in the side of the wall and ushered her through. Her eyes widened as she went through, not quite believing that she was actually inside the city. The gate closing behind her made her feel nervous, like there was nowhere to run to now, and she was trapped inside the walled city forever. She took deep breaths, reminding herself she was here for a purpose, and it helped to calm her hammering heart. Houses immediately rose up around her, nicer and less worn down than those outside the gates.

"It's just up here." Anders gestured with his arm as he turned up a side street and led her along, each side of the street lined in comfortable small houses, each sharing a wall with the next house. It was a bit cramped, but Kalina was reassured by the small flower boxes in the windows and colorful curtains closed for the night, the light inside sending bright multi-hued squares onto the cobblestones.

Anders turned left into a small house with blue and white flowers in a window box and blue curtains on the windows. He pushed open the door and light poured out, drenching Kalina in it's welcoming warmth. She cautiously followed, keeping an eye on the door behind her, ready to flee at the first sign of danger. The house was cozily appointed, soft cushioned furniture with bright blue and white scarves thrown over them. The living room hosted a fireplace, a couch, and a table, and it bled into the small kitchen with a wooden table and chairs and a small sink. By the sink stood a plump, very pretty, young woman in a yellow homespun linen gown, who looked to be about 8 months pregnant. She turned, her rosy cheeks and curling brown hair making her possibly the loveliest person Kalina had ever met. Anders kissed his wife on the cheek and gestured to Kalina.

"Well, my dear, I found this poor thing by the gate. Nell was trying to steal her away so I snatched her up and brought her here." He smiled broadly at Kalina who ducked her head in equal parts shame and shyness. She had never been shy in her life, but being in these people's home felt odd, and yet, strangely comfortable. "She's new to the city and doesn't have any money so I thought she could help you out with washing and cleaning and mending and we could give her a few pennies and a place to sleep." Anders' wife nodded, giving a warm smile to Kalina.

"What's your name, dear?" Her voice was like a melody and she gestured for Kalina to sit at the rough kitchen table. Kalina sat before answering.

"I'm Kalina, m'lady." She had never been taught the proper titles for people of higher rank, so she went with what she'd heard a noblewoman called by Gwen once.

"Oh, my dear, I'm no lady! You may call me Calla." She smiled and lowered herself into a chair. "I'm glad my Anders found you, Kalina. I'm finding that I sure could use the help more and more these days." She ran a smoothing hand over her protruding belly.

"When are you due?" Kalina suddenly flushed, realizing that her question could be considered rude, but Calla just chuckled.

"I'm about 8 ½ months along. Won't be too much longer now till the baby comes." Anders put a hand on Calla's shoulder and squeezed. She looked up at him lovingly and touched his hand. "You better get back to your shift, my love." Anders nodded and then bent to kiss his wife on the mouth. Kalina looked away, not used to seeing such public displays of affection. In fact, besides a handful of times Gwen had given her a hug for a scraped knee or a twisted ankle, or Delisa giving her a hug, Kalina had never received much physical affection. Her kissing Talon's cheek was as far as it went. Something stirred in her chest at the thought.

"I'll see you both at half past midnight." And with that, he left the house, the room feeling slightly larger after his absence, and Kalina realized just how small the house was. Calla looked Kalina over.

"Have you eaten?"

"No, ma'am. I haven't eaten since yesterday morning." Calla's eyes went wide.

"Well, then let's get you something to eat and then we can make you up a bed." Kalina nodded gratefully and watched awkwardly as Calla got up from the chair and began ladling a bowl of soup and slicing a generous hunk of bread and placing it, with a large pat of butter, on the table before her. Kalina's eye went round at the sight and her stomach growled so loudly that it startled Calla into a laugh. "Oh my! You must be hungry!" Kalina nodded.

"Thank you, Calla," she mumbled around a mouth full of hot stew.

Once her belly was full, she took her plate to the sink where she washed and dried it, placing it back on the neat little shelves above the sink. Calla disappeared into the upstairs and came down a moment later dragging a pile of blankets and a pillow. She dumped it on the floor beside the small fireplace, her face shining with sweat.

"I could have helped with that!" Kalina said.

"You can help drag down the rush mattress then. You'll have to fill it with fresh rushes in the morning, I'm afraid it's a bit moldy." Kalina nodded and followed Calla back up the stairs to find the small rush mattress in a hall closet, and dragged it down the stairs. Calla relaxed on the small couch, watching Kalina set up a little nest of blankets for herself. Calla smiled indulgently and Kalina felt a warmth in her belly from the kindness of the woman and her husband.

"Thank you again, Calla," Kalina said as she snuggled down and Calla began to make her way up the stairs to her own bedroom. Calla turned and smiled.

"Of course, dear." Kalina closed her eyes and slept the best sleep she'd ever slept.

Chapter 9

KALINA WOKE TO SUNLIGHT streaming in through the front windows, the curtains billowing slightly in the morning breeze. She sat up, rubbing her eyes, and her hood slipped off her head, taking her head scarf with it, the inch or so of bright silver hair capping her head reflecting the sunlight, the rest a dull brown hanging to the middle of her back. A gasp sounded from the kitchen and Kalina spun to see Calla standing with her hand over her mouth, gaping at Kalina's silver hair. Kalina quickly tucked it back into her headscarf, fear clawing its way up her throat.

"No, please, your hair is so lovely, don't feel like you have to hide it from me!" Calla said, reaching out as if to touch the silver locks from across the room. Kalina paused, her heart pounding in her chest, and pulled off her scarf. It felt good to have it uncovered. She unclasped her cloak and struggled out of the covers, the morning sun warming the room enough that she no longer felt the need for the cloak. She walked into the kitchen, Calla's eyes on her the entire way.

"Do you know who I am?" Kalina felt a desperate hope building in her chest, that this woman knew about the Valdir, and could tell her.

"I know of your people, I think." Calla gazed at the silver inch of hair. "You can, of course, keep it uncovered in our house, but I think that maybe you were right to be cautious. I will get you a prettier scarf to cover it when you are out in the city, alright?" Kalina relaxed, pulling out a chair at the table to sit, Calla coming over beside her and slicing her a piece of bread. A knot of excitement squirmed in Kalina's chest.

"Can you tell me about my people?" Kalina buttered the bread and began eating, her stomach rumbling at the food. Calla nodded and began pouring some warm goat's milk into a mug for Kalina.

"I only know what my mother told me, and what I remember as a child." Kalina gestured for Calla to continue. "There once were dragon riders, the ones who tamed the beasts and rode the winds. They were a tough folk, brave, living in the wild with their mounts, living off the land. And each of them was said to have silver hair." She reached out to brush the silver atop Kalina's head. "But none of them have been seen for well over a decade I thought, and yet, here you are." Calla looked at Kalina, a small smile on her face. "Where are you from?"

"I'm from Hywell Abbey, in the Deep Glen Forest. I was abandoned there as a baby. Beyond that, I don't know where I'm from, or who my people are." Something made Kalina tell the woman the truth. Calla nodded.

"There are no more dragons, for that matter. No one has seen one for almost fifteen years, at least not around these parts." Calla began washing the breakfast dishes and Kalina got up to help dry.

"What happened to the dragons?" Kalina put away the last of the dishes and went to tidy her corner of blankets and to pull out the rush mattress.

"Well," Calla sighed and sat down, putting her feet up on a chair and stroking her belly. "The dragons disappeared after the Long War ended. You know the one," Kalina shook her head. She only knew bits and pieces and she wanted to hear what this woman knew. "Well, almost seventy years ago a war started between Askor and Ethea. The dragon riders, your people were called the Valdir, fought as mercenaries alongside our kings. We fought Askor for the resources that the Great Grey Mountains have. Askor is a barren, cold country full of ice and tundra. Their only land suitable for farming was in the south, in the lake lands that butt up against the mountains. Ethea had mining communities throughout the mountains, mining everything from precious metals to iron and coal. It was what powered our country, and brought us great profit in trade. But Askor felt it was theirs by right and they began raiding our mining towns, taking over the mines, and killing our people.

"Our king paid the Valdir in gold and iron to get rid of the Askorians, and the fight raged on for fifty years. Finally, the king of the Valdir, for they had a king, despite not having a kingdom, had had enough. He had had an agreement with the king for his only son to marry the princess, but the king of Ethea signed a peace treaty with Askor and gave his daughter in marriage to their youngest son. The king of the Valdir was offended, and his people had been poorly paid, generations of his young fighters had been killed, along with a decrease in the dragon population. So he ordered his people and his dragons to withdraw, never to be heard from again. Some speculate they are somewhere in the Great Grey Mountains, biding their time, and hoarding the gold and iron for themselves. Some say they disappeared south into The Wastes and whatever lies beyond. No one really knows. And the Great Grey Mountains have remained abandoned except for a few small mining towns on the borders, neither Askor, nor Ethea owns them now. No one does. And our country and economy have suffered for the lack of mining and the prosperousness we once enjoyed."

Calla finished and glanced over at Kalina who was sitting amidst her blankets, a far off look on her face. "Oh, now look at me, going on about some long-dead war. Let's get your mattress some new rushes and we can get to our washing." Calla hoisted herself up from the couch and motioned for the still stunned Kalina to follow her. Kalina jumped up out of the nest of blankets and dragged her mattress with her.

She spent that afternoon refilling her rush mattress and helping Calla do the laundry of the house. Her mind raced over the information Calla had given her while she worked, pulling apart and piecing it together until she felt like maybe, just maybe she might fit somewhere in the story. Perhaps she was the child of some Valdir who couldn't take her with them, or who died in the fighting and sent her to the abbey. But that still didn't explain the prince's obsession with finding her. Another thought struck her and she paused in her washing. Perhaps the prince still felt threatened by the Valdir, and since she was the only Valdir that anyone knew of, that was why he was after her.

She found that Calla also took in washing for the neighborhood in order to make a few extra pennies, and Kalina helped her with the neighbor's washing. Calla had found Kalina a pretty green scarf to wrap around her head to hide her silver hair, and as the day went on, Kalina found herself growing more and more fond of Calla and Anders. Calla talked of Anders like he was the only thing in the world that mattered, and Kalina felt a soft longing begin in her breast. She hoped one day she would find someone to love the way Calla had.

Anders came home not long after dark from his shift and he helped Kalina make dinner for Calla while Calla rested on the couch with her feet up. Kalina and Anders joked and chatted, and she found him to be a decent man, who cared deeply about his wife and the people he encountered every day. He told her a story about an old woman who came begging daily that he often bought lunch for. Or the young beggar children who ran the streets just outside the wall, and how he often found small errands for them to run so they could make some extra coin.

The first few weeks passed in a comfortable blur for Kalina, and soon she realized she had lost her purpose for being in Ravenhelm. She had begun to learn small bits about the part of the city where Anders and Calla lived. They lived on Waterside, just north of the seaside and the docks. It was full of working-class people, all working hard to survive. Kalina had walked down to the quay with Calla one sunny afternoon and had finally stood on the edge of the boardwalk and looked out onto the great blue-grey expanse of The Emerald Ocean. She had felt free standing there, listening to the gulls cry overhead and hearing the lapping of the waves below her on the quay. It reminded her longingly of flying on Savath. Her chest ached as she realized she had focused so much on blending in with Anders and Calla's lives that she had forgotten all about Savath and the dragons. She felt ashamed that even Calla's story had not occupied her mind more frequently than it had, but it had been so nice to be wanted and cared for that she hadn't wanted to think of leaving.

Temple day dawned misty and cool, one of the last vestiges of winter, and Kalina knew she needed to find her way out into the city. Calla invited her to go to the temple with them, and she agreed, knowing that it might be a good way to learn a bit more of the city layout.

Calla had bought Kalina a new dress earlier that week because Kalina's was ripped and stained from her time with Savath in the woods and her time working hard in the Abbey. It was a pale green, like spring grass and it matched her headscarf nicely. She twirled in the middle of the kitchen, admiring the way the dress fell and how it felt on her body. She had also begun to fill out a bit since joining Calla and Anders. Calla smiled indulgently as she watched Kalina twirl, resting a hand on her now dropped belly. Kalina glanced over and thought about that baby, and how it wouldn't be long now. It would be good for her to find the answers she sought because she would bet that once the baby came, she would be forced back out onto the streets. No matter how useful she was, no one wanted an orphan girl around when there was a brand-new baby to care for.

The three of them walked to the temple in the center of Fort Heights, the richest area of town. Kalina looked around in awe at the huge houses, walled off on their own, tourettes and towers peaking up behind the walls, and large columns of rock adorning the front gates. There were flowers everywhere once they entered the temple street, and the crowds grew thicker. Kalina became a bit claustrophobic at the press of people around her, and she reached for Calla's hand in fear of getting separated. But Calla's hand wasn't there. Kalina looked around in panic, trying to spot Ander's dark unruly hair or Calla's pregnant belly in the crowd. But all she saw was a mass of bodies, each one looking the same as the next and her chest began to tighten, her breathing coming faster. She had to get out of there and into open space or she felt she might burst apart.

She pushed her way sideways through the crowd, away from where the press of people were going into the temple proper, and instead, she made for a tree she saw in a side courtyard. Finally, the people around her thinned and she didn't have to fight her way through anymore. Her breaths were still ragged and she stumbled as she ran towards the tree. She clung to its trunk, squeezing her eyes shut and feeling the scrape of the rough bark on her cheek. The sounds began to fade around her and she heard only the sound of her own heartbeat.

She had never seen so many people in one place, and the press of bodies along with losing Calla and Anders made the experience all the scarier. Suddenly, there was a soft hand on her back and her eyes flew open as a figure came into view.

"Kalina?" The voice was familiar and as her panic began to lessen, Kalina recognized the young, boyish face before her.

"Talon?" Her eyes were bright with tears, both from the panic she'd endured and from finding a friendly face. She broke away from the tree and threw her arms around him, gripping him tight as if he were her lifeline. He laughed awkwardly and began to pat her back.

"I thought that was you!" He pushed her away a little and she let go, embarrassment replacing her relief. "How did you get here? Did Savath fly you here? Where are you staying?" His questions were rapid fire and Kalina reached out a hand to slow him down.

"Can we sit?" Her voice was pleading and Talon nodded, leading them to a nearby bench beneath the tree. Kalina sat gratefully and sighed before turning to her friend. "Yes, Savath flew me here. I've been here for almost two weeks already, staying with a guard and his wife."

"Two weeks? I can't believe I ran into you!" Talon's voice was a comfort to Kalina. She felt squeezed from all sides, the sounds of the temple district too much for her to handle. She took slow deep breaths, focusing on Talon as her anchor. Soon the darkness around the edges of her vision began to fade and she felt grounded in her body once again. She realized she'd lost track of what Talon had been saying and she focused in on his voice. "....and after Sir Dyelan brought me back to Ravenhelm he beat me and then made me work in the stables. I wasn't allowed a break or a day off until today." Kalina nodded, trying to fill in the gaps of his story.

"What happened at the abbey?" Her voice was steadier than before.

"Your High Father was livid. He wouldn't stop yelling at Sir Dyelan, calling him all sorts of names you wouldn't think a High Father knew! He was so angry you had gotten away." Talon paused, eyeing her. "Were you a prisoner there Kalina?"

"No, I suspect he was more worried than angry." She couldn't forget the conversation she'd overheard Father Martin saying to the stranger, that he had wanted to protect her from the prince; and while she wanted to make that choice for herself, she understood why he had hidden it from her.

"Oh, well, good," he said rather awkwardly. Kalina looked around the square. The temple crowd had gone, all the worshipers now inside the great stone building dedicated to the Freyre, the benevolent Mother. She vaguely wondered if Calla and Anders would be worried about her absence. But she knew her way back to their house and if all else failed, she'd meet them back there. "So!" Talon's voice pulled her from her thoughts. "What are your plans now that you are here?"

"Well, that's kind of complicated." Kalina wondered whether or not to tell him the truth, about who she was and the danger she was in. She sat for a moment, eyeing him. His face was open and sincere, and he had managed to keep her secret this far, claiming he was trying to stop her when she'd fled on Savath. She needed help and perhaps he could help her. "Talon, do you have access to the royal archives and library?"

"Of course! I go there to meet with my tutor every morning when we are in the capital." She let out the breath she hadn't known she was holding.

"Do you think you could get me access as well?"

"Well, you have to be a scholar or scribe to have access or a nobleman." Kalina's face fell. There was no way she'd be able to gain access that way. "But perhaps if we get you a job inside the castle you could sneak into the library." Kalina brightened.

"Really? Oh, that'd be amazing!" She gripped his arm. He laughed.

"It'd be a big risk," he said slowly. "What do you need access for?"

"I know it'd be a risk but I promise it's worth it." She turned to face him fully, adjusting her headscarf slightly, self-conscious all of a sudden. "I need to find the dragons and my people."

"The dragon riders?" he scratched his head, thinking. "Makes sense. Our library is bigger than the one at the abbey. But aren't you putting yourself in more danger by being here? Right under the prince's nose, where Sir Gregan might find you?"

"I doubt they'd expect me to be here. Besides, Sir Gregan has never seen me up close." She could only hope she was right.

"Well," he said, eying her. "Let me see what I can do."

Chapter 10

KALINA PUSHED THE DOOR TO Anders and Calla's house open, hoping to find them home, but instead found an empty kitchen. She collapsed onto her bed, her body and mind exhausted from the excitement of the day. It was strange how something as simple as being in a crowd like that took more out of her than a hard day's work. Homesickness washed over her, and suddenly she was longing for the company of Delisa and Gwen and the freedom of the forest at their backs.

She had always just run out to the woods whenever she felt trapped or hemmed in. Freedom, open spaces, and solitude had always called to her. Living in a city, while exciting, was constantly draining her. She laid back, throwing an arm over her eyes. And she had just asked Talon to get her into the castle, one of the busiest places in the kingdom. What had she been thinking? She hadn't managed to hide her hair here in this house with Calla and Anders, how was she going to hide it everywhere else? At the abbey, her hair had been a novelty, one that Gwen helped her hide with dyes, but the people who dwelled in the forest didn't know the significance of her hair color. In a city, and in the castle, filled with scholars, the king, the prince, and Sir Gregan, she would stand out like a sore thumb. She had to find more dye.

Two hours later Calla and Anders came home. Calla came into the room, worry and fear written on her round, pretty face. She was clutching her belly and breathing hard, Anders directly behind her.

"Slow down, love. Take a seat, I'm sure Kalina is alright." He tried to steer her towards a chair but she pushed him off, calling out instead.

"Kalina? Are you here?" Kalina who had fallen asleep, sat up from her bed in the corner, rubbing her eyes, her headscarf partially slid off her head.

"Yes, Calla, I'm here." Calla let out a huge sigh of relief and sat heavily in the chair Anders had pulled out for her.

"Oh, thank the Mother." Kalina smiled and came over to her, taking her hands and rubbing them softly. "We thought something terrible had happened to you when we lost you in the crowd. Anders said you'd probably just stayed in the back and we'd find you afterward, but when you weren't there waiting, I feared the worst." Her voice was getting steadier and her breathing was slowing down. Anders looked less concerned now and turned his attention to the girl.

"What happened? Where were you?" Kalina blushed slightly. She hadn't meant to worry them. Calla didn't need anything stressing her out this close to her pregnancy.

"I got separated from you in the crowd so I made my way to that big tree in the courtyard. And then I saw an old friend. He stayed with me and helped me find my way back here." She bustled to make some tea while she talked, hanging the kettle to boil over the fire in the hearth, throwing on another log. Anders helped Calla put her feet up on another chair.

"What friend?" Calla asked, running a hand over her belly. She was so large now that walking for any length of time was a challenge. Kalina had been doing the washing the last few days herself as Calla's belly dropped and her back began to hurt more.

"I knew him back in the Abbey. He said he can get me a job in the castle, help me learn a bit more about my heritage." Calla looked up sharply.

"Is that smart, Kalina? Telling someone about who you are?" Her voice held concern but it put Kalina on the defensive.

"Of course. I trust him." Calla looked away. Anders just stood there, unsure how to intervene. "Besides, I will be careful. I was hoping you'd help me dye my hair tomorrow Calla," she said, changing the subject. Calla nodded, not looking at Kalina.

"Some Mountain Alder would work I should think," Calla said smoothing her dress around her legs and rearranging her feet on the chair before her. Kalina smiled as she pulled the steaming kettle from the fire and began to pour it into mugs. Anders came over and placed the tea leaves into the mugs, a pleasant aroma of rose and mint filling the small room.

"I'll get some from the market tomorrow." Kalina handed a mug to Calla who finally smiled back.

"We were just very worried, Kalina. I know you have only been here for a short time, but you've become a part of our little family." Anders smiled and nodded beside his wife, a hand on her shoulder.

"Thank you." Kalina felt a lump form in her throat looking at these two lovely people. She didn't know how she'd gotten so lucky as to find them but her heart swelled to see them. She'd never been a part of a family before, and while Calla felt more like a wise older sister than a mother, she was still so grateful for the simple fact that they worried about her well-being.

Kalina fell asleep that night with her heart full, looking forward to the next day.

"I found the Mountain Alder." Kalina burst into the house, clutching a small cloth bag in her hand. Calla turned from the pot of water she had boiling on the stove.

"Give it here." Kalina excitedly handed it over and watched as Calla crumpled the bark into a mortar and ground it to dust. Then she took a small measure of the hot water and began adding it to the powder, working it into a paste. "Now, take off your scarf and come over here." Kalina obliged, unwinding her scarf and letting her long silver locks fall down her back. Calla settled an old sack across her shoulders to protect her dress from the dye and then she began covering her hair inch by inch in the strange, woody smelling paste. "We have to wait at least an hour for it to settle into your hair and then we can rinse it out," Calla said, rinsing her hands in some clean water. Her skin was already turning a light brown until the water washed the dye away.

"How long will it last? How often will I need to re-dye it?" Kalina resisted the urge to touch her head which felt wet and warm and heavy. Her scalp itched just behind her ear and it was beginning to drive her crazy, but she resisted the urge to scratch.

"This may last a month if you don't wash your hair too often. But by then you'll begin to see some growth at the top and we'll need to cover it up." Kalina nodded, hopping down off the stool she had been perched on and began helping Calla clean up.

"So, every two weeks?" This dye lasted longer than the one Gwen used.

"Yes."

They busied themselves cleaning up the house while Kalina's hair set. Calla had her hang her head over the sink as she poured warm water over her scalp, scrubbing until the water ran clear. Just as Calla was wringing out Kalina's hair she grabbed her belly and let out a grunt as water splashed onto the floor below her.

"Oh. Kalina, dear, I think the baby's coming." Kalina grabbed her hair, winding it tight and letting the water drain off as she stood up straight, fear shooting coldly through her body.

"What do I do?" She tried to keep her tone even but her own panic was beginning to show. Calla, however, was calm as could be. She breathed deeply through her nose and out her mouth, one hand holding her belly, the other braced on the table.

"Go down the street and take a left at the butcher's shop. Two doors down on the left is the midwife. Bring her back here." She grunted again and began breathing fast as she slowly made her way towards the couch. Kalina put an arm under her and helped her sit before she ran out the front door and down the street. It didn't occur to her that she was actually outside, with her wet light brown hair streaming behind her and no headscarf until she was turning onto the butcher's street. It was freeing.

Ten minutes later Kalina burst through the door, an older woman in tow. The woman came in and placed her bag on the table as Kalina went to Calla who was panting regularly now.

"How are you doing, Calla?" the midwife said as she rinsed her hands in a basin of fresh water she'd poured.

"I think it's coming fast, Gadelle." Calla's voice was strained as she pushed her words out between breaths. Kalina sat beside her, holding her hand.

"Girl!" Gadelle's voice was commanding and sharp.

"My name is Kalina."

"Fine. Kalina then. Go fetch some fresh linens. We will need something to catch the blood and something to wrap the baby in." Kalina's face blanched at the words but jumped up to obey. She ran up the stairs and opened the old wooden wardrobe Calla and Anders had in their bedroom. When she returned carrying the clean bed sheets, Gadelle had helped Calla down to the floor and was checking up her dress. Kalina placed the stack of linens on the couch.

"What can I do to help?" Gadelle looked up, her eye softening at Kalina's obvious nervousness.

"Lay one of those out on the ground here, beside Calla. Then boil us a kettle of water to start." Kalina jumped to obey, the busy work helping her to keep her mind off Calla's grunts that were turning into moans and cries of pain.

"Now, lift your bottom dear while I put this beneath you." Gadelle's voice was calming, soothing as she worked. "There you go. Now, this baby is coming fast, unusual for a first pregnancy but it's nothing to worry about. On your next pain, I want you to push!" Kalina swung the kettle over the fire and turned in time to see Calla bearing down.

Calla pushed for an hour and despite the midwife's prediction, the baby seemed to be content to stay where it was. Gadelle frowned and reached to check once again. She felt all around and pushed her fingers into Calla's swollen belly, the frown deepening on her face. Kalina paced, constantly checking and rechecking the boiling water, refilling it as it boiled off.

"Calla, I think your baby might be the wrong way around." Calla was covered in sweat, her face bright red and her chest heaving as she rested between contractions. "We're going to have to move the baby if we can." Calla nodded. Kalina hovered behind the couch, wringing her hands in nervousness. She had seen calves and foals being born and had watched a dog giving birth but never a woman. And once, she'd helped the stable master when a foal was stuck. It had almost killed the mother and the baby had come out with a broken leg. The stable master had to put the foal down as the leg couldn't be fixed. She prayed to the gods it was different with human babies.

Gadelle pushed on Calla's belly, trying to rotate the baby. Kalina watched as the bulge on Calla's belly began to shift slowly. Gadelle was breathing hard now, and Calla was crying out in pain as the midwife continued to push and prod her belly, shifting the baby so that it was facing the right direction.

"Your baby was sideways Calla, that's why it wouldn't come out. I think I've got the head in position now. On your next contraction, push as hard as you can. I need him out." Kalina came around the couch and knelt beside Calla, offering her hand to grip. Calla looked at her gratefully before pushing. "That's it, girl, that's it. I can see the head!" Kalina looked excitedly at Calla.

"You hear that, Calla? Your baby's almost here!" Calla cried out as she pushed again, her grip on Kalina's hand grinding the small bones together. Kalina gritted her teeth against the pain and kept encouraging Calla.

"Slowly now, Calla," The midwife was inspecting the baby's head carefully, concern clear on her face. "Now push, Calla, push." Urgency was in her voice and Calla responded, fear blossoming on her face as she bared down, sweat pouring off her brow.

Suddenly, there was gushing and the baby came free, Gadelle catching the tiny body and Kalina watching as she unwrapped the cord that had wrapped around the baby's neck. Calla was panting, her head drifting back against the couch behind her. Kalina rubbed her hand rhythmically, both to comfort Calla and herself. There was no cry, no wailing from the newborn baby, and Gadelle stuck her finger in its tiny mouth, trying to clear its airway. When that didn't work, Gadelle gently flipped the baby on its belly across her arm and began rubbing it's back vigorously.

A few horrible moments passed by with no sounds but Calla's labored breathing and the crackling of the fire.

"Why isn't my baby crying?" Calla's voice was weak but it didn't waver. Kalina squeezed her hand, completely unsure of what to say. Suddenly, the quiet was broken by a loud cry from the small body in Gadelle's arms. Kalina let out a breath and smiled broadly at Calla.

"Your baby is going to be fine!" Kalina said, and her heart soared as Gadelle began wrapping the baby in a clean linen sheet, wiping away the blood and mucus that covered it.

"Congratulations, Calla dear, you have a baby girl." Gadelle handed the small form to Calla's open and waiting arms. Then she turned to Kalina. "Kalina, I need you to run and get Anders. Tell him his wife has had a rough birth and that he needs to come swiftly. Kalina nodded and ran from the house, a mixture of excitement and the remaining fear thrilling through her.

She found Anders at his usual post by the gate, laughing and joking with his fellow guards. She came running up, a small cloud of dust from the road rising around her. She panted hard as she halted, putting her hands on her knees. Anders turned to look at her, worry and confusion crossing his face.

"What is it, Kalina?" An edge of fear entering his voice. Kalina held up a hand as she willed her breathing to slow.

"Calla had her baby," she panted. "It was a rough birth. You need to come home." Anders sprang into action, turning to his fellow guards and ordering them to watch the gate, then grabbing his cloak from the guard house. Then he ran past her down the street. Kalina lifted a hand. "I'll follow behind!" She wasn't even sure he heard her in his haste to get to his wife but she didn't care. She followed more slowly, letting her body recover from hours of tension and the running.

Chapter 11

THE NEXT FEW DAYS WERE A blur for Kalina. She had worried that she would get in the way within Calla and Anders' household once the baby was born. That somehow, she wouldn't be important anymore or needed, and they would be excited for her to leave and go work in the castle. But she was wrong. Every time the baby cried, especially in the middle of the night, it was her job to get up with Calla and put the kettle on for tea. Calla preferred to sip hot tea while nursing, it helped to keep her awake and helped her replace her fluids. Sometimes she asked Kalina for a little toasted bread with butter or jam as well. Kalina was only too happy to help the new mother but she was becoming rather sleep deprived.

One morning about a week later, as Kalina was washing the dishes, there was a knock on the door. She wiped her hands on her apron and answered the door, surprise crossing her face as she saw Talon standing on the doorstep. His face lit in a wide grin as he beheld her light brown hair.

"Well, that certainly works as a great disguise!" Kalina laughed and stood aside, letting him in. Calla sat on the couch; the baby cradled in her arms as she rocked her to sleep.

"Calla, may I introduce Talon. The boy I told you about." She and Calla had had many conversations over the last week and Kalina had told the woman everything, including those bits about Talon. Calla smiled at the young man.

"Pleased to meet you, young Talon. Won't you come in and have some tea with us?" She gestured to Kalina and she jumped to heat the kettle. Talon seemed to have been growing, and he tried to fold his lanky body into a chair at the table.

"Thank you, Mistress Calla. Kalina, I got you a job at the castle!" He burst out with it as if he couldn't hold the news in any longer. "It's working in the kitchen as a scullery maid but it will get you a spot in the castle and access to the libraries." His face was so hopeful Kalina couldn't resist.

"That's great, Talon, thank you." Kalina handed him a cup ready for the water once it was boiling.

"When does she start? And how much does it pay? Does she get days off?" Calla asked as she placed the baby in a small rocking bassinet and came to sit at the table across from Talon. Kalina continued to bustle around setting out a small plate of shortbread biscuits on the table.

"Well, the woman who runs the kitchen is named Mistress Aynne and she's a decent sort. She works her girls hard but she's not cruel. I figured with your experience in the abbey's kitchens this job would be simple for you." Talon gestured towards Kalina as she poured the steaming water from the kettle into their mugs, the sweet aroma of chamomile and lemon wafting in the air. "You would sleep there; they have dormitories but you'd have one day off a week to come into the city if you wanted." He looked to Calla, who was eyeing him thoughtfully. Kalina took a seat at the table, brushing her hair back from her face. "It really is a good color on you Kalina." Talon hedged.

"So, when do I start?" Talon grinned at her.

"Tomorrow morning, just after dawn. She said report to the kitchen. I'll come by and pick you up at the front gate just before then and walk you up there." They sat together sipping their tea, Calla asking questions to get to know Talon and Kalina asking questions about the castle. Finally, as the sun began to set, Talon left and Kalina helped clear the dishes as Calla breastfed the baby.

"Do you trust him?" Calla asked again.

"Yes of course. Like I said before. I trust him." Calla sighed.

"I just want to make sure. He's risking his life and his job to help you get into the castle." Calla's voice was soothing. Kalina weighed her words carefully before responding.

"I know. I'll be careful."

"Will you come visit?" The question took Kalina off guard.

"Of course, I will."

"I wondered. You've been with us for only a short time, we didn't want to expect anything." Calla smiled warmly at her.

"You are family," Kalina said, barely managing to keep her voice steady.

"Oh, Kalina." She held out her arm for Kalina, her other still cradling the baby, and for the first time, Kalina embraced the woman. It felt strange, holding this woman as though she were her mother. This embrace was different from any other she'd experienced. Calla smelled wonderful, like milk and honey, and Kalina imagined this was what her own mother would smell like. She felt a hard, knotted place within her unfold a bit as she held Calla, the soft sounds of the baby beside her.

She pulled away and sat, watching the baby.

"Have you come up with a name yet?" Calla had hesitated on naming her little girl for fear of losing her, but Gadelle had assured her the day before that the baby was healthy and gaining weight properly, despite the rough birth. Calla smiled down at the sweet face and brushed a finger across the baby's cheek.

"I think I have. Anders and I talked about it last night and we're going to name her after his mother. Issa." Kalina smiled and reached out to stroke the fine baby hairs on the baby's head.

"Hello, Issa." She whispered.

The next morning came too quickly and too early for Kalina, who was still waking up multiple times a night to help Calla feed Issa. She struggled out of bed, packing what few things she'd acquired over the weeks into a small carry sack that Anders had bought for her. She had two dresses now, a few head scarfs just in case her roots were showing, and a few odd items that Calla had bought her in the market. She wished she had a pair of pants like boys wore but Calla had insisted that a young girl, and now a scullery maid, wore dresses. One day maybe she would wear pants so she could really run, or ride a dragon.

Perhaps, if she was able to discover where her people and dragons were, she could get pants for the journey. The thought made her smile. Riding Savath had been difficult enough with her skirts from the abbey. Pants would have made it so much easier.

She said a sleepy goodbye to Calla and Issa, and then Anders walked her through the quiet streets of Ravenhelm, the market stalls just being put up in the city center, the vendors quietly bustling around. Anders placed a comforting hand on her shoulder as they approached the gates, the sun just beginning to turn the sky to the east a light pink. Kalina stopped before the huge oak gates, with guards standing at attention on either side and swallowed hard. Where had her bravery gone? She had been so brave to leave her home at the abbey and fly away on Savath, and then again when she'd entered the capital, but this? Maybe she had grown too comfortable with Calla and Anders. Maybe feeling like she finally belonged made it that much harder to walk away. She could see them once a week on her day off, but this castle felt like a million miles away.

Anders spoke to the guards, and soon the gates were swinging open to reveal a short tunnel through stone, and beyond, a great dirt road leading up to the castle proper. Kalina stared, her stomach fluttering with what felt like dozens of bees. Anders stood before her and placed both his hands on her shoulders. He bent down, his brown hair was getting long, falling into his face as it was in need of a cut. His green eyes shown with pride.

"I've never met a braver girl than you, Kalina. You will do great." He pulled her in for a hug and Kalina breathed in the leather and dust smell of him, trying to fix it in her mind. An unexpected lump formed in her throat. "Don't forget to visit us. And be careful." Kalina nodded into his shoulder. He stepped away from her as she looked at the gate entrance and saw Talon waiting there for her.

"I'll see you both in a week!" She waved at Anders as she walked towards Talon, anticipation churning her gut. As she walked under the archway, she felt like there was a shift, some sort of change, and she squared her shoulders, ready to take on whatever was thrown at her next.

Chapter 12

KALINA AND TALON STOOD outside the door to the kitchens in mildly awkward silence. Kalina wasn't eager to go inside and Talon said Mistress Aynne would come to meet them. She glanced down at her homespun dark green woolen dress and smoothed it with her free hand. She wasn't nearly as nervous. Talon had been right; this was a job she knew how to do. Talon looked at his shoes beside her, bending to rub some dirt off.

Suddenly the silence was broken when the old kitchen door was pushed open and a stern looking woman with curling black hair pulled back from her round face stepped out. She was in her late 40's; a few grey whips around the edges of her hair gave her a dignified look. She was plump, as all good cooks should be, and her hands looked like those of a fighter, scarred and calloused. Kalina stepped forward.

"Mistress Aynne, this is Kalina," Talon introduced. "She's the girl I told you about." Kalina wondered vaguely what Talon had said about her as she reached out her hand to shake the cook's hand. Mistress Aynne looked her over from head to toe.

"You look capable enough, not too skinny. You never know what you will get these days in terms of help, and I'm glad I won't have to feed you up before putting you to work." She stepped back into the doorway motioning for Kalina to follow. "Thank you, Talon. Be sure to come by after lunch for a treat." Talon grinned before loping away across the courtyard, waving vaguely to Kalina. "Now, child, have you worked in a kitchen before?" Kalina nodded as she followed the woman over the threshold and into a bustling, noisy kitchen.

The smell of baking bread and cooking meat hit her, and despite having eaten a piece of toast with jam before leaving Calla and Anders' home, she was suddenly hungry. She had forgotten how welcoming and comforting kitchens could be. This kitchen was four times as large as the kitchen at Hywell Abbey and had almost twenty scullery and kitchen maids bustled around chopping veggies, carrying wood, kneading the dough, and cleaning dishes. The cook's second stood in the midst of things, ordering the maids about. Kalina was struck by how everyone seemed to know what to do and when.

Her abbey had never been this organized.

"Good." Mistress Aynne was still talking as she pulled her apron off a hook by the door and put it on, tying the cords behind herself. "You can put your things in the dormitory after breakfast has been served. For now, put them over by the door and grab an apron." Kalina hurried to do as she was told, using a spare ribbon to tie her hair back into a braid and out of her face before joining the cook at her workbench.

"What can I do for you, mistress?" She was suddenly eager to get started. The sooner she knew her way around the job, the more comfortable she would be. And then she could start looking for her family.

"Your job for today is to haul wood for the ovens, keep the water buckets filled, and empty the slop buckets. This is Margy, she will show you where everything is." A round girl twice Kalina's size appeared almost out of nowhere beside the cook. Her brown eyes were bright as she smoothed away a stray brown hair and motioned for Kalina to follow her.

"Thank you, Mistress," Kalina said as she hurried to follow Margy.

They passed across the kitchen to another door and out into the chill morning air. The sky was now a pale blue above them as they made their way towards a wood pile.

"What's your name?" Margy asked as she and Kalina began filling their arms with pieces of wood.

"Kalina."

"That's a pretty name," Margy said, smiling sideways at Kalina. "Not like my name. Margy. So clunky!" She laughed at herself as she bent to pile more wood in her arms.

"I think your name is very pretty." Kalina smiled back at Margy; perhaps she could make a friend after all.

"Thank you for that, but I don't think so." Margy's smile was strained as she began walking back towards the kitchen. "So! What brought you to the castle?" Kalina concentrated on walking down the few steps into the kitchen with her arms full of wood before answering.

"Well, I really just needed a change of pace. I was working with my mother doing laundry but it was time to venture out on my own."

A small lie, and one that warmed her more than she knew. Calling Calla her mother felt comforting.

"Are you from Ravenhelm then?" Margy looked over her shoulder as she led Kalina back to the door after dropping off their armloads of wood.

"No, originally we're from the Deep Glen Forest, but we moved here a few years ago." It was always best to keep some truth in your lies. She had learned that from her days in the Abbey. Father Martin had always been very good at detecting her lies but she had learned to inject small truths and had begun getting away with things more often. She let a small smile cross her lips in remembrance.

"Oh! What's that like?" Margy led her back to the same courtyard and this time Kalina noticed the well with buckets against one wall. Together they put a bucket on the hook and lowered it down to be filled.

"Well, it was definitely a shock coming to Ravenhelm if that's what you're asking."

"Yea, I bet. Me, I've lived here all my life." Margy hauled the bucket over the rim, carefully setting it on the ground before letting Kalina put a second bucket on the hook. Kalina noticed the girl had large muscles for someone so young, but she supposed hauling heavy buckets of water and armloads of wood would make you that way. She contemplated whether she was going to end up with muscles like Margy.

The girls hauled wood and water until there was no need for more, and then they emptied the slop buckets, hauling them out a different door and down a hallway and through another outer door at the base of some stairs. Through that door were the stables and a pig pen where they dumped the buckets of potato peelings and vegetable ends. Happy, fat pigs gratefully slurped up the leftovers as Kalina and Margy went back for a second round.

By the time lunch came around both girls were exhausted, Kalina more so than Margy, as she hadn't worked this hard in weeks, not since she had been at Hywell Abbey. She sat on a bench along one side of the kitchen and gratefully accepted the bread that Margy brought her, piled high with sharp cheese and slices of cold turkey. The food made Kalina feel more alert, and the warmth of the kitchen was beginning to make her sweat and feel sleepy.

The lunch and dinner rush passed in much the same way. Margy and Kalina rushed back and forth carrying wood and water and emptying buckets into the pig pen or into the pile near the pig pen for the garden. Kalina was dead on her feet by the time she slumped onto a bench in the servants' mess hall next to Margy and ate her hearty potato and leek soup with a slice of lamb and a piece of crusty bread. Her stomach was growling so loudly that Margy heard it and the two of them giggled together, Kalina's turning into an almost manic giggle as her exhaustion took over. Margy helped her gather her things and head up the stairs to the first floor, where there was a dormitory for all the female serving staff. Margy helped her find an empty cot and Kalina barely had the energy to stow her meager belongings before falling into bed.

The next day was much the same, and by the end of the week, Kalina wasn't so exhausted, her feet didn't hurt as much, and her back didn't protest at every load of wood she carried. She knew she was getting stronger and she marveled at how her arms began to stand out with muscle, and her stomach became taught, all remnants of baby fat gone with the labor.

Her first day off came, and Kalina practically ran from the castle to Calla and Anders' house, her chest almost bursting with excitement. This must be what it felt like to go home, to belong someplace, and she marveled at the foreign feeling.

"Calla!" she called as she burst into the house. Anders was coming down the stairs and Calla was nursing the baby by the fire.

"Kalina! So glad to have you back! We've missed you!" Calla held out an arm for Kalina and she collapsed into the woman, her heart feeling so full. Anders came around the couch and pulled her into a hug when she was released from Calla's arms.

"How is the castle?" Kalina told them all about her first week of work and they listened intently as she spoke.

"Any progress on getting into the library yet?" Calla asked as she put Issa into Kalina's arms.

"Not yet, but I've been adjusting to the workload and learning the schedule of the other servants. From around midnight until 4 am almost everyone is asleep. That is when I'll be sneaking out. I need to get in touch with Talon first, have him ask where I should start, and the best way to sneak in."

"Just be careful." Calla smoothed back Kalina's hair. "We need to dye this again next week. I'll pick up some mountain alder at the market and have it ready for your next day off." Kalina nodded, grateful.

Chapter 13

I<small>T WAS A STRUGGLE FINDING</small> pen and paper to write on, and then to find someone who knew who Talon was. Kalina had to ask ten servants before she found one who owned a pen and had a scrap of paper for her to borrow, as not many servants knew how to read or write. Kalina didn't truly know who she could trust, or what was safe to write, so she kept it short and sweet.

Talon,

My first week in the kitchens has been great. I'm tired but I'm learning a lot.

Thank you for getting me the job. Can we meet? I'd love to catch up.

How about the gardens during my lunch break tomorrow?

Yours,

K

She found a page boy walking down the hall by the kitchens and bribed him with a warm pastry to take the note to Talon. She was very grateful that Father Martin had insisted on teaching the children of the Abbey to read and write, otherwise, this entire task would have been useless.

The hours until their meeting the following day seemed to drag on forever and Kalina found herself getting impatient and antsy while waiting. She wasn't fully paying attention when Margy explained the details of how to start the hearth fire that morning and accidentally ended up dumping a load of black soot all over her dress and the floor. She was forced to sweep it up while Margy set the fire properly and shot her disapproving looks. Margy was nice, and Kalina felt they could be friends, but as she had no real plan, no idea how long she'd be in this castle, she was hesitant to get close to the girl.

Finally, her lunch break came just after the rest of the castle had finished eating their lunch, and she ran for the public gardens, passing through the grounds easily as if she knew the place by heart. Her apron marked her as a scullery maid and she was allowed access to all the public grounds and main hallways of the castle. It was when she wandered from those paths that guards stopped her to question her. Luckily, she just blamed it on being new to the castle, which

Mistress Aynne had confirmed on more than one occasion when a guard had found her wandering out of the acceptable zones.

She slowed as she reached the border to the garden, the high hedges blocking her view of the fountain where she hoped she'd see Talon. She could hear voices as she approached, and paused just behind the shrubs, straining her ears to hear. She didn't want to have her conversation with Talon overheard so she would have to wait until the coast was clear to really talk to him about getting into the library.

"The Prince doesn't know what he's up against." The voice was male and deep, and it made Kalina pause, her heart beginning to race at the mention of the prince. "He's just waiting for me to declare war on Wostrad. He already has a legion of ships in Black Harbor, little more than pirates, men he's recruited from Askor and he pays them to harry our coast. Although he thinks I don't know about it." The voice paused. "But I chose him for my daughter to marry. That's on me."

"Your Majesty, you can't let him get away with this... this... insolence!" A higher, more nasally male voice responded. "He must be put in his place, taught what is acceptable, otherwise when you're gone, he'll run this country into the ground with war. Your daughter is a very capable ruler, but I have my suspicions about the Prince and how he treats her. You already know those concerns."

"Yes, I know Balor. But I risk causing a war with Askor if I put him in his place, and I risk causing a war if I don't. He's backed me into a corner and I'm searching for a way out." The king sounded defeated, sad even, at his predicament. Kalina swallowed hard. This wasn't a conversation she was meant to overhear, but she was frozen to the spot. She prayed the king and his companion, Balor, did not leave the gardens, but instead continued walking, otherwise, she'd be discovered. "Perhaps if I sent him to the coast, to fight against his own men, and send Sir Dyelan and Sir Gregan to keep an eye on him. It would get him out of the way and give my daughter some peace and quiet."

"Brilliant plan, your Majesty." Soon their footsteps faded from her hearing. She let out a long sigh and moved into the gardens, hoping Talon hadn't missed her and left. She wondered vaguely about the possible conflict between Ethea and Wostrad, their southern neighbor, but it was replaced when she beheld the gardens before her.

She rounded a stunning fountain, watching the burbling streams of waterfall gracefully from the open mouths of small Wyverns and dragons statues cleverly carved from marble splash into the pool. In the pool swam large orange, white, yellow, and black spotted fish. Some had long graceful tails, and some had short stunted tails. There was a large black fish with gold along its fins and tail. It was one of the most beautiful creatures Kalina had ever seen, next to Savath, of course. She looked up from the water at the sound of footsteps and there was Talon, the gravel of the walkways crunching beneath his booted feet.

"Hi, Kalina! I'm so glad you sent me a message! I was wondering how I'd get to see you again." His grin was catching and Kalina grinned right back. For a moment she wondered whether she should hug him. Talon seemed to be contemplating the same thing as he stood before her awkwardly for a moment before sitting beside her. Bees buzzed in her stomach at seeing him again.

"It's good to see you."

"Yea, you too." Their conversation lapsed into an uncomfortable silence before she decided she couldn't take it anymore.

"Can you help me access the library tonight?" She cut right to the chase, no reason to delay it, and she couldn't stand the awkward silence. Talon's face fell a bit at the question, as if he'd been hoping she'd say something else.

"Of course, I can. I know of a little-used side door. It's dangerous. Sometimes the Princess or Prince are roaming the halls, and sometimes there are scholars nearby the entrance, but it's our only option." Kalina nodded, trailing her fingers in the fountain, laughing delightedly when one of the fishes came to gently nibble her fingers. "Those are koi. They come from some islands across the Emerald Ocean. The king had them shipped here in great barrels full of water!" Kalina continued to trail her fingers, letting more of the pretty fish nibble her fingertips.

"Would midnight work? That's when the majority of the servants are asleep. I think I can slip through the castle easily enough. I have been caught a few times; the guards now know I have a tendency to get lost so it won't be strange if I'm found where I shouldn't."

"Great idea!" Talon rubbed the back of his neck self-consciously. "Midnight would work, but I'm usually asleep by then."

"I am too, but for this, I'm willing to lose some sleep." She winked at him. They made a plan to meet by the kitchen staircase at midnight. They then sat in companionable silence, all awkwardness gone, tickling the friendly fish until the giant bell down in the city that chimed the hours, half hours, and quarter hours told her that her lunch hour was up.

"Thank you, Talon. For all you've done and are doing for me," Kalina said sincerely. She leaned forward and with her stomach flip-flopping, gave Talon a soft kiss on the cheek. He turned bright red and stuttered something while Kalina stood to leave, smiling to herself. "See you tonight." With a small wave, she left the way she'd come, leaving Talon sitting on the edge of the fountain, a hand pressed to his cheek and a bemused expression on his face.

Chapter 14

THE CLOCK STRUCK MIDNIGHT with a resonating gong that echoed down the deserted halls of the castle. Kalina crouched in the shadows, watching and waiting for Talon to appear. She had dressed in her dark green dress, leaving off the stark white apron. If she was caught tonight, being a confused scullery maid wouldn't save her.

Minutes ticked by, each slower than the next. Finally, faint footsteps echoed down the hallway and Kalina stiffened. Was it Talon or a guard come to take her away? She had a flash of concern, worry that Talon had perhaps betrayed her running through her mind. She dismissed this quickly just as a lanky figure came around the corner. Talon walked right past her hiding spot and she stepped out, placing a soft hand on his arm. He jumped, covering his mouth as a very uncharacteristic squeak came from his lips. Kalina covered her own smile, fighting down the laughter at the surprise on his face at her appearance.

"Kalina! Oh, my gods! Don't scare me like that!" Kalina giggled quietly, her laughter shaking her belly as he put his hands on his hips, his expression as stern as could be.

"I didn't even mean to scare you!" she whispered between shaking breaths. "But the look on your face was perfect!" She continued to laugh as he scowled at her and began walking down the hall. "Wait, Talon, don't be mad!" He waved her on with a hand and she followed, trying to control the laughter still bubbling up.

They walked softly and quickly through hall after hall. Kalina glimpsed through large open doors at parlors and game rooms, small meeting nooks, and ballrooms. These they passed quickly and in shadow as some were still occupied. They passed without incident until Talon suddenly pressed her into an alcove behind an old suit of armor. She almost protested when she heard the clattering of booted feet coming down the hall. She pressed herself into the darkness of the alcove, holding her breath in anticipation as a knight with an ornate sword at his belt came into view.

"Sir Gregan," Talon said, bowing low. Her blood ran ice cold at the sound of the man's name. She froze, watching from her dark hiding place. The knight looked at Talon appraisingly, a stern look on his rugged and scarred face.

"Page Talon. What are you doing out of bed so late?" His voice was gravelly, like boulders grinding together. Kalina could see a jagged scar across his throat.

"I was running a final errand for Sir Dyelan and then I was going to snag a book from the library to read before bed." His explanation had Kalina looking at him with newfound respect. A lie mixed with enough truth to be believable. The older man nodded, still eyeing Talon up and down.

"Well, run along, Talon. Sir Dyelan and I have a meeting early with the King and will require your services immediately following." Talon bowed low again and stepped to the side, allowing the knight to stride past. He waited until the knight had turned the corner and then turned to Kalina. She sighed in relief, her heartbeat slowing down, and came out from behind the suit of armor.

"That was too close for comfort," she said with a shiver. Talon sighed as well, his shoulders sagging.

"Let's hurry then." Kalina gestured for him to lead the way and together they practically jogged down the corridors.

"What happened to his throat?"

"The scar? No one really knows, but Sir Dyelan once told me when he was more than a little drunk that Sir Gregan got it while in the war. But Sir Charles told me it was from a lover he scorned." He shrugged as they jogged.

"Interesting."

The door into the library was hidden behind a tapestry, and the hinges were well oiled. It was clearly used for servants and scholars who wished not to disturb the silence of the stacks that stood beyond the door. As soon as Kalina stepped through, she let out a little gasp, her hand covering her mouth at the sight before her. Books and scrolls were piled on top of one another in row upon row, stacked twenty feet high in every direction, as far as she could see into the gloom. Glass globes of light were set into niches on the walls, their light only illuminating the first few feet of every stack. The corridors outside had been dimly lit, but it still took a few moments for Kalina's eyes to adjust to the darkness of the library.

She turned to Talon, who stood smirking in self-satisfied delight beside her.

"How big is it?" Her awe was unmistakable.

"It stretches the rest of this floor, the floor below, and two floors above. It's the biggest in the kingdom and fourth biggest in the entire known world!" His pride shown through.

"What are those?" She pointed to the glass globes.

"Those are alchemical globes from Alben. They make them there and ship them to us in padded containers. No one really knows what they have inside but unless they are broken, they give off light without heat." Kalina grunted her understanding. It made sense; torches would be too dangerous around the books.

"How will I know where to start?" She was suddenly overwhelmed by the sheer number of books available, and she was uncertain she would ever find the information she needed.

"I'll take you to the section on Dragons. It's my favorite." He began walking left down the stacks, checking each row before walking forward. "You can probably find a mention of the Valdir in there and then you can branch out! Each section has reference books, so if you find a subject that's interesting it can help point you to the next section," he whispered as he walked. In the utter silence of the space, his voice still seemed to carry for miles. Kalina winced. Any noise in this place would alert others. She would have to be careful coming back here.

"Is there a map? Or some way for me to find where the other sections are?" Talon paused before her and let her catch up to stand by his side. He pointed up at the tops of each row.

"See those numbers and letters there?" She nodded noticing the white numbers painted just below the top shelf. "Those denote section and subject. We are at the E's, and this is the 6th section. We want D23." They continued walking and rounded a corner, the numbers continuing down the next wall. Kalina was beginning to feel nervous that they wouldn't find the right section when she checked the tops of the rows again and saw D40, and beside that ahead of them, D39. They were getting closer and she sped up, almost walking side by side with Talon.

"Here it is." Talon slowed as they reached D23. He looked down the aisle and then turned looking at the spines of the large leather-bound books. Kalina followed suit, looking at the titles. She saw books that were titled Dragons and How to Raise Them, Draconica, The Encyclopedia of Dragon Breeds, Adventures with

Dragons, and so forth. She was sure she'd find plenty to read here that would lead her to the Valdir.

"What about Wyverns?" She asked out of curiosity.

"They are listed in a subset of dragons, down at the end. The Valdir might be listed in a subset as well, but I've never looked."

"How many books on dragons are there here?" Talon shrugged. "Probably thousands." Kalina stopped. Thousands? How was she supposed to search thousands of books? "It's okay Kalina! I will help you when I can!" She nodded and kept looking at the shelves, the daunting task rising over her head.

They spent the next hour pulling random books from the shelves and skimming through them. They couldn't risk sitting at a table in the open center of the library. While the comfy looking chairs and soft glowing lamps called her name, Kalina wouldn't risk it, although Talon said it was perfectly safe, that only a skeleton crew ran the library at night and they mainly spent their time in their offices up near the main doors, transcribing old books into new ones.

Kalina started with Adventures with Dragons, by Alfredious the Great. She sat uncomfortably on the cold ground and opened the book in her lap. It was full of adventures of a man named Alfredious the Great who traveled the world in search of dragons. He met a great many, but by his descriptions, Kalina suspected more than a few of them were Wyverns and not dragons. The book was written over eight hundred years previously when dragons roamed the world in more frequent numbers. She put the book aside after finding only a few vague mentions of him meeting a Valdir, but no location, and picked up another.

Hours and many books later, Kalina was too tired to keep her eyes open and she found she'd read the same paragraph three times and still didn't know what she'd read. She looked over and saw Talon had fallen asleep on the floor amidst a small pile of books. She sighed and closed the one in her lap, marking its title so she could start there the next time. She realized sadly that she couldn't do this every night and still expect to perform her job. She would have to find a balance between sleeping and searching. She shook Talon awake and together they began putting the books back on the shelves.

Talon walked her back to her dormitory. She stumbled into bed, falling asleep the moment her head hit the pillow.

Dawn came entirely too early for Kalina. She was groggy and exhausted, her entire body ached and by lunchtime, she had a pounding headache. She spent her lunch hour catching a nap in the gardens under the shade of a willow tree. Margy asked her what was wrong and Mistress Aynne made her clean all the dinner dishes by herself as punishment for falling asleep while stirring a pot of stew and letting the bottom burn. She wanted to go back to the library but she desperately needed rest, and despite her best efforts, she slept all the way through that night, not waking until Margy shook her the following morning.

Chapter 15

KALINA DEVELOPED A SYSTEM for searching the library. She would go after midnight every other night, search a few books, and then take a few books with her. She hid those books in a canvas bag in the garden where she spent most of her lunch hours. Then, whenever she had a spare moment, she would go to the garden and read, being careful not to damage the books in any way.

One night, a few days into this new system, she was quietly reading a book called Dances with Dragons when she heard soft footsteps coming towards her. Her heart began pounding and she quickly put the book on a shelf and ran for the center of the library. The footsteps stopped at the end of her row and began to slowly advance down it. She crouched, frozen, her back against a quilted armchair, as the footsteps came to the end of the row and stopped. From where she was, she could see all the way down the center of the library to the enormous oaken doors at the front. All that stood between her and those doors were hundreds of rows of books to pass by, and dozens of arms chairs, sofas, and couches, all placed in little circles meant for people to sit and discuss books. The doors were small in the distance, but there was no way she could run to them without being discovered. She felt like her heart would beat out of her chest as she waited for the stranger to walk away.

"Kalina?" A hesitant whisper came from behind her and she sagged in relief and stood up.

"Talon?" She came towards him and pulled him back into row D23, dragging him further into the gloom. "Don't scare me like that! I thought I was caught for sure!" Talon looked sheepish for a moment.

"I had to come find you. Sir Dyelan and I are being sent to the coast, to Blackwater." He looked down at her hand on his arm. "I didn't know when I'd see you again, so I wanted to come wish you good luck." Kalina squeezed his arm in gratitude.

"Next time send me a message on where to meet you." She grinned to lessen the blow of her words. "Be safe, will you?" Talon nodded and pulled her in for a hug. Kalina kissed him on the cheek and then laid her head on his shoulder. It felt good, even natural to be touched in this way, and for a moment, she was sad when he pulled away.

"I've got to go pack. We're leaving first thing in the morning." Kalina waved goodbye as Talon trotted off down the rows of books, disappearing into the gloom.

The following day found Kalina in the garden, reclining on a soft bed of grass underneath a large rhododendron bush in full bloom above her. She was reading a rather unwieldy leather-bound tome, scouring the pages for a mention of the Valdir. She breathed in deep, letting the fragrance of the gardens wash over her when her eyes caught the word silver. She caught her breath as she slowed down to read the sentence. Just as she started to read, the sounds of footsteps coming hurriedly down the path towards her hiding place made her slam the book shut and sit up, her face red with guilt, her heart fluttering in fear at being caught.

Her head struck the branches beneath the bush, making it shake and she clutched her head, leaves and flower petals falling around her. That was when she noticed the footsteps had stopped, right beside her hiding spot. Kalina slowly turned towards her left where the pathway and the footsteps were and jumped back as her eyes met a pair of vivid green ones.

A laugh rolled through the bush towards her as her heart threatened to pound out of her chest. She scrambled back until she pressed against the gnarled trunk of the rhododendron, no easy escape in sight now that she had been spotted.

"No need to hide from me." The voice was a woman's, soft, and lilting, and it struck a chord in Kalina's heart that she did not understand. "Come on out and we can talk." Kalina quietly put the book back inside its carry sack and stuffed it behind the bush before climbing out. When she straightened, she saw a beautiful blonde haired woman before her, dressed in a simple yet elegant purple silk gown that bunched just under her breasts and then fell sweepingly to the ground. Her hair was swept up in graceful waves and held in place by a simple golden circlet upon her brow. Kalina stared in wonder at the woman's straight nose and strikingly green eyes. "And who might you be?" The woman cocked her head and looked at Kalina's now very boring brown hair and light blue eyes. A flash of what might have been recognition crossed the woman's face, but it was gone as soon as it appeared. She waited patiently for Kalina to clear her throat.

"My name is Kalina, your Majesty." She was hedging a guess but only a queen or some sort of royalty would wear a circlet as fine as the one this woman wore. The woman's smile spread, making her seem even more lovely than before.

"Kalina. What a lovely name." She motioned for Kalina to follow her to a nearby bench. "I am Princess Cherise."

Kalina stood and curtsied to the princess, excitement and fear warring within her.

"What were you doing under that bush?"

"Reading. I spend my lunches there, your Highness," she corrected. She felt an odd urge to tell this woman the truth but knew she had to keep her secrets close to her chest. This woman was married to the prince. She was treading on dangerous ground.

"And where do you work?"

"The kitchens, your Highness. I'm a scullery maid." The princess frowned at that answer and Kalina worried that her low status was not acceptable and she would be punished for being in the gardens or for even speaking to the princess.

"The kitchens? Really? Someone as capable as you?" Kalina nodded, forgetting to sit back down. "Is that what you want to do?" Kalina found herself shaking her head no, unsure why she was suddenly compelled to tell this woman the truth. "Then what would you like to do if you had the opportunity?"

"Work in the library!" Kalina burst out and then she covered her mouth, appalled at her forthrightness. The princess laughed delightedly.

"The library? Don't you want to be a lady's maid?"

"No, your Highness," Kalina spoke softly, embarrassment welling up within her, her cheeks going pink. "I don't like sewing or gossiping. I prefer reading and learning." The princess nodded sagely, like she truly understood Kalina.

"Well then, I will see what I can do." Kalina looked up sharply, her eyes meeting the princess'.

"Why?" Why in the world would a woman like this, high born and royal, want to do her a favor. Suspicion began growing in her stomach as she eyed the woman.

"Why? Well, because I like you, Kalina. I can't explain why, but you remind me of me when I was your age. I know how tough it is to move up in this world, and I do enjoy helping others when I can." A warm smile accompanied her words, and despite Kalina's trepidation, she liked this woman.

"Thank you, your Highness." Kalina curtsied once again. "My lunch hour is almost over and I must get back to work." The princess stood.

"Until we meet again, Kalina," Kalina curtsied and ran down the garden path, only turning to look over her shoulder at the gate to the gardens. The princess stood there, watching after her, a sad look upon her beautiful face.

Chapter 16

KALINA WAS HARD AT WORK kneading bread dough the following afternoon when a hush fell over the busy kitchen. Kalina pushed her hair back from her eyes and looked up, expecting to see Mistress Aynne or someone about to make an announcement, but instead, she saw Princess Cherise standing in the doorway to the kitchen. Kalina hastily wiped her hands on her apron and tried to smooth her stringy hair back from her sweaty face. The princess surveyed the room, her eyes briefly alighting on Kalina before she spotted Mistress Aynne come in from the larder.

"Mistress Aynne." The princess' voice rang out across the now silent chamber. "I wondered if I might have a word?"

"Of course, your Highness!" Mistress Aynne bustled across the room, motioning for the princess to follow her into her office that stood just off the main kitchen. Once the door had closed behind them, the buzz of the kitchen started up again, women whispering about the princess and her reason for coming down. Kalina tried to block out their talk but she couldn't ignore Margy, who sidled over to stand next to her.

"What do you think that is about?" Kalina shrugged. She had a suspicion but she pushed down the hope that soared within her.

"Probably the princess wanting a certain dish made or to complain about the food," she offered. Margy shook her dark curls.

"The princess has never once complained about the food. In fact, a few times she's come down here to thank us all directly for our work." Kalina raised her eyebrows at the girl.

"Really?"

"Yeah!" Margy went on excitedly. "She gave us each an extra penny for our work and spoke to us individually. Her husband may be a troll but she is really very kind, for a royal." Kalina stood there, eyeing the Mistress' closed door, contemplating this woman who had wanted to help her. She went back to kneading bread dough, determined not to worry about what the princess might be saying to Mistress Aynne.

Soon, the door to Mistress Aynne's office opened and out came the mistress and the princess. Together they stood, speaking quietly, and soon Mistress Aynne curtsied to the princess and the princess left without a second glance in Kalina's direction. Mistress Aynne came over to answer one of the nearby kitchen maid's questions. Kalina felt her stomach drop an inch. Perhaps the princess hadn't been there about her. She was surprised at herself. She hadn't realized how much she'd been wanting the princess to let her work in the library. It would have made her research that much easier.

As she was finishing up the last ball of dough that evening, covering it to rise overnight for baking in the morning, she looked up to find Mistress Aynne at her shoulder.

"Kalina. May I see you in my office once you have finished with your task?" Kalina gave a shallow curtsy.

"Yes, of course, Mistress Aynne." She finished covering the dough and went to scrub her hands and forearms the sink filled with warm water for washing. She removed her apron as was only proper for a formal meeting, and tucked her hair back from her face. Then she squared her shoulders, a small worm of fear squirming in her stomach as she walked into Mistress Aynne's office.

The office was modestly appointed, a nice rug on the floor, much worn but well taken care of. It showed the rank that Mistress Aynne held and how she cared for what she owned. Kalina smiled and realized that she quite liked the mistress of the kitchens. The woman sat behind a large oak desk, shuffling lists of foodstuffs. She paused her shuffling and looked up at Kalina.

"Please, sit." She motioned towards a rounded back wooden chair that sat before her desk. Kalina obediently sat, quietly waiting to be told why she was there. "You saw the princess down here earlier?" Kalina nodded, her stomach leaping into her throat. "She was asking about you and your work here in the kitchen. I told her you are an exceptional worker and are steadily moving your way up the ranks of my maids." Kalina was shocked. She knew she had been given tasks with a bit more responsibility but she hadn't realized she was actually moving up. She had only been in the castle for a few weeks. "The princess thought you might make a good scribe and wanted me to have you transcribe my lists of supplies to assess your abilities. She wants me to send you to the head librarian if your skills prove to be good enough." She reached into her desk and drew out a pen and a few sheets of paper. Then she handed them to Kalina, along with the stack of foodstuffs and supplies. "Sit here and copy these out and when you are finished, we shall speak further on the matter." Kalina sat stunned for a moment, unsure of what to do. She slowly reached for the pen, dipping it in the pot of ink that Mistress Aynne set before her. Slowly, she began to write, doing her best to write down everything in her neatest hand.

A half hour later she had transcribed all the papers and Mistress Aynne stood before her, pacing back and forth as she read over the lists, searching for mistakes. Kalina was confident there were none but that didn't assuage her fear. She sat as still as she could, resisting the temptation to squirm or wring her hands. Soon, the Mistress looked up, an appraising look on her face.

"It seems you have a passing fair hand, Kalina. I would like to promote you to Kitchen Scribe so that I may better assess your abilities." Kalina nodded and curtsied slightly. "Now, go get yourself some supper." She obeyed, running to tell Margy her news.

She spent the next week working in Mistress Aynne's office, transcribing list of foodstuffs, doing an inventory of their pantries and cellars, as well as calculating their weekly budgets. The night before her next day off, Mistress Aynne called her into her office while Kalina was finishing tallying the number of bottles of wine they had. She asked Kalina to sit in the chair before her desk.

"It seems I have no choice but to recommend you to the head librarian." She didn't seem overly happy about the idea, but Kalina's heart leapt. She had gotten very little research done that week, and what she had found on the Valdir only mentioned aspects of their culture, not where they resided, and every text she found was over a hundred years old. "I will discuss your appointment with him tonight, and tomorrow morning you will report to his office in the library. I will send Margy with you to show you where to go. You will take all your belongings with you, as you won't be sleeping in our Dormitory after tonight." Karina's breath came out in a whoosh. She kept her face straight as she stood and curtsied to the woman behind the desk.

"Thank you, Mistress Aynne, both for the opportunity to work here in the kitchen but also for allowing me to move on." Mistress Aynne sniffed at her words but nodded. Kalina turned to leave.

"Kalina." She hesitated, turning back to the mistress. The older woman looked worried, scared even. "The library is a very different world than the kitchens. If you ever find you are not thriving there, this position will always be open to you." Puzzled, Kalina curtsied and thanked the woman. "Now go to bed."

Kalina nodded and left the office, her steps lighter than they had been in days. She could ask the other librarians and scribes about the Valdir and dragons without it being suspicious. For the first time in the weeks since she'd left her Abbey, Kalina woke with excitement and a smile on her face, ready for what the future might hold.

Chapter 17

KALINA TOOK A DEEP BREATH before opening the large oak doors that led to the front of the library. Margy had walked her there and the girl had cried a bit as she said goodbye, telling Kalina she would miss her. Kalina felt a pang of sadness as well but her excitement at starting this new adventure far outweighed it.

It was a very different experience seeing the inside of the library during the day, and with permission rather than sneaking around at night. The main hall was brightly lit, glowing glass orbs on every shelf held alchemical lights. She had walked into a sort of reception area complete with a small desk that she assumed was usually occupied. No one was currently there so she walked in further, coming even with the wall. She could see all the way to the far side of the library in the distance, and to her right and left along the wall with the main door were doors, all leading to offices, she assumed. Mistress Aynne had said the first door on the right, so Kalina hefted her small bag and went to the door. It was carved with an intricate vine and leaf pattern and she marveled at it as she knocked lightly on the wood.

"Come in." A voice sounded from within, muffled by the thick door. Kalina pushed open the door to find a cozy office, almost every surface crammed with books, including all available chairs and the large desk that stood in the middle of the room. Sheets of paper covered what surfaces the books didn't and it had a comfortable sort of chaos that Kalina was instantly drawn to. The lone chair that sat before the desk was occupied, as was the comfy looking armchair behind the desk. Kalina stopped as the princess turned from her seat before the desk and smiled.

"Oh, Kalina. So glad you could join us." Cherise gestured for Kalina to come inside. She did, setting her bag down on the floor and stepped up beside the princess, looking at the old man behind the desk. His skin was wrinkled like crumpled paper, his back stooped and deformed from years bent over a book, and his gnarled hands were permanently clenched into half-formed fists that allowed him to clutch a quill but nothing else. This man had obviously this library his life's work. Kalina curtsied to him as she did the queen. The old man smiled up at her, intelligence shining from his eyes. She realized he was old but not demented, which was a good sign.

"Master Buckner, this is the girl I was telling you about." Princess Cherise smiled at her and Kalina smiled back, the familiar fluttering back in her stomach. She wondered if she would ever go into a new situation and not feel that sensation.

"Ahh yes. Kalina. Come here, child." He held out his gnarled hands and Kalina hesitated before placing her own into his, stepping behind the desk.

He looked down at her hands rather than up at her face, turning them over and regarding the calluses that had been there all her life from hard work in the kitchens. That was when she noticed the small cot behind the desk, tucked into a corner. It was piled rather neatly with folded clothing, black robes that the librarian seemed to prefer, and blankets. To one side was a small side table with a few candles and a number of old books. Kalina realized this was not only his office but his bedroom. She wondered if he had rooms elsewhere as well when the old man patted her hands and gave them back to her.

"So, you want to be a scribe?" Kalina nodded, going back to stand beside the Princess. "Your hands tell me they've only done manual labor. The work of a scribe is considerably more sedentary and quieter. It will be the exact opposite of the hustle and bustle of the kitchens." His voice was pleasant and calming.

"I want a change of pace, Master Buckner. And if I crave the hustle and bustle, I'm sure I could stop by the kitchens on my lunches. Besides, my family lives in the city, and I can go visit them for some excitement on my day off." The princess looked at her curiously at the mention of her family. The old man nodded.

"Very well, then. Mistress Aynne did speak highly of you and your transcribing talents. We shall put you to work right away. You will start by getting to know the stacks." Kalina didn't quite know what he meant but he reached for and rang a small golden bell at the edge of his desk. A moment later a young boy in black scribes' robes, ink stains on his hands, and a rather rushed look, appeared in the doorway. "Dillion, this is Kalina. Would you please show her to an empty office and then give her a tour of the stacks? She is to start with organizing and getting to know our system, and then she can be given books to transcribe." The boy bowed to the master and then eyed her sideways. "Now, Kalina, how old are you?" Kalina hesitated for a moment, glancing at the princess.

"Around sixteen." The man nodded.

"Good, then you will have plenty of time to decide whether or not this is where you want to stay permanently." He gestured for her to follow the boy. Kalina curtsied to the head librarian and then turned to the princess.

"Thank you, your Highness. How will I ever repay you?" The princess beamed at her.

"Nonsense. Just do your best. I'm sure I will see you again, Kalina." The way she said Kalina's name made her pause and make eye contact with the woman, but Princess Cherise's face revealed nothing but serene calm as Kalina grabbed her bag and followed the scribe out the door.

The boy Dillion led her in silence left of the main doors and a long way down the row of offices until they came upon the last one in the corner before the wall turned right. Kalina looked around them and realized the secret door she and Talon had used was nearby, only a dozen rows down the right-hand wall. She smiled as the scribe Dillion produced a key and unlocked the door.

"This is your room. You sleep here and do your work here but we all eat in the second-floor dining hall." He sounded bored and he scowled at her as he spoke. Kalina nodded. She had eaten in the first-floor dining hall with the scullery maids and knew the second-floor dining hall was directly above it. It wouldn't be too hard to find. "Come back to the reception desk once you've settled in. A new set of scribes' robes has been set out on your cot." He gestured for her to enter and she did, stepping inside her room.

Dillion handed her the key and then hurried away down the hall created by the stacks of books on his left and the wall on his right. She looked around bemusedly, equal parts confused, excited, and afraid. The room was small, similar to the Head Librarian's but on a much smaller scale. There was a lit lamp on the small desk against one wall, a small window that opened onto the stacks, and against the far wall, a cot. Kalina moved inside the room, placing her bag inside the tiny closet that was built into the corner of the room. On the bed lay a pair of black robes, black pants, and a black shirt and vest. It seemed that the female scribes wore the same uniform as the boys. She smiled as she looked at the pants; she had always wanted to wear pants and now, in this strange twist of fate, she was suddenly allowed to do so.

She arrived at the reception desk 10 minutes later after changing her clothing and stowing her items. Dillion sat reading a book and he frowned slightly when she presented herself before him.

"What is my first task?" She was eager to get into the stacks and continue her research. Dillion sighed and closed his book with a quiet thump. He stood and motioned for her to follow him. He led her to the closest left-hand row of books. He pointed to the number and letter painted up top.

"Do you know how our books are organized?" Kalina bit her tongue before she could answer and made a show of staring at the number and letter before answering.

"But subject? Alphabetically?" Dillion nodded. He looked bored and thoroughly annoyed at having to teach her.

"Each letter represents a subject, and each number a row within that letter. Each row has a side A and a side B. Starting from here, the left-hand side of every row is A, the right-hand side B. Within each subject, within each row, the books are arranged by author, and those are arranged alphabetically." Kalina nodded. It made the most logical sense. But she had to ask a question she had asked Talon.

"In that case, what about subsets of subjects? Would Wyverns be listed under Dragons, subset Wyverns? Or under W for Wyverns?" Perhaps she had been searching in the wrong place for the Valdir, perhaps she needed to look in the V's on the floor below.

"No, they would be listed as a subset of Dragons." She breathed a sigh and hoped she'd come across a mention of them soon. "But some things might be considered their own subject. Take flying, for example, there is a small section under F listed for flying and that may contain some references to Dragons, but also to certain contraptions made by scientists in the past." Kalina's head began to spin. "There are also reference desks at the end of most rows. These can help you find specifically which subject you are looking for." He led her forward and Kalina watched carefully as Dillion opened a small wooden desk that was built onto the shelf. She had never previously looked hard enough to see this. Inside the desk were small paper cards, each with a book title, an author name, and all subjects listed therein, along with references to other sections of the library where you might find those subjects or most books by that author.

Kalina's heart jumped. This. This was how she was going to find her Valdir, not aimlessly looking through the books on the shelves. The system was more complicated than she had originally imagined, so when Dillion sent her on a hunt for a specific book by a specific author with only a vague hint of the book's contents, she was eager to oblige. She wanted to learn the system, and quickly.

When she returned to the front desk before heading to dinner, Dillion frowned at her.

"You don't belong here." His voice was cold and it took Kalina by surprise. She could tell he didn't want to be stuck teaching her, but this was different. There was malice in his voice and face and it made his boyish demeanor look ugly.

"Yes, I do."

"No. You don't. Just don't forget I told you that." And then he stalked off into the gloom, leaving her standing by the front desk, confused.

Chapter 18

KALINA FORCED THE BITE of potatoes down, its heat searing her throat. She sat alone in the second-floor mess hall. Around her, the scribes, librarians, scholars, and other workers and servants of slightly higher rank than the kitchen help and gardeners, who ate on the bottom floor, ate in small knots and cliques of people. The black robes of the scholars stood out in the sea of other colors and Kalina felt for the first time since coming here that she stood out, that she was not like the others around her.

Her first meal in the mess hall had made one thing abundantly clear. Scribes were not female. Every other scribe that worked in the library was male, all the librarians and scholars who frequented its halls were male. She hadn't realized it the first few hours working in the library because the place was so large you rarely encountered other people, but in the mess hall, her otherness stood out like a sore thumb. She had discovered during her first meal what Dillion meant, and things had only gotten worse from there.

She tried to eat her food as quickly as possible, shoving the roll of bread given with every meal into her pocket to be eaten later, so she wouldn't have to stay longer. As she cleaned her plate of potatoes and started on the roast beef, another tray clattered down across from her and she looked up. Dillion was standing before her, his tray piled high with used dishes, and before she could even say a hello he began speaking.

"Here, scullery maid, take our dirty dishes away for us." He smirked at her and walked away, as his little group of friends filed by, dropping their dirty lunch trays down in front of her. She sat motionless, staring straight ahead, a stony expression on her face. A few groups of scribes nearby smiled and began whispering, and her ears began to burn at the attention. Dillion and his friends laughed as they walked together out of the mess hall, leaving Kalina amid a pile of dirty dishes, her own meal partially forgotten before her.

She heaved a sigh and began to stack the dishes more neatly until she had them all on two trays before her. She would have to make two trips to place them in the tubs at the far end of the hall. Resignedly, she stood and carried them one at a time to the tubs, her face and neck turning a bright shade of pink as she passed by tables filled with scribes who all pointed and laughed or whispered to their neighbors. She heard taunts of "scullery maid," "whore," and "suck up." Some even whispered things as she passed. "Wonder what she did to get that position." It made her blood curdle in her veins.

Dillion had made it clear to her on her second day in the library that she was not only not welcome, but that she must have done something in order to get the job. He proceeded to casually accuse her of doing different favors for the head librarian, all of which were vulgar and made Kalina's stomach roil. He had seen the princess the day she'd started so he even began suggesting she was the illegitimate child of a nobleman, or that she had parents who had sold her to the princess, or even that she was a disgraced lady's maid. Kalina gritted her teeth at each suggestion, each insult, and focused all her efforts, all her free time to working in the library, transcribing the books she'd been given, and researching about dragons and the Valdir.

One afternoon she was working in a section near the far back of the second floor when she heard a small noise. In the relative darkness and quiet of the library, any noise was cause for concern and made her feel jumpy. She turned slowly, looking around her, peering down the row of dark books for the source of the noise. A shuffling off to her left made her swing around, a book held up as if it was a weapon when something hard slammed into her gut. Kalina doubled over, the book falling heavily from her hands to thud on the floor. She let out a small grunt, the breath completely knocked out of her. A second blow came down at her from her left, knocking her onto the ground. Blows from all angles ensued, her assailants above her quiet and stealthy, the only sound their labored breathing as they punched and kicked at her for a few brutal moments. Kalina curled into a ball, her arms covering her face trying to protect it but failing as one brutal kick caught her own hand, smashing the small bones into her own face, bloodying her nose and making her eye sting terribly.

The beating was over as quickly and quietly as it had begun, and Kalina lay on the ground, curled around her aching middle, soft sobs finally coming from her throat as she was finally able to get her wind back. No one came to her rescue, and she lay for what felt like hours, feeling the bruises form on her body, the blood dripping from her nose finally coming to a stop and beginning to crust over and dry. A second, small noise sounded from above her and she looked up sharply, her muscles tensing to take a second beating, but instead of an assailant, there was a large grey tabby cat with bright green eyes staring at her curiously.

She pushed up onto her elbows and she and the tabby stared at one another for a few moments, the cat seeming to assess her and her current state. He came towards her and rubbed against her face, a loud purr rumbling out from him. And despite her sorry state and obvious pain, Kalina smiled at the cat. She sat up and scooped him into her chest, cradling his soft warm body against her, burying her face in his warm fur, letting his warmth and purring comfort her as she began to cry, hot tears rolling down her already blood-stained face.

Was this the price she would have to pay in order to have access to the library? She hadn't even found one whisper of the Valdir yet and she'd been at this for over a month now, working herself into exhaustion every night, enduring the chaos of the kitchens, and the bullying, and now beatings from the other scribes who felt she wasn't good enough to have her position.

She looked down at the cat in her arms and noticed it had a small leather collar and a name tag dangling down. The name tag read Moose and she smiled. He was a rather large cat, and she wondered at the person who loved him enough to give him such a strange name. She hugged him to her once again before placing him gently on the floor and standing up, wincing at her body's protest. She put the book she'd dropped back on the shelf and then limped her way back to her room, the cat following behind her the entire way. At the door to her room, she paused, looking back at the cat who rubbed his cheek along the doorway and paused to gaze up at her with those green eyes. She smiled and opened the door wider, standing aside as the cat sauntered in.

The following day was her day off, and although Kalina had been looking forward to going into the city and seeing Calla, Anders, and baby Issa, she couldn't stomach the looks on their faces when she arrived covered in bruises, a swollen nose, and a black eye. She had woken up, stiff and sore, every part of her protesting as she went to the small mirror above her basin of water that served as a sink. She had examined the puffiness of her nose, concluding that while it was sore and painful, it wasn't broken. Her eye was turning a nice shade of purple. She pulled down the neck of her sleeping shift and saw the beginnings of bruises on all the parts she could see.

They hadn't beaten her so badly she had broken anything or ruptured anything, but her ribs were sore and taking deep breaths sent sharp pains through her chest and back and she suspected they may have been badly bruised or even cracked. She took off her shirt and stared down at her body, which was turning lovely shades of purple, black and blue with some tinges of green. Her black robes would cover the majority of the bruises but she couldn't hide the ones on her face and hands.

Instead of going into the city, she sent a note to Calla and Anders asking their forgiveness and saying she had things to take care of now that she was a scribe. Then she went in search of the solitude of the gardens, hoping for some time alone. The cat, Moose, had slept with her all night and departed when she'd left her rooms, sauntering off into the gloom of the library, tail flicking above him. Kalina smiled after him, taking a roll out of the pocket of her green dress she'd put on for her day off, and crunching down on the slightly stale roll. She wanted to avoid the mess hall today and planned to stop by the kitchens, to see Margy and hopefully beg a bite to eat.

The kitchens were a bustle, as always, when Kalina entered. The scullery maids and cooks barely looked up at her presence, and she wound her way in between them, smiling at those she knew until she made it to Margy's side. The girl looked up through her curls and squealed when she realized who it was. Kalina laughed and smiled as Margy threw her arms around her. Normally, Kalina wouldn't have allowed Margy to touch her, but today, after the bullying and pain of the last few weeks, she needed the comfort and contact. She bit her lip as Margy squeezed her, pressing on the bruises. Margy pulled back, looking at Kalina's face, her jaw hanging open as she took in the swollen nose and bruised eye.

"What in the Mother's name happened to you?" she exclaimed, pulling Kalina to the side of the kitchen, out of the earshot and pathways of the majority of the maids. Kalina tried to shrug the question off.

"Oh, just a bit of a run in with some not so nice people."

"Clearly." Margy took her hand and inspected the bruise that had spread black across the back of it from the kick to her face. "But who did this to you? Did you report them?" Kalina shook her head.

"No point. They wouldn't get punished, there was more than one. It's my word against theirs and I'm the only female scribe." Kalina took her hand back. "I don't suppose I could trouble you for some food? Eating in their mess hall has proved somewhat of a challenge." Margy's face went cold.

"Kalina, you listen to me, whoever did this to you had no right. And if you want, we can report it to Mistress Aynne. She won't let anyone, even scribes, get away with this." Kalina shook her head again.

"It's not worth it. It will only make them hate me more. It's fine, Margy, I promise."

"Fine. But from now on, you can come eat here in the kitchen with me. I'll tell Mistress Aynne it's because you miss me." Margy smiled at her rather wickedly, and Kalina suddenly regretted not letting this girl in a little more. Kalina smiled back.

"Thank you, Margy," she said gratefully. Margy flounced off into the kitchen, coming back a few moments later with a cloth napkin filled with a hunk of sharp hard cheese, a small loaf of bread baked full of nuts and fruit, some apples, and a small flask of juice. Kalina hugged Margy again in gratitude and promised to come back for the evening meal. Then, she left out the side door, wandering towards the gardens, looking forward to an afternoon in the sun.

Chapter 19

KALINA LAY IN A SMALL grassy grove, surrounded by towering oaks, branches spreading overhead, dappling the grass around her. She lay back, eating a piece of cheese, one arm beneath her head, watching the sunbeams dance through the trees overhead. Despite the last few days, she was surprised she felt this relaxed and content. Something about being out in nature surrounded by trees, like at her abbey back home, gave her a nostalgic and comforting feeling. Eating a meal without being harassed was rather pleasant as well, and she found she finally had an appetite.

It wasn't long until the silence and solitude of her little grove was disturbed. A soft footstep had her sitting bolt upright, fear thrilling through her, her body taut with the anticipation of being hit again. Before her, quietly walking through the glade, was Princess Cherise. Today she wore a pale green dress, flowing and graceful around her, her blonde hair up in intricate braids circling her head.

"I didn't mean to disturb you, Kalina." The princess stopped before her, hesitant to approach. Kalina realized her face had drained of color, as the blood came rushing back and she relaxed, taking a deep breath. She jumped to her feet and curtsied.

"No, of course, your Highness." She gestured to the grass beside her, unsure of how informal she could be with the princess. "Would you care to join me? I only have a little bread and cheese and a few apples but you are welcome to it." Princess Cherise came forward, smiling at Kalina and they both sat down, the princess fanning out her skirts on the soft grass.

"Thank you." The princess reached over and took a small piece of cheese and nibbled on it delicately, eyeing Kalina's bruises out of the corner of her eye. "Who did that to you?" Kalina ducked her head, letting her brown hair fall to cover her face. She shouldn't be spending time with the princess with bruises all over her face. How would it look if someone else saw them? But she couldn't bring herself to leave.

"No one, your Highness," Kalina said, reaching for one of the apples.

"Please, call me Cherise when we are alone." Kalina swallowed and nodded. "Now I know that's not true, but I understand keeping your secrets." Kalina was grateful she hadn't pressed.

"You mentioned your family in the city, tell me more about them." Cherise looked sideways at Kalina who began fidgeting with the hem of her dress. The two of them looked like two sides of the same leaf, each in a different shade of green.

"They aren't really my family." Kalina took another bite of her apple before continuing. "I was raised in a town in the Deep Glen Forest. But I left and came to the capital and when I arrived, a nice guard saved me from a man who wanted to hurt me. He took me in, and he and his wife became like family to me. Usually, on my days off I am with them." She gestured at her face. "But under the circumstances, I decided to stay away." Princess Cherise reached out a fine-boned hand and delicately touched the bruise around Kalina's eye. Kalina almost pulled away, stunned by the sudden contact, but remained frozen to the spot as the princess looked at her with such compassion and kindness, she didn't have the heart to swat her hand away.

"They sound like lovely people, to have taken you in and helped you." The princess reached for an apple as well and bit into it, the juices running down her chin and she laughed as she wiped it away, Kalina joining with her. Once their laughter had subsided the princess continued. "How did you get a job in the castle?"

Kalina considered. Should she reveal her relationship with Talon? Had word spread of Sir Dyelan and the Wyvern at Hywell Abbey and Talon letting a girl fly away on its back? She wasn't sure how much of her own story had gotten around the court, but she also couldn't lie outright to the princess. She chose a partial lie instead.

"I met Talon when he and his knight-master came to our town. He talked about the capitol so much that I felt I had to come here. He helped me get the job with Mistress Aynne in the kitchens."

Princess Cherise seemed to consider her words carefully, her face a serene mask despite a small crease between her eyes.

"What about you, Cherise?" Kalina asked, stumbling over the princess' name.

"What about me?" The princess smiled sideways at Kalina.

"Tell me about yourself," Kalina pressed. "Tell me about your father and husband and your life!"

Cherish laughed before answering.

"Well, I grew up here, in this castle. These gardens were my playground. That's why I keep coming here, even now." The princess continued to eat her apple as she spoke. "My father, well, he means well, and he tries his best, both with the country and with me. But he's getting on in years and knows I'll be taking over the crown soon so he spends much of his time instructing me in the ways of politics and running the kingdom." Kalina listened raptly, hoping the princess would give her a bit of information about the Prince. Something to back up what she'd heard in the gardens. "My husband is an ambitious man. He's from Askor, and we had an arranged marriage for political reasons. Our marriage ended the long war." Kalina noted that the princess did not light up while talking about her husband. It was a loveless marriage, then.

"Is he kind to you? Are you happy?" Kalina was surprised at her own boldness.

"He cares about me an awful lot."

"That doesn't really answer my question," Kalina said, a small smirk on her lips. The princess smirked back.

"I know." They lapsed into a comfortable silence. Kalina thought of all the questions she could ask this woman about the kingdom and about the Valdir when the crunching of footsteps on a nearby pathway broke their silence.

A man in his early 40's, dark hair surrounded by a circlet of gold, and dark eyes, stepped into the clearing, his eyes instantly going to the princess and then alighting on Kalina. His face, which was unremarkable and placid before, turned dark. Kalina's heartbeat quickened and she stood quickly, curtsying low.

"Cherise." The princess beside Kalina stood as well, giving a small curtsey to the man.

"Husband." Kalina's pulse jumped even higher and she had to actively work not to fall into that familiar panic.

"Who is this?" The prince's voice was cold, and his words did nothing to warm the chill that was spreading down Kalina's spine. Kalina stood there, eyes downcast, waiting for the Royals to speak to or dismiss her.

"This is Kalina. She is a scribe in the library. We ran into each other and decided to chat." The princess did not cower beneath the man's stare, nor did she become defensive.

"A female scribe? How peculiar." His eyes roamed over Kalina, making her start to sweat, and the urge to run was almost overwhelming. She didn't respond, opting for silence in case speaking gave her away. Friendship with the princess was not only dangerous, but it was also deadly. "You are dismissed, Kalina." He sounded bored when he released her. The prince flicked a hand at her and she stooped, scooping up her remaining lunch and with a quick curtsey, murmured goodbye to the princess as she hurried out of the sun-dappled glade.

Behind her, she heard the prince say "I thought I told you that you weren't allowed to wander these paths alone?" Kalina wondered at a man who could order a princess around, regardless of him being her husband. Didn't she have the right to wander the paths of her own gardens? Kalina was soon out of earshot and she took in deep breaths, relieved to be away from that man, her heart finally settling into a normal rhythm. She had thought that the prince was on the coast with Sir Dyelan, Sir Gregan, and Talon. Her heart leapt with excitement this time as she realized Talon might be back.

As she rounded the last bend in the path and the fountain came into view, Kalina saw someone sitting on the edge. The figure jumped up and came towards her as she saw with delight who it was.

"Talon! When did you get back?" She threw her arms around him, grateful for at least one person in this castle who was fully on her side.

"This morning! I knew it was your day off, and when I stopped by Calla and Anders on my way through town and saw you weren't there, I knew I might find you here." Kalina laughed as he released her. His handsome face was tanned and weather-beaten as if he'd spend the entire trip camped out on the beach, which Kalina supposed he had.

"Well, you found me." He held her at arm's length, his mouth dropping open as he surveyed her bruises.

"What in the gods' names happened to you?" Kalina blushed slightly at his attention. Everyone seemed to be overly concerned about a few bruises.

"Nothing. Just a run in with some scribes who don't like me."

"Scribes? Why would scribes beat up a kitchen maid? Did you tell Mistress Aynne? We can't allow this to happen!" He took her hand and began pulling her towards the entrance to the garden and back towards the castle kitchens.

"No, Talon, wait." She pulled him to a stop. "Something happened while you were gone." Talon frowned at her, as if he were prepared to receive more bad news. Kalina smiled at him. "I was promoted. To scribe." Talon dropped her hand and took a step back.

"Scribe? How?" His voice trailed off.

"I met the Princess. She liked me and thought I would be better off as a scribe so she pulled some strings and got me the job." Talon took the few steps back to the fountain and sat down.

"The Princess? Princess Cherise? THE Princess?"

"Yes. Cherise." Kalina sat down beside him, putting down her bundle of half eaten food. "She is very nice to have gotten me the job, and trying to research while actually in the library for work has been much easier. But the problem is that the other scribes hate me." Talon stood up suddenly.

"Then I will put them straight." Kalina laughed at his gallant effort to protect her. She didn't need protecting. She grabbed his hand, holding him in place.

"No, Talon. I am handling it my own way." She decided to change the subject. "What was it like on the coast? With the Prince?" Talon sat finally beside her and sighed heavily.

"The Prince is... cold. Sir Gregan and he often were alone, leaving Sir Dyelan and myself to handle the pirates. It wasn't a very pleasant business. We had a contingent of men with us, but it still took us two weeks to track down the leader of the pirates. His name was Black-eyed Bill." Kalina snickered at the name. Talon rolled his eyes. "I know. Stupid name, but not a stupid man. He was holed up in a backwater inn, his ship out to sea, manned by a skeleton crew. We almost didn't find him, but then a dockside whore he'd slapped around the night before gave him up and we were able to corner him and take him down. His fleet of ships followed."

"And the Prince didn't get his hands dirty at all?" Talon shook his head.

"Nope." Kalina snorted.

"Typical." She linked her arm in his. "Anyway, now that you are back we can do some research together." His presence alone would be a balm to her, easing her constantly on-edge nerves whenever she was alone in the library.

"Yea!" His face lit up at the prospect. "Starting tonight."

Chapter 20

KALINA RUBBED HER BLEARY and burning eyes as she put down yet another book. Her heart sank with every new book, every time she didn't find anything useful. There were plenty of mentions of the Valdir, the food they cultivated for years in the Great Grey Mountains, what the dragons ate, how they governed themselves. But nothing from the last decade, let alone the last hundred years. Talon and she had been at it for hours, gathering a huge stack of books from both the dragon section and the flying section in hopes of cross-referencing something useful. Beside her, Talon was diligently reading away. Kalina smiled softly at him and stood to stretch.

"I'm going to wander a bit, see if I can think of another tactic." Talon looked up at her and nodded in a distracted way. She began meandering down the rows between the stacks, grateful that she was at home here. There had to be more information about the Valdir but they had searched in the V section, the Flying section, the Wyvern section, and the Dragon section. All of them came up empty with recent references. As she wandered towards the flying section again, wondering if they'd missed some obscure reference, she heard raised voices. She paused in the darkness of the aisle and pressed herself against the books, listening.

"I'm telling you, there's more here!" She recognized that voice and her blood ran cold.

"Your Majesty, I have brought you every single book within this library with any reference to the Valdir going back a hundred years! I don't know what child you seek, nor do I know of any mention of one being born!" The shrill voice of a much older man and Kalina's stomach twisted. She desperately hoped the prince wouldn't hurt someone who sounded so old and frail.

"That's not good enough. Bring me every genealogy on the Valdir, along with every book that mentions them."

"All the books, your Highness?"

"Yes. All of them, Alexil," the prince snapped out. There was a flurry of movement and an old man in black scholar robes hurried past her hideout. Kalina quietly slipped farther down the row to where the light globes barely reached. Footsteps sounded and she watched as the prince paused before her aisle. His face was cold, devoid of any emotion, and Kalina knew in her bones that he would kill her the moment he found her. Finally, the prince turned away and strode off into the darkness, but it was a few minutes before Kalina felt like she could breathe once again.

Clearly, Scholar Alexil was the man to talk to about the Valdir. She walked as quickly as she could to the front desk where she asked the attendant in charge where to find Scholar Alexil.

"Why would you want to talk to that old coot?" the young man there scoffed, eying her with disdain.

"Just tell me where he is," she said impatiently. The boy pointed down the long hall lined with offices.

"Last one on the end." Kalina thanked him and set off.

Scholar Alexil's office was much like the Master of the library: every surface was piled with books. While the Master's seemed haphazard, Alexil's seemed to have some sort of order, a method to his seeming madness. Kalina knocked softly before entering.

"Scholar Alexil? Are you there?" The old man popped his head out from behind a pile of books, his white hair floating around his head.

"Yes? Oh! You must be Kalina, our newest recruit. Please, come, sit." He gestured for her to come sit at the seat before his desk. When she was settled, he spoke. "What can I do for you, my dear?"

"I was hoping you could help me find out about the Valdir." It was a dangerous move. But she knew she could lie her way out of it. The man's eyebrows rose so high they almost disappeared into his white hair.

"And why, may I ask, do you want to learn about them?"

"I only just heard about them. I overheard two other scholars speaking of them and I grew curious. Do you know where I should start?" Alexil eyed her suspiciously, before answering.

"You start with the dragons." Kalina smiled even as her heart sank. She knew that already.

"Thank you so much, Scholar Alexil." She placed the reference card back into the box.

"Dragons are a particular favorite of mine." A voice sounded behind her and the scholar. Kalina turned and saw Princess Cherise standing in the doorway.

"Princess." The scholar bowed deeply and Kalina stood and

curtsied a moment later. Her heart leapt at the sight of the woman.

"Thank you, Scholar Alexil. I think I can help Kalina from here."

"Of course, your Highness." Alexil bowed low and winked at Kalina. Kalina smiled and followed the princess from the room and back into the library.

"Your Majesty."

"Please, Kalina. Cherise when we are alone." Kalina looked around, seeing no other scholars or scribes nearby.

"Cherise." The princess nodded in approval and motioned for Kalina to sit with her at some nearby chairs. Kalina sat, nervousness making her bounce her leg. "Are you alright?" She asked the royal.

"Of course. What makes you ask that?" Kalina looked down sheepishly.

"The prince, he seemed cross with you when I left yesterday." Cherise smiled disarmingly.

"He was just worried about me is all." Kalina watched as the princess tugged absently on the sleeves of her dress.

"So, you said you like dragons?" Kalina sat forward, trying to change the subject as it clearly made the princess uncomfortable. The princess brightened.

"Yes! I have always been fascinated by them. I have even met a few when I was much younger. Not much older than you in fact." Kalina brightened.

"Wow! Where?" She couldn't keep the eagerness from her voice.

"Here at the castle. Just before the war ended. The Valdir were a regular presence until the war ended and they disappeared." Finally. Someone mentioned the Valdir.

"What were they like?" The princess looked up at her, a look Kalina couldn't read on her face. "The dragons?" She clarified.

"Huge. Bigger than a house, and scaled in what looks like jewels. But their scales are deceiving, they are in fact as strong as the strongest metal, capable of withstanding arrows and crossbow bolts. Their wingspans are hundreds of feet long and cast a shadow as they fly by." Kalina listened in wonder to the princess' descriptions. She tried comparing them to the size of a Wyvern. Savath had barely been larger than a large ox and its wingspan was only about forty feet wide.

She could have carried Kalina and maybe Talon but no more, and Kalina wasn't exactly large for her age, and neither was Talon. A dragon must be able to carry ten men, or even twenty.

"I've met a Wyvern before." Kalina burst out, unable to hold back her own experiences.

"Have you? What was it like?" The princess leaned forward, eagerness lighting her beautiful face.

"It wasn't nearly that big, or that majestic, but its scales gleamed like emeralds in the sun and it was surprisingly intelligent."

"You spoke to one?"

"Yes." Kalina was suddenly self-conscious. She was giving a lot away. The memory of Sir Gregor and the Prince making her stop short. "Only a few words." She wanted to steer the conversation back to the princess. "So, these dragons, what colors do they come in?"

Kalina and the princess sat and spoke for hours, discussing the variations on coloring and surmising what color dragons would come from the coupling of a red and green dragon and whether it would be brown, or would take the stronger genetics as humans did. Kalina asked if it was true that dragons could breathe fire.

"But there are some legends that say they can. Although nothing in recent history supports that theory." The princess nodded in agreement.

"Yes, you are correct. Only in legends."

They parted ways as the dinner bells sounded and Kalina found her stomach was rumbling. She needed to grab a bite to eat with Margy and then enlist Talon to help her go through more books. She curtsied a goodbye to Princess Cherise and ran down the hall to the kitchens.

After dinner, Kalina and Talon carried armloads of books over to the largest table on the bottom floor of the library and began sorting through them. Hours later they headed towards her room, bleary-eyed and exhausted. Talon waved goodnight as he trudged down the hall and Kalina entered her rooms. The cat, Moose, sat on her bed as if waiting for her to come home. It comforted her in a way she couldn't express. So much about the palace was foreign, empty, and alone. It was nice that with Talon, the princess, and Moose she had a few she could count on.

Chapter 21

KALINA HAD SUCCESSFULLY avoided Dillion and his cronies for about a week. She had eaten every meal in the kitchens with Margy and had spent her free time in the library. Now that she knew the prince was actively taking books on the Valdir from the library, she hurried to read all she could. One afternoon, right after her day off, she was running her fingers through her freshly dyed hair, wandering down the rows of books looking for a book Master Buckner had sent her to find and transcribe when she heard the scuffing of feet behind her. She whirled, suddenly frustrated with herself for being lost in thought and letting her guard down. Her heart pounded in fear and anger but she stood her ground.

Dillion and three other scribe boys stood in the aisle. Dillion had a smirk on his face. His cronies smiled viciously at Kalina. Four against one. Her stomach churned at the thought of what they could do to her. She backed up slowly, reaching out to the side for a book or something to use as a weapon.

"What's a girl like you doing in a place like this?" Dillion advanced, almost sauntering towards her. "I thought we made it clear with our first beating that you weren't welcome here." Kalina swallowed, trying to find the right words to respond with. She kept backing up, one foot behind the other, her hands trailing the shelves. Her bruises had barely begun to heal, turning a nasty shade of yellow. Her eye had gone back to normal and her nose, while still sore, was no longer red or swollen. She wasn't sure she could handle a second beating.

Suddenly the boys froze. Kalina strained her ears for what had stopped them, glancing behind herself for the reason, risking taking her eyes off them for a moment. The sounds of voices coming near reached her ears, and when she looked back at the group of boys, they had gone, scattering as quickly and quietly as they had appeared. Kalina sighed in relief, listening to the arguing voices of two scholars coming closer, one aisle over from where she stood. She froze, listening hard as a word reached her ears.

"...all traces of the Valdir. It's impossible! But the man sure is trying." The first voice she didn't recognize but the second belonged to Scholar Alexil she was sure.

"I don't understand his obsession with the Valdir. He has come to me again and again, searching for them and the girl, but he hasn't seemed to have found them yet. I'm not convinced she exists, and perhaps they fled the continent altogether. " That was Kalina's greatest fear. There was no way she'd find them then.

"I keep bringing him books whenever I come across mentions of them, but he still isn't satisfied. He once asked me to write a letter to the chief librarian of Alben, trying to see if they have heard of the Valdir to the south." Alben was their neighboring country to the southwest, as Askor was to their North and Wostrad to their south. Perhaps she needed to search in the histories of other countries to find mention of them. Kalina held her breath as the scholars walked past her hiding place in the next row.

"Well, surely the Prince has an extensive private collection by now?" Scholar Alexil sounded annoyed.

"He does indeed. And he won't allow me to even transcribe a second copy of those books. He just insists on keeping them for himself."

Kalina let out her breath as their voices faded into the distance. The prince had all the recent books about the Valdir. That was why she hadn't been able to find a single mention of them in the last hundred years anywhere in the library. All her hours of searching felt fruitless. She still wondered why the prince was so concerned with little old her.

Kalina sighed. She needed to find a way into the Prince's rooms. Those books could hold the key, some clue as to where her people had fled, where they hid, Whether they were even still alive. It seemed she had one piece of the puzzle, and the prince possessed the other.

Late that night Kalina slipped from her rooms, pausing for only a moment to pet Moose on the head before heading into the dark corridors of the castle. It was a fairly normal sight to see a scribe wandering the halls late at night, and with her dark clothing, she was hard to detect when she slipped into shadows as people passed her by. She carried a book about dragons in her arms, and in her pocket was a map of the castle she had found in castle records in the library. She knew that the prince's rooms were in the east wing on the third floor, next door to the princess' rooms. She didn't really have much of a plan, but she knew from the records that he had an outer chamber, an inner bedroom, a sitting room, and a bathing room, all connected by doors. The bedroom and the bathing room were farthest from the outer rooms and she reasoned he must keep his books in his outer rooms or his sitting room.

Around her, the castle was as quiet as the grave and she padded softly down the eastern corridor to the ornate doors that were the entrance to the prince's rooms. To her immense surprise, there were only two guards on duty. She remembered the servants' stairs had doors to each sitting room where most of the royals took their meals, and after contemplating whether there would be a guard stationed by the servants' entrance, she hurried to the entrance to the servants' stairs at the end of the hall.

It was dark except for the light of a torch on the stair, and the short passage to his sitting room was pitch black. She stepped just inside the passage, waiting until her eyes had adjusted to the darkness and she could make out the faint outline of a doorway in the gloom. She paused before it, took her hair and tied it up on her head, getting it out of her face and somehow making her feel more prepared for whatever waited beyond that door. She paused to listen, but there was no noise and no guard.

She pushed it open, having tucked the book on dragons into her pocket, and with a quick look to make sure she was alone, stepped inside the room. It was lit by a single candle burning on a table by two floor-to-ceiling double doors. The furnishings were beyond astonishing. Kalina had never seen anything so decadent in all her life, not even Father Martin's rooms had been this well-appointed, this luxurious. There were tapestries on the walls and rich deep carpets on the floors. Each piece of furniture was elegantly made and some even looked to be trimmed in gold leaf. There were bookshelves that stretched to the ceilings and a large table surrounded by chairs that was piled with papers and books. Kalina crept forward, her feet luxuriating in the plush carpet beneath them despite her thin-soled shoes. Scribes wore slippers so that their steps were soft and quiet in the library.

She stood beside the table and focused on its contents. The dimness of the room made reading exact words difficult so she took a small stub of a candle from her own pockets and went to light it on the one burning by the doors. Pausing to listen, she could hear someone's deep and even breathing from beyond the door and with a cold feeling settling in her stomach, she realized the prince must be asleep beyond those very doors. There was a set of smaller doors on the opposite wall that she assumed led to the outer receiving room. Along the wall opposite where she had entered, there were large windows, and as she watched, the moon that had been previously hidden by clouds became suddenly visible, lighting the room with a silvery glow. Her foot hit a loose floorboard and she froze at the resulting squeak, terror pounding through her. The snoring paused for a moment before continuing and after a few moments, she breathed a light sigh.

Kalina went back to the table and, without moving the books and papers, began to read what was written there. Most of the books were on the Valdir and her heart leapt to finally read their names on the papers. The prince had highlighted different passages, each referencing the Valdir in a different part of the country. Some mentioned the Borderlands, some the Great Grey Mountains, some the Deep Glen Forest, and even some the Wastes. There was a large map pinned to a wall, with colored pins all over, each she assumed meant something but one, in particular, was silver, the only silver pin on the board, and it was stuck deep into Hywell Abbey. Her abbey. She stood frozen. The prince knew where she was, and perhaps even who she was; had Sir Gregan known her name? She couldn't remember if the townsfolk had revealed that much. Fear churned in her gut and she forced herself to turn back to the table and search.

She began picking up and moving the books, reading and flipping through the passages, trying to set them down as she had found them. One book mentioned that all Valdir children were born with silver hair. Her hand went to her own hair, grateful it was still dyed. She was on week two and knew that soon she'd be heading into town on her day off so Calla could dye it for her again.

She left the prince's rooms that night more confused than she had been before she'd found the books on the Valdir. She had looked at his bookshelves as well, not daring to take down books in fear of making noise, but didn't find anything that would lead her to the Valdir. The prince's map stuck out in her head as she trudged back

to her room in the library. He knew where she had been. She just
hoped that she wouldn't run into the prince again, in case he had
somehow figured out who she was.

She fell into bed exhausted, knowing the next day of work
would be difficult due to so little sleep, but just before she drifted off,
she knew she'd be going back the next night to search the prince's
rooms further.

Chapter 22

KALINA QUIETLY PUSHED OPEN the door to the prince's rooms again, but this time she carried an already lit candle with her. The room was darker than the night before, no candle left burning this night. She crept forward, heading for the table stacked with books.

She had just sat down at an already pulled out chair, a book before her that discussed the end of the war and speculated on what had happened to the Valdir, when a blazing light and the sudden clomp of boots made her leap up, knocking the chair back onto the floor, and knocking her candle over. The flame lit the edge of a sheaf of papers on fire, and as Kalina took steps backward away from the table, rough hands grabbed her and held her; someone came forward in the dark, swearing as they quickly put out the small fire. Kalina's heart raced and she struggled in the hands that held her, trying to turn towards the partially open servants' doorway, hoping to escape. She didn't know what had happened, or how in the world she had been caught, but now that she was, her heart sank into her feet. This was it. This was the end. The prince had caught her and she was going to be killed.

The bright light that had blinded her so became a bright flame, as someone went around and lit the braziers and candles in the room, lighting the space as bright as daylight. Kalina blinked as she took in the scene around her. Two guards in green and gold palace livery held her arms. Sir Gregan and another guard stood at attention by the doors to the prince's rooms. The prince himself stood by the table; his hands black with soot from the fire he had just put out.

"A mouse was going through my things last night, and I thought perhaps it would be back tonight." He smiled a snake-like smile at Kalina, who kept her eyes down. She didn't know what this man wanted, so she would play it safe and wait and see. "I was lucky my little trap worked." He took a few steps towards her and tilted her chin up, noting her blue eyes and her brown hair. He eyed her roots for a few moments as if searching for the silver that wasn't there. "You're that scribe my wife introduced me to. Katrina was it?"

"Yes, your Highness." She didn't bother correcting him. Either he knew who she was or he didn't. No reason to play right into his hands.

"Hmmm." He began walking around the large table, his hands clasped behind his back. "Now the question is, who are you and what to do with you?" She didn't know what she hoped for. She had spent all her life in the abbey, and since she'd been in Ravenhelm she hadn't learned as much about the world as she felt like she needed to know right at that moment. She just hoped she wouldn't die. She had to keep her relationship with Talon secret. The prince already knew about the princess and her, but not the depth of their budding friendship. She swallowed as the man continued to pace the room, eyeing her thoughtfully. "While I decide your fate, you will spend your time in our dungeon as our guest." He waved a hand in dismissal and Kalina was dragged from the room, Sir Gregan leading the way. She struggled; if only she could get away, she could run for the library or the gardens, two places where she knew she could outrun and hide from the guards, but they had a solid grip on her arms.

They dragged her down hallways and flight after flight of stone stairs until there were no more hallways and only tunnels, dark but for torches set into the wall every ten feet or so. It was growing colder and damper the lower they descended, and soon the tunnels opened out into a large underground chamber. There were cells set into the walls here, going the entire perimeter of the chamber; the center of the chamber was open, a chair bolted to the stone in the center with straps. Kalina's heart rose into her throat as the men dragged her past that chair and into a cell. She had a feeling she knew what that chair was used for.

The guards threw her unceremoniously onto the floor of a cell, skinning her knees on the rough stone, closing the iron gate behind her with a dull clang. The far wall was made of stone, and the two sides were iron grates so that you could see your neighbors if you had any. There was no cot, only a bundle of ratty old blankets, and a chamber pot in one corner against the wall. She sat up, rubbing her bruised hands, and looked around, fear growing in her chest. The only light came from across the large chamber where torches lit the walls. She could hear shuffling, sniffing, and sobbing coming from somewhere off to her right, but she could only see a few cells down before it disappeared into the gloom.

It was cold. Bone deep cold and Kalina shivered as she crawled towards the pile of dirty blankets. She unraveled them, finding them mostly full of holes and smelling of urine and sweat, and she put them back down, unsure whether she had reached a point where she was willing to wrap herself in them. She pulled her black scribes robes around her more firmly, tucking in her hands and arms, and pulling her feet into her chest. She put her back to the wall, as there was a slight draft coming down the tunnel and into the chamber, and sniffed. She might never see Talon, or the princess, or Calla, or Anders, or Issa ever again. She already missed them terribly, and a few tears slid down her cheeks at her fate as she pressed her head into her knees and waited.

Time had no meaning in that dark place. Kalina knew she slept at some point but had no idea how long. Her joints and bones had begun to ache and she was contemplating getting up and walking her cell to get the circulation moving when she heard footsteps coming down the tunnel.

The prince stepped into view and Kalina's blood ran cold. This was it. She was going to end up in that chair. Two guards flanked him as he approached her cell. His cold face seemed even colder down in this damp, dark place. His unremarkable features suddenly seemed grotesque to Kalina as she waited for whatever was to come. The prince stopped before her cell and watched her for a few moments before nodding to the guards. Sir Gregan stood beside his prince. They came forward and unlocked her door and hauled her up and out into the main chamber. They dragged her as she began to fight in silent horror as they forced her to sit in the chair. Kalina could see old blood staining the wooden arms of the chair and the dark stain around the base of the chair was unmistakable. Her stomach rose into her throat and for a moment she was grateful she hadn't eaten in hours; her bladder cramped uncomfortably as though she might mess herself. She stank of fear.

The prince approached her and withdrew from the sleeve of his coat a long, sharp blade. Kalina began to sweat, fear twisting her gut as her mind raced to hold on to each thought. He smiled at her terror.

"I plan to ask you a few questions, Karina. If you answer them, and I am satisfied with those answers, you won't receive a cut. If you don't answer them, then I will cut you." He grinned at her, his dark eyes sparkling in the gloom. Kalina swallowed and nodded her understanding. Her breath was so shallow she wasn't sure she could speak, but she knew she had to. She was beginning to feel lightheaded, that familiar panic setting in. She struggled to hold herself together, to think clearly as the prince lay the knife on her forearm.

"Who are you?" What could she tell him? If she revealed who she was, would they kill her? If she lied, would he know? She decided she would rely on her trusty old habits of weaving truth and lies together.

"I'm an orphan." The prince's eyes lit at her answer but she continued. "My parents died of the pox when I was a child and I was sent to Whitepoint Abbey." That abbey was farther north than her own, but their High Father, Father Sidall, had come to visit their abbey two years ago so she knew enough about that abbey to pass. If she said Hywell, then Sir Gregan would know instantly who she was. "I came to Ravenhelm a few years ago and worked in the kitchen of the White Dove Inn." Her voice shook as she spoke. She mixed in familiar landmarks with a believable story. The prince narrowed his eyes, glancing up at the roots of her hair.

"Whitepoint, you say?" He sounded like he almost didn't believe her. She swallowed and held her breath as the prince stepped away from her, removing his blade and beginning to pace. "Why were you in my rooms?"

"I heard you had books on the Valdir. I wanted to read about them but knew I couldn't come to ask you directly."

"Why are you so interested in the Valdir?" Kalina desperately wanted to ask him that very same question but she swallowed and answered.

"They sound interesting. I read an old text that talked about their culture and I've been quite fascinated with them since." There, another nugget for him to parse out. "When I couldn't find any information in the library, I asked a scholar. They said you had all the books." The prince looked at her suddenly, his eyes flashing.

"What scholar?" Kalina swallowed, her mouth dry.

"I don't remember his name, your Highness. I'm new at the library and I have met so many scholars." The prince narrowed his eyes at her once again. Somehow, he was buying her story, but she wondered for how long. Her eyes flicked to Sir Gregan beside the prince. His eyes were narrowed in suspicion.

"So, let me get this straight." Kalina's stomach churned again. "You read a fairy story and decided to risk your life and your job to break into my rooms and read my books?" She blinked. He didn't buy her story. She clenched her hands on the arms of the chair, her knuckles going white as the prince came close. His blade flashed out, slicing a long cut down her forearm. She hissed as the blood welled.

"Yes, your Highness. I wasn't thinking, I-" she broke off as the prince slashed out again slicing her from her hairline down to her chin on her left cheek. She cried out, as the pain hit her a moment later, and blood began to pour down her face. She could taste copper in her mouth and knew the knife had cut through her cheek.

"I don't believe you." His voice was cold as ice. She sat gasping, her hair falling into her face, blood dripping down to fall into her lap. Pain like she had never experienced, a burning sensation lancing through her head, and it was all she could do to keep breathing. "Put her away." Footsteps retreated up the tunnel as hands fumbled at the leather straps that held her to the chair. She was limp in the guards' arms as they dragged her back to her cell. They were much gentler when they lay her on the cold stone floor and locked the door behind her. She barely knew what was happening when the door behind her opened a few moments later and one of the guards came in carrying a fresh stack of blankets. They weren't soft or comfortable, but they were clean and dry. The guard took away the old pile and closed the door behind her once again.

She was alone and shivering violently as she pulled the blankets towards her and wrapped them around herself. The blood was beginning to crust over, matting her hair and making her dress stiff. She spit into the chamber pot beside her, her spit red with blood. She put her head back against the cold stone and wished, for the first time since leaving the abbey, that she was back there, in her little cot in the dormitory, listening to Delisa snore away beside her. Maybe this whole adventure had been one big mistake.

Chapter 23

LONELINESS AND DESPAIR were Kalina's constant companions over the course of the next week. All her efforts over the past months, all her fear and anxiety, the abuse from Dillion, and the lengths Talon went to in order to get her into the castle, seemed fruitless. As the days dragged on she both wish for and was terrified that the prince would come back and question her. But it seemed he was content to let her rot in the prison cell. She slept as often as she could, and when she was awake, she counted the bars on her cage.

She struggled to wake, feeling like she was swimming up through a dark, dense sea. Her face throbbed as she swam into consciousness, and she winced as she moved. Her body was stiff and painful, the result of many hours asleep in that dark place. She wondered if prisoners ever survived long down here. If a wound didn't fester, they surely would die of exposure or lung rot. At the entrance to her cell, a tray of food had been placed, but Kalina watched while two rats feasted on the pitiful food that lay there. Her stomach churned at the sight and she moved to a slightly less painful position.

The rats scattered as she moved but it was then that she caught the soft sounds of footsteps coming down the tunnel. Her heart leapt into her throat once again. The mere thought of the prince coming to question her made her bowels turn to liquid and it was all she could do not to spiral down into panic. A small part of her, however, felt relief that it might all be over. But she steadied her breathing, focusing on the pain in her cheek, and realized it was just one set of footsteps, perhaps a servant come to take her tray. But the figure that came through into the large, dimly lit underground chamber was the last person she expected to see.

Princess Cherise hurried over to Kalina's cell; her arms full with a large bundle. She unlocked the door with a key and came inside, kneeling before Kalina. Kalina drew away, not wanting the princess to see her like this, but also highly suspicious. As much as she liked Cherise, the woman was married to the prince.

"Come here, let me clean your wounds." The princess laid out her bundle and unwrapped the edges, revealing a number of things that Kalina barely paid attention to. She watched, rapt, as the princess prepared to clean the wounds. First, the princess reached for her forearm, gently cleaning the wound with a hot cloth. Then she reached out towards Kalina's cheek and as the heat came into contact, Kalina flinched away. "You'll need to be still so I can clean it. We don't want it to fester." Her voice was soothing, encouraging. Kalina nodded and clenched her teeth, digging her fingernails into her palms as Cherise wiped away the crusted blood as gently as she could. The pain was almost unbearable but Kalina bore it without making a sound, her breaths coming ragged from her chest.

"How did you know I was here?" She managed to ask, her voice a mere croak. The princess' face fell as she rinsed out the cloth.

"Last night, my father died." The princess, no... the queen stopped talking, swallowing visibly. Kalina's heart hurt for this beautiful woman before her. "But just before he died, he sent me a message, saying you had been taken to the dungeons by my husband." Kalina was shocked. How had the king known she was there and who she was? Why did he care? "So, I waited until my husband was asleep, and came down here." She returned to wiping Kalina's face. Soon the water was tinged pink with her blood and her face was throbbing something fierce. "I'm sorry I didn't know sooner." She sounded so incredibly sad that Kalina put a hand on the woman's cheek. Cherise looked up, meeting Kalina's eyes for a moment before returning to her work. Kalina could barely bring herself to speak, but a question was nagging at her.

"How did he die?" The queen sniffed softly.

"I don't know. He was fine yesterday." She sniffed louder this time, and Kalina saw a few stray tears run down the woman's pretty face. She wanted to reach out and embrace her, take away her sorrow.

Queen Cherise picked up a salve and dipped two fingers into it, smearing it along the long cut on Kalina's face. "Did it break through into your mouth?" Kalina nodded, wincing at the slight sting. "Then you need to rinse your mouth really well after eating okay? Any food particles will get stuck and can cause infection." Kalina nodded.

"Thank you." She paused, wondering why this woman was risking her husband's wrath to help her. "Why are you helping me? He's just going to do it again."

"He'll never do this to you again, my darling." Some part of

Kalina unraveled at the words.

"How do you know?"

"Because I'm getting you out of here." With that, she tied up what remained in the bundle. Kalina had failed to pay attention but she took it when the queen handed it to her. "Now, I'm going to lead you to a secret passage in the wall. It takes you out into the gardens. There, you will find Talon who is ready and waiting to help you flee the city." Kalina's mouth opened and closed in astonishment. "But you can't stop, not even to say goodbye to your family in the city." The queen's face was deadly serious.

"But why not? The prince can't find me there, can he?"

"The prince knows more than you think. And he will find you if you stay." She stood and began hurrying through the cavern, Kalina hot on her heels. "Remember when we were speaking of the Valdir before?"

"Yes." Kalina was wary now and she slowed her steps. The queen kept walking, gesturing for Kalina to follow her into the dark tunnel.

"I know you're looking for them. I know they are your people." The queen looked back, pointedly at her hairline which was slowly turning silver. "You will find them in the Wastes. Go to the Wastes."

"But there's nothing in the Wastes. Most of the books say so."

"I promise you, Kalina, you will find your people in the Wastes." The queen was so serious that Kalina could only nod in agreement.

"Then I will go to the Wastes." The queen led her down a twisting side tunnel that Kalina hadn't noticed on her first trip down to the dungeons. It stopped at what seemed to be a solid brick wall. But the queen pushed her hand through and Kalina realized it was an optical illusion of some sorts, two tunnels leading off to either side.

"Go to the right and the final door will take you to the gardens. You know where to meet Talon." Kalina nodded. The woman reached out and pulled her suddenly into a tight embrace. Kalina hesitated before embracing her back, her arms going around Cherise's slim waist and squeezing hard. Cherise pressed a kiss to Kalina's head before releasing her, her beautiful face serious and so sad.

"I'm so sorry about your father, Cherise," Kalina said,

squeezing the queen's hand.

"Thank you." Cherise's voice almost broke but she held it firm. "Now go, my darling, before anyone catches you. But be careful, I wouldn't put it past my husband to send someone after you." Kalina nodded. She knew who he'd send. She let go of the queen's hand and ducked into the illusioned passage.

"Goodbye, my Queen." Her voice echoed off the stones around her and she glanced back and thought she saw a tear slide down the queen's face as she waved goodbye.

The passage wound around to the right and then there were stairs. She took them two at a time, the bundle the queen had given her bouncing against her back as she carried it over her shoulder. At the top of the stairs was an old rusted iron door. She had to shove her shoulder against it until it slowly creaked open and when she stuck her head through, she saw it was overgrown with ivy and very well hidden. She tried her best to cover it back up once she was through but she didn't want to waste any time.

Her journey through the night-darkened garden was uneventful. It was nearing midnight by the tolls of the bells. Guards patrolled the perimeters of the gardens but not the center. She paused before she reached the fountain and looked through the bundle. Inside she found not only food suitable for traveling, but she also her spare dresses and a few other things including a hand-drawn map of the Ethea, with the Wastes clearly marked in the eastern part of the country. It was a long way away, an entire country away, and she was expected to outrun pursuit and make it there and then find the Valdir and dragons. It all seemed so unbelievable, so unattainable and she felt a crushing sense of impossibility settle over her.

She pulled out her dark green dress and quickly changed into it, shoving her blood-stiffened scribes' robes into the bundle. She would have to wash them as they could eventually come in handy, and then she continued on her way to the fountain. Quietly she approached, keeping her footsteps as soft as she could on the gravel of the path but Talon heard her and turned around, a mixture of fear and relief plain on his face.

"Kalina!" his whisper sounded as loud as a shout in the quiet night. "I'm so glad you are okay." She drew closer and he noticed the cut on her cheek, his hand coming up to gently touch her face. "I guess you aren't really okay." Kalina smiled at his touch and was surprised at herself. Six months ago, she wouldn't have let anyone touch her, let alone touch her face in the way Talon was, or hug her the way the queen had. She felt suddenly like she had come a long way from that girl at the abbey.

"We have to go. Do you know a way out?" Talon's hand dropped from her face and he nodded.

"This way, through an unused postern gate in the wall." He began moving, grabbing his own large pack from beside the fountain.

"Are you leaving with me?" Kalina asked in confusion. "I thought you were just getting me out of the city." Talon turned to grin at her as he led her deeper into the gardens.

"Yes, I'm coming with you. You are special to me, Kalina. Besides, the queen herself asked me to take care of you. That's more important than serving a knight master." Kalina blushed at his words and kept walking, unsure how to answer. Her heart swelled at the thought of not being alone on her trek across the country, in search of what felt like a fairy tale. But he was giving up any possibility of being a knight now, and she wasn't sure she was worth that.

They came to an overgrown wall and a door, similar to the one Kalina had passed through earlier, embedded in the stone of the wall. It was covered in vines and leaves. Talon had to remove his belt knife in order to cut away the branches enough to haul open the door. Kalina shifted her weight from foot to foot, her eyes constantly searching the dense, dark gardens around them. There was a sliver of a moon in the sky, just enough to see by, but she hoped not enough to shine on them. She dug into her bundle and pulled out the green scarf that the queen had somehow recovered for her from the floor of the prince's rooms. She wrapped it around her head, hiding any traces of her hair.

Talon went through the door first and then motioned her through. They came out into a dark alley behind some towering houses, and together they ran down the nearest break between buildings, winding and weaving their way deeper into the city and farther from the prince's grasp. Kalina realized with a sickening jolt as they rounded a corner and saw the gates of the city before them that he wasn't the prince anymore. He was King. He was married to the Queen. He now had all her considerable resources at his command. Her blood ran cold as they neared the gates.

It was with a huge sigh of relief that she spotted Anders on night duty. She ran to him and when he saw her, he burst into a smile, until he noticed the gash on her cheek. He grabbed her shoulders and gently but firmly turned her cheek to him.

"Who hurt you, Kalina? Where have you been?" He was stern, but Kalina could hear the fear and concern behind his words.

She grabbed him and pulled him away from his fellow guards who stood talking by the gate.

"The Prince. Or should I say, the King hurt me." Anders' eyes widened at her words.

"What do you mean?" Kalina hesitated to tell him the entire truth but she knew Calla would be worried sick if she didn't explain. She was beyond grateful he was even at the gate tonight.

She told him a shortened version of what had happened, leaving out the more gruesome details. She told him to keep himself and Calla safe.

"I have to go now, to find my people." If Anders was ever brought in for questioning, he might be able to admit who she was, but he wouldn't be able to give up where she was going. Anders' face was serious and sad as he looked down at her.

"Are you going to be alright?" He didn't press her about where she was going.

"Yes. I have Talon with me. But you need to let us through the gate." He nodded and pulled her in for a hug, kissing the top of her head. She squeezed him back tightly. "Give Calla my love and baby Issa." Anders nodded and let her go, walking to the gate and to his fellow guards.

Kalina stood back with Talon beside her as they watched Anders converse with the other guards, then he motioned to them.

"This is my adopted daughter, Kalina. She needs to get through to our relatives in Wostrad through Beachwood harbor. If they don't leave now, they may miss their ship." The other guards nodded and opened a smaller postern gate for Kalina and Talon to slip through. Kalina reached out and squeezed Anders' hand as she went by, pouring all her gratitude and love into that one touch. In one swoop, the man had thrown those guards off her trail. With any luck, the king's men would follow them to Beachwood while they headed south along the Greenfall River to Long Lake.

The dark road stretched before them, heading across fields rich with crops, and through dense forests. Kalina felt her spirits lift slightly. She still felt like she was chasing a dream, a fairy tale, but she was free, and she was on an adventure.

Chapter 24

KALINA AND TALON RAN across the farmland, following the Greenfall River south. Kalina had to stop as the sun peeked over the horizon of the Great Grey Mountains to the North. Her body ached and her face throbbed from the cold air battering it as they ran. She stumbled a little as she slowed. If their pursuers were on horseback, they would be overtaken. They needed transportation, and fast. Talon stood beside her, his hands on his waist, breathing heavily as Kalina doubled over, clutching her stomach. She hadn't eaten in at least two days, for that was how long she estimated she had been trapped in the dungeon.

She pulled her makeshift pack off her back and dug through it. She wondered how many of her things from her scribes' room the queen had managed to grab. She untied the edges and began sifting through the contents, setting aside her blood-stained clothing and her extra dresses. She pulled out a piece of jerky and began chewing on it as she dug through the rest of the food and found a smaller package wrapped beneath. Inside was a small amount of money in a pouch, as well as the small green pebble that Savath had given to her. Her heart leapt.

She had completely forgotten about the pebble. What had Savath said? To hold it to her chest and call its name? If ever she'd needed the Wyvern's help, now was the time. She clutched the pretty stone to her chest and called loudly.

"Savath?" Talon looked at her quizzically. "Savath?" she called again, hope blossoming in her chest. The king would be waking up now and she would bet he'd be sending people after her within the hour if he hadn't already. Nothing magical happened. She didn't feel any deep power at work. All she could do was hope, that Savath came before they had to move on and before they were caught.

"What was that?" Talon was digging in his own pack now, pulling out jerky and a water skin which he handed to her.

"Savath gave me that rock and said if I ever needed them to hold it and call their name. I don't know if they will come but it was worth a shot." She took a swig of water, careful not to drink too much in case she vomited, her stomach cramping. "We aren't going to outrun pursuit at this rate." Talon nodded in agreement, his sweaty brown hair falling into his eyes.

They sat for twenty minutes, catching their breath and eating bits of jerky, but Kalina was itching to get moving, and soon she found herself tying up her bundle and slipping the green stone into the pocket of her dress. Talon stood with her and without another word, they began walking as fast as they could down the road.

They stopped just after noon as they reached a grove of trees. Kalina and Talon pushed their way through the underbrush, hiding their trail as best they could before settling down for a nap. Kalina was too tired to care if anyone was pursuing them, and she used the bundle as a pillow and slipped into a deep sleep.

She walked down the road alone. No pack hung on her back; no Talon walked beside her. She could only see the road before her, otherwise, the entire landscape was obscured by a thick layer of fog. She walked without urgency, wondering vaguely at the strangeness of her surroundings, when suddenly the fog swirled and she could hear hoofbeats coming towards her, echoing through the fog. Her heart began to race, and she felt dread flow through her and threaten to swallow her up. She began walking more quickly, slowly breaking into a jog, and then a run as the hoofbeats got louder and louder. She could not let them catch her, she had to get away. But the faster she ran, she did not seem to move any farther down the foggy path. The scenery around her never changed, and the hoofbeats continued to grow louder and louder. She kept looking behind her, over her shoulder into the swirling fog, waiting for a dark shape to fly out of the fog and snatch her up, or flatten her. Right as she thought the hoofbeats were on top of her, her feet flying across the perfectly even ground, she woke up.

Kalina sat up suddenly, gasping for air. She looked all around them frantically, searching for pursuers. The grove of trees was empty but for her and Talon, the sun beginning to set in the west. But Kalina could still hear the pounding, and it took her a few moments to realize it wasn't hoofbeats at all, but the pounding of great wings! She reached over and shook Talon awake excitedly.

"Talon, wake up! Savath's here!" He woke groggily, confusion muddled with sleep on his boyish face. Kalina smiled over at his messy hair and bemused expression. Hope took root in her stomach, and she stood to greet the great, green Wyvern that was settling in the road beyond their grove.

"Savath!" Kalina cried and she threw her arms around the chest of the Wyvern. A rumble emanated from the Wyvern, almost like a cat's purr. Talon stood a few feet away, watching the scene with a small smile on his lips. "I wasn't sure you'd come."

"I was very far away and it takes time for me to fly here." The Wyvern's voice rumbled against Kalina's ear and she felt the words all the way in her toes. She pulled away from the Wyvern and looked up into the scaled face.

"We need to get as far southeast as you can take us. All the way to the Wastes if you can."

"I can't take you that far, little one. I have a family now that I must take care of." Surprise lit Kalina's face.

"Do you have eggs, Savath?" The giant beast huffed in agreement.

"I have children I must attend to. I can take you as far southeast as the long lake, but no further."

"Any help is appreciated. Thank you, Savath." Kalina hugged the beast again and then she and Talon climbed up onto the scaled back, just behind Savath's wing joints. Kalina hung on to a spiked ridge and Talon put his arms around her waist. She felt his warmth press up against her and realized this was the closest they had ever been to each other. Her stomach flip-flopped at the thought as Savath rose onto her hind feet, spreading her wings out to her sides.

"Hang on tight, little ones." And with that, it launched itself into the air with a mighty sweep of her wings. Kalina's stomach dropped out beneath her and she felt Talon's arms tighten to an almost crushing degree around her. He gasped in her ear and Kalina smiled as the world dropped away beneath them, the rising moon before them, the setting sun behind them, and the sunset-kissed land stretching out before them.

Now that Kalina knew she was Valdir, she noticed how easily flying came to her. She instinctively knew how to move with Savath in the air, knew the wind currents that passed beneath the Wyvern's wings, and felt any fear dropping away as they soared. Talon still clung to her waist, his head buried in her shoulder, her hair torn free from its wrapping and slapping him in the face.

They flew into the night as it descended upon them, the sun

slipping below the far horizon, and the world below them became blanketed in velvety darkness. Kalina sighed as the night wind ran through her hair, the moon shining off her silver roots, making her feel more alive and at home than she had in months.

They landed beside a silver lake, the darkness of night still surrounding them. They had passed miles upon miles and were now close to the Borderlands. She wished Savath could have flown them farther, but knew that the Wyvern was doing them a favor as it was. And considering her size, it had already flown the two of them farther than Kalina would have thought possible. Savath's sides heaved as the beast took in huge breaths. Kalina and Talon slid off her back, Talon having to have Kalina pry his hands apart. They had locked around her middle in his fear of flying and were stiff. Kalina felt rejuvenated while Talon looked exhausted from fear.

"Thank you, Savath. I know that wasn't easy for you, carrying two of us this far." The Wyvern dipped its head before trundling down to the lake to get a drink. Kalina turned to Talon who was stamping his feet to get the feeling back into his limbs.

"We have to be careful here. The Borderlands are full of bandits," he said, looking into the trees, searching their surroundings. The Wyvern came up the bank, its big head dripping wet to stand beside Kalina and Talon. Kalina put her arms around the animal's neck once again, feeling the smoothness of the scales and the heat that radiated from within against her cheek. The Wyvern hummed in satisfaction for a few moments before pulling away.

"I have to go see to my children." The Wyvern dipped its head as if to say it was sorry to leave.

"Thank you, Savath. You really have given us a fighting chance." Together, she and Talon waved goodbye as the Wyvern swept its wings down in a great thrust, propelled itself into the night sky and disappeared into the north, towards the forest and the mountains.

Kalina turned to Talon and smiled.

"Well, might as well keep going until the sun is up." Together they began walking southeast, down the great road that followed the Rolling Run River out of the Long Lake and towards the Wastes.

Chapter 25

KALINA SAT, HER BACK against a large oak tree with branches that stretched out over the Rolling Run River beside her. Her feet dangled in the icy water, the cold taking away the ache of walking for hours. They had spent two days walking mostly at night and avoiding the roads during the day, but that was getting more and more difficult as they began to near towns. Wandering into a town trying to buy food after midnight did not go over well with most farmers and traders, and all the shops were closed. She and Talon had walked all night and all day and the sun was setting behind her as she soaked her feet.

Talon came into view from fishing down-stream, a string of fish dangling from his hand. He was suntanned, his skin a warm brown, his brown hair shining with golden streaks in the dappling of late afternoon sunshine coming through the trees. He grinned at her as he plopped down beside her and began gutting and cleaning the fish.

"Can you gather some firewood, Kalina?" Kalina jumped up to search and soon they were roasting skewered fish over a fire, laughing as the juices ran down the sticks and onto their hands and the fire popped and jumped as the oils fell and hissed into the flames.

Kalina gently scrubbed the healing gash on her cheek, trying not to dislodge the tender scabbing. She rinsed her mouth thoroughly with water whenever they stopped walking, making sure to get the road dust as well as any particles out of the wound that still pierced her cheek. She leaned over the river, Talon cleaning his fishing gear further down the bank, and looked at her reflection. She hadn't seen how much damage the prince had truly done to her face and she flinched back at the ghastly sight. The cut went from her hairline all the way down her cheek and to her chin. It was healing rather nicely but it would still leave a large scar for the rest of her life. Her heart fell, and she glanced over at Talon who smiled over at her. How could someone love her with a face like this? Dejectedly she finished cleaning herself and then went about collecting firewood for the night as darkness fell around them.

They relaxed side by side that night, a small open patch of sky showing bright stars above their makeshift bed of pine boughs.

Kalina sighed. If they weren't in such danger, if they weren't being pursued, she would feel utterly at peace lying like this in comfortable silence with Talon. He shifted beside her and his hand brushed hers. Suddenly, she warmed, a smoldering starting in her belly and rising up to her face. She had always thought Talon was handsome, but somehow, on a night like this, their bellies full, the stars shining bright overhead, and his closeness made her want to turn and kiss him. She hesitated, wondering if he possibly felt the same, or if her scarred face would make him turn away. Her stomach twisted at the thought.

That's when she felt his warm hand envelope hers, sending goosebumps up her arms and down her spine. She smiled, and as they watched the heavens turn above them, Kalina drifted off to sleep, her head slipping down to rest on Talon's shoulder.

The next morning, Kalina woke to a cold bed. The warmth of the night had burned off and Talon was nowhere to be seen. That was when she heard the yelling. She bolted upright, the blanket falling from her and looked around. The sound was coming from the nearby forest, their bed neatly hidden by the large oak tree near the river. She could hear movement in the trees and hear individual voices now, some rising in anger. Kalina crept forward, careful to keep herself hidden by the trees and undergrowth. Finally, she saw what was happening and froze.

Talon was being held by three large men in green and gold palace livery. Behind them stood four horses, one laden with goods, the others saddled for travel. The two soldiers holding Talon had his arms pinned behind him, a scrap of cloth shoved in his mouth to keep him from crying out. The side of his face and eye were already turning a sickening shade of purple where she was sure someone had hit him. His eyes were hard, and Kalina would bet if he wasn't prevented from speaking, he would be slinging curse words. The man pacing before him seemed familiar somehow but she could only see the man's back. It wasn't until he spoke that she knew who he was.

"You must have a camp around here somewhere, boy. She must be nearby." It was Sir Gregan. He paced in front of Kalina's hiding spot, just out of arm's reach. She tried to think, desperate for a way out of the situation. She had to get Talon away from Sir Gregan, who would take him back to the capital and the king's justice or kill him outright for helping her escape.

She watched the man question Talon for a few more moments, analyzing her options. She could burst in, but she wasn't much of a fighter, despite how brave she was, and she doubted her ability to overpower Sir Gregan, even with surprise on her side. She could try to distract them, draw them away from Talon but then what? Or she could wait, and see how the scene played out, waiting for an opening. She opted for the latter.

"Tie him to that tree. Olic, you stand guard and Poe and I will go search for his camp. It can't be far since we just found him pissing in the woods." Sir Gregan gave the orders and the two men behind Talon tied him bodily to the tree where he stood, trussed up like a pig for slaughter. Sir Gregan and one of the men left, looking for her and their camp. Kalina briefly wondered if she should run back to their camp and hide their packs, but it was far too late now. Instead, she watched the man Olic as he began to pace the small clearing. He was big, not as big as the knight, but he was much larger than either she or Talon. If she could sneak around and get Talon untied, the two of them could possibly overwhelm him, so she started to move. It was hard, not making noise in the dense underbrush but it seemed that Olic himself was making enough noise as he paced and he never even turned in her direction as she circled around him to the back of the tree Talon was tied to. She touched his hand lightly and whispered in his ear.

"I'm right behind you. Don't move so I can untie you." Talon had jumped at her voice but he settled down as she began to work at the knots. They were well tied and she had to use her teeth and even the small knife Talon kept on his belt to loosen them. She waited to let them drop until Olic was faced away. Then she whispered in his ear again. "I think the two of us can knock him out and run. What do you think?" Talon nodded in agreement and she felt his body tense. She dropped the ropes and together they raced up behind Olic.

Kalina leapt onto his back, clawing and kicking at him. The man bellowed and as he began to thrash, Talon knocked him soundly on the head with a rock. The soldier crumpled to the ground, Kalina rolling off of him.

"Nice shot." She smiled up at Talon, rubbing her sore bum. He reached out for her hand to help her up and she let him pull her into the underbrush. They crept towards the river, taking a very roundabout route. They could hear Sir Gregan and the other soldier crashing about in the woods, searching, and as they approached the open river bank, they could see their packs still sitting on the ground where they'd left them. They quickly gathered their things up and waded across the river, holding their packs above their heads as the water came up to their chests.

Kalina was soaked and chilled in the slight breeze but knew once she started walking, she would feel better. They both looked back across the river from the opposite, higher bank and saw Sir Gregan standing, his hands on his hips, glaring at them as they retreated into the woods as fast as they could. She felt good for having thwarted Sir Gregan but his face told her he wasn't done, that he would pursue her to the ends of the earth for his king.

Chapter 26

SIR GREGAN AND HIS MEN pursued them north into the woods. Having spent all her life near the woods, Kalina was fairly adept at getting them through, but their pursuit barely allowed them a moment's rest. Her heart fell farther every mile they trudged north. They should be heading southeast, towards their destination but it was too dangerous that way.

Sir Gregan had crossed the river on horseback not long after them, gaining whatever advantage they had thought they had. They had been forced to stay in the deepest parts of the woods, where it was hard for horses to follow. They kept pushing north until one morning, after barely getting a few hours' sleep in a deep hole between two enormous roots of a tree, Kalina realized she knew where they were. She recognized the woods around them.

Hywell Abbey was not far away. Sir Gregan may have been pushing them there on purpose, or he may have just been following them regardless but Kalina wondered if this would give them an advantage. Talon sat beside her, pulling small rocks out of his boots and retying them. He looked awful, exhausted and worn down. She knew they needed help of some kind.

"Hywell Abbey isn't far away," she said, hoping he might be open to the idea. "We could go there. I think Delisa, or Gwen, or even Father Martin would be willing to help us." Talon looked at her sideways, assessing her.

"Are you sure? Do you think that's wise? Wouldn't Sir Gregan expect us to go there for help?"

"You could be right, but we can't keep going like this. We need to get back to the Great South Road, and if Father Martin can help us, I say we do it." Talon nodded.

"How?" Kalina let out a breath.

"I have my old scribe robes. You will dress in those. I will wear your clothes, putting my hair up and acting as your servant. That will get us in until we can gain an audience with Father Martin to ask for help." She began digging through her bag, pulling out her old, blood-encrusted robes. She grimaced. "We may want to clean these first." Talon took them from her gingerly, holding them at arm's length.

"I'll go wash these and my extra set of clothing. You find us something to eat."

That evening they approached Hywell Abbey from the road. It was a huge risk, and Kalina kept looking over her shoulder, searching for their pursuers. Luckily, none came as they walked into town. Her hair was tucked up under an old hat of Talon's and she carried both packs on her shoulders as if she was Talon's pack mule. She felt a bit ridiculous, but no one would believe a scholar or scribe would be traveling alone with a girl.

The town around them was winding down for the night, the taverns and inns still open for business but the food stalls and shops all closed for the night. She felt strange, walking through such a familiar place. She had changed so much since leaving the abbey, that this place no longer felt like home. They passed the open doors of the tavern on the town square; the same one where she and Talon had gotten drinks on St. Martin's day. Light and music came from within and a few young men and women loitered around the entrance. Kalina watched them curiously, searching for familiar faces when she almost dropped her packs in excitement.

Delisa stood, her back against the open door, a boy of about her age leaning in to kiss her. Kalina gasped, and Delisa looked over, momentarily distracted from her kiss. She frowned at the sight of Talon and Kalina, but after a searching look, her eyes lit up in recognition. She squealed and pushed the boy away; he backed off, confusedly. She ran down the steps of the inn and grabbed Kalina up in a hug, swinging her around.

"You're here! I've missed you!" she said. Kalina laughed as Delisa dropped her back down. In the months she'd been gone, Delisa had changed. Nothing major, but slight changes, like she began curling her hair, and wearing more form-fitting dresses. Delisa really was trying to land herself a husband. Kalina smiled, holding her friend at arms-length as Talon stood nearby, watching. A frown furrowed Delisa's brow and she raised a hand to Kalina's cheek, tracing her scar. Kalina tried to distract her.

"You look amazing!" She took Delisa's arm and began to lead her away from the tavern. "We need your help. We need to get into the abbey and we need to see Father Martin. That knight, Sir Gregan, is pursuing us. He's not far behind." Delisa glanced down the road behind them before turning back and nodding.

"Right. Let's go." Kalina grinned, and together, she and Talon followed Delisa up to the abbey in the dark.

Delisa took them in through the kitchen, its familiar smells washing over Kalina, and making her feel a bit overwhelmed for a moment. Gwen stood at the large table in the center, kneading bread for the mornings baking. She looked up, curiosity on her face when Delisa entered. The moment the woman laid eyes on Kalina, she cried out, wiping her flour-covered hands on her apron and running forward to embrace her. Kalina laughed a bit at the woman's outburst. Gwen had always been kind but never loving towards her, so this display was a bit out of the ordinary.

"We have been so worried!" she said, squeezing Kalina tighter.

"What happened when I left?" Gwen stepped away finally, inviting them to sit at the table, getting them each a slice of bread with jam and a warm bowl of leftover potato soup from the evening's meal. Kalina dug in, the fear twisting her belly not enough to deter her from eating the first warm meal they'd had in a week.

"We didn't know you'd left until that knight and his men came bursting in here," Gwen said as she bustled around, finishing the bread dough. "He demanded to see Father Martin. Father Martin was terrible mad, yellin' and ragin' about the knight trying to kill one of his wards. He wouldn't hear any of the knight's explanations, he just gave him an earful and then kicked him out of the abbey." Kalina smiled at the image of Father Martin kicking Sir Gregan out. She wished she'd been there to see that. Delisa was sitting beside her at the table, eying her.

"Sounds like the knight had it coming." She looked over at Delisa. "What?"

"You've changed." Delisa smiled. "In a good way."

"I hope I have, honestly. I've missed you all." She wasn't completely sure she was glad she'd left, but if they found the Valdir then it was all worth it. After their bellies were full they followed Delisa through the darkened and quiet abbey, all the orphans in their dorms for the evening or out in the town at the taverns. The silence of the hallways brought Kalina back to calmer days, spent sneaking to the kitchens for a late-night snack, or to the library to borrow more books.

Father Martin was in his office when they knocked, the candles burning low. His face looked ten years older when he opened the door, his short greying hair a little disheveled. His eyes widened as he beheld Kalina. She pulled the hat from her head, revealing the few inches of silver hair, the rest faded to a pale brown that spilled down her back.

"Kalina," he breathed before reaching for her and pulling her into a hug. She stood there, stunned for a moment. He had never hugged her before, always keeping her at an arm's distance. She felt surprisingly okay with the contact and finally squeezed him back.

"It's good to see you, too," she said, her voice muffled by his robes. He released her and ushered them inside his office.

She took a seat in his small sitting area by the large fireplace that dominated the modestly appointed room. Talon stood behind her chair, Delisa taking the other empty one. Father Martin paced before the fire. Finally, he stopped and looked her and Talon over.

"You're that squire, who was with Sir Gregan." Talon nodded. "What are you doing with Kalina?"

"I was Sir Dyelan's squire, not Sir Gregan's. I helped her escape on the Wyvern," Talon clarified. "And we reconnected in the capitol. I helped her escape." Kalina launched into an explanation of their situation, leaving out some of the details.

"My question, Father Martin, is why you never told me I was a Valdir. Why keep it from me? I never really understood the importance of keeping my identity hidden." Father Martin slumped into a chair, placing his head in his hands. He looked like a man defeated.

"It's a long story, and not one I'm sure is mine to tell. But I'll tell you what I can." He looked up and met her blue eyes with his own watery ones. "Your grandfather sent you here to keep you safe. Again, the reason is not mine to tell. I knew the moment I saw your silver hair you were Valdir, but they had just disappeared and no one knew where. Your grandfather would have sent you to them if he'd known where they were but they left no trace." He paused, rubbing his hands down his face. Kalina shifted in her seat. "I didn't tell you because I thought I could keep you ignorant and safe. I didn't want you growing up knowing that fear and the burden it placed on you. And it seems in that I was wrong. Perhaps if you had known, we could have avoided this whole situation." Kalina nodded in agreement. She understood.

"If we find the Valdir, then all of this was worth it. I appreciate you telling me what you can."

"Why did you come back here?"

"We need help. Can you get us to Wolfhold? Sir Gregan is less than a day behind us, blocking our way south. But if we can get to Wolfhold, we can make it to the Wastes." Talon chimed in. Father Martin was quiet for a moment.

"I think that can be arranged."

Kalina wished they could have stayed the night, sleeping one last time in her small cot in her dormitory, the soft snoring of the other girls around her. But they couldn't afford to waste any time. Father Martin and Father Nic bundled them into the back of a cart and piled it with goods for trade in Wolfhold. Father Nic and Delisa piled into the driver's seat and after quick and tearful goodbyes to Gwen and Father Martin, they were off down the dirt road that led from the abbey and through the town.

Kalina watched through the barrels of goods as the only true home she'd ever known dwindled into the distance. Talon beside her reached out and took her hand, squeezing and shooting her a quick smile. Kalina smiled back and reached up with her free hand to grab Delisa's hand through the wooden slatted seat. Delisa twisted to smile down at her. Maybe they would avoid Sir Gregan and they could breathe for a moment. She let her head fall back against the sack of grain she was leaning against and looked up at the stars above her. She let the rocking of the cart lull her to sleep.

Chapter 27

THREE DAYS LATER THEIR cart rolled into Wolfhold at sunset. They hadn't encountered Sir Gregan on the road and Kalina could only hope he and his men were still slogging through the woods. Wolfhold held a small garrison of the crown's men, their green and gold livery making Kalina feel nervous. She hastily tucked her hair farther up into Talon's cap. She opted to stay in men's clothing, as no one was looking for two boys, one a scholar.

Lights were just coming on, the sun having just dipped below the horizon as they entered through the main gates. Father Nic drove the cart into a crowd that seemed oddly joyous and celebratory. Kalina turned to Talon.

"What day is it?"

"Not sure, but it seems to be a festival day." He tapped Father Nic on the shoulder and asked him. Father Nic smiled.

"It's the Festival of Flowers." Kalina gasped. That meant it was now full summer, and more time than she thought had passed since St. Martin's Day. The father was right, and as they moved further into the city they could see flowers strung up everywhere, on all the market stalls, the storefronts a profusion of colors. It was the day meant to celebrate the Mother and all her bounty. It fell at the beginning of summer when the majority of flowers were in full bloom.

Father Nic stopped at the center of town, where the crowd was too thick for him to pass and turned around.

"You'll have to find your way from here, I can't get the donkey and cart through any farther." He smiled at them both and handed Kalina a small bag of coins, enough to help them on their journey. "Be careful here, it's full of soldiers." Kalina nodded and stood in the wagon to hug him. Delisa hopped down with them and walked them toward the edge of the crowd to an overhang outside a tailor's shop. She hugged Kalina fiercely.

"I won't see you again, will I?" she asked, her voice husky from emotion. Kalina shook her head.

"If all goes right, no you won't." She kissed her friend on the cheek. "Take care of Gwen for me. And find yourself someone sweet." She smiled rather sadly as Delisa walked away back toward the wagon and Father Nic who was conversing with a nearby stall owner.

Talon led the way into the crowd; he had previously stayed at an inn in the center of town and thought they could get a room there. Kalina followed a step behind, her eyes darting this way and that, watching the soldiers at the gates and the soldiers who ambled through the town, some entering taverns, others buying things at shops, the rest strolling in pairs, obviously out on their rounds. The townsfolk were enjoying their night; plenty of food was being sold, along with trinkets and flower bouquets galore. Earlier in the day there would have been contests for best flowers and best arrangement, as well as a contest for best pies. It was one of Kalina's favorite holidays and she was sad she had missed it.

Her stomach began to growl at the smells coming from the nearby stalls. Her favorite Festival of Flowers treat was honeycomb dripping with blackberry jam. But they didn't have time to stop.

"Sorry." She grimaced and clutched at her stomach as Talon turned to eye her. "I'm just really hungry." Talon laughed.

"We'll be there soon. It's just the next street over." Kalina nodded and followed him farther into the darkening city. The inn they approached was bright with noise and music spilled from its open door. The painted sign above that swung in the summer breeze said The Lively Lilly. Kalina smiled at the delightful name and followed Talon into the warmth of the inn. It was crowded and for a moment as she entered, the familiar panic that often came over her when she was surrounded by pressing bodies and walls seemed to cage her in. But she focused on Talon's back pushing its way through the crowd and began taking deep breaths, and soon the panic retreated and she felt increasingly more solid in her body as they reached the bar.

She turned to face the crowded common room as Talon tried to get the attention of the barmaid. There was a small band of musicians in the corner by the large, cold hearth. The door remained open and Kalina sighed as a slight evening breeze moved in across the room. The tables had been shoved up against a wall, and people danced in an open space, while others sat around drinking, eating, and talking. Despite her earlier panic and her dislike of crowds, the energy was catching and soon her foot was tapping to the beat of the music.

Talon finally got the attention of the barmaid and ordered them dinner and a room for the night. Kalina's heart began to race at the thought of spending the night in a room with Talon. Somehow the presence of four walls made it seem more intimate than sleeping beside him in the great outdoors.

Talon took her hand again and led her to an empty table. Each time he touched her hand, Kalina got another thrill in her stomach. Talon had begun holding her hand as often as he could since that first night by the river, and Kalina wondered if he liked her in the way she was realizing she liked him.

Their meal came hot: braised pork with potatoes and cabbage and a large slice of country bread, still warm with butter on top. Kalina dug in like she hadn't seen food for years, with Talon doing the same beside her. The stress of the last few days on the road had made their appetites scarce. They both continued to watch the common room and after they had finished eating, the barmaid showed them to their room. Kalina stood in the doorway as Talon entered. There was one bed just large enough for two people, a basin of fresh, steaming hot water, and a small wardrobe. Kalina's eyes kept returning to the bed.

"Is there anything else you need, miss?" Kalina jumped at the barmaid's voice. She floundered for a second before remembering something she really wanted to do.

"How much for a bath?" Talon stepped forward.

"Make that two, please."

"Two pennies a piece. I can have the bathing room at the end of the hall ready for you in no time. I'll knock when the first bath is ready." Talon handed her the money and she closed the door, leaving them alone. Kalina turned, and a blush spread up her cheeks as she surveyed the bed once again. He cleared his throat.

"I can sleep on the floor if it's too uncomfortable for you." She shook her head.

"No, it's big enough for both of us." He nodded, a blush of his own warming his cheeks and forcing Kalina to look away. She busied herself laying her bundle out on the bed and pulling from it her spare, clean dress. They would have to wash her boy's clothes, so in the meantime, she'd wear her extra dress. This one was a dark blue with small pink roses embroidered by Calla on the sleeves. Kalina fingered the little flowers, suddenly homesick for Calla and Anders' house and the little bed by the fire. Things had felt so simple, even then. Before the search for the Valdir, the castle, the princess and the prince had swept her up.

"Are you okay?" Talon touched her shoulder. She turned to face him, the dress still in her hands.

"I just miss Calla and Anders and Issa. I guess I'm a little homesick for when life was simpler." She chuckled sadly. Talon smiled at her. "But I can't really go back now, can I?"

"Nope. You are well and truly stuck." Talon went to unpack his own pack. "Let's get you a real pack in town tomorrow. That thing won't hold up much longer." Kalina looked at her bundle. It was dirty and wearing thin in some places, and the edges were fraying. As she stood looking at it, she realized with a shock that the bundle was a blanket folded over. She dumped her things on the bed and unfolded it, revealing an intricate pattern of symbols embroidered onto the material. The background pattern was simple, small leaves knitted into neat rows. But forming a kind of dance across the fabric were symbols of flowing silver and gold, each one delicate, intricate, and unique. Kalina wondered at it, feeling as though she'd seen these symbols before in a book or somewhere.

The blanket looked old, and she would bet it was precious to someone, but then why would the queen give it to her and wrap her things in it? She wondered at it and decided that she would keep it and maybe one day, give it back to the queen in thanks.

The bathwater turned brown by the time Kalina was done scrubbing herself from the top of her head to her toes. The dye was slowly coming out of her hair and it looked rather grey on the ends instead of brown or silver.

Talon bathed after her, and when he returned to the room Kalina was sitting in bed, looking at the blanket the queen had given her as it hung over a rack by the window to dry after being washed. Talon's wet hair flopped in his face and he grinned at her as he dried it with a towel. She pretended to focus on the blanket in front of her but her eyes strayed to his. He flopped down beside her on the bed.

"What do you think those symbols are?" he asked. Kalina sighed.

"I don't know, but it feels important somehow. The Queen gave it to me." Talon studied it for a few minutes, squinting as if it would help him decipher the symbols.

"It's certainly a mystery. Kind of like you." He poked her playfully in the side. She laughed. "Maybe it's a secret message saying that you are actually a long-lost princess," he joked. But Kalina's heart began to race at the prospect.

"What? No. I doubt it. And if I am, I'd be a Valdir Princess and I doubt Valdir royal blood counts for anything in Ethea. Only Stanchon royal blood matters." Talon shrugged and rolled onto his back to stare at the ceiling.

"It's a possibility." She rolled her eyes and shoved him to the other side of the bed and climbed under the covers, her mind wandering, considering the possibility, no matter how absurd.

He blew out the lamp that stood on a small table by the bed and got under the covers. She was almost too distracted to remember to be nervous by his closeness. He reached over and took her hand gently, pulling her back to the present as if she was coming up for air after diving too deep in a lake.

"Goodnight, your Highness," he said, no mocking in his voice, only warmth, and sleep.

"Goodnight." Kalina managed to squeak. It took her awhile to fall asleep, her mind reeling at his closeness and the possibilities, but soon Talon's regular deep breaths pulled her into sleep.

Chapter 28

THE NEXT DAY TALON and Kalina ventured into the city. The celebratory atmosphere of the night before seemed to be continuing, for it was market day and the streets were packed with vendors. Kalina had only really ever seen her abbey and its neighboring town, and Ravenhelm, so Wolfhold was a different experience altogether. She saw more farmers than she had ever seen in her life, huge caravans of traders who sold strange and exotic things, and so many soldiers that she felt distinctly uncomfortable whenever they passed by one. She kept searching their faces for those of Poe, Olic, and especially Sir Gregan. She found herself constantly ducking her head, trying to hide her scar. The green wrap kept her hair hidden nicely enough but her scar was impossible to hide.

They needed supplies and so decided to stay one more night in the town, stocking up on extra clothing, a new pair of shoes for Kalina as her soft scribes' slippers had worn through in a few places, as well as food fit for traveling. Kalina felt more and more uncomfortable as the day wore on. They had no idea how far behind them their pursuers were, neither did they know how far they truly had to go to find the Valdir. They could be running across the country for months before finding them if the Wastes didn't pan out. The ever-present fear that perhaps the Valdir had left the continent altogether nagged at her.

It was four days to the last town before the Wastes, and Talon was also hoping to find them a ride on the back of a wagon. He spent much of his time that afternoon in the inn, going around to different groups of people, asking if anyone was traveling south to the town of Wildhelm. Kalina sat in a corner with a book she had borrowed from the inn's small library, sipping on tea, watching the room around her for any signs that someone recognized her. The inn filled up and musicians filed in to play as the sun went down. Kalina's anxiety continued to grow and she wished with all her heart that it was time for them to go to bed. Talon was still socializing, making his rounds of the room. She fidgeted, unable to really focus.

He sat at a table by the fireplace, a group of men and women around him. They looked like traders, a few of them clearly hired to guard a caravan as it made its way through the countryside. He glanced over at her and gave her a thumbs up which made her smile. It seemed he had gotten them a ride with the group. Kalina was settling back into reading the book, some of her anxiety lifted when the door opened and in stepped a familiar figure. Kalina froze, the book halfway up to her face, covering her partially as she looked over its pages and into the face of Sir Gregan.

He was flanked by Olic and Poe and behind them, a few of the soldiers from the local garrison. The men surveyed the room and Kalina ducked behind her book. She prayed Talon was still facing away from the men, otherwise, he'd be noticed right away. Sir Gregan then walked to the bar and the men sat down, facing away from the rest of the room. Kalina lowered her book just enough to keep an eye on the men while she tried discreetly to get Talon's attention.

Talon kept talking animatedly at his companions, causing Kalina to panic as she watched the men at the bar with one eye. Finally, after what felt like hours, Talon turned to glance at her again and saw her motioning for him to look at the bar, panic clear on her face. He glanced over his shoulder and stiffened at seeing the knight. His face went white and he slowly turned back to the people in front of him who were looking at him with curiosity and concern. He leaned forward and whispered a few words. One of the men in the group nodded and stood up, Talon joining him. The man began laughing and put an arm around Talon's shoulders, effectively hiding his face as he dragged him across the room to where Kalina sat in the corner near the stairs. The man bent down to speak as they passed.

"Follow us in a minute but keep your nose hidden in that book." Kalina nodded. The man and Talon made it up the stairs and Kalina waited, her heart pounding with each passing second, fear and worry making her nauseous. Finally, she felt a minute had passed and she stood up, holding her book before her face with one hand, the other grabbing her new cloak off the back of the chair and wandered up the stairs, resisting looking towards the bar.

She made her way to their room as fast as she could where, she found the barmaid, the man, and Talon. Talon was speaking while hurriedly packing their things.

"We need to get out of the inn without being seen. That knight and those soldiers are after us." It was a gamble, revealing that they were wanted by the law, but Talon seemed to trust the man and the barmaid. The barmaid nodded as Kalina entered the room.

"There is a back stairway that leads down into the kitchens and from there you can make your way out through the stables. We keep the door locked but as this is an emergency and Jaycob here is one of our best customers and makes a point to stay here as often as he can, I will unlock it for you both." The man turned to Kalina and smiled. He sketched a little bow to her.

"I hear your name is, Kalina, miss. I'm Jaycob." Her smile in return was shaky.

"Nice to meet you."

"My group and I are going to get you both to Wildhelm if you'll let us." Kalina practically sagged in gratitude. With Sir Gregan downstairs pursuing them, the thought of trying to make it on foot to Wildhelm and the Wastes was daunting.

"Thank you." She meant it.

Talon handed her the bag and Kalina looked around the room wistfully. Then they followed the barmaid and Jaycob down a set of dingy, dark stairs and into a small but warm and bright kitchen. There was an open door that looked out into the common room and Kalina couldn't help but glance into the space, her eyes seeking out the familiar men at the bar.

It was a mistake. Sir Gregan looked up from his mug of ale and made solid eye contact with her as she followed Talon out the back door. Horror rose in her chest as she realized that he had recognized her. She ran to grab Talon.

"He saw me." Her voice was strained. Talon grabbed her hand hard and turned to Jaycob.

"Where can we hide?" Jaycob motioned them into the barn. He pointed to a wagon heavily laden with items.

"Underneath that wagon is a false bottom." The barmaid looked sideways at Jaycob with raised eyebrows. "Don't look at me like that, Lacy. You know I might need to hide someone or something from bandits." He walked them over and slid quickly under the wagon. There was a small noise and a trap door fell open. He slid back out and pointed. "Climb in and stay quiet. They might search the barn but we will do our best to put them off your scent." Kalina crawled on the hay-strewn floor and looked up into the dark opened space underneath the sturdy wagon. She pushed her bag into the space and then climbed in, every part of her protesting being trapped in there with no way out. Talon climbed in behind her and she heard the small click of the locking mechanism behind them. Jaycob's voice drifted through the wood sides. "There are breathing holes and holes to see through on each side of the space. And a release for the lock by the door. Don't come out unless you really need to." Then he and Lacy wandered off towards the front of the barn, chatting amiably while Kalina and Talon tried to adjust themselves in the confined space. There was only enough room for them to lie down and roll over, and for their bags. She could only raise her head about a foot off the floorboards before she banged into the ceiling.

So she lay there, in the dark, Talon breathing heavily beside her, her heart still racing so hard she could feel it pulsing in her ears, waiting to be found or to die of the panic still swirling inside of her. It was harder to get a grip on the panic in this small, enclosed space and it felt like a long time before she was able to breathe easy. Talon scooted over to stare out a peephole beside her, watching the now empty barn.

Kalina had just started to fall asleep, the adrenaline fading away and making her drowsy when the sound of the barn door opening jolted her awake. Talon reached out a hand and laid it calmly on her chest. Kalina froze. She knew it was dark and he couldn't possibly have known where he was placing his hand but he kept it there and her blood ran cold as she realized that Sir Gregan must be standing feet away. Images of that rusty chair in the dungeon flashed before her eyes, Sir Gregan standing there, grinning while the prince cut her. She had to take slow deep breaths to steady herself. She strained her ears to catch a sound, any sound.

She could hear the soldiers rummaging around in various wagons, including their own, and she squeezed her eyes shut when they shifted the boxes and baskets above her head. But they soon seemed not to find what they wanted and began talking.

"Well, either they are doing a damn good job at hiding, or they got away," said one voice.

"If that barmaid hadn't waylaid us, we could have been out here sooner. They could be hidden by now." Kalina recognized Sir Gregan's voice next.

"If we had rushed out here after them it would have alerted every single person in that inn. Besides, I wanted them to think they had gotten away, to let down their guard. The King has high expectations." There was a grunt of ascent from his men. "Now. I want you searching every inn in this town, have your soldiers spread out to the surrounding areas and check every cart in and out of the city." With that, the voices moved off towards the front of the barn and Kalina slowly let out the breath she'd been holding.

Talon removed his hand from her chest and moved over so that his mouth was next to her ear.

"I've seen what Sir Gregan does to deserters and cowards in the army," Talon said quietly. Kalina swallowed hard, bile rising in her throat at the images that statement conjured. "We'll have to be extra careful."

Kalina sighed as the barn around them grew quiet and even the peepholes began to grow dark. A wave of tiredness washed over her, the stress of the last few hours catching up. She realized that they'd probably be in the wagon all night so she dragged her pack over and used it as a pillow, drifting off to sleep as the growing heat within the space and Talon's breathing lulled her.

Chapter 29

KALINA WOKE AS THE wagon began to move. Fear and confusion lanced through her but she realized that the space was much lighter and she could make out Talon's face in the gloom. He grinned over at her and she started to relax, the jostling of the cart making her suddenly pounding headache and upset stomach even worse. She gritted her teeth as she tried to find a more comfortable position.

Outside she could hear the voices of many people, the sounds of clopping hooves and the general noises of the city passing them by as the wagon trundled out into the countryside. Kalina wondered vaguely if they were even going south, or if there was possibly a bounty on her head and they were being carted back to Ravenhelm. She clutched at her stomach as it rolled and roiled and soon drifted back into a sweat-soaked sleep.

A cool hand on her brow woke her later and she realized that the wagon had stopped moving. Her thoughts were groggy and listless as Talon checked her head.

"Can you get out of the wagon, Kalina?" His voice sounded concerned. She nodded and struggled to pull herself over to the door. Talon climbed out before her and as she practically fell out of the secret space his arms caught her, gently lowering her to the ground. A welcome, cooling breeze brushed across the stray strands of silver and grey hair that had escaped her headscarf, taking away some of the heat in her face.

Another cool hand touched her forehead and cheek. She wondered vaguely why so many people were touching her. She turned her head away, not wanting to be touched anymore.

"She has a fever and is dehydrated." The voice was kind and female. "Let's get her into the back of the wagon and see if we can't get her to drink." Many hands touched her and she squirmed, moaning as they lifted her into the cart. Kalina felt soft blankets envelop her and someone dribbled cold water between her cracked and parched lips. She drank greedily until the water was pulled away. It felt soothing on her mouth and throat, but as it settled in her stomach she began to wretch, vomiting up bile and water all over herself, gentle hands rolling her onto her side.

"What's wrong with her? How did she get like this?" Talon's voice was very far away and Kalina frowned, wanting to comfort him.

"Stress can cause this, as can being in a space that's too hot, or food that's gone bad or an infection. Who knows what caused this." Kalina drifted back into sleep as the wagon began to move once again.

When Kalina woke again it was dark, the stars above her head bright. Her fever had broken and despite the pounding in her head and her upset stomach, she felt much less delirious. She sat up slowly, the pile of blankets on top of her sliding off, to look around. Jaycob's group had stopped for the night and were spread out along the side of the road, a campfire lit not ten paces away, the group of people gathered around it chatting and eating. Kalina stood unsteadily and reached down to wrap a blanket around her shoulders. That was when she realized her hair was falling loose around her face. Fear lanced through her stomach. Strangers had seen her hair and potentially knew who she was. What had Talon told them?

She tucked it behind her ears, taking a deep breath before approaching the fire, spotting Talon's lanky figure sitting beside it. She cleared her throat and everyone's face turned to look at her.

"How long have I been asleep?" Her voice was a ragged croak and she swallowed hard. An older woman in her 60's stood and came towards her. Her hair was long, wavy and grey, and she was pleasantly plump. She had her shirt rolled up to her elbows and she put out an arm, gesturing for Kalina to follow her.

"Come." Kalina took a few steps forward, as there was nothing else she could do but obey. The woman's warm arm went around Kalina's shoulders and she drew her towards an empty seat at the fire, settling her down on an upturned stump. Then she went to the fire and scooped up a small bowlful of some flavorful stew. Kalina almost declined but decided she might as well try to sip on the soup and see if it would settle the stabbing ache in her belly.

"You've been asleep for two days." Talon's voice was hesitant. "Are you feeling any better?" Kalina nodded as she took a tentative bite of the soup and chew it slowly.

"Yes, much." The woman sat down beside her and took up her own bowl of stew.

"You were very sick there for a while and we weren't sure you'd make it through." Her voice was as soothing as Jaycob's was and Kalina looked back and forth between them, concluding that this woman must be the man's mother. "I'm Straya, by the way." She smiled at Kalina who smiled back.

"Thank you, for taking care of me." She looked around the fire at each of their faces. "I doubt I would have survived if you hadn't been there." Talon looked down at his bowl. Kalina realized that her declaration came as an insult to his abilities to keep her alive. She would apologize later she decided, as the first bite of stew began to settle her stomach.

"How far south are we?" Kalina had finished her stew and some of the men had wandered off to see to the horses and secure the wagon for the night.

"We're about a day outside Wildhelm." Talon looked at her sideways and she gave him a tentative smile.

"Great." She looked at Straya and said sincerely. "I don't know how we can repay you." Their little bag of coins was needed to buy supplies in Wildhelm before making the final trek to the Wastes. By all accounts she had read in books, the Wastes was an empty high desert with little to no resources. Doubt wormed its way into her heart at the prospect of finding the dragons there.

"Every now and then we travelers do a good turn for someone without expecting anything in return." Straya patted Kalina's knee before turning to wash the dinner dishes.

Kalina lay in her bedroll that night, the headache a vague pounding, her stomach finally settled and full, and watched the night sky. She had met so many people since setting out from her little abbey. Most of them had been good, but a handful, like the prince, like Dillion, like that first man at the main gate, like Sir Gregan, had been bad. Kalina was eternally grateful for people like Calla and Anders, Talon, Delisa and Father Martin, Margy, Queen Cherise, and now Jaycob and Straya. She knew in her bones that she and Talon wouldn't even be alive right now if it hadn't been for their help.

The next day as the sun set, their wagon trundled into Wildhelm. Kalina and Talon stayed with Jaycob and his people as they made their way into the center of the town. They picked a small inn on the edge of town with an easy escape out the back into the nearby woods. Kalina and Talon weren't entirely convinced Sir Gregan hadn't followed them here and Jaycob was perfectly happy to oblige their paranoia. Kalina and Talon shared a room on the first floor, while the others slept on the upper floors.

Kalina couldn't get to sleep, and sometime in the night, Talon rolled over, an arm flopping over her middle. She lay on her side, her back towards him, and she unconsciously snuggled into his warmth. Talon woke up, and she could feel him shifting behind her as he lifted his head. She squeezed her eyes shut and let him curl the arm around her, tucking her body against his. She listened carefully as his breathing steadied again and he fell back into sleep. It was then that her frayed nerves finally settled and she was able to sleep.

The silence of the Snoring Fox Inn was shattered as Kalina and Talon's bedroom door was forced open. Kalina jolted awake, Talon leaping from the bed beside her and drawing the short sword he had acquired from Jaycob. He stood before the bed, looking at the door wild-eyed as Sir Gregan stepped through. The man stood, a torch burning in his hand, a grin upon his scarred face. Kalina's blood ran cold as she scrambled from the bed and grabbed their packs, clutching them to her as she backed towards the window. They had chosen this room because the window allowed an alternate escape route. While Talon stood between her and the knight, she scrambled to get it open and throw the packs outside to the dirt of the stable yard.

"Don't think you can hide from me any longer, Valdir filth." Sir Gregan's voice cut through her fear, making her pause. The King truly did know who she was then. She turned back to the room and snarled back at him.

"You haven't caught me yet." And she lunged for the window, hauling herself outside and dropping to the ground. She turned to look back at Talon who made a slash at the man who lunged for her. Behind Sir Gregan, Poe and Olic entered the room, swords drawn. Kalina watched through the window in horror as Sir Gregan dropped the torch and reached for his blade. Talon slashed again, attempting to give her time to flee but Kalina stood rooted to the spot. She desperately wanted Talon to come with her, not let her flee.

Talon made to strike Sir Gregan a third time and the big man came up with his sword, its tip tearing a huge gash in Talon's thigh;

his scream made Kalina's heart stop. She began yelling at the top of her lungs.

"Fire! Fire! The inn's on fire!" Sir Gregan paused over Talon and looked up and out the window at her, his face sneering. He gestured to his men and together they went out of the room and into the hall, no doubt to come find her. But by that point, the inn was stirring and people were beginning to yell. Indeed, the torch Sir Gregan had dropped had managed to catch the bedspread on fire and the room was filling with smoke. She climbed back in through the window and grabbed Talon, urging him towards the window and fresh air. Smoke filled her lungs as the fire spread and she began to cough violently as she pushed and hauled Talon out the window.

She could barely pull herself back out when Jaycob's face appeared in the window and he reached in, pulling her through to safety while the fire roared behind her. She fell to the dirt with a loud thud, coughing and gasping in the clear night air outside.

"What happened?" Jaycob was inspecting Talon's injured leg as Kalina caught her breath. Talon answered through gritted teeth.

"They found us. We fought. I lost." He winced as Jaycob tore a strip off his own shirt and used it to create a temporary bandage around Talon's still profusely bleeding thigh.

Kalina finally caught her breath and turned back towards the inn when she saw Sir Gregan and his companions come around the side of the building.

"Look!" She yelled, jumping to her feet and grabbing their packs. She slung one over each shoulder and then began bodily hauling Talon up off the ground. "We have to run!" She looked pleadingly to Jaycob, who stood as well. He reached for Talon's sword, taking it from him. He hoisted it in his fist, his usually gentle face now steely.

"Go." He nodded towards the woods as he turned back to face the on-coming Sir Gregan, Olic, and Poe. Kalina was terrified for him but she heeded him anyway, dragging the limping Talon with her. They half ran, half stumbled into the nearby trees, the clash of metal on metal beginning and then fading behind them as the trees swallowed them up.

Chapter 30

THE DENSE TREES CLOSED in around Kalina and Talon as they hobbled farther away from the clashing sounds of Jaycob fighting with Sir Gregan, Poe, and Olic. Kalina's breath was getting ragged with effort as she half dragged an increasingly heavy Talon through the trees. Their trail would be easy enough to follow and Kalina glanced down at Talon's leg, realizing they would have to stop and properly dress it if they had any hope of making it to the Wastes.

She slowed as she reached a large tree and gently lowered Talon to the ground, dropping their two heavy packs beside him. She stood panting and knew there was no way they could keep going like this. She couldn't carry both of their packs and Talon. She dragged open the tops of both packs and dumped them on the ground. She dug through, finding a clean linen shirt. This she began tearing into long strips for bandages. Then she re-packed their bags, putting the essentials into one bag, the rest into the other.

She took only her green headscarf, her blanket, and the rock from Savath. The rest of the things she discarded. It was with sadness that she set aside the dresses from Calla. But the extra weight would only slow them down. She did the same with Talon's pack, discarding the majority of his clothing, keeping only the necessities. The packs were relatively small but she was able to fit what little food they had in them. They had been planning to resupply the following day and were dangerously low on food. Kalina pushed that concern from her mind, choosing to focus on helping Talon and getting far away from Sir Gregan.

Talon was clutching his leg in pain, the gash going from the outside of his right knee up to almost his hip bone. It was bleeding steadily but not spurting blood and she hoped he would stop bleeding soon.

"Take your pants off," she ordered as she continued to cut strips. Talon gawked at her as if she had two heads. "Take them off or else I can't properly clean the wound." She pointed to another pair of his pants. "You can use those afterward." He hesitated before complying. Pulling the pants down over his wound made him cry out and despite Kalina's fear of being discovered, she knew she needed to focus. She didn't know much about taking care of wounds but she knew it needed to be cleaned and dressed if they were going to survive. In a situation that felt completely out of her control, this was something she could control.

She used a little of their precious water and poured it on the wound, cleaning it, Talon wincing and gritting his teeth in an effort not to cry out. Then she began to wrap his leg in the clean bandages, trying not to tie it too tight. Once he was fully bandaged, she helped him put on his clean pair of pants, gently dragging it over his thigh. Then she hoisted their one remaining pack and offered Talon a hand.

"We have to run. Can you keep up?" Talon's jaw clenched but he nodded. "Lean on me if you need to and we'll find you a walking stick soon." Talon put his hand on her shoulder, putting a little pressure there but not as much as before. Kalina looked sideways at him as they began walking south. She suspected he was still in immense pain but that he didn't want to wear her out or let her know just how bad it really was.

The sky began to lighten as the trees before them began to thin, making way for short shrubs and stunted, wind-blown trees. The wind had begun to pick up over the last half mile or so, and as they cleared the relative protection of the trees, the wind blasted them in the face, carrying with it the smells of this plateau. The Wastes stretched out before them, vast and empty but for shrubbery, dirt and stunted trees. Kalina stopped, Talon breathing heavily beside her, his leg clearly still bleeding, but he kept one hand over the wound. She looked out over the expanse, and then north towards the Great Grey mountains. There was nothing here. No dragons cavorting in the skies, no sign of human inhabitants anywhere. Her heart sank, her stomach twisting as she lost what little hope she'd had. She'd been pushing them for the last few hours trying to outrun danger, with the expectation that when she got here, to this place, that there would be safety, not this barren, empty expanse with danger close on their heels.

Talon squeezed her shoulder and she looked at him, her eyes brimming with tears as her heart shattered inside her.

"They'll be here. I can feel it. Besides, we have to keep going. We don't have an option." He gestured behind them. There was no sign of pursuit yet but Kalina knew in her gut that Jaycob had only gained them a head start, not a reprieve. She nodded. There was nothing else they could do. She began walking, Talon limping at her side, the trees getting ever farther behind them.

They stopped that night and ate the last of their meager food before curling up on the ground in their own cloaks and Kalina's blanket, having left their bedrolls back at the Snoring Fox Inn. They huddled together for warmth as the temperature dropped despite it being a clear, summer night. They had no fire for warmth, the sagebrush was the only available fuel. Talon was very warm beside her and she placed her hand on his cheek, feeling the heat burning there. Her heart twisted again. If they didn't find help soon, he wouldn't make it. He was bright with fever.

The following afternoon the sun blazed overhead as the wind howled in their ears. Kalina paused to breathe and to give Talon a moment to rest. She turned in a circle, once again looking at their surrounding landscape, searching for life. In the north, the Great Grey Mountains were a hazy blur, to the east and south there was nothing, but to the west, from where they had come, Kalina could make out movement. She froze, her hand going out to Talon's arm.

"We're being followed." Her voice was low and desperate. Talon turned to watch their pursuers coming steadily closer. Soon, Kalina could make out three distinct shapes on the horizon and knew that Sir Gregan had found them. "We have to run." There was no other option. Sir Gregan and his men were clearly on horseback, their silhouettes becoming clearer with each passing second, while they were on foot. She turned to Talon, her eyes desperate. "I'm sorry I dragged you into this. You should go, go north, towards the mountains, away from me." She began to step away from him. If he wasn't with her, then perhaps the King would not punish him. But Kalina knew in her stomach that if they were caught together, they would be punished together. The King wanted her, but who knew why. Talon was innocent in this. He had chosen to come along because of her, not because he was a part of this. Talon grabbed her hand, his fingers caressing hers, his cheeks bright with fever.

"I'm here with you, Kalina. And I'll stay with you. I choose you." Kalina's eyes began to water, her chest swelling. She didn't know why Talon had chosen her, but she didn't care. She squeezed his hand back and turned south.

"Then let's run." Together, they ran, fast as they could, Talon doing a sort of limping jog behind Kalina.

They ran for what felt like hours, and every time Kalina looked behind them, Sir Gregan and his men were closer. Her lungs ached and burned, her legs felt like jelly, and the pack that carried only a few things began to feel like it weighed a thousand pounds, but she kept moving, Talon falling farther and farther behind. Finally, Talon's leg gave out and he fell to the ground. Kalina turned back, helping him up and putting her arm around his shoulders.

"Lean on me," she gasped between heaving breaths. Talon's head rolled back on his shoulders as he tried to breath. She glanced behind them and saw their pursuers were maybe a mile away. They didn't have much time.

"I can't go much farther, Kalina." His voice was breathy and weak. "Maybe we should surrender?"

"Not yet." A desperate hope burned in her chest and she had to keep going. She half dragged, half carried Talon for another quarter mile until her lungs could not take it and she couldn't take another step. She wished now she had saved her pebble to call Savath, but even then it would have been too late. She collapsed to the ground, Talon gratefully falling beside her to the dirt. Kalina desperately wished they had water but they had drunk what they'd had the night before. Her stomach roiled, her lips were cracked and bleeding, and her muscles screamed. They were done for. She laid back on the dirt and looked up into the light blue sky, a few distant clouds rolling by overhead. Her breathing steadily slowed as she listened to the approaching hoofbeats of their pursuers. Beside her, Talon's breaths came out raggedly and she saw his face was scrunched in pain, his chest rapidly rising and falling. Kalina wanted to help him, but her own body was betraying her and refusing to move.

The hoofbeats got louder and louder and Kalina could almost feel the ground moving with their thunderous approach. She looked at the sky again and noticed a black dot hanging above them. As she watched, it plunged and she noticed two more dots with it. They slowly grew larger and larger until Kalina could make out their vague shape, and her heart leapt. Perhaps Savath had come, after all, bringing her children with her. She tried to sit up but failed, and all she could do was shakily point skyward.

"Talon." Talon looked up and gasped. The shapes got bigger

and bigger until they created shadows on the ground. Kalina suddenly realized with a mixture of horror and excitement that these shapes were much bigger than Savath. They were as big as a large house. "Dragons." She whispered, completely in awe. The creatures descended upon them, and as their huge bulks hit the ground near where Kalina and Talon lay, they sent up a huge plume of dust and scattered sagebrush. Figures leapt down from the enormous dragons and just as they stood over Kalina and Talon, she lost consciousness.

Chapter 31

KALINA SLOWLY SWAM BACK into consciousness. Her body was warm and she felt as though she was floating on a bed of clouds. Her eyelids were heavy and she wanted to slip back into sleep. But the events of the previous days came flooding back and she knew she had to wake up, to see whether she was still in danger or had been saved. Her memory of the dragons descending felt like a dream, and she wasn't entirely sure it was real.

She cracked open her eyes, the sleep flaking away making her eyes feel gritty. Above her was the dark ceiling of what seemed to be a cave, and while her body was nice and warm, a cool breeze played across her face. She struggled to sit up, the layers of blankets and furs piled on top of her sliding off her torso. She was in a small chamber carved into the rock. Her bed lay in the center of the chamber, and a piece of colorful cloth covered the hole that was a door. Her heart began to pound. She didn't understand where she was, but her gut told her she was with the Valdir. Excitement warred in her empty stomach with the desire to run. She took a deep breath and tried to settle her nerves.

The fabric was pushed aside suddenly and a woman with bright silver hair stepped through, her arms full with a tray full of food. The woman looked up and smiled; her slightly wrinkled appearance told Kalina that she was in her late 40's or early 50's. Her tanned face was tattooed with small lines and dots, and Kalina drew in a deep breath.

"Oh good, you're awake." Her voice was pleasant and kind and put Kalina more at ease. The woman knelt beside Kalina's bed and placed the tray of food on her lap. "Eat up. You'll need your strength for what comes next." Kalina frowned, tucking her silver hair behind her ear.

"What do you mean next?" The woman smiled at her indulgently.

"For the flood of information coming your way, dear. There's so much to tell you, and you'll need your strength." Something occurred to Kalina as she picked up a piece of bread and began dipping it into what smelled like a spicy broth.

"Where's Talon? My friend?" The woman put a hand on her

heart; it was an odd gesture but it made Kalina think she was apologizing for something.

"He's recovering in another room. His leg was infected when we got him here and he was beginning to burn with fever." Worry filled Kalina.

"But is he alright? Will he be okay?" The woman put her hand out in a placating way.

"Yes. I believe he will." The woman gestured again. "Now eat." Kalina obeyed and once the first few bites hit her stomach, she realized she was ravenous and she began to eat the food with gusto. The broth was spicy and filled with chunks of meat she thought was beef. The bread was light and airy and it felt familiar somehow. There was also a bowl of greens tossed in some sort of vinegar that had a delightful zing. Kalina ate until she was overfull and then drank three cups of water from a carafe the woman brought in. Once she was well and truly sated, she sat back on her bed, leaning up against the rock wall and eyeing the woman who was sitting quietly in a corner.

"Where am I?" The woman moved forward, gathering up her dirty dishes.

"You are with the Valdir, my dear. Your people." Kalina's gut flip-flopped. Finally. Finally, she had made it here, to her own people. The victory felt bittersweet, however, since Talon was injured, and she wondered if Jaycob had survived his duel with Sir Gregan. She hoped against hope that he had survived and wasn't yet another casualty of her quest to find her people.

"And who are you?" The woman executed a small bow while sitting beside her.

"My name is Eira. I am your aunt." Kalina froze.

"My aunt?"

"Yes, I believe so."

"How in the gods' names do you know?" Her heart was racing. If she had an aunt, perhaps she had parents as well.

"Approximately 16 years ago my brother fell in love with a girl and she got pregnant. Not long after that, we were forced to flee and never knew what happened to the babe. My brother believed you were dead, never born." Eira reached out and brushed the hair from her face. "But you look so much like him." Her voice was tender and Kalina felt something blossom in her stomach. She wanted to meet this man who was supposedly her father. A part of her wouldn't believe it until she saw him. But something else was more pressing.

"I'd like to see Talon." The woman smiled and nodded.

"But first, what shall we call you?" Kalina started. Of course, they wouldn't know her name.

"Kalina."

"Kalina. Follow me." Eira offered her arm to Kalina who tentatively took it and stood, her legs wobbly and achy despite the time spent in bed.

Eira led her down a dimly lit hallway made of stone and Kalina realized that they must be inside a mountain. The stone was a light color, a yellowish red. Kalina wondered at what type of stone it was as she realized that it was not the same as the cave she and Savath had stayed in on their flight from the abbey to Ravenhelm. So, they weren't within the Great Grey Mountains, but where were they?

Eira stopped before another chamber, its entrance also covered with a piece of fabric for a door. She gestured for Kalina to enter first and Kalina entered without hesitation. It seemed to be a mirror of her own chamber: it was small, and in its center was a bed, Talon lying atop the covers, his leg bandaged, his torso and other leg hidden under a light blanket. He was breathing shallowly and calmly and Kalina realized he was asleep. She knelt beside him and took his limp hand, squeezing it, letting him know she was there. There was no answering squeeze and Kalina looked up at Eira in alarm.

"He is drugged with the valerian root. He won't wake up for a while." Kalina looked down at Talon and reached out to smooth the brown curls of sweat-soaked hair that had fallen onto his forehead. He looked even younger in his sleep but Kalina noticed the stubble that was growing on his cheeks and chin. She smiled.

"Kalina." She turned to look at Eira. "There is someone I think you should meet." Kalina nodded and stood, following Eira from the chamber. She glanced over her shoulder one last time at the sleeping Talon.

They wound their way through the stone corridors until they entered a series of much larger chambers. These chambers towered over her head, and Kalina found herself falling slightly behind Eira, as she looked around in awe. The first chamber had small pools throughout, little rivulets of steaming water, and as she looked, she realized with an embarrassed start that this was a bathing chamber. All around the room, in different pools, were naked women. Every single one of them had long, silver hair. Their tanned skin shone in the light filtering through holes in the ceiling and Kalina saw that all the pools emptied into a deep channel that tumbled out of the chamber through a hole in the ground.

Her embarrassment at their nakedness was short-lived, however as she realized that their skin was tattooed with symbols very similar to those on her blanket and those on Eira's face. Whirls of black and grey and red circled their bodies. Some were covered head to foot, some only had the tattoos on certain parts of their bodies. She wondered as she passed, as she saw most of their faces were tattooed like Eira's.

The second chamber they entered had people sitting at tables dug out from the stone, where you stepped down into it to sit and eat. Kalina could smell food floating in the air and the chatter of people around her made her feel surprisingly at home. Why this felt so different from all the times she'd been in a crowded room before she didn't know. Perhaps it was knowing these were her people, or perhaps she had changed. Some people looked up and called to Eira but the woman gently waved them off with a hand on her heart and motioned for Kalina to follow. Kalina jogged to catch up.

The third chamber they entered was even larger, the ceiling so far away Kalina almost couldn't see it in the gloom. But this chamber was different. It was open to the air, large cave entrances dotted the rock, and beyond them Kalina could see out into the gathering dusk, the sun slowly setting in the west. She realized they were looking north, and as she continued walking forward, she looked out and down, her stomach lurching as she saw how high up they were.

That's when the roars caught her attention. Soaring in the air around the mountain, dragons of all colors and sizes flew. Some were smaller while others were larger, but all bigger than Savath. Kalina's mouth dropped as she watched them circle before coming into land. She realized with a jolt that this was the main entrance and that they were going to be feet away from her in a moment. She backed up quickly, stumbling over the uneven ground of the cave until Eira caught her and held her steady.

The woman grinned a fierce grin above Kalina as the dragons

came in for a landing, each choosing a different entrance, and each hit the stone edges, their claws scrabbling for purchase, gouging grooves in the soft outer stone, sending up a plume of dust and debris. They folded their huge wings and crawled in through the openings, their large bulks making the chamber seem to shrink. Kalina gasped in wonder, the setting sun glinting off their scales, sending a rainbow of colors dancing off the stone.

Then she noticed the riders atop the enormous beasts. They each wore leather covering most of their bodies excluding their heads, the leather dyed a rich red-brown. The nearest dragon was also the largest, its deep sapphire scales so blue it was almost black in places. The man atop this dragon had long braided silver hair, a serious countenance, and tattoos criss-crossed his face. His vivid blue eyes looked down at her and he dismounted his dragon, removing his leather gloves as he strode towards them. Kalina's heart began to pound as he stopped before her and looked down.

"So, this is my daughter."

Chapter 32

KALINA'S LEGS BUCKLED at those words, but Eira kept her standing. Her father stood before her, eyeing her critically.

"This is Kalina. Kalina, this is your father Hakon, King of the Valdir." Kalina's mouth went dry as she looked into his fierce blue eyes, her eyes. The more she looked at him, the more she realized that she looked a lot like him. They shared the same eyes, nose, and hair. Her mouth and frame she must have gotten from her mother.

"Kalina. Of course, she would name you that. That was my grandmother's name." Kalina had no words. His deep voice rolled over her as she stared. "Is she dumb?" his sharp question startled Kalina even more.

"No Majesty, just in shock I think." Eira pinched her lightly. "Say something, dear." Kalina swallowed hard.

"Nice to meet you, your Majesty." She curtsied a bit awkwardly.

"No need to stand on ceremony here." His voice was gruff but a bit of warmth was seeping into it. "You are my daughter, after all." He held out a hand to the enormous dragon waiting behind him. "This is my dragon, Kaya." The dragon's head snaked forward, her large scaled nose a mere foot from Kalina. Her large yellow eyes were narrow slits like a cat's and she looked down at her with such intelligent interest. Kalina briefly wondered how similar dragons were to Wyverns.

"Kalina," she huffed, her warm breath stirring the hair around Kalina's face. Kaya's voice rumbled the earth beneath her. She found herself smiling as she gazed up at the dragon.

"Hello, Kaya. Wonderful to meet you." The dragon snaked out her tongue, tasting the air around it. Kalina reached out a hand, holding it beneath the dragon's nose, allowing her to catch her scent.

"The honor is all mine." The dragon shifted back. "I will go to the den, Hakon." The king nodded in dismissal, one hand brushing the beast's neck in farewell. Kalina finally noticed the other riders had dismounted as well, their dragons having left the chamber, and they stood in a small knot a few feet away. Hakon waved them over.

"You should meet my entourage." The others came forward to

169

stand beside their king. There were 7 of them in total, each in red leather, each tattooed and silver-haired, with various types of weapons strapped to their waists. Most wore their hair braided back and away from their face, but all wore it long, men and women alike.

"This is Geir, my second in command." Her father gestured to a very large man. His grey eyes looked her over, assessing her. Kalina stood tall and nodded her head in greeting. The big man nodded in return and she thought she detected a slight change in his eyes that looked like approval. "This," Hakon said, gesturing to the woman beside Geir. "Is Asta." The woman stepped forward and bowed to Kalina. Kalina smiled and nodded back. She was lean and wiry, and older than she looked from afar. "This is Arvid." He gestured towards another male who bowed to her. "And Ingvar." Another male about her father's age. "This is Kari." This was a much younger woman, only maybe ten years older than Kalina and she grinned at Kalina as she bowed. Kalina found herself grinning back.

"Pleased, your Highness." She winked at Kalina and Kalina instantly felt a kinship with the woman. Hakon cleared his throat and continued.

"This is Rangvald." The next was a younger man who looked very similar to Kari, sharing the same nose and bright blue eyes. Kalina wondered if they were siblings. "They are your cousins and Eira's children." Hakon then gestured to the final member of the seven. "And this is Leif, Geir's son and new to my entourage." Kalina's breath caught as she looked at the last person. He was young, only a few years older than her, and he had his father's same grey eyes and muscled build. His face was handsome, and Kalina felt her face flush as she looked at him. Suddenly, she felt self-conscious before him and very conscious of her scar and the dirt that crusted her body. Leif bowed low to her and looked up, his eyes meeting hers. She nodded at him as he straightened.

"Nice to meet you, your Highness." His voice was like honey and Kalina felt something move in her chest. Eira squeezed her shoulder, bringing her back to herself.

"Yes. It's very nice to meet you all." She made herself look around at them all, including her father. "It seems I have a lot of people to meet and a lot to learn about." She smiled at her father, who smiled back. He placed a hand on her shoulder.

"Yes, you do. Shall we discuss things over an evening meal?" Kalina nodded. "Then I will meet you in my rooms in two hours, once we've all had time to tend to our mounts and wash up." He dismissed his entourage and they all bowed, filing out of the cavern, talking and laughing together. Kalina stood rooted to the spot, unsure of what to do. "I will see you soon Kalina, daughter of mine." He smiled warmly at her and Kalina smiled, warmth blossoming in her core. So, this was what it felt like to finally belong.

Eira guided her away from her father and back through the dining hall and into the baths. Here she led Kalina to a bench cut into the wall and sat her down. She disappeared for a few moments and Kalina looked out over the bathing pools in a slight daze. The bathing room wasn't as crowded as it had been earlier but there were still a few women sitting around in the tubs chatting. A few threw glances in her direction but none came over to talk. Eira reappeared with a bar of soap in one hand and a fresh towel in the other. She put the towel on the bench and offered Kalina the soap.

"This is the women's bathing chamber. You are safe here. Please, undress and pick a tub." Kalina did as she was told, peeling off her dress that she now realized was crusted with dust, blood from Talon's wound and sweat from running across the Wastes. She suddenly felt belated shame at having met her father in this state but there was nothing to be done about it. She lowered herself gently into the hot water, her skin instantly turning pink at the scalding temperature, and sighed. She let the heat wash away her aches and pains and settle her mind. A hand tapped her on the shoulder and she cracked open an eye to see Eira handing her the soap she'd forgotten. She smiled and took it gratefully, scrubbing her body until there wasn't a trace of dirt that she could find.

When she finally emerged from the baths, her hair shining silver in the torchlight that now lit the cavern, her body pink and clean, Eira stood waiting with a small pile of fresh, clean clothing. Kalina dried off and then inspected them. There was a pair of soft red pants, an off-white cotton shirt. A leather vest with a brown belt accentuated her hips and thighs. Overall, Kalina thought it was rather flattering.

Eira handed her a pair of soft leather boots that were a little big but otherwise finished the ensemble. She looked down at herself and felt powerful, strong, not at all like she felt when she'd worn her dresses, Talon's clothing, or even her black scribes' robes. She smiled in satisfaction.

"Now, let's go see your father." Kalina followed Eira out of the bathing chamber through a different doorway that she hadn't noticed before and up multiple winding staircases and down several halls.

Eira pushed back a piece of fabric to reveal a large room. This room was different from the others, much more richly appointed, but not gaudy. There were rugs and throws on the floor, and an actual bed frame and bed. There were even wooden tables, chairs, and a couch. Kalina took it all in, self-conscious in her new clothing and about spending alone time with her father. Her father stood by a window that looked down onto the empty Wastes. There was a slight breeze coming in through the window that blew stray wisps of her father's silver hair back from his strong face. She swallowed hard and stood behind Eira.

"Hakon, your daughter." Kalina bowed slightly to her father as he turned to survey her.

"Thank you, Eira. We will take our meal as soon as it is ready." Eira bowed slightly and left, leaving Kalina standing before her father, twisting her hands behind her back. She continued to look around the room, unsure of where to look or what to say. "You do look a lot like your mother, despite my hair and eyes." He strode closer to her, his large rough hand pushing back a lock of her hair. His hands were calloused from years of fighting. "But you got my nose, how dreadful." He winked at her and stepped past her. Kalina smiled a small smile and turned to follow him. He gestured for her to join him at the table, where she sat across from him. "Now, I want to hear all about you."

Kalina hesitated before answering. "What do you want to know?" She had a moment of fear lance through her as she contemplated an answer. Who was she now that she'd found her family? She supposed that wasn't what mattered. What mattered was who she had been.

"Everything." He put his chin on his folded hands, elbows resting on the table top as he watched her, blue eyes twinkling. So Kalina told him. She told him about her upbringing in Hywell Abbey and Father Martin and Father Nic and Delisa and Gwen the cook. She told him odd stories of St. Martin's feasts and helping in the kitchens and the time she and Delisa had stolen a basket of apples from Gwen and then let the Abbey's ponies out of their pens so they could ride them, instead of causing chaos and making the ponies sick on apples. She even told him about Mari and her bullying and how that led to her meeting Savath. She told him about every detail she felt was important to know. And he listened, a rapt audience who genuinely seemed interested in what she, an orphan from nowhere had to say. Dinner arrived while she spoke.

"So," he said when she had finished. "You made your way all the way to the Wastes with just Talon and the word of the Princess to guide you?" Kalina nodded, taking a big swig of her water. Their meal lay eaten and forgotten before them.

"Well, she's the Queen now." His eyebrows rose at that. Kalina realized she'd left out that detail of the story. "The night she helped me escape, her father had died." Hakon cleared his throat and sat up straight.

"There's something you should know about her." Kalina put her water glass down and watched her father as he looked at her uncomfortably. "She's not just the Queen, she's your mother."

Chapter 33

KALINA'S MOUTH DROPPED open. The queen, her mother. That couldn't be right.

"What do you mean?" Her mouth had gone dry and she reached for her glass again. Her father reached for his own glass, taking a swig before answering.

"Yes, she's your mother. Before she married her husband, your mother and I met and fell in love. We were very young, foolish even. She became pregnant, but before she gave birth I was called back to my people. My father had died in battle and I was forced to leave my position as an emissary to the King to lead my people. The next thing I heard, the child was stillborn and your mother had been wed to the youngest prince of Askor to broker a peace treaty." He paused letting Kalina gape for a moment, taking the flood of information in. "That was when I convinced my father's entourage to flee. There was nothing left for me here and with the war winding down, I wasn't about to put the rest of my people in danger again. We had already lost so many capable men and women, so many of our children were without parents, I couldn't let us keep suffering. So we left, to find a place where we could be safe and free." In the silence that followed, Kalina's mind raced.

"Did you love her?" Her voice was small.

"Yes. If her father had followed through on his original promise, we would have gotten married. My father supported the union, especially as it furthered our wealth and status within the nation, but her father had other plans. He didn't want an alliance with a barbarian people, especially not when he had a war to end. He sold her to their prince as soon as she was no longer pregnant." He put his glass down in disgust. Kalina realized that he hadn't supported the war at all, and he would have done anything for her mother, but he was undermined. "So, I fled with my people. Broken-hearted into the Wastes. So far that no one else knows this mountain existed and together with the dragons, we dug ourselves out a home." He gestured to his room, lit with candles all around.

"But then I heard a rumor from our spies which we had sent out into the kingdom, years later, that there had been a silver-haired child. But I didn't pursue it, with no way to search, I didn't look because I was broken and sure you were dead." His blue eyes now pleaded with her, begging her to understand why he'd left her. She swallowed and stood, coming around to her father's side of the table. He looked up at her, unshed tears standing in his eyes, and she bent down, putting her arms around him. He wrapped his around her and soon Kalina could feel him weeping against her. Tears came unbidden to her own eyes and she fought to keep them down, but years of neglect and loneliness and feeling like an outsider got the best of her and soon she was crying too. They stayed like that for a while, a father holding his long-lost daughter until both had let their feelings out and could think again.

Hakon was first to pull away. He held her out in front of him and looked at her. Kalina's hand went to her cheek, where the long scar still stood out, purple against her tanned skin, self-conscious. Hakon reached out and removed her hand.

"Every scar has a story, a lesson learned, a meaning. Never be ashamed of your scars." Kalina nodded, something welling up in her chest. "All I know is that you are my daughter, and a Princess of two realms, and I am so happy you are home." He put an arm around her shoulders and squeezed, and despite her fear of the unknown, she leaned into him and let his embrace suffuse her with warmth. "Now, that's enough for one night. We will have plenty of time to catch up. Go get some rest." He kissed her forehead and sent her off out of his room and down the stairs. Eira awaited her near the bottom, and she took Kalina back to her rooms.

Kalina slept fitfully that night. Dreams of dying a horrible death kept waking her from sleep. Soon she sat up, unable to sleep any longer and went in search of Talon's rooms.

The halls were dark as she wandered down them, the only light the rare torch set into the stone wall. Kalina wondered at such a place, dug from the ground by dragons and humans alike to create a home. It took a few tries but finally, Kalina found Talon's room. He still lay asleep on his bed, a few candles burning and a pitcher of water and a glass beside him. Kalina knelt next to him and smoothed his hair out of his eyes. She gently shook him, hoping that he would finally wake and that they could talk.

He stirred, opening his eye groggily and looking up at her. His eyes went wide as he saw her and he attempted to get up but Kalina put a hand firmly on his chest and kept him down.

"Don't get up or you'll hurt yourself." She laughed quietly at his determination. "I just came to check on you, see how you were doing." He coughed and reached for the water. She beat him to it and poured him a glass. He gulped a few swallows before answering.

"Are you alright?" he croaked. She grinned. Talon had always looked out for her. A lump rose in her throat as she thought about all he'd done to get her here.

"Yes. I'm fine. More than fine, actually." She reached out and took his hand. "I found my family. I have an aunt and cousins and a father." Talon's eyebrows rose at that last statement. "And, brace yourself." He grinned at her. "Queen Cherise? She's my mother." Talon's jaw dropped as he stared at her. Kalina smiled and tucked her hair behind her ear. "Yea, my father told me the story." And she quickly told him the story of her birth. Talon frowned.

"So, he thought you were dead? How did no one know the queen had given birth to you? It wasn't even gossiped around the palace!"

"I know, it must have been a very well-kept secret," she said, a slightly bitter edge entering her voice. If she hadn't been so well hidden, perhaps her father would have found her sooner. But then, so would the prince. She brushed her thumb across Talon's hand. "Anyway, it turns out I am royal like you said." That night at the inn felt like months ago, not days. Talon nodded. Then with a huge grin on his face, he gave a small awkward bow from where he was propped on his pillows.

"Your Majesty." He grinned up at her and she lightly smacked his arm.

"Stop that. I'm still the same old Kalina."

"Kalina, Princess of the Valdir and Ethea," he said. That hit her hard. She hadn't dared to name herself out loud but it made it all the more real.

"Holy gods, I'm a princess!" She looked at Talon's grin and laughed out loud in genuine bewilderment. Never had she thought that an orphan girl from the middle of the Deep Glen Forest would turn out to be the princess of two realms.

"You were always my Princess." Talon's voice had gone soft, and Kalina looked down at his boyish face in the candlelight and felt that fluttering in her stomach start. He had a look on his face that Kalina couldn't quite fathom, but she felt the urge to lean down and kiss him. She swallowed, her lips parting slightly as she leaned forward, their lips touching softly in a gentle kiss. She squeezed her eyes shut, her stomach going wild at the warmth of his lips on hers. The kiss ended too quickly and both of them sat there, looking at each other in awe.

"I've got to go to bed. You get some sleep and I'll see you tomorrow," she said suddenly, everything that had happened that night too much for her to handle. He nodded, disappointment in his eyes, but he let her pull her hand from his and leave with a small wave. Kalina made her way back to her room, her mind preoccupied with other things when she ran into a solid figure in the hallway.

"Sorry, Princess," a deep, male voice said as hands clasped her arms so that she wouldn't fall over. Kalina looked up into the grey eyes and handsome face of Leif. She squeaked out a reply and hurried past him to her room. He turned to watch her scamper down the hall.

Kalina tossed and turned when she got back into her room but she finally fell asleep as the sun began to rise out over the Wastes.

Chapter 34

KALINA WOKE TO EIRA SHAKING her. She blearily opened her eyes and sat up, wondering what time it was and how long she'd slept; she didn't think it had been long. Eira sat back on her heels before Kalina.

"Your father wishes to speak with you and asks that you join him for breakfast." Kalina nodded tiredly and began to get dressed. She found that she really liked the soft fabrics and colors that the Valdir all wore. She pulled on her soft boots and followed Eira out the door. They arrived at her father's rooms just as someone brought a tray of steaming food. Kalina's stomach grumbled as they entered, and she barely noticed her father speaking with Geir and Leif. She froze when she saw them, her eyes darting between the two men and her father. Leif gave her a sideways look, the corner of his mouth lifting slightly.

"Ah, here's my daughter!" Hakon broke away from his men and strode towards Kalina. She smiled up at him, still getting used to the idea that this man was her family. "I hope you slept well?" She looked up at Leif but the young man gave away nothing as she turned towards her father.

"I slept fine, thank you." Hakon waved away Geir and Leif.

"I'll speak with you both later." The two men bowed and left the chamber, Eira close at their heels. Hakon guided Kalina to the table where there were pieces of bread, meats, fruit and a kind of porridge that smelled wonderful. Kalina sat and began putting berries into her porridge. Hakon sat across from her, eyeing her as she began to eat. "I have something important to talk to you about." Kalina paused, her spoon partway to her mouth, and looked up at her father.

His blue eyes sparkled as he continued. "We have a tradition within the Valdir that dates back millennia. It's our rite of passage if you will. Once a young Valdir is old enough to fight in our army and pick a dragon, they must go through this ceremony. You are not allowed to know about the rite beforehand, it is taboo to speak of it to young members of the tribe and you will be sworn to secrecy once you have completed it, but it will be difficult and you will need to be brave." He paused and watched her. Kalina had stopped eating and put her spoon down, her stomach now roiling with uncertainty. "Will you do it?" Kalina watched her father, realizing that this clearly meant a lot to him and that he must have been wanting to ask her since they parted last night. Slowly she nodded.

"Yes. I will do it." Hakon beamed at her.

"Excellent! I will make the necessary arrangements and you will do it tonight!" Kalina almost choked on her water.

"Tonight? So soon?" She wiped the water dribbling down her chin. Her father nodded enthusiastically.

"Yes. The sooner the better. I want to make you a part of our tribe, a member. You are the princess after all and it would go a long way towards dispelling any doubts or mistrust." Kalina was taken aback. She had no idea there might be those who didn't trust her, but then again, she'd only met a handful of people, not enough to really instill confidence in her. She sighed.

"Fine. Tonight then." They finished their meal, chatting about small things, still getting to know one another, and then Kalina was sent to spend the rest of the day in contemplation for the rite.

Eira led her to a small chamber with a large window that overlooked the Wastes. She left Kalina there to contemplate the rite, and what it truly meant to be a part of the tribe, and said she would fetch her at sundown for the ritual. Kalina sat on the floor and looked out at the wide-open expanse of the Wastes.

She felt like everything had been so rushed, had happened so quickly. She was surprisingly grateful for the hours spent alone to contemplate and breathe and let the fact sink in that she was home, with the Valdir, with part of her family anyway, and no longer an orphan. Instead, she belonged, and she was slowly beginning to feel whole. The night's ritual didn't scare her at all. Whatever it was, it couldn't kill her or else her father wouldn't be so excited for her to do it. If it meant becoming a part of this tribe, a part of a proper family, she wouldn't hesitate. And if it meant she could choose her very own dragon? She would walk through fire to get a dragon.

An hour before sunset Kalina heard steps on the stairs. She shook herself, the day having passed more quickly than she'd realized. She wondered who was coming to see her as she stood up to greet whoever came through the door. To her immense surprise, Leif entered, carrying a tray of food. He smiled at her as he set the tray down on the floor before her.

"I thought you might want something to eat before the ritual." Kalina's mouth had gone dry but she saw a pitcher of water on the tray and she sat to pour herself some.

"Yes," she said after letting the water clear her throat. "Thank you. Will you join me?" She didn't know what they'd talk about but it seemed the polite thing to do and she was getting a little lonely.

"Technically you are supposed to spend this time alone." Leif sat down opposite her and took a piece of hard white cheese from the tray.

"And yet, here you are." Kalina continued to sip her water. Those darn moths were back in her stomach and she wondered if it was due to Leif's presence or the impending ritual. Either way, despite her hunger she only nibbled on the food.

"Yes." Leif chuckled. "Here I am." He took another bite of cheese, his grey eyes looking her over. "So, what's your story, Princess?" She was still struggling to get used to being called that.

"Well, it's rather complicated actually." She told him the bare bones, leaving out many of the details. She was surprisingly sick of telling her own story. She wanted to make a new story so she could stop telling the old one. No one cared about an orphan girl. But being a princess? Riding on dragons? That was a story worth telling.

"This must be a shock then, coming to a place like this. Very different from city life or even abbey life." She shook her head.

"It's not so different. I'm no stranger to hard work, and I'm learning to really enjoy the hive mind."

"Hive mind?" His eyebrow raised quizzically.

"Yes, hive mind. Everyone working together for the common good? Like honeybees."

"Ah. That makes more sense." Kalina chuckled.

"What about you?" Leif looked up at her from his cheese. His grey eyes were a bit unnerving but Kalina looked him in the eyes for as long as she could stand it.

"I was born here. Raised here. My mother died in a skirmish to protect our borders when I was very young, while my father was off at war. But once he returned, everything sort of settled. Honestly, you're the most exciting thing to happen in this place since the war. And everyone is talking about it." He smiled at her. "No pressure." He winked.

"Oh well. That's why my father was so insistent on the rite of passage." Leif nodded.

"You are important. And this will give people a chance to get to see who you are, what you are made of."

"I'm not sure what I'm made of. Up until a few months ago, I was just an orphan."

"And now you are a Princess. This is the price you pay."

They lapsed into silence. Kalina picked at the food before her, her appetite was completely gone.

"Will it be scary? The ritual, I mean."

"It takes someone brave." That didn't really answer her question, but the one thing she knew for certain was that she was brave. It had gotten her into a lot of trouble, but it was one of her redeeming qualities. Leif looked out the window at the setting sun. "It's about time." He looked at her sympathetically and reached out to place a warm, calloused hand on her arm. "I'll be right there with you." She nodded. Somehow that declaration made her feel better, braver. She smiled at him, the butterflies in her stomach calming, a warmth spreading from her center outwards at his touch.

"Thank you."

"I'd better go before Eira catches me." With that, Leif took the tray and left. Kalina turned back to the setting sun and took a deep breath, feeling grounded and more solid in who she was.

Eira came for her as the sun dipped below the horizon, a torch held aloft in her hand. She motioned for Kalina to follow her, and Kalina did so in silence. They wound through a series of halls, and Kalina was lost within a few minutes. They stopped in a small chamber where a group of old Valdir women awaited her. They took her into the center of their circle and began to paint her with a reddish-brown paint. Kalina didn't know what to do, but let them do as they would. She closed her eyes as their cool fingers made swirls and lines, dots and symbols on her face, neck, chest, and arms. Then they sat her down and braided her silver hair. It had grown even longer over the last months, reaching well past the middle of her back, and their expert fingers deftly tied it back from her head. When they finished, Kalina wondered at how she must look. She imagined she must look like a true Valdir now. Eira led her from the room once again.

Soon she could hear a low chanting, almost like a song, as she entered a well-lit chamber with Eira before her. This chamber was packed with people and was huge. Along the far walls, there were even dragons perched. The only thing missing were the children, which she realized were not allowed to know about the ritual. She took a deep breath, calming the rising panic at the number of people, the press of bodies. She had to do this, and she wasn't going to let her panic get the best of her.

The crowd parted, allowing her and Eira to pass through and into the center of the chamber, where they came to a stop before her father. There was a circle formed in the center of the floor and a dark, glittering substance covering the space. Kalina glanced at it but didn't understand it before turning to look at her father.

He stood on a raised rock platform, a long, painted robe flowed from his shoulders to the ground, covered in the same symbols as her blanket, as most of the Valdir had tattooed on their bodies. Kalina still didn't know their meaning but knew that she would learn in time, now that she had found her home. She would have all the time in the world to get her questions answered. Her father put his arms out, raising them up for silence, and the chanting around the chamber died. In the silence, his voice was like the boom of a drum, loud and sonorous.

"People of the Valdir," he began, turning slowly in place in order to see the entire crowd. The dragons shifted in their places along the walls. "We are gathered here today to witness the rite of passage. My daughter, Kalina, Princess of the Valdir and Ethea, will go through this rite in order to be considered a full Valdir, a part of our family." Hakon looked down at her, a fierce smile on his face. Kalina found herself grinning fiercely back at him. "Let the ceremony begin!" With that, the crowd cheered and the chanting began anew, renewed, louder, and it seemed to fill her up and vibrate along her bones. She turned to the dark circle. Two people came forward, one was Eira, the other Geir, both carrying torches. Together they bent and put their torches on the floor, igniting in a whoosh whatever dark substance lay there.

Soon, the circle was alive with flame, fire dancing along its edges and sparking into the middle. Kalina's heart dropped into her stomach as she looked at the ring before her. She looked to her father who had stepped down beside her.

"What am I to do?" She asked him quietly. He placed a hand on her shoulder and pointed at the ring.

"You are to walk through the fire, my dear." Kalina gulped at those words. Could she really walk through fire to gain the tribe's respect? To gain a family? To gain her dragon? She leaned down and removed her new leather slippers as she didn't want to ruin them. Her feet met the cold stone and she winced. She steeled herself, her mind focusing on what it felt like to fly, and she looked up, her eyes making contact with Leif who stood across the circle from her. He grinned at her and nodded.

Kalina stepped forward.

Chapter 35

THE FIRE BIT INTO HER FEET and licked up her calves. The coals beneath her soles were sharp and Kalina gritted her teeth as she felt them slice into her tender feet. She wondered if full-blooded Valdir had thicker soles than she did but it took every bit of strength she had to keep from crying out, from leaping from the fire. The flames were calming down but the coals still smoldered red hot beneath her. She bit her lip to take away the pain from her feet, biting until she drew blood and a coppery taste flooded her mouth. The crowd's chanting continued to fill her, making her feel more alive at that moment than she had ever felt in her life.

She tore her eyes away from her feet and looked up at Leif. He anchored her in the room, gave her a destination, a goal, and as much as Kalina wanted to walk slowly, she knew she needed to move quicker. She picked up her pace and before she knew it she was across. She stumbled and fell as she reached the far side, Leif catching her in his arms. Quickly he scooped her off her feet as the crowd around her cheered.

Kalina let out her held breath in a whoosh, and despite the almost blinding pain in her feet she managed to look over at her father and see the pride that beamed from him. The cheering turned to chanting once again and Kalina could make out her name among the words. She grinned, her heart full and free as her people began to embrace her. Leif carried her through the crowd, each person she passed reaching out to touch her arms, her legs, her hands, her head. Each one a welcoming gesture, and for once she didn't feel overwhelmed by the sheer number of people or their touches. She felt whole.

Finally, Leif reached the edge of the chamber and Eira. The woman kissed her on the forehead before Leif placed her on the ground. She cried out as her feet struck the stone, and Eira's arm went under hers as she helped Kalina limp from the chamber. Back into the small chamber with the old women, she went, but this time the women bathed and bandaged her feet. Eira spread a salve over Kalina's feet and she felt a blessed coolness move up her legs, the pain receding.

"You will have trouble walking for a few days, but this salve will help it heal nicely." She placed the jar of salve into Kalina's hands. Kalina feared her feet would never heal, but she knew that all the Valdir who went before her were currently walking, so she gritted her teeth at the pain. Eira helped Kalina up, walking her back to her own little chamber. Kalina practically fell into bed and was asleep as soon as her head hit the pillow. The previous night's lack of sleep and the stress of the ritual finally caught up to her.

It took three days of applying salve three times a day and limping before Kalina could walk relatively normally again. She'd spent the first day in bed, allowing her feet to heal. Talon had limped in to visit her, and she explained her foot injuries were from a coming of age ritual. Eira had come to her that morning and made her swear an oath of silence about what the ritual entailed, and despite how much Talon begged, Kalina did not relent. She respected her new tribe and family more than that. Leif had come and sat with her, waiting while she rested. Once she could walk again, Kalina found she still had trouble sleeping.

She spent the sleepless nights roaming the halls, getting to know the passages and rooms but also looking for the dragons. She was curious about where they rested when their riders were inside the mountain, and where the eggs were. She found the dragon cavern on her third night wandering the halls. It was the sound that alerted her, as she turned a corner in a corridor she hadn't traveled before. There was a din, a general noise full of shuffling, whispers, and the flapping of wings. During her research at Ravenhelm, Kalina had learned an awful lot about the dragons. They knew many languages and were quick learners. Their own language was spoken much like those of birds or bats, a combination of whistled songs, chirps, and buzzes, paired with echolocation. They could hear sounds that humans couldn't and much of their speech was silent.

She followed the noises down a set of steps and out into the largest cavern she had seen yet. It was open to the elements at one end, a true cave with an opening just large enough for one dragon at a time to enter and leave. The ceiling was too high for Kalina to see, at least at night, and she couldn't make out the far wall, just a blackness filled with the sounds of the dragons. All across the floor were dips and holes, most large enough for one dragon to curl up in, but some large enough for many, or small enough for what she assumed would be baby dragons to curl in. Most of the dips and holes were occupied. Kalina gasped, her eyes wide at the sheer number of dragons that filled the space.

She had never expected that after months of searching, and hearing that dragons had disappeared from the land, she would find hundreds of them. It occurred to her that perhaps not every Valdir was paired with a dragon. It also occurred to her that she didn't truly understand how that pairing worked, since the prince, or rather king, had taken all books regarding the Valdir from the library. She vowed to ask Eira or Leif or her father the following day about how it all worked. She wandered the edge of the room, watching the sleeping dragons. Most looked like huge jewels set into the reddish stone, and she marveled at the varying shades. There wasn't just green, or blue, or red. But rather, crimson, and grass green, sapphire and sky blue, vermillion and chartreuse. Every shade you could imagine within the realms of blue, green, yellow, red, orange, purple, and even black and white existed. She spent the next hours sitting on a large rock by the edge of the cavern, watching and marveling.

Her father found her the next day as she was walking from the bathing chamber to get her morning meal. Hakon always seemed mildly excited when he saw her, like he was on the edge of his seat, waiting for the next thing to happen. It made her smile as he approached, a grin beginning on his face in response.

"Hello, my dear." He winked at her and fell into step beside her. "I was hoping we could have another meal together, and then I have a surprise for you." Kalina eyed him suspiciously, a small smile on her lips.

"Oh?" They went to grab trays of food from what served as the kitchens. "What kind of surprise?"

"One I hope you'll like." Kalina rolled her eyes at his response as they went to find a place to eat. They sat at the end of a table, stepping down into the depression that served as a seat.

"Father, can you tell me about the dragons?" Her father smiled at her, a twinkle in his eye.

"Of course, I can. What would you like to know?"

"Everything." Kalina could barely keep the excitement from her voice. "Like, how do you choose one? What is the pairing? How does it all work? Are you paired for life? What happens if one of you dies? What is flying like? Can I ride one?" She fired off questions, her father's grin growing as she spoke.

"Woah, slow down, Kalina." He put up both his hands in placation. "I will answer them all in due time. But first, I have a request." Kalina closed her mouth, about to ask another question. "Part of being a part of the Valdir, and part of being a princess, includes training. You will train in diplomacy, in politics, in how to lead these people, and in our history. But you will also train in the fighting arts. How to fight with bow and blade, spear and ax, and hand to hand. Most Valdir fight with long spears, better for fighting on a dragon, you see. You will learn to fight atop a dragon and alongside it. These tattoos-," He pointed to his own face and then the faces and of those around them. "You earn those as you master these arts. They stand for courage, wisdom, life, love, clarity, speed. Each symbol means something different to the Valdir." Kalina pointed to the three dots above his right eye.

"What does this one stand for?"

"That one stands for wisdom." He gestured to three lines beneath his right eye. "And these stand for strength. They can be placed anywhere on the body that it is meant for. This one is meant for strength of mind." He tapped his temple and winked at her. "All this and more you will learn if you agree to be trained. You may have the title of Princess, but no one will force it on you." Kalina was quiet for a minute. A large part of her wanted the responsibility, the reason to live, the belonging, but she knew the responsibility would be immense. Her father guessed her trepidation. "You make your own destiny, Kalina. Your own future, your choice." Kalina nodded and swallowed before answering.

"I will do it. I want to do it." Hakon beamed at her, laughing and reaching out to squeeze her hand.

"I'd hoped you would say that!" Kalina's heart swelled at his approval. "Now, let's finish eating so I can give you your surprise!"

He answered some of her question about dragons during their meal. He gave a brief explanation about the deep magic that runs through all magical creatures in their world.

"The deep magic allows the dragons to choose one human to bond with for life. It feels as though a lock has clicked into place in your heart and suddenly, this dragon is yours, and you are theirs." Kalina felt a thrill in her stomach at the prospect.

She followed Hakon into the main chamber beyond the dining hall where she'd first met him. Kaya stood on the stone, her sapphire scales gleaming in the morning light. Hakon paused before his dragon, reaching up to stroke her nose. Kalina wondered if it was soft like Savath's had been.

"The surprise I have for you is that we are going for a ride." Her heartbeat quickened.

"On Kaya?" The dragon snorted.

"Yes, on me, Kalina. I will give you a taste of the wind." Her blood thrilled through her veins as her father flashed her an untamed grin. She responded in kind. He helped her up into a leather saddle. Kalina hadn't noticed them before when she'd seen her father ride in on Kaya. It had two seats, meant for two riders, and there were straps to hold her into the saddle. She thought back to her rides on Savath and realized how unstable and unsafe she had previously been. The saddle made her feel safe, grounded. Hakon climbed up behind her and placed his arms into straps before her, pushing her slightly forward.

"Grab on to these." He indicated the second set of loops on the straps he held. Kalina did as he instructed. "Now, hang on!" She could hear the excitement in his voice and as Kaya lumbered towards the edge of the mountain, the open air before them, wind whipping her braided hair behind her, her heart leapt in anticipation. She suddenly understood why the Valdir braided their hair back from their face. Kaya paused on the edge, her wings tucked into her sides for a moment before plunging into the air. They fell for a few seconds, Kalina's stomach rising into her throat before Kaya snapped out her wings, catching the wind currents and soaring out into the blue sky, the sun shining off her sapphire scales. Kalina whooped in delight as they leveled out, Hakon laughing behind her at her joy.

They flew together for hours, Kaya catching spiraling currents up high into the air, so high Kalina had trouble breathing before dropping down, down, down, her wings snapping out what seemed like mere feet before the ground. They danced through clouds and skimmed across the mountain top. Kalina drank in the world, orienting herself in space. The mountain that the Valdir called home was a great mammoth sandstone that rose out of the barren Wastes. All around them, all the way to the horizon, was nothing but flat expanse. Kalina could see a few lakes in the distance, but even the Great Grey Mountains were smudges to the north. She marveled at how far the dragons and Valdir must have flown to find peace.

Chapter 36

KALINA WAS WIND-BLOWN, her lips chapped and bleeding, her cheeks pink and her eyes watering as they set down hours later. Her adrenaline still pumped through her veins as Hakon helped her off Kaya. She shook feeling back into her fingers and toes, hopping around, a huge grin on her face. Hakon laughed a hearty laugh at her joy. Kaya grinned in a very dragonish way, her mouth open, copious teeth and fangs showing, her tongue lolling.

"That was the best thing I've ever done! It doesn't even compare to flying on Savath."

"Flying on Wyverns is more, tame. They can rarely carry as much weight, and their wings are thinner and not as strong as dragons'. They cannot handle steep dives and maneuvers with a rider on their back. On their own, however, they are very agile." Kalina nodded.

"When can we do that again?" Hakon laughed.

"We can do it every day if you'd wish. But starting this afternoon I want you to begin your training." Kalina nodded. They went to get some lunch before she started training. Then Hakon brought her to the same chamber she had fire-walked in. In the center of the room stood Geir. His grey eyes were solemn as Kalina and her father approached. She swallowed, her anxiety rising.

"Kalina, you remember Geir?" Kalina nodded and Geir bowed. "He will be teaching you your hand-to-hand combat, your fighting arts." Hakon motioned Kalina forward. "He will explain how training will go, and why it is important. Eira will handle your diplomacy, history, and other training." Her father left her to Geir's teachings.

Geir eyed her up and down as if assessing whether or not she would make a good warrior, a good Valdir. Kalina found herself straightening, squaring her shoulders, hoping she looked fierce enough. Geir's mouth quirked in what Kalina thought could have been a smile, but it was gone just as quickly as it arrived. He began to circle her, and the anticipation grew in her stomach making her a little nauseous. Finally, after what felt like an eternity, Geir stopped in front of her.

"It's obvious you've done hard labor before. But you are still too skinny, too soft. We will have to work on building your muscles and endurance before we can get into the meat of hand-to-hand combat." Her heart fell. She knew she wasn't much of a fighter, especially considering how many times Mari had given her a black eye, or the time Dillion and his friends had beat her up. She knew how to take a beating, that was for sure. Geir continued. "First, you must learn how to fall." Kalina rolled her eyes.

"I already know how to fall."

"Then show me." Geir pushed her so unexpectedly that she stumbled, tripping over her own feet and falling hard on her bottom. Geir smirked at her as she sat on the hard stone, a scowl creasing her forehead in frustration.

"Fine. You show me then." She stood slowly, her tailbone smarting. Geir gave her a grim smile and went into a crouch. Then he fell, but he fell with a purpose. His body crumpled, tucked in on itself, his hands slapping the ground as he rolled. Soon, Geir was back on his feet, as though he'd never fallen over in the first place. He certainly wasn't rubbing his bum like she was. Kalina watched him closely. "Show me again." Geir grinned this time, as he showed her over and over until Kalina got into a crouch, keeping her center of gravity low, and tumbled rather than fell. That was a better word for it. She tumbled in a controlled motion, ending up back on her feet, no worse for wear.

"Good. Now you must learn to do that in all directions. You must practice this until it becomes second nature, until you could do it no matter where you are, no matter the circumstances. I will be testing you when you least expect it, as will others. This is the first lesson we teach our children." She realized that this was a lesson they taught their children, not their seventeen-year-olds. She stopped dead. Seventeen. She had turned seventeen sometime in the last months. She had known it was approaching when she was back in the castle, searching the archives, but with everything that had happened, she had forgotten to mark the day.

"Do it again." Geir stepped towards her. She was still partially lost in thought as he shoved her shoulder once again. She half fell, half-remembered to tuck and roll at the last second, falling awkwardly on her wrist. She came back up to standing, clutching her wrist and massaging it. It ached something fierce but it wasn't broken. "You see?"

"Yes, Geir. I get it."

"Then practice." So she did. She tumbled and rolled over and over and over until every inch of her body ached.

Kalina slept well that night but woke the next morning with bruises in places she didn't know she could get them. She was waiting in line for breakfast when someone shoved her from behind. She fell, tumbling at the last second, only her pride hurt and a few of her new bruises twinging. She stood and looked up to see Rangvald grinning at her. Behind him stood Kari, a smirk on her face. Kalina grinned back and got back into line.

"Want to eat with us?" Kari said from behind her. Kalina turned, looking into those familiar bright blue eyes of her family.

"Sure." They got their trays of food and sat together at a table. Kalina began to eat rather awkwardly, unsure of how to interact with her own people.

"So, you were raised as an orphan? What was that like?" Kari was inquisitive and a bit brash but Kalina liked her despite her own awkwardness.

"Ummm, different. Nothing like what it must have been growing up here."

"It was boring." Kari's voice was drawn out. "Nothing exciting ever happens here unless we make it exciting. You-," she pointed her knife at Kalina while she buttered a roll. "Are the most exciting thing to happen here, probably ever."

"So I've heard."

"Living this far removed from the rest of the kingdom has been a challenge." Rangvald seemed the more level headed of the two. "Kari here likes to make trouble just for trouble's sake." Kari grinned maliciously at her brother. Kalina found herself grinning back.

"It wasn't any more exciting growing up in an abbey. Mostly it was me getting beat up on the regular by an older girl, or me getting into trouble with Father Martin. The most exciting thing to happen was when I left on the Wyvern." Kari's eyes lit at the mention.

"Is that how you found out you were Valdir? Did you discover it when you realized that flying was second nature?" Kalina smiled.

"No, I found out from Father Martin, at the abbey. Then, later from a woman in Ravenhelm. She told me what my silver hair meant. Before, living in the abbey, my hair was just an oddity, something to make fun of, something I had to hide."

"Make fun of? Do other people not have silver hair?" Rangvald was serious.

"No," she giggled. "Only those who are really old have silver hair." Kari looked at her with a confused look.

"So, no children are born with it?" Kalina was utterly shocked that Kari and Rangvald didn't know anything about the outside world. But she realized that neither had she before she had left Hywell Abbey.

"Nope. We are special in that way." Kalina realized she'd just included herself as part of the Valdir. She smiled slightly.

"What about the boy who came in with you?" Kari's eyes twinkled and Kalina felt a blush travel up her neck.

"You mean Talon?"

"Speaking of." Rangvald pointed with his fork to the cavern entrance. Kalina spun around and saw Talon standing there, his dark hair standing out like a black sheep among a flock of white ones. She waved at him and he grinned, limping over, his injury clearly visible as he approached.

"Kalina! I've been looking everywhere for you!" Kalina motioned to the seat beside her. Talon eyed the depression in the earth dubiously. "I'd better go get some food before I attempt to sit." He left them to grab a tray of food. Kalina watched him walk away, aware of how young he seemed compared to someone like Rangvald or Leif. She supposed she must look that young as well but she didn't really feel it. Not anymore.

Talon joined them a few moments later and Kalina stood to help him down to his seat. Once seated, Talon looked around at Kari and Rangvald and smiled.

"I'm Talon." He stuck out his hand for them to shake but both of them frowned at his palm.

"I'm Rangvald. Kalina's cousin. And this is my sister Kari." Rangvald broke the awkward moment, reaching to shake Talon's hand.

"I can introduce myself, brother." Kari elbowed her brother in the ribs and then gave Talon a sickly-sweet smile. "I'm Kari, and I'm the best person here." Kalina snorted into her food, Rangvald grinning over at her. Talon chuckled nervously.

"Good to know." He began eating, shooting glances at Kalina and then at Kari. "You certainly are related." He gestured between Kalina and Kari. "Same eyes, same nose."

"Their mother is my father's sister," Kalina explained. Talon nodded.

"You mean Eira?" They all nodded. Kari began asking Talon about Ravenhelm, firing off questions left and right. Kalina was grateful for the distraction. Soon other Valdir had migrated over and begun talking to Kari and Rangvald, and Talon turned to Kalina. "Where have you been these last few days?"

"With my father." She updated him on her recent adventures in a low voice.

"So you really have a father." Talon shook his head in wonder. "What's it been like?"

"It's been so great Talon. I finally feel like I belong somewhere." Talon frowned slightly.

"You can tell your mother, the Queen, now can't you? Take up your place at her side, as the rightful Princess of Ethea?" Kalina shook her head sadly.

"The King would kill me on sight. As much as I want her to know about me, I think I'll have to content myself with this family." Talon didn't seem satisfied with that answer but at that moment Geir arrived at their table.

"It's time to train, Princess Kalina." Kalina shrugged in regret to Talon and followed Geir from the dining hall.

Kalina trained every morning and afternoon with Geir. The mornings were spent learning combat, while the afternoons were spent strength training and running through the vast underground complex, building up her endurance. Her evenings were filled with instruction from Eira, and Kalina slowly learned about her own history and how her father ran the Valdir.

Once Geir was satisfied she had learned to fall, he began throwing punches, teaching her first to dodge and then to block. Her progress felt slow but Kari assured her later that she was a natural and that she had overheard Geir telling Hakon that Kalina was the best fighter he'd trained in years. Kalina wished Geir would tell her that instead of just giving her more work once she'd mastered a move.

Her body began to change slowly. Her arms became muscled, her legs growing larger and denser, her stomach tight with muscle. She found she was much hungrier and ate much more than Talon who now met her for every meal. He commented on the changes during her third week of training.

"You're getting bigger than me!" he joked but Kalina could see the frustration in his eyes and hear in his voice that his injury was holding him back. She knew he hated working in the kitchens, washing dishes after every meal, not being allowed to carry anything heavy or walk long distances. His healing was going slowly and he chomped at the bit to move.

"You'll be joining me in no time," she assured him, hopeful she wasn't lying.

One afternoon, Kalina was covered in sweat as she cycled between leg lifts, squats, and jumps, with Geir watching over her, when her father entered the chamber. He watched her in silence for a few moments until she had finished her set and then he wandered over.

"I see you have improved since I last came to watch your training sessions." Kalina realized suddenly that apart from a few dinners eaten together, and another couple flights, she hadn't seen her father much in the last weeks.

"I should hope so." Geir's voice was gruff but Kalina could see the small smile in the corner of his mouth that she had come to see whenever she did a move particularly well.

"Yes!" Hakon clapped Geir on the shoulder. "You have done a fine job teaching our Kalina." She smiled at the praise, wiping the sweat from her brow. Her father approached her, putting a hand on her shoulder. "I have not come only to congratulate you. I have come to say goodbye." Her stomach dropped.

"Goodbye?"

"The King of Ethea has sent a small contingent of men into the Wastes. They are well provisioned and seem determined to find us. I doubt they will ever make it as far as our mountain but I, Geir, and a small contingent of soldiers must fly out to intercept them. It has been a long time since we've had to fight for our freedom, but we knew it would happen eventually." He turned rather sad eyes to Geir who looked back solemnly.

"Can't I come with you?" Kalina knew she sounded desperate, pleading to accompany her father, but she didn't want to say goodbye to him so soon after finding him, even if it was only for a little while.

"Oh, my darling." He put an arm around her and kissed the top of her sweaty head. "I will be back! It is a small group and we have our dragons. It shouldn't take more than a day or two and we'll be back before you know it." He released her and her stomach settled. "Now, while we are gone, Rangvald will be taking over your training." He squeezed her once again. "Train hard now. Soon, you will need it." And then he left her, Geir following soon after.

Chapter 37

KALINA THREW HERSELF INTO her training. Hakon, Geir, and
Leif had left with a contingent of Valdir soldiers for the edge of the
Wastes toward the King's men. Kalina couldn't sleep unless she was
so exhausted from training that she practically fell asleep during her
evening meal.

Eira patted her on the back one evening days later as Kalina
anxiously stared at a scroll. Most of the Valdir's records were written
on scrolls, easier to carry when traveling, and easier to store. Books
were heavy and cumbersome, the binding process beyond the
Valdir's ken while living in such an isolated place. Eira told Kalina
that their people traded with other nations. Ethea and Askor hadn't
seen the Valdir in decades but their neighbors far to the south, beyond
the wastes, were well acquainted with Valdir traders.

"Ethea and Askor became too dangerous for us. The King of
Askor wanted to enslave or kill us, while the King of Ethea felt we
owed him our allegiance and obedience. We felt we were our own
people, with a duty to no kingdom but our own. So we fled, so far
that this place isn't on the maps of any countries. We are a kingdom
unto ourselves, although Ethea claims that the Wastes fall within
their domain." Kalina listened, trying to pay attention. She had
worked extra hard that day with Rangvald, her body sticky with stale
sweat, her muscles, and bones aching sweetly. She longed for her
bath and her dinner but knew she needed to focus and get through
Eira's lesson.

"We couldn't survive here without help, so we began flying
south, to where no one had heard of dragons or the Valdir, and we
began trading goods with the villages and towns on the edges of the
Wastes within the borders of Wostrad and Alben, our neighbors to
the south. We have outposts to the north throughout the Great Grey
Mountains where most do not dare to live. We raise cattle and do a
little farming in the foothills, careful not the reveal our presence to
the King. We trade with them for fabric, varying foodstuffs like flour
and sugar, and we give them animal hides, shed dragons' scales and
skins, and pottery." Eira eyed her suspiciously. "Are you paying
attention, dear?" Kalina sat up straighter.

"Yes, Eira. The Valdir traded dragon scales and pottery," she repeated, trying to sound like she knew what was happening. Eira sighed.

"Go get some food in you. We'll try again tomorrow." Kalina jumped to her feet, hugging Eira fiercely before running off towards the dining cavern, the woman laughing in her wake.

When Kalina entered the cavern she immediately noticed that things were uneasy. She looked around, expecting her father to have returned. But she didn't see a sign of him. She could hear murmurings and she went to the nearest table.

"What's happening?" she asked a stout older woman. The woman looked up at her.

"The dragons were spotted on the horizon flying for home." Kalina's heart leapt at the news. Her father would be here soon. She grabbed a roll from the serving area and then ran from the hall, her sore muscles protesting as she raced to the entrance cavern. The space was already filled, crawling with man and beast alike. Dragons bellowed, calling for water or food, or for help with an injury. Men and women bustled about, some carrying buckets of water, others bandages, and other items for healing. Kalina looked over the crowds, searching for a familiar face.

A hand landed on her arm and she jumped, turning to look up into the handsome face of Leif. Kalina started to smile at him before noticing that his face was bloodied and worn. He looked exhausted. Kalina lifted a hand as if to touch his face but hesitated.

"Are you alright?" Leif took both her hands in his.

"Kalina…" His voice trailed off and she saw utter sorrow there.

"Is it Geir?" Her voice was small. Surely, he hadn't lost his father in the fight. But Leif shook his head, swallowing hard.

"No." Kalina sagged in relief.

"Good. Where's my father?" She began to turn to search for him again, but Leif tugged her back to look at him.

"Your father," he paused, seemingly unable to get the words out. "Your father is dead, Kalina. Kaya too."

Kalina just stared, her mouth opening and closing, her body going from hot to cold as goosebumps rose up her arms.

"What did you say?" she squeaked out, a rushing sound starting in her ears, the edges of her vision wobbling.

"I'm so sorry, Princess." She tried to pull away from him,

disbelief and dread heavy in her chest. Her father couldn't be dead. He was king. He was a Valdir warrior. He had Kaya. Leif pulled her back towards him, wrapping his arms around her as she began to shake. Kalina breathed in the smell of leather, sweat, blood, and the musty smell of the dragons. It reminded her of her father. Panic rose within her, the same familiar panic she had always known. Her legs buckled, her stomach rebelled, her head swam and her breathing came out in short shallow breaths. Above her, Leif murmured to her but she had no idea what he was saying.

She had only just found him, only just begun to get to know him, only just begun to belong somewhere. And now, without warning, without reason, he was just gone. She would never see those laughing blue eyes she had come to love so much. She realized with mounting horror that she'd never told him she loved him. She'd never gotten the chance. She began to sob uncontrollably, her chest feeling like it was caving in. Leif held her, eventually picking her up and carrying her away from the busy cavern and into her quiet bedroom.

She slept for three days. Leif, Talon, Eira, Kari, Rangvald, and even Geir each took turns watching at her bedside, proffering a cup of water and a small roll of bread stuffed with nuts or cheese every time she awoke. She would occasionally drink the water but usually, she just rolled over, ignoring them all.

"She's never endured a loss like this before," a voice said quietly one night when Kalina awoke. Her head pounded but she didn't want to reach for the glass of water six inches from her nose. "She'd only just found him. And to lose him so suddenly..." the speaker trailed off. She wasn't sure if it was Talon or Eira speaking the voice was pitched so low. But she didn't care. The very thought of her father made her want to bury her head under the covers and never come out.

She knew she was being selfish, childish even. Would her father want her to wallow in bed like this? Refusing to eat? She doubted it. But she felt bogged down, mired in sadness, a black cloud hanging over her head. And she felt guilty. She didn't even really know why, but it was there, lurking behind the sadness, rearing its ugly head whenever she thought she might pull herself out.

"But will she recover? She has a crown to take up, and a people to lead." This voice she was sure was Talon's.

"She will. When she's ready. Until then, it's okay for her to grieve." The two voices went silent and she drifted back into her dreamless sleep.

The next time she woke she was alone. She sat up, rubbing the crusted tears from her eyes. Her body ached in a way it never had when she was training. Her head pounded and she downed the water glass beside her bed in two gulps then looked around for more.

She left her room, practically dragging her body down the corridors and halls and upstairs until she found herself outside her father's rooms. The door was shut, and Kalina stood before it, fear of what awaited her inside twisting her gut. But finally, she pushed aside the door and stepped inside.

It smelled like him. The old book smell mixed with leather and the mustiness of dragons made her chest go hollow. She pushed forward, forcing herself to take in the room and its furnishings, wandering from corner to corner, picking up small items and discarding them. These were his things, his treasured possessions. And she missed him terribly. Missed him like she had never missed anyone else. She didn't miss her mother this badly, or even Calla or Anders, or Delisa this much. Her father had begun to make a home in her heart and now there was a huge hole where he had been

The door opened as she stood looking out the window. She didn't turn. She didn't care who it was behind her. She watched the sun rising in the east, footsteps approaching behind her.

"Princess?" Leif's voice was gentle. She didn't turn. Silence reigned for a few moments.

"What do I do now?" Her voice was small, diminished, broken. Leif sighed behind her. He stepped forward and put his hand into hers, gently squeezing her fingers. She looked up into his grey eyes. Sadness lingered there. He smiled.

"You lead, your Majesty."

To be continued...

Ready for more? Born of Stone is up next.

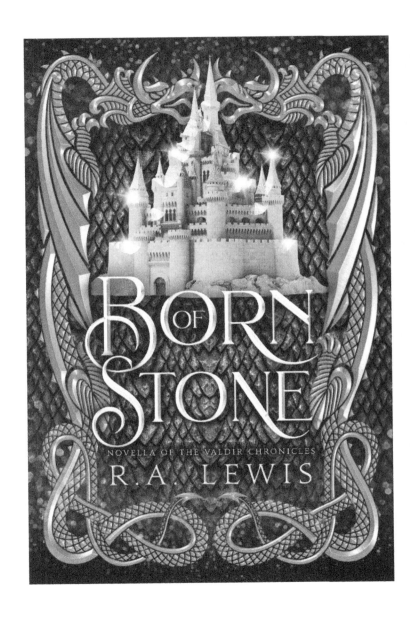

BORN OF STONE

NOVELLA OF THE VALDIR CHRONICLES

R. A. LEWIS

Born of Stone

A Valdir Chronicles Novella

Dedication

To overcoming the odds.

Chapter 1

CHERISE HURRIED DOWN THE HALLWAY straightening her bodice and skirts as she made her way towards the entrance hall of Ravenhelm Castle. She couldn't believe she was late yet again, and her hands worried at the pins holding her blonde curls away from her lovely face and green eyes. Just that morning her father had pulled her aside to reprimand her for spending so much time in the library or out riding her mare instead of sitting with him in council. He didn't understand how boring she found sitting in council, surrounded by stuffy old men discussing Ethea's politics. He didn't understand how trapped she often felt, or that her alone time reading or riding was the only freedom she ever got as the princess of the realm. But she had been reading a book in the library when she'd knocked a full teacup onto her skirts and was forced to rush back to her rooms to change.

Today was an important day. It was the day that the King of the Valdir, a race of dragon riders, and his son were to arrive at Ravenhelm castle. They were coming to solidify the alliance between the Valdir and the Etheans, to strategize for upcoming battles against their northern neighbor Askor, and to renegotiate their current arrangement with her father. Cherise knew how important it was for her to be there on time, but she couldn't stand the idea of showing up in a stained dress.

Turning the corner of the hallway in a rush, her eyes on her skirts, she ran straight into something very solid, and very much alive. Cherise let out a small cry as she fell but just when she was about to strike the ground, a hand snagged hers and pulled her to her feet. She looked up, startled, into the brightest blue eyes she'd ever seen.

"Oh, excuse me, I'm so sorry..." she trailed off as she looked at the young man that stood before her. His clothing was strange: a white linen shirt and a dark red leather jacket and pants that looked like some kind of strange armor; his bright silver hair hung long, braided back from an intricately tattooed face. She let out a small gasp as she righted.

"No, I'm sorry. I should have been paying attention to where I was walking, but I was caught up in this tapestry here." The young man gestured to the wall beside them. Cherise barely turned her head, more interested in the Valdir that stood before her than in the tapestry. His handsome face was lit with a warm smile. He bristled with weapons, which was strange since her father usually didn't allow armed men into the castle unless they were palace guards, but clearly, this man had permission.

"It's not a problem," she said breathlessly, smiling back and regaining her composure. "I'm Princess Cherise." She gave him a small curtsey, since she wasn't quite sure who he was among the Valdir, but she knew by his silver hair he certainly was a Valdir. He smiled more broadly and gave her a low bow in return.

"I'm Hakon, son of King Natan of the Valdir."

The King's son. He was the Prince of the Valdir. She flushed furiously as Hakon captured her hand and kissed the back of it gently. Fire raced up her arm and a shiver went down her spine at his touch.

"Pleasure," she said breathlessly. "I was just heading to the entrance hall to greet you and your father. Am I too late?"

Hakon smiled and gestured behind himself and the empty corridor.

"You are a bit, actually. Our fathers are already in the council chambers. I opted to explore instead of sitting through formal reviews of our troop movements."

Ethea had been at war with its northern neighbor, Askor, for decades now, since Cherise's grandfather's time. It showed no signs of stopping either, not unless major changes were made, treaties signed, and compromises accomplished. But her own father was just as stubborn as his father, and her grandfather had been, and he also wasn't one for upsetting the status quo by making life altering decisions. So she doubted he'd make the changes necessary to end the war.

"Well then, I'm glad I ran into you. My father would have been furious if I'd just burst in on them." She reached out and took his elbow. "How about a tour?"

He smiled broadly at her, his white teeth dazzling against his tanned skin and contrasted nicely with his silver braids and bright blue eyes. He really was the most beautiful man she'd ever seen.

"I would be honored." He held out a hand before them. "Lead the way!"

Cherise beamed at him, swept her blonde curls over her shoulders and led the way down the hallway, making for her favorite place in the castle: the gardens.

"I'll let you in on a little secret," she said as they strolled along the cobbled pathways of the gardens, surrounded by broad-leafed trees and early spring flowers. It was a bit cool outside, but as long as they kept moving, she wasn't too chilled. Plus, it gave her an excellent excuse to stay close to the Prince. "This is my favorite place in the whole world. And it's the only place I can get a little privacy." She nodded behind them to the soldier who followed just within eyesight. Her father was a paranoid man and always had at least one soldier tailing his daughter when she left the castle.

"But we're being followed," Hakon pointed out, smiling at her bemusedly.

"Not for long." Cherise snagged his arm and began to run, quickly turning a corner in the path, the soldier momentarily blocked from view by the shrubbery. Then she dragged him into the bushes, not worrying for one moment about her elaborately braided hair or her pretty dress. She could always have her maid fix any tears later. After a few moments crashing in the underbrush, she crouched down, pulling the tall Hakon with her.

She put a finger to her lips, both of them breathing hard as running footsteps sounded on the cobbled pathway a dozen feet away.

"Princess Cherise?" a voice called. Cherise covered her own mouth to stifle a giggle and Hakon's blue eyes sparkled in the dappled light beneath the shrubbery.

Soon the footsteps trampled off and Cherise let out a bark of laughter. Hakon grinned as she took his hand again and led him deeper into the lush garden. Perhaps it was a stupid idea to be alone with a man she didn't know, but something in her gut told her Hakon was a good person.

"Won't you get in trouble for that?" Hakon asked as they pushed through the undergrowth and out into a small clearing, where the ground was covered in soft moss and sunlight streamed through the canopy overhead. Cherise flopped down onto the grass and let out a sigh.

"Probably. But it just means my father will put more guards on me for a while."

Hakon sank to the ground beside her, crossing his legs beneath him. He fiddled with a stick he found, occasionally looking up into her eyes with shy interest.

"So, tell me about the Valdir," Cherise said, flinging a small leaf at him. He grinned.

"What do you want to know?"

"Do you really ride dragons?"

"Yes. My dragon is named Kaya and she's the most stunning sapphire blue you've ever seen."

"Can I meet her?"

"Perhaps. She and my father's dragon are outside the city at the moment with our soldiers. But maybe we can go to visit her."

"Can you take me flying?"

"If Kaya decides she likes you, then yes." He smiled at her, clearly pleased with her boldness and sense of adventure. "You said this is your most favorite place in the world. Have you seen much of the world then?"

Cherise's smile faltered and she looked away.

"No, I've never left this castle really. Only on festival days and occasional days out riding in the country. But I've never been far." She lay back on the moss and closed her eyes, bathing in the sunlight that filtered in through the trees. Her heart felt heavy in her chest. She knew she'd never leave Ravenhelm, not unless forced to. Her job was here. "But I've never needed to leave. I have everything I need here

210

and a library to tell me about all the other places."

When Hakon remained silent, she cracked an eye and looked at him. He, too, was looking up to the sky above, but with a wistful look on his face. Finally, he answered.

"That's a little sad if I'm being honest. I've flown everywhere from the Great Grey Mountains to south of the Badlands and the border with Wostrad. I've flown across the Eastern Wastes and across the straights to Ablen's shores. There is so much more of the world than this castle, and so many beautiful things to see."

Cherise sat up then.

"I guess you'll just have to show me then."

Hakon's eyes met hers and he grinned.

Chapter 2

CHERISE SUCKED IN A BREATH as her knee brushed Hakon's beneath the huge council room table. She and the Valdiran Prince were sitting on one side, the Valdiran King on the other with his closest advisor, a big man a little older than Hakon named Geir who had given Cherise the once over before sitting down at the table. He had unsettling grey eyes.

Her father, King Osian Stanchon of Ethea, sat at the head of the table, his hands crossed over his chest. The rest of the seats were occupied by the other members of the Ethean council. Cherise's favorite was a tall, slim and serious-looking man sitting beside the Valdir delegation. He was the Spymaster and Cherise knew that he always had the best gossip and the best tidbits of information. She couldn't say how many times Lord Illeron had helped her get out of trouble with Mistress Aynne, the new head of the kitchens.

But right now, all of her attention was on the small spot of her knee where it had touched Hakon's. It seemed to burn, sending a shiver all the way up her spine. She darted a look at the young Prince. He was very handsome, his silver battle braids pulled back behind his head into a tail, tied by a colorful piece of fabric. It made his sharp cheekbones and blue eyes stand out in the dim chamber. Cherise let out a small sigh.

She couldn't believe how much she liked this young man already. She had never been crazy about boys before, though her friends were. They often spent hours talking about the various eligible bachelors among the noblemen's sons, extolling their virtues and comparing them. But Cherise had always been separate, outside that. Partly it was because she knew she was destined to be Queen, and probably marry for political gain rather than love, but she'd always thought most of those noblemen's sons to be quite silly and shallow. Especially Lord Astin's son, Averil. He was a few years older and still unmarried. He was handsome enough, but he always seemed eager to suck up to those in power. She hated how he was always trying to impress her father when he was around.

She was pulled from her contemplation of the woeful courting pool by a comment made by King Natan of the Valdir.

"Askor is getting bolder, your Majesty. They are not only attacking Blackwater, but they have marched farther into the mountains, and have taken over the Breven Mines. They killed everyone there, including the women and children in the nearby mining camps. I know you have your forces keeping them back along the coast and Blackwater, but I need reinforcements in the mountains. My people are stretched too thin trying to protect not only Treyville and Cragmeer but our own high camps as well. I have already had to evacuate one camp near Breven in fear of them being attacked. And what if Askor launches an attack from the east? How will we counter that?"

The King of Ethea frowned and steepled his fingers in deep contemplation. Cherise knew that look. She had seen it every time she'd gotten into trouble as a child. Usually, it meant he was trying to find a suitable punishment but sometimes it meant he was trying to find a good solution. She and the other council members waited patiently for his answer. Cherise slid a sideways look at Prince Hakon and found his bright blue eyes watching her too. She quickly looked away, letting her blonde curls fall like a screen in front of her face, a small smile playing across her lips.

Finally, her father spoke.

"How would we provide for an army within the mountains? That is why we have enlisted you and your people. You are used to living there, you have the resources to survive. My armies do not. How could we march them through the mountains and keep them supplied?"

Cherise watched the King of the Valdir's face fall, emotions playing across it. He wasn't the best at hiding his feelings it seemed. She looked at Hakon again and his face wasn't nearly as open as his father's.

"What if we had the Valdir fly in a force and supplies? The dragons are strong enough to carry that. We could delegate some dragons for supply runs if we have the support and help of Ethean soldiers," Hakon spoke up, offering a solution. Cherise beamed at him as he spoke before looking eagerly to her father.

Her father sat back in his chair, his eyes narrowing as he thought.

"That could be an option. We will discuss the details tonight over dinner. In the meantime, let's discuss the crop yield so far this year, and current stores to get us through till fall harvest." He turned to Lord Renfort, a man of middling years and a dour countenance. Cherise had only had limited interactions with the man and his wife but they were both very serious people.

"Thank you, your Majesty. Crop yields this last fall weren't as we had hoped and our stores are much depleted. We don't have enough young men in the fields to help harvest, and so some food spoiled before it could get picked and then distributed. But the castle has a substantial store from years past and could potentially share some of the bounty with the army or the people, if necessary." He paused to clear his throat. The King of Ethea's face had hardened. "But of course, the army takes priority."

That made the King's face relax a bit.

"And what about so far this spring? How are we doing?" the King said.

"The early harvest has only just begun and so far, the production is far less than previous years at this time. Partly it was the cold winter lasting so long that stalemated us, but we're facing a pretty serious shortage this next winter. Rationing will need to start much sooner than other years."

Cherise's stomach clenched at the thought. She looked to her father's already gaunt face. Every winter they all lost a bit of weight as rationing had increased, but this year had been especially hard and she had watched her father eat far less than even his servants. She wondered if he would even make it through too many more winters of rationing if things got much worse.

She remembered when she was a child that food had always been scarce. Some years there had been large banquets and celebrations, and food was often found in the council chambers. She used to sneak in just before the council started and steal pastries off the pretty plates then scampered out before her father could catch her. But there hadn't been enough food for that in years. The banquets had become much less opulent and parties had finger foods only, no large meals. Things were changing, and it made Cherise nervous. The war had lasted a hundred years, and while there had been years of plenty, the years of food shortages now outweigh the years of plenty. Ethea had once traded profusely with Ablen, and Wostrad to the east and south, but as the war dragged on, and Askor's power grew, their trade lines had deteriorated along with their stores. Each year was leaner than the last, each generation smaller than the last, and their current trajectory was not sustainable. Cherise knew something had to give.

"Well, there's nothing can be done to help that. We've survived worse than this. We will survive again," her father said putting his hands down on the table. "In the meantime, we will discuss the problem of rationing and supplying an army force within the mountains. Council is dismissed for today."

Cherise stood with Hakon and the other council members. She watched them speaking softly as they exited. Hakon left with Geir in tow and Cherise followed not far behind. She paused in the doorway and saw her father still sitting at the table, Lord Illeron now beside him, talking softly. For some reason, her father's hunched body language made her pause.

She turned to watch Hakon and Geir turn the next corner. She wanted to follow them, to chat about the war and get to know the Prince a bit better but something about her father's countenance made her linger, listening at the open council door, just out of sight of those within. The King and Lord Illeron were speaking in hushed tones but she could still hear.

"This war is interminable," her father's weary voice said. "I'm not sure how much longer Ethea will last if we keep this up."

"It will end one day, your Majesty. We just need to find the right solution."

"Have any of your little birds told you anything we can use?" Her father sounded hopeful and it wrenched at Cherise's heart.

"No, your Majesty. Other than that, the King of Askor's new wife is pregnant with her second child. But that's no surprise."

There was a soft thump from the room and a groan of exhaustion.

"What do you think of the young Prince's plan? His father didn't seem too keen on it," her father asked, his voice slightly muffled.

"He's a smart young man. I think it's worth discussing."

Cherise smiled at that. Hearing the Spymaster endorsing Hakon meant a lot to her. She looked down the corridor to where the Prince had disappeared, a part of her hoping he would come back around the corner, looking for her. But her father's next words made her breath catch in her chest.

"He is a smart man. When we promised his hand in marriage to Cherise, she was just a baby, and him a child. I was always skeptical about the match, but she's smart as well. Perhaps they will go well together."

Suddenly Cherise found it hard to breathe. She couldn't seem to draw air in or out. Promise to be married? She was already betrothed to Hakon? Why hadn't her father ever told her? Why wasn't this common knowledge? Did Hakon know? She couldn't imagine he did, he hadn't mentioned it when they'd met. But they had only just met.

"It was a wise decision to let them meet and get to know one another before announcing it. But we really should make it official soon. I have the paperwork drawn up in my office when you are ready." Lord Illeron sounded happy at the prospect.

"In due time. I have my reasons for keeping it between us and his father."

Cherise couldn't handle it any longer. She pushed away from the wall and practically ran away from the council chambers and down the stone corridor, her slippered feet slapping the stone. She didn't stop running until she was in the garden, under her favorite

216

willow tree, hidden by its drooping branches. Only then did she feel safe enough to think and feel freely.

How could her father, Lord Illeron, and King Natan have kept this big piece of information from her and Hakon? What was she supposed to do now? How was she supposed to act around him? She put her head into her hands, the thoughts and feelings too much, threatening to overwhelm her.

Chapter 3

CHERISE DRESSED CAREFULLY FOR the day ahead. Her father had arranged for her and Hakon to go riding together in the country just outside Ravenhelm. Normally riding was one of her favorite pastimes, but her stomach was in knots as she laced up her leather riding boots and donned her split-skirt riding dress. She had barely talked to either her father or Prince Hakon since the council meeting the other day and she was twisted and conflicted inside.

On the one hand, she'd always known she'd have an arranged marriage. And she'd known it was coming soon since she'd reached her majority a few months prior. But knowing that her father had made a verbal agreement for her marriage long before she could even have a say in it was frustrating. She was both angry and resigned.

But when she walked into the stables and saw Hakon standing there, his father's young advisor, Geir, standing beside him, and she melted a bit inside. She remembered how kind he had been the first day they'd met, and suddenly, the prospect of a ride with him in the countryside didn't feel as strange.

"Are you ready to ride?" she asked as she approached, pulling on her leather riding gloves. Hakon beamed at her but Geir just scowled slightly. She had a feeling Geir was a very serious young man.

"Surprisingly, I've never ridden a horse. A dragon, yes, but never a horse," Hakon said bemusedly, and turned to look at a beautiful black stallion in a nearby stall. Cherise's mouth dropped open but she snapped it shut.

"Never?"

"Nope. Never had a need. But I'm excited to learn. So is Geir here, although he doesn't show it." The Prince lightly punched his grey-eyed companion playfully. Cherise grinned as Geir rolled his eyes.

"Well. Good thing I'm an excellent rider. I can teach you." She walked importantly over to the stall where her horse, a palomino mare named Aura, stood waiting. She opened the stall and walked in, checking Aura over before leading her from the stall. As the Prince and Geir looked on, she placed a saddle and bridle on the mare, tightening the straps and explaining everything as she went.

"Sometimes," she grunted, elbowing Aura in the ribs, "she won't let you cinch the waist strap tight enough. So, you have to let them know who is boss." She finally tightened the strap and Aura shifted her weight, letting out a small grumble. Cherise smiled and straightened, wiping the sweat and stray blonde hairs from her face.

Both Hakon and Geir were watching her, mouths slightly open. Finally, Hakon smiled and let out a laugh.

"I'm afraid you'll have to walk me through that step by step."

Cherise let out a sigh and moved to help them both saddle two geldings, one a dapple grey, the other red. By then her own guards were saddled and ready, waiting for her and the Valdir in the courtyard. She mounted up onto a patiently waiting Aura and turned to watch and giggle as Hakon and Geir struggled to get into their saddles, trying to get their mounts to obey. Finally, they were all seated and Cherise led the way out of the courtyard and down the main road to the castle gates.

The ride through the city was stressful, her guards on either side, protecting her from any rabble. As their little group passed, people came out of nearby shops and houses to watch and call greetings, creating a crowd for them to wade through. Despite the stress of navigating the crowd, Cherise loved her people. She loved chatting with merchants and shopkeepers and laundresses, finding out the gossip of the city and letting them know that their Princess saw and heard them.

It was with a sigh of relief that they passed between the outer gates of the city and the countryside finally surrounded them. Rolling green hills of farmland and the deep green smudge of the Deep Glen Forest in the distance greeted them for as far as the eye could see in every direction, a ribbon of blue winding through it. Watching Hakon and Geir grip their reins with white knuckles as they jostled around in their saddles made Cherise smile. The guards around the two royals dropped back slightly, letting Hakon and Cherise ride side by side.

"Look, you're holding the reins all wrong," she said, reaching across the distance and readjusting his fingers. When they touched, a thrill moved through her.

"I'm just trying not to fall off!" Hakon said with a laugh.

They rode along in silence for a few minutes, enjoying the spring breezes and the sun on their backs. Cherise watched the Prince out of the corner of her eye as they moved down the road and across the field. Soon she found her frustration at her father for keeping his arrangement with the King of the Valdir a secret dissipating. She was enjoying the movement of her muscles as Aura bunched and moved beneath her.

Soon they passed beneath the shadow of the forest and a cool darkness descended. Cherise drew Aura in, slowing down to a walk. Hakon awkwardly tried to rein in his horse as well but in the process only managed to bounce around the saddle and then get thrown forward. He clutched at the horse's mane, hauling himself upright as Cherise hid a laugh behind her hand.

"I was hoping your first impression of me wouldn't be as an awkward newling trying to find its legs!" he said, grinning sideways at her. She smiled back as they settled into a walk.

"My first impression was me bumping into you and almost falling over. Not much better, I'm afraid."

"Aren't we a pair?" he asked. She grinned back, her heart lifting. Perhaps, despite her frustration, being married to this young man wouldn't be so bad. He was handsome, and he was kind as far as she could tell. Maybe she could give him a real chance.

They stopped for lunch in a lovely glade, the guards producing small satchels with bread and cheese, and small pastries filled with lemon tart. These were Cherise's favorite and Mistress Aynne, the cook, knew it. She always sent a few along whenever Cherise went out riding.

"Tell me about your mother," she said as she leaned back on her elbows and watched Hakon's lanky form reclining beside her. She saw him swallow as he rolled onto his side to face her, propped on one elbow.

"Well, my mother is dead actually. A few years now."

Horror spread through her and she put a hand to her mouth.

"Oh," she said before reaching across the distance between them and placing her hand on his arm for a moment. "I am so sorry. I didn't know."

His throat bobbed but he smiled at her, albeit a little sadly.

"It's perfectly fine. You didn't know. And despite how painful it is, I want to talk about her."

"Then tell me," she said gently.

"Her name was Katla and she was beautiful. She taught me how to fly. My father was off fighting in the war. In fact, this is the most time I've spent with him since I can remember. But she was always there when I was growing up. She taught me to fly and to fight and to hunt. She taught me about my people, and what was required of a leader. I would be nothing without her."

Geir spoke up for the first time. He was sitting a few feet away, sipping on his water flask.

"She taught me to fight, too."

Cherise looked over at the grey-eyed Valdir. Somehow, she knew in her heart that he missed Hakon's mother as deeply as the Prince did. Hakon looked at his friend and smiled.

"She did. Your mother was gone, and your father wasn't around much. She practically raised us together." He smiled into the cup of wine he held. "I miss her every day."

"What happened to her?"

"She died when a sickness ran through our camp. She tried to hold on, but I was already a grown man. I told her it was okay to go."

Cherise watched the sadness and pain play across his handsome features.

"I lost my mother to that same sickness," she whispered.

Three years earlier a fever had run across the land, striking down young and old alike. One day her mother had been fine, helping the sick servants in the castle's infirmary, and then the next day she was lying alongside them. It burned her from the inside out until she no longer made any coherent sentences and didn't know her own daughter. Cherise fought back tears as she thought about her mother and she knew as she looked into Hakon's eyes that he understood.

He reached across the gap between them and took her hand into his, holding it and squeezing. They stayed like that, watching each other's faces for a few minutes until Cherise wiped her eyes and let out an awkward laugh.

"That's enough sadness for one day. Let's head back, shall we?" She got to her feet and shook out her riding skirt. Hakon smiled up at her, one corner of his mouth quirking up at her.

"Yes, let's."

Chapter 4

THE RIDE BACK THROUGH THE forest was quiet, each of the young people lost in their thoughts, the guards riding a few dozen feet back, quietly chatting amongst themselves. Just as they were about to break through the trees and into the open fields, there was a whizzing noise, and Aura shied, rearing up. Cherise cried out, trying to hang on and not fall off. More whizzing sounds filled the forest, followed by more thunks as arrows hit home in tree trunks.

Cherise frantically searched around her as she got Aura under control. Beneath the darkness of the trees was chaos. Hakon and Geir struggled to get their mounts under control, while Cherise's guards raced to her side. Around them in the trees were figures, some mounted but most not, all armed.

"Bandits!" she yelled, kicking Aura into action. She drew the dagger that she always kept in her bodice, ready to fight, but in the meantime, she kept Aura moving. A moving target was harder to hit.

She watched, her heart rising into her throat, as Hakon leapt from his horse's back and drew the long sword he wore at his waist. He charged into the shadows, Geir not far behind him. As her guards engaged the nearest bandits, she watched in amazement and horror as Hakon and Geir fought, each taking down three bandits. Within a matter of a few minutes, the forest was quiet once again, except for the moaning of injured men.

Hakon and Geir made their way to her through the gloom. Hakon wiped his bloody blade on the edge of his tunic before sheathing the blade. Cherise noticed he was limping and she dismounted a still nervous Aura to go to him.

"I'm fine," he said with a smile. But she didn't believe him. He has a nasty gash along his eyebrow in addition to the limp.

"Let me help," she insisted, putting her arm under his and helping him to sit beside a tree. She looked up to her now bloody guards. One was combing through the dead bandits among the trees, one was wrangling the horses, and a third was digging through saddle packs for bandages. "Bring me the bandages and some water," she called to a nearby guard, who quickly brought her what she needed.

Geir sat heavily beside them underneath another tree, and then leaned back. He was sweat-soaked and panting but she didn't see any visible injuries, so she focused her attention back on the Prince. She used the water and a clean bandage to wipe the sweat and blood from the cut on his brow, being as gentle as she could. Her heart was still pounding, and she knew that if she didn't focus on the task at hand then she might lose it. So, she gritted her teeth and made quick work of the wound before wrapping his head in a piece of the bandage.

Their eyes met as she finished, and Cherise felt a sudden urge to kiss him. They were mere inches apart, their labored breath mingling between them. She sucked in a breath and then sat back on her heels, putting distance between them. There would be time for kissing later, she reasoned, despite how much she wanted to.

"How did they find us?" Geir asked, wiping his face.

"Bandits are always a risk in these woods. They come up from the Borderlands. They seem to be ranging farther every year. But this is too close to the castle. We have to ride back and warn my father. He'll send out a squadron to hunt down whatever is left of them because there are always more." She stood and brushed her hands off on her skirt, looking around nervously.

"Our camp isn't far from here," Hakon said, standing too and wincing. "I know the dragons would love to help hunt them down. We could stop by there on the way back, and send out our own party. It'd be faster."

Cherise bit her lip. It was a tempting offer. Finally, she nodded her assent.

"Let's go to your camp."

The guards helped her mount up, then helped Hakon with his twisted ankle, and they rode north through the trees.

Within a half an hour, as the trees thinned and a natural clearing came into view, Cherise gasped in awe at the unfamiliar sights and sounds of the Valdiran camp. Dragons as huge as houses roamed the clearing, or curled in tight balls beneath the tree canopy, their scales a dazzling array of colors. Their deep voices rumbled around her. All around her were tanned and silver-haired Valdir. She sat in her saddle, following Hakon and Geir as they wound their way through the tents and dragons, calling greetings to Valdir on the ground. Her heart raced at the sight of the dragons and she couldn't take her eyes off them.

Finally, Hakon came to a halt beside a beautiful sapphire blue dragon. He dismounted and limped to her side, her great head snaking down to meet him. He barely reached the top of her head when he stood beside it, one hand stroking the scales between her dark eyes.

Cherise slowly dismounted, utter joy running through her at the sight of this beautiful creature. Hakon smiled and gestured her over, but she approached slowly, nervousness squirmed in her belly. The beast was huge, and as she approached, it opened its mouth, displaying impressive, deadly teeth as long as her arm, wickedly sharp.

"Don't be afraid. This is Kaya, my dragon." Hakon reached out a hand for Cherise which she took hesitantly. He pulled her close and the blue dragon raised her head to inspect the princess.

"Hello, Kaya," Cherise said hesitantly. She knew very little about dragons but her curiosity was beginning to override her fear.

"Hello, Princess." The dragon's deep voice surprised her. Hakon let out a sharp laugh at the look on her face.

"Don't seem so surprised. I know you've read books about dragons before," he said, stepping aside so she could get a closer look at Kaya.

"I have, but somehow, you aren't quite what I expected."

"What did you expect? A large, dumb cow?" the dragon said, grinning and showing all her teeth. Cherise was shocked for a moment before she joined Hakon in laughing.

"Maybe, but you are more beautiful and more intelligent than anything I could have expected." She stepped up beside the dragon. "May I?"

"You may. I especially like scratches under my chin." Then Kaya lifted her head, proffering her favorite spot to Cherise, who laughed some more while she scratched the scales there. She was surprised again by how the scales felt. They were at once hard as stone, but supple, allowing for movement. She stood there marveling for a few minutes. Then she stepped back, remembering the reason why they were there in the Valdir camp.

"Hakon, we need to find those bandits."

The Prince nodded and gestured for her and Kaya to follow. They made their way through the camp until they found Geir and an older grey-eyed Valdir. Cherise knew in an instant it was Geir's father.

"Commander, has Geir been filling you in on the situation?" Hakon asked as they approached, his limping gait concerning Cherise.

"Yes, your Highness. I am organizing a group to search the woods now." He turned to Cherise and gave her a bow. "Your Highness, I am glad to finally meet you. I am Sci, the commander of the King's army. Would you show me on a map where the bandits usually hide?"

"I'd be happy to, Commander." She followed him inside a tent where a small table was covered in maps of Ethea and the Great Grey Mountains. She looked over them curiously, for some of the maps held locations and names she had never heard of.

"The bandits come from the Badlands to the south of us. But sometimes they range north into our woods. They attack the town of Pinefair on the coast at least once every fortnight." She pointed to parts of the map south of Ravenhelm, the capital of Ethea. "I would start just south of us and then sweep west."

"Thank you, your Highness. I will let my men know."

"Commander, I wonder if I might ask a favor?" she asked as he began to leave the tent. He paused and turned back to her.

"Of course."

"Could I have a copy of these maps? They contain places unknown to me, and I'd like to study them."

"They contain places only known to the Valdir, your Highness. But I think I can arrange to have copies sent to you." He bowed to her and left the tent. She stayed for a moment, admiring the maps, and then rejoined Geir and Hakon outside. Kaya was now a dozen feet away chatting with a large red dragon.

"Would you like to go for a short flight to the castle? Your guards can take back the horses," Hakon suggested.

Cherise's heart leapt in her chest, butterflies taking flight in her stomach.

"I would be honored," she whispered, too excited and scared to speak. Geir went to tell her guards, one of whom insisted on flying with Geir. Soon, the four of them were mounted atop Kaya, and Geir's red dragon, Enola. Cherise's stomach was flip-flopping inside her as she clutched at Hakon who sat astride Kaya. It was difficult to sit astride so large a beast in a riding skirt, but for the first time in her life, she didn't care one wit for propriety. She was on a dragon!

The flight to the castle courtyard was possibly the best and worst moment in Cherise's life. She was thrilled to be flying, but the act of flying was terrifying. She hadn't known how afraid of heights she was until she was a few thousand feet up with nothing but a few leather straps holding her in. She clung tightly to Hakon, who laughed breathlessly and tried in vain to pry her fingers loose. When they landed with a jarring thump in the courtyard, a cloud of dust rising around them, she let out a long sigh of relief and finally loosed her grip on his middle.

"You about crushed the life out of me," he laughed, rubbing his sore ribs. She smiled sheepishly.

"I'm sorry. As it turns out, I'm absolutely terrified of heights." She laughed at herself.

"Then we'll just have to get you used to flying."

Her stomach flipped over violently at the thought and she swallowed hard against the bile that rose in her throat. She nodded hesitantly, but in her heart knew she'd never get on a dragon again unless she had to.

A man came running into the courtyard and Cherise recognized him. He slowed to a quick walk until he was near them.

"What is it, Lord Illeron?"

The tall man bowed to her before speaking.

"Your fathers request your presence in the council chamber, your Highnesses. There's been news," he addressed both her and Hakon. They looked at each other before saying goodbye to Kaya and Enola and followed Lord Illeron, Geir not far behind.

Chapter 5

"THE ASKORIANS HAVE ATTACKED the Cragmeer mines and are holding some of our people hostage. They've already killed one dragon and a few miners, but the rest are being held within the mine. One of our villages is only a few hours away on foot," King Natan of the Valdir said once the council chamber was full. Cherise shot Hakon a look and she could see he was held as taut as a bowstring.

"That is the furthest into the mountains they've managed to get a force," King Stanchon said rubbing his eyes. "We need a different plan. Their ships are attacking Blackwater as we speak and soon they'll make their way south. If they attack here, at Ravenhelm, then we've got very little in the way of protection for the citizens of Ethea."

Cherise could see the worry and fear in her father's face. She knew how much he cared for his people, even if he didn't always show it. She wished with all her heart that she could do something. But all she could think of was that she could help in the infirmary or the kitchens; small things, nothing of any real consequence. She and Hakon had already reported about the bandits, but this was a more pressing issue. Finally, Hakon spoke up.

"Father, why don't you and Sci go there now. You can evacuate the village and then attack the mine. Surely we can save at least some of the trapped miners and Valdir." He looked genuinely worried for his people and Cherise's heart gave a small flip in her chest.

"That's a good idea, your Highness," Lord Illeron said. "Once the Cragmeer mines are freed, then your force can drive westward and help Blackwater. Perhaps we can stall their march south."

"Most of my people have so far refused to evacuate," King Natan said, looking at his son. "But what you say has wisdom. I will go, but you and Geir must stay here. I will leave you a few guards and I expect a report every week. You need to be my eyes and ears here as well as my mouthpiece." He turned to King Stanchon. "Assuming that is alright with you, your Majesty."

"Yes, yes." Cherise's father waved his hand in agreement. "The Prince will stay and you will go free our people. But I expect to see you at Blackwater by the end of a fortnight."

Cherise watched Hakon's father's face harden for a moment before he bowed slightly in response.

"Of course, your Majesty."

It was strange to realize exactly how beholden the Valdir were to Ethea, Cherise thought, watching Hakon and his father making plans. What was their stake in this war anyway? Yes, the Prince was engaged to her, although she wasn't sure even he knew it. But couldn't the Valdir just get on their dragons and fly away, find someplace safe? The Great Grey Mountains had always been their home, and although Ethea technically had control over those mountains, the Valdir had always been separate. Was this about land? Or just about power? It troubled her that she didn't really understand why King Natan was fighting Ethea's battles, but she supposed she was grateful anyways.

When the council was dismissed, Cherise wandered out into the hall, lost in her own thoughts. A light hand on her shoulder had her pull up short. Hakon stood behind her, his handsome face a mask of worry.

"Could we go for a walk?" he asked and she nodded in agreement, taking his arm and leading him away. He still limped but it seemed to not be bothering him as much. Geir followed behind but Cherise didn't mind. She liked the grey-eyed Valdir.

She led him down the corridors, aiming for her second favorite place in the castle, a place they hadn't yet been. Hakon was silent as they walked, clearly lost in his own thoughts. Cherise let go of his arm finally and pushed open the huge oak doors to the castle library. Hakon finally seemed to come out of his thoughts and he looked around with interest.

"This is my other favorite place in the castle," she said, reaching out to take his hand. When his skin touched hers she had to suppress a shiver of delight.

"It's huge! I've never seen a place so big in all my life!" Hakon exclaimed as he followed her into the dim interior.

A small desk sat before the door and behind it sat an old man with a cloud of white hair that stood out from his head in all directions. He had on spectacles and a long black robe covering his thin frame. His smile was warm and kind.

"Hello, Alexil. This is Prince Hakon of the Valdir. Hakon, this is my good friend, Scholar Alexil," Cherise said cheerily.

"Pleased to meet you, your Highness," Alexil said, giving the Prince a deep bow from his chair behind the desk, the top of his head almost touching the desk's surface. "I've always loved meeting Cherise's friends." He beamed at the Princess and she smiled back.

"Alexil has always been there for me," she explained to Hakon. "He taught me to read and write, and he taught me about dragons." She winked at the Prince, who chuckled. He knew as well as she did that much of what she had learned about dragons from books was useless. Reading about them and seeing or speaking to them was a completely different matter.

"Scholar Alexil, I have a few volumes I'd like to add to your library if you wouldn't mind me bringing them by later? One is an account from a Valdir perspective on the lifespan of a dragon, and the other was dictated to a Valdir by a dragon. That one is historical in nature," Hakon said politely. Cherise's and Alexil's eyes went wide at the thought.

"Why, I would be honored, your Highness! Just honored!" Alexil said in awe.

"This evening, then." Hakon gave the scholar a smile and then looked to Cherise. She shook her head in astonishment and then gestured for him to follow her.

"I'll take you to my favorite place."

She led him through rows and rows of books, stretching out as far as the eye could see in the gloom of the ill-lit library. While they walked, she explained why the library was so dark, and why there were only small lamps on the tables that dotted the center of the room.

"It's so that none of the pages get faded in the light, and also so that the risk of fire is low," she said.

"Do you have to worry about it getting damp?" he said as he admired the stacks.

"No, there are ventilation shafts all over the library, spanning all three floors. It ensures that there isn't too much moisture."

They stopped before a small table at the far corner. It was tucked away from the rest of the tables and two very plush chairs were pushed up beside it. Cherise reached down and used the small box of matches to light the lamp there and then sat down, a small puff of dust rising around her. She laughed and then coughed which made him laugh and cough.

"Tell me what's on your mind," Cherise said as their coughing finally subsided and they sat together in the silence of the library. Geir had taken a seat a way down the line of shelves, just out of earshot, and in the dim grey light, he was hard to make out. Hakon let out a long sigh.

"I am afraid, Cherise."

She sat back in her chair, shocked. She would never have guessed that a man as brave as him could be afraid.

"What are you afraid of?"

"The responsibility. My father going back into the thick of the fighting. I was so relieved when he said we were coming here. It meant he'd be safe. So would Geir and Sci. But now, I'm expected to help him lead from afar. Who will watch his back?" He put his head into his hands. "What if Askor succeeds? Then our ancestral home will be taken from us."

Warmth bloomed in Cherise's chest. She felt so privileged that the Prince of the Valdir was confiding in her. So, she decided to return the favor.

"I'm scared, too," she admitted. He looked up at her then, his bright blue eyes boring into hers. "I'm scared that I'll inherit a throne to a destitute and empty kingdom. I'm scared we will lose everything. And I'm scared for your father, too."

He nodded while she was speaking.

"I'll be here for you as much as I can, Cherise," he said, reaching across the small table and taking her hand in his. She smiled.

"And I'll help you however I can. Just tell me, and I'll make it happen."

He returned her smile, and then his eyes drifted to her mouth. Cherise's heart began to race, as he shifted forward, bringing them within a foot of each other, leaning over the table. Cherise leaned forward too, bringing their lips closer. Her heart pounded so loud she was sure that Geir could hear it. She shot a look sideways, searching for the silver-haired Valdir in the gloom but was pulled back into the moment by the feel of Hakon's cool hand on her cheek.

She looked into his blue eyes for a moment before leaning all the way forward and pressing her lips to his. The kiss was gentle at first, longing and sweet, but soon it deepened and she found herself tilting as if she was going to fall into an abyss that she couldn't get out of.

Abruptly she pulled away, breaking the contact and panting slightly. Hakon grinned at her and she lightly touched her lips. They felt different than before. She'd kissed other boys, noblemen's sons mostly, but none of them seemed to change her. Not in the way the kiss with Hakon had. She stood and made an awkward curtsey, as Hakon continued to grin at her.

"Thank you," she said and then fled the library.

Chapter 6

A FEW DAYS LATER, AFTER A particularly grueling council meeting to make decisions on what kinds of foods to send to the Valdir fighting in the mountains, King Osian Stanchon called Cherise as she was about to leave.

"Cherise, please stay and speak with me," he said as she paused in the doorway, looking back.

"Of course, Father." She came to sit beside him, Lord Illeron nodding to them both as he left the chambers. Cherise caught sight of Hakon lurking outside and she waved him off. She would go find him later. After their first kiss in the library, they'd met there or in the gardens every day. There had been more kissing, but mostly talking and enjoying each other's company.

"I'd like to talk to you about the Prince," her father began as Lord Illeron closed the council room doors behind him. Cherise's back stiffened.

"What about him?"

"There's something I've been meaning to talk to you about since you've reached the age of majority."

Cherise waved a hand in the air.

"I know about the engagement with Hakon, Father," she said, trying to stall whatever he was going to say. "And I have to say that I'm surprisingly happy with the match." She smiled down at her hands as she said this. But her father cleared his throat.

"No, that's not what I meant. Hakon is a nice boy, Cherise. But as Princess of Ethea and my only heir, you have certain responsibilities. Marriage is not meant to be fun. It is not based upon love, not for us anyway. It is a duty. And one that you will enter into willingly." He was getting more serious by the minute. "I am not sure anymore that a marriage to Hakon is the right move. We may have to look farther afield. Wostrad maybe, or Ablen, or perhaps even Askor. You need a strong king by your side, and we need allies."

Cherise didn't know what to say. She was so shocked by his

words she could barely put two thoughts together. Why would he change his mind so suddenly? Hadn't Hakon shown his worth in the council chamber? Her heart began to race in her chest.

"I know that you like him, Cherise, but don't get too attached. The Valdir are invaluable to us, and they are fierce fighters, as are their dragons, but I'm not entirely convinced that they will be the key to victory," he continued, rubbing his forehead again.

But this time, Cherise didn't feel any sympathy for his plight.

"I won't marry anyone else, Father," she said, her conviction clear.

"You will, Cherise. If I tell you to marry a pig, you will obey me."

Cherise stared at him, anger and sadness warring inside her. How could he force this upon her? But as she watched, she saw the sadness that he carried within him as well. She saw what this war was costing him.

"You would marry me off to Askor if it would end the war?" she asked softly.

"Yes. I would. And I intend to send the King of Askor a letter."

Her face fell, defeated. She was empty inside. It was too late to not get attached. She already felt for Hakon something she'd never felt for anyone else. How was she going to tell him?

"May I go now?" she whispered, staring at her hands and willing the threatening tears not to fall.

"Yes, of course. Just keep that in mind." Her father waved his hand to dismiss her and then turned back to the empty council chamber, his face sullen.

She stood swiftly and left the chamber, hurrying down the hall and making first for Hakon's suite of rooms. She hoped he'd be there, or perhaps down in the practice ground. When he wasn't with her, those were his usual haunts within the castle.

She was lucky that when she knocked, Hakon answered. She strode into his rooms without an invitation and sat down on the edge of his bed. He softly closed the door and came over to her, frowning. He knelt, taking her hands in his.

"What is it?"

"My father just told me not to get too attached to you. That our engagement might not happen!" She burst out with it, unable to hold her anger and sadness inside. Hakon sat back on his heels but never let go of her hands.

"What engagement?" he asked, bewildered.

"Your father and my father agreed, when we were small children, that we should marry. It was one of the reasons the Valdir continued to fight for Ethea." Cherise knew it wasn't the only reason the Valdir fought for Ethea, but the other reasons didn't matter just then.

"How long have you known about this," he asked. His voice was cold now and she looked up in surprise at his face. But his anger didn't seem to be for her, rather for his own father, as hers was for her own.

"I overheard them speaking about it the day after you arrived. At first, I was angry, but-" she trailed off, looking into his eyes. "Now, I know in my heart I don't want any other."

Hakon sucked in a breath, his handsome face searching hers for the truth of her words.

"I don't want anyone else either, Cherise." He looked down at their entwined hands. "I've been wanting to say this ever since the bandit attack. I love you."

Cherise's breath hitched and she let out a small sob.

"I love you too, Hakon. But my father-"

He interrupted her by standing and gathering her into his arms, burying his face in her blonde hair.

"Your father is only doing what is best for his country. Not what is best for you." She began to sob harder at his words. "And as much as I want this engagement to be real, to be set in stone, there's nothing we can do about it. We each have a responsibility to our people, to the realm."

"Run away with me," Cherise said through her tears, pushing back from him and searching his face. "We can run away then, find someplace where you and I can live together with Kaya, in peace."

Hakon gave her a soft smile, full of love and understanding. He put his hands on either side of her face and gently kissed her, not caring about the tears that continued to flow down her cheeks. She felt as though her heart was both full and breaking inside her at his kindness.

"I'd love to, my darling, but we can't. We have a duty."

Cherise cried harder then, burying her face into the Valdiran leathers that he always wore. He smelled of dragons, wind, leather, and woodsmoke. He smelled wild and yet familiar, as if he was her home. She wished she could stay there forever, in his arms. Hakon stroked her back and whispered in her ear about how much he loved and admired her.

She was trapped. There was no way out. She had to do whatever her father decided even if it meant losing Hakon and what happiness they had managed to find together. And it wasn't fair.

Chapter 7

CHERISE SWIRLED AROUND THE dance floor, her pale gold dress spun out behind her as she twirled, the music a crescendo in the background. Hakon was equally resplendent in Ethean style clothing, a close-cut dark green jacket with a gold waist sash and gold trim on the hem and cuffs. It was perfectly tailored and fit his broad shoulders nicely, and as Cherise twirled, she admired the figure he cut on the dance floor.

Other nobles danced around them, their attire creating a beautiful rainbow of colors. It reminded Cherise of a nest full of colorful dragons, each preening and flapping its wings to be noticed. She smiled at the mental image of the noble men and women around her roaring and flapping their arms like fledgling dragons.

"What are you grinning about?" Hakon asked as he drew her close once again.

"Oh nothing," she said with a small laugh.

Tonight, she was light as a feather. She loved parties, but she especially loved this one because Hakon was by her side. She knew that their love was neither wise nor prudent, but she didn't care. Her father kept giving her meaningful looks across the ballroom but she ignored him. The only person she had eyes for was the one holding her as they danced.

The song came to a close and she grabbed Hakon's hand, tugging him off the dance floor and behind a hanging curtain into a small alcove, away from prying eyes. She put her back to the cool stone wall and pulled him to her, pressing her lips to his. They were both sweating, the room hot with the press of so many bodies, and from dancing multiple songs together. But she didn't care. She didn't mind the slightly salted taste of his lips as she drew his body against hers, feeling the hard planes of his body come in contact with her soft ones.

If this was all she was going to get, these few stolen kisses, these few private moments, then she was going to make the best of them.

Every time the possibility of his leaving, of her losing him, of her being married off to some stranger crossed her mind, she shoved it aside violently and remembered the taste of his tongue and the feel of his hands as they roamed her hips and thighs.

Finally, they broke apart, each breathing heavily. Cherise looked into his eyes, now bright with desire and love. Her heart ached but she refused to acknowledge the reason for that ache. Instead, she pulled his head down and whispered in his ear.

"I love you, Hakon."

"I love you too, Cherise," he whispered back, pressing a soft kiss to the spot below her ear and just behind her jaw. It drew a small gasp from her, and she almost begged for him to kiss lower when a trumpet sounded from the ballroom. She stiffened as the sounds of panicked people reached her ears.

"What is that?" Hakon said, pulling away from her.

"I don't know but we'd better go check," she said sullenly, taking his hand and pulling him from the shadowed alcove.

The dancing and music had stopped. Noblemen and women were standing around, watching something that was occurring near the entrance to the ballroom. Cherise stood on her toes but couldn't make out what was happening so she politely pushed their way through the crowd until they were at the front and could see what was going on.

A travel-worn and weary messenger in Ethean clothing stood before her father, handing the King a note. King Stanchon tore open the seal, quickly reading its contents, his face getting harder the further he read. Cherise's heart began to pound in fear. When a messenger interrupted a ball, it was never good news.

"Please, everyone, continue enjoying the party," the King said, gesturing for the band to resume playing. As the nobles around Cherise and Hakon began to move back onto the dance floor, and talk started up again, she pulled him closer to the dais where her father stood, still frowning at the letter. When they approached, he looked up at them.

"Oh, good, I'm glad you're here, Hakon," King Stanchon

gestured for Hakon to climb the dais steps. The Prince looked to Cherise and she nodded, urging him to find out what was happening. As Hakon approached her father, Cherise felt a presence at her side. It was Geir, and he looked worried.

"Do you know what this is all about?" he asked, crossing his arms over his barrel chest. Cherise shook her head, worry churning in her gut.

"I have no idea. But it can't be good news."

They watched as the King put an arm around Hakon's shoulders and spoke to him in a low voice as he walked the young Prince from the room. They exited out a side door, Lord Illeron following. The Spymaster looked over his shoulder at Cherise and gestured with his head for her to follow. Cherise squeezed Geir's arm before following her father, Hakon and the Spymaster from the ballroom.

When she went through the side door, she found herself in a small antechamber. It held only an ornate mirror and a bench for waiting, a plush carpet on the floor. Her father still had an arm around Hakon's shoulders but now Hakon was crying, his handsome face buried in his hands. Icy dread washed over Cherise. She stood rooted to the spot, unsure of whether she should run to Hakon and comfort him, or stay where she was. Her father had seen them dancing and noticed their closeness, but did he suspect how close they'd become?

"What happened?" she asked instead. Her father turned towards her, concern on his face.

"It seems that King Natan of the Valdir, along with his dragon, has died in battle," he said somberly.

Her hand flew to her mouth.

"No!" she uttered, unable to fathom what Hakon must be going through.

"The missive I just received says that while executing a particularly difficult aerial maneuver, an Askorian soldier shot an arrow into his dragon's wing, causing her to swerve. In the close quarters of the high mountain peaks, it slammed them both into an unforgiving rock wall and they plummeted to their death. Sci was right behind them and saw it happen."

"Is Sci okay?" She asked, knowing that Geir would be just as anxious to know his father was alright.

"Yes, he was able to fly out of range in time."

"Was the mine freed? Or do the Askorians still occupy it?" Lord Illeron asked from where he leaned against the wall by the door.

"No, they weren't able to free the mine."

"What am I to do?" Hakon asked, interrupting the questioning about the mine. "Do I go to be with my people?" His voice was shaky with emotion, but the tears on his cheeks were already drying. Cherise felt a surge of pride at the sight of him being so strong, even in the face of such devastation.

"Commander Sci asks that you stay here, and continue to negotiate troops and resources for now. But I'm sure you will go to your people soon," her father said, shooting her a look heavy with unsaid words.

She understood his meaning. Hakon wouldn't stay here forever. He had a duty to his people, and with his father dead he would soon be crowned their king. Her heart sank in her chest. Their time was even more limited than she'd originally thought.

"May I go, your Majesty?" Hakon asked, straightening his spine.

"Yes, of course." Her father waved them away and Cherise came forward to take Hakon's arm and lead him from the ante-chamber and out into the deserted castle hallway.

As soon as they were out of eyesight of the King of Ethea, Hakon's shoulders slumped, as if a great weight had settled there, and Cherise supposed that in a way one had. A weight that she knew would one day be on her own shoulders. She took his hand in hers and led him to that deserted corner of the library where she knew they would be alone and undisturbed. Geir had not followed, neither had any of her guards.

Once she had him seated, she dragged her own chair around the small table until their knees were touching, then she pulled his head to her shoulder and wrapped her arms around him.

"I am so sorry, Hakon," she whispered.

A soft sob escaped him and she gently stroked his hair and back as he cried for the loss of his father, his last living parent. Finally, after a few minutes, his crying subsided and he went quiet.

"What am I going to do without him?" he whispered. "I'm not prepared to become King."

"Yes, you are, Hakon," she said pushing him up so she could look into his eyes. "You are the bravest and kindest man I've ever known. You will be the best King the Valdir have ever had. I know it in my bones."

He looked at her, his mouth hanging slightly open. And then he was kissing her, desperate and passionate kisses, his need clear as he pulled her across the small gap between them and settled her across his lap, pulling her skirts up so she could straddle him.

Cherise gasped at his sudden passion, his nearness and the unexpected fire that seemed to run through her at his touch. But she gave in, trying to convey every ounce of love she had through each touch and kiss.

When they finally parted, they were both panting with desire and need. Cherise stroked his face, pushing his silver battle braids back from his forehead and kissing it. He closed his eyes, his hands tightening on her waist.

"I'm going to ask your father for permission to marry you. I am a King now, no longer a Prince. Perhaps that will be enough to sway him."

His words sent a shiver down her spine and hope bloomed bright in her chest.

"You'd better have a plan to win this war then, my King," she said, bending to kiss him slowly, sensually on his already kiss-swollen lips. "Because he won't give me to you easily."

"I already have a plan."

Chapter 8

CHERISE STOOD BY THE DOOR to her father's study, Hakon standing nervously beside her. Her father was busy penning a letter to this noble or that and he had asked them to wait while he finished. But the waiting was killing her. All she wanted was for her father to throw his arms wide and accept Hakon as her betrothed, but she knew that was not likely. So, she stood as patiently as she could, her face downcast, staring at the floor.

Hakon was nervously fiddling with a loose thread on his tunic sleeve. Today he was back in his red Valdiran leathers and she knew he wore them like armor. He was expecting a fight, just as she was, and he'd come prepared. They'd stayed up most of the night talking about what they wanted, what their future would be like, and how best to convince her father that they deserved to be wed. Hope had spurred them on, and even now, hope was what kept them rooted to the spot, waiting on the whim of a King.

Finally, after what felt like an eternity, King Osian Stanchon put down his quill, stoppered his ink bottle and set aside his letter to dry. Then he looked up at them and interlaced his fingers on the desk before him.

"What can I do for you today, Hakon?" His voice was very business-like and it put Cherise on edge. Hakon cleared his throat and stepped forward.

"Well, your Majesty, I wanted to speak with you about the matter of your daughter," he began. But the King held up a hand, stopping Hakon.

"If you are referring to the spoken agreement between myself and your father upon Cherise's birth, then I regret to inform you that no formal documents were signed."

"Yes, I know that. I understand that it was a verbal agreement only, but I believe that the marriage is a solid plan. It would serve to strengthen the bond between the Valdir and the Etheans. It would give the Valdir all the more reason to fight with your soldiers to free the Great Grey Mountains and Blackwater from Askorian control."

"You have a point, young King," her father said. Cherise's heart skipped a beat at his words. "But how do you propose we end this war? If I make a marriage alliance with another country, then I'll have their added military might at our backs. But I already have the Valdir's loyalty."

Hakon stiffened at those words and dread pooled in Cherise's stomach.

"You make a good argument, your Majesty. But I believe that I know of a way to end this war once and for all."

Her father sat back in his chair and gestured for Hakon to continue.

"Then do tell."

Hakon cleared his throat before continuing.

"I propose to take a small force of fighters and fly north to Winterreach Castle, the capital of Askor, infiltrate it, and kill the King of Askor. No King, no war."

Cherise's blood froze in her veins. He hadn't told her his plan to end the war, just assured her he'd come up with one. But not one that risked his life. She stepped forward.

"No, Hakon, you can't-" she began, but her father raised a hand to stop her.

"No, Cherise. It is a good plan, a solid plan. And I'd like to see him attempt it." The King of Ethea's eyes narrowed as he looked at Hakon's determined face. "Fine. You may marry my daughter, but only once the war is over. Until then, you may consider yourselves betrothed."

At those words, Cherise's heart soared, all thoughts of Hakon risking his life gone with the simple knowledge that he was hers. She was practically dancing on her toes with excitement.

"Thank you, your Majesty," Hakon said, bowing low, a grin spreading across his face. Cherise burst forward and threw her arms around her father's neck, kissing his cheek.

"Oh, thank you, Father, thank you!"

Her father gave her a crooked smile and then waved them off.

"Now go. Hakon, I expect a full report tomorrow during the council meeting. You and your force will leave tomorrow night for your camp. And I will want regular reports back on your progress."

Hakon nodded to the King of Ethea and then reached for Cherise. She beamed at her betrothed, joy filling her to the brim. Together, hand in hand, they left her father's office and ran down the hall, both of them laughing and talking at once.

"Let's go tell Kaya," Hakon said excitedly.

"Oh, yes, let's," Cherise agreed. Together, they ran through the halls and out through a side door on the first floor. Ever since she'd flown them back to the castle after the bandit attack, Kaya had stayed on the castle grounds. Cherise's father had allowed her and Enola, Geir's dragon, to stay in one of the smaller parade grounds.

"Kaya!" Hakon said excitedly, running up to his lovely blue dragon who was napping in the sun. She opened one night-dark eye, speckled with stars, and looked them both over.

"What has happened, Hakon?" she said in her deep, rumbling voice.

"The King has agreed that I can marry Cherise," he said breathlessly.

"That's wonderful!" Kaya exclaimed and then snaked her head down to right in front of Cherise. "Welcome to the family, little one." She grinned a toothy grin at Cherise who grinned back, putting out a hand to touch the dragon's nose.

"Thank you, Kaya."

"Shall we go for a ride?" Hakon asked, pointing to Kaya's back. Cherise hesitated. She hadn't really enjoyed her previous ride, but she was going to marry a dragon rider. She should probably get used to it. So, she nodded and took Hakon's hand, letting him help her onto Kaya's back. Once she was situated in the saddle, her legs tied into the leather straps, Hakon climbed up in front of her and she buried her face in his Valdiran leathers.

"Kaya, take us someplace private."

Cherise smiled into Hakon's back at those words but soon was gritting her teeth as Kaya launched them skyward, her great wings beating a staccato into the afternoon air. Soon they leveled out, however, and Cherise knew she'd have to get used to heights, so she cracked an eye, her stomach swooping inside her. One moment it was in her toes and the next it was in her throat. She could barely string two thoughts together as they winged north along the coast, the sparkling blue of the ocean on their left, the vast green of the Deep Glen Forest to their right.

It wasn't long until Kaya was descending, circling down until they landed in a small cove with a white sandy beach. She landed with a great thump, a cloud of sand flying high and settling into Cherise's elaborately braided blonde hair.

She slid down off of Kaya's back, grateful to be on the ground and fought the temptation to kiss the sands below. Instead, she took a few wobbly steps towards the crashing surf and took deep breaths. Her stomach settled as Hakon slid down behind her and approached.

"I figured we could spend some time alone here, just us," he said softly in her ear, snaking his arms around her. She smiled, feeling much more grounded and at peace.

"It's perfect, Hakon." She turned and wrapped her arms around his waist, pressing her fingers to his well-muscled back, enjoying the feel of him as she pressed her face into his chest. His arms engulfed her and she relaxed, hope and joy and fear all mixed together inside her.

They were alone, truly alone for the first time. Kaya flew up to the top of the cliffs that rose above them and lay there on the rocks, sunning herself, eyes closed. No one was here to watch them. No one was here to stop them. She looked up into Hakon's bright blue eyes and saw desire there. She felt the same flame kindle in her own stomach and she took his hand, leading him to a particularly white stretch of beach. There, she slowly removed her outer dress, unlacing the bodice and slipping its blue satin folds from her shoulders. Hakon's eyes roved over her as she disrobed down to her underdress. He drew in a breath when the fabric finally slid to the sand.

"Come, my King," Cherise said, holding out a hand to her betrothed. For she knew this was probably the last night she'd get with him for many months to come. He took her hand and together they fell to the sand.

Chapter 9

THE DAY HAKON, CHERISE CRIED for hours. They had spent the entire night together on those white sands, enjoying each other's company and talking about their future. They dreamed of the children they would have and the kingdom they would run. They talked of the different laws they would enact and how they would incorporate the Valdir into Ethea. They both so desperately wanted to live in peace.

But instead, here she was, whiling away the hours, waiting for something to happen. She read in the library, and had long discussions with Alexil about politics and governing. She even spent an intense few weeks learning about the Valdir and trying to figure out how she would play a role in their community. There had never been a marriage between a Valdir and an outsider, at least not in any written history that she or Alexil could find. So, their marriage would be a first, it would be historic.

She spent days daydreaming of their wedding, what kinds of flowers there would be and what flavors of cake they would eat. But when all that had been daydreamed about until she was sick with longing, she found herself pacing the hallways, bored and restless.

One day a few months after Hakon left, when the late summer sun was beating down on the castle and on Ravenhelm, a Valdiran messenger arrived. Cherise had sent multiple letters to Hakon, but so far, each one had gone unanswered.

She waited, pacing back and forth in front of her father's office, wringing her hands and waiting for the messenger to come out. When the door finally opened, she stopped pacing, her heart pounding and her stomach churning in knots. She bit her lip to stop from immediately accosting the young Valdir who exited, but she couldn't help herself.

"Excuse me, sir. Is there, perhaps, a letter for me? I'm Princess Cherise." She waited as the young man eyed her.

"Yes, there is in fact." He dug in his pocket and brought out a small envelope with her name printed on it. He handed it over. Cherise clutched it to her bosom tightly.

"Thank you, sir," she said quietly. She waited until the young Valdir had turned the corner of the hallways before she tore open the envelope. Inside were three pieces of paper. One was from Hakon and her heart leapt to read his words.

My Dearest Cherise,

I will soon be sending you a gift from Kaya and me. I know you will love it. Thank you for your letters. They have brightened my days here in camp. I leave soon for Askor, but we just managed to free the Cragmeer Mines from Askorian control. Too many died, including Geir's father, Sci. I'm sorry I haven't written more. I have been so busy, but you have never been far from my thoughts. Please, think of me, and we will be together again soon.

Yours,
Hakon

It was short, and she couldn't help but be a little disappointed at its stilted sentences. She read it three times, memorizing it. Every word was like music she could hear in her heart and she gently kissed the paper before folding it back up.

The second letter was from someone named Eira who said she was Hakon's younger sister.

Dear Cherise,

My name is Eira, and I am Hakon's younger sister. He has been so busy lately that I knew the only way he'd respond to your letters was if I made him. So I did. You're welcome.

I also wanted to write and welcome you to our family, no matter how small it is. I hope to one day soon come visit you in the capitol and read in your library. My brother says it is the biggest library he's ever seen. I am a keeper of stories and records here with the Valdir, and so I'd be interested to get in touch with your head scholar so we

may trade information. Would you mind passing my other letter on
to him? Open discourse can only make our two peoples stronger,
don't you agree?

I'd love to hear more about you. My brother has told me quite
a lot but I'd still like to hear the story from the dragon's mouth, so to
speak.

> *Your sister,*
> *Eira*

The third letter was indeed a missive to the head scholar.
Cherise tucked it into the pocket of her dress to give to scholar Alexil
later. But for now, she wandered back to her rooms, an inexplicable
sadness filling her. She missed Hakon. She missed Kaya. She even
missed Geir and the grumpy scowl he always wore. She wondered
how she'd ever get through the next few months until she saw him
again.

The weather was slowly changing, cooler winds blew down
from the north, and each morning the ground in the gardens was crisp
with early frost. Cherise was wandering its paths, a light shawl pulled
up around her shoulders, hoping the cool air would calm the nausea
that had been plaguing her, when her maid, Ellena, appeared on the
path ahead. She was running, her slippered feet kicking up gravel as
she slid to a stop before Cherise in a very undignified and unladylike
manner.

"Whatever is the matter with you, Ellena?" Cherise asked,
bewildered. Ellena's dark hair was unraveling from her tight braid as
she huffed and puffed, trying to catch her breath enough to speak.

"There is a delegation just arrived, your Highness," the woman
gasped out, grabbing at a stitch in her side.

"What delegation?"

"From Askor. It includes a Prince. At least, that's what the other
maid said," Ellena said, trailing off as Cherise began running. There
was only one reason a delegation from Askor would even be allowed
on Ethean soil.

She raced back to the castle, her guards and Ellena close on her heels. She didn't stop when she hit the stairs and arrive in the entrance hall just in time to see her father walking up the grand staircase with a young man not much older than she beside him dressed in Askorian colors.

She paused, gasping for breath, her nausea all but forgotten. Her mind raced, wondering how she was going to listen in on their conversation. Then she ran straight for the servants' stairs, startling two maids as she ran up it, hiking her skirts high and taking the stairs two at a time. Soon she was walking swiftly down a dark hallway, trying to calm her galloping heart.

The servants' door to the council chambers was only a few feet away and she paused, brushing away the errant curls from her sweating face and trying to compose herself. She needed to be quiet in order to hear anything so she approached the door silently and pressed her ear against it, straining to hear the voices inside.

"Thank you for coming, Prince Terric," she heard her father say. A Prince. Ellena had been right. Cherise tried in vain to slow her pounding heart.

"It is my pleasure, your Majesty. My father was eager to send me once we'd received your letter."

"Ahh, yes, my letter. I do wonder what he thought of my proposal?" Her father sounded almost cheerful. Her gut churned with fear and the nausea returned.

"He thought the proposal of a marriage alliance between your daughter and myself a delightful prospect." The Prince's voice was slightly nasally like he was just getting over a cold. Cherise didn't like the sound of it at all.

"And does he accept the terms?"

"Yes, he does. He will cease this war, and give you back your mountains and mines. In exchange, I will marry your daughter, and we will have exclusive trading rights with your country."

"Exclusive? I will still need to trade with Wostrad and Ablen," her father began but the Prince cut him off.

"If you want peace with Askor, your Majesty, then there will need to be some sacrifices. We are giving up the mountains. You must give up your trading rights."

"And my daughter," she heard her father mumbled. But the Prince didn't reply. "Fine. Let's draw up the papers tonight and you can meet my daughter tomorrow."

"Perfect," the Prince responded.

Cherise was sick to her stomach now and she raced from the door, running down the servants' hallways and up another flight, barely making it to her own rooms and her bathing room before vomiting onto the floor. She sat against the cool stone wall, tears streaming down her face.

Her father had sold her. Sold her like some prized pig to the highest bidder. She realized in dismay that there hadn't been any papers signed with Hakon. Nothing was made official. Her chest felt like it was caving in, all traces of hope gone.

Ellena came into the bathing chamber to find Cherise slumped against the wall, vomit on her dress. Cherise stirred when Ellena tried to lift her.

"He sold me, Ellena. He sold me to Askor."

"Shh, hush now. Let's get you cleaned up," Ellena said helping her towards the tub and opening the tap to fill it with hot water.

"I have to tell Hakon."

"And you will. You will write him a letter as soon as you are clean."

Chapter 10

SNOW FELL SOFTLY OUTSIDE RAVENHELM castle, covering the castle grounds in a white blanket. Cherise stood at the window looking north towards the Great Grey Mountains, invisible in the falling snow. But she knew they were there, watching over her. She smoothed a hand lovingly over her now bulging belly.

"One day, you will play in that snow, and you'll be free, little dragon," she whispered softly to her belly.

She withdrew a much-folded letter from her dress pocket and opened it, reading for perhaps the hundredth time the words within.

My love,

I am heartbroken. I cannot fathom the sadness and anger you must be feeling. You know I love you with all my heart, but since our betrothal wasn't official, there is nothing I can do to fight this injustice.

My people are broken and afraid. The mountains are no longer safe for us. What was once our ancestral home has become a barren battleground. We no longer feel safe here, our enemies to the North and Ethea to the south, both laying claim to a wild country that the Valdir have inhabited for centuries. My people deserve freedom. They deserve to rebuild in peace, just as Ethea deserves peace.

We received a summons from your father to attend him at court. Once we would have responded to the call with Ethea as our ally, but I do not want to be beholden to Ethea any longer. There is no gain for us, especially now that he has broken a promise to my people.

I am leaving and I am taking the Valdir and the dragons with me. We will find someplace safe, someplace to call home, and once we do, I will send you a letter. But until then, my darling, you must do your duty to your people. You must end this war. And you must wear your crown.

Yours forever,
Hakon

The note had arrived with the most beautifully wrought crown she'd ever seen. It was made of a dark iron, and along each delicately carved point were cleverly placed dragon scales in shades of sapphire, the same shade as Kaya. A second smaller note had been folded beneath it.

Dear Cherise,
Please keep this and wear it on the day you are crowned Queen. Although we are far apart, you will forever by my one and only love.
Yours completely,
H.

As it turned out, her nausea hadn't just been because she'd been sold to Askor that day many months ago. It had been morning sickness. And now, as the Midwinter festival approached, she wandered the castle alone and pregnant. She had never responded to Hakon's letter. She had never told him of his child. He was a King now, and he had his own people to think of. This child was her responsibility. But she hoped it had his blue eyes and his silver hair.

Her father had made excuses for her, sending Prince Terric home for the winter, and encouraging him to return once the spring had melted the snow. Because by then, she would have given birth. She could then marry the Prince of Askor with no strings attached. She had raged at her father for the betrayal. But he hadn't listened. He had told her it was her marriage or the loss of the entire kingdom. The end of the war was more important than her happiness.

Now she understood, even if she didn't wholeheartedly agree. She understood what her father was up against, how the pressure of ending a hundred-year long war had weighed on him. She understood that sometimes one had to sacrifice the few for the betterment of the many. But it had taken her months to figure that out.

Ellena entered the bedroom and saw Cherise standing by the

window.

"Is there anything I can get you, your Highness?" she asked coming to drape a warm shawl around Cherise's shoulders.

"Could you fetch Lord Illeron for me please?" Cherise asked, looking down at her rounded belly. She was still a few months away from giving birth but her pregnancy was unmistakable.

"Of course."

The door opened a little while later and Cherise turned to see the lanky form of the Spymaster in the doorway. He smiled at her as he entered.

"How are you today, your Highness?" he asked as he took a seat at her small table. Cherise came to join him.

"I'm really well, actually, thank you." She reached across the table and put a small envelope in front of Lord Illeron. "I heard back from High Father Martin of Hywell Abbey today."

The Spymaster took the letter and read it before looking back up at her.

"It sounds like good news. What would you like from me?"

"I want you to be the one to take my baby there. I trust you to keep that secret for me." Lord Illeron had always been kind to her. He'd always given her tidbits of information about the world outside, and he's always indulged her as a small child. Growing up, he'd been her favorite nobleman, and she'd always looked forward to their talks. If anyone would be able to take her baby and hide it away from prying Askorian eyes, she knew it would be him.

"Me? You want me to take the babe to Hywell?"

"Yes. This child will be my true heir, my firstborn child. It will be a child of the Valdir as well, and therefore different. If Askor gets wind of its existence then I fear what they will do in order to ensure it doesn't inherit the throne. It is imperative that it be kept safe." She paused, her eyes filling with tears. "If something should happen to me, should I die, then this child will be next in line for the throne. It will be up to you to retrieve it and put it in its rightful place on the throne of Ethea."

"How will I prove the babe's lineage?" he asked, a slight frown on his long face.

"I will have papers drawn up, signed and sealed. You will take them with you to the Abbey and leave them with Father Martin."

"Of course, your Highness. I would be honored."

"Good. Then you may go."

Lord Illeron stood and took her hand, bending low to kiss it. It warmed Cherise slightly, the tears now threatening to spill down her cheeks.

Once she was alone again, she stood and went back to the window, both hands cradling her protruding belly. The tears fell fast and thick now, small sobs shaking her frame.

"I love you, little dragon," she whispered through her tears.

To be continued

Ready for more? Born of Embers is up next.

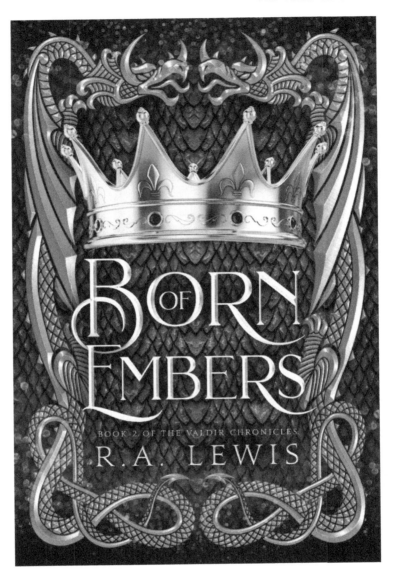

RA Lewis

258

Born of Embers

Book Two
Valdir Chronicles

Dedication

This book is dedicated to all those aspiring authors who think they can't do it. I promise you, you can. Never stop dreaming. I didn't.

RA Lewis

262

Chapter 1

KALINA STOOD IN THE SMALL waiting chamber, sweating like mad. It was the tail end of summer and the mountain air around her was almost unbearably hot. She looked down and straightened her new red leather broad belt, making sure it wasn't riding up. Her palms were sweaty but not because of the heat. It had been two months since her father Hakon, the king of the Valdir, had died in a battle along with his dragon Kaya. They had been at war with Ethea ever since. Kalina was now taking up his crown.

Eira, Kalina's aunt, entered the chamber, her silver hair elaborately braided back from her lightly wrinkled face, her red Runark tattoos and bright blue eyes matching Kalina's. She smiled at her niece and set down the small wooden box she carried.

"You look beautiful," she assured, brushing a hand over Kalina's scarred cheek. "Are you ready?"

"Not really. But I don't have much of a choice do I?"

"You always have a choice, my dear."

Kalina gave a nervous smile back.

Her own father had said something similar. That she had a choice in her future, she didn't have to do anything, be anything she didn't want. But she knew in her gut that her father would approve of this, be proud of this. So, it didn't really feel like she had much of a choice.

"Okay," she breathed, "I'm ready."

Eira smiled, picking up the small wooden box. Kalina followed her aunt from the chamber, patting her own intricately braided silver hair, making sure everything was still in place. Leif, Kalina's second in command and Geir's son, met them in the hallway, his handsome face smiling softly as she approached. He reached out an arm and Kalina snaked her arm through his, resting her hand on his muscled forearm. Eira led them into the crowded chamber.

Silver haired Valdir filled the entry chamber, making Kalina's body feel hot and cold all at once with fear and panic. She clutched Leif's arm, trying to ground herself. She had gone from an orphaned nobody, to finding out both her parents were alive, to becoming

Princess of the Valdir, and now she was to become queen. It was a lot to handle in such a short amount of time.

Her friend Talon, who'd been with her on this crazy journey, stood at the front of the audience, his floppy brown hair standing out vividly against the sea of silver hair that surrounded him. He smiled at her, giving her a subtle thumbs up. She gave him a weak smile and continued to the raised platform at the front of the chamber. Her cousins, Kari and Rangvald stood beside Talon, grinning. Leif walked her to the center before patting her hand and stepping back. Suddenly she was alone, in front of the entire crowd. She took a deep breath in through her nose, releasing it slowly through her mouth. The commander of her Valdiran armies, Geir, stepped forward, and together, he and Eira flanked her. A hush fell over the chamber.

Eira raised a hand in the air.

"Today, we gather here not as individuals, but as one tribe, one family, to support and raise up one of our own. Kalina, daughter of Hakon, wishes to take the throne vacated by her father."

Kalina swallowed down the lump of sadness that rose at her father's name. Eira turned to Kalina, opening the box. Geir came forward and took it from her, allowing Eira to pull a crown from its depths. It was made of beautifully twisted iron and jet-black stones that sparkled with some inner fire in the sunset light that filtered through the openings that dotted the side of the mountain. Eira raised the crown into the air for all to see.

"This crown represents the hardships and toil of our people, the living we eked out of the ground before the long war, and what we fought to protect for Ethea during it. It represents the bond we share with the dragons, and their role in our culture and our lives. It is not an easy burden to bear, it is supposed to weigh heavy on the one who wears it. But it is supposed to also bring them strength, because they are supported by the strength of their people." She turned to Kalina who felt vaguely like she was going to be sick right there in front of everyone. "Kalina, daughter of Hakon, I present you with this crown. Do you swear to serve your people in everything you do?" Kalina swallowed again, trying to wet her dry mouth before answering.

"I do." Her voice came out strong, much to her surprise.

"Do you swear to put your people's needs before your own, to work towards the common good, and protect the safety of our people and culture?"

"I do."

"Then I crown you Queen Kalina, Daughter of the Valdir."

Eira lowered the crown onto Kalina's elaborately braided hair. It settled there, the weight strange and foreign to her. As Eira stepped back, the crowd erupted in cheers and chanting. Kalina surveyed the gathered people, searching for familiar faces, for friendly ones to bolster her up. But her eyes fell on the faces of a group of men and women standing off to the side. Their eyes were stony, their mouths set in grim lines. She did not recognize any of them, but the anger and distrust radiating off them dulled the joy that was in the rest of the chamber. Finally, Geir raised his hands for silence.

"Tonight, we will celebrate while the Queen is fasting and preparing herself to serve her people."

She had almost forgotten about that, in the excitement and fear of the day. The crowd began to disperse and she took Leif's arm once again and left the chamber. She glanced behind her, making eye contact with a stocky, muscled and bearded man at the forefront of the small knot of unhappy Valdir. He glared at her; arms crossed before him. She watched until a curve of the tunnel blocked him from view.

"Who was that?" she whispered to Leif as he led her to her isolation chamber.

He looked down at her with his soft grey eyes.

"Who?"

"The group of Valdir who seemed angry I was crowned."

His grey eyes went cold and hard as stone.

"Jormungand, Halvor and their people. They came from Windpost, a small village along the Great Grey Mountains. They have been spreading dissent since they arrived, trying to convince us that you shouldn't be crowned, that you aren't true Valdir since you were raised elsewhere." He squeezed her hand. "Don't worry about them now."

In the months since her father had passed, Leif had been one of her staunchest allies and they'd begun to build a friendship that Kalina treasured. She trusted his opinion and if Geir wasn't her second in command, his son would have been. They arrived at the same small chamber that she had sat in before her coming of age trial by fire. It had one small window and a bench carved from the rock. Leif took her hand from his arm. Eira was within earshot but Leif spoke quietly in Kalina's ear, his breath tickling the little hairs at the base of her neck.

"I will come by to check on you later." He winked at her and then left, walking off down the hallway carved from stone.

Eira ushered her inside.

"You will remain in this chamber until tomorrow night, when I will fetch you for the final choosing ceremony." She handed her niece a pitcher of water. "Anything you need me to do before you are left alone?"

Kalina shook her head.

"Thank you, Aunt Eira."

Suddenly, she was alone, for the first time in what felt like years. But she distinctly remembered feeling very alone just months ago. The moment her father died she had felt alone, unsettled, like now that he was gone, she didn't belong. She knew it wasn't entirely true, but with the mounting pressure of being queen, she was feeling more and more isolated. She settled herself on the stone bench, trying to find a comfortable position to sit and wait out the day.

Concern about Jormungand sowing dissent among her people bounced around in her head. Being a queen was so much more than she had originally thought, and for a moment, she wished she could go back to just being a nobody orphan. She had thought she was more of a figurehead, but she was now involved in so many decisions she could barely keep track. But as much as she longed for the simplicity that her old life held, she wouldn't trade the adventure she'd had in the last few months for anything. And tomorrow, after she fasted, she would get to pick her very own dragon.

Chapter 2

KALINA TOUCHED HER TENDER FACE gingerly as she followed Eira down to the dragons' chamber. When her fasting was over, she had been taken to a room with incense and candles burning, giving it a hazy look and making her feel lightheaded. The elder women of the Valdir made her lie on the floor of the chamber and then they had tattooed her face and body with the Runark symbols many Valdir had. She knew that now she finally looked like she belonged; her face looked similar to her aunt's, or even to Leif's.

Each Valdir who was of fighting age had reddish tattoos covering their faces and bodies, each a different Runark with a different meaning depending on where it was placed on the body. She now had a series of lines circling her right wrist that represented responsibility. They had tattooed her with the symbols for wisdom, cunning, and strength on her face. Wisdom was three dots above her right eye, strength of mind was three lines below her right eye, and cunning was the top part of a triangle above her left eye. They had even tattooed the Runarks for strength, courage, and grace along her spine.

It had hurt. Hurt more than even walking through the fire had. But the pain had since faded to a dull burning, an ache she cherished because it meant she was a part of something. The old women had chanted and sang as they worked, giving the entire scene a sense of unreality. Kalina felt as though she were floating, the pain the only thing anchoring her to the earth.

On the nights she couldn't sleep, which was often since her father had died, Kalina wandered the halls of the mountain, often finding herself here, on the edge of the dragons' chamber, imagining today, the day she got to pick an egg for herself. Dragon eggs only hatch once the deep magic is activated, and finding a Valdir rider was something that triggered that magic. No one really understood it, although Kalina had asked. All the elders referred to it as a mystery, something to be grateful to the gods for. Eira did mention the god Skaldir whom the Valdir worshiped above all others, and that he had gifted it to the Valdir when he made them.

The dragons however worshiped their own pair of dragons, and their story states that the first dragons recognized that their children were lonely, and therefore breathed the deep magic into existence in order to allow their children to bond with the Valdir, and have a partner for life. This ensured that if a dragon or a Valdir never found a mate, at least they had each other.

At this exact moment in time, as she wound her way among the gathered dragons and Valdir, following Eira to the egg pit, Kalina didn't really care how or why there was the deep magic. She just wanted to meet her dragon.

The egg pit was a huge sandy depression in the center of the chamber, similar to the holes the dragons dug for themselves. The sand was naturally warm, heated from deep within the mountain by some hot spring, its heat radiating up through the ground. Eira stopped on the edge of the pit beside Geir, Leif, Rangvald, and Kari. Kalina swallowed before stepping down into the soft sands, letting their warmth fill her up as she descended. Soon she stood at the very bottom of the pit, looking up at all the Valdir faces above her, the eggs ranging around her in different shades of color. The Valdir began to chant in Valithan, the language of the Runark and Skaldir. Much of the language was lost to time, but their symbols and a few words remained. They chanted "Lay-atha" over and over.

Kalina put a shaking hand out, laying it on the nearest egg which was a rich reddish orange in color. When nothing happened, she moved on to the next egg, and then the next, making her way in an ever widening spiral up the pit. Her stomach began to drop as she moved farther up the pit without anything happening. She didn't even know what to expect if she did manage to find her dragon.

When her hand alighted on an emerald green egg, a shock spiraled up through her body, making her gasp. It was like nothing she had ever felt before in her life. Energy seemed to sing along every muscle and tendon, along her very bones, and a connection settled deep into her chest; a bond that felt like coming home, like a warm hug, like the adrenaline and joy of flying. She fell to her knees before the egg, which was about as high as her waist, and watched, fascinated and in awe as micro cracks fissured out from her hand. Finally, she was forced to take her hand away as the egg burst apart, and a dragonling about the size of a dog spilled out into her lap, legs and wings all akimbo.

The crowd around her began to cheer, but Kalina barely even

heard them, so entranced was she with the creature in her arms. The dragonling pushed itself upright into a sitting position, putting its soft claws against the skin of her forearm, and looked up into her eyes. Suddenly, she felt as though she were falling into an endless sky of stars. For a few unending moments they gazed at each other. The dragonling's eyes were a deep black from edge to edge, speckled with lights. Finally, the dragonling hiccupped and Kalina began to laugh in utter joy at the creature. She gathered him up, for she felt in her gut that it was a male dragon, and carried him from the pit, up through the still cheering crowd, and down the long corridors of the mountain until they were finally alone in her quiet room.

She spent the remainder of that night watching the dragonling, which acted much like any newborn creature. He ate the meat Eira had brought with a voracious appetite before curling up like a cat in Kalina's blankets and sleeping. Leif came to her rooms not long later, carrying her first meal in two days. Two huge slabs of beef from the farms the Valdir had in the foothills of the Great Grey Mountains along the edge of the Wastes, each cooked to mouth watering perfection, were on the tray he bore. A bowl of roasted potatoes and carrots, as well as a pitcher of water, made Kalina's stomach rumble loudly. She put a hand on it, laughing softly as he set the tray on the large table that dominated the other half of her room.

"I guess I was so distracted that I forgot how hungry I was," she said as she joined him.

Leif sat at the table and pulled one of the plates of food towards himself.

"That happens with everyone when they choose a dragon. I think I forgot to eat for two days, I was so caught up feeding and taking care of Arikara."

Kalina smiled as she chewed a mouthful of beef, the juices running down her chin. She wiped at it with a sleeve and gestured with her fork to Leif.

"How did you come up with her name?"

He shrugged and kept cutting his steak.

"It's a family name. My great grandfather's dragon was named Arikara."

"Do you know if my family has any?"

"Yes. You have a few famous ones. Your grandmother's dragon was named Sike, and your great-grandmother named hers Maska. I think your great aunt had a dragon named Dohasan. Do any of those ring for you?"

One did.

"Maska. It just feels right somehow."

He laughed a bit.

"Yes, that's often how it happens. One just seems to fit."

"Maska," she said, rolling the name around in her mouth, getting the taste and feel of it. It seemed to match her little green friend. She watched him from across the room, a strange longing welling up in her chest. "Does it always feel like this?"

Leif smiled at her sympathetically.

"No. Not always. The connection is still there, and they are your greatest companion, but those intense feelings seem to be there at the beginning for a reason. It's like the love a parent has for their child, and it makes them care for that child. The deep magic makes our feelings almost overwhelming at the beginning so we bond deeply with our dragons."

"Huh."

Kalina had stopped eating at this point, staring at her bonded dragon asleep on the covers, twitching slightly at some dream. A cool hand touched hers and she jumped, coming back down to reality and the man before her.

"It gets easier. Now, eat, before you fall over," Leif said, a soft smile on his face.

Suddenly, she realized just how exhausted she was from the last few days. She dug into her food with zeal, finishing off her last potato in record time.

That night, she slept through the night for the first time in months, comforted by the little warm body beside her, lulled to sleep by Maska's tiny whistling snores. All her fear at becoming queen, and all her grief after losing her father, temporarily forgotten.

Chapter 3

MASKA GREW QUICKLY. Kalina fed him daily and soon he was eating huge sides of beef for every meal and still begging for more. She realized she'd never thought about how the Valdir fed the dragons, and when she asked Leif, he laughed, saying they had villages along the foothills to grow their crops and raise cattle. One village, called Harrowing grew their crops in huge swaths of fields. The other village was called Windpost and had vast herds of cattle that the dragons helped keep safe. That was the village run by Jormungand and Halvor, he explained.

"What if Jormungand and Halvor decide to cut off our beef supply?" She remembered the look on the young man's face.

"He may not be happy you were crowned, but he is actually your cousin and he cares for your people. He won't cut off the mountain."

Leif seemed so sure, but Kalina wasn't. This man was competition, and if she was being honest with herself, if it came down to it, she might give up the crown.

"How are we related?" The young man's eyes had been the same blue as hers, her father's, and Eira's. The same as Rangvald and Kari.

"His mother is your father's aunt."

Kalina nodded, worry churning her gut. She tried to take her mind off it, for there was nothing she could do to convince Jormungand she was a good queen.

She stroked Maska who lay curled beside her, full and satiated from his meal. Eira had warned that all young dragons did was eat and sleep since they were busy growing. Maska had almost doubled in size in the week she'd had him, and was rapidly approaching the size of a pony. Eira had also told her that it took about six months for dragons to gain adolescence and be able to fly with a full-grown human. They didn't possess the size and speed and agility of a full-grown dragon, but they were large enough to bear their riders weight at that size. Most dragons grew as large as a house, but some stayed smaller. It varied from dragon to dragon.

Maska was doing wonders in terms of keeping Kalina's mind off the recent death of her father. She hadn't had much time with the man, but what little time she'd had, she'd begun to feel like she had found her place, like she belonged here. When he died, she'd been flung into an alien world where nothing made sense anymore and she felt more lost than ever. Her heart ached every time she thought of him, but Maska's warmth and rumbling purrs comforted her when she cried at night for his loss.

Talon came to visit her every day. Most days they talked about the dragons, or her struggles as queen. But some days Talon was withdrawn and moody, and Kalina had to poke and prod to get him to speak. One afternoon he came wandering into her room as she was playing on the floor with Maska. The dragon was big and clumsy, still learning how to use his large wings to help him maneuver both on the ground and in the air. He was beginning to fly, but only using his wings to propel himself across a room in a long leap, or to jump to the top of the table to eat. Kalina was throwing a soft ball high into the air and letting him chase and catch it. He was getting quite good.

Talon crossed the room and sat on the floor beside her, his mood lightening slightly as he watched Maska leap and jump across the room. Kalina watched him from the corner of her eye. He was dear to her, her best friend and someone she cared deeply for, but the fond romantic feelings she'd once felt for him had begun to fade after her father died.

"What's bothering you?" she asked, throwing the ball high.

He sighed heavily.

"I don't really fit in here, Kalina."

She knew. Once he'd recovered from his injuries, he'd tried to make friends by training with the Valdir, but many of the Valdir were wary of outsiders and he'd never quite integrated himself. Rangvald had tried, taking him on flying patrols but flying was not Talon's favorite activity.

"I know," she said, laying a hand on his arm. "It's been difficult for both of us." She was thinking of Jormungand.

"Why don't you come back with me? We can tell the Queen who you are and you can take up your place as heir?" The light seemed to flood back into his eyes at the thought. "I'm sure she would accept you back."

She was shaking her head before he even finished speaking.

"I can't, Talon. I can't leave my people."

His face fell. She watched his jaw clench.

"And the King would still try to kill me. I'd die by some accident or something."

"Well, I can't stay."

They were both quiet for a time, watching Maska play.

"Where will you go?"

He couldn't go back to the capital. The king knew he'd helped her escape, and she was sure if he returned, he'd be stuck in the dungeons.

"Anywhere else. Perhaps back to your abbey. They seemed nice and I bet I could get a job in their town." She nodded.

"I'll write you a letter for Father Martin."

A sadness settled over them both. Sadness that their friendship was changing, coming to an end. He would always be her friend, she knew, but his absence would still hurt.

He left a week later, Leif flying him to the edge of the Wastes. Kalina cried when he left, adding another loss to the list that seemed to keep on growing. She spent the remainder of the day training hard in the training chamber with Geir, using her sadness and frustration to fuel her spear and bow practice. She was getting very good; her spear throws accurate to within a few inches of the target dot Geir had painted on the stone. Her bow shots were also well grouped and her shoulder muscles were building nicely. But it was the twin axes she preferred to fight with. They felt the best in her hands, like extensions of her arms, and she performed the best when she fought with them.

Maska was down in the dragons' chamber with his own teacher. Dragons spoke their own language first, and then the human's many languages. They learned fast and Maska was already picking up on the words she would say to him.

Towards the end of the training session Leif entered. Geir was still her second in command, but Leif was her closest ally and friend under the mountain. Kari and Rangvald were close, but neither of them seemed to possess the patience and understanding that Leif had. She paused as he approached, panting from the effort.

"You've really improved," he commented.

273

She smiled, wiping sweat from her eyes.

"I'd hope so."

"Why are you here?" Geir said, approaching and taking Kalina's bow and quiver of arrows.

Leif's face fell. Whatever he had to say wasn't good.

"There's been a report of a small host approaching the mountain across the Wastes. They are using wyverns to drag their supply wagons and it's clear they are in it for the long haul." Kalina put her hands on her waist, a stitch in her side, hurting. She hadn't seen a wyvern since one named Savath had flown her and Talon to Long Lake. They were smaller than dragons, and did not possess front legs, only claws on the ends of their wings that they used for crawling along the ground. If they were using wyverns, then they must have extremely heavy wagons to transport, for there were other, more land friendly beasts to pull them.

"Who reported it?"

"Nash. He was flying patrols this afternoon." Leif gestured behind him.

Kalina looked over to the young man who was waiting by the entrance to the cavern, hands held behind his back. She hadn't noticed he was even there. He was about her age, perhaps a year or two older, his hair was braided back from his face like most Valdir warriors and he had laughing green eyes. He smiled at Kalina as he approached.

"Report," Geir barked at the Valdir soldier.

Nash swallowed, looking up at the much larger man. Geir crossed his muscled arms, waiting.

"I was flying over the Wastes to the west of us and saw a dust cloud. I flew lower to investigate and saw a host of about five hundred along with enormous wagons being pulled by captive wyverns. I flew straight back here to report."

Kalina's blood began to run cold, a chill traveling up her spine. Since being crowned she had focused on Maska, on training, and on winning her people over slowly. Eira had cautioned her against rashness, advising her to do things like attending birth celebrations, name days, dragon bonding ceremonies and the like, in order to get to know her people and show she cared. This was her first big decision, and her knees wobbled when Geir and Leif looked to her for leadership. She swallowed, running a hand down her face.

"Gather the council in my chambers."

And then she left them, breaking into a run the moment she left their sight. She bathed quickly and asked the kitchens to send up some food, all the while she worried over the decision she had before her.

Her chambers held a large stone table with chairs set around it for her council members. It was the same table she and her father had sat at and eaten their meals for the few months before he died. That thought made her sad. The council members filed in as Kalina finished braiding her wet hair in the traditional manner of her people.

She strode to the head of the table, looking at each face in turn. To her left was Geir, her first in command, and to her right was Leif. Next to Leif sat Rangvald and Kari, both watching her with their familiar blue eyes that caused a pang to run through her at the reminder of her father. The others around the table were her teachers and mentors among the Valdir. Eira, her aunt, sat beside her children, and on the far side of Geir sat Arvid, Asta, and Ingvar. All were previously her father's council members and captains in the army.

Arvid was the youngest of the three and a fierce fighter. When Geir was unable to train Kalina, Arvid often took over, teaching Kalina dirty tricks to outsmart or incapacitate her enemies. Asta was older, wiry, and wise. Ingvar was Geir's right hand man. He never did anything without Geir's approval and the two had become close since Kalina's father's passing. They were all good people, all solid. But Kalina still felt like an outsider. Despite the position she held, she didn't quite fit in. She hoped deep in her heart that one day that would change.

She cleared her throat before speaking.

"I called you all here to hear what Nash saw on patrol."

Everyone sat up a little straighter, interest and some trepidation lighting their faces. She called Nash in from the corridor and made him give a more detailed report. When he finished, the room went quiet. Everyone's faces were horror struck when she finished speaking.

"That's the largest force the King of Ethea has sent against us to date." Geir said over the murmurings of the rest of the group.

"We can't let them just waltz into our territory unchallenged."

Kari's strong voice broke through. "Let's crush 'em!" She pounded her fist into her palm and smiled viciously.

Kalina tried to hide her own smile. Kari was always rash and the first to jump into a fight. Beside her Rangvald rolled his eyes. They were two sides of the same coin.

"Caution is going to be our best ally. Send out a small group of scouts, watch them for a while, identify some weaknesses," Rangvald said, ever the cautious thinker.

Kalina nodded.

"I agree with Rangvald. But we can't just sit back. Let's start with sending a few other riders to investigate further. Once we have their reports and know what we are up against, we can organize a larger force."

She looked to Geir and Leif who had remained quiet on the subject. Geir nodded his approval.

"Can you choose a few riders to go? I also need to know what those large wagons contain. Supplies? Or more catapults?"

"Supplies seems likely if they are planning to make it to the mountain and attack us. They would need supplies for a siege," Arvid said.

Kalina scratched her chin, thinking. Leif nodded at her, his calm grey eyes watching her steadily. She looked away, her cheeks warming with his attention, and refocused. Finally she spoke.

"The rest of you, assess the number of fighters we have and begin to develop a defensive strategy. We will have to confront them soon and we'll need to act quickly." Heads nodded around the table. Being authoritative had never been her strong suit but she was brave, and that bravery allowed her to pretend she was in charge, in control.

Everyone filed out, talking amongst themselves, and she let out a long breath, trying to settle the shaking that had started in her middle. She wished suddenly that Maska was there with her. Leif stayed behind, going to the tray of food that had been left for her. Kalina joined him, picking up a piece of bread filled with dried fruit as he poured her a glass of milk.

She took the glass gratefully, finally filling her empty belly with much needed food. Once the edge of her hunger was abated, she turned to Leif, eyeing him. He had grown up even more since she'd first met him. Not so much physically: he'd always been tall and muscled with a strong jaw. But since dealing with her father's death and being placed in the higher position he was in, he had grown much quieter, more circumspect, more reserved. They'd both had to grow up these last months: trial by fire.

"How are you?" His voice was quiet, soft, caring.

Kalina grimaced slightly.

"I'm surviving."

He smiled sideways at her.

"You look like you're doing more than surviving. That was a great show of leadership back there." He said, nodding towards the table.

She shrugged.

"I decided to fake it and hope no one noticed." She laughed softly. She took her milk and sat down on the couch. "Besides, I knew if I faltered, you'd be there to pick up the pieces."

Her heart was fluttering in her chest, the aftermath of public speaking and pretending she knew what she was doing combined with Leif's nearness. He sat beside her, the leather, wind, and dragon smell of him wafting to her. Most Valdir smelled mostly the same, like the musty dragons, dirt and rock, leather, and the wild wind they rode through over the wastes. But the smell always reminded her distinctly of her father.

She took a deep breath and let it out in a sigh, trying not to let memories and sadness overwhelm her. Being queen was proving to be a serious challenge, and the time between finding out she was a princess to becoming queen had been only a matter of a few short months. She went from orphan raised in a remote abbey, to kitchen maid, to scribe, to enemy of the crown, to princess, to queen. And she was barely seventeen, young even by Valdir standards. She was overwhelmed and constantly exhausted, and she was always wondering when life would resume some form of normalcy, if that was even possible. She didn't know what normal was anymore.

Leif was watching her as these thoughts ran through her mind. She wondered what he was thinking. Finally, he finished his own milk and stood to leave, but turned back to look at her.

"You are doing fine, my Queen."

Kalina smiled at his retreating back. She didn't really believe him.

277

Chapter 4

KALINA'S HANDS SHOOK SLIGHTLY as she tightened the leather straps of the saddle on Arikara's back. All around her in the entrance chamber, dragons and their riders were preparing for battle. Leif was securing water skins to the saddle and making sure their weapons were ready.

She had opted for a bow with a short draw and arrows so she could easily wield it from dragon back, and the traditional long spear of the Valdir. Once they were on the ground, however, she had chosen the twin axes that were currently strapped to her back in leather sheaths that stuck up over her shoulders for easy access. Her armor included a thick leather vest with chainmail that covered her shoulder joints. Chainmail also hung down across her lap, protecting her vital parts but still allowing her to move. She wore stiff red leather leggings and bracers on her arms. She remembered seeing knights at the castle clanking around in heavy metal armor. Hers seemed to provide more movement but also less protection.

The noise in the entrance chamber began to overwhelm her and she wished with all her heart, not for the first time, that Maska was big enough to ride. She stood with her eyes closed, leaning against the slightly reassuring bulk of Arikara, trying her best not to imagine the battle looming ahead. If she did, the fear would overwhelm her. She had never fought someone to kill them. She'd been in her fair share of fights and scrapes but none where she was responsible for her peoples' safety, or the dragons'. None where she was the queen and was expected to lead.

Her name being called jolted her from her quiet meditation. Her long silver hair was half braided close to her scalp; the rest pulled away in twists to keep her face clear. She wore her dark red leathers, along with her entire army but on her head, instead of the traditional leather band to hold the hair back, Kalina wore her crown. She had argued against wearing it but Eira insisted it was tradition. She had told Kalina that it would help her people to see her on the battlefield and to easily identify her. It seemed an unnecessary risk to her but she didn't argue.

Leif stood waiting for her, the entire chamber going quiet as she stepped up beside him and Geir, her second in command. She surveyed her warriors faces, trying to shove down her own trepidation and fears and be seen as the queen she knew they expected. Sometimes it was exhausting having to be so in control all the time. That was why she treasured her time alone with Maska, where she could be herself.

"People of the Valdir." She tried to look into each of their faces but they began to blur. "Think about what we are fighting for. Our people, our home so hard won and carved out of the rock. Our very freedom. This peace we've had for more than a decade is over." Every person's face looking at her held a fierceness she couldn't quite fathom. Somehow, her words were working. "I don't want to ask you to fight, to sacrifice what little ground we have regained, but preserving our life, our culture, is of utmost importance. We must fight for that." In the following silence a cheer went up from the crowd and they all began to mount their dragons.

Kalina felt relief flood through her as she followed Leif to Arikara. Her job was done now. She had placed command of the army into Leif and Geir's capable hands. The father-son duo had been holed up for a day making a battle plan after they got the reports back from their scouts. She was just along for morale and for the ride.

Leif helped her up onto the double saddle, she seated behind him. Once he was mounted and settled, Arikara's huge claws dug gouges across the floor of the entrance chamber as she made her way to the edge of the mountain. Below them, the plains of the Wastes stretched away into the distance. Without warning, Arikara launched herself out and fell, snapping her wings out just when it seemed they'd hit the ground. Kalina's heart was in her throat as they caught the air currents and soared into the sky behind the rest of the advancing army.

The Valdir army made an impressive display, as close to five hundred dragons filled the eastern sky, the sun bouncing off their varying scales, creating a riotous rainbow of color. Kalina's breath was taken away, and despite the sheer force and might spread out before her, she still felt small and fragile somehow. She always prided herself on her bravery; it had gotten her this far, and she hoped it wouldn't fail her again, but her fear had been building steadily over the last few months. She felt she was only a few moments away from breaking apart.

Geir lead the charge through the skies. They all stopped at a rocky outcropping and each dragon grabbed a large rock with their powerful forelegs. These were to be dropped on the enemy in an aerial assault. Kalina had asked Geir why they hadn't used this tactic before, and he told her that during the long war, they were often the aerial support of troops on the ground, and it was too dangerous to drop projectiles since they never knew where they would land. But now that they knew none of their own were on the ground, he agreed to implement the tactic.

Within an hour they were flying over the approaching Ethean army. The Valdir circled once, releasing the large boulders their dragons carried down onto the unsuspecting heads of the soldiers below, before descending, and her heart began to pound as they drew closer to their target. The soldiers on the ground had not expected the attack from the sky, but after a moment gathering themselves, they began to scatter.

At first, Kalina thought they scattered in fear, but just as they came within shooting range, she realized they were scattering with purpose. From the top of the three large wagons sprang catapults, huge ones, large enough to take down a dragon. None of their scouts had seen this coming. They had reported on a fairly innocuous army filled with foot soldiers. But now Kalina saw the truth, and it filled her with a cold dread.

She screamed, trying to call her people back, to fly higher and gain some distance from the death machines. But Geir was too far away, and too close, the first wave of their aerial legion at his heels. Leif, seated in front of Kalina, realized a moment after her the danger his father was in. He dove, Arikara tucking her golden wings and plummeting, desperate to get to his father in time. Kalina screamed again, fear clawing at her throat as they fell. The wind whipped her face, making her eyes stream with tears as they raced to warn their people.

The catapults released. Fiery projectiles flew through the air, and it was a blur of motion before the first one struck home. Kalina watched in horror as it struck Geir and his red dragon, Enola. The second and third projectile hit home and her army scattered. The number of dragons between Kalina and Leif and Geir became too many, and she could not see what had become of him and his dragon. Were they lost? Fallen? Or were they alive, struggling to gain altitude? She searched the skies for a flash of red, fear and panic beginning to cloud her mind, the same panic she had grown up with, that she thought she had begun to master. Where was he?

She took some deep breaths, pushing the panic to the back of her mind. It took tremendous effort, but she knew her family, people she loved were in danger. She finally pulled her bow from its spot on the saddle and notched an arrow. She called to Leif and they dove, the world dropping away. Arikara was smaller than many of the other dragons which meant she could weave in and out of the aerial chaos happening around them. Kalina pressed herself flat against Leif's back, trying to make herself small in the howling wind, the gold dragon's wings were tucked in tight, the air rushing over them.

The battle field below her came into view. Many of her people had landed on the ground, fighting atop their dragons like a mounted legion. A few were attacking the catapults, trying to dismantle them.

The scout, Nash, was fighting beside his brown dragon, who was deadly when confronted. His dragon was atop a siege tower, the neck of the catapult in her massive jaws. Soldiers swarmed around her, trying to hack at her near impenetrable scales. Nash was beside her, fighting, men falling around him.

Kalina, Leif and Arikara flew in to join them, her bow string twanging as she fired arrow after arrow, Leif's doing the same beside her. Each one found its mark, Ethean soldiers falling left and right. Arikara landed on top of the main structure of the catapult. She used her smaller talons to snap the ropes and pulleys holding the catapult together. The long arm Nash's dragon held was now worthless. She yanked it, and it snapped from the main mechanism.

Leif paused his shooting, breathing heavily, as Kalina killed the remaining soldiers atop the siege tower. Nash stood and looked to his queen, a grim, wolfish smile on his face. Kalina sent him a strained smile back.

The battle raged around them. Their original plan had fallen apart when the catapults had sprung. Rangvald and Kari had disabled the catapult to their right and Kalina could see Eira and Arvid trying to take down the third. She pointed, yelling to Leif.

"Should we help them?"

281

Leif followed her arm and nodded, and Arikara plunged down the side of the tower and out across the battlefield. As they approached, Kalina notched an arrow, taking aim over Arikara's shoulder and let it spring away from her as they flew by the second catapult. It plunged into the neck of a soldier that was about to attack Kari from behind. He fell without a noise.

The third tower rose into view before them and Kalina swallowed as they rose above it with a few strong wingbeats. Arvid and Eira were struggling, Arvid locked in battle with two opponents, her long battle braid swinging as she fought. Eira was trying to dismantle the catapult as Arvid's and her dragons fought off attackers.

Arikara dove, crashing with her full weight onto the catapult, smashing it in half. Kalina continued to pick off soldiers until suddenly there were no more left atop the tower. She paused to breathe, surveying the Wastes around them. Small knots of men and dragons still fought, but it was clear now that the battle field was slowly going quiet, their enemies defeated. The Valdir had won.

They followed Eira and Arvid as they began a sweep of the field, searching for survivors. Kalina began to shake as the adrenaline that had been pumping through her moments before began draining away, leaving her exhausted and cold. She and Leif landed on the battlefield, dismounting Arikara and stretching their aching muscles. She was cramped and sore from gripping the dragon so hard during their headlong dive and fight.

A young man came sprinting up, his silver hair soaked in red blood.

"Captain!" He gasped, bending over to catch his breath, pointing away behind him to the first siege tower they had dismantled. "We found your father." He said between gasps.

"Where?" Leif's voice was hoarse when he spoke.

The man pointed back over his shoulder towards one of the other catapult towers. Leif gripped the young man's shoulder, squeezing before vaulting up onto Arikara's back, Kalina groaning as she followed him up. Arikara leapt into the air, skimming along the ground until she was close to the base of the tower before landing at a run, her huge claws digging deep into the churned up and bloodied earth below. Leif slid off her back, Kalina following, her heart racing, hope blooming in her chest. There was a small knot of people gathered around the red hulk of Geir's dragon. But as Leif pushed his way past the people, he fell to his knees, a sound like a wounded animal escaping him as he beheld his father's mangled and dying corpse, crushed beneath his own dragon's enormous body. Kalina's hand flew to her mouth at the scene before her.

Geir was alive, but barely. Leif reached out to grasp his father's hand. Geir's eyes, bloody and clouded with pain searched for son's face.

"I'm here, Father."

Leif's voice was barely audible. Kalina knelt beside him, placing a hand on his back. He lowered his head until his forehead pressed against his father's, the blood mingling with their sweat and tears. His father's breathing was labored, and wet, a sound that tore at Kalina's heart. Leif's father tried to speak but couldn't as blood bubbled up through his lips. Leif hushed him.

"No need to speak." Leif's voice cracked as he spoke. "I love you, father."

Kalina's heart shattered within her. She didn't think she had enough heart to shatter anymore. The loss around her was too great.

Geir's eyes went wide, his eyebrows rising as he flicked his gaze between Kalina and his son, but Leif seemed to know what he was asking, communicating in the ways only fathers and sons could.

"I'll take care of her. I promise. You don't have to worry."

Geir's body relaxed in Leif's arms at those words, his eyes drifting shut, his breath becoming shallow. Leif gripped his father's hand more fiercely but the man slipped away, going limp, his chest no longer rising and falling.

"Goodbye," Leif whispered.

Kalina longed to hold him as he had held her when her own father died. But she hesitated, her hand still on his back. She hadn't been a queen then, and they hadn't been in public, so she tried to convey her support through that one touch. Perhaps later, when they were alone, she could hold him and they could cry.

Eira came through the crowd, laying her comforting hands on Leif's bowed and shaking back, rubbing in small circles. She smiled at Kalina as if to say I've got this.

"He is with the gods now, Leif. He died honorably, in battle, as

283

all Valdir should. Not old and alone in bed. You should be proud of him and his death. It was a good death."

Leif relaxed slightly at her words but Kalina didn't. Her people believed that death was not a bad thing, not something to fear. They believed that when your physical body died it went to join the gods in their realm, to feast and fight by the gods' side. She knew Geir and his dragon Enola were now feasting with Thrane and Thrire, the gods of death, but that didn't stop the pain.

"Thank you, Eira," Leif said before turning back towards Arikara who waited for him just outside the circle of onlookers. Arikara had her head low, in sadness.

Kalina stood and followed him. He paused beside his dragon, putting out a hand. Then he raised his grey eyes to look at Kalina. She nodded, knowing what he needed from her. She turned to face the gathered crowd.

"You know what is needed." She looked to the chained wyverns. "Release them, and then return home as soon as possible. There's a storm coming." She glanced up to the gathering grey clouds in the sky. They had been building all day.

Then she turned and mounted Arikara with Leif. The dragon pumped her golden wings fiercely until they were high in the sky, and skimming the low, dark clouds.

Chapter 5

KALINA CRIED THE WHOLE WAY back to the mountain, tears streaming down her cheeks and away behind them and she was grateful she was sitting behind Leif. She couldn't imagine what he must be feeling. She was utterly spent, all her bravery gone for the day. She knew Geir was dead. She knew many of her people had died in the battle. The appearance of the catapults had been an unwelcome surprise as well. A mounted aerial legion with highly trained fighters and dragons the size of a house usually crushed whatever it faced.

But her own father had died in a skirmish with this king's soldiers, and now so had his second in command. Leif's father. He looked so defeated sitting before her, his body hunched over the saddle. When they landed and dismounted, she looked at his face, covered in dirt and blood, and drawn in a way she had never seen before. It scared her down into her bones. Her first instinct was to hold him, tell him it was alright, as he had done for her. But he was now her second in command, so she hesitated.

"I'm sorry."

He turned to look at her. His grey eyes, so like his father's, were filled with such sorrow it nearly broke her heart.

"I'm sorry," she said again, searching for the right words to apologize.

But she didn't have them. How could she make him see that she, too, was heartbroken and lost. That the pain and fear had battered her until she felt like she was going to blow apart. There was no way to say that. Leif nodded at her swallowing and Kalina could see that he just needed time. So instead she laid her hand on his cheek.

He looked down, as though she was some foreign thing, before reaching to take her hand and press his face into it briefly before squeezing. She let him drop her hand and walk away then. She looked sideways at Arikara and the dragon's golden eyes peered down at the queen. She reached out and patted the golden dragon, suddenly longing desperately to go find Maska and spend some time alone with him.

Kalina sighed and left the chamber, letting Leif be alone with his dragon. She made her way down the deserted halls of the

285

mountain, the brewing storm rumbling the air outside, reaching her as she travelled deeper. A storm like this could destroy part of their mountain home, but Kalina felt like the weather matched the way she felt inside.

The storm hit just as the rest of the Valdir made it back to the mountain from the battlefield. Over five hundred had left to fight and only four hundred had returned. Kalina wanted the warmth of the dragons, their musty smells, the quiet rustlings and murmurs. She needed their quiet distraction from the gaping hole of loss within her. The air grew warm as she descended, the many large bodies of the dragons heating up the space and sending it throughout the tunnels. Their heat, plus the hot springs that naturally ran through the mountain, heated the mountain just fine.

Kalina came out into the dragon cavern, its enormous ceiling rising above her, deepening into a velvety darkness. The musty smell of the dragons hit her and she breathed deeply, letting its calming scent wash over her. She opened her eyes and searched for Maska's small green form but he was impossible to spot amongst the full-grown dragons in the chamber. She began weaving her way through the dragons, trying to avoid stepping on tails, or getting jostled or squashed between their huge, hulking bodies. She politely asked to be let through and the dragons obliged. Finally, she made it to a large outcropping of rock and paused, her back pressed up against it. She was about to yell for Maska when she heard a voice.

"Your Majesty."

The voice sounded young and male and Kalina whipped her head around, trying to spot the speaker. Finally she looked up and saw a lone figure in riding leathers sitting atop the rock. In his hands he had a loaf of bread and it looked like he was eating his evening meal with the dragons. His silver hair was hanging down in his face, his battle braids partially unraveled, and he was still spotted with battlefield gore. He seemed familiar and finally it came to her.

"Nash?"

The Valdir smiled, his bright green eyes flashing.

"Good to see you again, your Majesty."

Kalina flinched slightly at the title. Today in particular she didn't feel much like a queen. He sat back, tearing the bread in his hands and biting a chunk out of it.

"What are you doing down here?" she said.

She continued to look for Maska among the dragons but so far was unable to find him. She had come for peace and quiet but instead, this interloper was disturbing her hard won calm.

"Well, I live here. And this is my dragon, Sitala."

He gestured to a chocolate brown dragon, almost fully grown, beside the rock outcropping. The dragon raised her head from where she was lying and eyed Kalina with two dark pools for eyes. Kalina nodded to the dragon in greeting and then looked back at Nash.

"I meant, what are you doing down here. No one ever comes down here." She meant that only she did, and she wanted to be alone.

He grinned at her.

"I come down here all the time. I like it better than being up there."

He motioned to the mountain above. She understood that sentiment.

"I just don't fit in with them. I'm different." His green eyes came to rest on her own blue and she shivered, both in profound understanding and sorrow.

"I understand," she whispered.

"Besides, if I had been up there how would I have been able to talk to you?" He abruptly slid down off the rock, his sudden nearness making Kalina freeze. "You still have blood on you."

He reached out gently and brushed a fingertip along her left temple. Kalina shivered at his touch. For some reason, in light of recent events, she wanted someone to touch her and she missed it when he removed his finger.

"I haven't had time to bathe since the fight."

He smiled and gestured down at himself.

"Neither have I."

His nearness was making her feel strange, a little light-headed.

"I should go and bathe. Long day tomorrow." She tried to turn, and made to leave the chamber.

"But you didn't see your Maska."

She froze with her back to him. How did this stranger, know her dragon?

"He's just over there."

She turned to see Nash pointing just past his own dragon.

"I can take you to him if you'd like."

She shook her head.

"No, thank you. I can find him." She marched past him, her battle braids flying out behind her as she hurried to get away from him.

"Nice to meet you, Queen Kalina," he called after her cheerfully.

She rolled her eyes and rounded a large grey dragon to find Maska, already curled in a small emerald ball, asleep. Kalina stood near him, a hand on his warm side as it rose and fell, feeling his heat soak through her. She needed sleep too. Every muscle in her body ached and the caked blood was becoming uncomfortable, irritating her skin.

"Maska," she whispered. He only raised a wing, inviting her into the space between his wing and his side. She slid in, forgetting her desire to take a bath, and lay with her back against his warm belly, letting his heat permeate her as he covered her with his wing. She closed her eyes and let out a long sigh.

Chapter 6

KALINA'S CHAMBERS WERE COLD and slightly wind-whipped. Freshly washed, she shivered, her silver hair wet and plastered to her clean linen shirt. She curled up in her bed, pulling the thick covers over her head and slept. Her dreams were filled with the blood and screams of her people. She saw Geir and his red dragon falling from the sky over and over, and when she tried to save him, she saw him lying dead on the battlefield, and felt helpless.

Sunlight streaming in her window, falling across her face, woke her. She stretched, her entire body aching from the fighting the day before. She took her time making her way to breakfast; once she was finished, she would have to face her council, and right now, she wanted to be alone. She went to visit Maska in the dragons' chamber before grabbing food. He told her he preferred it there because he was with his own kind. It tore at her heart, but she knew he was getting too big to fit on her bed anyway and soon he wouldn't make it into her rooms at all, he was growing so fast.

The dining cavern was crowded but quiet, the whole mountain subdued after the loss they'd suffered. Her people watched her as she crossed the chamber, heading for the food line and then for her rooms. Kalina couldn't stomach eating in front of them, their eyes on her, judging and questioning her ability to lead, to be their queen. What kind of queen leads her people into a slaughter?

Her council members filed in a half hour later. She had barely touched her food, pushing it around her plate and nibbling. Her stomach was churning from the previous day's events, for Geir's loss, and for what her council might say. Everyone's faces were set as they entered, taking their seats around the table. Kalina sat at the head, her back stiff, her stomach churned with anxiety. Leif was the last to enter. Rangvald and Kari looked sympathetically at the commander but Leif's face remained cold, frozen in a mask. Kalina's heart clenched at the sight, threatening to break apart, but she tried to hold herself together.

Arvid looked angry, and as Kari looked back towards the table her face held the same expression. Ingvar, usually quiet and mild tempered also looked ready to tear something to shreds. Asta and Eira looked calm, but sad. Finally, Kalina spoke.

"I think we need to recognize Geir's loss in a public way, and the loss of the others on that battlefield."

Heads nodded around the table. Asta spoke up.

"It used to be Valdir tradition to fire a burning arrow onto a funeral pyre. Perhaps we should build a large funeral pyre on the top of the mountain and light it. Give people a chance to publicly grieve."

Kalina smiled. It was perfect.

"Yes. Let's do just that. Honor the old traditions, before we came to this mountain, as well as show our people that we care. Remind them we are mourning alongside them."

Leif looked up at her as she spoke, his face still stony but Kalina could see in his eyes that he was grateful.

"There is news. Some of our people left yesterday. Fled the mountain for Windpost and Jormungand," Rangvald said into the silence that followed the funeral plans.

"What? Why?" Kari spoke up.

Kalina was stunned and she sat back in her chair as Leif explained the situation.

"Even though the catapults were not Kalina's fault, some of our people are worried about the path we are heading down as a people." He looked at Kalina, apologies swimming in his eyes. "They think that Kalina coming here and being crowned Queen has placed us in danger. Danger we haven't faced before."

They weren't wrong, which was what hurt her so much. It was her fault people were dying. Kalina glanced at Leif but his handsome face remained closed.

"Then what are we going to do about Ethea's King?" Kari's voice was sharp, cutting through the tension in the room, fraying the ends.

People around the room shifted. Kalina knew she was queen, that she needed to have a plan, but she didn't. She felt completely lost. She felt that all too familiar panic beginning to rise in her, flooding her body and making her brain feel fuzzy and stuffed with cotton, like she couldn't think straight.

"What, no one has a plan?" Kari looked at them all incredulously. "Fine. I have one. Let's attack them, go right to the source, right to the capital. Take the throne by force."

The table erupted in talk, voices flying everywhere. Rangvald was of course against it, and he began citing the ways in which it could go wrong. Eira and Leif were quiet. Leif reached under the table and took Kalina's hand, his warmth helping to dispel the panic welling up. Kalina needed to lead, no matter how badly she wanted to run from this room. Releasing Leif's hand she stood, he shouldn't be the one comforting her right now. The voices around the table went quiet, and Arvid and Ingvar's eyes darted to her. She braced her hands on the table top, putting pressure on them until they turned white.

"We won't be taking the throne. Not now, maybe not ever."

Kari's voice rose in protest and Kalina just raised a hand. Rangvald put a hand on his sister's arm, forcing Kari into silence. The girl's face hardened in anger and Kalina worried for a moment if Kari would do something reckless. But she felt her own conviction in her guts. She had no desire for the throne of Ethea. Only for peace.

"We will put permanent patrols along our borders, and we will send a small contingent to stay with our farmers in the foothills of the Great Grey Mountains. I won't risk being unprepared, or leaving our people vulnerable." Her eyes cut to Leif who sat beside her. He offered her a small smile and a slight shrug. She knew he didn't entirely agree with her course of action.

"With respect, your Majesty," Kari said, her voice like ice.

Kalina had never heard her sound this distant, this cold. Kari was always a bundle of energy and usually had a joke to crack, but this Kari was sick of losing people and clearly wasn't going to just let it go.

"This won't end until the king is defeated. We all know that." She looked at each of the advisors in turn. "Just patrolling our borders, going on the defensive, will only drag this war out, make it last for years. We can't survive a war like that again. And frankly, you always playing it safe is just going to get us all killed. If you won't listen to your advisors, then why even have them?"

Kalina clenched her fists at her cousin's words, digging her nails into her palms, trying to calm her own frustration and fear. She knew Kari was right, but knowing she would be sending people into the heart of the country to die, for her, she just couldn't justify it. She couldn't lose any more people, and her gut told her to wait.

"I understand. I will search for a way to make peace, but I won't attack Ravenhelm." Kalina turned and walked from her own rooms. "Council is dismissed."

The others stirred behind her as she crossed the threshold and began to head down through the mountain towards the dragons. Emotions rolled through her, churning her gut, making her head ache. She longed for Maska and the open skies and, not for the first time, wished he was big enough to ride.

A general din filled the dragon's cave, and despite the noise, Kalina felt her heart settle slightly at the sight, sound, and smell of them. She began weaving her way through the dragons, asking a few if they'd seen her Maska, making her way towards where she'd seen him sleeping the night before. She had to pass that same rock outcropping where she'd met Nash.

Kalina tried not to look like she was searching for him, but when her eyes alighted on his lanky figure lounging atop the rock, she immediately pretended she hadn't seen him. A soft laugh echoed across the chamber, blending with the sounds of the dragons.

"Tough morning, your Majesty?" Nash's voice rang out.

She winced before turning to face him. He was always so happy, smiling. It annoyed her but her own chaotic feelings felt strangely calmed by him. Nash stood atop the boulder, a rag in his hand. It looked like he had been cleaning his dragon's saddle.

"You could say that," Kalina said.

She began to walk past, not really wanting company, when he hopped down beside her. He placed a hand on her shoulder and she stiffened.

"Sorry," he said quickly, withdrawing his hand as if she'd burned him. "I just thought that you could maybe use a friend."

She relaxed slightly and turned back to the young Valdir. His handsome face was full of concern as he watched her blue eyes. She let out a heavy sigh, and rubbed the space between her eyes.

"Maybe you're right. Maybe I do need someone to talk to."

She realized she had no one, that she was alone in this mountain. Normally she would have talked things over with Leif, or even Kari or Rangvald, but Leif was grieving, so were Kari and Rangvald, and Kari had made her stance abundantly clear at the meeting. Kalina felt like she had no one she could turn to. Talon was gone, and Eira was burdened enough as it was with her own children.

"Want to sit?"

He gestured towards the top of his rock and Kalina nodded. Nash's dragon lowered her chocolate head, letting him and then Kalina climb on, and then she lifted them to the top of the rock. Kalina looked the warm brown dragon in the eyes.

"Thank you, Sitala."

The dragon smiled lazily.

"You are more than welcome, your Majesty."

Sitala then turned in a circle and laid down in a slight depression in the rock floor. Kalina often wondered at the similarities between dragons and cats. She distinctly remembered Moose, the cat from the library at the capital doing the exact same thing. It made her smile as she settled onto the warm rock beside a lounging Nash.

"So, what's on your mind?"

She hesitated before speaking. If she told this man what her problems were, would it be proving that she wasn't ready to be queen? That she wasn't meant to be here, leading these people? That those others were right to leave and join Jormungand? Would someone like Nash tell others that their queen had doubts and they would then lose all faith in her? Her stomach began to churn at the thought and she remained quiet. Nash shifted beside her.

"It's okay, your Majesty. You don't have to tell me anything. We can just sit here. In silence."

He smiled at her, his eyes laughing. She finally smiled back, his humor helping to melt away her stress.

Before she could answer there was a faint whistling sound and something struck her shoulder, a sharp pain lancing through her. She gasped, falling backwards into the rock, looking around her wildly. She saw a figure running through the dozing dragons, silver hair and dark leathers marking them as a Valdir, but they were too far away to identify. Nash was yelling and the dragons in the cavern were waking up. A few began to fly off, and Nash cradled Kalina's head. She looked down at her chest, a black arrow protruding from it. She looked at it curiously.

She looked up into Nash's green eyes, wondering vaguely why he was so angry, the pain from her shoulder clouding her mind. The edges of her vision were slowly going black and with a sudden panic she wondered where Maska was and began to ask for him.

"Shh, your Majesty. Just lie still. Help is coming," Nash said above her, his face filled with fear and worry.

Finally, she sank into a soft, velvety blackness.

Chapter 7

WHEN KALINA WOKE, HER SHOULDER was throbbing. Every little movement sent pain shooting up her neck and down her spine. She opened her eyes, searching for Maska, for Nash, for Leif. But Eira sat beside her bed, her wizened face drawn in worry. Kalina swallowed, her mouth dry and sticky. She tried to talk and a croak escaped her, alerting Eira. Eira sat up in her chair, reaching for the pitcher of water beside the bed and handed Kalina a mug of water to drink. She downed the whole thing in just a few gulps, handing the mug back for more.

"How long?" she managed to croak out. Her throat hurt vividly when she spoke.

"Three days."

Eira poured her another mugful and Kalina drank it gratefully before allowing Eira to help her sit up, propping pillows behind her.

"What happened?" She had vague memories, just flashes of an arrow, Nash's green eyes and a figure running out of the cavern.

"It seems you were shot by one of our own. An assassination attempt while you were down in the dragon's cavern."

"Did you catch them?" Eira shook her head sadly.

"No. They got away. We suspect Jormungand, but no one has been able to prove it."

"Jormungand? Why would he do this?"

Her pain-muddled brain tried to make sense of the move. She knew he was unhappy she was queen, but to try to assassinate her? It didn't make sense. Why not challenge her openly?

"It's just a theory." Eira patted her arm and changed the subject. "Feeling up to some food?"

Just then, her stomach growled loudly, making them both laugh. Kalina's laugh devolved into wincing though as pain shot through her. Eira stood.

"I'll be back with something to eat."

Kalina lay back against the pillows and closed her eyes. She longed for Maska but knew he was safe in the dragon's chambers. Leif came with her food a little while later, helping her to sit up and eat a thin broth. It hurt to move but she knew she needed to eat.

"What happened to Nash?" she asked after she was done eating.

RA Lewis

Leif took the bowl away and set it on the side table next to her bed.

"He was questioned. We didn't know if he'd been a part of the plot or not but his answers checked out with the story of the dragons nearby."

She relaxed back; glad Nash wasn't being blamed.

"Where's Maska?"

Leif smiled at her.

"He was nearby when you were shot and he was there when we found you. He's been asking after you every day."

"I need to see him." She tried to sit up further, making as if to climb out of bed, but a wave of pain hit her and she fell back onto the pillows. Leif was there in an instant, supporting her and helping her to lay back down. The feeling of his hands on her back and arms distracted her from her pain momentarily.

"You need to recover. You'll be up and about soon enough."

Kalina sighed as the pain subsided and she relaxed, resigned to her fate as a bed warmer.

Leif launched an investigation while she recuperated, throwing himself into the work to distract from his own grief at losing his father. But it dead-ended after Nash's and the dragons' questioning. No one had seen who the assassin was, just that they were Valdir. It frustrated Leif that he couldn't keep her safe as he had promised his father. So he had taken to pacing her rooms, constantly on the lookout for any more danger. Kalina doubted they would try to come back and finish the job when everyone was on such high alert.

They held a funeral honoring Geir and their dead warriors. Atop the red rock mountain from which they had carved their home was a graveyard of sorts. It contained markers for every Valdir who had died and pyres for the burning of bodies.

Kalina wore her cleaned and oiled red leathers along with a new white linen shirt for the ceremonies. Leif stood tall beside her, his own clothing equally pressed and clean. Kalina swallowed and reached to touch his hand with her good arm as they stood before the tallest pyre. Geir's body was laid out, surrounded by the discarded scales of his blood red dragon. The night before, the dragons had carried out their own ceremony, sending his dragon Enola to their gods. Now it was the Valdir's turn to send Geir to be with theirs.

Leif let go of her good hand as he was handed a lit torch. Kalina saw his throat bob as he stepped forward and lit the pyre, watching the flames spread hungrily along the fuel. Soon, Geir's body disappeared into a towering inferno of flame, and Kalina was forced to take a step back from the heat.

Almost every single Valdir within the mountain was attending, making the flat plateau atop their mountain seem dangerously crowded. Kalina had to take deep breaths to calm the panic within her, all while trying to stem the flow of tears that slid down her cheeks. But she was undone when she saw Leif's own grief-stricken face and she let her sobs come. She couldn't imagine a life without Geir, and yet, here they were.

They burned the other bodies of their fallen that day as well. The mountain's grieving filling up each room and hallway until it was an almost palpable thing. Kalina tried to move past her grief but small things continued to send her into spasms of sobs. Eira told her to focus on healing, and Kalina tried her best.

It took three more days for her to heal enough to walk without pain, and another three weeks to be able to use her shoulder. It was a long process and one that Kalina was impatient to finish. She grew more and more anxious as the weeks dragged on, and she knew she needed to find a way to distract herself. Eira had a small library full of books and scrolls containing relevant Valdir histories as well as some histories about Ethea and neighboring kingdoms. When Kalina could walk she spent hours in the small chamber where the books were kept, poring over manuscripts, partly out of boredom and partly in an effort to understand her own history and that of Ethea's. As much as she was accepted by the majority of the Valdir, she was also heir to the Ethean throne.

Leif sat with her for hours discussing the ways in which she could keep her people safe, how she could win back those who were defecting daily to Jormungand's village. Every morning when Eira brought her breakfast, she reported that another few people had left during the night. The Valdir numbers within the mountain were dwindling, and Kalina felt helpless to stop it. The responsibilities were piling up and she was overwhelmed. Sometimes she wanted to run away herself, but her duty kept her in place.

"What about setting up a warning system? Along the Grey Mountains," Leif said.

Kalina looked over at him. He sat beside her in the small library chamber one evening.

"What kind of warning system? What can travel faster than a dragon can fly?" she said, turning the pages of the book on Askor before her.

They had been discussing the king's ties to Askor, and what help they could provide the king via the sea.

"Fire. Light travels faster."

Kalina sat up straighter at this, listening.

"It takes two days for a dragon to cross from one end of the mountains to the other. If we put two people atop the mountains within eyesight of the next and have them rotate watches, we could signal down the mountains within a few hours. They could dispatch a rider from the last post directly north of us. They could be here in half a day."

Kalina mulled the idea over. They had the resources to do it, and it wasn't a bad plan. It would give them a heads up if the king called for aid. Askor was known for its military might, but they were an icebound land hemmed in by the sea on three sides, and the Great Grey Mountains on the fourth. The only way they could provide significant help was by sea or by crossing the mountains themselves; either way the Valdir would know about it.

"It's not a bad idea. Regardless of whether we attack the capital, it's a good idea."

Leif stood and stretched. He then broached a subject he'd clearly been mulling over for a while.

"I am allowed to appoint a second in command. I'd like to appoint Rangvald."

She nodded in agreement.

"He's a good choice."

Leif began to leave the chamber but turned to face her.

"I'll go tell him." He waved as he left the room.

Kalina finished reading the chapter she was on before standing and stretching herself. She wanted to see Maska.

Maska was laying atop the rock she'd been shot on, Nash and his dragon Sitala with him. She hesitated before approaching, the very sight of the rock making her feel anxious. But she wanted to see her dragon so she pushed forward, through the crowd of heated, scaled bodies until she was below the rock.

"Maska?" she called up and soon an overly large green head stuck out over the edge of the rock, followed by Nash's beaming face.

"I was hoping I'd see you here."

She shrugged in response, a small smile on her lips.

"Well, here I am."

Sitala snaked her head around the rock and offered Kalina a lift up which she took gratefully. Once atop the rock she ran forward a few steps, throwing her arms around Maska's neck. He had grown so much in the last month, he was almost the same size as Savath, the wyvern Kalina had first flown on. It wouldn't be long before they were learning to fly together.

"I've missed you," Maska rumbled, his voice seeming to settle into her bones, making her feel like she'd finally come home.

"Me too." She stayed there for a few moments, Nash letting her and Maska have their time. Finally, she drew away and sat down beside her dragon who sprawled across the rock, his bulk almost taking up every available inch of space, forcing her and Nash to sit side by side, their knees touching.

"Thank you," she said awkwardly, unsure of how to thank the man sitting beside her.

"You're welcome. It's the least I could do for my Queen." He nudged her slightly. She rolled her eyes.

"You're the only one. It seems everyone else either wants me dead, or doesn't trust me." She thought of Jormungand and her people leaving the mountain.

"You still have the majority of the Valdir behind you," he said encouragingly.

"I guess." She paused before continuing. "I don't know really how I'm supposed to feel. I want to be a good queen, serve our people, but I'm an outsider too," she said, turning to look at Nash. "I don't quite fit in. I didn't grow up here and they don't trust me or know me. I went from a nobody orphan to a queen in a matter of months and, honestly, I'm still reeling from it. And now, I'm expected to fight a war, unite a country, keep my people safe, and be a good queen. It's too much to expect of me, too fast!" Her voice rose as she spoke, frustration and fear making her emotions high. "All I want is to see my father again. I was happy when I found my family, where I belonged, but I was thrust into a role I'm ill fit for and now all I can think about is wanting space, freedom."

Nash nodded in empathy as a tear slid down her scarred cheek. He reached out and wiped it away, his calloused hand brushing her skin. She pulled back slightly, looking at him with wide eyes.

She didn't let strangers touch her that way, not so intimately. It made her feel uneasy but as she watched his kind, handsome face, butterflies began to beat in her stomach. Could someone like her? Even in this state? Scarred and emotionally drained? Leif had been pulling away since his father had died, and yet, here was a man who genuinely seemed to like her.

"Then why don't you leave?"

His question was so frank it caught her completely off guard.

"What?" she asked incredulously.

"Leave. Wasn't your father always going on about deciding your own fate? I remember him giving speeches about that a few times over the years. You can make your own future. If this isn't the one you would have chosen for yourself, pick a new one!"

His advice was sound. Her father had told her to make her own fate, and if she wasn't happy here, she could leave. But she had a responsibility, a duty to these people as their queen. She had made a vow when Eira had crowned her. She smiled and waved at Nash in dismissal, her heart clenching in loneliness and doubt.

"I doubt that's quite what he meant." She stood to leave. "Thank you for the company, and for letting me vent. I feel much better now."

She wanted to spend time with Maska alone. Maska stretched beside her, ready to follow. Nash stood as well, dusting off his hands.

"Any chance you'd like to go flying with me and Sitala tomorrow?"

He sounded hopeful, and despite her own frustration, Kalina was grateful for his company, and his words. She smiled at him.

"Sure. I'd love that."

Chapter 8

KALINA SPENT THE EVENING TALKING with Maska, telling him what she had found in the books she was reading. He allowed her to relax a bit and for the first time since she'd come to this mountain, forget that she was someone important, forget that she was a queen with responsibilities. He was turning into the perfect partner for her and, not for the first time, she was grateful for their bond. He allowed her to be the book-obsessed little orphan she had always been at heart.

The next day she raced out of her rooms, eager for her flight with Nash, when she almost ran right into Kari outside her door. Kari looked like a malignant thunderstorm: on the one hand she looked like she was going to yell and scream, but on the other hand she looked like she might puke on Kalina's feet. Kalina motioned for her to come into her rooms.

Kari crossed the room and sat on the sofa, putting her head into her hands. Kalina sat beside her, not entirely sure how to help her cousin. So she just waited, hoping Kari would speak up and tell her how she felt. Finally, after a few minutes had passed, Kari looked up at Kalina.

"He's gone." Her voice was hollow.

Kari and Rangvald had lost their own father many years ago, and Kalina knew that Geir had often stepped in to fill that role for them. Her own heart ached at Kari's pain. She knew what that felt like. Geir had begun to fill her own father's shoes in the months since her father had died. She felt an emptiness in her own chest, that sometimes threatened to swallow her whole.

"I know."

She patted Kari gently on the back, her own heart clenching.

"He was like a father to me-" Kari's voice trailed off in a sob, tears streaming down her cheeks now. "I wish I knew what he'd want me to do."

"About what?"

Kari gestured at the world in general.

"About everything."

In that moment, Kalina realized how much pressure her cousin was under. Being on the council and helping to lead the people was

301

a larger burden than she had realized. She searched for the right words to say.

"I think I understand. But I know he wouldn't want us rushing off blindly into battle. We have to be more cautious than that." She said it gently but Kari's face hardened.

"Don't you think I know that?" Kari's words were harsh and sharp and Kalina sat back at the venom in them. "Don't you think I know what Geir would have wanted? I've known him all my life!" Kari stood suddenly and started pacing towards the door. "You've barely known him for ten minutes."

Her words stung Kalina, and she felt her heart sink. Just because she'd known Geir for less than a year, didn't mean he wasn't important to her, precious to her. He had been her first trainer, he had taught her how to fight, how to fall, and even how to fly. She had every right to mourn him too.

"I loved him too, Kari." Her voice was low and she stood from the couch, her back stiff and straight. "I am doing what I think is best. What he and my father would have approved of. Not the rash, impulsive thing."

The last bit was meant to hurt. Kari's eyes blazed at her cousin as they stood across the room from one another.

"Fine. Do the safe thing. You're just going to get us all killed."

Kari turned and stormed from the room. As soon as the door slammed behind her, Kalina regretted every word. She only had a few people here she was beginning to trust and get close to, and Kari was one of them. If she alienated everyone she knew, then she truly would be alone. She already felt isolated from everyone else, why would she make it worse? Silent, hot tears slipped down her cheeks and her chest felt hollowed out.

She realized suddenly that she was now late to meet Nash for their flight, and despite the urge to curl up in a ball, she knew that she needed the time in the sky. Flying never failed to make her feel better, so she grabbed her crimson leather jacket and made her way down to the dragons' cave wiping tears from her face. She found Nash waiting with Sitala and Maska. She smiled tightly at him while she climbed into the saddle behind him. Maska spread his wings beside them, eager to fly.

One thing she knew she could count on was that Nash would

make her laugh. He cracked jokes the whole time they flew over the vastness of the wastes. He and Sitala enjoyed doing aerial acrobatics which, while dangerous, put a huge smile on Kalina's face and she began to push aside her own fear and frustration and just enjoy the moment.

"If you could do anything with your life, what would it be?"

Nash's voice flew back to her on the wind, the only other sounds the loud thumping of the dragons' wings that was more like a concussion to the air than an audible sound, and the whistling wind. She laid her cheek on his back, thinking. Who would she be if she hadn't followed this path? Probably just some orphan, still working in the Abbey kitchens, serving the High Father. She grimaced inwardly at the image. She was grateful she had left. Life was infinitely more interesting now, but was queen what she wanted? What if she could walk away from it? Who would she be?

"I'm not sure. Probably a scribe or a scholar. That's what I was at the castle before coming here. I love reading and writing."

She smiled. A part of her longed to be in a quiet library again reading a book with Moose the cat curled beside her. Nash looked over his shoulder.

"What about you?" she asked, looking up into his green eyes that turned amber in the fading sunlight.

"I would be a merchant. Make my fortune trading with the countries south of us, where the king of Ethea and Askor don't hold sway. Where we can govern ourselves."

Kalina noticed his use of 'we.' She looked at him questioningly.

"We?"

She raised an eyebrow at him and for a moment his face was blank as he realized what he'd said. Then he grinned back at her.

"Yea. We. Maybe. You don't have to do this." He gestured at the mountain as they approached. "Any of this. We could leave, go south. I could sell anything, and you could procure books. The Valdir don't really have a library but I think they should. And you should help build it!"

Kalina froze, her heart pounding in her chest. Beside them, Maska looked at her, soaring on his wings, letting the air currents hold him up. Kalina knew he was listening. Part of the ancient magic that bonded dragons and the Valdir was that they never really had to speak, they just sort of always knew what the other was feeling. She would say a few words, he would respond, and then they'd lapse into silence, spending time together on a deeper emotional level than she could with any human.

Nash had a point. They could leave. She didn't have to do this, be a queen. She could leave and immerse herself in books. He was good company too, and for a moment, she wondered if it was possible, if they could do it. But the moment passed as she thought of her people, and the responsibilities looming over her head. The small smile that had lingered on her face faded.

"It's a beautiful idea, Nash," she said. "But I don't think it's something I can do."

His face fell slightly at her words but then brightened.

"That's fine. I'm just happy I get to spend time with you like this."

He gestured to their dragons and the general open sky around them. She nodded in agreement.

They flew until the sun was dipping below the horizon, turning the high scudding clouds orange. When they had landed in the dragons' cave and took the saddle off Sitala, Kalina turned to Nash, ready to ask him to fly with her the next afternoon as well when she came face to face with him. His green eyes watched her intensely as he reached for her waist. Her heart began to pound at his nearness, his touch.

Nash's face was determined as he stepped in close to her, pulling her towards him. She took a step back, her back coming up against a wall. She pressed her hands against the rough stone of the cavern, feeling the coolness there, and allowing it to take the edge off the panic she felt welling in her at his nearness, at his touch. She liked Nash, in fact, she liked him very much, but it was so rare for people to touch her that it still sent her into a panic. She closed her eyes and breathed.

His breath was warm on her face and he smelled faintly of vanilla. She swallowed and removed her hands from the wall, resting them lightly on his upper arms. He continued to look into her eyes as they stood there, breathing each other's breath.

"Are you okay- with this, I mean?" He spoke in a near whisper.

She nodded, her stomach doing flip flops as he leaned closer, his lips gently brushing hers. She had been kissed before, by Talon. The most recent time had been just after her father's death; and the kiss, and Talon, were so tangled up with that grief that Kalina hadn't really known if she had enjoyed it.

Nash's lips were soft and light as they brushed over hers once, twice, three times. He trailed kisses along her jawline, her breath speeding up, the panic with it. She gently pushed him away, breathless and anxious.

"Thank you," she said rather awkwardly as they took a step back from one another. "Would you like to go flying again tomorrow?"

Nash's face brightened at the invitation.

"Absolutely, my Queen."

He bowed and winked at her and she found herself smiling.

She began to walk away, towards the tunnel up into the heart of the mountain when a movement made her look up. Standing in the doorway, his face stony, was Leif. Her heart dropped into her toes at his face as she realized he'd seen everything. But before she could call out to him and hurry to his side to explain, he turned and disappeared up the tunnel. She sighed as she trudged after him. She would have to explain why a queen seemed more interested in kissing a lowly soldier than running her country and it wasn't a discussion she was looking forward to having.

Chapter 9

KALINA RESUMED HER TRAINING SESSIONS, but instead of training with Leif, he assigned her to Arvid, effectively cutting off any conversation they might have had. At first her shoulder hurt intensely, pain shooting up her back and across her chest with every movement, but the more she worked the easier it got. Eira gave her a salve to rub into the still pink scar.

"You have to break up the scar tissue in order for the muscles to work properly again."

So she did, rubbing the salve in after her nightly bath, and working hard in the training chamber with Arvid to loosen and strengthen the muscles there.

Kalina spent three days trying to decide whether to track Leif down to talk or let him be. They had crossed paths a few times in the dining hall and the training cavern, but he had only nodded at her and turned the other way, determined to avoid any awkward conversations that Kalina was intent on having. Finally she decided she'd had enough and she bugged Rangvald to tell her when Leif was running a patrol.

When he entered the entrance cavern, she was waiting for him. Maska stood beside Arikara, the two of them having a discussion, but they broke off when Leif entered the room. Kalina stood nearby and she gave him a tentative smile as he approached.

"I thought I'd join you today on your rounds of the sentry outposts."

Leif paused, looking as if he wanted to run away. She knew he wouldn't appreciate that she was forcing this on him when he clearly wasn't ready to talk, but she refused to drag this on any longer. Perhaps this time would be good for them. He continued forward, pulling himself up into Arikara's saddle and checking that his weapons were strapped into place.

"Sounds good, your Majesty."

He reached down and offered her a hand up. His face remained stony and her own bright face fell a little as she climbed up to join him. Maska followed Leif and Arikara out of the cavern and onto the ledge. Together both dragons tucked their wings and leapt from the ledge, plummeting towards the earth far below before snapping their wings out and catching the strong updraft that always seemed to exist just beyond the mountain. Every time she left the mountain her eyes strayed to the growing graveyard that crowned it. Sadness threatened to overwhelm her and she buried her face in Leif's back. She didn't want to think about her father and Geir up there. Or the thousands of other Valdir laid to rest atop the mountain.

They flew in silence, both of them getting used to each other's presence once again. Leif kept looking over his shoulder at her repeatedly until finally she began laughing. He grinned hesitantly in return at his own ridiculousness and she settled in, the tension broken. Perhaps he had realized that she could kiss whomever she liked.

The first sentry outpost they came to was nestled into an outcropping of rock that jutted up from the edge of the wastes, creating a natural hideaway and barrier for the Valdir soldiers and their dragons stationed there. They circled the area from high above several times, searching for Ethean soldiers before diving quickly to earth. Two soldiers came running to greet them as they landed just east of the rocks, motioning for them to follow them in. The dragons lumbered over the earth, leaping high to climb between the rocks and into a natural depression in the ground. They jumped to the ground in a cloud of dust.

"Bjorn, Erland, how goes it here?"

Leif removed his red leather gloves and ran his fingers over his braids, smoothing the small pieces of hair that often tried to pull loose during his flights. The two men before them bowed low to their queen before answering their commander.

"Nothing so far, General," Bjorn answered.

He was a big man, well-muscled and in his early thirties. Erland was the same age but much leaner muscled. They looked to be a formidable pair when they fought which Kalina assumed was why Leif had chosen them to be stationed here together.

"We thought we spotted a small patrol a few days ago to our north." He pointed towards the Great Grey Mountains. "But when we went to investigate, we saw no sign of them. We've been making daily passes since with still no sign. I suspect it was just a large herd of deer."

Leif raised an eyebrow at this last statement. Bjorn shrugged.

"I saw the movement, General," Erland said, rubbing the back of his neck. "I was tired, and it was at sunset, so I can't be sure if it was my eyes and the light playing tricks on me."

Leif smiled and clapped the man on the back. Kalina stayed quiet, letting Leif do his work. He seemed to command respect with her people, something she hoped one day she could do as well. She was there to observe anyways.

"I understand. Why don't you show me your food reserves and give me an inventory of what you need."

He left Kalina with the dragons and followed his men into the structure they had built into the rock for storage. The dragon's large claws were good for digging and they had gouged shelves into the rock for storage of food. Kalina settled in, leaning against Maska for comfort and observing the small out posting. Maska shifted beneath her and looked up.

"Look," he said, staring into the bright blue sky above.

She followed his gaze and saw a dragon hovering high above, waiting to come in to land.

"Leif!" she cried out, pointing into the sky where a small, dark streak dove towards them.

Once the dragon's wings snapped out to slow their fall, Kalina recognized Kari and her purple dragon, Yurok, before they landed with a thud. Kari slid from Yurok's back, her face pink from the wind. She glanced at Kalina and nodded briefly before turning to Leif.

"Your Majesty, General. There has been another attack."

Leif pushed the inventory into Erland's arms and strode to Kari's side. Kalina joined him, worry churning her gut.

"What do you mean? Where?" Kari's face twisted.

"The northern tribe. The village of Harrowing has been attacked and they've called for aid."

Kalina's head swiveled north, the same direction Erland and Bjorn had thought they'd seen a host moving. The two men stood stock still, their faces drained of color as they listened to the exchange.

"Take the queen with you back to the mountain, and then I want you to join me in Harrowing with a contingent of men," Leif commanded.

"I'm coming with you."

Kalina stepped between Leif and Kari, refusing to be left behind. These were her people too. Kari eyed her for a moment before finally offering a small smile. Kalina would take that as a win.

"My brother already has a small host flying north. We can join them," Kari said turning back to Leif.

She always seemed to relish a fight, and Kalina had come to realize that it was her own way of handling the shock and horror that war and fighting brought. Leif turned to look at Kalina beside him.

"Are you sure you are up for another fight, my Queen?"

She shifted uncomfortably at his and Kari's watchful gazes before nodding resolutely.

"Let's go."

Leif turned back and gave strict instructions for Bjorn and Erland to patrol the skies, searching for returning soldiers, before he climbed back into Arikara's saddle, helping Kalina up behind him.

Together, the three of them raced north, and before too long, a big plume of smoke rose into the air before them.

Chapter 10

THE THREE DRAGONS CIRCLED BEFORE coming in to land. Below them, Rangvald's host was already on the ground and they could see Valdir soldiers and dragons roaming the decimated village. Kalina couldn't make out whether there were any survivors, but the army that had destroyed the small farming village was nowhere to be seen. This hadn't just happened; it had happened at least a day ago. It was like they had come and gone in shadow, vanishing without a trace.

The fires were out, the houses smoking ruins. Arikara landed with a thump, blackened dust rising around her and Leif. Maska alighted beside them, his own dust cloud rolling over them. Kalina coughed, covering her nose and mouth in the thick, smoke-laden air. Around her, Valdir soldiers worked with a purpose putting out fires, their dragons helping to scoop dirt over the still smoldering parts of buildings and to dig through the wreckage for survivors. Maska snorted beside her.

"These poor people. Where are their dragons?"

His deep voice reverberated through her, and her own heart twisted. Together they walked through the village, Leif having run off to give orders to his men, Kari and her dragon jumping into the rescue effort. A large wooden structure loomed out of the drifting smoke clouds, its roof half collapsed, a smoking charred skeleton of a building. It was large enough for dragons and Kalina realized with a shock of disgust that the damage must have come from the flaming catapults Ethea had been taking into battle. The devastation of the building was absolute where the dragons had been.

They rounded the corner of the burned-out structure and Maska let out an anguished roar as they beheld the broken, burned, and bloodied bodies of dozens of dragons. Some still lay curled into their makeshift nests, as if they'd died in their sleep. Kalina fell to her knees, her heart felt like it was shattering in her chest at the sight. Tears obscured her vision before spilling down her cheeks and beside her, Maska stumbled into the wreckage. She was too devastated to call him back. He nuzzled the corpses of his fallen kin, as if trying to revive them.

The Valdir were a dwindling people, having most of their

population wiped out in the long war, but the dragons were a dying species as well. They had been hunted into extinction on other continents, and only the Valdir had discovered the deep magic that could bind a dragon and a Valdir together. On this continent the Valdir were bonded with the only population of dragons as far as anyone knew. There were no more wild dragons in existence, according to the texts. Kalina empathized with Maska's sorrow.

She searched the wreckage and found a few fallen Valdir just inside what was left of the doorway. It looked as though they had been trying to warn the dragons, to save them, but the flaming projectiles launched too quickly, and they hadn't made it out alive.

Leif found her standing at the doors, tears making tracks down her cheeks that were now stained with the ash that floated through the air. He placed a hand on her back and she looked up into his grey eyes, seeing the sadness echoed there.

"Come. I want to show you something."

Kalina left Maska there to grieve his people and followed Leif numbly through the village. She saw men and women carrying charred bodies on makeshift stretchers from the wreckage of houses and laying them side by side in the field beyond. The land here was on the edge of the wastes, the Great Grey Mountains rising high above them and there was much more vegetation here along a small river. It was perfect for growing crops. Leif led her to the edge of the small village to great swaths of burned land.

"What was planted here?" she said.

Her voice was hoarse from the smoke, her throat tight from crying. Leif's face was stony as he kicked at a clod of smoking plant matter.

"Crops. There were fields of wheat and barley, and beans and potatoes. But this one here-" He gestured to the one before them. "This was our only existing crop of Emberweed."

She looked at him in shock and confusion. Emberweed was mythical, something spoken about in hushed whispers or told about in stories long since ended.

"I thought Emberweed didn't exist?!"

Eira had told her about their history when she was still training to be princess. The older woman had mentioned Emberweed, otherwise known as Valdiserum, had once been grown and cultivated all across Ethea. The Valdir fed it to their dragons before battle and it allowed the dragons to breathe fire. But none had been seen in hundreds of years, and it had passed into legend. Dragons didn't breathe fire anymore.

"Last year, before you came to us, your father discovered that a trader from Saldor to the far south had come across some seeds. He sent me with a small contingent of men to find this trader and pay him whatever he wanted for them. We brought them back here and planted them. This was our only crop. It wasn't fully grown yet, but once it was, we were going to feed it to a few volunteer dragons to see if it truly made them breathe fire."

Kalina's heart sank. If Maska could breathe fire, it would give her a greater advantage in battle. It would give them all a huge advantage over the king of Ethea.

"Did I do this, Leif?" she asked, walking down the smoking rows. "Is this my fault?"

She didn't turn to look at him. She couldn't. If this devastation was her fault, she would never forgive herself.

"No." His answer was definitive. "There's no way you could have known he would attack here. We didn't even know he knew of this village."

She paused on the edge of the field, her hands clutched across her stomach, as if she could hold herself together. She felt like shattering, blowing out across this expanse. She hurt so badly for her people.

"But if I had agreed to attack the capital-" she trailed off. Leif turned her toward him, his fingers digging into her arms.

"Not even then. You were right to be cautious. He had probably already sent this group of soldiers. There was no way to stop this."

Kalina didn't believe him. But she appreciated he was trying. She was queen, she was supposed to lead these people, and she was failing. He let her go and she walked a few steps away.

She looked down at her feet and noticed a flash of bright green among the charred remains. She bent down, brushing away some fallen ash and dirt to find a small plant, a seedling really. It had barely broken the surface of the ground, so it had been protected from the fires. Hope bloomed in her chest as she scooped the tiny plant from the ground.

"Leif."

She wanted to leap in joy but the combination of the lump in her throat and her own trembling excitement caused her to barely whisper. He turned and saw the tiny green plant. He rushed over and gently unfurled her fingers to inspect the seedling.

"One survived," he breathed.

"If one did, perhaps others did as well," she said excitedly.

Leif called his men and a few came running.

"Dig up this entire field. We found a seedling, and where there is one, there may be others."

His people got to work. Kalina continued to cradle the Emberweed seedling on the edge of the field while people bustled around her. She felt numb, the adrenaline of the last few hours beginning to wear off. Her body felt heavy and she was exhausted.

Gentle hands took hers and she looked up into Leif's kind eyes. He had a small burlap sack that he had filled with a bit of dirt. She gently buried the seedling in the dirt before he tied a loose knot in the top, leaving plenty of room for airflow and then handed it back to her. She took it gratefully, gently and hugged it to herself, afraid to let it go.

"You should go check on Maska."

He gave her a small push back towards her dragon. She could see Maska and other dragons working together to dig large pits for burying the bodies. Normally the Valdir would burn their dead, but as many of these bodies were already burned, and there were so many, hundreds, they opted for burial. Maska's dark eyes found her and she buried her face into his warm scales. Just the dragon's presence made her feel calmer. She showed Maska the Emberweed, hoping it would lift his spirits.

"We're going to fly it to a new home," Leif said as he joined them a few minutes later, Arikara beside him, her golden scales reflecting the sunlight.

"Where will we take the seedlings?"

Leif pointed up into the Great Grey Mountains.

"Somewhere the King of Ethea cannot find us."

Kalina looked up and beyond to the distant peaks of the mountains before them. She had only been in them once, almost a year ago with Savath when the wyvern had taken them there for a night. She hadn't been back since but she did remember the wind and the cold.

"Can it grow there?" she asked, doubtful.

"There are high valleys that are inaccessible from the ground that have rich soil. We've had our cattle there before." Kalina knew that the Valdir had once lived in these mountains, before the war with their northern neighbor Askor forced them to flee south to the Wastes.

"What are we waiting for?"

She turned to look at the two dragons and Leif. He gave her a small smile and nodded. They mounted Arikara, strapping the bags with the dozen or so seedlings their men had found and launched themselves into the air, leaving the majority of the host on the ground with Rangvald and Kari.

Chapter 11

KALINA DUG A SMALL HOLE IN THE GROUND, reverently placed her small Emberweed seedling in the depression and covered it over. The high meadow around them was lush and green, wild flowers in their final bloom in a profusion of color as if they were all saying goodbye to summer. The mountains towered above them, their snowy peaks reflecting the sunlight, making the valley bright. It was a perfect place to plant the seedlings. With luck, there would still be a few more months of the growing season left.

There was a small hut along the edge of the meadow and as they landed an old Valdir couple had emerged. The couple dragons lay basking in the warm sun on an outcropping of rock, their pale green and yellow scales reflecting the light and making it bounce across a small pond. It was an idyllic setting and Kalina wished that the Valdir still resided in the mountains. She had never really understood why her father had chosen to move his people south to the Wastes.

The Wastes were a lonely, inhospitable place and being there forced their people to be separated from one another. The mountains were unsurpassable enough that the majority of fighting forces could not penetrate, which was why the king of Ethea had ordered the Valdir and their dragons to fight for him in the treacherous mountain passes and the deep valleys during the long war.

Her father had called it more of a series of small skirmishes than an all-out war, as no sizable Askorian force had made it through the mountains. But Kalina supposed the Valdir had needed to disappear, and if they had been seen flying through the mountains then the king of Ethea would have known where to find them and could try to force them into his army once again.

The Valdir had groups of people, small enough to avoid detection, stationed all along the mountains. This couple had a herd of sheep which provided wool and meat for the greater Valdir forces when needed. They would be perfect for protecting the Emberweed until the crop was mature enough to experiment with.

Leif came to stand by her side as the old man and woman approached. Kalina was grateful to have him with her. Together they tasked the couple with farming the Emberweed, promising provisions and other Valdir to help. The couple were gracious and kind, setting her mind at ease. One less thing for her to worry about.

"There is another village south of here I want to check on. Warn them about the attack," Leif told Kalina, looking at her over his shoulder as they strapped themselves back into the saddle.

"Good. I want to see more of our people."

Leif studied her for a moment, as if assessing her sincerity. It didn't surprise her. She hadn't chosen this job, but they all relied on her so much. They took to the air and she relaxed as the mountains melted away beneath them until they soared out over the vastness of the Wastes once again before turning east. Flying always helped to clear her mind, and think more freely.

The town of Windpost was nestled between two foothills, a stream cutting it off on its south side, mountains to the north and hills to the east and west. It was well protected from discovery. The Valdir there raised large herds of cattle which they drove across the plains and into the surrounding foothills with their dragons. Leif and Kalina circled overhead and he pointed out the moving brown swaths of what she thought was land below them, showing the vastness of their herds.

Their dragons landed in a cloud of dust, the few soldiers they'd brought with them from the first village landing beside them. When Kalina slid from Arikara's back she saw familiar faces. Halvor and Jormungand, the unhappy Valdir from her coronation, the men suspected of orchestrating her assassination, were striding towards them. Her aunt's cousin stared at her, his blue eyes hard and angry. She clenched her fists, restraining herself. He had tried to have her killed but she knew that in order to win her people she'd have to play nice and show some self-control.

"Halvor, Jormungand, we have news," Leif said, holding out his hand for them to clasp.

Halvor clasped his forearm in a tight grip. Jormungand stood off to the side and gave Leif a tight nod, not taking the proffered hand.

"Have you met our Queen, Kalina yet?" Leif gestured.

Both men turned but unsurprisingly neither one bowed.

"We don't recognize her as our Queen," Jormungand said.

Kalina stiffened at those words, her blood running cold as she looked at the two men, taking in their straight backs, their hands on their swords, and the hostile look in their eyes.

"She is a stranger to us, and an outsider. She didn't grow up here, she doesn't know these people." Jormungand gestured to the gathered villagers around him, not a single friendly face among them, but Kalina recognized a few of them. They had previously been at the mountain, before her father died.

"She is Hakon's daughter. She is your cousin. She is our Queen," Leif pronounced. He stared the man down- a clear challenge. Halvor put his hands out placatingly and stepped forward, putting himself between the two men.

"I don't doubt that she is. I mean, just look at her. We aren't contesting her parenthood. We are contesting her right to lead us. It should be someone who knows the people, who knows our history, our struggles. It should be Jormungand."

Leif's eyebrows rose as whispering erupted all around them. Kalina's gut clenched. He wasn't wrong. She was a stranger here. She stepped forward, going against her better judgement.

"I understand your hesitation to trust me, Jormungand. I know I wasn't born here. I don't know everything there is to know about the Valdir. But I didn't choose to be raised as an orphan. And now that I have found my way home, I am willing to learn. If you feel I am lacking, then teach me."

It felt like the right thing to say, and a few people in the crowd shifted uncomfortably. But Jormungand and Halvor and many others began to shake their heads.

"That's very nice of you, girl."

Kalina bristled at the informal address.

"But we aren't interested in some upstart who knows nothing leading us. Perhaps in a few years, once you've learned the ways of the world."

Jormungand's tone was mocking and Kalina's face began to redden as he spoke.

"Perhaps I'll name you my heir!" he said jokingly, getting a few laughs from the crowd.

Kalina clenched her fists and tried not to punch him square in the face. A queen wouldn't punch her subject, but she really wished she could.

"For now, we will answer to Jormungand. We don't answer to you." Halvor said.

"You will answer to your Queen," Leif said, keeping his voice level, his tone cold as he stepped forward until he was face to face with Jormungand.

The two of them stared at each other, the tension rising. Kalina's heart began to race. Finally Halvor stepped between them again, a firm hand on each man's chest, forcing them to step apart.

"We are all Valdir," Halvor said. "With that being said, this village and its people will not answer to her."

He nodded at Kalina. Kalina had a feeling that if it was just Halvor involved that they could convince the man to recognize her as queen. He seemed a reasonable man, but Jormungand was young and headstrong, and he was ambitious.

"This isn't over, but in the interest of time and safety, we have come to warn you that the village of Harrowing, west of here, has been burned to the ground, destroyed. Everyone dead. Ethea may push east and attempt an attack on your village as well."

"Thank you for the warning, General," Halvor said respectfully to Leif who nodded curtly.

"They won't attack us," Jormungand said with confidence.

"Any why's that? What makes you so special?" Kalina said, a challenge in her voice.

Jormungand eyed her for a moment before answering.

"Because we have patrols out daily. Ingvarold up in Harrowing was lazy, more interested in farming than keeping his people safe. I won't be that stupid."

His lip curled as he watched her. Guilt flooded her at his words. She hadn't been able to keep Harrowing safe. She had barely known they existed. Was this her fault?

"No. Of course not." Leif's tone was sarcastic as he turned away from them.

Kalina clenched her jaw to keep everything in her head from spilling out of her mouth.

"After you, your Majesty."

He motioned to their waiting mounts. Maska was clearly agitated, pacing from foot to foot behind them. Dragons have infinitely more patience than most humans but it seemed like the events of the day had been too much for both dragon and rider. Kalina nodded and walked to Maska as Leif turned back to

Jormungand and Halvor.

"You will regret turning against the crown. Mark my words."

And then he turned and vaulted up into Arikara's saddle, offering a hand up to Kalina who reluctantly broke away from Maska to join him. He motioned to their small group of riders and with the village watching, they launched into the skies.

Kalina's main concern just then was keeping everyone safe, and Jormungand posed a serious threat. They controlled all of the Valdir's beef supply, as well as their milk and butter supply. And with Harrowing gone, so was the majority of their fresh produce. She was suddenly overwhelmingly grateful that she had noticed the Emberweed seedling. Without that plant, then they had no hope of ever defeating the king of Ethea, let alone sooth the growing dissent within the Valdir ranks. Perhaps if she could find a way to bring Jormungand back into the fold, she could prove to her doubters that she was a good queen, worthy of ruling. Although her own self-doubt was rising, and she was struggling to manage it.

The sun was beginning to dip below the horizon, shooting the blue sky with ribbons of orange and pink. The mountain rose before them in the gathering dusk and Kalina was grateful to be home. She was so tired. But she was a queen now, and being queen left little time for rest.

Chapter 12

THE COUNCIL TABLE WAS SILENT AS Kalina and Leif entered. She was nervous, her stomach squirming with anxiety as she searched the gathered faces. Eira gave her an encouraging smile, as did Rangvald, but Kari was looking at her hands, and the rest had determined looks on their faces. Leif sat but Kalina remained standing for a moment before sitting- it took a moment to gather her courage to speak but finally she took a deep breath.

"What we found today was nothing short of a tragedy, not only for the Valdir but for the dragons." She searched their faces. Many nodded around the table. "But we can't use this as a reason, an excuse to go to war. We must play this more carefully, think through our options."

At that talking erupted around the table. She knew it had been a gamble. She knew the attack would make people angrier, and would only incite Kari. What small peace the two of them had earlier was once again shattered.

"What?" Arvid said, almost standing from her seat.

"We can't just sit here and let them do this." That was Kari, Rangvald placed a hand on his sister's arm.

"We can't run in without a plan either, Kari." He looked at her with his eyebrows raised.

Kari scowled at her brother but sat back for a moment.

"Our crops are destroyed, how can we just let that lie without retaliation?" Ingvar said, his face red with rage. "Women, children, our farmers, all dead. They deserve to burn for this."

Arvid nodded in agreement. Eira remained quiet.

"At the very least we must send more of our warriors to the villages, for protection." Asta put in.

"Look," Rangvald chimed in again, his voice causing the others to go quiet. "I agree that we need to do something. But I think Kalina is right, we need to exercise caution. Perhaps this was meant to draw us out, bring down our resources, weaken us. Spreading ourselves even thinner won't help."

He looked to Asta as he said the last part. Leif nodded and spoke up.

"I agree. We shouldn't send more of our forces north. We need to keep them here, protecting the majority of our people."

Ingvar looked angrier than ever.

"What about Harrowing and its people? What about those still vulnerable in the mountains or in Windpost?" he said, naming Halvor and Jormungand's village. "They deserve our protection."

"Windpost doesn't recognize me as Queen," Kalina said, standing to place her hands on the table. She cleared her throat. "And those in the mountains are better protected than we are. I agree with Leif and Rangvald. We will not be sending our troops elsewhere."

"What if they attack again?" Arvid spoke up.

"Then we will respond, provide support to our people."

"That is not enough!" Kari finally said, slamming her fist on the table top. "That is not enough. Our people were already suffering before, during the long war. And now you expect them to just lay down and take it? Suffer once again? How long, your Majesty do you think they will follow you if all you do is bandage their hurts and tell them you are sorry?"

Kari's anger was an almost physical thing, raging so hot Kalina took a step back from the table. Her words stung. Already, people were leaving the mountain for Jormungand. Her cousin wasn't wrong.

"What do you expect me to do?" she whispered. She felt helpless, trapped, pushed into a corner where her only two options were to lie down and die or plunge into the fray with no hope of escape.

"We take the fight to them, to the capital. We take the throne from them and put you on it. We unite our two kingdoms."

Her face was filled with such conviction, such passion. Kalina wished with all her heart that it was a viable option, but storming the capital was a suicide mission and it felt like she was the only one who knew it.

"I will not attack the crown and forcibly take it from my mother. Nor will I declare myself heir. It is her crown. I don't want it."

That declaration was followed by silence. Finally, Arvid spoke up.

"Well, we've discussed it before, but this is a perfect opportunity to do so again-" Arvid began.

Kalina sat back down, blocking out the conversation around her as panic began to build inside her. She had done so much better at managing it lately. Having Maska and flying with Nash had helped but right now she couldn't very well go see Maska or go flying. Leif reached out and snagged her hand, squeezing, but she barely felt it. She felt like she'd gone deaf, the world around her a dull buzz, the only thing she could hear was the pounding of her own heart. She squeezed her eyes shut, taking deep, measured breaths, trying to calm her heart.

Sound came rushing back as she was able to calm her nerves, but it wasn't what she wanted to hear. Rangvald and Kari were standing, face to face, arguing. Rangvald was trying to reign his sister in, but Kari was hot-tempered and wasn't having it. The rest of the council was angrily weighing in on their argument.

For the first time in her life, Kalina felt like she was the only adult in the room. She stood and slammed her hands on the table, the loud smack reverberating through the chamber. The arguing stopped abruptly and all eyes turned to their queen. She was barely holding herself together now.

"Everyone out."

Her voice was quiet and low, but it carried. Kari looked at her in disbelief and began to speak but Leif held out a hand.

"We will make plans later. Let's take a break," Leif said.

Everyone filed from her room, but Kalina still stood at the table, her hands splayed out on the rough wood, focusing on her breathing and the feeling of the grain beneath her fingers. Eira was the last to leave. While Leif was speaking quietly with Rangvald by the door, Eira came around the table and put a gentle hand on the back of Kalina's neck.

"Don't let their passion and fear sway you. You are Queen. Do what you think is best for your people." She kissed Kalina's cheek gently and then left the room. But Kalina didn't respond. She didn't know how she felt. Leif came towards Kalina once they were alone.

"You too," she said. "Out."

He paused mid-step.

"Are you sure? I'd be happy to stay-"

"Yes. Out."

He turned and walked out the door, leaving her standing alone in her room.

She collapsed into her chair, her legs shaking and weak from the rush of adrenaline that had caused her to tell them to leave. Suddenly, she didn't feel like she knew who she was anymore. Where was the girl from before her father died? The one who wanted to belong, to lead her people, to be a part of something bigger than herself? Everyone wanted something different from her. Talon had wanted her to come back to Ravenhelm with him to take her place as princess of Ethea. Leif wanted her to be a good leader and queen. Kari wanted her to be more decisive, bolder, more vengeful. Each council member wanted her to be something she was not, and wasn't sure she could ever be. Jormungand wanted her off the throne and the king of Ethea wanted her dead. Did anyone want her just for herself?

Nash.

Nash didn't want anything from her besides spending time with her. Nash had wanted to run away with her, to start a life where no one was trying to pull her left and right, where she could do whatever she wanted. Hadn't her father told her it was her choice? Her future?

The dragon's chamber was dark and warm when she entered an hour later, a bag slung over one shoulder. Most of the dragons were asleep for the night. She carried a torch to light her way but she abandoned it at the cave entrance. For the first time all her night time wandering had come in handy and she'd managed to make it to the kitchens and then the dragon chamber without being seen. Maska wasn't quite old enough to fly her, a few more weeks of growing and he would be the size of a small wyvern and could begin carrying her, so her only hope was to find Nash and his dragon Sitala.

She found him asleep atop the rock outcropping with Sitala curled at its base. She gently tapped Sitala, pointing to the top of the rock. The full-grown dragon sleepily helped the young queen to the top. Nash sat up groggily from his sleep, his braids lightly mussed. He grinned when he saw her.

"To what do I owe this late-night visit, your Majesty?"

"Please, call me Kalina."

She hesitated before going on, still nervous and unsure.

"Were you serious about running away?"

His green eyes went wide at the mention, but he nodded.

"Of course."

"Then let's go. Right now."

Her skin was itching with the need to be free, to feel the responsibility fall from her shoulders. He chuckled.

"Right now? I haven't gotten any food-"

She held up the bag she'd packed.

"I brought plenty. Now let's go."

His face fell, suddenly aware of how serious she was.

"Give me five minutes." He leapt from the rock and ran back up to the passage. All the while he was gone, Kalina's heart threatened to pound out of her chest. What if he was going to wake Leif? Or tell Eira? What if he was just going to leave her there? Soon he was back, and she climbed from the rock, sliding onto Sitala's back. Maska was nearby, and she hurried to his side.

"We're going away," she said as she stroked his smooth green scales. "I need to get out of here."

He could sense her anxiety and stress so he simply snorted a breath of warm air over her and rubbed his head against her side.

"Let's go then."

He followed them as they left the dragon's cave, treading carefully, trying not to disturb any other dragons. She didn't want anyone being alerted to their departure until long after they'd left. Together, she and Nash loaded a small saddle they put on Maska, before climbing into Sitala's saddle. Then they launched into the air, climbing into the night sky, the moon reflecting off Maska's green scales. Jormungand could have the damn throne if he wanted it so badly, she thought as they left the mountain behind.

She had left a note on her bedside table, along with her Valdiran crown. The note contained an apology. She wasn't quite sure who she was apologizing to, she was letting so many people down. But as she'd written it, she'd imagined Leif reading it. She was glad she wouldn't be there to see the sadness on his face.

As they traveled south, the direction she pointed them in, she felt the anger and fear, stress and anxiety, the responsibility of being queen to the Valdir slip from her shoulders, and for the first time in months, she felt like she could finally breathe.

Chapter 13

THE COASTAL TOWN OF AMBERHARBOR was set into the sides of cliffs, the houses clinging precariously all the way down to a slim quay, a sandy beach, and a small harbor. It was known for the way the lights of the buildings up the cliffs reflected off the bay at night, bathing the beach in an amber light. It was primarily a trading post, where ships came to unload and load cargo, sending trundling caravans up the steep switchback road to the top of the cliffs and then out across the southern plains of Ablen and south, to unknown parts of the world.

It wasn't the most anonymous place for two young Valdir and their dragons, but Kalina didn't see another option. She had wanted to continue south, to where no one that was loyal to Ethea would know who they were, but Nash had other ideas. He wanted to begin trading here. He said that the Valdir would need support from the south, especially with Ethea attacking their villages along the Great Grey Mountains. He wanted to be their southern emissary and merchant extraordinaire. He wanted to be their savior. Kalina just wanted some space, some peace and quiet. However, as the days wore on, she wasn't entirely sure what she wanted anymore.

She walked down the crowded narrow street cut into the side of the cliff, a letter clutched tightly in her fist. Eira had told her that the Valdir sent letters through Wildhelm, and that they weren't as cut off from the rest of the country as she had thought. So here she was, making her way towards the small post center in Amberharbor, a letter addressed to Leif pressed against her stomach, guilt making her hurry.

She had brought a decent sum of money with them when they'd left, her plan to buy more books, useful books, for the Valdir's library the only thing that had kept her going the last few days. She spent all her spare time in the local book shops, perusing their meager selections, trying to find texts that might somehow help the Valdir. She'd found an obscure book on growing Emberweed, as well as a few tomes on farming, but nothing else worth spending the money on. Nash had spent his time down on the quay, trying to forge connections, buying merchants drinks, and discussing trade deals. He planned to write to Jormungand once he'd established contacts and convince him to send goods to trade. It was a slow process and to Kalina it seemed he just spent most of his time drinking.

The post center was cool and damp when she entered, the small bell above the door tinkling. Everything on the coast smelled slightly like mildew and she suddenly missed the warm smell of the mountain and the dusty rock they all had lived under. A short, round shopkeeper came out of a back room where she could hear the soft cawing of birds. She raised her eyebrows in surprise. The short man laughed, taking a cap off his balding head and wiping the sweat from it. It was still rather warm here in the south.

"Oh, yes. We use all sorts to carry letters here." He eyed her silver hair before turning his attention to the letter she still clenched tightly. "For one that size I'll need two silver pennies. It will have to go with a raven. They can only carry so much." Kalina nodded, slowly loosening her fingers and handing the letter over before digging in her purse for the coins.

"Have I addressed it correctly?"

The man eyed it, and nodded.

"Yes, everything seems in order."

He went into the back and came out with a stunning black raven on his arm, its feathers so black they were almost blue. He rolled the letter and slid it into a small, lightweight tube attached to the bird's leg. Then he walked to the open window and let the bird launch from his fist, out over the harbor, before turning west across the straights. Kalina stood and watched it for a few minutes before turning back and thanking the man.

The street outside was crowded as she trudged back up the switchback to the top of the cliff. She paused, looking out over the blue straights, Ethea a greyish smudge on the horizon. She dreaded the long walk up the coast along the cliff to the small cave where they were staying with their dragons. They were forced to keep their dragons hidden. Valdir and silver hair stood out enough, but dragons would make them stand out even farther and might put them all in danger. So, she trudged up the cliff through the shrubs and stunted, windblown trees, looking around to ensure she wasn't followed before ducking down a steep path to a small cave carved into the side of the cliffs.

Maska greeted her, snaking his large green head to sniff her clothing thoroughly as she entered. He was getting restless at being cooped up here, but Sitala did her best to keep him entertained. He was still growing fast, and was finally large enough to begin flying with her but she and Nash had deemed it too risky here, where the ships that frequently sailed the straights might see them. Feeding them had been a challenge, too, but Nash had rigged a fishing net to hang into the water below their cave and every day it was filled with enough fish to feed them all.

It was full dark outside, the only light a small fire she had built to cook her dinner. She was getting sick of fish. She was lying on her makeshift bed, her blankets pulled up over her head, when Nash came back. He was stumbling slightly when he made his way into the cave, collapsing onto his own bed before the sounds of his snores filled the cave. She remained awake, unclenching her teeth as he began snoring.

The first few days with Nash had been great. He'd taken her flying every evening until they had seen a ship and had to fly high into the clouds where it was hard to breath. He'd taken her to restaurants along the quay, and they'd talked about their dreams, Kalina finally letting herself begin to wonder at a life where she wasn't a queen, where she could decide what she wanted from life.

But that had been short lived. After she had gone through the local libraries and bookstores, realizing how small a selection there really was, she began to doubt the decision. And Nash had begun spending nights at the taverns with the local merchants and she was suddenly left alone in an unfamiliar town. The excitement wore off and soon the guilt of leaving her people, (and Leif) behind began nagging at her.

So, she'd written him a letter, trying to explain herself. It'd taken her ten tries before she'd finally landed on words that might make sense. And now, waiting for a response was going to drive her mad. Especially if she had to listen to Nash snore every night while she waited. Finally she closed her eyes and drifted into a fitful sleep.

A week passed with little excitement. The small bookshop on the quay smelled like leather, paper, ink, and dust. It was a comforting smell for Kalina, and despite the anxiety and guilt that was plaguing her daily, she felt herself relax as she entered. The small bell above the door tinkled and she moved into the gloom of the shop, books almost immediately rising around her on either side in tall stacks that rose to the ceiling. The shop owner was named Dhalen, and he was a kind man, which was partly why this shop had quickly become her favorite. He bought and sold books that came in off the ships, and he had promised her that his inventory changed weekly. So she kept returning, hoping to find something good.

He bustled around the corner, his small stature and large bespectacled eyes making him seem owlish as he approached.

"Ahh, Kalina. Glad to have you back. I have a few books over here that might spark your interest."

He walked right past her, gesturing for her to follow. He led her to a large counter at the front of the shop where books were stacked. He went around the other side of the counter and pulled a small stack of books towards himself. He plucked off the top one and handed it to her.

"The History of The Rise of Ethea," she read out. She looked up at Dhalen, an eyebrow raised. "I've already read many histories on Ethea. How is this one different?"

Dhalen was ginning at her now. His enthusiasm for books never failed to bring a smile to her own face.

"This one recounts how the Valdir and Askor played a part in the long war, and what their influence and power was during that time. The war was the beginning of the fall of Ethea, it was considered a great kingdom before the war. This book talks about how it got to be so great."

She nodded, opening the front cover of the book, glancing over the first few pages.

"Excellent. Thank you."

He beamed at her and reached for the next book but just then, the door behind her opened and someone stepped inside the small shop. Dhalen looked up and greeted the newcomer.

"Come in. Look around but don't hesitate to ask questions." Then he returned to the book before him, showing it to her. The hairs on Kalina's neck began to rise when she realized the newcomer wasn't moving from the doorway, and suddenly she felt trapped. She turned slowly to face the stranger trying to seem natural. He was an unassuming man, blonde hair, blue eyes, mildly handsome. He smiled placidly at her, making eye contact. She smiled tentatively back before turning back to Dhalen.

Once she had seen and purchased the books from Dhalen she turned to leave and found the stranger standing right where he'd been before. He stepped aside, gesturing to the door so she could pass but he remained too close, too near, and her heart pounded as she squeezed by him and out the door. Once on the front step, she paused, breathing in deeply. She heard the stranger behind her asking Dhalen for a book on Wostradian Poetry before the door swung closed.

Chapter 14

ON HER WAY BACK TO THE CAVE SHE checked in at the post center, asking the shopkeeper Graycen if there were any letters for her. She and the man had become familiar, since she now checked in daily for letters from Leif.

"Ah! Yes, I finally do have a letter for you Miss Kalina."

He held up a finger, indicating she wait as he rushed into the back of his shop. Her heart began to pound in anticipation, excitement, and fear at what Leif might say. Graycen handed her a small letter and she cradled it to her as she stepped back out onto the busy early evening street of Amberharbor. She barely noticed the blonde man from the book shop until she ran right into him, dropping her books and the letter.

She bent to pick them up, mumbling apologies, but they nearly bumped heads. She looked up at the blonde man, her eyes wide in fear. The man was smiling broadly at her.

"Sorry, Miss! I didn't mean to startle you." His voice was deep and melodic, but it put her immediately on edge.

"It's fine," she mumbled, gathering up her books and Leif's letter.

The man offered her a hand, which she briefly took as she stood, then dropping it like it had burned her. Something about him unsettled her. Maybe it was the fact that he'd stood and waited in the shop, or the fact that in a town full of people she'd bumped into him again. It made her nervous. She muttered a quick thank you and then hurried on up the street, glancing behind her every few feet to make sure she wasn't being followed. The sun had gone down by the time she hit the top of the cliff, and she was able to relax slightly. Her fear of being followed slipping away as she disappeared into the dark.

She leaned back against Maska. The light of a small fire filled the cavern with warmth, as she stared at the letter from Leif. She was working up the courage to open it, to read his words. What if he didn't forgive her for leaving? She hadn't had the will to eat her dinner that night, her stomach rolling. And she was grateful that Nash wasn't there. He didn't know she'd sent Leif a letter in the first place.

Finally, she slipped her finger beneath the wax seal and broke it, opening the stiff paper.

Dear Kalina,

While I don't pretend to understand your reasoning for leaving, I, of course, forgive you. I know your father always talked about people making their own future, and having the freedom to choose. So, I can't say I blame you for choosing to leave.

Maybe we weren't fair to you. Maybe we didn't support you enough. Whatever the reason, and whatever my failing, I'm sorry.

Things are tense here. Jormungand has claimed the crown in your absence and more people than ever are leaving the mountain for the foothills. There's only the old and very young left here, and a small contingent of your loyal soldiers. We all hope you will one day come back to us, but we won't force you.

Eira received word from her contact in the capital that your mother, the queen, is pregnant, and being confined to her rooms. The King continues to obsess over you and your claim on the throne, and continues to send men to Wolfhold where he now has a large garrison stationed, ready to attack us. I have Rangvald and Kari organizing our defenses but with so few left to defend the mountain, we aren't taking any risks. We're trying to hold things together but Arvid, Asta, and Ingvar have left us and the council. Only the four of us remain.

I hope you will decide to come back to us. Maska should be raised around more dragons, and hiding isn't really your style. We miss you and hope you are safe and doing well.

Yours,
Leif

Tears were streaming down her face by the time she finished reading. It seemed her crown and people were falling apart. Hadn't she wanted Jormungand to take over? Hadn't she wanted freedom from the responsibilities? She wondered if Leif himself missed her, and the thought that he might not have made the tears come harder. The fact that he blamed himself for her leaving made her already bruised and battered heart break further.

Kalina cried herself to sleep that night, and when she woke, Nash was back in the cave, snoring away on the floor, stinking of alcohol. She stood over him, hands on her hips, wondering where she'd gone so wrong, how she'd ever thought it was a good idea to run away with a man she barely knew. She gave him a nudge with her boot, trying to rouse him from sleep.

"Wake up."

She nudged him again. He snorted a bit and rolled over. This time she kicked him in the thigh, enough to startle him awake.

"What?"

He sat up, his braids a mess on his head. He looked up at her, confused.

"What is it?"

"We need to talk," she said, and stalked away to the campfire where she stirred the coals to life, dumping an extra branch on to cook breakfast.

Nash blearily got out of bed and came over to sit by the fire. The mornings and evenings were getting cool, autumn finally descending on the coast.

"What did you want to talk about?"

He stretched as he spoke and Kalina wished, not for the first time, that Nash was Talon or Leif. She missed their easy company, their support, their candor. Nash was funny and impulsive, which made for a good time, but he was also quicker to anger than she had realized and his impulsiveness could put them in danger. She reached for the small bag of tea leaves and scooped some into two mugs. Then she set a pot full of water to boil.

"What is our plan?" she asked without looking at him.

"What do you mean?" he asked while he began mixing water and oats in a second pot and placing it on the fire to cook. "You know my plan. I know yours." He shrugged.

"I don't feel like I do know your plan anymore. Drinking all day in the taverns with merchants isn't going to gain you customers and connections. You don't really even have a product."

Nash eyed her, scowling.

"I sent a letter to Jormungand. He's agreed to give me beef, wool, and dragon scales to trade."

Kalina stiffened at her usurper's name. Then she forced herself to relax. Was he really a usurper if she had left? She supposed not, but that didn't make Nash's statement feel less like a betrayal.

"Jormungand? Really?" She stood up and began to pace before the fire. Maska raised his head to watch his rider for a few moments before lying back down.

"Are you kidding me? You can't be angry about that. You left. They aren't yours to govern anymore. You let Jormungand take the crown," he pointed out.

His words stung, making her guilt burn even brighter. She went silent for a moment, trying to wrestle her own emotions under control. She had given it up, abandoned her people. She deserved this, didn't she? She swallowed.

"Fine. But you're drinking away all our money."

His face stayed stony at her remark but he paused briefly in his stirring of the oats.

"I'll cut back."

She nodded and went back to pouring their tea. They ate breakfast in silence and then Kalina left for town. She spent the day in a small tea shop, watching the world go by and reading through a book she had picked up from Dhalen's small book shop that morning that detailed one man's adventures on the sea and the creatures he discovered there, some sounding suspiciously like dragons or wyverns, but that dwelt in the water. It sent her imagination reeling. What if Ethea's dwindling numbers of wyverns and dragons weren't alone? They were certainly the most well-known and well documented thanks to the Valdir. Kalina became lost in thought.

She thought she had seen the blonde man leaving the tea shop when she'd first arrived, but she had dismissed it. Here, there were plenty of blonde people; it was probably just any other blonde man. She sat at a small table in the sun, enjoying the sounds of the city around her. She realized that she had truly come a long way. A year ago, large crowds had made her nervous, sending her into massive panic attacks. But here she was, craving the hustle and bustle of the town after weeks spent in a lonely cave. The mountain where the Valdir lived was always full of the buzz of activity, and she was never truly alone, a person or dragon around every corner. She'd grown used to it, and now that she was away, she missed that feeling of being a part of something.

A melancholy settled over her as the day wore on. She missed her friends and family, she missed the dragon cave, she missed training. She looked down at her body. They'd been forced to trade their leathers for more common clothes. She still dressed in pants, her hair making her stand out enough that wearing pants wasn't strange. Plus, many of the ships had women on them, and they wore pants. The clothes they'd bought when they arrived were becoming loose, her recent muscle loss making her feel empty and hollow. She vowed to exercise that night.

With a heavy heart she trudged back through town, to the top of the cliffs. There, she stopped and watched the sun dip below the horizon of inland Alben. She felt lost and confused, unsure of what the right next step should be. Should she go home to the Valdir and pick up whatever pieces were left? Or should she stay here and try to find some sort of happiness?

The cave was dark when Kalina approached. Usually, Maska waited for her on the edge, but this time, the cliff edge was deserted. The cave was empty when she entered, and for a brief moment, she began to panic. It wasn't that strange for Sitala and Maska to go hunting at night, when they were less likely to be seen by ships. But as the hours passed, and they didn't return, she started to worry. She couldn't fall asleep that night, and instead stayed up, stoking the fire, hoping the light would bring Maska back.

Chapter 15

NASH ENTERING THE CAVE WOKE KALINA, and she realized she'd fallen asleep. She sat up, stretching, and looked around the cavern, still empty of dragons. Nash wasn't drunk this time, which made for a welcome change.

"No dragons tonight? Are they out hunting?" he asked casually, sitting down at the fire and pulling some leftover food to him. Kalina shook her head.

"I don't know." She stood and walked to the edge of the cave. "They were gone when I got back just after sunset and I haven't seen them since."

Nash's head jerked up in alarm.

"That long?"

She nodded, fear wriggling in her stomach, her heart leaping in her chest.

"I'm scared something's happened."

Nash stood and began pacing.

"I'll go into town and see what I can find out. You stay here and wait for them."

He raced off, leaving Kalina to wait, alone in the dark, her fear growing by the minute.

The next few hours were some of the worst she'd ever spent. The dragons had never been gone for more than an hour or two, preferring to hunt nearby. But this felt different, and she began jumping at every sound, that old familiar panic rising in her chest, threatening to drown her.

Pebbles clattering on the cliffside announced Nash's arrival. He ran into the cave, his breath coming in ragged gasps from running up the cliffside from the town. He stopped, hands on his knees, heaving breaths rasping from him. Kalina wrung her hands, waiting for him to speak.

"They've been drugged and taken," he gasped out. "Water."

She leapt to grab him their water skin. He took a few deep gulps before continuing.

"They've been loaded in the hold of a ship in the bay, due to leave just after sunrise."

Her eyes went wide. That was barely an hour or two away.

They had to act fast. She couldn't fathom the idea of losing Maska. She jumped into action, allowing the movements and planning to take her mind off her anxiety.

"What ship?" she asked as she dug out their weapons that they'd stashed in the corner of the cave.

Nash came up beside her and dug out his own. Together they strapped on sword belts, and Kalina strapped her axes to her belt, one on each side for easy access.

"A ship called The Swift. It's part of a Wostradian trading fleet out of Harris Bay," he explained as he spoke.

"How in Skaldir's name did you even find them?" She looked at him sideways as she braided her hair back.

Nash shrugged.

"I have my sources. I haven't been drinking in taverns just for fun, you know. I have made connections. I merely spoke to some of my sources about what they'd heard of two dragons being bought or sold or transported. One of them was drunk enough to tell me." His scowl deepened as he strode from the cave. "He won't be feeling well in the morning."

Kalina barely caught these last words but she could imagine what Nash had done to the man. She followed him at a quick pace, trying to hold herself back from running and tiring herself out.

The cliffside town was quiet, only the occasional sound from a nearby tavern or house disturbing the cool autumn air that blew in off the ocean, scented with salt. If she hadn't been rushing to save her dragon, Kalina might have enjoyed the quiet, lovely night. The moon hung overhead, almost full, giving them plenty of light to see by. But it also meant that others could see them, so they stuck to the shadowed alcoves and overhangs of buildings, trying to remain inconspicuous. Their silver hair reflected the moonlight like a beam so they used their cloaks to cover their heads.

The quay was quiet, only the soft lapping of waves against the loading dock breaking the silence. Kalina and Nash crouched behind a stack of barrels ready to be loaded onto a nearby ship. It was a triple masted monstrosity, clearly meant to move a large amount of cargo. But there was no sound or sign of the dragons. There was one lookout above decks, and Kalina assumed the rest of the crew were asleep below decks.

"What's the plan?" she whispered to Nash.

He looked at her, his eyes wide and round with his own fear, as if to say 'I got us this far,' and she realized she would have to make a plan.

"Fine. Here's the plan."

She outlined it for him in quick, short tones, anxious to get to Maska, and then they split up. Nash put his weapons away in his belt, staggering out from behind the barrels, making his way up the gangplank of the ship, acting as though he was belligerently drunk. Kalina saw him pull a small flask from his vest, taking a swig to make the act more believable.

"Hey! You!" he called out to the lookout as he stumbled on deck. He tripped over his own feet, falling flat on his face. The lookout came running over.

"Sir, this is a private ship, I'll need you to disembark."

The man helped Nash to his feet, and back towards the gangplank. Nash neatly pulled himself from the man's arms, stumbling across the deck once again.

"Is this the Maiden's Hair? I remember when I sailed on that ship. She was a beaut, much like this one."

He stumbled off, leading the lookout on a rambling tour of the ship, talking about his previous voyage. Kalina stifled a laugh. Despite how desperate their situation was, despite the last few weeks of frustration and guilt and anger, Nash still managed to make her laugh. She vowed to tell him later that he'd missed his calling as a player.

With the lookout thoroughly distracted and at the far end of the ship now, she snuck on board, making for the shadowed doorway to the hold. The moon lit the deck, but once she pushed open the door with a soft creak, she was plunged into utter darkness. Darkness had never scared her, and she recalled all the times she'd wandered the forest at night, or the halls of the castle, or the library, or the halls of the Valdir's mountain. This was her element, something she was used to. She kept her twin axes in her hands as she slowly felt her way down a very steep staircase. At the bottom was a hallway, doorways to cabins coming off each side, and at the far end another staircase descending into the hold.

She crept past the open door to a kitchen, a large man dressed in a stained white apron asleep on the table, his hand around a tankard of ale. The doors were closed along the rest of the hall and she tiptoed down the last set of stairs. She had no idea how she was going to get a full-grown dragon, that probably took up the entire hold, out of here, let alone two dragons, but she had to try. The hold below was huge, the entire length of the ship. A large bulk took up the majority of the space, and suddenly, Kalina regretted not bringing a light.

"Sitala? Maska?" she whispered into the dark.

The bulk moved slightly; a groan echoed around the chamber. Kalina edged forward, putting an axe into her belt. She had a hand out, feeling for dragon scales. Finally, her fingers touched the smooth scales of a dragon, its side rising and falling as if in deep sleep. She felt along it, searching for its head. Finally she found it, and tried to lift it, tapping between its eyes to wake it up.

"Wake up! You've been kidnapped! We have to get out of here!" she whispered fiercely, praying to the gods for them to wake up, but Sitala didn't move. Maska shifted, but didn't wake. Suddenly, there was shouting from above on deck, which echoed below. She froze, fear lancing through her. There was a shuffle of movement from above and then the pounding of feet on the deck. Kalina pulled her second axe from her belt and turned to face whatever was coming for them.

Someone hurtled down the stairs, a lantern in one hand, and a sword in the other. Kalina saw the glint of the sword and she didn't hesitate. She lunged forward, striking with her axe, trying to catch her opponent off balance. But they were quick, leaping sideways and catching her blow on their blade. Despite their agility, they had to fight with a lit lantern, and it made them slower. She attacked again, whirling her axes with both hands, slicing from above and below, a move meant to force your opponent to react to one or the other, making them vulnerable. The man before her blocked the higher strike but missed the lower one, her blade sinking into his hip.

A scream ripped from his throat, and he fell to one knee, almost dropping the lantern. Kalina backed off for a moment, unsure if she should risk a fire in the hold, or give him enough time to put the lantern down. Finally, he put it on a nearby crate and forced himself to his feet, his face tight with pain. His blonde hair finally caught the light and Kalina recognized him with a jolt. He was the man from the bookstore, from outside the coffee shop. He must have followed her to the cave. Her momentary hesitation gave him an opening and he swung his sword at her, catching her high on the shoulder. She screamed and staggered away, her scream finally waking the nearest dragon. The green of Maska's scales reflected the weak lantern light as he struggled up, letting out a roar Kalina had never heard before. He was tethered to the floor of the hold but he broke the metal chains easily enough, the restraints snapping at his strength. He lunged forward, his enormous jaws clamping shut around the torso of the blonde man.

Kalina leaned against the nearest wall, horror filling her at the utter surprise on the man's face before he disappeared into the dragon's maw. Maska crunched down, the sounds of bone snapping making her stomach churn. Blood spilled from between his jaws before he released the man, his lifeless, broken body slumping to the floor.

Maska swung to look at her, his eyes still groggy from whatever he'd been drugged with.

"Kalina," he rumbled.

The pain in her shoulder suddenly became overwhelming as the adrenaline began to fade and she looked back at her wound. The man's blade had cut deep, and she was bleeding heavily. She needed to get Maska and Sitala out of here and somewhere safe.

"Can you wake Sitala?" she asked her dragon as she clutched her wound, trying to staunch the bleeding.

"Of course." Maska turned and began releasing the chains around Sitala's large, brown form. Kalina grabbed the lantern and began searching the hold for a release on the doors above them. Finally, she found a lever that she pulled, grunting at the pain and effort. Two great doors overhead creaked open, allowing the weak early morning light inside.

"Maska," she begged.

Sitala sat up, blinking her eyes blearily.

"Help," Kalina begged with a grunt.

Maska climbed the few crates within the hold and shoved at the doors, opening them wide. There was shouting from up on deck and more pounding feet.

"We have to go," Maska said, nudging Sitala up towards the

doors and the open sky beyond. Kalina struggled towards him, using her good arm to haul herself onto his back, dropping her axes in the process. She immediately missed their weight but knew she had no choice. Maska was only just big enough to carry her, but she had no other option.

"Go." Her voice came out as a whisper, all her strength focused on hanging on with her legs and her one good arm. Sitala climbed from the hold and with a jerky bound, Maska followed.

Chapter 16

THE DECK OF THE SHIP WAS IN CHAOS. Kalina couldn't see Nash anywhere, but she didn't have the energy to worry. All she could focus on was keeping them moving. They had to get out of there. Sailors were running around, gathering weapons. A few bodies lay prone on the wood, blood spreading out in dark puddles around them.

Maska ran to the edge of the ship, trying to gain enough space away from the rigging ropes and lines to spread his wings. But when he paused before leaping out over the water, he turned back. Kalina was blinded by pain, unable to think straight, but she searched the deck as best she could. Sitala was using her massive bulk and tail to clear away the sailors who were fighting her. Kalina finally saw Nash in combat with a large sailor; they were locked in hand-to-hand combat, grappling against one another. His silver battle braids streamed out behind him as he fought, struggling to incapacitate the man and get to Sitala.

Kalina's heart was in her throat as she and Maska waited and watched. At any moment someone could recapture them and take Maska away from her, and it took everything in her to stay and wait for Nash to make it to Sitala. Nash's face was bright red, the man's massive arms bearing down, threatening to squeeze the life out of him. Kalina didn't see Nash's weapons anywhere. Sitala's tail lashed out, hitting the center mainsail, snapping the huge beam in two. People screamed as it began to fall, the huge canvas sails, along with tons of ropes, came crashing down. Kalina and Maska launched into the sky, trying to avoid the collapsing ship. Fear clawed its way up her throat as Maska banked and came back around to watch the wreckage.

Sitala was struggling her way out from under the huge canvas sail that had unfurled as it fell. Nash was nowhere to be seen but Kalina could see the large sailor sprawled on the deck, unmoving. Finally, she saw Nash's head pop up from beneath the fallen sail and he clambered out, struggling to get to where Sitala was trapped. He helped her unpin her trapped tail before he climbed onto her back just as the large sailor began to stir.

"Nash!" she called, urging him to move faster.

Sitala launched them into the air and soon Maska and Kalina were following them up the coast line, away from the harbor town, the ship, and danger. Kalina's arm and legs were shaking as Maska came in for a landing, her adrenaline fading, her breath ragged with pain. The moment his feet hit the ledge of their cave, she fell from his shoulders, hitting the dirt hard. Nash was off of Sitala's back in an instant, rushing for her. He pulled her to her feet and urged her inside. Her silver braids hung matted with blood. He lowered her to the ground beside their now cold campfire before rushing around the cave, digging through their packs and pulling out things for bandages, a needle, and thread.

Kalina laid back, her shoulder throbbing with a dull pain now. Her right hand hurt more than her left shoulder now, the strain from holding on to Maska bright in comparison. She let her head rest on the dirt of the cave floor and realized vaguely that she had finally flown on Maska. If she hadn't been in so much pain, and so exhausted, she would have been elated. But the edges of her vision were growing dark, and she couldn't bring herself to be excited or worried about anything as she slipped into warm blackness.

When she woke, the cave around her was dark, the sound of Maska's snoring a sweet melody to her ears. The fire was burning low, the embers casting just enough light to see the bare details of the cave around her. Sitala and Maska lay asleep across the cave entrance and Nash was sprawled beside her, an arm flung over his face. Kalina tried to sit up, but the pain of her shoulder caused her to slump back to the ground.

They weren't safe here. The blonde man had had help drugging and capturing Maska and Sitala. She was still mystified at how he'd done it. But it didn't matter now, what mattered was they needed to get out, get away from Amberharbor. Word would get across the straits, and the king of Ethea would send his soldiers to track them down, torture them, and get information on her people. Then he would kill her. Fear began to overtake her as she lay there in the dark. She felt helpless, lost, alone, and in pain. In an effort to distract herself, she forced herself to sit up, pushing through the pain and gritting her teeth.

She stoked the fire, putting on a pot of water to boil. Her hair was stiff and matted with her own blood, and once the water was hot, she used it to gingerly wash her hair one-handed. Her left hand hung down, partially useless. It frustrated her, but she grimaced and pushed through it, getting her hair clean. When the sun rose a few hours later, she was still awake, sipping on a cup of hot tea, waiting for Nash to wake up. When he yawned and rolled over to face her, she smiled grimly at him. He sat up.

"Good morning. How are you feeling?"

She gestured to her useless arm.

"How   do   you   think?"
He bit his cheek before getting up to come over and inspect the wound. He peeled off the bandage he'd put on her the night before.

"It doesn't look too bad," he commented as he began to clean it, using the hot water she had used to make her tea.

She hissed as it touched her tender, stitched skin. She couldn't bring herself to look down, so she watched as the dragons began to wake.

"Kalina?" Maska said as he woke, searching for her.

"I'm here, Maska. I'm fine."

The dragon's worried green eyes softened as he watched her.

"What happened?" She couldn't help herself. She needed to know.

Maska turned to look at Sitala who had woken up beside him. Sitala looked away and Kalina thought she saw shame on the dragon's face.

"It was a silly mistake," Maska started.

She knew he was young. But Sitala was a few years older, and should have known better. Or so Kalina thought.

"What mistake?" she demanded.

Sitala was still not meeting Kalina's eyes. Nash stood, hands on his hips.

"What mistake, Sitala?"

Finally, the brown dragon turned to face them.

"For the last few days, someone has been leaving a pile of fish on the rocks below the cliff. I've been eating them. There's not nearly enough food out here, our nets have been empty, and we can only do so much fishing at night..." it sounded to Kalina like the dragon was whining, begging to be forgiven.

"So, you ate fish that a stranger left?"

It turned Kalina's blood cold. It meant someone had noticed their presence here days ago. They hadn't been nearly as careful as she'd thought.

"I didn't think it would be poisoned." Sitala hung her head, sadness and shame evident in her voice. Kalina suddenly felt sorry for the dragon.

"I didn't think it was a problem either," Maska said, trying to stand up for his friend.

Kalina stood and walked to her dragon, laying her good hand on his side and leaning into him.

"It's okay. Neither of you suspected they would drug you and take you from us." Nash had gone to Sitala to comfort her.

Kalina let her head drop onto Maska's warm scales.

"We flew," she whispered to him. He grumbled a purr at her in agreement.

"Let's do it again."

His response made excitement flair in her breast and for a brief moment she forgot the horrors of the previous day. But when Nash walked back to the fire, digging through the packs for some food, she stepped away from Maska, determined to make a plan.

"Now what?" she said, joining him at the fire. "We can't stay here anymore."

Nash paused in his searching, as if thinking. Abruptly he stood up and walked to the small pile of wood along the cave wall, stacking a few in his arms.

"I'm not abandoning all my hard work," he said, his back turned to her. She couldn't read his face.

"Well, I can't stay here. It's not safe, and I'm not willing to risk myself or Maska again."

He shrugged at her words. Suddenly, she was angry. Why was he acting as if their almost dying wasn't a big deal? Why would he continue to put her in danger by staying here? She had thought he liked her, cared for her, but suddenly she felt more alone than ever. Maybe it would be better if she went back to the mountain. At least Leif and Eira cared about her, even if she was no longer queen.

"Fine." She turned to her dragon. "Let's go, Maska."

"Where are we going?" he asked.

"Home."

Chapter 17

KALINA STRAPPED HERSELF INTO THE SMALL saddle that barely fit Maska. Suddenly it was time to say goodbye, her bag packed with the few books she'd bought and some meager food supplies. Nash stood awkwardly before her, twisting his hands.

"I'm sorry, Kalina."

She nodded, tears pricking her eyes. They hadn't really known each other when they'd left, and she knew she'd treated him unfairly. But she was so unhappy, and needed to leave.

"I'm sorry I couldn't make you happy."

That cut her, her chest hollowing out. She felt like she was losing someone all over again. Like Geir. Like her father.

"I know," she barely croaked out. She leaned forward, putting her arms around him and resting her head on his shoulder. "This just wasn't the right decision. I have to go home. I have to fix this."

He nodded against her head, his chin bumping her lightly.

"Go be a queen. Don't let Jormungand bring you down."

She smiled as tears slipped over and spilled onto his leather vest.

"Thank you."

She and Maska launched into the bright morning, the sun sparkling off the water below them. It was their first official flight together, and she felt a thrill of exhilaration as he flapped his wings to gain altitude and turned them back north, across the straights to Ethea.

Maska was barely big enough to carry her, but he did his best. They had to stop after a few hours for him to rest. Kalina was impatient to get home, suddenly anxious to see Leif again, and to take up her crown again if they'd let her. Her expectations, however, weren't high. All she really wanted was to feel like she belonged. It was the feeling she'd been searching for all her life. She'd almost found it with Calla and Anders back in Ravenhelm, the couple who had so kindly taken her in after she'd left the abbey where she'd grown up, and then again in the Valdir's mountain before her father died. She'd left in search of it once again and only found loneliness. Maska was the only bright light in all of this mess she had created. She only hoped she could find her way out, and maybe now was the time to listen to her advisors instead of her own heart and head.

The mountain loomed out of the vastness of the Wastes as the sun set on the third day and suddenly her heart was filled with nostalgia and longing. She couldn't wait to land and see Leif. She had been gone now for almost two months, and who knew how much chaos had reigned in her absence. Leif's letter had been brief so she hoped things were not worse.

The entrance cavern of the Valdir's mountain was empty, dark, and cold when they landed, the autumn breezes more frigid here than along the coast. Kalina shivered as she dismounted, keeping her hand on Maska's neck.

"Where is everyone?" he whispered, snaking out his long neck and peering down one of the nearby tunnels.

"I don't know." She patted him gently. "Why don't you go down to the dragon hold and get yourself something to eat and some rest."

He nudged her tiredly with his head before diving from the cave mouth. She straightened the red leathers that she'd donned for the trip, hoisted her bag of books, and made her way through the mountain. It felt as though she'd never left, and was once again doing her usual night time wanderings. The tunnels around her were quiet and dark, the usual torches set into the wall every dozen or so feet, cold to the touch. Alarm began to grown in Kalina's chest as she got closer to the dining chamber without finding a single person.

The soft murmur of low voices finally reached her as she entered, along with the glow of torch light flickering along the high walls. She relaxed slightly as she approached, recognizing Leif, Kari, and Rangvald sitting around a table, eating a late-night supper. It looked to be some tough looking meat, a few root vegetables, and some bread. She approached cautiously, her own stomach grumbling at the sight of food no matter how humble the fare. A loose rock shifted under her foot, causing Leif's head to snap up, his handsome face turning towards her, his grey eyes going wide at the sight.

He coughed on his food as he tried to speak, Rangvald turning to slap him on the back before noticing Kalina standing just outside the torch light. He jumped to his feet, Leif a second behind. Kari remained sitting, but a small smile turned her lips.

Rangvald's hug enveloped her as he squeezed tightly. There was a cracking noise, and suddenly the tension in her back eased. She laughed breathlessly as she squeezed her cousin back. She hadn't realized how much she'd missed him and his quiet way.

"I've missed you," she said as he stepped back.

Leif was right behind Rangvald's hug, but his felt much different. His arms encircled her waist and she placed her hands on his shoulders. He lifted her from the ground briefly as he held her to him. Warmth blossomed in her core and spread outwards, thawing some of the loneliness she'd felt since she'd left. She breathed deeply as she buried her face into his neck, trying to let his scent drown her. He was warm, and familiar, and a different sort of longing started deep within her at his touch. When he finally put her down, she felt the loss of his touch like a flower feels the loss of the sun.

Finally, Kari stepped forward. Her hands were crossed over her chest, and she eyed Kalina. Kalina swallowed before speaking.

"Kari, I-" but before she could even squeak out an apology, the woman was embracing her.

"We've missed you. I'm so glad you are safe."

Kalina returned the hug, grateful that Kari seemed to have forgiven her for the moment, but she knew she owed this brave woman more than just some lame excuse. She owed her an explanation. She owed them all that.

"I'm so sorry that I left." She paused, unsure how to truly express her feelings for these people. She put her hands out. "But I'm back for good. I'm done running. I'll serve the Valdir however I can, even if it's not as your Queen." She looked around at them, her family and friends, and realized suddenly, she was home. The thing she'd been searching for all along was right here, waiting for her while she was mourning and feeling lost. She just hadn't allowed them in, hadn't allowed them to be that for her.

Kari broke into a grin and she put her arm around Kalina's shoulders.

"We're glad to have you back, your Majesty." She led Kalina away. "Someone else has been dying to know where you've been."

They rounded the corner into the bathing chamber and Eira stood up from where she was helping an elderly woman from a tub. She placed her hands over her mouth and came running, folding Kalina into an embrace. Tears sprang unbidden to Kalina's eyes and she hastily wiped them away with her sleeve, grateful Rangvald and Leif couldn't follow them into the women's bathing chamber.

"Kalina."

Just the sound of her name on this woman's lips made her feel more at peace.

"I'm sorry-" she began before breaking down into tears and collapsing into Eira's arms.

The woman held her as she cried, Kari graciously taking her leave, the bathing chamber slowly emptying until the two of them were alone. Eira was her aunt by blood, and the first Valdir she'd ever met. This woman had trained her, answered all her stupid questions, and been the first to stay up all night with her after her father had died. Eira was like a mother to her, since her own was locked away across Ethea.

"I know, child," Eira said in a soothing voice, brushing her hand down Kalina's head. "Hush now, you are back with us and that's all that matters."

That night, Kalina slept the best she'd slept in months, back in her own bed, in her own room. And when she ventured down to the dining cave for breakfast, she encountered a sight she never thought she'd see. The Valdir began clapping and cheering as she entered the room. The only ones left were those who believed in her, many of them very old or very young. The rest had followed Asta and the rest of the council members when they'd left the mountain for Jormungand's village.

She smiled and waved at the bright faces before her, so full of hope. Leif approached, the small box that contained her crown in his hands. As she stood before her people, he presented it to her, opening the box and looking into her bright blue eyes with such expectation, such trust, that Kalina only hoped she could live up to his, and their, expectations. She reached into the box and pulled the iron and stone crown from it, placing it atop her braided silver hair.

A cheer went up as she lowered her hands. She was once again their queen, but a queen of what? Of the old and infirm? Of children? She smiled at their hopeful faces and turned back to Leif, trying to calm the fear squirming in her guts.

"Council meeting, my chambers, twenty minutes." And then she turned, smiling and greeting people as she walked back across the room, her appetite suddenly gone.

Chapter 18

LEIF WAS THE FIRST TO ARRIVE, A SMALL tray with bread and a hard-white cheese in his hands. Kalina reluctantly tore off a piece of bread and nibbled on it as she sat, waiting for Rangvald, Kari, and Eira to join them. Once they had all arrived and were seated, she realized she actually preferred a smaller council. People she knew she could really trust. She surveyed their hopeful faces.

"I need someone to tell me what's happened since I left. How exactly did Jormungand take control? And what can be done about it?" She looked to Leif, steepling her fingers beneath her chin.

"When you left, everything was fine for a few days. We held the people together; said you'd gone on an overnight to clear your head. But when you didn't return, they began to panic. The second week you were gone, Jormungand and Halvor showed up with a contingent of men and took control. They gave speeches in the dining cavern and in the great hall. They trained with the men and spent hours in the dragons' cave. They convinced most of the Valdir to leave and join their village, stating that they needed soldiers and farmers for their herds of cattle. Promising land to farm, houses to live in." He paused and looked over at Rangvald to continue.

"I scouted out the village a few weeks ago. Many of our people are living in tents, or sleeping on the ground because they can't build housing fast enough." Rangvald took a swig of water from the glass before him. He looked as if he was preparing himself. "But despite that, Jormungand does have a right to the throne. He has them convinced he can bring them home to the mountains, where we can once again live in peace. And the fact that the King of Ethea hasn't attacked in weeks doesn't help. It has only served to convince the people that since you left, they are safer."

Kalina looked at the table. The truth was, they were safer without her as queen. But she couldn't let that derail her. Jormungand was selling them a false sense of security. There was a reason the Valdir had fled to the Wastes, that reason hadn't vanished because she'd left.

"So now what? How can I win back my throne and our people?" Kari grinned at her, excitement coloring her sharp features. The blue eyes she shared with Kalina sparkling. Kalina smiled grimly back.

"You must fight him." Eira's voice rang into the silence. "Valdir tradition states that if two people claim the throne then they must fight to the death. The winner is the better warrior and has been chosen by the gods to keep the Valdir safe."

Kalina's gut twisted just thinking about it. She had become a competent warrior since she'd found the Valdir, but ten months of training was nothing compared to a lifetime. She looked up at Leif beside her, his handsome face drawn with worry.

"I'm willing, but I'm not sure I have the skills."

"If you choose to challenge Jormungand and fight, then only the gods' mercy will tell us who is to rule. It's not a matter of skill, although that is how it would seem. It is a matter for the gods."

Kalina shivered. She'd never really been religious, despite being raised in the abbey. Father Martin had taught her the basics about their gods, but he'd never insisted she worship. The Valdir worshiped the same gods as most Etheans, only they often put emphasis on the Warrior Skaldir rather than The Mother Freyre. Skaldir created the Valdir, formed them from the mud of the mountains to fly alongside dragon kind. They were exceptional warriors, and he showed them his favor by allowing them to survive battle. If she managed to survive this fight, it showed that Skaldir looked favorably on her.

She nodded finally in resignation and determination.

"I'll do it." Leif's face fell slightly, worry creasing his brow, but there was also a fierce pride in his eyes as he watched her. Rangvald nodded slowly, and Kari grinned at her.

Kalina's shoulder was slow to heal but as soon as she had movement back she began training, getting herself back into fighting shape. She spent the days training incessantly with Kari and Leif, reconditioning her body and learning the skills she'd need to hopefully beat Jormungand. She fell into bed every night too exhausted to be worried, but one morning she woke to find Eira sitting beside her bed. Panic rose in her chest, fear that something bad had happened once again.

"Is it Maska?" she asked, about to jump out of bed.

Eira put her hands up.

"No, no. Maska is fine. He's training, out on maneuvers with

Arikara."

Kalina relaxed back into her pillows, suddenly red with embarrassment at getting worked up so quickly.

"I came to discuss your crown."

Kalina's eyes slid to the box she kept the crown in while she slept, tucked away on her bedside table.

"What about my crown?"

Eira sighed and got up to pace to the small window that overlooked the Wastes.

"Do you really want it?" She kept her back to Kalina as she spoke, allowing her the privacy to think.

Kalina stayed quiet for a few moments. Of course, she had every right to ask this. Kalina had been anything but consistent since her father had died, and then she had left.

"Yes. I do, Eira." She got out of bed and began to pull on her pants and boots as she spoke. "I didn't really know that I wanted this until the day I got back, to be honest. I was scared, alone, and suddenly taken from orphan to Queen in a matter of months. But now that I'm back, I know I'm back for the right reasons. This is my family. These are my people. I didn't really understand that before." She came to stand beside her aunt. "This time I want to be here for me, not for my father, not for you, not for anyone."

Eira finally smiled and turned back to her, putting her wrinkled hands on Kalina's shoulders.

"Now, that, I believe."

They sent a letter to Jormungand, warning him of their arrival and her intention to challenge him, but despite the weeks she'd had to prepare, Kalina still felt like an amateur wielding her axes. She flew on Maska across the wide-open wastes, Leif, Kari, Rangvald, and a small contingent of soldiers behind them. Eira had elected to remain back at the mountain with the rest of their supporters. Kalina was poorly equipped for the task ahead, but she knew there was no other way. Not if she wanted to be queen.

They landed as the sun was just above noon, the village of Windpost busy with farmers, cattle herders, vendors selling and trading goods, and people going about their daily lives. A crowd formed as they dismounted. Leif beside her put his hand on her elbow, squeezing gently, letting her know she was not alone as she took deep breaths to calm the panic and fear welling up inside her.

Jormungand and Halvor stepped out of the crowd, her former council members flanking him. Asta, Arvid, and Ingvar eyed her warily, confusion clouding their faces. Clearly, Jormungand had kept their letter to himself and not told his new council members of their plan to challenge him.

He stood before them, his arms crossed over his chest, eyeing them. He smirked when he took her in, the crown on her head. It would be his crown by the end of the day if Skaldir didn't favor her. She swallowed hard before stepping forward. Maska and the other dragons stayed where they were, giving the Valdir space.

"So, the prodigal Queen has returned to her people," Jormungand said with a mocking tone.

The gathered crowd laughed nervously around him. He smiled, his blue eyes sparkling as he watched Kalina.

"The only problem is, they aren't your people anymore."

Silence fell over the crowd. Kalina cleared her throat. She knew she had only so much time to prove she was worthy of the crown.

"Yes, I abandoned you," she addressed her people, her voice ringing out. "But I returned because I knew I had made a huge mistake. Before, I thought that I was an outsider, that I didn't belong."

"And you were right." Jormungand tried to undermine her but she ignored his comment.

"But I returned because no matter where I came from, you are my people. I was so blinded by grief that I didn't see it at first, but now I see it all too clearly. So I have returned to challenge Jormungand for my throne, and if Skaldir favors me, I will rule you not as my subjects, but as my own family."

She finished, and there was a general shuffle and murmuring around the gathered crowd. Beside her, Leif smiled. She didn't have to win her people with speeches, she needed to win the coming fight.

"Jormungand, I formally challenge you to fight for the throne of the Valdir. May the most worthy fighter win."

She stuck out her hand for him to shake. Jormungand grinned then. He grabbed her forearm, his skin hot against hers.

"Let's begin."

His voice made her shiver.

Chapter 19

A DEPRESSION WAS CUT INTO THE EARTH, its sides carved with benches for seating, the center a flat expanse, a stage of sorts. Kalina stood at its center, the benches filling up around her, a buzz of chatter from the hundreds of silver-haired Valdir that lined the walls. Dragons and more of her people stood along the brim of the bowl, looking down. All eyes were on her and it made her want to run, the panic rising inside her in a crescendo until she could barely hear anything but her own heartbeat. But she was here for a reason and she wouldn't lose sight of her goal again.

Jormungand stood across from her, Halvor and Arvid by his side, all three of them eyeing her, trying to size her up, find a weak point. Arvid leaned towards Jormungand, a hand covering her mouth and spoke to him. He smirked, Halvor grinning beside him. Kalina swallowed hard and began focusing on her breath, hoping it would calm her racing heart.

Suddenly, a spear was shoved into her hand and someone grasped her shoulders roughly, turning her. Leif's face swam before her, helping to block out the sight of Jormungand stretching, his heavily muscled body on display. She was nothing, no match for such a man, and the thought of fighting him, to the death no less, terrified her beyond words.

"Kalina," Leif's voice cut through her disordered thoughts. She focused on his fierce, grey eyes. "You have to focus now. You can beat him. Do you hear me?"

She nodded numbly.

"Play to your strengths. Remember what my father taught you."

She finally looked at him sharply, her panic suddenly pushed to the background. Geir had taught her the basics until it was second nature. Arvid and Asta had been her teachers as well, but they had taught her spear and knife. Geir had taught her hand-to-hand, how to fall, how to be quick. Those were lessons that she could use against someone as big as Jormungand. She nodded at Leif, her anxiety settling into a hard rock in her stomach as she adjusted her grip on the spear.

Each fighter was allowed a spear, preferred among the Valdir, as well as a short sword and a knife. Kari strapped the latter around Kalina's waist and looked her queen in the eyes.

"You better come out the other side of this. I don't know who else I'd scream at until I turned blue."

Her words were meant as a joke, to lighten the moment, but they helped bolster Kalina as Kari left the area, joining Leif along the first tier of benches. Jormungand stepped forward. Both fighters wore the signature red leather armor of the Valdir, and it shone in the sun from overhead. Kalina was sweating despite the cool air as Jormungand began to circle her, forcing her to move.

She watched his feet closely, waiting for any telltale sign that he was going to make a move. Better to bide her time, let him tire himself attacking than to be the aggressor. Suddenly, with a slight shift of his feet he lunged at her, the spear outstretched to give him maximum reach. She leaned to the side, the tip of the spear brushing the edges of her leather vest, barely leaving a mark. He stepped back, his breath coming harder than before. He was testing her. She began to move, forcing him to circle this time.

She waited, circling, her spear held at the ready until once again he shifted his feet forward, the spear flying towards her. This time she ducked and rolled, the spear passing harmlessly overhead. He'd overextended once again, and as she came to her feet in a crouch, her own spear still clutched in her hand, he was within easy reach. She lashed out, the tip of her spear sinking deep into the flesh of his leg. He grunted and almost dropped his spear and she took his momentary distraction to dart away, putting distance between them again.

He gritted his teeth, almost snarling at her before running at her, limping slightly as he came on, as swift as a charging bull, his injury barely slowing him. Kalina had known he wouldn't make the same mistake twice so she was ready. She waited for him in a crouch, her spear at the ready. He yelled as he charged, his spear held in both hands before him, ready to impale her. She tensed as he came within striking distance and then danced out of the way, the spear slicing her side this time, drawing blood but not impaling her as he had intended. She spun and ended up behind him as he stumbled to a halt, her own spear at his back. He turned and knocked her spear aside, discarding his own as he moved towards her, almost too quickly for her to react. Suddenly there was a hand around her throat, and she was lifted bodily from the ground.

Kalina kicked frantically for a moment, desperate to make contact with some part of Jormungand's body as he held her there, his face twisted with rage and desperation. She was small compared to him, barely larger than a child. But she wasn't without defenses. She reached to her waist and pulled at the short sword, her fingers fumbling with the sheath. Finally it rang free, the blade giving her just enough reach. She stabbed out blindly, the edges of her vision beginning to go black as she tried in vain to suck in air. The blade hit something and Jormungand cried out, dropping her to the dirt. He doubled over, clutching his side where she'd stabbed him.

She gasped, drawing ragged breaths that seared her throat as she looked at him, down on one knee, clutching his side. She stood, brushing some errant strands of sweat soaked silver hair from her face, her own blue eyes hard on his as she approached, her sword held out, coming to rest against his throat. He winced as he straightened, his hand still clutching at his side.

The queen glared down at her subject, willing him into submission.

"Say it," she demanded.

He glared at her, hating the humiliation.

"Just kill me already." He spat at her.

She ignored the slight and pressed her blade harder into his throat, drawing a drop of blood.

"Say it loud."

His blue eyes were cold and full of an emotion she couldn't identify.

That's when she heard it, the distant screaming. Her head jerked up, as did Jormungand's to the sound coming from beyond the gathered crowd. In the first row, Leif whispered to Kari before racing up the stairs to the top, shoving people aside. Kari stayed, her brother beside her, watching Kalina and her opponent in the ring.

An arrow hit the ground beside Kalina and she jumped back, and for a moment, there was utter silence before chaos erupted. Her people began fleeing, most drawing their own weapons as a volley of arrows rained down upon them. Kalina thought fast and ran to a nearby discarded shield in a pile of weaponry and grabbed it. She used it to block the raining arrows as the screams became louder, some from Valdir and dragons alike.

Maska's big bulk landed in the depression beside her, followed by a huge red dragon. She glanced over and saw Jormungand climbing onto the dragon's back, his spear in his hand. She'd forgotten her spear but a bow and a quiver full of arrows was sitting beside the ring, waiting for some warrior to use. She grabbed them and leapt atop Maska. Jormungand was still bleeding, his face grey. He looked over at her and nodded. They had a job to do, to protect their people. Their own feud could wait.

Maska launched into the air above the battle that raged below them. The town of Windpost had been surrounded by an Ethean host. They had those deadly catapults on the edge of the city and were firing at buildings and dragons. Kari and Rangvald were already aloft but Kalina couldn't see Leif's golden dragon in the sky around them. She searched the field, spying Leif and Arikara fighting side by side on the ground, protecting a small group of women and children from the onslaught of Ethea's soldiers.

"There!" she cried out, pointing with her bow.

Maska dove, followed closely by the others. They landed with a boom that shook the ground, the soldiers scattering, sewing chaos for just a moment. Kalina leapt from Maska's back to join Leif, realizing a few moments later that Jormungand was beside her.

"Protect the children!" she yelled at him.

The man nodded and hoisted his spear, a grimace of pain crossing his face. Leif looked at her gratefully as they and their dragons formed a circle around the women and children, those who were not trained to fight. The soldiers charged, and for a while, Kalina didn't know how many she killed or how much time passed. She only knew that she fired arrows until there were no more, making sure each one met its mark. And then she swung her sword until her arm felt like it was going to fall off, the bodies falling around her. Beside her, Jormungand fought his hardest, his injuries slowing him down.

A soldier pushed past the man's defenses and Kalina saw him go down. She was already so tired she wasn't sure how much more she could fight, but she needed Jormungand to guard her left side, as Leif was guarding her right, so she plunged through the bodies to his side, slicing the enemy's soldier's throat and then reaching for

Jormungand's arm, hauling him to his feet. She put her arm under his shoulder, holding him up as he looked at her gratefully, his breath coming hot and hard against her cheek. She helped him limp towards his red dragon who had the women and children huddled under its outstretched wings. She lowered him to the ground beside his dragon and then turned, expecting to have to fight until she couldn't stand, but the battlefield before them was empty of opponents. Only the groaning and bloody bodies of those fallen in battle lay before her; the few standing Valdir, victorious.

A cheer rose from the Valdir and their dragons at their victory, but Kalina couldn't bring herself to cheer. She looked down, seeing the faces of the men and women who had died in the battle before her, their mangled bodies fallen across one another. It made her sick, and she turned to the side, vomiting into the dirt. This had been her first real battle. The last one had been fought on dragon back, and she'd felt removed from the action. But this time she'd seen their faces as they'd fallen, their humanity, and it made her stomach twist violently. She put a hand out to steady herself, finding the solid side of Maska before her. She wiped her mouth on her sleeve as she straightened and looked up at her brave dragon. His green scales were smeared with bright red blood, his own maw dripping with gore but his eyes were kind as he looked down on her.

"I'm glad you are alright, Littling."

He intoned, his deep voice spreading some measure of warmth deep into her bones. She leaned her head against him, heedless of the blood, and let his radiating heat seep into her.

"I'm not so sure I am," she whispered into his scales.

A tap on her shoulder made her turn and suddenly Leif was there, wrapping her in his strong arms. She clung to him, her breath coming in short, sharp gasps as she tried to hold herself together, even if just for a little while longer. But she was so exhausted she had no room for tears. Not yet.

"Your Majesty."

The words drew her away from Leif. Jormungand stood, one hand clutching his bloodied side, the other using his spear as a crutch to hold himself up. His red dragon stood behind him.

"Jormungand."

"They are yours, your Majesty," he said, genuine respect and admiration in his eyes now. "As am I."

He sank to his knees before her, bowing his head in reverence. Another crowd was gathering as they stood there.

"Tradition says you take his head," Kari whispered to her as she came to stand beside Kalina, her face smeared with blood, her hair coated in it. She shrugged. "But I've never much liked tradition." She grinned at her cousin and Kalina found herself grinning back.

"Rise, Jormungand." Kalina stepped forward, limping from the ache in her bones and the myriad of injuries she hadn't begun to take stock of. "I could use someone like you on my council, if you'll accept."

Jormungand's blue eyes widened.

"I need someone who has lived in the villages, who knows my people's hardships, and who isn't afraid to question me." She held his gaze. It took every ounce of strength she had left to do this, hoping she had just gained a powerful ally.

"I would be honored, your Majesty."

He bowed his head and then struggled to stand, grunting in pain. Kalina clapped him on the shoulder and then turned to the gathered people, fighters and villagers alike.

"We may have won this battle, but we haven't yet won the war. But I won't sit in that mountain any longer and watch as my people suffer. We will attack them where it hurts most. We will take back our kingdom and Ethea. Together, as one people."

A cheer went up at her words and Kalina's insides began to shake. She was completely exhausted but she smiled and waved before allowing Kari to help her to a still standing building. It took everything she had to walk upright through the door, but the moment it closed behind her, she collapsed to the floor.

Chapter 20

KARI HELPED HER QUEEN TO A CHAIR at a rough-hewn table, and Kalina sat with a grunt of pain. She winced as her cousin's deft fingers began to loosen the straps that held her leather armor in place and let out a sigh of relief when its weight was lifted from her shoulders.

But that's when Kari hissed. Kalina looked down, the cotton shirt she wore beneath the armor was soaked in red, spreading out from a wound in her side. She vaguely remembered Jormungand's blade slicing her side but she had thought it was just a flesh wound, not the gaping hole this felt like. Kari lifted her shirt and poured water on the wound washing away the blood and Kalina had to look away, her head swimming with pain.

The door to the little house banged open and Leif stood in the doorway, Jormungand close on his heels. Leif's eyes were full of concern as he entered, going to a knee before her and clutching her hands.

"Is it bad?"

Kalina wanted to laugh at the concern in his voice, but realized a laugh might not be appropriate in that moment. Perhaps the stress and strain of the last few hours were getting to her after all. She gritted her teeth as Kari inspected the wound.

"Not that bad. It's a bleeder, but not too deep. No organs damaged. I'll sew it up and she'll have another new scar!" She said this last part with delight, slapping Kalina on the back.

The breath whooshed out of her lungs and it took a moment to catch her breath as her cousin chuckled and began to sew the skin back together.

"How many did we lose?" Kalina asked through her teeth.

Leif's face fell as he stood and began to pace. Behind him, Jormungand sat heavily in a chair and began removing his own armor, placing it by the small fireplace. Kalina realized with a jolt that this must be his house, his home. And here she was, bleeding all over it.

"At first glance, maybe a hundred, perhaps more. This was a small raid, only five hundred men attacked with siege weapons."

He went quiet as he thought. Jormungand was trying to clean his own wounds but he spoke up.

"Perhaps it was a diversion. You moved the Emberweed, correct?" Leif paused briefly in his pacing as Kalina's heart rate shot up at the prospect of Ethea destroying their meager crop. But Leif waved a hand in dismissal.

"There's no way they know about that. Only a handful of people know where we planted it. But that's a good point. Either they are testing us, picking us off, or it's a diversion. But a diversion from what?"

Kalina thought while Kari finished the neat stitches in her side. It was now a dull ache, one that she could, with effort, shove to the back of her mind. She stood, motioning for Jormungand to take her place and let Kari sew his wounds as well.

"Where else would they attack-" she trailed off as horror flooded through her.

"The mountain," she and Leif exclaimed at the same time.

They had left with most of their small force of warriors, leaving Eira to keep the women, children, and elderly safe. It would be the perfect place to attack, while they were away.

"We have to get there. Now." She began to buckle her own armor back on, wincing as it put pressure on her wound. Leif put a hand on her arm, stopping her mid movement.

"Yes, but not you. You need to stay here. Stay safe."

His eyes were warm grey pools, holding her in place. But she deliberately removed her arm from his hand.

"I will not abandon my people. Not now when this is all my fault."

Jormungand stood, trying to pull his shirt back on.

"It's not your fault, my Queen. It's mine. If I hadn't challenged your rule, split our forces, and forced you into taking this action then we wouldn't be in this mess." He began to reach for his armor. "I'm coming with you."

Kari grabbed his hand and pulled him towards the small bed in the corner.

"Oh no you don't. You have lost a lot of blood. You need to rest. Leave the heroics to more able-bodied people." She grinned at him and grabbed her weapons off the table where she'd left them. "After you, your Majesty."

Kalina grinned back at her cousin, grateful that whatever bad feelings had been between them over her leaving were finally dissipating. Leif huffed in frustration but followed them out, giving a few orders to Rangvald who had just joined them.

Kalina limped to Maska's side, checking him over for any major wounds. Suddenly she felt guilty for not doing it sooner, but she would have known through the deep magic that bound them if he had been severely injured. She paused for a moment, pressing her forehead into his scaled side, breathing in the musty, wind-kissed scent of him, letting it ground her before pulling herself stiffly up into his saddle.

The village of Windpost had still been in war torn chaos when they'd left. But Leif had insisted that Jormungand and his second, Halvor stay to help their people pick up the pieces. As Kalina waited for her commander to give orders, she sat atop Maska and watched as her people dragged the bodies of Ethean soldiers into one giant pile, ready to light on fire. With a shock, she realized these were all her people, the Etheans and Valdir alike. She'd killed her own men on the battlefield. The thought made her sick. Not even the wind in her face, cooling the sweat that lingered on her skin helped remove the horror of what she had done.

Suddenly, more than ever, she wanted an end to this madness, this conflict, this war. She wanted to unite her people and take back the Ethean throne from its king. Her mother might even be grateful. She needed to talk to Eira once she was back about getting a message to her mother through Eira's contact in the castle. But first they needed to secure the mountain.

Four hundred Valdir flew with them south through the Wastes to the mountain. The sun was going down, setting the barren plains before them ablaze. If she hadn't been so utterly terrified of what they might find when they arrived, she would have thought it was the most beautiful sight she'd ever seen.

The sun had set by the time the mountain came into view, but they didn't need the sun's rays to see what was happening within the mountain. Light and fire blazed from every cave opening, shouts and the clash of steel rang out across the distance as they flew in. Kalina and Maska made for the entrance cavern at the top of the mountain. Beside her, Leif shouted orders for half their forces to land in the dragon's cave at the base of the mountain. Kalina was focused on landing and saving her people. The dragons couldn't navigate the small corridors so as soon as Maska's claws hit the stone, Kalina vaulted off, her spear held tightly in her grip.

"Go help the other dragons fight down below."

She sent him off, and he launched himself from the cliffside and dove. Her heart climbed into her throat at sending him off alone to fight, but she knew she didn't have a choice. Suddenly, the Valdir's decision to settle here, in a mountain with small corridors and spaces for enemies to hide, seemed ludicrous. The Valdir were meant to fight with their dragons, not alone.

Leif landed beside her; the entrance cave oddly quiet. Finally, the sounds of screaming drifted to them from down the corridors. Once a few dozen warriors had gathered beside her and Leif, she motioned for them to follow and then she led the way into the mountain, aiming for the main dining cavern.

The halls were dark but Kalina knew them like the back of her hand. She'd spent enough nights wandering them that she knew every nook and cranny, every hiding spot. Leif had sent some men down different corridors, splitting the forces to come at the Etheans from all sides. This was their territory, and they knew it better than anyone.

So, when the clash of weapons suddenly filled the passage, and the sound of running feet met them, Kalina motioned to the Valdir who melted into nooks in the walls and nearby rooms, effectively disappearing in the gloom. Bodies hurtled by, the ragged breathing and jangle of metal told Kalina these weren't the Valdir. They were Etheans with their metal armor. She stuck out her foot from her small alcove and tripped a soldier, the men behind him falling heavily to the floor, shouting at the one who had fallen. Someone lit a torch and as the fire blazed up, Kalina leapt from her hiding place, spear at the ready.

"For the Valdir!" she screamed, her people pouring from their hiding places and attacking the fleeing Etheans.

Within moments they were slaughtered, Kalina having run two men through with her spear before they stopped coming. And suddenly, the tunnel was quiet once again. She shoved down her disgust at slaughtering her own people and pressed on, wanting to find Eira.

Chapter 21

THE DINING CAVERN WAS FILLED WITH people, soldiers from each side clashing with one another. Kalina led her people into the fray, slicing left and right, a hoarse cry coming from her lips as she fought, searching the faces of the Valdir frantically for Eira. Surely, she would be here, with the majority of her people.

Finally she broke through to the other side of the chaos, the bathing chamber only a few dozen feet away through one of the many hallways that branched from this cave. She couldn't hear anything above the clash of weapons and screams of dying men and women behind her but she pressed on.

Steam rose from the dozens of pools cut into the rock as she entered the women's bathing chamber, making it hard to see. Bodies moved in the swirling darkness, the torches either extinguished or the Valdir hadn't had a chance to light them before they were attacked. Holes in the roof let in the occasional beam of dim moonlight, and in the darkness, Kalina began to feel exposed and alone. Neither Kari or Leif had followed her here, and she stood there alone. Fear crawled its way up her throat as she stood wrapped in the darkness, the steam making her lungs feel wet and heavy. Just when she thought she might turn and run out of the cavern; a hand alighted on her shoulder. She jumped and almost ran Leif through, but he stopped her blade, knocking it aside easily. He held a finger to his lips and pointed to the far side of the cave where Kalina's straining ears could now make out sounds of battle. Together they ran through the cave, avoiding the sunken, steaming pools until they were on the far wall. Past the door was a long hallway that led to many rooms beyond

Flickering lights played along the tunnel, and the clashing of many blades rang clearly. Kalina slunk down the passageway with Leif close on her heels. She wondered vaguely if two of them would be enough to fight off whatever force lay before them, but it didn't matter now, there was no time to go back. A large room opened onto their right where the fighting was coming from. Kalina slowly peered around the doorway before ducking back, breathing hard.

Leif looked at her questioningly. Kalina shook her head and reached up, pulling his head down so her lips were on his ear. His nearness made her shiver but she whispered urgently in his ear.

"Eira is in there with a few women and children. She's fighting off five men."

Leif nodded, drawing back, his eyes fixed on hers. For a heartbeat she thought he might kiss her, but then she took a step away, readying her sword. This wasn't the time or the place. She nodded to him and then she stepped through the doorway.

Eira was single handedly holding off five Ethean soldiers with a single Valdiran spear. She looked haggard and exhausted, her silver hair unbound from its usual braids, and blood dotted her face and neck. Kalina's heart swelled at the sight of her aunt and she rushed forward silently, taking the first soldier by surprise. Leif was hot on her heels and within a few moments, the two of them, with Eira's help, had dispatched the five men.

Eira threw an arm around Kalina, hugging her fiercely before letting her go. She handed her spear to a woman behind her before turning back to them.

"They came in just before sunset. We didn't have the men to run proper patrols so we didn't see them approaching. We were careless, thinking we were safe way out here in our mountain." She paused, catching her breath. "There are about two hundred of them. Now go, find the rest and take our home back."

She nodded to the door, and after braiding her hair back quickly, she took the spear back from the woman and stood before the women and children behind her. Kalina squeezed her aunt's arm before turning with Leif and running down the corridor, searching for more soldiers. She handed her own spear to the woman who'd been holding Eira's and drew her own short sword. She wished, not for the first time, that she had her twin axes. She turned to the woman who stood stoically beside her, her strong features cast into sharp relief by the flickering torchlight.

"What is your name?" Kalina asked.

"Hilde, your Majesty." The woman executed a short bow.

"Help Eira keep these people safe, Hilde."

Kalina clapped the woman on the shoulder before turning to nod to Leif to lead the way. Behind her, Hilde stepped up beside Eira, Kalina's spear clutched tightly in her fist. Most Valdir are taught to fight as young children, but not all continue to fight. Many went on to have other professions and specialties. Kalina briefly wondered what Hilde's profession was.

They worked their way down to the dragon hold, killing soldiers as they came upon groups of them throughout the mountain. When they entered the chamber from the stairway, they saw a pile of bodies in the middle of the floor, dragons arranged all around it. Maska was there and he came running over, his powerful muscles gleaming in the light from the torches that always burned along the walls. Kalina threw her arms around him, grateful and relieved he was alive and unharmed.

"What happened?" she asked as Arikara came over to join them.

Maska looked back over his shoulder at the bodies before lowering his huge head to her level.

"We found intruders in our nest. So, we destroyed them."

His deep voice rumbled through her, making her insides quake. She was exhausted, every inch of her so tired of fighting she could barely stand.

"Good." She barely managed to whisper. She put a hand out onto his warm scales, using him to hold herself up. Her side ached horribly, and it felt sticky. She was sure the stitches Kari had given her had been torn. She looked up and saw Leif's grey eyes watching her.

"We need to check the mountain, make sure they're gone." His voice was kind.

He knew how much he was asking of her. She nodded dully and followed him back up the long stairs.

They checked the gathering chamber and found dead Valdir and Etheans but no living enemy. They found the rest of their army gathered in the dining hall, most of the soldiers sprawled out on benches and tables, exhaustion written in every line of their bodies. She had asked so much of them. Today they had fought two battles, and many of their people had died. She couldn't just walk away without recognizing it.

As Leif began to organize food and water for the soldiers as well as the survivors, Kalina walked among her men, nodding to them, squeezing a shoulder or hand here and there, murmuring a thank you occasionally. She was so tired but this she forced herself to do. Finally, she made it through the group to where Kari sat against a wall, her spear broken beside her. She smiled grimly up at Kalina, and Kalina collapsed to the floor beside her, using the wall to help control her rather un-queen-like fall to the dusty earth.

Women of the Valdir walked around, offering food and water, and Kalina had to force her own hands to rise and accept them. Her muscles felt like lead. Leif stood before the group and began talking, thanking the men for their hard work and for saving their people but Kalina's eyes began to drift shut, and soon she was asleep against the wall.

She woke in her own bed, the mattress soft beneath her, the sun shining in through her window. She tried to sit up but hissed in pain, a hand going to her side. A fresh bandage encircled her side, her bloody clothing gone. She searched the room and found herself alone, but just as she was contemplating getting up, the curtain over her door flew aside and Eira entered, a tray in one hand and a stack of fresh clothing under an arm. She smiled tightly at Kalina as she set the tray on the nearby table.

"Good. I'm glad you are awake. We need to change your bandage."

Kalina scooted to the edge of the bed and allowed Eira to sit beside her. Eira took Kalina's arm and propped the elbow on her shoulder as she unwrapped her queen's bandages. Kalina's side was red and swollen, the angry slash freshly sewn closed. It was seeping a little blood which Eira gently washed away and applied a strong-smelling salve. It reminded Kalina of the salve they'd used on her feet when she'd walked through the hot coals. When she was re-wrapped Eira smiled again and reached over to the pile of clothing, handing Kalina a white, loose shirt.

"Are they waiting for me?"

"Yes. As soon as you are decent, they will come in. Jormungand arrived in the night with much of his village in tow."

Kalina looked up at her aunt, curiosity as a brief flash of fear ran through her. Was Jormungand there to beat her while she was down? Or was he there to support her? They had left so abruptly yesterday in the aftermath of the fighting that she wasn't sure she could be completely confident of his loyalty despite his declaration. But she nodded and pulled the shirt on, then reached for her pants. Once they were buttoned, she stood, wobbly on overly sore legs, and straightened her back.

"Let them in."

Chapter 22

KALINA STOOD ON THE EDGE OF the cliff, leaning against the red rock beside her, watching the sun set over the Wastes. Maska lay behind her, basking in the disappearing sunlight, his green scales reflecting a golden glow. His tail flicked back and forth lazily and Kalina looked at him over her shoulder, smiling. The council meeting had been a hard one. Jormungand had been as good as his word. He had brought his men back to the mountain, leaving Halvor to bring the rest of the Valdir home, while only a skeleton crew of soldiers stayed behind to tend what herds of cattle they had left.

Kalina was cautious of his support, but knowing he wouldn't let her run away again made her feel a bit more confident. She had allowed Asta, Arvid, and Ingvar back onto the council, but it made her skin itch when they spoke. She didn't trust them after they abandoned her but she realized that she had abandoned them first, and they had every right to leave. It bothered her that even after she returned, they had chosen to stay with Jormungand.

Kari had once again suggested they attack the king directly and take back the throne for Kalina, and she finally agreed with her cousin. But it wasn't a thing to celebrate. Her stomach twisted as she thought about her decision. Now the hard work would come. She felt like she barely had a hold on the Valdir, and now she was expected to somehow take over an entire kingdom, one with a large army and considerable resources. Besides, Askor to the north was loyal to the king, since he was its youngest prince. If she did by some miracle manage to take the crown, could she convince enough of the nobles and commanders to follow her? A long road stretched before her and she wasn't sure she was equal to the task but she would surely try. She owed her people that much.

Rocks skittered across the ground behind her as a boot scraped along the rock floor. Kalina tensed, turning to see who was behind her. Leif stood there, watching her, his muscular arms crossed over his chest. He smiled as she met his grey eyes and he approached, coming to stand beside her on the edge of the entrance cavern. She smiled, relaxing in his presence.

The setting sun glinted off a ring of golden dragon scales around Leif's wrist. It was something Kalina had never seen before and she impulsively reached out to touch it, taking his hand in hers. His hand was warm and calloused and she heard him suck in a breath as she held his hand, turning his wrist this way and that.

"Are these from Arikara?"

He nodded as she looked up, suddenly acutely aware of his nearness, and his eyes searching hers. She couldn't seem to forget the closeness of his body and breath the night before in the tunnel either. It was an effort to hold herself apart from him and not lean towards his warmth, his solid, reassuring frame.

"Her discarded scales. I was bored one day and decided to shoot one with an arrow. It bounced right off."

Her eyes went wide and she looked at Maska. She knew dragon scales were tough, as dragons rarely came out of a fight covered in cuts and slashes. Their wings however were often punctured. Maska raised his head, listening.

"I realized that perhaps we've been too hasty to give them away as a trade item. Our tough leathers stop most things, but what if we could have armor as tough as the Ethean's metal armor but lighter? That's the main reason we haven't used metal. It's too heavy for the dragons to carry, and too hard to move in. But dragon scales-" he grinned, taking the bracelet of scales off his wrist and showing her how easily it was manipulated and how light it was. "They can be manipulated and moved in any direction while still providing protection."

She looked up into his face, alight with passion and excitement. It was in that moment; she knew she felt more for him than just the friendship they'd been building for the last months. She wanted to see him this excited and happy all the time. She wanted to be the reason.

The scales were cool in her hand, like water made solid. She marveled at their lightness and movement. Could it really be possible?

"Leif," she breathed. "This is genius. Have you made anything else besides this?" She handed it back to him and he clasped it back onto his wrist.

"I'm working on a shirt but I don't always find all of Arikara's scales."

"Just walk around the dragon cave. I'd bet you'll find enough for a dozen shirts." He smiled.

"Yes, then it wouldn't look uniform." He looked out at the setting sun, a small smirk on his lips. "It wouldn't match Arikara."

Kalina let out a surprised and delighted laugh.

"You're worried it won't match your dragon?" He shot her an amused look.

"Yes, I know it's silly. But it feels important."

Kalina grinned but she thought she might understand. He'd look handsome in gold, his silver hair, a gold dragon scaled shirt, and golden Arikara beneath him. He'd strike a formidable figure on any battle field.

"Could you make me one?"

He looked at her, his eyes searching.

"Of course, my Queen."

She waved away the title. She both hated and loved when he got formal with her.

"How soon can you have one ready?"

He looked her up and down, as if measuring her. It made her flush and she looked down, suddenly self-conscious under his scrutiny.

"Give me a few weeks."

Her eyes snapped up.

"That fast?"

"You aren't that large, Kalina."

He gave her his half smile, his eyes sparkling. She noticed in the fading golden light that his grey eyes had a small ring of gold in the center, so faint you could only see it in a certain light. His gaze made her shiver slightly. He frowned.

"Are you cold? I can go get you a blanket."

She straightened, embarrassed that he'd noticed her reaction.

"Just the wind."

It wasn't really a lie. Fall was settling over the Wastes and the wind that whistled around the mountain was cold. Leif left a few minutes later to get dinner and meet with Rangvald a few minutes later to discuss moving the herds into the mountain. Kalina went over and sat down against Maska's warm scales, running her hands over their smooth surface. It surprised her that they hadn't thought to use the scales as armor. Some scales, like those along Maska's sides and underside were almost as large as her hand, but those along his tail, legs, neck, and face were smaller, ranging in size down to the size of her smallest fingernail.

"How often do you shed?" she asked Maska, suddenly curious.

"We shed our scales every few months. We never have the same scales for long. But if scales are damaged, they shed faster."

Her eyebrows rose at this revelation. She had no idea that Maska shed his scales that often, but then again, she'd never had a reason to pay attention. She relaxed back once again.

As night closed in, she began to doze, content in the warmth radiating from Maska's side after hours sunbathing. The stress of the last few days melted away as she enjoyed the cold breeze on her face and his warmth behind her. Maska rumbled a purr.

Light blazed through her closed eyes and she felt Maska shifting beneath her as the sound of running feet reached her. She opened her eyes groggily, a bit annoyed at being disturbed. She'd been having a lovely dream about flying on Maska through a star flecked sky.

"Kalina!" Kari's voice was breathless, her torch held high, its flickering light casting long shadows.

"What is it, Kari?" she said, standing slowly, stretching stiff muscles. Her side pulled sharply and she winced, letting out her breath in a whoosh.

"Come quickly. We've found something."

Chapter 23

KALINA FROWNED BUT FOLLOWED HER cousin out of the entrance cave, glancing back at Maska who stood as well. He watched her go and she shrugged, not for the first time sad that he couldn't join her in the smaller caverns and hallways of the mountain.

Kari led her down the halls until they were before the door to her rooms. She paused, putting a hand out to stop Kalina from entering. Kalina frowned, confused.

"Kalina. The patrols we sent out to make sure the King hadn't sent anymore forces found someone wandering the Wastes." Kalina opened her mouth to speak but Kari held up a hand, her normally smirking face serious. "It was your mother, the queen."

Kalina's stomach felt like the floor had dropped out from beneath her. She shoved past Kari and threw aside the door covering. The room was brightly lit, and a group of people stood over her bed. She strode forward, ignoring the hands of Leif and Eira attempting to stop her, to slow her down. She pushed aside her council members until she stood over the figure lying on her bed.

Her mother Cherise's blonde hair was dark with dirt and grime, twigs and leaves stuck throughout it. Her beautiful face was drawn and thin, too thin, for beneath her torn and dirty dress, her pregnant belly stretched. Her eyes were closed and she breathed heavily and deeply, clearly in a fitful sleep. Kalina sank to her knees, taking her mother's frail hand.

Her council stood behind her, the silence in the room heavy with unsaid words. Finally, Leif murmured and they all left, leaving her alone with her mother and Eira, who sat on the other side of the bed. Kalina's eyes pricked with tears, her audience finally gone. She felt like her chest was going to cave in at the sight of her mother, but another, smaller part of her was ecstatic that her mother was here, with her.

"What happened to her?" she said, her voice barely a whisper.

"When the King found out she was pregnant with his child, he locked her away. My contact in the castle wasn't sure if it was to keep the baby alive for fear she would kill it, or if it was just another effort to control her."

Kalina nodded. It almost didn't matter what the reason. Her

mother had suffered enough at the hands of that man and now she was finally free.

"Did you know about this?" She gestured to Cherise's prone body, the state it was in. Eira shook her head sadly.

"Alexil didn't know what had happened to her until it was too late."

Kalina's eyes shot to her aunt.

"Alexil? The scholar?"

Eira nodded solemnly.

"He was my friend once upon a time. And he was a particular friend of your mother's." Her tone was soft.

Kalina looked back at her mother's face. She barely knew this woman, and the foreign feeling made her stand and drop her mother's hand.

"I knew him," she said as she began to pace the room, thoughts racing through her mind.

"Yes," Eira agreed. "And he knew who you were the moment he met you."

Kalina looked quizzically at Eira.

"Did he tell you?"

Eira shook her head.

"He didn't want to give me false hope. He told me later, once you'd left to find the dragons."

"What did he do to her?" Kalina's voice was barely a whisper as her eyes roamed over her mother's face.

"He is not a nice man. He abused her for years, always trying to undermine her authority in council. Alexil wrote to me of how often she came to him for council. He advised she leave, or even, have him killed, but she refused. I don't know the reasons why exactly."

Kalina was confused and torn. She didn't know how she was supposed to feel with her mother, the Queen of Ethea, now here in her mountain and the king all alone on the throne of Ethea. She had suspicions that the king was conniving, and manipulative. Why had her mother run? Was he more abusive than Kalina had originally thought? Why hadn't her mother fought back? Disgust ran through her.

"Tell me when she wakes."

And then she turned, leaving her mother in the capable hands of her aunt. Nervous energy ran through her and she wasn't quite sure what exactly she wanted but she needed some sort of release. Perhaps flying on Maska would get rid of the itch that seemed to crawl beneath her skin.

Leif was in the dragon caves, spending time with Arikara and updating her and Maska on the situation. Kalina almost walked right past him, ignoring him altogether but he snagged her arm, pulling her up short. She almost wrenched her arm from his hold, anger boiling up within her. She wasn't even sure why she was angry. Angry at the king for his mistreatment of her mother. Angry at the world for her losses. She wanted to lash out but his calm eyes and cool touch stopped her in her tracks.

"Kalina."

Hearing him say her name caused goosebumps to raise on her arm. Suddenly, the months of tension that had been building beneath her skin turned to electricity and she looked up into his storm grey eyes. He seemed to feel it too, because he turned and pulled her close, their bodies touching and their breaths intertwining. Kalina's heart began to race, and the pull she'd felt towards him since the moment she'd met him became overpowering. She reached one hand up and slid it behind his head, cupping the back of his neck.

His breaths began to come faster as she touched him and his hands tightened on her waist. She took a sharp breath in before standing on her tiptoes and pressing her lips to his. At first the kiss was soft, sweet, but soon, the electricity crackling between them, it became deep and passionate. She opened her mouth for him and suddenly she couldn't get enough of him. She wanted every piece of this man who had supported her since the beginning, who had been unwavering even when she had doubted everything about herself.

It was several minutes before they broke apart, shaky and laughing softly. Kalina's heart was slowly calming down, the anxious energy finally dissipated. She touched her lips softly, surprised at their swollen feel. She wanted more from him, so much more, but knew it would be a mistake to ask for it tonight. She still had too much to deal with, too much before her to complicate it further.

She stepped away from him, smiling softly, his grey eyes

following her as she went to Maska and climbed onto his back without a saddle. He climbed onto Arikara and together they flew from the cave into the cold night air, their only warmth the memory of their kiss and the dragons beneath them.

Chapter 24

CHERISE WOKE THE NEXT DAY. Kalina was in the training chamber practicing her archery when Kari came to fetch her. Kalina took her time putting her bow away, dread filling her at the prospect of speaking to her mother. She didn't entirely know why. This was her mother, a woman she was supposed to love and care about but all Kalina could see was a coward. She stopped at the kitchen and took a tray of food with her when she went back to her own rooms.

Cherise was sitting in bed, her face and hair freshly washed and combed out, a shining halo around her head in the early morning sunlight that filtered in through the window. Kalina forced a small smile when she entered and set the food on the bed beside her mother. Cherise held out a hand and Kalina took it hesitantly, sitting down beside her.

"Kalina. So good to see you again." She squeezed Kalina's hand and some slight warmth spread through Kalina.

"As it is to see you, Mother." She hesitated on the last word, almost not saying it. Cherise noticed and winced slightly.

"Ahh, yes. That. I am your mother, Kalina. And I'm sorry I couldn't tell you before."

Kalina looked down at their entwined hands.

"But you have to understand, I was trapped between a rock and a hard place."

Kalina shook her head, frowning.

"Why didn't you leave him? Why didn't you have him killed? Anything?" she asked desperately, finally looking up into her mother's blue-green eyes. Cherise's face turned sad, and she smiled sadly at her daughter.

"When it all began, I thought he was nice enough. It wasn't until he had sunk his claws in that I began to realize he wasn't the Prince I'd married. And when he began to control me, he'd already paid off all my guards and maids and I wasn't allowed any close friends." She reached up and stroked a few of Kalina's stray silver hairs. "And then you don't know how to get your own power back. You feel useless and alone. I didn't think I had the strength to defy him."

"But you could have had your father do something when he was alive." Kalina was grasping for something, anything to put the blame on her mother but the anger within her was slowly unraveling.

"My father was many things, but he was not assertive with my husband." Cherise sighed. "He had a country depending on him, and he couldn't risk angering Askor to the north. He was stuck as well." She smiled again and squeezed Kalina's hand. "I wish I had been strong enough to insist I marry your father, or that I had had the guts to leave with him when he asked. But I was young and scared and didn't want to leave the life I had always known." She went quiet and Kalina studied her mother's face, a new sort of understanding growing inside her.

"Then why are you here now?"

"Because of you, my girl. My husband, King Terric, locked me in my rooms, insistent on my never leaving my bed once he found out I was pregnant. He stationed guards outside my door all day and night. But I knew about the back exit and a secret passage between our rooms. I would pace it at night and listen to his conversations with his council members. I heard him and Sir Gregan in conference one night discussing the war with you and your people."

Kalina shivered at the mention of Sir Gregan's name. She remembered all too well him chasing her across the kingdom and how many times he had almost caught her.

"I heard him say he was planning to attack your villages and then attack your mountain while you were distracted, killing all your people. His entire goal has been to wear you down, thin you out until you and your people are too weak to attack him. So, I left. Hopeful I could make it here in time to warn you." She shrugged helplessly. "But it seems I was too late." A tear leaked out and slid down her cheek as her voice cracked. Kalina leaned forward to wipe it away.

"But you made it here, and now you are out of his clutches. We plan to act quickly and take him down. Soon you will be back on the throne, without him to govern you."

Her own heart leapt at the realization that with her mother here, with her, she could easily set her up as queen once again after she'd taken the crown. She realized with horror that she'd never really considered her mother's feelings or life in any of her plans. She vowed to do so in the future. But her mother was shaking her beautiful head, her eyes sadder than ever.

"And as soon as I have given birth I will take over as Queen."

Kalina looked down at her mother's swollen belly.

"How long?"

"A few weeks, if that." Cherise smoothed a hand over her belly, a gesture Kalina knew all too well. She remembered Calla, the woman who'd taken her in in Ravenhelm, sitting by the fire, her feet up on a chair, smoothing her hand over her belly. She smiled softly at the fond memory. Cherise smiled back at her.

"There is plenty to talk about. Perhaps after I've eaten and taken a nap we can talk with your council?"

Kalina nodded and patted her mother's hand.

"Of course." She stood, about to leave her mother alone.

"Later, I'd like to hear about you."

Kalina smiled and left the room. Her heart was calmer than before. At least she understood why her mother had never left, even if she didn't agree with it. And having her mother here, after her father's loss, was a balm she hadn't known she needed. The anger at King Terric had grown, however, and all she could think about was riding into Ravenhelm and settling her axes into his spine.

Thinking about her axes made her travel to the armory, searching for new ones. She hadn't replaced the ones she'd lost in Amberharbor. The armory was a large room off the training cavern that held all manner of weapons and was run by a man named Skaldrik. He had huge arms, and he told her that when they lived in the mountains, he'd had a forge that burned day and night, and allowed him to make the most beautiful weapons. Now, he was stuck repairing old ones. With no regular fuel to burn besides pitch for torches and what little wood they had going to the kitchens, new weapons were a luxury the Valdir couldn't afford.

Kalina entered, her hands behind her back as she wandered the walls, searching for a new pair of axes to swing. Skaldrik stood from his place by the door and followed her around, his gruff demeanor something she found oddly comforting. That was when she caught sight of a familiar face sitting at a table in the corner polishing a short sword.

"I didn't know you worked here, Hilde," Kalina said as she approached the woman.

Hilde gave her a tight smile and gestured to Skaldrik.

"Skaldrik is my husband."

Kalina looked to the huge gruff man and noticed the softening of his eyes as he looked at his wife. Kalina had to hide her smile.

"Glad to know you are in such good hands, Skaldrik." Kalina patted the huge man on the upper arm, which was as high as she could reach, before turning back to perusing the walls of weapons.

"How about these?" She pointed to two smaller axes hanging crossed on the wall. He grunted and took them down, handing them over to her.

"They aren't what I'd make for you, but they'll do in a pinch," he grumbled.

She raised an eyebrow at him while she swung the blades, feeling their balance and weight.

"Oh? And what would you make me?"

He grunted again and stalked across the room to a wooden crate. He had a small stack of papers there, as well as a quill and a bottle of precious ink. Kalina followed him curiously, still swinging the axes through the air slowly.

"I'd make you such blades that anything else you ever wielded would feel like a child's toy." He handed her a rough sketch drawing of twin axes, their blades shaped differently than any she'd seen except in ancient drawings of Valdir weaponry. They were double sided, their blades long and wide and covered in Runark, like the tattoos that covered her face and the faces of most adult Valdir. They were perfect. Kalina grinned at him over the sketch.

"They're perfect. What do you need to make them?" She handed the page back.

Skaldrik took the drawing and tucked it away, his face a permanent scowl.

"A proper forge. Nothing we have here."

Kalina nodded and looked at the other twin axes. She held them up.

"These are good enough. Thank you, Skaldrik."

"My pleasure, your Majesty."

The big man bowed to her, making her feel strange. Among the Valdir, bowing was not common. Her subjects rarely bowed, except to show the deepest respect. It touched her that he felt that way about her. She smiled at him awkwardly and took her axes from the cavern.

Chapter 25

KALINA HAD SLEPT THAT FIRST NIGHT on her couch but tonight she knew she couldn't stay there. Tonight, she'd go spend the night with Maska down in the dragon cavern. Having her mother here was great, but she had grown used to having her own space, her quiet time and now suddenly she had someone who wanted to talk with her every moment. She needed some quiet time with Maska, who never asked her to talk unless she wanted to.

Kalina's council met in a smaller chamber, since her mother was still recuperating in her own rooms. She smiled to herself while her council members spoke around her. They'd been going around and round for an hour about the best way to attack the capital. Kalina and Leif had agreed on a plan, but Jormungand and Kari disagreed. Jormungand and her cousin had looked at each other with wary respect when they realized this fact and Kalina had to hide her smile. Perhaps the two of them were well matched and could be friends.

Suddenly, the door flap was pushed aside and one of Leif's officers stepped into the chamber.

"Pardon the intrusion, your Majesty, but there is news."

Kalina stood with her council members.

"What is it, Bjorn?" Leif asked.

"There's a messenger."

"Let them in." Kalina said, motioning.

The council members all sat once again, waiting. Bjorn disappeared for a moment before returning with a familiar face. Nash stood in the doorway. Kalina gaped at him before walking forward. He smiled tightly at her and embraced her as she reached for him.

"Nash! I didn't think you'd come back."

She stepped back and held the man at arm's length. He shrugged, his green eyes darting around the room, taking in each face.

"Is there a place we can speak in private?"

Kalina frowned.

"This is my council. Whatever news you have, I'm sure they must hear."

He nodded and stepped forward to address them all while Kalina went back to her chair at the head of the table. He cleared his throat awkwardly before speaking. Kalina wondered at his strange

379

demeanor. This wasn't the Nash she'd left a few months ago back in Amberharbor.

"After our Queen left me in Amberharbor I was captured by King Terric's men." His declaration was met with utter silence, the entire council chamber in utter shock at his words.

Finally, it was as if some spell broke the tension building in the room and everyone began talking at once, questions firing at Nash faster than he could answer. But Kalina raised a hand and everyone went quiet, looking to her.

"How did you escape?"

The most important question. Nash finally made eye contact with her.

"He let me go."

Kalina sat across from him and frowned. Kari, who sat on her left, seemed a ball of energy, full of questions. Kalina laid a hand on her cousin's arm. To her right, Leif spoke up.

"Why?"

Nash seemed to rock forward on his toes, as if getting ready to run.

"For this."

His hand whipped forward, and a flash of silver spun through the air. Kalina barely had time to gasp before something thudded into her and knocked her to the floor. Chaos erupted in the chamber as she lay there, trying to comprehend what had just happened. Leif was immediately by her side, as was Rangvald. That was when Kalina realized that the thing that had knocked her down, that was keeping her pinned to the floor, was Kari. Rangvald gingerly pulled his sister off of his queen, and Kalina sat up with Leif's help.

That's when she saw the dagger sticking out of Kari's right shoulder. It was in deep, up to the hilt, blood seeping through her shirt. But Kari was awake, her eyes wide in anger and shock. Kalina's head whipped around, searching the room for Nash, and when she found him, he was held between Ingvar and Arvid, Jormungand behind him, a knife pressed to his throat.

"Wait!" Kalina cried out. "Don't kill him."

Jormungand looked up in disbelief but took a step back. Kalina struggled to her feet, briefly pressing a hand to Kari's back in gratitude. Leif never left her side as she walked towards Nash. She was actively trying to hold back tears of anger and betrayal, but she had to stay calm. When she was face to face with him, she searched his green eyes, finding only pain and sadness there.

"Why?" she asked him again, her voice barely above a whisper. Nash's face crumbled and he sagged in his captor's arms.

"They have her. They have my Sitala."

His voice broke on her name and suddenly Kalina understood. She swallowed the lump in her own throat and the panic that threatened to crawl its way out and nodded to Ingvar and Arvid, Bjorn standing behind them in the doorway, shocked.

"Take him away and lock him up."

They dragged him from the room with Jormungand, Asta, and Bjorn on their heels. Nash cried out, calling for Sitala, begging to see her, begging for forgiveness. Kalina squeezed her eyes shut, digging her fingernails into her palms and focusing on the pain there. Why hadn't he stabbed her when she'd first hugged him? He had seemed in shock when she approached him but Kalina couldn't figure out why. Leif placed a hand on her shoulder, his gentle heat spreading through her. She longed to turn and bury her face into his chest and let herself fall apart but now was not the time. She took a shuddering breath and turned back to the room where Rangvald had helped his sister into a chair and was removing the blade.

Kalina went to her cousin's side and took her hand. Kari looked at her fiercely and for the first time, Kalina realized just how much this woman felt for her. Kari was truly her friend, willing to take a blade for her, willing to die for her. And with a small jolt, Kalina realized she felt the same way.

"Thank you, Kari. Words are not enough to express my gratitude."

She tried to make her feelings known through her touch and her eyes. Kari smiled and then gritted her teeth as Rangvald began wrapping her shoulder with a bandage. Eira came forward then, taking Kari's hand and helping her to stand.

"Let's go get you fixed up, my darling."

And then she took her daughter out of the room, her son trailing behind and leaving Kalina standing alone with Leif. She turned to face him.

He stepped forward, his arms going around her and she melted into him. As her arms wrapped around his muscled torso, she realized she could feel him shaking and she drew back for a moment, looking up into his handsome face.

"I thought-" he trailed off and then cleared his throat. "I thought you were dead."

Kalina nodded silently and pulled him close once again. She let a bit of her fear and anger out in a small sob. She was so incredibly lucky. If the dagger had flown true it would have hit home, in the center of her chest. She had come so close to dying and suddenly all she wanted to do was live.

"Come with me."

She wiped her eyes with one hand and took Leif's other and led him from the cave and down the darkened hallways.

They came out into the dragon's cave where she made a beeline for their dragons who were lying side by side. Kalina woke Maska gently, placing her head against his. She whispered to him of what happened and felt his frustration and anger at the fate of Nash and Sitala. As much as they hadn't been good matches for her and Maska, they had been their friends. Kalina and Leif put their saddles on their dragons and then mounted up. Together Maska and Arikara launched them into the air and out of the cavern, the wide-open expanse of the Wastes opening before them.

Kalina was tempted to just keep flying until they were far away from here. But the last time she had tried to run from her problems they had resulted in Nash being captured and then trying to kill her. So instead, she lost herself in Maska's aerial acrobatics, the setting sun and cold air stinging her face and taking away the fear that had been consuming her and making her heart race in exhilaration. Leif and Arikara frolicked beside her, savoring the joy of their queen and her mount.

Chapter 26

KALINA SPENT HER DAYS WITH KARI when she wasn't with
her mother, keeping her company while she healed. With Kari she
plotted revenge on the king, the various ways in which they would
kill him. It put a grin on Kari's face and was an outlet for Kalina's
anger. She trained in the evenings with Leif, working hard until her
side no longer pulled in pain and she once again felt strong. She still
slept in the dragon's cave but now Leif joined her and together they
would curl up side by side, their dragons around them in a protective
ring. She hadn't slept so well in months.

A few weeks after the attack, when Kari was in the training yard
with her, working slowly and carefully with her shoulder, Eira came
to find Kalina. When she had finished her sparring session with Leif,
sweat pouring down her face, she walked over, meeting Eira halfway.

"Aunt." She wiped her arm across her forehead, smearing the
sweat. "Is everything alright?"

Eira smiled and reached out, tucking a stray piece of Kalina's
silver hair behind her ear.

"You do look like your mother, you know." Kalina smiled.

"She asked for you this morning."

Eira walked with Kalina from the training cave and into the
darkened hallways. With winter descending, the mountain was
cooling off. Hallways and caverns that used to be humid with heat
were now chill. The drying sweat on Kalina's skin made her shiver.

"I'll go right after I bathe. I'll bring her dinner."

Eira nodded in satisfaction and squeezed Kalina's arm.

"Good."

An hour later Kalina stood outside her rooms, a tray of food in
her arms. She took a deep breath before pushing aside the door
covering and entering. Cherise was sitting up in bed, her beautiful
blonde hair braided to the side, like the Valdir wore theirs.

"Hello, mother."

The title still felt foreign on Kalina's lips. She had been an
orphan for so long, and she'd known about her parents for so short a
time, she still wasn't used to addressing someone as the title mother
or father. Her heart sank at the reminder that she would never see
her father again. Cherise smiled broadly and held out a hand for her

daughter.

Kalina searched Cherise's face when she sat beside her. Her mother had filled out a tiny bit since she'd arrived, finally eating food, and Kalina could see that they did share certain facial features. Kalina had her father's blue eyes, and high cheekbones, but she had her mother's softer brow, straight nose, and full lips. Her mother's green eyes sparkled with joy at seeing her daughter.

"How have you been feeling?" Kalina asked.

They had talked about her past, and she had told her mother about most of her life, but she still felt like she still barely knew her.

"Better. Eira has been taking great care of me. Strange, to think that in another life, she would have been my sister."

She smiled sadly, before dropping her gaze to the tray of food Kalina had brought. She reached forward and grabbed a small, shriveled apple.

"Oh, I love apples!"

"Me too."

Kalina took another of the apples and bit into it. It was a bit sour, but it was full of juice which ran down her chin. She wiped it away, struggling to figure out what she wanted to ask her mother. She remembered the last time they'd eaten apples together, in the garden at Ravenhelm Castle where they'd first met.

"Tell me about you and my father." She asked finally.

Her mother paused mid-bite and smiled.

"That's an easy question. Let me see, where do I begin?"

"When did you first meet?"

Kalina relaxed back onto the end of the bed and watched her mother's face as it brightened. She smoothed her hand over her huge belly and sighed.

"It was the beginning of summer and I was rushing down the hall because my father had asked me to come greet the King of the Valdir. But I spilt tea all over my dress and had to change so I was late. I was passing the council chambers, hoping they were still in the entrance hall, and straightening my skirt when I ran smack into your father." She paused and laughed at the memory. She looked over at her daughter at the end of the bed. "He helped me up and was gracious and kind. We got to talking about our people and he told me what it was like to be the Prince of the Valdir. Over the next few weeks we spent every moment that we possibly could together. He introduced me to Kaya, his dragon and even took me flying. My father did not like that." She paused again with a small laugh.

Kalina cleared her throat.

"What made him decide to break your engagement?"

Cherise smiled sadly.

"Well, there was only a verbal agreement with Hakon's father that we should wed. The agreement had been made when Hakon and I were born, during the middle of the war, and then when we were old enough, his father came to the capital to solidify the marriage but my father refused. Askor had already been sniffing around, looking for a way to end the war and my father wasn't sure what was the best course of action. So, after he realized that Hakon and I were falling in love, he knew he needed to make a decision."

"And he decided to marry you off to the Askorian Prince?" Kalina said, bitterly. She wouldn't have been raised an orphan if her parents had been allowed to wed. She blamed her grandfather for that.

Cherise reached out and patted her daughter's hand.

"Don't blame your grandfather. He didn't feel he had a choice. The war was taking a huge toll on the Valdir and our people. Our resources were dwindling, and Askor was harrying our coast, so trade ships weren't getting through from other countries. He made a tough decision."

Kalina still frowned. She understood it, but it wasn't fair. It wasn't fair she'd been deprived of love and affection. But there was nothing she could do to change the past.

"I just can't believe he forced you into a marriage with a man like Terric."

Cherise looked down at her baby bump, a sad smile on her lips.

"One day, Kalina, you may understand the importance of a political marriage. Before I even knew I was pregnant with you, my father sat me down and told me his reasons. I knew I had a duty to my people above all else, so I agreed to the marriage. As Princess of Ethea, and Queen of the Valdir, you too may find yourself in a situation where you must decide between a man you love and a political alliance." Her eyes were serious as she watched her daughter.

Kalina shifted uncomfortably. She had never really thought of that possibility. Surely, she wouldn't be forced to marry someone from another country just for political gain? The war with Askor was over and once she took back her kingdom, or rather, her mother's kingdom, the war between the Valdir and the Etheans would be over and she would be free to marry whomever she wished. A vision of Leif in a white suit swam before her and she had to hastily shake her head to dispel the image. Finally, Cherise patted the bed up by her head.

"Come, let's think about something happier. Any ideas of what I should name your little brother?"

"How do you know it is a boy?"

Cherise winked at her daughter with a cunning smile.

"I just know, my darling."

Kalina grinned and moved up the bed to sit beside her mother. Together, they spent the next hour discussing different names for her half-brother.

Chapter 27

KALINA WAS IN THE DRAGON CAVERN, spending quality time with Maska discussing the events of the last few days, when Jormungand came running down the stairs. He burst out of the tunnel and into the cavern, heaving breaths. Kalina stood, one hand on Maska's side. She wasn't sure if she was restraining him or reassuring him but Maska was suddenly tightly wound beside her. After the events of the last few months, Kalina didn't know what to expect.

The man was doubled over for a second, catching his breath but finally he straightened, his silver hair a bit disheveled.

"My Queen," he huffed out. "We just got word from the mountains. Askorian ships have been spotted on both the west and eastern coasts. They are heading south."

Kalina's blood ran cold and she looked sideways at Maska. For a few moments, she wasn't sure what to do but finally she motioned for Jormungand to join her.

"Come. I'll fly you up to the top of the mountain and we will call a meeting."

Together they climbed onto Maska's back and the green dragon launched himself into the air, skimming just over the heads of the other dragons and out into the sky. Cold air hit her like a wall and Kalina was momentarily gasping for breath. Winter was here and, soon, the Wastes would be covered in frost every morning. When Maska landed in the entrance chamber, Kalina had formed the outlines of a plan.

"Call the council. Immediately."

She snapped out the order to Jormungand who nodded and raced off as Kalina strode towards her rooms. There she helped her mother out of bed and into a dressing robe and then to a chair at the table. Just as they sat, her council members began to arrive. Kalina gave Leif a meaningful look and together they stepped off to the side.

Kalina laid out her plan to him, eager for his input. He scratched the silver stubble on his chin for a moment before answering, his face deadly serious.

"It could work. But you'd be asking people to die."

Kalina clenched her jaw and nodded.

"We'll ask for volunteers then. I'm done playing safe."

Leif nodded, and they turned to rejoin the group. Kalina gestured for Jormungand and Rangvald to report.

"We set up an early warning system all along the Great Grey Mountains as you asked. Its purpose was to let us know if anything was happening on our coasts," Rangvald explained.

Jormungand jumped in.

"We just got word that Askor has sent two fleets of ships, one down each coast and we think they are coming here. I would hazard a guess that they are planning to come at us in a pincer movement, from both sides."

Rangvald nodded beside the man. There was a general murmur around the room.

"We can't stay here. We must leave. We are so few already." Asta objected, her eyes wide in fear.

It was the first time Kalina had seen fear on the warrior's face and it scared her, right down to her bones. Panic began to rise, but beside her, Leif noticed her stiffening posture and reached a hand below the table, squeezing her knee. Kalina slowed her breathing and focused back on the task at hand, the plan she had formulated. She let her breath out and stood.

"Then we flee. We take the women and children and those too old to fight into the mountains. We send them with the majority of our forces. But we leave a skeleton crew here, enough to draw Ethea and Askor in and encourage them to fight. Then while they are distracted, fighting, we infiltrate the capital and take the throne for my mother, and then use Ethea's military to drive the Askorians out."

Asta, Arvid, Ingvar, and Jormungand looked at her with renewed respect. Eira frowned, but Kari let out a small cheer. It was what she'd been pushing for all along.

"But who do we ask to stay?" Rangvald piped up, ever the calm negotiator. "It would be asking them to go to their deaths."

Kalina nodded gravely.

"We ask for volunteers. I won't force my people to fight a battle they know they can't win."

Jormungand stood suddenly.

"I volunteer, my Queen." He was always so formal with her. "I will stay here and lead whatever soldiers choose to remain behind."

Kalina nodded to him in thanks. Asta beside him stood as well. "I will stay too, my Queen."

Kalina was taken aback. This meant that the woman respected her.

"Good. We must begin the evacuation tonight. Rangvald, I'm placing you, Kari, and Eira in charge of getting our people to safety in the mountains. Leif, you and I will go with Asta and Jormungand to ask for volunteers. The rest of you, help where you can." She dismissed them and they filed from the room.

They gathered their soldiers in the gathering cavern, the space becoming crowded with bodies as they filed in. Kalina and Leif stood on the rock formation that her father had stood on when she had walked through fire for her initiation. Word had spread like wildfire about the evacuation, and the Valdir fighters before her were restless with anxiety. She cleared her throat when Jormungand nodded to her that they were all present.

"Valdirans. We have asked you all to gather here for a reason. Our home, this mountain, our people are being threatened. We must protect them. But we have two paths ahead of us, one more dangerous than the other." She paused, unsure of how to continue, how to convince these men to give up their lives for her plan.

Leif stepped up beside her and continued.

"As you all have heard, we are evacuating the mountain. We are sending our people back into the Great Grey Mountains, to hide and, hopefully, to settle. Askor is coming, and they will attack us within the next few days, probably with the whole of Ethean's forces beside them. This is our opportunity to get back at them. Most of our forces will go to the mountains to protect our people. But we will need a force to remain here, under the command of Jormungand and Asta." He gestured to the two people before them. "This force will draw the armies in, force them to fight on our ground, and take out as many as possible."

He paused, and Kalina cleared her throat.

"While a force fights here, I will be leading a force into the capital of Ravenhelm, while their armies are busy, and I will take back the Ethean throne."

People began talking around the cavern. Kalina didn't blame them. She was asking them to make an impossible decision. One man in the audience piped up.

"So, you're asking us to die here while you take the capital?"

Kalina nodded.

"I am asking you to make a sacrifice for your people. Not for me. Volunteering to stay here and fight might mean death, but it will ensure your people make it to safety, and it will give us our best hope to end this war and take back a throne that belongs to us. It will allow peace to reign once again."

She hoped her own desperation didn't enter her voice but she was too emotional to tell.

The murmuring around the room continued and Kalina clenched and unclenched her jaw, waiting for an answer. Leif stood stoically beside her. Jormungand stepped into the crowd, closely followed by Asta and together they began making their way around the cavern, stopping to talk to people here and there. Finally, a hush fell over the group and a man stepped forward. He was older than most soldiers, in his fifties and scarred from battle. He looked up into Kalina's eyes.

"I will volunteer. Not just for you, or for my family, but because your father, Hakon, had faith in you to lead. And I trusted my friend."

Kalina's heart clenched at the sound of her father's name, and tears came unbidden to her eyes. She swallowed, a lump forming in her throat as she nodded at the man.

"Thank you."

Suddenly there was a flurry of men and women stepping forward to fight, many of them older, until a force of about eighty stood in the front of the cavern. Jormungand eyed the group thoughtfully before turning back to Kalina.

"This will be enough."

"Thank you all for your sacrifice. As for the rest of you, your work is not over. Get your families packed and ready to go, help those who don't have anyone and help me get our people to safety."

She hopped down off the rock and walked through the volunteers, shaking hands where she met them, and thanking them individually. She tried to learn their names and memorize their faces, but they quickly began to blur together. Finally, she was clear of them and making her way down the hall, Leif at her heels. All she wanted to do was to curl into a ball and cry, lose herself in the fear that was constantly threatening to consume her, but she knew she couldn't. She had to keep going, her people were counting on her. So, she swallowed the fear, letting it settle into a hard knot in her stomach, and made her way back to her rooms, dodging the chaos of her people packing around her.

Chapter 28

HER ROOMS WERE IN CHAOS. Cherise was hobbling around, trying to pack a few items into a bag, and Eira was there packing Kalina's things. Kalina didn't much care for anything besides her riding leathers, her weapons, and her crown, all of which she was currently wearing, but Eira was insisting on adding spare clothing and her books. Kalina sighed and began helping them pack, dismissing Eira to pack her own items.

But as soon as the older woman left, Cherise collapsed to the floor. She cried out as she fell, and Kalina dropped the extra pair of pants she'd been folding, and rushed to her mother's side.

"Eira!" she yelled, holding her mother up with both arms.

Cherise was huffing and panting now, one arm under her large belly. Her aunt stuck her head back into the room, a worried look on her face. Kalina was beginning to panic as she helped her mother sit on the edge of the bed.

"The baby, it's coming," Cherise panted.

Kalina's heart began to race. Eira came and took over for her, helping Cherise to lie back on the bed. This was the worst possible time for her mother to go into labor, but they didn't have an option. Kalina jumped to her feet.

"I'll go get some hot water and linens."

She remembered what the midwife had done when Calla had given birth so she knew at least some of what was needed. As soon as she exited her rooms she leaned back against the wall of the hallway. Tears leaked from her eyes and she began to tremble. This was all too much, too much for her to handle. She put the back of her hand against her mouth to stifle the sob that escaped her lips. She needed to pull herself together.

Many deep breaths later and a few pacing steps back and forth down the tunnel and she finally felt in control. She took off down to the kitchen where she asked a woman to boil water and bring clean linens. Then she went to find Leif. He was in the entrance cavern, supervising the loading of Skaldrik and his weapons. Skaldrik's dragon was enormous and deep red in color and, not for the first time, Kalina wondered if the dragons grew proportional to their rider's size. Maska was slowing down in his growth and was likely to remain smaller than other dragons. Kalina herself was small. But that was a question for another time.

"My mother just went into labor," she blurted out to Leif, as he pulled her aside to speak. "She can't be moved."

Leif could see the fear in her eyes.

"We just got word from the scouts we sent out that the ships are moving fast. The western ships are already moving up the river, and the eastern ships will make landfall by morning. We have less than a day before they attack."

Kalina suddenly felt like she couldn't breathe.

She put a hand out and grasped Leif's. She didn't care who saw them. He seemed to have decided he didn't either because he drew her into a tight embrace. She took deep, shaky breaths, trying to get herself under control. Their evacuation had just become dire. Finally, she was able to pull away, wiping her wet eyes on her sleeve.

"Get them all out and tell Jormungand to be ready. We will need to be gone by morning."

Leif held onto her arm.

"What will you do?" His voice was gentle, low.

"I'm staying with my mother until she can be moved. Then we will flee."

Leif nodded as if he'd made up his mind.

"I will stay with you."

Kalina let out a breath in gratitude.

"Thank you."

Then she jogged away back down the hallway to her rooms where the hot water and linens had arrived.

The night seemed to fly by. Kalina stayed by her mother's side, holding her hand and encouraging her as she pushed. Messengers came and went, alerting her to the evacuation progress. Many times, Kalina found herself locking eyes with Eira, worry etched in every line of their faces. Even if Cherise gave birth quickly, it was likely she couldn't be moved for at least a day, maybe two. And they couldn't be here when the mountain was attacked.

Her mother was quickly losing strength as the sun rose over the Wastes. Kalina was dozing with her head on the bed, her body slumped over. A hand on her shoulder made her sit up, rubbing the sleep from her eyes. They felt like sandpaper but she blinked it away and looked around the room. How had she fallen asleep? She couldn't remember putting her head down. Wouldn't her mother's birthing cries have woken her? Her mother lay quiet on the bed now.

Eira stood beside her. The older woman motioned for Kalina to follow her out into the hall. Kalina nervously adjusted her weapons belt.

"Your mother is dying."

There wasn't any time to sugar coat it but Kalina still felt like she'd been hit in the gut.

"What do you mean?"

"She stopped pushing a few hours ago, and her breathing is very labored. I think," she paused, anguish on her own face, to match Kalina's. "I think the baby inside her may be dead. But the only way to know is to cut it out of her."

Kalina's heart stopped, skipping a beat. She began shaking her head slowly.

"No."

Eira reached out and tried to take Kalina's hands but Kalina took a step back.

"No. You can't cut into her. It will kill her."

Eira held out her hands in a helpless gesture.

"We don't have another option. She is going to die either way. And the baby might already be dead. Either we cut her open and try to save at least one of them, or we let them be and lose them both."

Kalina's head was so full of thoughts she couldn't catch and hold on to any of them. Eira finally caught hold of her arm.

"Let's go wake her and ask her."

She was pleading with Kalina, but Kalina could barely bring herself to listen. Eira steered her back into her rooms where the only sound was the labored breathing coming from the bed.

Eira leaned over Charise, taking a small jar with a pungent aroma that Kalina could smell across the room and waved it beneath the queen's nose. Cherise's blue-green eyes shot open and she let out a little cry. Eira ran a hand over the woman's brow, murmuring soft words. Kalina had to steel herself in order to come back to the bed. It was heartbreaking to see her mother like this, so weak and fragile.

"Cherise," Eira began but Kalina reached out and put a hand on her arm, shaking her head slightly.

Eira stepped aside and Kalina took her place beside her mother. Cherise's eyes roamed the room, feverishly before alighting on Kalina.

"Oh, Kalina."

Her mother's voice was weak and thready, no heavier than the beating of a hummingbird's wings.

"Mother." Kalina had so rarely spoken that word but this time it almost broke her already cracking heart in two. "Mother, you are sick. And we think the baby may be dying."

She tried to be gentle, but with the sun rising, the evacuation finished, and an army on it's way, they didn't have time to coddle. Cherise frowned.

"The baby?" She seemed confused until she looked down at her own swollen belly. "Is he going to die?"

Kalina almost choked on the words.

"He might. But we can rescue him." Cherise's hopeful gaze fell back on her daughter. "But it would involve cutting into your belly." She paused, unsure how to break the news. "It will mean that you would die, mother. However, your baby might live. Otherwise, you both will die."

Tears were streaming down her cheeks now, and soon matching tears were leaking down Cherise's cheeks.

"But you can save him?" She asked, her voice trembling.

"Yes." Kalina nodded.

Cherise swallowed hard and then nodded. Despite the fear in her eyes she wanted to save her baby.

"Do it. Save my baby."

Kalina let out a little sob and clutched her mother's hand. Eira ran from the room and Kalina knew she only had a few moments before her mother died.

"Mother, I promise, I will protect the baby. I will take back your kingdom and I will be as good a Queen as I can be."

She wanted to make sure her mother knew that her country and her child would be in good hands. Cherise smiled dreamily; she was slipping back into unconsciousness.

"I know you will, my love." She reached up and gently patted Kalina's cheek. "I know you will." And then she was gone, asleep, the only sound her labored breathing once again.

Kalina wiped her eyes angrily. She was angry at this situation. She was doomed to be an orphan forever. As soon as she'd found either parent, she had lost them. And it wasn't fair.

But she knew that life was never fair. And as Eira entered the room with a knife and a bowl, Kalina sat on the edge of the bed, ready for whatever came next.

Leif entered a few moments later and paused, assessing the situation in the room. Kalina looked over at him hopelessly.

"Everyone is gone except for us and Jormungand's force."

Kalina let out a sigh of relief at his words. At least the majority of her people were safe.

"We need to leave."

She nodded.

"And we will. But not without the baby." She gestured towards Eira who was heating the knife over a candle flame.

Leif's eyes widened at the knife.

"What are you going to do?"

Eira gave him a strained smile.

"Cherise is dying, and so is the baby. We have to cut it out or else we will lose them both."

Kalina took Leif's hand and pulled him onto the edge of the bed.

"Will you get the dragons ready? Have them in the entrance cavern, and pack our stuff. As soon as the baby is born, we will need to flee."

He nodded; fear written in every line of his body. She grabbed his face in hers, locking eyes with his grey ones.

"We need you. I need you."

Leif swallowed and nodded again and she drew his face in, kissing him fiercely for a moment before letting him go. He ran from the room and Kalina turned back to her mother.

Eira eyed her for a moment before turning back to the laboring woman before her.

"I'll need you to hold her down."

Kalina nodded weakly but did as she was asked, putting her body weight across her mother's chest.

Chapter 29

KALINA DIDN'T REALLY KNOW WHAT happened next. She shut her eyes against the images and focused on holding her mother down. The Queen of Ethea started to convulse as Eira cut into her, a wailing scream escaping her lips, even though her eyes stayed squeezed shut. Kalina was sobbing as she put increased pressure on her mother's shoulders.

It felt like the screaming, crying and sounds too horrible to describe went on forever. But suddenly, like the wind abruptly dying from taut sails, they were over and Cherise lay still beneath Kalina's hands. She leaned back, tears making her mother's face blur, but she knew in that instant that her mother was dead. She released the pressure on her mother and began smoothing out the hair that had gotten caught on her mother's sweat soaked brow. She pushed the blonde waves aside, arranging them on the pillows in a sort of halo.

Behind her a baby's cry rang out across the cavern but Kalina didn't turn. She couldn't bring herself to look at the child that had caused her mother's death. She knew it was irrational. The baby was innocent but right in this moment, she wanted to say goodbye, not hello. Eira seemed to understand and she left Kalina to tend to her mother as she washed and wrapped the baby, getting it ready to travel.

Leif came running into the room, his own brow covered in sweat. He paused, looking around the room.

"The armies have both been spotted. We have to leave. Now."

Eira used an old bed sheet to wrap the baby and secure it to her own body before gathering the last of her things. The woman paused beside the bed, laying a hand on Kalina's shoulder.

"We must go. We can't take her with us."

Kalina knew that. But she wanted her mother to look beautiful nonetheless.

"I'll meet you in the entrance chamber."

And then Eira left her alone with her mother, Leif standing awkwardly in the doorway.

Kalina leaned down and kissed her mother's forehead, whispering something that was meant for her mother's ears only. Then she stood, throwing a final blanket over the bloody scene on the bed, covering it and making it look like her mother was just sleeping. Her heart shattered inside her as she turned and walked away.

Her tears kept falling as she walked past Leif and into the hallway. They didn't stop when she made it to the entrance chamber and mounted Maska. Maska launched himself from the side of the mountain, Leif and Eira in tow on their dragons. Then they flew north, hoping the armies didn't notice three dragons' departures.

The flight north to the camp in the mountains was cold. By the time the foothills were below them, Kalina's tears had frozen on her cheeks and she had no more to shed. She was once again alone in this world with an entire nation and people counting on her to lead them. The temptation to run and never return was strong but she knew that she could never do that to them again.

She and Leif had decided to send the Valdir to the small mountain camp where they had replanted the Emberweed. It was remote but the valley floor had plenty of room for them to make camp. Winter would be descending soon, and she hoped with all her heart that the Emberweed was ready for them to try. If it worked, then it would give their dragons a huge advantage in the war.

The mountain valley where they landed was just turning to dusk, the sun having dipped below the high mountain walls that seemed to hem them in. Kalina stepped down off of Maska and stretched, her muscles aching from a day of flying and from the last day or so of not sleeping. She desperately wanted to lie down on the soft ground beneath her feet and sleep but the small cries of her new baby brother made her straighten.

She hadn't looked at him when he'd been born but Eira approached her now, the baby held in her arms. Kalina swallowed and held out her arms as Eira set the bundle in them.

Kalina had never seen anything so beautiful in her life. Not even Calla's daughter Issa stirred emotions like this within her. The baby boy, no matter who his father was, was her half-brother and carried a part of Cherise in him. And Kalina loved him for that. He opened his tiny dark blue eyes and looked at her, his face scrunching as if he was about to cry, but he didn't. It struck her suddenly that he must be hungry and she looked up at Eira in alarm.

"Who is going to feed him?" She asked, looking around for a goat or a cow to milk. Eira chuckled and stepped closer, smoothing the baby's few wisps of blonde hair.

"Babies don't need to eat right away. He will be fine until morning. I heard that Hilde finally had her baby. She has plenty of milk for them both." She smiled at Kalina. "Have you thought of a name?"

Tears came to Kalina's eyes unbidden. She and her mother had sat talking of baby names for hours. They had decided on one name. It was Cherise's father's name. Her grandfather's name.

"Osian Natan Stanchon," she breathed.

"Osian. Interesting." Eira raised an eyebrow before cracking a smile. "Will he be raised among the Valdir?"

Kalina frowned. She hadn't thought that far ahead. In the entire flight here she'd only been thinking about her mother, not what she would do with her brother.

"I don't know. He might be better off being raised here, where he's not in danger. But I know how that feels: being shipped off somewhere to be kept safe yet never really feeling like you belong. I'll let him choose, when he's older."

Eira nodded and took Osian from Kalina's arms just as Leif approached. They stood and watched as Eira took the baby down the small valley and towards the partially erected camp her people were setting up.

Kalina's eyes roamed the valley. A small patch of tilled up earth caught her attention and she gasped.

"Where is the Emberweed?"

She began running, ignoring Leif's shouts for her to stay, to slow down. She raced towards the patch of ground, where a few months earlier she had planted a seedling. They couldn't all be dead, could they? Finally, she tripped and fell over the first row, sending her to her knees in the dirt. She dug her hands in, searching desperately for something, anything.

Strong hands pulled her back and briefly she scrabbled at the air, not understanding. Dimly she began to listen to Leif's words through her panic filled haze.

"They have been harvested! The Emberweed is safe!"

She sagged in relief, turning to bury her now tear streaked face in his chest. They had worked so hard for this. They had lost so much. And she was so scared of losing what little advantage they had. Finally, her breathing slowed as Leif traced circles on her back. She took a step back, shifted, and looked around.

Some of her people had looked over curiously, but they went back to their tasks as she straightened and wiped her cheeks clean. She finally turned back to Leif who stood patiently waiting for her. Maska and Arikara had followed them down the slope to the garden patch. She made eye contact with Maska, letting him know she was alright and then motioned for Leif to show her the way.

He led her to the smaller of the two permanent structures in the valley: the hut the farmer and his wife lived in. Leif knocked before entering and Kalina followed, a bit of shame leaking in at her outburst.

The hut was cramped, full of a table and chairs, a large bed in one corner, hidden by a partially drawn curtain, and a fireplace for warmth along an entire wall. It was cozy and smelled of wild mountain sage, woodsmoke, and a smell Kalina could not place, somewhere between a crackling fire and burnt cinnamon. It was a spicy scent and as she took in the rest of the room, she saw drying racks along one wall. They contained small, pale green shriveled leaves.

"Are these them? The first crop?" She said, as she stepped forward to inspect them.

The farmer and his wife stood in the corner; their hands clasped behind their backs. The old man stepped forward.

"Yes, your Majesty. We harvested them just over a week ago, just before the frost set in."

"What about the seeds?" Kalina asked.

"Collected and put into those jars." His wife stepped forward and pointed to the jars along the mantle place. There seemed to be enough seeds in there to plant twice as many plants next spring.

"Excellent. This is all rather amazing," Kalina said as she finally picked one dried plant up. The leaves were green and broad with red veins travelling throughout. She wondered if it would do what all the stories said it would and allow the dragons to breathe fire and began walking outside. Leif quickly apologized to the farmers and followed her.

Night was descending swiftly as she approached Maska and Arikara. Her green dragon looked almost black in the darkening night, but she could still see his beloved face.

"Maska. I have some dried Emberweed. Will you try it, and see if you can breathe fire?" Maska leaned down and sniffed the leaves in her palm.

"It smells strange, like something I once smelled long ago and have only forgotten."

He took another whiff, and then delicately plucked it off her hand with his large claws. He dropped it into his mouth without another word, just as Leif caught up with them, the farmers in tow, their own dragons coming from their shelter to join. Maska chewed thoughtfully, swallowing hard.

"How does it taste?" Kalina asked.

"Like fire and brimstone. Like hot stones after sitting in the sun all day. Like sunshine and growing things," he said, rather cryptically, and suddenly Kalina wondered if Emberweed made dragons poets as well as able to breathe fire.

The thought was so funny she had to keep the smile from spreading across her face, but she couldn't. Suddenly she was laughing, the hilarity bubbling up from some strange and desperate place within her that needed to find something good and pure to laugh at. Leif began to smile, and soon all those around them were laughing too, including Maska.

Abruptly, he gave a loud burp, and a jet of flame flew from his nostrils. He reared back startled, and everyone around him screamed and ducked as the fireball flew over their heads. Kalina was the first to stand up and look at her dragon, who stood there sheepishly with his jaws clamped shut.

"Try that again," she encouraged.

Maska eyed her skeptically and let out a second burp, but this time he aimed high into the sky, away from anyone else. It didn't really sound like a burp, more like a dull roar but it was short, in a small burst. Kalina jumped up and down clapping and hugging Leif who was equally joyous.

"It works!" She yelled, feeling utterly triumphant.

Now, they had a chance at taking back Ethea. Now, they had a chance to avenge her father and mother.

Chapter 30

TWO DAYS WENT BY IN THE HIGH mountain valley. Kalina didn't sleep well, but there were no hallways to wander, only a crowded valley. She spent the nights sleeping out under the stars with Maska, her mind never ceasing to race. She struggled to quiet it as the various scenarios of what had happened back at the mountain in the Wastes played through her mind. Had Jormungand managed to thwart the attacking armies? The image of her mother lying dead in her bed also continued to haunt her dreams, often speaking to her, although her words never made any sense. Her mother's ghostly image often spoke of ice and snow, but Kalina had never experienced a winter harsher than a bit of snow on the ground.

The couple who lived in the small house had offered to let Kalina stay there but she refused. She might be queen, but she was used to roughing it. Leif slept nearby, curled up beside Arikara. Both dragons used their wings to shelter their riders from the ever-present wind and the chill that was unmistakable here. The first morning when Kalina had awoken, the ground was covered in a thick frost, her breath visible in the chilly mountain air. She thought it would worry her, since her winters at the Abbey had been mild in comparison, but it didn't. Instead she felt invigorated by the cold air. Her people were already in full swing, cutting trees for cabins to live in during the winter and smoking meat. Bjorn sent out hunting parties into the mountains and soon they were coming back with stacks of animal pelts and meat. Kalina and Maska spent their first day helping to haul logs from a nearby tree-studded valley.

The second day she and Maska flew with Leif and Arikara to a nearby warning outpost, high atop a mountain. The air was thin here, and once Maska landed on the landing pad carved into the side of the mountain she was forced to climb a set of stairs that snaked up to the flat top, just large enough to house a small hut and a large pyre of logs and brush. Her breath was coming out in gasps as they reached the top and she let Leif do the talking as she surveyed the mountain range around them, catching her breath. Finally, she followed the two Valdir who lived there into their hut for a cup of hot tea which helped her feel a bit better. Her head had begun aching their first morning in the mountains and had not stopped.

On the third morning as Kalina sat sharpening her axes, watching her people work on erecting buildings, a cry rose up over the valley. She put her axes back into their scabbards along her back and stood, searching for the source of the outcry. Finally her eyes found the small dark dots on the horizon that flew towards them.

Leif joined her as they waited for the dragons to land but as they came in close, Kalina recognized Jormungand and his red dragon, Shania. When they landed Kalina tried to count the numbers of soldiers left. Of the eighty that had volunteered, fewer than twenty remained.

"So many lost," she said, trying to keep her voice from shaking.

How many more were going to die in this war for her crown? How many people was the king willing to kill just to get to her? She had been an unknown orphan less than a year ago and now she was the most wanted person in the kingdom.

For a moment, she was overwhelmed by the idea that she might never find peace, that her people might all die before she found freedom from this man. She trembled as Jormungand dismounted in front of her. Leif saw her discomfort and came to stand by her side, sliding one hand to the small of her back. His touch helped ground her and by the time Jormungand had organized his men and was approaching to report, Kalina was standing tall once again.

"Your Majesty," Jormungand said, bowing deeply.

Kalina clasped his hand warmly.

"What happened?" She searched the faces of those still living, finding only pain and sadness etched there.

"They attacked within minutes of you leaving," he began. "Askor's force was small compared to Ethea's. I don't think they expected much of a fight. We lured them high into the mountain, fighting as we went. Then we fled, just as they realized it had been a trick." Jormungand knelt before her suddenly, making Kalina take a step back. "I disobeyed your orders, your Majesty."

"What do you mean?"

Leif took a step forward, placing a hand on his sword. Kalina put out a hand for him to wait. She wanted to hear his explanation.

"After we left the mountain we flew east, to the coast. There we cut off Askor's escape, setting light to their ships, destroying their supplies, and killing their guards. They won't know they've been stranded until their main army makes it back across the Wastes to the bay." He looked up at her, a tentative grin on his face. "They will have nowhere to go, no way across the wastes, no food, no water. Their forces will die, your Majesty."

Kalina almost sat down at his words. This was a mighty blow at Ethea's allies. It was both a good thing and a horrible thing he had done.

"What will Askor do when they find out what happened?"

Jormungand's face fell at the question.

"I didn't think of the long-term repercussions. Only what I could do to cripple them."

"Clearly. Askor has armies twice the size of the entire Ethean force. Do you think they will just back off if we kill a few thousand of their men?"

Jormungand shook his head at her words. Kalina began to pace back and forth. Kari and Rangvald had come to join them.

"We need to attack now. While their army is still returning from the Wastes. While the capital is unaware of our ruse, and vulnerable."

Kari all but cheered beside her, a grin spreading across her face.

"I'm ready when you are," she said.

Kalina gave her a strained smile. This was her least favorite part.

"I'm calling a council meeting." She turned to Leif. "Please inform the farmers we will need their hut."

She walked off in search of Eira and Osian. She wanted to feel her baby brother's weight in her arms and smell his hair before deciding to jump into battle to take back the throne. The throne was his if something happened to her.

The small hut was cramped and hot, despite the plummeting temperatures outside, as the sun began to set. Kalina looked around at them all, trying to decide who to take with her. Kari spoke up into the silence.

"I think our best bet is to take a force and fly straight into Ravenhelm. Take them by surprise before they are able to mount any defenses. Kill the king, take the throne, and dismantle those damned catapults."

She emphasized her point by slamming her fist with a loud

smack on the roughhewn oak table. Kalina smiled in response to her cousin's vehemence.

"I think we need more stealth than that. We don't want to terrify the people, put every soldier and guard within a hundred miles on alert. I think it would be better if we sneak in, leaving the dragons in the forest nearby, and quietly take over. We can force the King to renounce his throne and I will ascend it."

Kari snorted at Kalina's plan and she shot the woman a glare before continuing.

"It has minimal loss of life."

Leif nodded in agreement, scratching his chin.

"It could work. But how will we sneak in? How will we avoid the guards? Our hair alone makes us stand out," he said.

"Easy. We wear head scarves to cover our hair until we get inside," Kalina supplied. She hated doing it but it would work.

"What about when the King refuses to abdicate?" Jormungand asked.

"Then we take it by force. I'm sure there is proof somewhere of my birth. We can even bring Father Martin to the capital to testify on my behalf-" she trailed off.

What about the dark stranger, the one she had met in the Abbey? He had admitted to being the one that had brought her to Hywell Abbey originally? Who was he? Could he prove her parentage? He had told the High Father at Hywell that he'd been following the wishes of her parents, so surely, he could prove who she was? But she had no idea how to find him.

Eira stepped forward.

"You look just like your father, Kalina. But you also look like Cherise. If anyone who knew her saw you, they would know."

Kalina frowned. Surely that wasn't true. Then how did the king not know who she was all those months ago? Perhaps because her hair wasn't silver, and sometimes you only saw what you wanted to see. He saw a scullery maid or a scribe. Not a princess. Not a queen.

"Fine," Kari said, propping her feet up on the table. "Who's going with you?"

Chapter 31

"I WANT KARI, JORMUNGAND, RANGVALD, and Leif with me. Eira, I leave you in charge of our people," Kalina said as she made eye contact with each person.

They were her inner circle. She surprised herself when she'd included Jormungand in that group but she realized that he was. She trusted him now to have her back. They all nodded in return. Asta, Arvid, and Ingvar all seemed resigned to the situation. She might value their opinions, but they had never been close to her.

"We leave at first light."

Dismissed, the council members filed out of the small cabin, leaving Kalina and Leif alone. Kalina eyed him from where he leaned against the small kitchen table. She didn't really know where they stood, what they were to each other, but as the crown of Ethea loomed ever closer, she struggled with wanting to cling to him for support and comfort, and to push him away in case it all went awry. She supposed it didn't matter now. They would leave in the morning.

"Leif-" she trailed off, unsure where to begin. Then she took a deep breath and continued, wringing her hands before her. "If I don't make it through this. If he takes me-" she couldn't finish the sentence. She shuddered slightly. She couldn't let herself think that way. She couldn't go down the path of panic and fear. She had to remain strong. Osian needed her, as did her people.

Leif crossed the space between them and enfolded her in his arms, his hands gently stroking her back. She buried her face in his leathers. This was her favorite place to be, in his arms, smelling his leather and sweat and mountain air smell. The mountains seemed to suit him.

"Nothing's going to happen to you. I'll make sure of it," he said reassuringly.

Kalina sighed and looked up at his handsome face and grey eyes.

"If something happens. I want you to be King." Her voice was soft but she meant it. "You know these people better than I do. They trust you. And you can raise Osian to be a good person."

Leif's grey eyes clouded over. He frowned down at her and she reached up to tuck a strand of silver hair behind his ear, cupping his face.

"You will do this for me, Leif."

He closed his eyes briefly, leaning into her touch.

"I will," he finally responded.

Kalina's heart felt better, more settled and she disentangled herself from him before heading out to find some food and Osian. She wanted to say goodbye.

Osian's tiny hands and feet, and soft skin made her sad, her heart breaking slightly at the thought of leaving him. But she knew there was no other way to end the war, to keep him and her people safe. So, she smelled his hair and rocked him gently before handing him back to Eira so that she could prepare for the next day. The rest of the day was spent preparing to leave and anxiety plagued Kalina the whole time.

They flew as high as they dared, to where the air was thin and it was a struggle to breathe. From that height, they would look like birds high in the sky to the casual observer on the ground. Kalina had instructed Eira to ready their remaining forces, and fly to the capital in three days, regardless of whether or not they had heard of her success. She hoped that they wouldn't need rescuing but she would rather be safe than sorry.

They landed in a grove just outside the road to Ravenhelm, hiding themselves amongst the trees. When Kalina dismounted she paused and rested her head on Maska's side.

"You'll be careful in there?" he asked.

He was worried about leaving her alone in the castle with the man who had been trying so hard to see her dead. Kalina smiled.

"I know my way around, Maska. Remember, I did spend a few months as a scribe in this castle. Besides, I'm more worried about you remaining undiscovered out here."

Maska huffed in response, still not satisfied with her answer. He snaked his tail around her and enclosed them within the green shelter of his wings. It was the closest thing to a hug he could give her. The space was warm and green tinged and it made her feel safe. She sighed heavily before stepping away from him.

"Stay out of sight for three days. Then fly to the gardens, we will meet you there."

She hugged her once more before breaking away and joining

the others who stood preparing. They all had tied head scarves around their distinctive silver hair and Kalina pulled out her green scarf, the one Calla had given her all those months ago, and covered her hair. It was a strange feeling to have it covered once again, to be invisible and a nobody once more. They had put on normal, dark clothing and capes, keeping their traditional red leathers in their carry sacks. Kalina was wearing men's pants and a loose shirt and vest, which were easier to fight in. Kari wore the same. Dark capes kept the rain and snow off as they traveled.

Kalina had debated wearing the dress Calla had made for her, with the flowers embroidered on the hem and the sleeves, but when she'd tried to put it on, she realized that it no longer fit. All the training she had done had changed her body. She was full of muscles now, and if she had forced the dress on, she would have burst the seams. So instead she had packed it away and put on the men's clothing. Calla would understand.

They decided to travel separately rather than one large group. A group of people, all with head scarves, would raise attention but individually they might be able to make it to the gates of the city unnoticed. Kalina and Kari together went first. The road was crowded as it had been on Kalina's first trip into Ravenhelm, full of merchants, travelers, and farmers. Kalina and Kari didn't look horribly out of place, as many people were bundled against the cold, their hair hidden by hoods or shawls.

The shanty town outside the gates of Ravenhelm had grown, the poor unable to sustain life within the walls, or the unsavory unable to conduct business within them either. The makeshift buildings and tents had expanded around the city, and the smell as they approached was worse than ever.

Kalina paused beside a cart overflowing with partially rotten vegetables that an old woman dressed in rags was trying to sell to passersby. Kalina vowed that if this worked, if she was able to take the Ethean throne, she would find a way to end these people's poverty. The old woman was talking with her friend, an equally bedraggled and run down woman whose profession was unknown.

"Look at all them hopefuls. Going up to the castle like it'll be their salvation." The old woman spat. "Don't they know they'll just end up back out here with no food, nowhere to stay, and no promises?"

The younger woman beside her scoffed.

"They thought it was bad in the country, with the army takin' everythin' they 'ad. The King won't give them no handouts."

That's when both women spotted Kalina eavesdropping.

"What are you looking at, missy?" The old woman made a shooing motion. "Off with ya, unless you're plannin' to buy me wares!"

Kalina shuffled off, pulling Kari with her into the slowly moving crowd.

The huge gates loomed before them, and Kalina looked everywhere for Anders, the guard who had taken her in the first time she'd stood before these gates. He had helped her get in to the capital last time, and the last words he'd said to her was that she was his adopted daughter. She desperately needed to see his friendly face. But every guard was unknown to her so she pushed on, ignoring the fear rising up in her gut.

They were briefly questioned by an uninterested guard and then sent through the gates. As soon as they passed under the stone archway, Kalina sighed in relief. Their first hurdle was crossed. Now they needed to wait for the others. They made their way to a tavern Kalina remembered from her first time in the city. It stood on the corner of two streets in the area of the city where Anders and Calla lived.

A sign with a wyvern hung over the entrance and Kalina smiled as they entered. The name, The Wandering Wyvern, was strangely fitting for their mission. This had all started with a wyvern, and now it would end with one.

The tavern was dimly lit, with a few tables unoccupied and a few workers sitting at the bar. Kalina led Kari to a table by a window, one where they could easily watch both the street and the door for trouble. A small regiment of soldiers marched by the window and Kalina's heart jumped into her throat. Kari stiffened beside her until they had marched out of sight. They both ordered mugs of ale and sat sipping the bitter brew while they waited for Jormungand, Leif, and Rangvald to appear.

Kalina jumped slightly as the front door opened and a figure stepped through. The light from outside temporarily obscured his face but as he closed the door and her eyes readjusted, she leapt up from her chair.

"Talon!"

She ran forward and threw her arms around the man before her. Talon was confused and he pushed her back briefly to get a good look at her face. Then he began laughing as he embraced her fully. Gone was the awkward, gangly youth she remembered from months ago when he'd left the Valdir. He had filled out, a light brown beard coming in to cover his cheeks and jaw, all traces of baby fat gone. He also looked like he had grown a few inches.

"Kalina!" he laughed as he set her down and took a step back to inspect her. "What on earth are you doing here?"

She grabbed his hand and led him over to their table where Kari stood to give Talon a brief hug in greeting. Kari's face held a mischievous grin. She had always teased Talon when he had been with them in the Valdir's mountain and it seemed she meant to restart.

"Well, it's a long story," Kalina began, pausing as the bar keeper brought over another ale for Talon.

Talon shrugged out of his heavy winter coat and looked Kalina up and down.

"I've got time. I just got off work and came here for a pint. Anders usually joins me about this time." He turned to survey the room, as if the older man would be there, waiting.

"Perfect. I can talk to him too."

That was when she noticed Talon's livery that had been hiding under his coat. She reached out and touched the symbol on the chest. Two crossed swords on a field of green and gold. She looked up into his face.

"You're a palace guard? Like Anders?"

Talon had been a squire for Sir Dyelan, slated to be a knight. Being a castle guard was a huge step down. Talon smiled at her and patted his chest.

"What a better place to gather information for the Queen than within the guard?" He winked at her. Kalina's face fell and his followed.

"Did she get you the job?" Her voice was quiet as memories of her mother flashed before her eyes. Had it really only been a few days ago that she had died? It seemed like a lifetime ago.

"Yes, as soon as I came back Anders smuggled me into the castle gardens where she met with me. Turns out, she'd been in close contact with Anders since you'd left. She made me a guard, and stationed me to her advantage- outside the Prince's rooms."

Kalina's eyes went wide at this bit of information. He continued on, grinning.

"I was her spy. The king's doors don't block out the sound, so I kept an ear out and reported his movements and plans to her when I could. Anders did the same from the city, since he's particular friends with most of the guard." He reached out and took her hand. "But she disappeared a month ago, and no one's seen her. She mentioned she was going to try to get you a message, to warn you, but..." he trailed off at the sadness in Kalina's eyes.

"She made it to the Wastes."

Tears spilled over and fell from Kalina's eyes. She hadn't really taken the time to grieve. Not for her father, nor her mother. She wiped them away with the sleeve of her shirt.

"She was very sick, and she was too late to warn us of the attack."

Talon let out a long sigh.

"She died, Talon. Giving birth to my half-brother."

His eyes rose to meet hers at the declaration.

Anders chose that moment to walk in through the front doors. Talon stood and ushered him over to the table. Kalina hastily wiped her eyes before standing to embrace the man. Anders laughed and hugged her so tightly she felt her back pop with the force.

"I can't believe it's you!" he said, as he joined them at the table a few moments later, ale in hand.

"Anders, this is my cousin, Kari." Kalina introduced the two, worry churning her gut.

She realized she really didn't want to retell her entire story just then. So, she gestured to Talon who nodded. He told Anders about the queen in hushed tones. Anders' handsome face fell, a serious expression replacing the joy he'd shown at seeing Kalina.

"Are you here to take back the throne then?"

Anders' face was deadly serious. Kalina nodded slowly and watched with mild horror as Talon's eyes lit with an intensity she'd never seen before. She was finally doing what he'd pushed her to do months ago. All of this scared her, but she knew that she must push forward, for her own people.

It dawned on her suddenly, that Leif, Jormungand, and Rangvald were taking their time arriving at the inn. She stood, finishing off the last of her ale, thinking she'd have to go search the city as night began to fall outside, when the door finally opened, revealing the three Valdir. They hurried over, grabbing a second table and chairs to join the group already assembled.

Kalina gave quick introductions all around, although Rangvald and Leif already knew Talon.

"What we need, is a plan-" Kalina began.

She was still unsure how they would sneak into the castle and capture the king. Anders held up a hand.

"Say no more. Talon and I will get you in."

Chapter 32

"WHERE ARE YOU STAYING FOR the night?" Talon asked.

Kalina stood and walked to the bar.

"Two rooms for the night please, for myself and my four companions."

The barkeeper was a stout man with a balding head of dark hair. He eyed her curiously, and then his eyes flicked to her companions. Her gut tightened as she worried, he would ask them questions she really didn't want to answer. Finally he spoke.

"Any friends o' Anders is a friend o' mine." He gave her a wink and passed her two iron keys. "Will ye be wanting supper as well?"

"Yes, please. Thank you."

She pushed over a whole gold coin, more than enough to pay for their rooms and their meal. He tapped the side of his nose and then disappeared through the back door into what Kalina assumed was a kitchen. She rejoined her friends.

"All taken care of."

Anders stood, finishing his ale.

"I'm going to grab Calla. We can all eat dinner here together."

He left in a hurry and Kalina watched him go. Talk buzzed around her, but she barely participated as her friends discussed the best ways to enter the castle. She was too caught up in memories to pay attention. Finally the door opened and Calla stepped through, her long black hair curling down her back, her cloak gathered around her, keeping baby Issa safe and warm in her arms. Anders entered the tavern behind her and closed the door. The sound of the shutting door made Kalina jump and she stood, making her way to Calla.

"Oh! Kalina!" The woman's arms embraced her tightly from the side, Issa against her other hip. Issa had grown and Kalina looked down at the baby in wonder. A mop of curly black hair covered her head but her eyes were those of Anders. Kalina was reminded painfully of Osian back in the mountains and she realized with a pang that she missed him terribly. Calla unceremoniously put Issa into Kalina's arms before removing her own cloak and taking the seat beside Talon, squeezing the young man's shoulder as she sat. Kalina didn't sit right away, instead she smelled Issa's head and clutched the little girl to her.

"The country has gotten worse since you left."

Anders was speaking as Kalina sat down, bouncing Issa on her knee. The baby gurgled and babbled, making her smile. But she looked up at Anders, listening to his recounting.

"When the old king died and you escaped, the new King brought in Sir Gregan as his commander. He's been recruiting all over the city, pulling men from their homes, even recruiting boys as young as twelve or thirteen."

That made Kalina's heart lurch. They were just children. Valdir children grew up knowing how to fight but they weren't allowed on the battlefield until they were sixteen.

"Where are the armies stationed? We heard there was a contingent in Wolfhold, but I haven't seen many soldiers here, only the castle guard," Rangvald said.

"The King and Sir Gregan sent all their forces south. They have a large camp set up just outside Wildhelm, and they maintain themselves by taking from the local population. Farmers have been forced to give up their crop yields, their women have been raped, their cattle slaughtered, their sons taken, all to maintain the King's army," Anders responded, his face a mask of anger.

Kalina swallowed. This was all her fault. How many people were going to die because of her? That was why she was here; she had to stop the madness.

Dinner was served while they talked of the atrocities the king was exacting on her people. For the second time in a few months, Kalina realized that these were all her people. Not just the Valdir, but every citizen of Ethea. And she needed to protect them. Her resolve to take the throne solidified in her stomach as she watched her friends talk.

"So how do we get into the castle?" Kari asked.

Kalina was suddenly, overwhelmingly grateful for her friends. She knew she couldn't have done any of this on her own.

"We could sneak you in through the kitchens," Talon suggested. "Mistress Aynne wouldn't mind. She hates the King. As do most of the castle servants."

"What about the library? Kalina, didn't you mention you were a scribe in the library?" Leif asked, turning to look at her.

The intensity in his eyes softened as he beheld her holding Issa.

414

Kalina smiled at his sudden attention and handed Issa back to Calla. She needed to focus.

"What about the secret entrance to the dungeons. The one I escaped from?" She looked to Talon who scratched his chin, thinking.

"Could work. If we can get you over the wall into the garden, then we can try it. If it doesn't work, the kitchens are right there and can be our backup option."

"There. That's the plan. Is Sir Gregan in residence?"

If the big man was there, it would make things much more difficult. Talon shrugged.

"I'm not sure. Last I heard he was running drills in the field with the new recruits taken from their homes in the surrounding towns."

He pointed to Leif, Rangvald, and Jormungand, who had stayed quiet throughout their discussion. Kalina had noticed that the man preferred to listen and observe, before making any decisions.

"You three better have a backstory, or feign an injury. All our young men are either working in jobs too valuable to leave, or forced to join up."

"We'll be breaking into the castle tomorrow night." Jormungand finally spoke up, waving his hand dismissively. "We only need to avoid their draft for one day."

Talon eyed the man before nodding.

"Your presence has probably already been noted." Anders piped in. "The guards at the main gate are instructed to tell Sir Gregan or one of his minions about all newcomers who are able to serve. I'd stay inside tomorrow if I were you."

They continued planning into the evening as the tavern filled up with late night drinkers. It was a quiet tavern though, no bard was visiting, so the crowd stayed relatively quiet. As the fire in the huge fireplace began to get low, Kalina finally stood, stretching. She leaned down and kissed Issa on the cheek, the poor thing having fallen asleep hours ago. She then kissed Calla as well and bid them good night. She squeezed Talon's and Anders' shoulders as she passed, making her way up the stairs to the bedrooms they had rented for the night. Kari stood behind her and followed.

Kalina didn't sleep well. Every sound, every creak of a footstep on the stairs, made her think it was Sir Gregan coming to get her, or the King sending guards to arrest her. Her heart raced every time she woke and it took long minutes to calm herself down enough to return to sleep.

So when morning sunlight peeked through the old lace curtains on the window, she was groggy and exhausted. The tavern's main room was almost deserted, only a grumpy looking Kari and Jormungand sat in the corner by the fire, moodily eating some sort of grain gruel. The tavern wasn't known for its food, but Kalina gratefully took the bowl the bar keeper proffered her and went to join them. At least the food was hot.

"Where are Leif and Rangvald?" she asked as she plunked down next to Kari and began spooning sugar into her bowl. The older woman kept scratching at her head scarf, clearly unhappy at being forced to wear it. Kalina gently took her hand and held it underneath the table, preventing her from scratching. Kari shot her a look before pulling her hand free. She started to scratch again but then thought better of it and sat on her hand with a grunt of frustration. Kalina pressed her lips together, trying to suppress a grin at her cousin's antics.

"They went out to scout the perimeter of the garden wall. Talon told them where it is." Jormungand mumbled into his food. "They were awful chirpy this morning."

"Chirpy?" Kalina grinned.

"Yea. Like a bird, you know? Early risers." He gestured outside to where the early winter sun shone down onto the cobbled street.

She suppressed her grin. She wasn't sure why everything seemed so funny this morning. Perhaps it was because she was almost home, almost done with all the running and hiding and fighting. An end was in sight and she couldn't help but be optimistic even if for just a moment.

"Well, I'll tell them not to be chirpy in the future," she said and went back to eating her breakfast.

Leif returned at lunch and sat heavily at her table. She was trying to keep her mind off what was coming that night by reading a book from the tavern's small library. She planned to go to Calla and Ander's house after lunch to help them make dinner for all of them, and to spend time with the woman who had become a sort of mother figure to her. She paused reading for a moment, realizing suddenly how many people had come to replace her parents in her life. First it had been Father Martin and Gwyn. Then it had been Calla and Anders. After her father died, Geir had taken his place, but when he'd died, she hadn't found anyone to replace him. Eira had been her mother's replacement, and still was even after her mother had died. She was grateful to all of them for loving her and teaching her. Without each of them, she wouldn't be who she was.

Leif eyed her as she sat there thinking. He poked her with his elbow and she looked over into his grey eyes.

"Copper for your thoughts?"

She smiled at the silly expression.

"I was just thinking about family." Was he her family now, too? She shoved him back. "Find anything useful?"

"Other than that, the garden section of the wall is poorly guarded, no." He propped his boots on a nearby chair. "Rangvald and I watched it all morning and didn't see one patrol. Should be easy to sneak over tonight."

Kalina nodded absently, her mind now racing ahead to all the possibilities of the evening.

"Where's Rangvald?" Jormungand had come down the stairs to join them. Kalina looked up, suddenly noticing Leif was alone.

"He stayed to watch the wall until dinner."

Jormungand frowned.

"Is that wise? With the draft?"

Leif shrugged in response.

"He knows how to be safe."

That evening, when Leif, Jormungand and Kari arrived at Calla and Anders' place, they realized collectively that Rangvald was nowhere to be seen.

Chapter 33

KALINA'S STOMACH DROPPED INTO her feet at the thought of Rangvald being captured by Sir Gregan's men. All they had to do was pull off his headscarf to know he was Valdir, and she could imagine how they would treat him then. The thought made her sick to her stomach.

Dinner was set on the table but none of them ate a bite. Talon walked through the door moments later and Kalina stood.

"Talon, Rangvald was taken. Recruited."

He froze in the doorway, his jacket partially shrugged off.

"I need you to find out where he's being kept. They must know he's Valdir by now."

Talon shrugged his jacket back onto his shoulders and turned to Anders who stood behind his wife, his hands on her shoulders.

"There are only two places he could be. The dungeons," he glanced at Kalina. "And the guard shack at the front gates. I'll check the front gates, but that means Anders will have to help you in through the dungeons. You can check those while you are in there."

They sprang into action, donning their dark clothing and shoving bread rolls into their mouths for quick energy. Kalina kissed Calla on the cheek, thanking her for the meal and promising that once this was all over, they would have a proper dinner together.

Anders led them through the slowly quieting streets of Ravenhelm. Darkness had fallen and most people were home eating dinner with their families. Only those on dubious business or heading to the tavern for a drink were out on the cold streets. Getting to the castle and over the high garden wall was easier than Kalina had guessed, but once inside the garden, there were patrols to avoid.

"These weren't here before," she whispered to Anders who crouched in the thick underbrush beside her.

"These must be new. They weren't there yesterday."

Kalina's stomach clenched at his words. It meant they knew who Rangvald was. It meant that the king might know she was coming.

They snaked their way through the garden, remaining quiet and low, not allowing even the weak winter moonlight to shine off their blades. Kalina had strapped her axes to her hips instead of on her back so that they were hidden by her cloak and less visible.

The wall that held the hidden door to the dungeons was still overgrown with ivy. Anders didn't know where it was so Kalina had been forced to lead them there. It was a painful few minutes as she stood, exposed against the rock wall, feeling around in the ivy for a catch, a seam, or a handle. She couldn't remember if there had been one when she'd escaped all those months ago. Finally, after what felt like an eternity, her heart racing the entire time, her fingers caught on the edge of something. She pulled and a small handle came loose, allowing her to pull the stone door open.

A rush of warm, damp air rushed out at her, startling her for a moment. She hadn't expected the underground dungeons to be so warm. It made her nervous but she entered, the others quickly following behind her, filing into the passageway. They didn't dare light a lamp of any kind, so Kalina reached back, taking Leif's hand into hers and then she pressed forward, her other hand outstretched to feel for the walls.

As they came to the final bend, the one Kalina remembered as where she'd last seen her mother's face on the day she'd escaped, a faint light appeared down to their left, towards the dungeons. Her stomach clenched at the memories and the scar on her face burned as if in response. An image of the king slashing at her with his knife made her take a step back and she had to fight to keep herself together. Leif's warm hands went around her from behind, holding her close in the dark for a moment. He kissed the top of her head briefly before letting her go. She took deep breaths before turning left, away from freedom and the castle above, towards whatever horror awaited them down below. They had to know if Rangvald was there.

The dungeons were just as she remembered them as they paused in the cave's entrance and surveyed the scene before them. Only this time instead of herself in the rusted iron chair held in by leather straps, it was Rangvald. His silver hair fell around his head in blood-soaked ribbons, his face and body a map of slashes and bruises. Before him stood Sir Gregan and the king, as well as a few guards. The sight of Rangvald looking so defeated and bloody tore at her heart.

As they watched, sizing up the situation, Sir Gregan reached into his belt and withdrew the very same knife he'd used to cut Kalina. It glinted in the flickering light from the torches set along the wall as Sir Gregan toyed with it. The King leaned down, placing a hand on either arm of the chair so that his face was level with Rangvald's. He spoke so quietly that Kalina couldn't hear him, but whatever he said must have made Rangvald angry, because next thing she knew he had headbutted the King, breaking the man's nose.

Chaos erupted then as Kari rushed out from the passageway to save her brother, and Sir Gregan put his knife to Rangvald's throat. Kalina called out to stop her cousin as Leif ran by her to help. Kalina ground her teeth, frustrated at not having a solid plan, and gestured for Anders to follow her as she unhooked her twin axes from her belt and ran into the cavern. The two guards met Kari and Leif head on, swords drawn, and when they clashed, the sound reverberated off the high cavern walls above them.

Within moments Leif had driven his sword through one guard's gut and Kari had sliced the jugular of the second. Suddenly they all stood before the King, his face bloodied and angry, and Sir Gregan, who smiled maliciously as he held his knife to Rangvald's throat.

"That's far enough." Sir Gregan's voice rang out across the space.

Kari froze, Leif beside her. Kalina kept walking, removing her headscarf as she went, knowing she was going to be the key to ending this. She took a deep breath before she stepped in front of Leif and into the torchlight. She needed to be strong for Kari, for Rangvald, for all her people.

"I heard you've been looking for me."

The King's eyes went wide at the sight of her, and then a look she couldn't really put a name to, something akin to hunger perhaps, came into his eyes. He wiped delicately at the blood still pouring from his nose and stepped forward.

"I've been hoping you would be stupid enough to come here."

He began to pace before her, his arms clasped behind his back. He wore a long coat with gold buttons down the front that flared out and split at his hips and fell to the floor. It billowed behind him as he walked.

"How fitting, that it should be here, in this room. Do you remember our last encounter?"

He smiled, gesturing to his cheek and ran his finger down it, mirroring her own scars path. Kalina tightened her grip on her throwing axes.

"I remember you were too stupid to know who I was," she said.

But she instantly regretted her words as Terric held up a hand and Sir Gregan pushed the knife deeper into Rangvald's skin. He cried out and a trickle of blood ran down his neck. Beside Kalina, Kari growled deep in her throat, her face a mask of hatred and anger. Kalina understood how her cousin felt. Every bit of her wanted to rip Terric apart.

"Interesting choice of words," Terric purred. "But not, sadly, the ones that will get your precious spy back."

He gestured to Rangvald. Kalina's mind raced. She had two choices. Rush the King and Sir Gregan and try to kill them, almost certainly killing Rangvald in the process, or offer him something he couldn't refuse.

"Then I offer myself in exchange."

Beside her Leif stiffened and took a step forward, looking at her. She gave him a weak smile. Terric grinned, and it sent a shiver down her spine.

"Well then, finally, something sensible." He waved a lazy hand and Sir Gregan loosened his knife against Rangvald's throat. Kalina held her axes out to her sides as she stepped forward. She watched as Sir Gregan took a step away from Rangvald, making his way around the chair to release her cousin. In that instant, Kalina threw one of her axes as hard as she could. It was like the spell over the room had been broken and suddenly Leif, Anders, and Kari sprang into action.

Her axe found its home in Sir Gregan's side and he fell, leaving Rangvald completely alone in the chair. Leif ran to free him and Kalina approached the downed knight, her other axe lifted and ready to throw.

"Stand and fight," she ground out.

She was angry now, and her anger boiled inside of her as she watched the huge man struggle to his feet. He pulled her axe from his side, panting as his own blood soaked his tunic and pants. Spit was hanging from his mouth and it sprayed as he spat at her. She smiled a grim smile before she went in for the kill.

Chapter 34

KALINA STOOD OVER SIR GREGAN'S BODY, both axes now covered in blood. She had managed to dodge his blow with her axe and come up under his guard, her smaller frame lending her an advantage the large man didn't expect. Her second axe had found its home in his chest, caving in his chest wall and stopping his heart.

Leif had managed to cut the leather bindings that held Rangvald and was now helping Kari and Anders wrestle a struggling King Terric into the leather straps. Kalina felt a sense of satisfaction at seeing the King tied to the chair. But as she watched this man struggle against his bonds, all the righteous anger began to ebb, leaving her feeling hollow and cold.

"What should we do with him now, your Majesty?" Kari said, her knife now held to the man's throat.

Kalina found herself hesitating. She wanted this man dead, she wanted him to pay for the torture he had inflicted on her, her mother, and her people. But that meant he got off easy, that he wasn't forced to pay for his crimes. It also meant another death, which if she was honest with herself, made her sick to her stomach. She didn't want to watch another man die, especially a defenseless one. But she couldn't help herself. She sheathed her axes and withdrew her knife. His eyes went wide in fear as she stepped up beside him. Slowly, carefully, she drew her blade down his cheek, marring his flesh as he had once ruined hers. Then she wiped her blade on his tunic and stepped away.

"Throw him in a cell. We have too many other things to deal with now." She turned and began to walk away.

The clang of a closing cell door echoed across the cavern and she paused at the passage entrance. Now came the part she had struggled with. How to take over the castle, the realm, the armies. It was after midnight, and later that day Eira and the rest of her army was due to descend on the capital. She needed to be ready.

Leif was behind her as they climbed the passage and came out into a deserted side hallway on the main floor. Kalina stopped for a moment, completely unsure of how to proceed. The sound of stomping boots made her heart race as a group of guards rounded the far corner of the hall and made their way towards her. She tensed and gripped her blood-soaked axes, ready for another fight as they came to a halt before her and her friends.

"State your business," the lead guard stepped forward and said.

Anders stepped up beside Kalina but she held out a hand, letting go of her axes. She tried to disguise how much her hands shook.

"I am Kalina, daughter of the late King Hakon of the Valdir, and daughter of the late Queen Cherise Stanchon. I am the rightful heir to the Ethean and Valdiran thrones and I have come to claim my birthright."

Whispering threaded through the group of soldiers.

"It's a coup," a voice said.

"Where is the Queen?" another called.

"How do we know you are telling the truth?" The foremost guard said, his hand twitching on his sword.

"Because I know it to be true, Callum."

Anders had stepped forward, addressing the guard. Kalina gave him a grateful look.

"Anders. How do you know?"

Anders swallowed and dug in his pocket. He pulled out a piece of paper Kalina had never seen before. As he unfolded it, she caught sight of the official seal and what looked like her mother's signature. She almost let out a sigh of relief but bit it back and looked the guard in the eyes. Callum stepped forward, taking his hand from the blade, and took the letter.

"This is a letter from the Queen," he said as his eyes began to skim. "It states that Kalina Stanchon is her one true heir. I recognize her signature." He held it out to his men, and eyed Kalina with a mixture of curiosity. "We never even knew you existed. Are you the reason for this war? For the King's obsession with the Valdir?"

She nodded.

"I never understood why he was pursuing me until I found out about who I was. He must have known, and knew I was a threat." She took a deep breath before pressing on. "My mother, Queen Cherise, died in childbirth just a few days ago."

Shocked faces greeted her statement. Finally, Callum glanced around, seeming to suddenly realize the strangeness of the situation. His eyes narrowed.

"Where is the King?"

"He is locked in the dungeon. I will see he gets a fair trial for the atrocities he's heaped upon my people. In the meantime, I must secure this castle and this city. Sir Gregan was in the dungeon too, and while he is dead-" Callum and the other guards looked at each other at this declaration. "- his men and the armies may still want to fight us."

"What about Askor?" Anders said.

"I don't know. They will be angry we deposed their Prince. But with my mother gone, I am the rightful heir." She wasn't entirely sure that was how Ethean rule worked, but it made sense. Osian was not the heir, as a second child, but did she have a legal right to take it from the king? She looked at the guards before her. She needed to know where their allegiances stood.

"How will you serve?" she challenged.

For a brief moment she thought Callum might pull his sword and attack. And he did pull it from its sheath, each guard behind him doing the same until about twenty swords were before her. A shout echoed from down the hall.

"Callum! Callum! She's your Queen you idiot!"

Talon came racing down the hall, his own sword bouncing against his side as he approached. Kalina was relieved to see him alive and well. He came huffing and puffing to stand between her and Callum. Callum eyed the sweat drenched Talon and then quirked an eyebrow.

"I know that, you fool."

He planted his sword on the ground and knelt before Kalina. Kalina allowed a small breath of relief to escape her lips as the remainder of the guards knelt as well, murmuring her name.

"Queen Kalina."

"Stand," she said, grateful her voice was steady.

"I want the city secured and any guards or nobles who outwardly refuse my rule placed in the dungeon for now. I will hold a coronation in two days, once the rest of my people arrive." She turned to Talon. "I need you to go recall my troops. Tell them the war against the Valdir is over."

Talon bowed slightly and ran off to do her bidding. Callum turned to his men and began barking orders, Anders joining him. Together they left, leaving Kalina with two palace guards, Leif, Kari,

Jormungand, and a limping Rangvald for company in the now quiet hallway. Kalina took off, heading for where she knew her mother's rooms were. She wanted peace and quiet. She wanted a few moments alone to scream, or wail, or even just process everything that was happening. When they arrived outside her mother's rooms she turned to her entourage.

"Leif, you know what to do." He nodded to her, curiosity flashing across his face for a moment before he turned.

"Kari, you will stand guard out here. You, what's your name?" He addressed one of the guards.

"Stan, sir."

"Stan, you will stay with her and guard your Queen. Jormungand, find the healers hall and get Rangvald some help. Then I want you to send for Calla. We'll need her to help organize the castle."

Kalina smiled. She admired his ability to take charge in any situation.

"Commander," she said and Leif turned, an eyebrow raised. "Go to Mistress Aynne in the kitchens and tell her to come to my rooms." She paused. "Tell her to bring Margy and Master Alexil as well."

He nodded and marched off down the hall with the other guard who he began talking with amiably. Jormungand threw Rangvald's arm over his shoulder and began hauling him down the hall.

Kalina turned back to the door to her mother's rooms. She didn't bother looking behind her at the doors to the king's rooms. Those rooms she would save for later. Someone else could tear those rooms apart for all she cared. She rested her hand on the ornate golden door handles and paused, letting out a heavy sigh.

"Are you alright, your Majesty?" Kari placed a surprisingly gentle hand on Kalina's shoulder.

"Yes. I'm fine."

She pushed the door open. Stale air smelling of dust and mildew, mixed with the soft floral scent that was uniquely her mothers, met her. Her chest tightened at the smell, but she stepped inside. It was dark, but soft moonlight filtered in through high windows falling across the enormous four poster bed. Kalina made her way to the bed and sat, a puff of dust rising around her. Her chest felt like it was going to cave in with sadness.

    She buried her face in her mother's pillow and before she knew what was happening, she was asleep.

Chapter 35

A KNOCK ON THE DOOR WOKE KALINA. She hadn't realized she'd fallen asleep and she got up feeling groggy, the events of the day crowding in, threatening to overwhelm her. When she opened the door, all thoughts were banished as Margy rushed in, enveloping her in a huge hug. Kalina laughed, hugging the girl back and moving back into the room to allow Scholar Alexil and Mistress Aynne inside. Mistress Aynne held a candle and taper and began lighting the lamps in the room until it was aglow with soft light.

"I knew you were someone special!" Margy said in Kalina's ear. "I just can't believe you are the Princess!"

"Good to see you too, Margy." Kalina gently extricated herself from Margy's embrace and nodded to Mistress Aynne and Alexil. "And I am glad to see you both. We need to talk about what has happened since I left, and how we can get this castle in order."

Mistress Aynne raised an eyebrow, her usually stern face trying unsuccessfully to hide a small smile. Alexil was grinning beside the older woman, his white hair sticking out in all directions.

"I take it you know I was in communication with Eira?" Alexil said, taking a seat at a small table that occupied a corner of the room. The others joined him.

"Yes, she told me that you were doing everything you could to help my mother."

Alexil's wrinkled face fell at the mention of the late queen.

"I was. Sadly, it wasn't enough." The sorrow in his voice was palpable. "Leif told us of her passing."

Kalina reached across the table and squeezed the old scholar's hand in empathy.

"You did enough. She was able to make it to us, and we helped her have Osian, my half-brother. He is safe and will be here in a few days."

Alexil brightened slightly at that.

"I'm sorry for your loss, your Majesty." Mistress Aynne finally chimed in. "But if I may, we need to get to the business of running your castle. There are still those who will challenge your right to rule, and the faster you gain control, the easier it will be to combat those who dissent."

Kalina smiled and nodded, grateful that the woman could stay on task.

"Just what I needed, Mistress Aynne. I am promoting you to Steward. I need your expertise and your planning abilities to help run this place."

Mistress Aynne's face blanched slightly before she steeled her features and made a small bow from her seated position.

"As you wish, your Majesty. But who will run the kitchens?"

Kalina turned to a stunned looking Margy.

"I was rather hoping you would do it Margy?"

"But Kalina, I mean, your Majesty, I don't know how to work numbers!"

"That's alright. I will teach you," Mistress Aynne said.

A terrified Margy nodded in acceptance.

"I also have a dear friend, Calla, coming to help but she will be my personal assistant until a better one can be arranged."

"What would you like me to do, Majesty?" Alexil piped up.

"I need you to go through the King's rooms and see if you can find anything useful to support my claim. Perhaps a mention of me in a book? Use the libraries as well. In the meantime, you may also put back every tome the King took from the library."

Alexil's eyes lit up at that.

She dismissed them after telling them a bit of her story. They deserved an explanation for her coming in and changing their lives so suddenly. Then she blew out the lamps and fell asleep again, exhaustion and stress taking over.

Kari shook her awake just after sunrise. "Get up. You're wanted in the council chambers."

Kalina jolted upright at her words, rubbing her eyes that felt like sandpaper. Kari left her alone to wake up fully. Her mother's rooms faced south and she could see the pink sky to the east. Her bundle of Valdir clothing had been delivered in the night and was sitting on the foot of her bed.

She donned her red leathers once again and carefully extracted the iron crown from where Eira had made her pack it. She went to the gold, ornate mirror that stood in a corner and placed it atop her freshly braided hair. She looked like herself again. This was how she felt most comfortable. She strapped her axes to her back and strode into the hall, Kari and the other guard following behind her as she made her way to the council chambers. They weren't hard to find, for when she turned the corner from the royal's hallway, a door stood open half way down the next hall, angry voices emanating from it.

As Kalina entered, the voices died down as all eyes turned to her. She was relieved to see Mistress Aynne standing in a corner as well as Jormungand, Leif, and Rangvald all seated around a crowded table. Rangvald looked haggard but definitely better, his wounds treated and healing. Extra chairs had been drawn up and seven stuffy old men sat on the opposite side from her Valdir council. Kalina had to suppress a giggle at how put out the Ethean noble men seemed.

These were the council members of the king, and she knew she would have to remove some of them from office. They wouldn't like an upstart young woman, let alone a Valdir, telling them what to do. She took the chair at the head of the table and sat down as Kari took her place beside her brother. Mistress Aynne opened a servant's door and in marched Margy, another servant girl in tow, with trays full of refreshments. They laid them before the nobles and the Valdir in almost complete silence.

Kalina let the silence stretch, allowing the tension to build as the Ethean noblemen eyed her, letting them wonder what she would do. Finally, as Margy retreated with a wink, Kalina spoke, breaking the tension in the room.

"Noble council members of Ethea, and my trusted council. Today is an exciting day." Her panic began to rise but she'd addressed a large group of people before. She always felt she must look ridiculous and sound ridiculous standing before them like this. But she belonged here. This was her birthright, and if she didn't take it now, they would take it from her by force. So she cleared her throat and kept speaking.

"Today the old ways die and a new order rises. Ethea is no longer just Ethea. It is Ethea and the Valdir combined as one people. My father was Hakon, King of the Valdir. And my mother was Queen Cherise Stanchon of Ethea. I am the marrying of two peoples, two races, two thrones. You sit before me divided-" she gestured to the fact that they were on opposite sides of the great oak table. "But you will part here one people. We are all Etheans."

She stood, placing her fists on the table before her. A few of the noblemen were looking at her with newfound respect. But a few continued to look at her like she had three heads, like she was dirt beneath their shoes and something that should be eradicated. Those she would have to eliminate herself.

"For the last century, my people, the Valdir, have been persecuted, treated as nothing more than hired blades, something to be thrown into battle so that upstanding men such as yourselves could stay home with their families. We have been conscripted, killed, and sold. My people were forced to flee at the end of the war because we had been betrayed. My grandfather promised my mother to the Valdiran King's son, and then reneged on that promise, forcing us into exile in order to save our people. Since then we have been hunted by the Askorian Prince who married my mother after I was born. He is no King of Ethea. My mother remained Queen until the day she died giving birth to my half-brother, Osian Stanchon."

Murmurs flew between the Ethean nobles at this pronouncement. Kalina let them whisper for a moment before taking control again.

"And now I am the eldest living child of Queen Cherise Stanchon. The crown is mine by rights and from this day forth, persecution of any kind towards a Valdir or even an Ethean is a crime. For the Valdir are now Etheans." She eyed the nobles one by one. Some looked away from her blue-eyed stare, but a few held her gaze.

"I will have a coronation tomorrow evening in the throne room. I expect all nobles and their families to attend to swear fealty to my crown."

Then she turned and strode from the room, not even giving them a chance to question her. There was a time and place for questions, for them to ask for her entire story, for her to soothe their fears. But it was not today. Whatever the reason for them gathering in the council chambers, she didn't care. There was enough to do without sitting and listening to grown men argue.

Chapter 36

CALLA ARRIVED WITH BABY ISSA strapped to her chest. She came into Kalina's rooms like a whirlwind, straightening the space, dusting, and opening drawers and wardrobes. That afternoon, Eira and Osian arrived, along with the rest of the Valdiran army. Kalina immediately sent for the majority of her people to join them as soon as possible for her coronation. Mistress Aynne was the perfect choice to supplant the stuffy old steward who had been loyal to Terric, and as the day went on, men and women who had been fired when Kalina's grandfather had passed, came flocking to the palace, eager to get their jobs back and serve her, their rightful queen.

Kalina did her best to be a part of everything: answering questions about food choices for the coronation, decorations for the throne room, meeting new servants that Mistress Aynne presented to her for approval, a few noblemen who sought her out to kneel and swear fealty prematurely, or to fawn over her which she found nauseating. Despite a visit to Maska, who'd arrived after they'd sent Jormungand to fetch their waiting dragons, she still found herself exhausted and overwhelmed by the time supper rolled around. Calla caught her in a darkened alcove, trying to catch her breath and calm the panic that seemed to be lurking just under the surface ever since she'd addressed the council members. The woman took her hand and drew her into the newly cleaned queen's chambers and sat her down for a cup of tea and a few cookies that Margy had sent up.

Kalina was grateful as she nibbled on the edge of a buttery cookie and took a sip of her tea. It was the first moment all day she'd had a chance to breathe. Calla had laid Issa in a small wooden cradle that Anders had brought for her and was rummaging through Kalina's mother's old gowns in the huge oak wardrobe. She pulled out an ice blue one and held it up. Rhinestones sparkled in the light of the setting sun outside.

"What about this one?" She said.

Kalina frowned at the dress.

"What do you mean? What about it?"

Calla turned to her, a slightly exasperated look on her face.

"For your coronation, silly."

Kalina's face drained of color. She had gotten so used to

wearing pants and leathers with the Valdir that it hadn't occurred to her that as queen of Ethea and the Valdir she would need to change her wardrobe back to dresses.

"But I can't fight in that-" she said, her voice trailing off.

Calla lowered her arms and gave Kalina a 'you know what you need to do' look. Kalina sighed heavily and finished her tea.

"What about something new?" She said, standing to approach the wardrobe.

"There's not enough time to make you a new one by tomorrow night. We will have to alter one of these gowns," she trailed off as she stuck her torso deep into the wardrobe that was full to the brim with dresses.

Kalina's hands grazed the fabrics, remembering her mother in a few of them during her months at the castle. Her mother had always looked good in blue. And her father's dragon was blue. Her fingers stopped on a dark blue dress in satin. She reached up and pulled it from the wardrobe.

"What about this one?"

Calla stood up from her search and looked at the gown, her dark curls a bit of a mess. It was the dark blue of the deepest lake. The satin shone in the setting sun, glittering off the silver embroidery on the bodice, neck and skirt. The neckline was a deep cut v, but the top above the breasts and down the long sleeves was a delicate lace. It was stunning and elegant as it fell to the ground in an A-line silhouette. Calla let out a low whistle.

"That would be just perfect. With a few modifications." She took it from Kalina and began to shoo her from the room. "Leave it to me. Go find something else useful to do."

Suddenly Kalina found herself standing in the hall, two fresh guards waiting to escort her wherever she needed to go. She sighed and moved off down the hallway, curious what her old room in the library was like, and if it was still the same as the day she'd left it. Her guards trailed behind her, giving her room and privacy to explore.

The library was just as dim, quiet, and cool as she remembered it. She moved among the books like she had found lost friends, her hands dragging gently along their spines. She recalled many happy times spent searching through books and translating them for the scholars. But she also remembered the times that the other scribes had bullied her. She frowned at the memory as she approached her old room. The door was unlocked and she pushed it open, coughing slightly at the dust cloud that rose.

She brought in a small lantern from a nearby table and illuminated the dark room and was suddenly shocked at how small and cramped it was. Had she grown so much in a year that she no longer fit in this space? Or was it that this space had always been this small, but that she had learned to accept its limitations?

She continued to wander the halls of the castle, visiting the kitchens and begging for a roll stuffed with cheese from Margy before making her way to the massive, ornate doors of the throne room. Gold filigree wound up the edges of huge oak doors, their surface intricately carved with twining leaves and branches. The more she looked, the more astonished she became. Among the leaves and branches she could see carved wyverns and dragons. Suddenly, she wondered if at some point in Ethea's past the Valdir had been on the throne.

She pushed the heavy doors open and slipped through. The massive hall of the throne room was dim and quiet, only a few torches lined the walls, sending flickering light to dance across a large golden wrought throne. Kalina's feet padded softly across the parquet floor and the closer she drew to the throne, the more certain she became that something grey was sitting in it. Finally, she paused a few feet away and broke into a huge grin.

Moose, the grey tabby cat she had grown so fond of while she'd worked in the library, was sprawled out on the throne's seat. At her approach, he began to purr so loudly it seemed to reverberate in the entire room.

He rolled over, exposing his underside, and she climbed the stairs to rub his soft striped belly. She picked him up and sat on the throne, still stroking the purring cat. It was then that she realized that she was truly sitting on the Ethean throne. Her heart began to pound as she surveyed the hall, taking in every inch of it and memorizing the placement of all the doors.

Tomorrow, when she was to be crowned, she might not have the forethought to plan an escape if everything went south. The prince still languished in the dungeons, guarded day and night by an

Ethean guard and a Valdiran guard. But that didn't mean he didn't have supporters. The noble men she'd addressed that morning were a wild card. Some seemed accepting while others seemed ready to kill her. She sighed deeply. She would find out soon enough, and she needed to focus on the things she could control.

She brought Moose back to her rooms and he curled up on her bed and slept with her all night. The following morning, she awoke to Kari saying that more of their people had arrived, those who hadn't wanted to remain in the mountains as winter descended. Kalina didn't blame them. Winter down here on the valley floor was harsh enough. She knew the Valdir had used animal pelts, primarily that of the huge wolves and bears that lived in the Great Grey Mountains, as extra warmth, but it didn't feel like enough after a few decades living in the warmth of The Wastes.

She greeted them in the entrance hall and assigned them suites of rooms. Her people were few enough that most of the families fit into the guest halls of the castle. One day she'd have to find them homes in the city, let them assimilate into the great Ethean people but for now she would keep them close.

The dragons gathered in the courtyards of the castle grounds and the gardens. Kalina and Maska had spoken the day before about building a new set of stables big enough to house the dragons of those who lived at the castle. That was when an interesting question presented itself to her. If she combined her peoples, knowing that some would intermarry and have children, children like her: half Valdir and half Ethean, what would that mean for the deep magic that bound the Valdir and the dragons? Would the dragons begin bonding to more and more diverse people? Would anyone with a drop of Valdiran blood be able to bond with dragons? Would her people fade into obscurity? It was a question that terrified her both in its implications and its possibilities. Maska was equally curious and concerned and he promised to talk about the possibilities with the other dragons so that when the time came, they could properly discuss it. Kalina promised to do the same, but not until after her crown was secure.

Finally, as the noon bells rang in the city, Kalina made her way from the gardens where Maska was, up to her rooms to get ready for her coronation.

Chapter 37

CALLA AND EIRA HELPED KALINA DRESS. When she saw the dress Calla had altered she had gasped. The bodice was altered to cling closer to the body and sections of the skirt were slit so that it was easier to move in. When Kalina put it on, the top fit like a glove, hugging every curve down to her waist before flaring out around her. She wore her red leather pants beneath and Eira came forward with an intricately carved broad belt to strap around her middle like a corset. They finished off the look with carved red leather bracers. Calla reached out and tugged at the waist where the satin skirt met the lace covered top.

"If you tug here, the skirt can be torn away. This is in case of emergency, mind, not so that you can ditch the skirt the moment you are crowned."

She gave a mock frown to Kalina, who laughed.

"I won't ruin your creation, Calla."

The woman softened and dragged her to a chair in front of a small vanity.

"Now for your hair, I was thinking intricate braids," Calla said, holding sections of Kalina's silver hair up.

Eira came up beside the younger woman. The two had become fast friends once Eira had arrived at the castle.

"Let me do it. It should be done by a Valdir."

Kalina knew how important battle braids and Runark tattoos were for the Valdir. Soon Eira's deft fingers were flying through her hair. Calla bustled around the room, digging through boxes until she let out a small gasp. Kalina and Eira turned to see Calla holding a bejeweled box, one hand to her mouth.

"What is it, Calla?" Kalina called and the woman looked up finally, a little flustered before coming over to them and presenting the box.

Kalina took it. Inside sat a stunning crown. It was wrought in a dark iron, not too unlike her own Valdiran crown, but along each delicately carved point were cleverly placed dragon scales in shades of sapphire. Kalina knew what this was before she found the note hidden beneath the crown.

Dear Cherise,

Please keep this and wear it on the day you are crowned Queen. Although we are far apart, you will forever be my one and only love.

Yours completely,

H.

A tear slipped down Kalina's cheek as she read the note that was written in her father's hand. He had made this crown for her mother even after they'd been torn apart. For all Kalina knew, this was the last thing her father had sent to her mother, their last communication. Her hands shook as she withdrew the crown from the box and placed it gently atop her own head to see how it looked.

She sat before the mirror clad in shades of sapphire and red. It suited her and complimented her silver hair perfectly. She nodded and removed the crown, placing it back in the box and handing it to Eira.

"I will be crowned with this."

Eira nodded solemnly and retreated, carrying the box. Calla came up behind Kalina and stroked her cheek before hugging her, their eyes meeting in the mirror.

"I know your mother couldn't be here with us today, but I will be out there, and so will Anders and Talon."

"Talon's back?" She had sent him to gather the army. Now she wondered if he had succeeded.

"He got back this afternoon. He rode ahead of the army but he assured me that it was all in hand."

Kalina let out a breath in relief and nodded, wiping a few errant tears from her cheeks, careful not to smudge the koal drawn around her eyes, and trying to settle her churning stomach. She glanced back at the mirror one more time. Her scar stood out against her pale cheek, as did the brown Runark tattoos that covered her face. She didn't think she looked pretty, her scar always making her feel self-conscious, but she looked formidable. Like an ice queen.

Once again Kalina shuffled nervously in the antechamber off the throne room, waiting for her time to enter. She could hear the gathered crowd of Ethean nobles and Valdir behind the small door that led to the throne and she was beyond nervous. A part of her wanted desperately to run. But she was here for her people, not to give in to her own panic.

Finally the door opened from the other side and she stepped

through. Silence reigned as she crossed the floor and climbed the steps of the dais and stood before the throne. She finally focused on the crowd and not her feet and saw the room utterly divided. Silver haired Valdir stood to her left, while the Etheans of all colors stood to her right. The Valdir watched her expectantly, with looks of reverence and respect. Most of the Ethean nobility watched her with expectation, fear, distrust, and some with hatred.

The head Priestess of the Order of the Mother Freyre ascended the dais and held out her hands for silence within the already silent room. Kalina struggled with the urge to vomit and instead, planted her feet, focusing on the feeling of her shoes on the floor, letting it root her to the spot. She held her head high and stared into the faces of her people.

"People of Ethea," the Priestess intoned, before nodding to the Valdir. "And people of the Valdir. Today we gather to witness the crowning of a new monarch. The changing of monarchs is always a time of upheaval, of great change. But change is often good. Kalina Stanchon of the Valdir and Ethea stands before you, ready to be the one to lead you through that change and into an even brighter future."

She paused then, looking through the room as if searching for a better candidate. Kalina did her best not to fidget.

"If anyone here has an objection to her taking the crown, now is the time to speak up, or be forever quiet."

A general shuffling and murmuring filled the chamber. Finally a plump man of middle age, dressed in a rich velvet doublet, stepped forward. Kalina recognized him from the council chamber.

"Lord Averil," the Priestess announced as he ascended a few steps up the dais.

He bowed slightly to the Priestess before eyeing Kalina and turning back to the gathered crowd.

"Lords and ladies of the court. I stand before you as a trusted member of the King's council. You have all known me for many years and trusted my opinion."

The crowd of Ethean nobility nodded in assent.

"I stand before you now, and I say, this girl is no Queen of mine. Our King languishes in the dungeon, forcibly deposed by this upstart, nobody girl who fancies herself a Queen." He said the last bit with sudden vehemence, his noble composure slipping. He pointed angrily at Kalina, who resisted the urge to take a step back. She had to stand her ground.

Sound erupted in the throne room, many of the nobility calling for her head on a spike, for all the Valdir to be eradicated from Ethea. Hatred spewed from many of their mouths. Kalina watched as her own people bristled and began to threaten back but when she made eye contact with Leif and Jormungand in the front row she shook her head slightly. Within a few moments, the Valdir were looking to her and she held out a hand for their silence. There was no use in fighting this hatred with more hatred. She had come here to end a war, not start a new one.

"People of Ethea," she said, stepping forward as an uneasy hush fell over the crowd.

Lord Averil turned towards her but he did not step down.

"People of Ethea. I include the Valdir in this, for they are my people, as are all the people who dwell in Ethea. I was born to Queen Cherise and King Hakon of the Valdir and I am of both people. I was raised right here in Ethea. In a small Abbey dedicated to the Mother." She smiled then to the Priestess who smiled serenely back. "I know what it is to suffer, to toil. And since I found the Valdir, I have known war. I have fought on the battlefields and seen young men and women die for a war they didn't choose, for a King who ripped them from their beds to fight. I will not do that." She held out her hands in a placating manner. "I am the daughter of an oppressed people, but I am also a daughter of Ethea. I promise as your Queen to be a just and kind ruler. I will fight for my people and take care of them."

She was cut off suddenly by Lord Averil.

"Promises are all well and good, Lady Kalina."

He emphasized the Lady to try to put her in her place. She was getting rather sick of this man's arrogance and of constantly being second-guessed.

"Your goodness isn't being debated here. Your right to rule is," he continued.

"I am the daughter of Hakon of the Valdir and Cherise Stanchon-" she began again.

Lord Averil began to laugh but she plowed forward.

"And I have proof," she interrupted, giving him her best glare.

She held out her hand to Anders who stepped forward, handing over the letter from the queen. Kalina marched to Lord Averil and handed it to him as the laughter died on his lips. He quickly scanned the letter, before looking up, frowning at her.

"This still doesn't prove anything. I could fake this signature."

He flashed the letter. Kalina was at a complete loss. How could she prove who she was? Would she have to take the crown by force? Instill fear so they would obey? It was the last thing she wanted to do.

"Is there anyone here who can corroborate your story?"

Lord Averil was still speaking as he began to pace the dais steps. Kalina looked ahead, trying to keep her focus on the back of the room and not let her audience see how much she was shaking.

"I can."

Chapter 38

A VOICE KALINA THOUGHT SHE recognized rang out in the hall, quieting all the murmuring voices of doubt. A tall slim man with dark eyes and hair that was going grey with age stepped forward, making his way towards the dais. Kalina realized with a jolt she knew who it was. Or rather, she knew she'd seen him before. He was the dark stranger who had met with Father Martin the day she'd learned she was a Valdir. The day everything had changed.

"You," she said as he approached the dais, taking the few steps up with a strange grace. He smiled a tight smile to her and nodded.

"Yes. I can vouch that she is in fact the daughter of both King Hakon of the Valdir and Queen Cherise Stanchon. She is the heir to both thrones and our rightful Queen now that Queen Cherise has passed on."

Lord Averil blustered for a moment before finding his voice.

"How do you know? Can you prove it?"

Lord Averil seemed to be turning an interesting shade of purple and for a moment Kalina was relieved that this stranger had stepped forward to vouch for her.

"Yes. I have here," he produced a scroll with an unbroken seal from his doublet. "A writ from his late Majesty, King Osian Stanchon stating that his daughter, Cherise Stanchon gave birth to a female child named Kalina Stanchon shortly before her marriage to Prince Terric of Askor. That child was named heir to the throne and then entrusted to my care. I placed her at Hywell Abbey with Father Martin, to be looked after until such a time as she was deemed safe. Prince Terric, however, learned of her existence and knew she could depose him and began searching for her relentlessly. Many of you knew of his obsession."

Many of the nobles around the room began to nod in agreement.

"I knew she had to remain at the Abbey. So I went back to check on her almost one year ago. My plan was to one day reveal her heritage and bring her back to the palace to live, but the High Father had different plans. He was fond of the child and wanted her to have a normal life. A few days later, however, that child disappeared and a few months later we learned she had taken the throne of the Valdir following her father's death in a battle with Terric's men. She has come back to Ravenhelm to claim her birthright, a birthright I fully support."

With that declaration, the man turned and knelt at Kalina's feet, his head bowed in deference. His story almost brought tears to her eyes, but she blinked them away and instead leaned down to take his hand and help him stand.

"Thank you," she said, her voice coming out a bit thick with emotion. "Who are you?"

The man smiled kindly at her, before bending to kiss her hand.

"I am Lord Illeron, Spymaster."

Sound filled the throne room until the Priestess held up both her hands. Lord Illeron stepped to the side, showing his support as Kalina surveyed her people. Many of the Ethean faces were now open with curiosity rather than closed with distrust. Lord Averil was still scowling but he had retreated back among the crowd to sulk. He would have to be removed from the council, Kalina knew. It was one thing to be questioned as Kari and Jormungand had done, and another to be outright opposed. He would be a thorn in her side.

"Without further ado, we will proceed with the coronation."

She gestured for Eira to step forward, the ornate crown box in her hands. She opened it and presented the crown to the Priestess who took it in her hands and reverently held it aloft before Kalina.

"With this crown we name you Protector of the Realm. With this crown we name you Keeper of All People. With this crown we name you Daughter of Freyre, Queen of the Valdir and Queen of Ethea."

She gently set the crown atop Kalina's braided silver hair. Kalina felt as though a physical weight much greater than that of the crown settled upon her shoulders. She was now responsible for so much more.

"All hail Queen Kalina!" the Priestess intoned.

"Long live the Queen!"

The crowd responded and as one, as if they were bent over by a rolling wave, the entire audience, including the Priestess, bent their knees before her. Kalina's heart swelled as pride lifted her up. She felt thankful that these people trusted her to take care of them.

She would try to be worthy of it.

To be continued…

Ready for more? The final book, Born of Blood is up next!

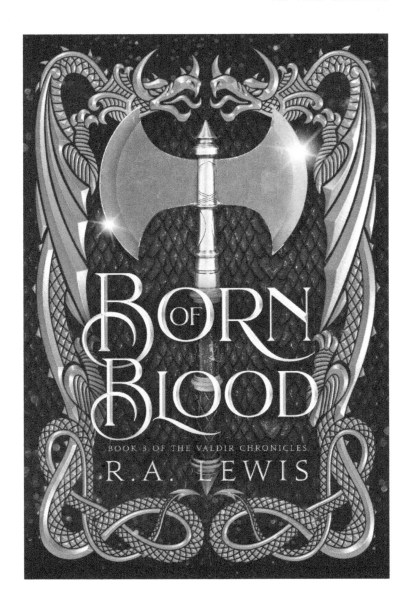

BORN OF BLOOD

BOOK 3 OF THE VALDIR CHRONICLES

R.A. LEWIS

RA Lewis

Born of Blood

Book 3
The Valdir Chronicles

Dedication

This book is dedicated to imagination. Never lose it.

RA Lewis

448

Part 1

Chapter 1

LATE AFTERNOON SUN FILTERED IN through the high windows of Queen Kalina Stanchon's sitting room in the Ravenhelm Castle, falling across the scattering of papers on the large desk. Kalina sat, her head in her hands, silver hair falling down around her, a crown with blue scales and silver scrollwork askew on her head. She was now queen of two peoples, both of Ethea and of the Valdir, and the pressure was building. She groaned just as someone entered through the ornate doors on the other side of the room.

"Oh, quit complaining," a voice rang out, making Kalina's head snap up. "You are the Queen. Things can't be all that bad."

"Easy for you to say, Delisa. All you ever see is the good stuff." Kalina gestured to the stacks of papers before her. "This is what it takes to actually run the country."

Her best friend paused in front of the desk, both hands firmly planted on her ample waist, her hip cocked out and an eyebrow raised.

"All I see is the good stuff? What about all the times in the last month that I've had to talk you out of running away? Again?"

The look she gave Kalina spelled no-nonsense, but the corner of her lip twitched in a smile. Kalina gave a small chuckle and sighed.

"You're right. I'm just feeling overwhelmed."

"Wasn't it like this with the Valdir?"

"No. The Valdir had limited writing materials in the mountain, and since their population was so small, it was relatively easy to handle. But Ethea is a huge country. There are so many more moving parts, plus I have to think about what's best for the Valdir, and they are having trouble assimilating."

"They did live in that mountain for more than a decade," Delisa said as she bustled around the room, straightening various items and stacking Kalina's discarded breakfast and lunch dishes. "Besides, cities weren't really meant for dragons."

Delisa's words were true enough. Maska, her huge emerald dragon, had come to her a week after the Valdir and the dragons had arrived at the capitol and mentioned feeling useless. They hadn't needed the Emberweed after all, and so he'd felt like he wasn't useful to her or the kingdom. Kalina had not flown with him in days, and without patrols to run and a mountain to guard, he spent his days lying in the sun of the gardens and getting fat on cattle that were brought to him. Many of the Valdir had left the city, back to the Great Grey Mountains, choosing to settle in their ancestral homeland rather than stay in the capital, Ravenhelm. More and more left every day. Kalina was sad to see her people leaving, but she knew it was for the best. They were never meant to live in the tight quarters of Ravenhelm, and she couldn't combat the wariness of the city's general populace at having such fierce warriors among them. The Valdir needed space and freedom, a feeling Kalina knew all too well, and she wasn't about to keep them tied to a city they hated.

"You're right," Kalina sighed and scrubbed at her tired face with her hands. "I'm just going to finish going over these reports about grain consumption and then I'll take a break for dinner."

Delisa grunted her approval and then went back to straightening up Kalina's office. Kalina had sent for Delisa not long after her arrival at the capitol, offering her a position as a member of her household, and her best friend had responded wholeheartedly. Now Kalina was beginning to appreciate her friend's ability to help her hold things together.

When she wasn't busy with her baby, Calla, the woman who had taken Kalina in the first time she'd stepped foot in Ravenhelm, often spent time at the castle. Together, Calla and Delisa had hit it off marvelously, the two strong women helping to keep Kalina in line whenever she tried to run off for a flight on Maska or to the training grounds instead of attending yet another infernal council meeting.

Soon, the lines began to blur on the page and Kalina found she was reading and re-reading the same sentence over and over and still didn't know what it said. Finally, she put down the papers and stood, stretching. Her muscles were stiff and sore and she vowed to hit the training yard early the next morning to help them loosen up. It was difficult to keep herself in shape when much of her job of running the country happened from behind her desk.

She spent the evening eating dinner with Delisa and Kari, the two women cracking jokes and poking fun at one another. Sometimes the two women flirted, furtive touches giving them away. Kalina eyed them sideways, a small smile playing across her lips as Delisa poked Kari in the side with a wicked grin on her face. Kalina would be very happy if two of her best friends in the world ended up together. But she wouldn't bring it up, she wanted to let them figure it out on their own.

The next morning was bitingly cold, winter giving its final grip on the city. Frost covered the ground, turning every blade of grass white. Kalina stood in the frigid air, her twin axes in her hands, as she moved through the warm-up sequence which Geir, her father's best friend and her previous commander, had taught her all those months ago. Every time she did them she thought of him and it brought with it a twinge of pain and sadness; although as time went on, the pain of losing him, her father, and her mother was beginning to lessen. Especially with the distraction of running a country. Besides, she'd spent more time with Geir, and his loss had seemed more painful somehow than losing either of her parents. Walking through the palace gardens always reminded her of her mother, and flying with Maska reminded her of her father and their first flight together.

She felt a presence behind her so she pivoted, her axes at the ready. She might be queen, but she couldn't let her guard down, not entirely. Beside her personal guards stood Leif, her commander and Geir's son, watching her with his grey eyes, his silver battle braids falling around his shoulders as she moved through her exercises. He smiled crookedly at her and she returned the smile.

"Thought I'd join you," he said as he moved to her side, pulling his own sword from its scabbard and beginning his own fluid dance. Kalina resumed her movements, and her chest filled with joy and pride.

Her own feelings for Leif had been growing steadily since coming to Ravenhelm. He had been her staunchest supporter, and more than once, when the pressure of being the Queen of two peoples began to make her feel overwhelmed, he had been there to hold her as she'd fallen apart.

"I haven't seen you in a few days." Her words came out in huffs and puffs as she exerted herself, executing a slow block and attack with her axes.

"I've been in the Valdir villages, setting up a small council there and appointing a leader to help run things like you asked. Since they are so far away, it's hard for you to be there to settle disputes."

"Good. Who did you appoint?"

"I wanted to appoint Skaldrik but he insisted on staying here as the chief metal worker. He said he has a surprise for you." He winked at Kalina.

She looked at him bemusedly. She was curious, but she didn't want to spoil the surprise for herself.

"So I ended up appointing Asta. She hasn't been happy here, so I took her back with me," he continued.

"That was a good choice. She has a solid head on her shoulders." The woman had been a part of Kalina's council since the beginning, and before that she'd been a part of Kalina's father's entourage and council. She and Kalina frequently butted heads, but Kalina felt confident the woman would take care of her people and do what was in the best interest of the whole rather than the few, especially if Eira, Kalina's aunt, was there to guide her.

"I have a surprise for you, too," Leif said, giving her a mischievous grin, as he turned to perform a slow attack on her with his blade. He stepped in close, pressing his body against hers. His nearness made her suck in a breath, tasting the tang of sweat in the air between them on her tongue. His sword and her axes were locked in a quiet and slow struggle, and for a few moments, Kalina got to savor the feel of his muscled body against hers before they broke apart.

"What is it?"

She began circling him, their individual training dances forgotten. He grinned across the gap at her, then stepped forward swiftly and raised his sword to attack her but she deflected it fluidly and stepped around in a circle, forcing him to follow.

"You'll see soon enough. It's something I promised to give you a while ago." He winked again. "There's your hint."

Kalina stopped dead in her tracks, a puzzled look on her face. Leif stopped too, lowering his sword. What had he promised to give her? So many things had happened in the last months that details were blending together and getting fuzzy.

"Don't hurt yourself," Leif joked.

Kalina snapped out of her momentary lapse in focus just in time for Leif to launch himself at her in a full-speed attack. She had to pull her axes up quickly in order to block his strike. He kept coming, forcing her back across the small practice yard until her back was pressed up against the wall of the training barracks. His face loomed closer and Kalina flicked her eyes to her guards. They were turned away, watching for outside threats, not worried about what Leif was doing. Leif was her commander after all.

He leaned across their straining weapons and pressed his lips against hers. Kalina relaxed at his touch, their weapons falling, discarded on the ground as Leif deepened the kiss. They were hidden from any spying eyes by the side of the building and the low overhanging roof, and Kalina felt comfortable enough for a moment to entangle herself with Leif, winding her arms around his neck and stroking it with her fingers. These stolen moments with him were what kept her going, even when she wanted to quit.

Finally, they pulled apart, both panting slightly. Luckily, their bright flushes could be attributed to their bout of fighting rather than the kissing as they made their way back into the castle, Kalina's guards falling into step behind her. Alone time was something she craved, and lately, the only alone time she got was when riding Maska. Even then, usually at least one Valdir was required to fly with her. She chose Leif when he wasn't busy, otherwise Kari or Rangvald. Neither of them would force their way into her alone time. They understood it better than most.

The interior of the castle was cool but not as cold as the early spring outside its walls. So far winter had been a busy affair, full of meetings with the Ethean nobles to discuss crop yields, the treasury, the army, recompense to families shattered by the war, and for the nobles to declare their loyalty to her. Kalina was heartily sick of sitting politely in a stuffy room with a whole slew of stuck up peacock nobility, all of them looking down their noses at her. She had found a significantly warmer reception from the common folk of the realm, and she'd spent time getting to know her people as much as she could. Each festival day, of which there were many in Ethea, she spent down in Ravenhelm, talking with people, learning their concerns and needs. Most of her council thought it was a bad idea, but Kalina didn't care. She had learned from her aunt Eira that the best way to be accepted was to get involved. So she had.

"You know, eventually you'll need a few of those nobles on your side," Eira had warned one afternoon when Kalina had come storming in after Lord Avril had once again insulted her for being a half-breed orphan. Kalina had thrown a pillow clear across the room and then immediately stripped her clothes off, not caring that she left her velvet purple dress in a pile on the floor, and donned her red leathers, eager to go to the training grounds to get her pent up aggression out.

She knew Eira was right, but it was so hard trying to connect with people who not only still didn't trust you, but thought you were beneath them and thought the way you did things was unacceptable.

Kalina sighed and put her axes away in their double sheathes over each shoulder. At least she still had a few allies, like Leif. She glanced sideways at him, as he prowled beside her through the stone corridors.

"Now, how about that surprise?" she said with a grin.

He returned it, wolfishly.

Chapter 2

KALINA STARED IN AWE AT THE GOLDEN fall of scales that made up the light chainmail shirt she wore. She ran her fingers down it, mystified at how light it was and how easily it moved with her as she stretched and twisted.

"All of these are from Arikara?"

Leif chuckled beside her, admiring the way she looked in the shirt.

"Every one. That's why it took so long. I could have made you a rainbow one out of randomly discarded scales but I wanted something special. Something beautiful, like you."

Every inch was covered in golden dragon scales. The sleeves reached down to her elbows, and it fell just past her backside, with slits in the sides to allow for easy movement. It covered all of her vital parts while still being functional, and glittered in the sunlight that bled in through the window.

Kalina looked up at Leif in awe. She couldn't believe he'd spent so much time meticulously fitting each scale to the shirt, all for her. She wiped away an errant tear as she turned back to the mirror.

"It's the most beautiful thing I've ever seen. You'll have to tell Arikara I said thank you."

"Tell her yourself."

He put his arms around her waist and turned her towards him.

"I wanted you to have the most beautiful armor in the world. There is no other like it in existence. When the rest of the Valdir hear about it, they will all want their own. So, cherish this one." He lifted her chin with his fingers and she stared up into his grey eyes. Her breath caught in her throat for a second before he lowered his lips to brush hers. She wished with all her might that they could stay that way forever. But they had a council meeting soon, and then she was meeting with Mistress Aynne and Margy to discuss the preparations for an upcoming ball that was being held to celebrate the Festival of Flowers.

That made her pause as she began to pull the dragon scale shirt off over her head. St. Martin's Day was only a few months away at the end of Spring. She marveled for a moment about how far she had

457

come as she pulled the shirt off and set it reverently on her bed.

"Maska is going to be jealous," she joked, pulling her leather vest back on and tightening the laces across her chest. "He'll be mad you didn't ask him for his scales."

"Green would have been nice, but gold compliments both of you perfectly." Leif held out her ax sheath and she pulled it on over her shoulders, buckling it across her chest. She never went unarmed anymore, even with constant protection in the castle. After two different assassination attempts, she wasn't taking any chances, especially since Terric, the former king of Ethea, was still imprisoned beneath the castle in the dungeons.

"Well, you will still have to apologize to him." She smirked over at Leif. "Now let's go see what Lord Averil has to complain about today." Leif laughed at her remark and together they left her quarters and made their way towards the council chambers.

Kalina's Valdir council members were already present, as were a few of the Ethean noblemen and one woman. That was the first thing she'd done once she'd taken the throne: allowed women on the council. She currently had only Lady Elise Renfort of Ethea on the council alongside her Valdir women. A stoic and sensible widow, Lady Renfort's husband had died in the Long War and she'd never remarried. She bobbed her elaborately styled grey head at Kalina as she sat at the large head chair.

Kalina's cousin Kari sat picking her fingernails with a dagger, a smirk on her clever face, and beside her, her brother Rangvald, who was much more reserved and practical, rolled his eyes at his sister's antics and lack of decorum. Kalina nodded to Jormungand who sat on the other side of Kari, the bearded and stocky man nodding back. Leif took his spot beside her and squeezed her leg beneath the table in support, as he'd always done. Lord Illeron, the tall and thin Spymaster, entered the chamber, bowed slightly to her and took a seat on her left-hand side. This man had delivered her to Hywell Abbey as a baby, hiding her away from Askor and its king's many watchful eyes. And he had been the first to stand up for her when she'd claimed the throne, deposing Askor's Prince, Terric.

Lord Avril entered the council chambers last, behind even Lord Tameron who always had a habit of being late to everything. When he finally took his seat beside Lord Illeron, Kalina was growing impatient. She steepled her fingers before her nose and looked at each council member, waiting for someone to open the discussion. She hadn't requested the meeting, Lord Averil had. Finally, the man cleared his throat and spoke.

"Your Majesty, I requested this meeting to discuss two things. First is the matter of the succession." He paused, swallowing as Kalina narrowed her eyes at him. She had heard mumblings about this before, but not directly from Lord Averil himself. She took a deep breath and let it out slowly, waiting.

"All of us here on the council want what is best for the Stanchon line, and for the good of the kingdom." Lord Avril's eyes darted around, looking at the others around him. Lord Tameron nodded beside him and seemed to be the man's only supporter, but Lord Averil wasn't daunted and he plowed on. "But some of us are concerned that you are still unmarried. With Ethea fresh out of a war, with Askor to our north, and the possibility of another war, we fear for the safety of the crown. We suggest that you consider finding someone to marry, and to get us an heir as soon as possible."

In the silence that followed his words, Kalina put her hands flat on the rough oak table before her. She clenched her jaw, trying not to let her frustration come out. Leif gripped her knee beneath the table and she used his touch to help leech away some of the anger that had boiled up at Lord Averil's suggestion.

"Lord, Averil. I respect you, and everyone at this table's, opinion. I even welcome hearing anything anyone has to say. But in this respect, I must politely decline. I have barely taken the throne, and I am still trying to stabilize a country fresh out from under the foot of a tyrant. Marrying now would create unneeded upheaval and would be but a mere distraction from our true goal: peace and prosperity."

"But, your Majesty, a wedding could be just what the country needs. It will prove that you are thinking about stability, and would set many minds at ease among the nobility that you are thinking of this country's future. Especially if that marriage is politically advantageous," Lord Tameron chimed in, backing up his friend Lord Averil. They made eye contact with one another and Lord Averil nodded. Kalina let out a breath.

"My Lords and Ladies, let's table the discussion of marriage for now. There is the upcoming Festival of Flowers celebrations, as well as Prince Terric's trial, to focus on. Marriage will come in due time." Kalina sat back in her chair, effectively ending that line of questioning.

Lord Averil cleared his throat again.

"Your Majesty, that brings up the second matter, Prince Terric's trial. It is my opinion that it be held publicly. He deserves to hear from his former subjects, hear their accusations, and stand trial for those crimes." Lord Tameron once again nodded vigorously beside him. Kalina had to struggle not to roll her eyes.

"Public? Doesn't that put Prince Terric at risk? Doesn't it put us all at risk?" Leif said.

Kalina narrowed her eyes at Lord Averil. She didn't entirely trust his motivations for making the trial public. She searched the faces of the other council members, who had remained suspiciously quiet thus far.

"I agree. What say you Lady Renfort?" she asked. The older woman shifted slightly in her seat before speaking.

"I don't disagree. I believe the man should answer publicly for his crimes against this country, but I am concerned about the guards' ability to maintain order and decorum among the masses."

"We will enlist the army's help," Lord Averil interjected, turning to Leif, an eager smile on his plump face.

Leif's face remained void of emotion. He was particularly good at keeping his emotions close to his chest. Kalina had never mastered that, she wore her emotions all over her face. She often wished she could be as stoic as him.

"I can, of course, bring in an extra squadron of my men but I don't think this is a good plan. Too many variables we cannot control, too many things that could go wrong. My Queen, I think this should be a private affair, with only nobility present."

Kalina agreed with him, but she could see from other's faces, they were in the minority. Kari had finally put down her belt knife and leaned forward.

"I agree with you, Leif, but I also agree with him." She squinted at Lord Averil. "That piece of scum deserves whatever is coming to him, and the ones he hurt most were her people. While he and the nobility sat up here in the lap of luxury, your people wallowed in poverty, giving up everything for a war he created out of fear."

Rangvald hesitantly nodded beside his sister. Kalina sat back in her chair. They weren't wrong. Her people had suffered more than she could fathom.

"We'll bring in a few squads and focus on controlling everything we can," Rangvald said, putting a hand on Leif's shoulder, placating.

Jormungand was sitting back in his chair, his arms crossed over his chest, scowling through his thick silver beard. Kalina nodded to him, encouraging him to speak his piece.

"It should be public. And the Valdir should be present. He butchered our people, slaughtered their relatives and friends. Dragons should also be present. He burned them alive. Besides, their presence should help keep people in line."

The only person who had been silent was Lord Illeron. Kalina rubbed the bridge of her nose, she could feel a headache coming on. Finally, she looked up at the older man and raised an eyebrow.

"What say you, Lord Illeron?" she asked. The man shrugged.

"It seems the majority want a public trial. While I would prefer it be private, I believe that your people would see it as a disservice, a way to keep them out. And right now, you need the public's approval more than anything."

He was, of course, right. Kalina sighed and stood.

"Fine. It will be a public trial. But let's finalize the details after the Festival of Flowers. For now, let's worry about celebrating and throwing a great party."

Chapter 3

KALINA RAN HER FINGERS ALONG THE rows of flowers added to the ballroom perimeter, enjoying their softness and the pleasant aroma that wafted from them. Streamers and ribbons hung from the ceiling and chandeliers, and flowers adorned every surface. The staircase that descended into the room had a garland of ivy, sunset roses, and daylilies, as well as maiden's kiss, and dragon's breath. Dragon's breath was her favorite, floating in the air like clouds of smoke, its pattern delicate and lace-like.

It reminded her of Maska and she decided that as soon as she was done with this meeting, she would go visit him for a quick flight. Delisa, Margy, Mistress Aynne, and Calla came through the main doors together, followed by a handful of servants. Kalina met them partway across the room. Delisa frowned at her outfit, putting her hands on her ample hips.

"I don't understand why you insist on wearing those old leathers instead of the dozens of beautiful dresses hanging in your wardrobe."

"Is that any way to address your Queen?" Mistress Aynne said, giving Delisa a disapproving look. Calla and Margy hid their smiles behind their hands, and Kalina pressed her lips together, trying to hold in her own smart retort and smile.

"Nice to see you, too," she said to the small entourage before her. She gestured to the partially decorated ballroom around her. "You all have done such a stunning job already, I'm not sure what feedback I have."

Mistress Aynne pulled out a clipboard and riffled through some papers on it until she came to the one she wanted.

"The decorations have been handled, your Majesty. We just need you to finalize this menu and make a decision on entertainment. Then we can go over the guest list one final time."

Kalina had to work hard not to roll her eyes. Party planning was the last thing on her mind. She was looking forward to celebrating the holiday but she had no desire to be a part of the planning. For this, she had leaned heavily on Calla and Delisa.

"Fine, what is on the menu?" She held out her hand and Mistress Aynne placed a list in it. Margy stepped up beside her and together they pored over it. A half an hour later, Kalina had approved food choices and realized as her stomach growled that after so much discussion of food, she was starving.

"Now, we have a band that will play all the traditional Ethean songs, but I wondered if there were any Valdiran tunes you would like played? We need to let them know by this evening if they are to learn them by the end of the week."

Kalina froze at Mistress Aynne's words. With so many battles since her arrival with the Valdir, there hadn't been much time to become familiar with the music. Suddenly, she felt like a horrible fraud. She was no Valdiran queen. She was just an orphan nobody from the deeps of the Ethean forests. Her cheeks heated as she cast around for a suitable answer.

"I may not be the best person to answer that. Eira, Kari, or even Rangvald or Leif would be better choices. They grew up with the Valdir and know the songs and their names."

Her heart sank at her own words. Suddenly, she very much wished she'd paid more attention to that part of her people's culture. But in the scheme of things, it just hadn't seemed important, not compared to fighting and surviving.

"Eira is not in the castle at the moment," Mistress Aynne began but Delisa interrupted.

"I'll sit down with Kari tonight and discuss music. Don't worry about that part."

Kalina was immensely grateful for Delisa stepping in. Mistress Aynne sniffed and looked down at her papers.

"Fine. I need it by tomorrow morning." She turned back towards the center of the ballroom. "Now, there is the matter of the theme. Are you sure you want to stick with a masked ball, your Majesty?"

"Yes. I have never been to one, and frankly, from what the other ladies of the court say, it sounds like so much fun."

"Excellent. Then I will leave you in Calla and Delisa's capable hands. Margy?" Mistress Aynne turned and began walking back towards the door. She had always been all business, which was why Kalina had appointed her castle steward. Margy shrugged and gave Kalina a "what can you do?" look before following after the Mistress.

"Now, what are you going to wear?" Calla said, taking Kalina's arm.

Together, the three women returned to Kalina's rooms to inspect the contents of her closet and discuss party dresses and costumes. For a few brief moments, Kalina felt like a young girl again. She had never been one for fashion and parties, but for the first time in a while, she looked forward to the occasion.

Kari eventually joined them, and she sat at the table in the corner of Kalina's rooms and watched Delisa like a hawk, a small smile on her face. Delisa flounced around Kalina's room, pulling out dresses and holding them up, discussing the merits of each. Kalina smiled at her friend's antics, indulging them whenever Delisa turned to her to ask a question. Calla sat on the bed and made notes in a small notebook, sketching designs. There were only a few days left until the Festival of Flowers but Calla could sew fast and Delisa had offered to help.

"What color do you want to wear, Kalina?" Delisa said, holding up a deep purple dress in velvet. Kalina winced and shook her head, laughing.

"Definitely not velvet, but purple would be fine."

Kari smirked and pulled out her belt knife to carve designs into the table. Kalina reached over and put her hand over her cousin's, raising her eyebrows. Kari let out a long-suffering sigh and sat back, using her knife to clean beneath her fingernails once again. It took everything in Kalina not to laugh. Kari must have the cleanest fingernails by now.

Delisa cocked her head to the side and looked at the dress she was still holding.

"Calla, what do you think? Should we give her a theme?"

Calla looked up from her notebook, her eyes were a little wider.

"Hmmm? What was that Delisa?"

"I said, should we do a theme? We need four dresses and perhaps we could make a play off a theme?"

"Spring. I've been sketching a few dresses based on that theme." Calla stood up from the bed and came to the table. Delisa put down the velvet dress she'd been eyeing and joined the three of them.

Calla laid out her notebook and spun it around so they could all see it. On the two pages, they could see were beautiful sketches of dresses, each with a springtime theme.

"See, this dress I've sketched for Kalina. It is based on a spring forest, all in hues of greens with a few delicate gold, silver, and white flowers embroidered on the hem of the skirt and the sleeves and bodice. The mask is a delicate filigree of green wire, like the sunlight filtering through the canopy above."

Kalina stared in awe at the dress Calla had sketched. The silhouette was very simple with a tight bodice to her natural waist and then a soft flow outwards with a long trailing train that would look like a bed of moss flowing behind her. She smiled and let out a soft sigh. She missed the woods, and Calla had captured its likeness perfectly.

"This dress I sketched for Kari. It represents the bonfires we light in our temple squares and on the hillsides. It represents life and the joy of dancing. All in shades of burnt oranges and reds. The mask is a metallic golden orange to reflect light."

Calla looked around sheepishly and they each clamored for her to turn the page and show Delisa's and her own gowns. Her elegant fingers slowly flipped the paper revealing two more gowns.

"This one is floral, representing the flowers we decorate everywhere, the colorful streamers, and the blast of life that spring brings. It will be in a profusion of colors and have a wide skirt." She pointed to the small bodice and flared skirt covered in flowers. "This is for Delisa."

"This final one will be in shades of blue, to represent a softly flowing stream, bringing life-giving water to the world. This one I will wear." The dress was soft, delicate, and flowing with a train behind it like Kalina's. It was perfect.

Kalina looked at Calla in wonder. Somehow the woman had managed to not only represent Spring but had also captured each of them perfectly in dress form.

"Calla, these are the most beautiful dresses I've ever seen. It would be an honor to wear mine at the ball." Kalina gave her friend a small seated bow. Calla blushed and looked down at the drawings before tucking them away.

"I'll have them ready by the afternoon of the ball if Delisa will consent to help me."

Delisa nodded eagerly.

"Let's get started."

Chapter 4

THE NIGHT BEFORE THE FESTIVAL of Flowers, Kalina couldn't sleep. She wasn't sure if it was the anticipation of the party the following day, or anxiety about the upcoming public trial of Terric, but she found herself wandering the halls of the castle, avoiding her guards. She had slipped out through the hidden servants' entrance to her chambers and down a pitch-black staircase to a lower level.

Kari had insisted on her front entrance being guarded but Kalina never mentioned the back one, for good reason. She wanted a way out. She had taken care of herself before when King Terric had been hunting her, and now she was at least better prepared, better trained. So she often wandered the halls at night, as she used to wander the corridors of the mountain in the Wastes, pondering the day's events, and thinking of the future.

That night, though, her ponderous footsteps brought her to the entrance of the dungeon. She wondered about Prince Terric below, wallowing alone in one of those cold, dark, and damp cells. She remembered her own time spent in those cells all too vividly. She wrapped her shawl a little tighter around her shoulders before she walked down the cold corridor towards the dungeon's depths.

She wasn't sure what drove her to put one foot in front of the other down the cold stone passage. It could have been morbid curiosity about how the former king was faring in the lonely dark, or that she needed confirmation that she was doing the right thing. Either way, she suddenly found herself standing before two Ethean guards, staring at her in her nightdress, her shawl wrapped firmly around herself, her silver hair undone from its usual braids and flowing down her back to the top of her hips. She had to stifle a smile at their bewildered faces. She couldn't imagine what they must think of her and what stories they would tell their fellow soldiers tomorrow about her strange appearance in the dungeons.

Cells lined the torch-lit the walls, while a leather-studded iron chair stood in the center of the cavern. Her stomach clenched at the sight of the chair, remembering when she'd been strapped to it, Terric standing above her, knife in hand. She remembered Rangvald, hanging limply, beaten down and tortured. That was her reason, that was her conviction that what she was doing was right. Everything Terric had done had hurt her people, and she was done just letting it happen, unanswered for. After the celebrations from the Festival of Flowers died down, she would have his public trial, and she would relish every moment of this man getting what he deserved.

A few cells away slumped a familiar figure. Nash sat against the bars, his eyes closed tight. He looked gaunt and hollow somehow, empty. Her heart clenched. She had once cared deeply for him. In fact, she still did. He had been there for her when she'd doubted herself as queen, and he had run with her when she'd asked. He and his dragon Sitala had been her friends. When they had moved to Ravenhelm Castle, she'd had him transferred to this prison, to sit in a cell alongside her enemy, Prince Terric. She had only then found out that the prince had killed Nash's dragon, Sitala, and when Nash found out, he'd gone mad. Many Valdir did when they lost their dragons. Many even died within a few days or weeks of their dragons' deaths. The sundering of the deep magic had that effect.

Kalina felt pity for Nash, but he had tried to kill her after he'd been captured by Terric, and his current mental state made him a threat to himself and those around him. She decided as she watched him that she'd see what other comfort she could get him, and then she moved farther into the gloom of the dungeons, searching for the prince's cell.

She approached Prince Terric on tiptoe. She had no way of knowing if it was the same cell she'd been thrown in all those months ago, but she knew it wasn't any more comfortable. The man sat huddled against the far rock wall, threadbare blankets clutched to his body, trying to hold in the warmth. His face, usually a hard mask, was gaunt, his dark eyes peering at her from their hallowed sockets. She drew in a sharp breath, but then let it out slowly. She wouldn't show this man any fear.

"Come to gawk at your prisoner? Your King brought so low?" His voice was just as oily as ever, just as menacing. It sent a shiver down Kalina's spine.

"I came to see who you truly are, Terric. And to ask you one question."

He raised an eyebrow at her, in a mock query. He didn't care what her question was, not really.

"Oh, and what is that, Princess?"

"Why?" Her voice rang through the silence of the cave, echoing off the walls, seeming to bounce around forever until finally, it faded into silence. It was almost like Terric was waiting for it to die out before answering.

"Why what? Why did I kill your father? Why did I keep your mother imprisoned? Why did I hunt you?" He smiled a sneering smile. "I won't answer any of those questions. You don't deserve one."

Despite the storm boiling inside her at his snideness, Kalina kept her face calm, something she knew Leif would be proud of. She picked at a loose string on her shawl.

"Then I won't tell you about your son."

She had tossed the bait and now waited as he swallowed it, hook, line, and sinker. His face slowly grew redder until finally, a dam seemed to break and he let out a long sigh. Her half-brother Osian, Terric's son, was currently safe with Eira in the Valdiran high camps. But the Prince didn't know that.

"I'll tell you why, if you can tell me about my son."

Kalina waited patiently, nodding at him to continue, her heart pounding in anticipation.

"I did all of this because that slu-" he took a deep breath and continued. "That woman scorned me before we were even married. I tried to get out of the marriage, tried to convince my father that it was folly, a lost cause, but instead, he insisted I marry her despite her transgressions." The anger was clear in his voice.

Kalina was shaken to her core. This man, this terrible, horrible, abusive and manipulative man, had done all this, hunted her to the ends of the continent, and did horrible things to the people she loved, all because some teenaged boy was hurt by a girl?

"So wait, you did all this because a girl liked another boy better?"

"That bitch was promised to me when she went behind my back and slept with your barbaric father and then begot you. You were a threat I couldn't abide. So I hunted you. Your father begged, you know, begged for his life, saying he would send me ten of his warriors in your stead. But I refused. I finally was able to bring your father back here and torture him."

Kalina froze, every bit of her suddenly going cold. She could feel it in her bones.

"What do you mean? I thought my father died with his dragon on the battlefield? We burned his body.." she trailed off. Whose body had they burned, if it wasn't her father's?

"His dragon died, yes, but your father lingered. Sir Gregan took his body from the battlefield and dressed another Valdir who was dead and badly burned in your father's clothes, leaving the crown nearby. Hakon was brought back here where I took my time killing him. Then I removed his head."

"You lie." Her voice shook as she spoke. She couldn't believe a word out of his mouth.

"Believe what you will, your Majesty-" he said in a mocking tone. "If only you hadn't killed Sir Gregan, he could have told you the gruesome details." He smirked at her. "You were only a few weeks too late to save him, too. If you'd come at the Fall equinox, he would still have been alive."

Kalina turned then, unable to hold in her anger, fear, and sadness anymore and stormed from the dungeons.

Cries of "What about my son? What about my boy?" followed her past the guards and up the passageway. When she came out into the lower hallways of the castle she stopped and leaned against the rough stone of the wall. Her breath came in hitches and starts, sobs breaking through. She felt as if she was going to blow apart into a million pieces.

What if her father had been alive all that time? Had he really been tortured and then beheaded? Terrible images raced through her mind and she pressed the palms of her hands into her eyes to try to get them to stop. He had to be lying. If he wasn't lying then they had burned someone else's body, and she maybe could have done something to save him. She could have had her father still: instead, she'd run away and ignored what was going on in her kingdom. That terrible possibility of 'what-if' hung over her head, threatening to drown her.

The sobs finally slowed and that old familiar friend, panic, began to subside. She pushed away from the wall, her shawl now trailing behind her, and made her way to the one place she knew she'd be safe and undisturbed.

When she got to the small room in the corner of the library, she was relieved to see Moose, the grey tabby cat, already curled on the small cot piled with blankets in the corner. Kalina wiped her face with her hands and closed the door behind her, feeling her way in the dark to the bed where she curled under the blankets around the softly purring body of the cat and fell asleep.

Chapter 5

MARGY SHOOK KALINA AWAKE, and she stared blearily around the tiny, cluttered library room. Her face felt sticky with shed tears, and a sadness lingered in her chest. Margy looked worried and slightly harassed, a candle held in one hand as she looked down on her wayward queen.

"Everyone has been looking all over for you." She stepped back, enough to allow Kalina room to sit up in bed. Her head was pounding but she knew she'd slept better than she had in weeks. Moose jumped down off the bed beside her and sauntered off into the library, probably to catch a mouse for breakfast. She often wondered where he went to the bathroom since she'd never seen him outside the library, but suddenly, she really didn't want to know. Kalina's own stomach growled at the thought of breakfast.

"Can I get some breakfast, Margy?" She asked as she followed the head of the kitchens out into the dim light of the library.

"Yes. But get yourself back to your rooms, today is the Festival of Flowers and you don't want to be late for your own party." Margy gave her a scolding look, but the edge of her lip was twitching, threatening to break into a smile at any moment. Then she turned away.

"Margy-"

The girl turned back to Kalina.

"Don't tell anyone about this room. It's my own secret."

Margy touched the side of her nose and winked before rushing off down the hall and out of the library. Kalina straightened her night dress and threw her shawl around her shoulders, debating taking the most direct route to her rooms, or going by the servant's passages so she could go unseen. Finally, she decided on the passages and slipped from the library, moving through the cool darkness of the stone hallways. When she finally arrived at her rooms, she peeked through the door, covered by a tapestry, where Kari and Delisa stood in the middle of her rooms. Delisa was pacing and Kari stood, her arms crossed, scowling. Kalina sighed and stepped through, making them both jump.

"Kalina!" Delisa chided, before collecting herself. She was

chastising a queen after all. "Your Majesty, you scared us." She gave a small curtsy before rushing to take Kalina's shawl. Kari continued to scowl, only this time it was aimed at Kalina. She had no such compunctions about addressing Kalina.

"Where the hell were you?"

Kalina was tired, and her head was pounding. She really didn't want to have to explain her nighttime wanderings to Kari right at that moment, so she dismissed the question.

"What time is the kickoff of the celebrations in the temple district?" she asked as she began to remove her clothing, leaving them on the floor while Delisa picked them up one by one, exasperated. Kalina entered the bathroom that was connected to her bedroom, a steaming bath already waiting there.

"In an hour. Now, wash quickly and I'll get your first dress ready."

Kalina sighed as she lowered herself into the waiting bath, letting the warm water wash away the tear stains and fears of the night before. She wanted to talk to Leif about what had happened, to have him reassure her that there was nothing they could have done to save her father. She wanted his quiet assurance and comfort. But first, she had to go celebrate with her people.

Delisa dressed her in a soft purple dress with delicate silk flowers sewn onto the bodice, long flowing sleeves and a soft train that stretched out behind that could be bustled for dancing. Her hair was elaborately braided atop her head in the traditional Valdiran style. Finally, a small circlet of silver was set atop her braids. It was her day crown, as she called it. It was understated and less heavy than the iron and dragon scale one she wore for special occasions, and instead it was delicate silver filigree.

"Is Leif nearby? Can I speak with him a moment about security while we are in town?" Kalina said, slipping a dagger into her bodice between her breasts and then strapping another to her calf above her soft slippers. She refused to go unarmed, especially in public.

Her cousin Kari gave her a knowing look before exiting to the drawing-room. Kalina followed. She rarely used this room, preferring instead the intimacy of her own bedroom, but it was perfect for meeting the occasional noble who came to call. And now, Leif was using it as a waiting space, along with Rangvald. Rangvald lounged in a chair, his long, lanky body stretched out and taking up far too much space. But as soon as Kalina entered, he sat up, pulling himself together. Kalina smiled at her other cousin before taking Leif's arm and leading him back to her now empty bedroom, Delisa already gone to finalize preparations.

"You look stunning, your Majesty," Leif said, his grey eyes twinkling with mischief. Kalina couldn't help but smile back, despite the worries running through her head. She pressed up against him and tilted her head back, letting him press his lips to hers in a sweet kiss. She wanted to linger there forever, in his arms, but she knew she had things to discuss with him.

Fear was still pounding through her. She couldn't stand the idea that she had sat idle, letting her father die. Horror flooded her as she realized that her mother had been here, just a few floors above, while her father had possibly been tortured. Had her mother known? For once, Kalina was grateful her mother was gone too; the knowledge that the man she'd loved was being tortured in her own dungeons would have ruined her. Finally, she pulled away and explained what was on her mind. Leif's face grew darker with every word she spoke until finally, she finished.

"Could I have saved him, Leif? Did any of our spies even suspect he was here?" she asked, her heart breaking within her chest once again.

"No. Kalina, listen to me-" Leif took her chin in his hand and forced her to look at him. "None of our spies heard he had been taken from the battlefield. If he had, it was during the battle itself, because they removed him immediately following the fight." He paused, searching her face, and she could see his own clever mind working behind his grey eyes. "I suspect the Askorian prince is just saying those things to get a rise out of you, to make you angry enough to make a mistake. You can't let him get to you."

He pulled her into a tight hug and Kalina buried her face against his black vest coat. That was when she realized, rather belatedly, that he wasn't wearing the traditional Valdiran leathers, he was wearing Ethean style spring clothing. It looked good on him. She breathed in deeply the scent of Leif, the same scent that reminded her of her father, and home. It was the scent she loved, and it was overwhelming her. Leif kissed the top of her head.

"Your father died valiantly in battle, surrounded by his men and with Kaya. Not in a dark, cold dungeon. We burned him atop the mountain."

Kalina glanced up at his face. He looked determined, but she could see the kernel of doubt there and knew he would investigate the matter. She closed her eyes for another moment, trying to use his warmth and feel to ground herself, and pull her away from the yawning abyss that was her grief for her father, mother, Geir, and everyone else they'd lost in this war.

"Let's go greet your guests, your Majesty." Leif held out a hand for her; she took it gratefully and followed him from the room.

They spent the afternoon wandering the temple district of Ravenhelm, her little entourage around them and a brace of palace guards led by Anders walking at their sides. Talon was still organizing the armies, having been knighted by her within the first week of her becoming queen. He and Leif had partnered to organize and train the soldiers in both aerial combat and ground maneuvers. Talon had been the first to point out that two riders per dragon, one Ethean, and one Valdir, would make their long-range weapons more effective. He was constantly coming up with new and inventive ways to use the Valdir and Etheans together. Kalina had even stumbled upon Talon chatting with Maska, discussing battle tactics, a topic her dragon greatly enjoyed. It turned out Maska often spent his days with Talon and the armies, strategizing and training. It was a good outlet for him and it made Kalina proud.

Calla joined them as the afternoon progressed, once she'd put baby Issa down with her new nanny. With Calla doing so much sewing and work at the castle, she had been forced to hire help. She winked at Kalina as she joined their little group, taking her husband's arm.

"The dresses are ready and being delivered to your rooms as we speak."

Kalina's heart fluttered in excitement a bit. Today was for lighthearted, spring fun, but tonight was when the real fun began.

She, Delisa, and Calla danced around the maypole, laughing delightedly, while Kari stayed off to the side staunchly refusing to participate. She might laugh and joke about some things, but girly things, like dancing around a maypole decorated in ribbons was a line she just wouldn't cross.

They ate honey cakes and candied nasturtiums and drank pear cider while watching silly puppet shows. Kalina was able to let her fears from earlier melt away as she enjoyed celebrating the beginning of spring with her fellow Etheans, greeting as many of her people as she could and getting to know the local vendors. Finally, as the afternoon sun began to move towards the horizon, their little party bid the locals good evening and went back to the castle for a much-needed nap before the ball.

Kalina collapsed onto her bed in a happy daze, for once feeling free enough to enjoy the day.

Chapter 6

THE BALLROOM WAS LIT WITH FAIRY lights that seemed to float in and out of the garlands of flowers that covered every surface and hung from the ceiling in swaths. The guests were already there, resplendent in their court finery, decked out in a rainbow of colors and each sporting ornately wrought face masks. Kalina was dressed no differently but she still felt every eye turn her way as soon as she entered.

She descended the formal staircase accompanied by Leif, her personal court traveling before her down the stairs. Her hair had been pinned and braided into an elaborate up-do, small white flowers woven through her silver locks. They were only visible up close but they added a delicate and earthy feel to the whole ensemble when paired with her mask and flowing dress. She felt stunning, her head crowned with an intricately woven crown of gold and silver filigree that seemed to mesh with her mask. Beside her, Leif looked equally regal in hues of gold with green trim, the light to her dark. Calla had given her a wink when Leif had appeared to escort her and Kalina had gasped at his close-cut jacket and pants.

Kalina was acutely conscious of every eye on them as they slowly walked down the stairs, she was focusing on putting one foot in front of the other, heart racing as they approached the ballroom floor. Mistress Aynne had come up to her rooms as she and her ladies were getting ready and coached them on how their entrance would go. She was to descend the ballroom steps and then open the ball by dancing the first dance with Leif. The other ladies of her entourage would join in with their escorts once the music was underway and, hopefully by the end of the tune, the rest of the guests would be dancing as well.

Kalina swallowed and squeezed Leif's arm as he pulled her around in a graceful arc until she was in his arms, facing him. He nodded to her, a small smile touching the corner of his lips, his grey eyes warm behind his mask, and he began to move just as the song began. She stumbled on the first few steps, despite having practiced with Delisa incessantly over the last few weeks, but she took a deep breath and turned her brain off, focusing instead on Leif's handsome face, and the feel of his hand in hers.

She watched out of the corner of her eye as Talon stepped forward with Delisa to dance beside them, Delisa's flowing floral dress a fine compliment to Kalina's green one. Kalina winked at Talon, her nervousness melting away at the sight of her old friend, back finally from training the troops. The knight grinned back and twirled Delisa around the dance floor. Next, Kari and Jormungand joined the fray, Kari's jaw tightly clenched. She had argued with Mistress Aynne about dancing but the stewardess was a stern taskmaster and, finally, Kari had relented, saying she would dance but she wouldn't enjoy it. Despite her grim expression, she absolutely glowed in the red and orange dress that flared around her like living flames. Finally, Calla and Anders cut across the dance floor, their matching ensembles in hues of blue a refreshing sight.

Soon the murmuring crowd was joining them and, as the first song came to a close and the next one followed on its heels, Kalina was feeling much more at home in the center of all the chaos and attention. She took Leif's arm and allowed him to escort her off the dance floor to a nearby table piled with various finger foods and delicacies. She picked up a few pieces of toasted bread spread with goat cheese and jam before turning to survey the crowd. Leif disappeared for a few moments and returned with two glasses of a bubbly wine that Kalina had never tasted.

"What is this?" she asked, "it's delightful." She took a few sips.

"Be careful!" Leif laughed, gently lowering it from her lips. "It's called Moonwine and it will go to your head faster than you think."

Kalina nodded and sipped more slowly.

"Where does it come from?"

"Somewhere on the southern continent I believe, but honestly, you know I know even less of the world than you do."

Kalina knew he hadn't meant that comment to sting but it did. She had run away to Ablen and traveled further than he ever had. She swallowed a sudden lump in her throat.

"I'm not going to leave again, Leif."

He turned to look at her, a little stunned.

"That's not what I meant, Kal."

He had taken to using a shortened version of her name when

they were in private and it surprised her to hear it spoken then, in a public forum. But she had just brought up a sensitive subject. She looked down at the floor in remorse. The last thing she wanted was to spark a fight.

"I'm sorry."

"I just meant, you'd traveled this world farther than me, and you have read far more books than I have, so you'd probably know better than me about the Southern Continent," he explained coming to stand beside her and placed a soft hand on her lower back, his warmth permeating through her. Kalina was conscious of the watching nobles around them, so she took a hesitant step back.

"I understand, sorry I got all dark on you. It's been a long day."

Leif smiled at her knowingly, and nodded, but put another step of distance between them. He might be a part of her entourage and the general of her armies, but seeing them so close together and familiar in public would start rumors flying. In fact, they already were. They didn't want to stoke the fire. She took a deep breath and focused back on the swirling colors of the dresses around her as the crowd ebbed and flowed, dancing to the music. She was determined to enjoy this party and not let Terric's words from the night before and the doubt sitting uneasily in her stomach ruin it.

She smiled as a familiar figure approached. Lord Illeron bent to kiss her hand, before straightening his lanky frame. He smiled back, his close-cropped greying hair and salt and pepper beard hiding the aging wrinkles beside his mouth.

"You look stunning, your Majesty," he said.

"Thank you, Lord Illeron. You look quite handsome yourself," she replied with a small curtsey.

He stepped up beside her and turned to the crowd before them.

"Have you given any further thought to Lord Avril's proposal?"

Kalina made a face at the man and he let out a laugh.

"Of course not. I've had entirely too much on my mind," she retorted. It struck her suddenly that here was a man who might have known about her father. Lord Illeron was her Spymaster but before he had been loyal to her grandfather and after her grandfather had died he'd disappeared, until the day she was crowned. Had he known about her father's presence in the dungeons? "Lord, Illeron, may I speak with you in private?"

"Of course, your Majesty." He offered her his arm and walked with her out the two huge double glass doors onto the large open balcony. There was a couple at the far end canoodling, and a set of guards at the door, but otherwise the space was unoccupied. It would become more crowded as the party continued, Kalina didn't doubt, so she took advantage of their momentary solitude.

"Last night I went down to speak with Prince Terric," she began, putting her clenched fists on the balcony railing and looked out over the expansive garden below them.

"Was that wise, my Queen?" Lord Illeron had never minced words with her. She'd only known him a few short weeks but knowing he was the only reason she was alive in the first place made her trust him at least enough to allow it.

"Probably not, but he suggested to me something that I can't quite believe." She swallowed and continued. "He said that my father was taken from the battlefield and brought back here to be tortured." Her cheeks were flushed, and she was trying to restrain her panic. "Do you think my father was in the castle? You have spies everywhere, even within this castle. Did you ever hear of Terric torturing a Valdir in the dungeons?"

Lord Illeron was quiet for a moment and when she looked at him she could see a war of emotions storm across his face for a second before he mastered it. Perhaps it was the darkness of the terrace, but she was sure she'd seen fear written there. Finally, he spoke.

"Your Majesty, I don't want to lie to you. But I also think that the details of the situation you've described would not be wise to discuss. It is a viper nest you don't want to unveil."

Kalina's blood ran cold at his words. He may not have said it outright, but he had all but confirmed her deepest, darkest fears about her father's death.

"I want to move the trial up to the day after tomorrow. Public, in the main parade ground. Can you arrange it?" Her voice was deadly cold, as everything inside her seemed to have frozen solid. Beside her, Lord Illeron nodded his consent.

"I can, your Majesty."

"Thank you. Now, I would like to be alone."

Lord Illeron bowed low and left her alone on the terrace, the other couple having gone inside some minutes before. Kalina crumpled onto a bench nearby, removed her mask, and dropped her head into her hands. She couldn't believe how everything she'd believed had been turned on its head in a matter of hours, all because she'd been stupid enough to visit the prince. Hot tears leaked from between her fingers but she angrily wiped them away, as hesitant footsteps approached.

Calla stood before her on the balcony, wringing her hands before her. Kalina wiped her tears away and put her mask back on before standing up.

"Thank you for the dress, Calla. It is the most beautiful thing I've ever worn." She approached the woman who had taken her in when she'd had nothing, and took both the woman's hands. "Let's go dance, shall we?"

Calla didn't say anything about having seen Kalina crying, she just took her arm and led her back into the fray, where they both danced and ate and drank the night away with Kari and Delisa.

Chapter 7

WAITING FOR THE TRIAL TO START WAS torture for Kalina. She sat on a wooden throne in the early afternoon spring sunshine, waiting for the crowd to finish gathering. She had slept most of the day before on and off, and when she wasn't sleeping and recovering from the ball, she had been preparing what she would say today during his trial. Her job was to play the judge. Her word was law, but her council was her jury, their job to present arguments about why they believed a punishment for a crime was acceptable.

The people in the crowd were there to bear witness. And although she had originally fought against a public trial, a part of her was glad that the people would get the chance to see her sentence a tyrant to life in prison. For that was what she planned to do. She wanted him to suffer, and she knew that a long time spent in those cells would break any man.

Dragons lined the edges of the parade ground, causing some of the gathered Ethean nobles and civilians to shift nervously, casting their worried looks as though they were concerned the dragons might suddenly decide to eat them. Kalina had reassured her people repeatedly that dragons had no interest in eating people, and that they preferred cows and sheep, but because dragons were big and scary with many rows of sharp teeth, the general populace still didn't quite believe her. Fear of dragons was ingrained into human's brains, just as primal as a fear of the dark. Even Kalina herself had been afraid the first time she'd seen a dragon or even a wyvern, but she'd soon learned to master her fear.

Maska stood directly behind her throne, his bulky green shape reflecting the bright sunlight and sending a cascade of green dancing lights over Kalina every time he shifted on his feet, which was often since he was impatient.

Lord Averil stood to her left, and he kept eyeing her and Maska as they waited. She tried her best to ignore him. He had tried to gain an audience with her the day before to discuss the trial, but Kalina had refused. She had even argued with Leif about the change in date. But she was determined. She wanted this over with and she wanted Terric to suffer.

"The Etheans seem shifty," Maska's deep voice rumbled behind her. She nodded slightly, her eyes moving from face to face.

"Do you think someone will try something?" She said out of the corner of her mouth.

"I'd like to see them try." Maska let out a rumbling growl in his chest and it made Kalina smile wickedly. She would also like to see them try.

Finally, the prisoner was led out of a side entrance and onto the parade ground by Slyvan, her head jailer. The gathered crowd immediately erupted in sound: boos and shouted insults were flung across the yard. Prince Terric seemed to physically flinch back from them for a moment before catching himself and standing up straight. He was flanked by his two usual guards, the same two that Kalina had encountered at the entrance to the dungeons a few days prior.

She sat up straighter in her seat, her heart pounding in her chest, threatening to burst out of her. She wasn't entirely sure why she was so nervous. She should be excited, even happy, but instead, she felt on the edge of tears. Her council members sat to her right under a large cloth awning, sheltered from the sun beating down. Kalina had no such protection, except from Maska's large bulk towering above and behind her, but she didn't mind. She wanted everyone to see her, to know she wasn't hiding. Maska snaked his head down until it was level with hers, his large clawed forelegs gripping the sides of her throne, gouging the oak.

"He deserves this, Littling. You know this."

She swallowed and nodded at his words and focused back on the scarcely contained crowd, her castle guards barely keeping them at bay with the shouted orders of Anders and Sir Talon. Right as Slyvan and his prisoner reached the stairs to her raised platform that was to serve as his trial spot, a weak spot in the guard's line broke, and a small crowd of commoners surged towards the two men, now exposed and unprotected.

Kalina let out a shout, and Arikara, Leif's huge golden dragon, suddenly descended on the crowd, her bulk enough to cause them to scatter, but not before some lucky person was able to get in a punch. Prince Terric of Askor lay in the dirt, clutching his stomach as though someone had delivered a blow to his guts. Slyvan hauled him up unceremoniously and then marched him up the stairs as Arikara, along with Leif now, helped Anders and Talon regain control of the crowds.

Kalina now felt a public trial might have been a bad idea, but she really had no other choice except to continue. She took a deep breath and looked over to where Prince Terric now stood, a mere half dozen steps away, chained, his elbows held on either side by a guard.

"Prince Terric of Askor. You have been brought here before your peers and your country, to answer for your crimes. You have been accused of treason against the crown, treason against your people, conspiracy to commit murder of a member of the royal family, attempted murder, unauthorized detainment of a member of the royal family, and genocide. There are many more charges, but I won't bother listing them now, as they will be listed on your formal writ of sentence."

Kalina was immensely grateful that her voice had not wavered. She turned to Lord Averil and Lord Illeron who stood from their seats. Leif had rejoined the council now and was watching her carefully. She gave him a small smile to let him know she was fine, before turning back to the two Lords.

"Lord Averil, Lord Illeron. It is my understanding that you each have prepared an argument both for and against the Prince's crimes?"

"We have, your Majesty." Lord Averil bowed low, and Lord Illeron followed suit beside him.

"You may proceed."

Lord Averil stepped up first and cleared his throat, speaking as loudly as he could so as to be heard over the continued yelling and jeering of the gathered crowd.

"Your Majesty, I hope you can find it in your wisdom to deal fairly with Prince Terric, and send him back to his father in the North. He was forced into marriage with a woman who was in love with someone else and who had already had a child out of wedlock with another. Surely, you of all people can understand how that might have soured him towards not only her and her child, but against the realm as well?" Lord Averil's face fell at his own words, his expression displaying a level of sympathy that Kalina knew in her guts was as fake as it could get. She of all people? She didn't understand the prince at all. Not one bit. Lord Averil's speech left her with a sick, slimy taste on her tongue and the last thing she wanted was to hear him talk further. But she nodded for him to continue.

"Please, continue to defend the traitor, Lord Averil," she said with a lazy wave of her hand. She didn't want him or Prince Terric to know how much he was getting to her. Her eyes flicked to the prisoner as Lord Averil continued. Terric's cheek was now scarred like her own, and she thought that would give her some pleasure, but it did not. He had tortured her, slicing her left cheek from temple to jaw, permanenting scarring her. But she could never stomach torturing him.

"All he wants is to return home to his own country, to live out the remainder of his life in solitude. At least you can give him that." Lord Averil spread his hands in supplication. Kalina let out a long sigh.

"Lord Illeron?"

The thin man nodded at her and stepped forward, his hands clasped behind his back.

"If your own father had beaten you, chased you to the ends of the earth, threatened to kill you, stolen your sons, and raped your daughters, would you just let him live out his days in peace? Prince Terric was supposed to protect this realm. He was supposed to lift his people up after a long war, and help them rebuild, creating a stronger and better kingdom. Instead, he preyed on the weak and starving, he chased its rightful queen across the realm and then started yet another war against an oppressed and already depleted people. Then he tore young men and women from their homes for his own personal vendetta against a child he'd never met, who'd done him no harm. A man like that doesn't deserve a quiet retirement. A man like that deserves death, but if you won't give him that, then he deserves to spend his life in the dark."

Kalina nodded approvingly. She looked to Lord Averil and raised an eyebrow.

"Do you have a rebuttal, Lord Averil?"

The plump man seemed to bluster for a moment before regaining his composure. He stepped forward once again, shooting Lord Illeron a menacing look.

"Prince Terric just wants peace, he no longer desires war or revenge." Lord Averil seemed to be almost pleading now.

Kalina couldn't believe it. She sat, looking at her council and seeing them with grim, determined faces. Just as she was about to respond, someone threw something from the crowd and it splatted just a foot away. She looked down at it distractedly, wondering why in the world a tomato was suddenly smashed beside her. Soon, fruit and even clods of dirt and horse patties began raining down from the skies, the crowd beyond the makeshift fence of palace guards launching them skyward, clearly aiming for Prince Terric. Kalina ducked her head and ran back towards Maska and the safety of his wings.

Her council began moving, each launching from their seats, and soon screaming and yelling filled the air around her as she ran. Suddenly something barreled into her from the side and she fell heavily to the ground. Someone landed atop her, straddling her, but instead of protecting her, they attacked.

She looked up through the barrage of missiles and saw that Prince Terric sat atop her, a small dagger shining in his chained hands. His scarred, bearded, and gaunt face grinned maniacally down at her as he raised the knife to stab her. Her blood seemed to freeze in her veins for a moment before she remembered her training. She bucked her hips, arching suddenly beneath him, throwing him sideways off of her. His eyes went wide, as he was dislodged and landed heavily on his side. Kalina was up in an instant, sliding away, putting distance between them and pulling her own knife from her bodice, ready for a second attack. Her council members were closing in, Leif just moments away from reaching her as the Prince stood. The knife was raised again above his head, ready to plunge downward, when a massive set of green jaws descended from the air overhead, engulfing Prince Terric's thin form.

A scream escaped him just as Maska closed his teeth with an audible snap, and the sound was abruptly cut off. Blood oozed from between his enormous jaws, his dark, star-flecked eyes searching the gathered crowd, now completely frozen in terror, all noise abruptly halted. It was as if, in one swift movement, Maska had frozen the entire parade ground. Not a single person moved, they just watched in abject horror as Maska opened his jaws and the mutilated and bloody corpse of the Prince fell to the cobblestones. Even Kalina's own stomach churned.

Then a scream shattered the silence from somewhere behind her, and sobbing filled the air. Kalina suspected it wasn't because Prince Terric was dead, but rather the horrific nature of his death that was causing this outburst. She finally felt like she could move and she stood, straightening her dress and stepping up to her dragon's side. Leif, bewilderment on his face, stepped up beside her. Arikara snaked her neck forward, clearly as a show of solidarity with the little group. Kalina cleared her throat and straightened her crooked crown.

"What Maska did was in defense of my life. Prince Terric attacked me with a knife, and Maska saved me. Nothing more. This trial is now over. You are all dismissed." Then she turned on her heel and walked towards the door that led back into the castle, Maska trundling along beside her. She felt like she was about to break apart into a million different pieces and she wanted to get out of the public's eye before she lost it. Finally, she turned to Maska and pressed her head against his warm, scaled chest.

"Thank you, my friend." He let out a growling purr that vibrated through her.

"He didn't taste very good. He hadn't bathed in a long time. So I spit him out."

Kalina let out a bark of laughter, tears of mingled relief and pent up fear rolling down her cheeks.

"I'll come see you tonight, and we can go for a ride." She patted his side and followed Leif into the castle. As soon as the cool darkness of the stone surrounded her, she leaned back against it, pressing her hands onto the rough surface.

Leif came to stand with her, looking out over the parade grown beyond the doorway. Kalina followed his gaze and watched as Anders, Talon, Kari, Rangvald, and Jormungand took control of the crowds and began herding them like cattle towards the exits. Lord Illeron was deep in a heated conversation with Lord Averil, who was a blotchy red color that made Kalina worry for his health. The remainder of her council was standing around, staring at the slowly congealing pool of Prince Terric's blood, and casting eyes in Maska's direction.

"Are you alright?" Leif finally asked, turning to survey her from head to foot before taking her face in his hands. "He didn't manage to stab you, did he?" She shook her head, unable to speak.

Leif let out a long sigh of relief and pressed his lips to her forehead before pulling her into a tight hug.

Finally, Kalina found her voice and she croaked out, "I'll be fine."

Chapter 8

"**NEXT TIME YOU'LL BE WEARING THE** armor I made you."

"Next time it won't be a public trial."

Kalina stood at the edge of the large balcony off the now empty ballroom. Maska was basking in the late afternoon sun behind her, seemingly unconcerned about the events of the morning. As he had described it: "there had been a threat, and he'd ended it." He'd given what Kalina could only equate as a dragon shrug. Leif was pacing the balcony, clenching and unclenching his fists. Kalina was still a little shaken by the ordeal, but a large part of her was relieved. The prince was dead, and he could no longer hurt her or those she loved.

"He had help. Someone gave him that knife, he didn't just have it on him." Leif paced towards Maska and then turned on his heel. Kalina turned away from the view of the gardens below and watched him. "That little distraction with the crowd was orchestrated, it wasn't random."

Kalina didn't disagree. She tried to distract her own racing mind by watching the lean, muscular lines of him as he prowled the stone balcony. She wished they could be alone, truly alone, away from all the hubbub and chaos of the court. But she was tethered here by her responsibilities and she had to see them through.

"We'll have Anders and Talon question the guards present, see who paid them or blackmailed them to allow the crowd through. Do you think this was another assassination attempt? Or just a lucky chance?" She rubbed the back of her neck. The stress was wearing on her body and she was suddenly looking forward to climbing into bed that night.

Leif's eyes flicked to her as he paced.

"If I had to guess, I'd say assassination. But I can't figure out what they thought to gain. If Terric had succeeded, there were enough dragons and Valdir there that you would have been avenged in a matter of moments. Terric was going to die either way. Someone must have convinced him it was worth it. Was it an attempt to get off a lucky shot at you? Or to start a war with Askor? Because those are the options."

Fear clawed its way up Kalina's throat. War with Askor. It was part of what she had been avoiding for months since she became queen. She knew her council members feared war, it was why Lord Averil had continued to pursue the idea of a political marriage for her, a way to forge an alliance like her mother and Terric had. But whenever she thought of marriage, the only face she saw at the altar was Leif's. And she couldn't just walk away from him for some Askorian, Ablen, or Wostradian princeling. Not that she had ever brought the prospect up with him, even the thought made her stomach clench in fear.

"I think we need to begin preparing for the possibility of war, then," she said and turned back to the gardens behind her, trying to hide her fear. Maska shifted on the stone behind them.

"I think you are right. I will leave tonight to inspect our troops and get a report from Rangvald. You should talk to Kari. She has something she wants to show you. I'll be back in a few days." He came up behind her and put his hands on her arms. She shuddered slightly at his touch, his warmth seeping into her cold bones.

"I'll miss you," she whispered softly. He squeezed her arms briefly before stepping away.

"I'll miss you more, my Queen."

She turned and gave him a soft smile.

"Until later."

He let out a piercing whistle, and within a few moments, large wing beats shattered the cool spring air. Arikara, his huge golden dragon landed on the ground a story below, her head poking up high enough to see Kalina, Leif, and Maska on the balcony above.

"Take care of him, Ari," Kalina said. The golden dragon gave her a long-suffering look, as Leif launched himself over the edge of the balcony, landing on Arikara's back with a soft "oof."

"I always do, your Majesty." The dragon winked and then shot into the sky, her wing beats concussing the air around them, forcing Kalina back a step.

She watched them as they flew south and east over the city until they disappeared into the blue of the sky. Maska let out a groan behind her. She turned and lay a hand on his large, emerald-scaled nose.

"I guess I'd better go find Kari." Suddenly she was conscious of how much he'd grown in the last year. He now dwarfed her, and she could lay her entire body along his nose and still only reach his eyes. "Thank you, Maska, for everything you did today. I would be nothing without you."

"That's not true. You'd still be Kalina, Queen of Ethea and the Valdir. But you certainly wouldn't be as interesting." Occasionally Maska cracked jokes, and they always made Kalina feel a bit lighter.

She found Kari just inside the glass doors to the ballroom, standing watch with another palace guard.

"Leif said there was something you wanted to show me?"

"Oh, yes. It's a little project I've been working on, that I hope you will appreciate."

Kari began walking away and Kalina shrugged at the other guard and followed. Kari led them down to a side practice yard attached to a small barracks. Kalina wondered what this had originally been used for before she and her people had taken over the castle. On the practice grounds, women, both Valdir and Ethean were practicing with swords and bows. They were led by Jormungand, who was walking the yard correcting posture and stance or shouting orders.

"These are what I've been calling, The Queen's Guard." Kari swept her hands out, a huge grin on her face. She was clearly very proud of what was happening but Kalina was just a little confused.

"Are they separate from my usual guard? What is their purpose exactly?" She watched the nearest woman, realizing with a sudden shock that it was Hilde, the blacksmith Skaldrik's wife. Kalina had encountered the woman a few times and knew she was a fierce and capable fighter.

"They are meant to replace your regular palace guard. It is comprised of women only, so they can protect you anywhere, any time that a man might not be able to. These are women devoted just to you, not to the realm, or to a general. They are willing to lay down their lives to protect you." Kari looked sideways at Kalina, a small smile playing on her lips. "I am their leader."

Kalina's eyebrows rose as she resisted the urge to tease her cousin. A small force of fighting women all her own? It was an interesting and, honestly, welcome concept. She did always feel rather strange with men standing watch outside her doors at all hours. Kari had always done her best to include at least one female on duty at all times but sometimes that wasn't possible.

"How many are there? How many are Valdir, and how many Ethean?"

They continued to watch the women train, some of whom had noticed their queen and their commander watching them. Kari grinned.

"There are about twenty-five in total. The numbers are about split down the middle, half are Valdir and half are Ethean. The Valdir, however, are more skilled and are currently each paired with one Ethean to help them train. Jormungand and I are doing our best to get them up to snuff but since Ethean women are rarely if ever allowed to fight, it has been a rather rough transition for them. But the heart and will are there, however untrained."

"I think this is a great idea, Kari. Thank you."

"I've already worked up a schedule with your current guard and plan to start rotating them in so that they can get used to their duties. But that means for a while you will have three guards with you at all times."

Kalina shrugged.

"What's one extra? May I meet them?"

Kari eagerly stepped forward and called for a halt of the training. Then she proceeded to introduce Kalina to every woman, giving a few sentences about what brought each woman to the Queen's Guard. Kalina couldn't remember each name and story but she made sure to memorize each face and vowed to get to know them individually over the next weeks and months.

Just as Kari was finishing up the introductions, a servant came running into the courtyard, looking around rather frantically before seeing Kalina. He then walked over as calmly as he could, but she could see he was bursting with news. He was young, probably one of the young men and women Mistress Aynne was recruiting for what she called the messenger service.

"Your Majesty." He bowed low.

"Yes, young man?" Kalina felt strange saying that as he must have been about 16 or 17, only a few months younger than she herself. But she felt years beyond him in so many ways.

"A letter just arrived from up the coast. An Askorian ship has been spotted out to sea, making its way south. It should be here by tomorrow afternoon."

Chapter 9

THE WIND WHIPPED AROUND KALINA as she stood on the deck of her ship, watching the mouth of Ravenhelm harbor. The Askorian ship was just sliding into view on the ocean, its red sails standing out against the dark blue of the water and sky. She clutched the railing before her, nervousness thrilling through her. Leif still wasn't back yet, although she'd sent word the moment they'd learned of the ship. And now she wasn't sure he would be back in time to accompany her aboard the Askorian vessel. Lord Illeron stood by her side, as did Kari and Jormungand. Behind her, she was flanked by a mixture of Queen's Guard and palace guards, along with Lord Averil who had insisted on attending, as well as Lady Renfort who stood straight-backed and resolute in the freezing wind.

Maska, along with Kari's purple Yurok and Jormungand's red Shania, circled overhead, swooping and diving through the air, looking for all the world like puppies playing. Kalina's mouth twitched in a smile. She knew they were enjoying themselves, but she also knew that each of them was ready in a moment's notice to kill. Kalina had insisted that a small supply of their precious Emberweed be kept on board, just in case they needed to have the dragons burn the Askorian ship to the waterline. But she hoped that would not be the case.

The large ship was a three-masted giant, clearly made for long voyages in comfort, judging by the number of portholes on the side and the array of passengers on the deck which could be seen as it came closer. The sails slowly furled, and Kalina could see sailors scrambling across the deck and rigging as the forward motion of the ship slowed. Kalina and her entourage watched in expectant silence as the foreign vessel dropped anchor and slid to a stop a few dozen yards off the port side of the Ethean ship.

Kalina could see a small party, not unlike her own, watching them from the deck of the ship. She wondered if the Askorian King, King Blackbourne, was aboard, or just a delegation. One ship was no threat against her entire country, but they could be a threat against her, which was why she had chosen to meet them on the water, and not in her own home.

"What do you think they want?" she said to Lord Illeron beside her. He stood with his legs apart, clearly at home on the rolling deck of a ship. He eyed the other ship suspiciously.

"My eyes and ears in the Askorian court have only brought me snippets of news regarding the King and his plans. It seems that while he may be upset that we killed a few troops and imprisoned his son, he has his own country and children to deal with. He recently remarried, this time to a much younger wife. He may be preoccupied, or he may just be playing it close to the chest."

"How many children does he have?"

"Six sons and seven daughters, although many of the latter are married off now and only a few even reside at court. This is his third wife, and who knows how many mistresses he's had or how many illegitimate children he has running around his castle."

Kalina's eyebrows rose at the number. She could barely imagine one or two children, let alone thirteen or more. She wondered if he would even care about Terric's death since he had so many other children to replace him. She guessed she would find out soon enough.

"Look!" Kari said, pointing at the Askorian ship. A green flag was being hoisted up their center mast.

"What does that mean?" Kalina squinted at it. There was a slight commotion behind her as she turned to watch her own sailors hoisting their own green flag.

"It means that they want to speak with us and that they mean peace," Lord Illeron said.

"Send over a boat then, and offer for them to meet us here. On our boat." She turned on her heel and walked aft to the large cabin. Kari and her small entourage followed, leaving Lord Illeron and the sailors on deck.

The room was already cramped with Kari and Jormungand, Lord Averil and Lady Renfort. They squeezed around one side of a large oak table, trying to still look regal and intimidating while squeezed shoulder to shoulder. Kalina adjusted the crown atop her silver braids, her nerves still playing havoc as they waited. Finally, Lord Illeron and a small group of the Queen's Guard returned, cramming into the room. He held out a letter that Kalina took.

"What does it say?" Kari asked, trying to sneak a peek over Kalina's shoulder.

"It seems they want to meet on land, outside the city." She looked up at Lord Illeron. "Is that wise?"

"There is a small cove just north of here with a wide beach and a steep stair to the top of the cliff. It would be a good place for a meeting. We can ask them to anchor there, which will remove them from our harbor, and guard the stairs. We could meet on the beach tomorrow at noon."

Kalina folded the piece of paper back up carefully, using the movement to help her think. Finally, she spoke, all the eyes in the cramped room on her.

"That sounds like an excellent plan, Lord Illeron. Please send them back a message with the plan, and we will return to shore." She stood and made her way towards the door, Kari and Jormungand scrambling to get out of her way in the tight quarters. "We will meet with them tomorrow."

She returned to shore with her entourage in a longboat, leaving her sailors and Lord Illeron to handle the execution of the plan. When she returned to the castle, a letter was waiting for her from Leif, saying he was delayed with the troops. There had been a problem between the training master and Rangvald, and Leif was needed to settle the dispute, but he would be back at her side as soon as possible. Her heart sank as she read it, knowing she'd be attending the morning meeting without him.

She stood before her bedroom windows that evening, watching the Askorian ship depart from the bay and turn north, anxiety, and fear of what the following day held churning in her gut.

The short boat ride to the cove the next morning left Kalina nauseated and exhausted. She hadn't slept well that night, and besides her quick foray onto the deck of a ship the day before, she'd never stepped foot onto a boat in her life. Lord Illeron stood beside her at the rail as she clutched it, trying to calm her bucking stomach.

"I can't imagine it is much different from flying on a dragon, your Majesty," he said, a slight hint of amusement in his voice. Kalina shot him a sideways glare before focusing on the horizon again.

"It is different. I can read Maska's muscles and anticipate how he's going to move. But this," she gestured at the ship beneath her. "It is constant and irregular at the same time, and I have nothing to focus on. I'd rather be flying."

Lord Illeron chuckled, making Kalina scowl further, clenching her teeth against the next wave of nausea.

"Perhaps you should fly in on your dragon then, your Majesty. It would make for an impressive display of might without actually threatening anyone. And it would give us the upper hand."

She considered this. She would absolutely rather fly than be aboard ship as it sailed up the coast. Finally, she nodded and called Kari over.

"I'm going to fly with Maska from here on out. Will you fly with me?"

Her cousin nodded and shouted orders to the Queen's Guard before following Kalina aft where they called their dragons down and mounted one by one. Soon Kalina was airborne as Maska rose higher above the sea. The fresh, cool air calmed her, settling the butterflies in her stomach.

They circled the cove high above while their Ethean vessel anchored and launched boats into the surf. A large white tent had been set up farther up the beach, and boats from the Askorian ship were making their way to the shore. Now was a perfect time to land. Maska slowly spiraled down, his massive green wings glistening in the midday sun and casting a growing shadow across the sand. Just as the small group of people departed the Askorian boats, Kalina and Maska landed beside the tent with a boom, a cloud of fine sand rising into the air.

Kalina watched with satisfaction as the small group of people cringed back, visibly startled and frightened of the dragons before them. Upon closer inspection it seemed the group was comprised of well-dressed nobles along with a few servants and soldiers. The women clutched at their fancy hats and dresses, while the men threw their hands up to shield their eyes from the flying sand. Fear showed on every face as she dismounted and straightened her dress, Kari close behind her.

Delisa and Calla had conspired with Kari to create a few outfits for Kalina that were both regal and functional. Both Delisa and Calla had insisted that a Queen wear a dress most of the time, but Kari understood what it was like to ride astride a dragon. She had helped them incorporate the riding leathers that Kalina needed, with the tight bodices and flowing skirts that were currently popular at court. Kalina had loved her coronation dress so much that she had also requested that more be made in other colors.

Now, as she walked towards the white tent lightly blowing in the wind, she wore a deep purple dress with a slit skirt so she could ride Maska, the Valdir red leather pants beneath it. She wore her red leather broad belt and bracers but no weapons beyond a few knives stashed in her belt, bodice, and boot. Kari and her Queen's Guard were fully armed, however, and they followed her into the tent, studiously ignoring the Askorian nobles who cautiously filed in behind.

Chapter 10

THE TENT WAS EERILY QUIET AS KALINA took her place at the head of the table, with Kari on her left and Lord Illeron on her right. She wished again that Leif was by her side, and sent up a quick prayer to Skaldir for his safety returning from the countryside where her armies were stationed. There was no room to house her entire army within Ravenhelm, so a temporary tent city had been erected outside the walls.

The Askorian nobles filed into the tent, taking their seats at the opposite end of the long table that occupied the space. Many of them looked supremely uncomfortable, their eyes darting around nervously. But one man was eyeing her, seeming to size her up. He was tall, with light brown-haired and dark eyed, and looked similar enough to Prince Terric to be a close relative, was eyeing her, seeming to size her up. An awkward silence stretched thin, the animosity from both sides palpable. Finally, Kalina cleared her throat.

"Welcome to Ethea, Lords, and Ladies. To what do we owe this unexpected but welcome visit?"

The dark-haired man across from Kalina stood and gave her a slight bow of his head, the kind you might give to visiting monarchs. His clothes were richly made of thick fabrics, but they also had seen hard use.

"Your Majesty. My name is Julian Blackbourne and I am a Prince of Askor. Prince Terric is my older brother. We have come to request that you release my brother to me so I may return him home, and also-"

Kalina held up a hand.

"Let me stop you there, Prince Julian. Your brother Prince Terric stood trial two days ago for his crimes against this crown, and during his trial, he attempted to assassinate me. He was killed by my dragon, Maska." She paused, watching the prince's face hardened for the briefest of moments before he mastered his expression. "We are sorry for your loss," she continued. "We'd be happy to give you his body for proper burial in your country."

Prince Julian laced his fingers before him. He was clearly a diplomat by the way he spoke, his hands were slender and fine-boned with no hint of calluses insight. Kalina held back a slight smirk. She had to admit it felt good to know that for once in her life, she was more powerful and more dangerous than a prince of Askor.

"Thank you, your Majesty. That is most generous of you." He cleared his throat. "We would be grateful for the opportunity to take him home with us." He sat back down, and Kalina could see his jaw clenching and unclenching. He wasn't happy.

"Was there another reason you came, Prince Julian?" she asked, raising an eyebrow at him. She saw Kari grin out of the corner of her eye. Prince Julian shook his head.

"No. We just came to collect my brother," he said. She didn't believe him.

"Very well then." She looked to Anders and Talon who stood to the side. She and her council had anticipated this when they'd spotted the ship and so she had made sure Prince Terric's body, or what was left of it, had been prepared for shipment. "Sir Talon will bring his body to your men on the beach. Now, I have a message for your king."

"Of course, your Majesty." The other nobles beside the prince shifted uncomfortably, each of them aware of how precarious and charged this whole situation was.

"Please tell your father, the King of Askor, that Ethea is no longer his to command. He no longer has a puppet on the throne. We are a free nation, and no longer under Askor's thumb. If he wishes to maintain the peace, please tell him to keep his ships out of my waters, and his soldiers out of my mountains. We will extend him the same courtesy."

Kalina stood, preparing to leave the tent when the prince's voice rang out.

"What about my nephew?"

She paused, dread pooling in her stomach. How had they heard about Osian so quickly? She turned back slowly, her face schooled into polite confusion.

"I'm sorry, what are you talking about?"

"My brother wrote to me just before you performed your coup and took over the castle that his wife was pregnant with his son. She is dead, is she not? That means the baby may have survived. Where is he?"

"I'm sure I don't know what you are talking about. My mother Cherise Stanchon, the late Queen of Ethea, died during a skirmish." Kalina turned away to leave once again.

"He belongs with us, his father's family."

"If there was such a child, he would belong with his mother's family," she said smoothly. "But there isn't. Good day, Lords and Ladies. Good day, Prince Julian." Finally, she turned on her heels and exited the tent, making a beeline for Maska, who lay on the warm sand waiting for her. She heard the prince yell as she left.

"We know he is alive. And we will bring him back to be with his people."

Cold shot through her as she leaped up onto Maska, turning to see Prince Julian and his nobles filing out of the white tent. Her own people ranged out in a line before her, Kari and Jormungand mounting their dragons behind her. Kalina had to bite her tongue to keep from responding. Instead, she told Maska to leave, and with a mighty sweep of his wings, they were launched skyward, leaving a sea of stunned faces below.

She considered staying to make sure the Askorians left, but she knew she could count on Lord Illeron, Anders, and Talon to see to that. She wanted to get back to the castle right away and to send Jormungand to the Valdir camps high in the Great Grey Mountains to check on Eira and her little brother Osian. She needed to know they were safe.

When Maska landed on the practice grounds of the Queen's Guard, a small contingent of her soldiers came pouring out of the barracks. A few began taking the saddle off Maska, while the others lined up behind her as she waited for Kari and Jormungand to land.

"I need you to leave now and fly straight to High Pass Camp," she said to Jormungand, placing a hand on Shania's side. "I need to know Eira and Osian are alright. Please," she said with desperation and fear in her voice. Jormungand bowed low from the back of his red dragon.

"Of course, your Majesty. We will leave as soon as we have grabbed provisions."

Kalina nodded, her mind already hundreds of miles away in a camp high in the mountains. There must still be snow on the ground up there.

"How could he know where Osian is? Or even that he is alive?" She said to Kari who had joined her. Together they walked back into the castle, leaving Jormungand to resupply and leave.

"I don't know, Kalina, but we will find out."

"In the meantime, we must prepare for war. That prince had murder in his eyes when I told him we were no longer under Askor's thumb. As soon as my council arrives, I want to meet with them."

"I will let you know when they return."

Kalina let out a long sigh. She needed something, a nap or perhaps a strong drink, after a day like that. Instead, she changed into her Valdiran leathers and went back down to the practice grounds where she, Kari, and a few of the Queen's Guard went through drills. Kalina worked until all thoughts of worry about her brother and Askor had left her mind, and all she focused on was the ache and fatigue in her body.

But lying in bed awake that night, after a frustrating council meeting, the fear returned. What had she just done? She had been so drunk on her own power, so focused on proving that she was better than Askor, that she had instead provoked them further and possibly started yet another war they couldn't afford. Her people had suffered enough, she was already struggling to feed the country, she couldn't possibly also feed an army on the move as well. But what choice did she had? Should she have just apologized, begged for forgiveness? That would have made her look weak, and she was already in a fragile position. No, she'd had no other choice, and now she'd have to live with the potentially awful consequences.

Fear for her younger brother also ricocheted around in her head, making sleep all but impossible. She wondered if leaving him in the highland camps with the Valdir had been a good idea, or whether she should have brought him here to live in the castle. She had wanted to keep him safe until he was old enough to decide for himself where he wanted to live. She wasn't sure where was safest, surrounded by dragons and Valdir trained to fight? Or in a castle surrounded by her own guards and high walls? Both seemed to have pros and cons. She finally fell asleep making a list of all the reasons why it would be a bad idea to bring him to Ravenhelm.

Chapter 11

KALINA WAS PACING THE COUNCIL chamber three weeks later. She was angrier than she had ever been, but she was also the most terrified. It had taken a week for word to arrive. She had expected Jormungand, only he hadn't returned from the mountains. Eira had come but had arrived empty-handed.

Her aunt had broken down in tears the moment she'd seen Kalina, and Kalina could see the barely healing burn on the woman's temple. She knew then that Osian was no longer at High Pass Camp. He had been taken by the Askorians. The ship and the meeting had been some kind of distraction, a way to make her think her brother was safe and to pull her resources to the coast. It had been a warning and a farewell.

Eira had told her about how a small force of men had been spotted in the next valley, so she had sent the majority of her fighting forces there to investigate. They couldn't prove they were Askorians, but what else could be? Then a fire near their Emberweed barn had broken out, and she had left Osian with a young girl named Bri while she had gone to help put out the flames. When she returned, Bri and Osian were nowhere to be found. She had launched a search party, but when her fighters returned, reporting they had slaughtered all the supposed Askorians, she didn't know what to think.

Jormungand had shown up the following day, and he had taken a few Valdir and Eira with him to track the enemy into the mountains. But somehow they evaded Jormungand and his search party. When they returned, Jormungand had sent Eira with the news and the reassurance that he and Halvor, his friend, would continue the search. Kalina had spent the last week and a half pacing it seemed. Either she was pacing her rooms, or the halls, or the practice yard.

Even Maska had taken to pacing the garden paths, wearing ruts into the cobblestones. He was just as worried as her. Babies were precious to both the Valdir and the dragons. Dragons only mated later in life, and only produced a dozen or so eggs in a lifetime. Not all of those dragons hatched or made it to adulthood, at least not in recent years with all the fighting. While dragon and Valdir culture had become so intertwined in the last few centuries that they were

501

virtually indistinguishable, the dragons still were their own people, with their own councils and leaders, their own conflict resolution. It was rare for the Valdir to participate in their affairs, just as it was rare for dragons to participate in human affairs. But they did share one purpose, and that was to protect all life, especially the lives of young ones.

Leif had returned finally the previous day. Kalina had made sure he was aware of the situation at the castle, but he had been forced to stay with the troops, first to resolve a conflict with Rangvald and another commanding officer, and then to inspect the troops for war. Kalina was grateful she'd had the foresight to send him there, but the entire time he'd been gone she'd missed having him by her side.

Now she waited for him and the rest of the council to join her as she paced the council room. There had been no word from Askor yet, and no sign of her baby brother. Even her Valdir up on the heights of the Great Grey Mountains hadn't seen anything since the Askorian ship had gone north. The silence was concerning. At least if there had been news she'd have something to do, some way to fight back or plan. But this interminable waiting was driving her to insanity.

Finally, after what felt like a lifetime, Leif entered the room, followed closely by a scowling Kari. Rangvald was still with her troops, along with Talon, and Jormungand was still searching the mountains to the north. Her council chamber would feel rather empty today. Leif came and took her hand gently, and she gave him a strained smile. She knew she could show Leif and even Kari how she really felt but the others, especially Lord Averil and his lackey Lord Tameron and even Lady Renfort needed to see strength from her. Any weakness and Lord Averil would find a way to exploit it, she knew.

So by the time he entered, Kalina was calmly sitting in her seat at the head of the table, awaiting their arrival.

"Lord Illeron," she began, addressing the man just as he took his seat to her left. "Is there any news from your spies in the north?"

The thin man cleared his throat before answering. Kalina braced herself for bad news.

"There is no news of Prince Osian, your Majesty, however, there is news that King Blackbourne is gathering his army at the coast. We don't know yet whether he intends to set sail south, but we do think the possibility is imminent."

Kalina let out a sigh and turned to her commander.

"Leif, how are our troops looking?"

He had already given her his report the night before when he'd returned, but now he needed to repeat it for the council.

"Our armies are tired and have gone unpaid for too long. Many were conscripted, and despite the Queen's reassurance that they may return to their families, many have opted to remain because it means three square meals and a roof over their heads. They also talk about sending what money they do make home to their families. Other than that, they are well trained and improving daily under the command of Rangvald and Captain Higgs. Sir Talon has left to join them and together they will march our army from Wolfhold to the coast. The only concern is housing them once they arrive in Blackwater."

"Lord Tameron, will you see to it that temporary garrison housing is built outside the city of Blackwater and prepare it for the arrival of our troops? As I understand it, your wife is running the city in your absence?" Kalina looked to the plump man who rapidly turned red under her scrutiny.

"Of course, your Majesty. I will leave at once to prepare." He began to get up, clearly a bit flustered, but Kalina held up a hand, a smile pulling at the edges of her lips.

"No need to leave immediately, Lord Tameron, it can keep until after the meeting. Commander Leif, will you let the Lord know what is needed?" Leif nodded, and Kalina could see the side of his mouth twitch.

"Lady Renfort, how are our crops looking? Winter still has a hold in the mountains but is beginning to let go here in the valley. Can we afford to feed our troops and provide for Ravenhelm and the outlying cities?"

Lady Renfort opened a small notebook she had with her and cleared her throat.

"Your Majesty, the harvest this year was the smallest it has been in the last decade, due to Prince Terric's forced draft taking our young men out of the fields, and in part to having to feed a huge army that was constantly marching into The Wastes. We will be hard pressed to make it through till summer, let alone the next harvest season." She closed her notebook decisively. "We will all need to make sacrifices in order to survive."

"Right then," Kari spoke up. "The Valdir will share what little we can, but in the meantime, I say we tighten our belts and give the poor some of what the castle consumes."

"I think that's a great idea." Kalina agreed, enjoying for a moment the look of horror that crossed Lady Renfort's, Lord Tameron's, and Lord Averil's faces. Lord Illeron smiled quietly beside her. "Mistress Aynne?"

One of the Queen's Guards opened the council door and Mistress Aynne swept in, her decisive air instantly seeming to calm the room.

"Mistress Aynne, I wonder if you wouldn't mind sitting in on the council, at least until Lord Tameron gets back from Blackwater, and until the remainder of my council returns from the field?"

Mistress Aynne gave Kalina a quick curtsey.

"Of course, your Majesty." She continued around the table and seated herself across from Lady Renfort, who gave Mistress Aynne a slight sneer. Clearly, Lady Renfort thought herself above the castle Stewardess.

"Mistress Aynne, can you give us a rundown of the state of our coffers? Can we afford to pay our army a bit more?"

"The kingdom's coffers are sadly lacking, your Majesty. It seems that Prince Terric and his council," she said this pointedly to Lord Averil, looking over her glasses at the man before continuing. "- spent the majority of the crown's money on the war effort, with little to no investment or return. We do not have the proper funds to fight another war with Askor, and as it stands, it will take years to replenish what was misspent."

Kalina chewed her lip and glanced sideways at Leif. She had known it was bad, but not this bad. Pretty soon her entire army might desert her if she couldn't afford to pay them.

"What about trade with the southern realms? That avenue has been closed for so long due to the wars but what about now?" She finally turned to look at Lord Averil. She hated that he was in charge of their trade agreements. He was partially the reason they were not in a good place politically with the rest of the world. Prince Terric had been a terrible diplomat, but so had Lord Averil. He had only cultivated the relationship with Askor, and for years, they had been cut off from Wostrad and Ablen and the other down realms. But that was going to change.

"It seems that Wostrad is reluctant to trade with us, given that we seem to be perpetually at war. They feel we don't have anything worth trading, and therefore are not interested in entering into agreements with us. Ablen may be more open to trade across the Cressport Straits but we need to be careful of Askorian ships attacking from the Ice Gulf to the north."

Askor had never admitted to having a fleet of pirates, but they either came from Askor, or from islands so far afield that no one in the southern realms had heard of them. They flew no colors and routinely attacked ships between Ethea, Wostrad, and Ablen across the straits. It was a gamble, but one Kalina needed to take.

"Please, send a trade delegation to Ablen. Include at least two Valdir, as my people have more to offer than you may realize. We need to figure out what we can trade that is cheap and easy to make in wartime that can be traded for food and goods in case Askor decides to attack." Her mind began racing, trying to come up with a suitable trading item. Dragon scales had been traded in the past, but now her people were hard at work collecting them to turn into armor. Dragons were almost invincible from all but the strongest catapults and projectiles, but their riders were vulnerable. They needed something else.

"Your Majesty, if I may." Lord Averil stood suddenly and bowed low to Kalina. "I think that we should continue to pursue a relationship with Askor."

Kalina began to object, Leif and especially Kari speaking up when Lord Averil pulled a stamped and waxed sealed envelope from his breast pocket.

"Before you deny me, I believe you'll want to read this."

Chapter 12

THE LETTER WAS ON HEAVY PARCHMENT, the wax seal bearing the snowflake and star emblem of Askor. Kalina's heart began to race as she took it from Lord Averil, glancing up at Lord Illeron, who frowned. Clearly, even her Spymaster knew nothing of this letter. That alone set alarm bells ringing in her head. She cracked the seal and opened the letter.

Dear Queen Kalina Stanchon of Ethea and the Valdir,

We are writing to you today with a proposition. Despite recent events and the loss of our son Prince Terric Blackbourne, we are prepared to extend an olive branch.

For many years, our two kingdoms have been united not only by a peace treaty but by marriage. The marriage of your mother to our Prince Terric, while not well matched, did ensure the safety of Ethea and prosperity for both our kingdoms.

Our proposal is this: come north to Winterreach, for peace talks with us, and we will try to come to an understanding that benefits both our countries. We also propose an alliance by marriage between yourself and our youngest son. Of course, you can wait to agree to the marriage until you've met him, but I think you will be satisfied with the match.

We await your prompt reply.

Sincerely,

King Remon Blackbourne

Kalina sat back in her chair, letting the letter rest on the table before her. Her eyes shot to Lord Averil's face, searching, but he seemed to be as ignorant of what the letter held as the rest of those around the council table.

The threat loomed that if she refused the invitation then he would launch his troops directly at her, as evidenced by his troops amassing on the northern coast. She was stuck between a rock and a hard place. Finally, she handed the letter to Lord Illeron.

"Lord Averil, are you aware of what is in that letter?"

"No, your Majesty. Only the rumor that it may contain a marriage proposal between you and a Prince of Askor."

"Threats. That is what that letter holds. It threatens war if I don't travel north to their capital and engage in peace talks, as well as consider a marriage proposal to his youngest son." Her mother had warned her that one day a political marriage might become necessary, but she'd hoped it wouldn't be so soon.

Lord Averil had been pushing marriage since the moment she'd been crowned, and she'd pushed his concerns off, sure that Osian would be her heir until and if she decided to get married. Besides, Leif had been the only man she'd even considered marrying, and politically, he wasn't the best match.

"It doesn't mention your brother, Prince Osian at all, your Majesty," Lord Illeron said, handing her back the letter.

Kalina let out a long sigh, slouching back into her seat. Leif gently took the letter from her hand and read it, with Kari reading over his shoulder.

"I know." Kalina chewed on her lip as she thought. "I'll need to think on it, at least for tonight before I make any decisions or send a reply." She stood, pushing her hands into the tabletop. "Council is dismissed."

As everyone filed out of the room, Kalina continued to lean on the table, letting the rough wood beneath her palms ground her. Lord Illeron paused beside her and laid a hand on her shoulder.

"I think there may be some merit to what Lord Averil has been saying all along. Marriage would take you off the market, and countries like Askor wouldn't be able to use that against you." He gave her a knowing look.

Kalina smiled at him gratefully but she knew he meant she needed a political match. Perhaps she should send to Wostrad or Ablen for a suitable match, perhaps with the might of Ethea and one of the southern realms combined would help to stop Askor from considering another war.

Kari and the Queen's Guards walked her back to her rooms where she collapsed onto the bed. She stared at the ceiling, all the possibilities running through her head.

She barely slept and the next day found herself wandering the halls in a semi-daze, worry knotting her gut. The last thing she wanted was to feel backed into a corner with no other options. But she supposed she had been wishing for something, anything, to happen and it had. Now she had to adapt and make a decision or drown.

She was so lost in her thoughts that afternoon that she didn't notice Leif coming up behind her as she paced the practice yard. Her bow hung forgotten in her hand, the target on the other side of the yard woefully empty of arrows. She thought shooting would help clear her mind, but instead, she kept getting distracted.

Leif's warm arms went around her waist, his chin resting on her shoulder, forcing her to stop moving. Her heart leapt into her throat for the briefest of moments before she recognized his scent. If he had been an assassin, she would have been dead. She promised herself she'd begin paying better attention, no matter how troubled her mind was.

"Copper for your thoughts?" he whispered in her ear, kissing her temple lightly before stepping away. Kalina frowned at him. He was always so calm. It was one of the things she loved best about him, but she often wondered how he remained so steady when events were swirling around them.

"This whole marriage thing. I don't know what to do."

She watched as his face fell slightly before he mastered whatever emotions were going on behind the steady mask he showed her. Disappointment settled in her gut. She wouldn't get an answer from him. At least not a straight one. Not one from the heart, not if he was already masking his emotions.

"You need to do what is best for the country, Kalina. Whatever that is." He stepped away from her, and she felt his absence like a blow to her gut.

What had she expected? For him to profess his love, go down on one knee, and ask her to marry him? No, that only happened in fairytales. That wasn't what happened to queens.

"Yes, of course. You're right." She raised her bow and placed an arrow on the string. In one swift movement, she brought her right hand back to her chin, setting the tension along her bones and then gently loosened her fingers. The string snapped forward, sending the arrow flying. It landed dead center of the target across the practice field with a dull thwack.

Leif grabbed his own bow from a rack by the barracks and smiled stiffly at her before joining her. Together, they shot arrow after arrow until Kalina's shoulders and arms were pleasantly sore. She let herself get lost in the quiet focus that was archery, her mind finally settling for the first time all day. Leif's presence often had that effect on her.

As the afternoon sun rose to its zenith overhead, she sighed and put away her bow.

"I'm going to send letters to Wostrad and Ablen. I think before I commit to anything with Askor I need to hear any proposals they may have," she said, turning back to Leif. He stood in the center of the yard, his bow held loosely in his fingers, the sun shining on his silver braids, the angles of his cheekbones standing out. He was achingly handsome, and Kalina's heart clenched to look at him. His calm grey eyes watched her as she spoke. She cleared her throat before continuing. "I think we'll need to accept his offer of peace negotiations regardless of the marriage proposal. I need to see what I can find out about Osian. We know he's there with them. I can't let him stay there to be raised by that monster."

"I agree. You should contact the southern realms. Perhaps they can help."

Kalina wondered if he really did agree. She wondered if he felt the same thing she felt for him. She'd never put it into words, but in her heart, she knew she loved him. Was he really okay with her possibly marrying a royal from a southern kingdom? Her heart clenched and her throat burned so she could barely speak as she nodded and walked away, leaving Leif standing alone in the dusty practice yard.

She found Mistress Aynne and had the woman help her pen two letters, one to each southern realm. She knew there were more kingdoms across the seas, but none that she knew enough about to send letters. Afterward she brought the letters to Lord Illeron to send. And then she waited.

Chapter 13

THE FIRST DELEGATION TO ARRIVE WAS from Wostrad. Three members of their court along with an entourage of both soldiers and servants, all finely dressed in light clothing, stood in Kalina's throne room. There were two men and a woman standing before her, all in their forties and all-black of hair.

The taller of the two men stepped forward and bowed low, his long braided beard that was almost touching the floor. His skin was tanned, his eyes equally dark. He gestured to his companions before speaking.

"Queen Kalina Stanchon of Ethea and the Valdir. We come as delegates and emissaries from Wostrad, your neighbor to the south. We come bearing gifts from our King, as well as his greetings." He bowed again, his arm outstretched.

A servant wearing robes of orange and red, much like his masters, stepped forward, a small chest in his hands. Kalina leaned forward slightly to get a better look. Despite her own trepidation at this delegation being here, she was curious what the southern realms would offer. Perhaps there would be a proposal she just couldn't refuse.

The chest was opened and she peered inside. It held all manner of bottles and vials full of different colored liquids. Some swirled, it seemed, while others held liquids so dark they sucked up the light. Kalina raised her eyebrows and looked at the dark-haired man.

"They are beautiful, but what are they?"

"Your Majesty," he said, with a yet another obsequious bow. "These are a selection of perfumes from our most famous perfumiers. Wostrad is well known for its scents and smells, and our King thought you might enjoy these as a token of his affection."

Kalina wrinkled her nose slightly. She'd never worn a perfume in her life, and she wasn't about to now. But she smiled gratefully, thanking him, and nodded to the servant who stepped back. A second servant stepped forward holding a small crate. She opened the top to reveal various types of what Kalina could only assume were exotic foods.

"Fruits from our jungle far to the south. They are the sweetest and most delightful thing you've ever tasted, your Majesty. We have

510

delivered crates to your kitchens and hope that you might serve them with our dinner tonight."

"That sounds delightful."

Her plan was to receive both sets of delegates, one today and one tomorrow, and each night have a small dinner party for them so they might get to know one another. At least new and interesting foods might make the boring evenings playing nice with nobles more entertaining. She nodded to the servant who stepped back.

"What does your King propose?" She realized belatedly that she didn't know the man's name.

"Your Majesty, our King proposes that you come to the capital of Wostrad to meet him. He would like to forge an alliance between our two realms, making them one strong and formidable force."

Kalina frowned slightly. She had known the King of Wostrad was unmarried but she also knew that he was in his forties, much older than she was.

"Doesn't the King have a son almost my age?"

"Yes, your Majesty, he does." The man bowed again. She had to restrain herself from rolling her eyes. His bowing and scraping was beginning to wear on her.

"Strange, that he would want me to marry him rather than his son."

The man's face blanched a bit at her comment but he recovered quickly.

"The King feels that you deserve to marry a king, not a prince. He has the necessary experience, knowledge, and strength to protect and guide your Majesty. He would be your safe harbor, your knight in shining armor. He wishes to pass his knowledge on to you so that one day you may rule your kingdom and his with wisdom and strength."

She frowned. He made it seem as though their King planned to take over ruling Ethea if she married him. She looked sideways at Leif and Kari, who stood nearby. Leif was studiously not making eye contact. He had, in fact, barely spoken to her since she'd mentioned she was going to see what other offers she could get. That had been over a week ago and Kalina was beginning to get worried. Kari was grimacing slightly. Kalina wondered if it was from the speech the man had just given, or because Kari hated standing around in court.

"Lord…" Kalina trailed off, finally stymied by the fact that she didn't know the man's name.

"Lord Galtero, your Majesty. And my companions are Lord Trevesani and Lady Eleadora. We are at your disposal." He accompanied this with yet another bow, his fellow courtiers doing the same. Lord Trevesani was just as dark as Lord Galtero but not as tall and lean. He was of average build and, frankly, unremarkable in Kalina's eyes. Lady Eleadora was stunning, her dark hair and eyes paired with her tanned skin making her exotic.

"Thank you, Lord Galtero. I look forward to speaking further with you about your King's proposal tonight at dinner." She gestured and her own servants and guards stepped forward to escort the Wostrad delegation to their rooms in the guest wing of the palace. Kalina sat back into her chair and let out a long sigh, rubbing the space between her eyes. This was going to be a long few days. Each delegation was set to stay a week and she already couldn't wait for them to leave. Especially Lord Galtero and his infuriating bowing and scraping.

That evening she met with the Lords and Lady from Wostrad in a small dining chamber, along with her council members and their wives (if they had any). Lady Renfort was a widow and did not bring a guest. Lord Illeron also came solo, but Lord Averil brought his rather docile and quiet younger wife. Lord Tameron had a wife just as short and plump as he was, but where he was a follower and did Lord Averil's bidding, his wife was clearly shrewder. Her eyes darted around the room, her red hair done up in an elaborate coif atop her head. She was constantly whispering in her husband's ear and he was politely smiling along.

Kalina was sat between Lord Illeron and Lord Galtero. Lord Illeron had the ear of Lady Eleadora and ignored Kalina all night but she didn't blame him. He was her Spymaster after all and Lady Eleadora was talking his ear off. She gritted her teeth and hoped he was at least getting some good information as she focused on speaking with Lord Galtero. She changed the subject to the King of Wostrad's offer.

"Lord Galtero, I wonder, does your King expect me to let him run my country? Is so, then he is sadly mistaken. I may be young, but you can ask any member of my court, I am hardly untested." She paused for a bite of her salad which featured a tart kind of fruit she'd never had before that she assumed was from Wostrad. "If I was to accept his proposal, I would need some assurances that my people and my country were mine alone to govern. He would have a say, of course, as my husband, but I would retain full autonomy."

That was something her mother had never had. Once she married Prince Terric, she had been overshadowed and forced to kneel to him. Kalina would never do that. She wanted a partner, someone to bounce ideas off, someone to talk to when she was frustrated and overwhelmed, but not someone to take the reins from her. This was her country to lead, no one else's.

"It sounds, your Majesty, like what you want is a consort and not a king. Our King has certain expectations of a wife, especially if she comes with a country in tow."

Kalina sat back in her chair. She hadn't even considered this possibility. Was having a consort even an option? They'd still be married in the eyes of the gods, but her consort would only be one of her lords, not her king. Was that what she wanted? She didn't hear what Lord Galtero asked next, so absorbed in her own thoughts that eventually he got bored and turned to his neighbor to chat.

Kalina bid her guests' goodnight after another excruciating hour sitting around sipping cups of black tea and politely discussing politics. Each of them was careful not to step on anyone's toes but it was clear that Wostrad was only looking to absorb Ethea, not help make it stronger. As queen, she would oblige the delegation to stay in the castle until their parting date later that week but she knew the answer she would be sending to their king was a resounding 'no.'

Chapter 14

THE ABLEN DELEGATION DIDN'T arrive as planned. Their ship had been delayed due to a storm that cropped up on the Cressport Straits and they had to wait an extra two days to sail. This left Kalina with an unexpected day to herself. She decided to spend her morning in the practice yard training with the Queen's Guard.

A young and eager Valdir named Asa had come to join her, along with Hilde. Another, older Valdir named Gyda had also joined them. The four silver-haired ladies paired off, Kalina with Hilde, and Asa with Gyda, each with their weapon of choice in their hands. Kalina withdrew her two twin axes, twirling them in her palms to settle them in her grip. It had been weeks since she'd practiced with them since Leif had been avoiding her and she'd had no one else to spar with.

As she and Hilde exchanged slow and deliberate blows, axes ringing against sword, Kalina's mind was able to wander and think about the Wostrad delegation and Leif. Thoughts flitted through her mind. Would Wostrad still be interested in trade and perhaps even an alliance if she formally turned down their king's proposal? Would Leif speak to her again if she did? She desperately missed her friend, her confidant. But she also missed his comfort and care. A part of her felt betrayed by him, but a larger part of her understood his putting distance between them. If she was going to marry someone else, he had to move on. He couldn't keep waiting for her, and she shouldn't be trying to kindle a romance when the probability of her marrying for political reasons grew ever more likely.

Hilde's sword slicing her wrist brought her crashing back to reality as blood dripped onto the hard-packed dirt of the arena.

"Your Majesty! I am so sorry!"

Hilde's normally stolid face had blanched white and there was genuine fear in her eyes. Kalina hissed in a breath at the pain that lanced up her arm. She slid her axes into their sheaths and then cradled her bloody arm.

"It's fine, Hilde. I wasn't paying attention. It was an accident." She gestured towards the open barracks. "Do you have wound care supplies in there?"

"Yes, of course."

Hilde put her sword away, the urgency of the moment finally making her move. She led Kalina into the quiet darkness of the barracks, where Kalina paused in the doorway, surveying the space. It was build in a longhouse style, with no walls or rooms, only beds on either side stretching from door to door. It looked like the dormitory she and Delisa had grown up in at Hywell Abbey. She smiled softly before following Hilde, who now sat on a nearby bed, pulling ointment and clean bandages from a small chest.

Kalina sat down opposite her, strangely aware that this was someone's bed, that these blankets belonged to someone who was willing to lay down their life for hers. It was a surreal feeling, and for a moment, she felt as though the roles should be reversed. She felt like a nobody, just a simple orphan girl. It should be her in these barracks fighting for a more deserving queen, not the other way around.

Hilde reached out and began to clean and then wrap Kalina's arm. Kalina watched the woman's face and realized there was a faint, almost silver scar that started on Hilde's forehead and stretched into her hair. The woman's battle braids were so intricate that they followed the scar, making it almost invisible.

"Are you happy here, Hilde?" Kalina asked. She knew Hilde was married to Skaldrik, who made weapons for the Valdir, and she wondered where the scar had come from and if the woman was living in these barracks to get away from something unpleasant at home.

"Yes, your Majesty."

"Please, call me Kalina. Most of the Valdir do."

Hilde looked up at her, searching Kalina's face for any deception. Kalina wondered what hell this woman had walked through.

"Yes, Kalina. I am happy here."

"I noticed you have a scar," Kalina pointed out gently, not wanting to force the subject.

Hilde's hand flew up to brush the silvering puckered skin. Kalina gave her a soft smile and touched her own scar on her cheek in empathy. She knew what it was like to have a scar on your face, to wonder if you were beautiful if anyone would or could ever love you looking like that. Hilde gave her a faint smile back.

"It was years ago," Hilde began, focusing back on Kalina's

wrist and wrapping it in the gauze. "I was just a girl, no older than you. I fancied myself in love with a man. We got married rather quickly, and soon, I realized he was not a man, but a monster. But by that point, I was trapped." She looked up into Kalina's understanding eyes. "Things got worse and worse until one night he threw me against a wall, splitting my head open. I don't remember much, but I am told Skaldrik was passing by and heard me scream. When I woke, Eira told me that Skaldrik had killed my husband."

She finished bandaging Kalina's wrist and patted her hand, smiling.

"It took a few years, but Skaldrik won me over. He is a good man and has always given me my freedom. When I told him I wanted to join your guard, he wholeheartedly agreed. I spend two days a week with him, and the rest of the nights I sleep here." She put a hand on her small cot.

"I'm so sorry for what you went through, Hilde. But I am grateful you are here. I couldn't ask for someone better by my side." Impulsively, she reached out and grabbed the woman's hand, squeezing. "Now, let's go outside. Asa and Gyda will be worried about us and think we've fallen asleep!"

The Ablen delegation arrived with little fanfare. Kalina was summoned from a nap in the library, where she was curled up with Moose the cat, to meet them in the throne room. She hastily donned a light pink dress, her least favorite, and entered the chamber. Leif was standing by her throne as usual, and as she ascended the steps she tried to catch his eye. He briefly made eye contact, nodded with a tight smile, and then turned back to face the newcomers. Kalina let out a sigh before she turned and sat on her throne.

The three courtiers before her could not have been more different than the Wostradians. They were all fair-haired and light-eyed, with pale skin. Despite this difference, they looked the most like her native Etheans. She watched them expectantly until a tall willowy female stepped forward and gave a deep curtsey, her fellows behind her following suit.

"Your Majesty Queen Kalina Stanchon. My name is Lady Dafina. This is Lady Ina and Lord Pierce. We come with greetings on behalf of our King and Queen. They wish to welcome you to your throne, and offer you these gifts as a gesture of goodwill." She gestured to her side where a small display had been set up. She walked over and began explaining. Kalina stood and walked down the stairs to the throne room floor so she could get a better look. Kari and Leif followed close behind.

"This is salt that we have extracted from seawater." She took a handful of black salt and poured it back into a small pouch. "This is barley from our many farms. These are our most common spices, and I hope your cooks will find a use for them in your kitchens. We have brought with us our own cook who is willing to teach yours a few Ablen dishes for you to try." Kalina nodded gratefully. "And these are samples of the textiles our country produces." They came in a rainbow of colors, many of them intertwining to create intricate patterns on the cloth. Kalina fingered the soft wool. It would be perfect for colder winters. She wondered if Calla could make her a cloak from the material.

"These are all lovely and precious gifts. Thank you." Kalina turned and returned to her throne. "Now, I would very much like to hear your King and Queen's proposal."

"Our King and Queen send their regards, and their condolences on your recent losses, your Majesty. However, they do not wish to extend a marriage proposal at this time for either of their sons. Instead, they wish to establish trade rights, which have been so cut off in recent years." King Terric hadn't been keen on trading with any but his father's kingdom, and it had resulted in widespread famine and poverty all over Ethea. Kalina was determined to rectify that.

"Their proposal is one I can happily accept. Ethea would be honored to re-establish trading rights with Ablen."

Lady Dafina smiled serenely at her.

"Then perhaps we could discuss this further over dinner."

Kalina graciously agreed and bade them go and relax. She would see them soon enough. The Alben delegation filed out, their servants following. She sat on her throne as the room emptied. Finally, as Leif turned to leave she called after him.

"Leif, please. Wait."

He paused, turning back to her. Hope fluttered in her chest before she saw his stony expression. Her heart clenched painfully in her chest.

"Why are you avoiding me?"

Leif seemed taken aback at her forthrightness. She watched as his hands clenched and unclenched.

"You are a Queen, your Majesty."

Kalina sat back. His unexpected formal address making her feel cold and alone, but she waited, hoping he had a good explanation for his strange aloofness.

"It is foolish of me to continue to lead you along when you are going to marry for political reasons. I can't continue to be a distraction for you if you are going to make the right choice for this country."

She wanted to ask him why it was so easy to walk away, why he hadn't spoken to her about it first, why she suddenly felt like a day old biscuit he'd tossed in the rubbish bin. She tore her eyes away from his hardened grey ones. She didn't want him to see her cry.

"Thank you for explaining it to me, Commander."

She stood, and swept by him, hoping she could make it to the privacy of her rooms before she began to sob. She couldn't understand how he could be so cruel, so distant. She felt like the last year had been just a lie. Had he not really felt feelings for her? Were all the private touches and kisses just a joke? She couldn't even figure out when things had changed, his behavior seemed to have taken a complete turnaround overnight.

Hot tears spilled down her cheeks, darkening the collar of her pink dress as she walked swiftly down the halls, Kari and Hilde following behind her throwing each other worried glances. Neither woman spoke and they let her slam her door in their faces when she arrived at her rooms. That's when the tears came in earnest.

Chapter 15

THE ABLEN DELEGATION LEFT A week later, after the Wostradians. Kalina had spent hours in the council chambers trying to smooth things over with Lord Galtero after she declined his king's offer of marriage. Then she had spent another few hours negotiating trade deals with Lady Dafina, Lord Pierce, and Lady Ina. Lady Ina agreed to return and become the trade ambassador for Ablen, and Kalina had promised to identify an ambassador among her own courtiers to represent their interests at the Ablen court.

They parted ways with a temporary agreement of peace, trade, and alliance in place. Despite her half-brother's disappearance, the threat from Askor, and Leif being so distant, Kalina was beginning to feel a bit more optimistic about the future of her kingdom as a whole.

One spring night she was sitting on her bed, bundled in a blanket and reading a book, when Delisa came bustling in. Kalina brushed her hand over the grey tabby cat Moose's fur and watched her friend curiously. Delisa sat on the edge of her bed and looked Kalina over.

"You look terrible."

"Oh, thanks so much." Kalina rolled her eyes.

"You look exhausted. I want you to sleep in tomorrow. No more meetings or plans." Delisa looked at her queen sternly. Kalina chuckled at her friend's admonitions. "And tonight, we're going to have a girls night."

Kalina raised an eyebrow and put her book down.

"What exactly is a girls night? We never did that in the abbey."

"That's because we were constantly surrounded by girls. And we were kids with no control over our schedule. But now, I'm in control of your schedule and I'm clearing it." Delisa stood and walked to the door with purpose. "I'll be back in a bit. You just sit and enjoy your book." Kalina shook her head bemusedly and returned to her book and her lightly snoring kitten.

An hour later her doors burst open and in came a literal horde of people. Kalina dropped her book and climbed out of bed, confused about what a girls night included but she was excited to find out.

Delisa was followed by Calla and a bundled up baby Issa, a scowling Kari, Hilde, and even Margy. Margy carried a large basket and a few maids followed her inside with trays piled with sweets and bite-sized foods in all varieties. When Kalina stared openmouthed at the food, Margy winked at her.

"Can't have a girls night without something to munch!"

Her table was cleared of maps and papers and piled instead with cakes and fruit and a variety of chilled fruit juices and a sweet wine from Wostrad that Kalina had taken a liking to since coming to Ravenhelm. Luckily, there was a small hoard of the wine deep in the castle cellars that Margy saved just for her. She joined the other ladies at the table and everyone helped themselves as the maidservants left them alone.

"Let's play a game!" Delisa announced. She leaned against Kari, who responded by wrapping her arm around the dark-haired beauty, a faint smile playing across both their lips. Kalina grinned into her cup of wine, finally happy that her suspicions of the two women's' relationship were confirmed. It made her heart happy to see her cousin and her best friend so happy together, and it seemed that their personalities perfectly complemented one another. Kari was sharp-tongued and extremely loyal, but she was also very solitary and preferred all things that had to do with fighting. Delisa was soft and feminine, and her outgoing nature helped to bring Kari out of her comfort zone. They challenged each other constantly, and from what Kalina had noticed, her cousin would do anything for Delisa.

"I hate games," Kari muttered. Delisa frowned at her partner.

"I bet you'll like this one once we start playing."

"What is it?" Kalina asked, curious. Beside her, Calla handed baby Issa over and Kalina began to bounce the baby on her knees.

Delisa grinned and pulled out a set of playing cards and began handing them out. Kalina swapped Issa to one arm in order to hold her cards.

"It's fairly simple. The goal is to get rid of the cards in your hands. You might have to lie in order to get rid of the cards but you can't let others know you are lying."

"I'm confused," Calla said. "How do we get rid of them?"

"So if I say I have two commanders, you can then put down two dukes, or three if you have that many, and then the next person can put down however many ladies they have, and so on. The trick is, what if it's your turn to put down a duke and you don't have any? Well, then you lie! You pretend you have one and hope no one catches you. But if I have three in my hand, I know you have none so then I'll call you out by saying 'liar!'"

"Okay, I think I've got it." Kalina shuffled through her cards. "Are we starting with dragons low or high?"

"High. In honor of the Valdir." Delisa grinned and Kari rolled her eyes behind her.

"Okay, I have two soldiers." Kalina placed her two cards face down.

Delisa eyed her but nodded and put down one card.

"I have one piker."

Kari put down two cards. "Two horsemen."

Hilde shuffled through her cards. She had been quiet since they'd all joined and Kalina wondered if the woman felt out of place playing cards with nobility and royalty. But she raised one eyebrow at Kari and then spoke.

"Liar, Captain."

Kari sat up straighter.

"No, I'm not!" She was quite offended.

"Well prove it then," Delisa said cheerfully. She reached forward to the pile of cards and flipped the top two over. One was a horseman, the other a piker. Kari scowled even deeper and laid back against a pillow.

"Fine. What now?"

"You take the whole pile and we start fresh." Delisa handed Kari the stack of cards and then turned back to Hilde. "Now you can start back at soldier."

The game went on for hours, each round getting more and more ridiculous the more they drank. Kalina found herself letting go of month's worth of anxiety and stress and began to feel lighter and freer. These women were her family, and she wouldn't trade that feeling for the world. They stayed up until the early hours of the morning until each of them fell asleep in a pile of pillows. Kalina let Calla have the bed with Issa and she curled up on the window seat, the sound of rain pattering against the window panes. She felt comfortable for the first time in months, all her worries about her brother and Leif pushed to the back of her mind, and the wine made her head feel slightly dizzy, her body light. It was a pleasant sensation and she fell asleep without a thought in her head.

The next day Kalina woke alone in her room. She sat up from the window seat she'd been curled on and peered outside, where the rain hammered on the window panes, the sky a dark grey. It was a gloomy day, but at least someone had cleared the mess from the night before.

Her head pounded slightly and her mouth was dry as a bone. She disentangled herself from her blankets and went to her bathroom. The stone chamber was slightly slanted to a drain in the center, and it didn't really help that she felt slightly unsteady on her feet already. A large tub stood in the center of the room. It wasn't until she had become queen that she'd realized the castle had hot running water. Working in the kitchens and as a scribe, all she'd had access to was cold running water, but the royal chambers were equipped with hot water from pipes that ran through the fireplaces down in the kitchens.

One of the first things she had done once she'd learned this fact was take a long hot bath. Going from an orphan to queen had been quite a culture shock, and going from queen of the Valdir to queen of all Ethea was an even greater one. Sure, she'd had large chambers within the Valdir mountain, but she had bathed with the rest of the Valdir women in communal bathing pools. Moving to the Ravenhelm castle meant she was suddenly showered with opulence and sometimes she wasn't quite sure how to react. She was given anything she wanted at a moment's notice. Her bed was cleaned and changed daily, her food cooked exactly the way she liked it, and she could have any dress made whenever she wanted. The change had been so abrupt and strange that she had done everything she could to limit the extravagances. She told Delisa, who was in charge of her schedule as well as her chambers, to only have the maids change the bedding every other day. She only took a bath every other day, and she only commissioned dresses from Calla when the woman was available. The last thing Kalina wanted was to overwhelm her friend.

All these people had helped to get her here, and she wasn't about to take advantage of their kindness. But this morning, with her head pounding, she opted for an extra-long hot bath with some pretty smelling salts. She called in a maid to prepare it as she sat and ate a few bites of bread and drank a glass of milk. Her stomach settled slightly as she climbed into the bath, sighing in relief as the hot water closed over her. She began to doze, the fragrant steam wafting around her and she only stirred at the sound of a soft knock.

Chapter 16

"COME IN," KALINA CALLED AS she finished tying the knot on a soft floor-length robe in a deep blue silk around her waist.

The door creaked open and a familiar figure stepped inside. Leif stood at the door, his hands fidgeting before him, his eyes averted. Kalina's hands went to her chest. She hadn't expected to see him, and suddenly she felt very naked and exposed before him. It was strange, she thought, how a few weeks ago she wouldn't have felt that way around him. Strange how the revelation that their budding romance couldn't go anywhere could change how they acted around one another. She had barely spoken more than a few words to him in the last few weeks.

"Yes, Leif?" His name on her tongue made her heart clench in her chest. He straightened slightly.

"Your Majesty." He bowed low, his many battle braids falling over his shoulders in silver ropes. Kalina took that moment to admire his sharp jawline and broad shoulders, but when he straightened, she struggled to control her emotions. If it didn't bother him to be so formal, then it wouldn't bother her. "I have a message from the council. They wish to meet with you at your earliest convenience."

Kalina let out a small sigh. Her head still ached, and hadn't Delisa ordered her to stay in bed today? But duty called, and she couldn't ignore it.

"I will be there within the hour, then. Thank you, Commander." She turned away, unable to keep her emotions from her face. She didn't turn back around until she heard the door click shut.

She sat heavily on the bed by her wardrobe, a part of her mind wondering what to wear: a dress, or Valdiran leathers, when a second knock broke the silence of her room. She stood suddenly, wondering if Leif had come back, her heart leaping into her throat. But when she said "come in," the person who entered wasn't at all who she expected.

Hilde stood in the doorway, her tall frame obscuring the outer hall. She bowed low and then stood, fidgeting nervously.

"How can I help you, Hilde?" Kalina said kindly, giving the woman what she hoped was an encouraging smile.

"Your Majesty, my husband, Skaldrik, asked me to speak to you on his behalf. He said he has a gift for you, and wondered if you might visit his forge whenever is convenient for you."

Kalina smiled at the woman. She had always liked Skaldrik. He kept the limited supply of weapons sharp and in good repair for the Valdir when they had lived in the mountain, and now he ran the smithy within the castle, making new weapons to outfit her army.

"Of course. I will come and see him after I am done at the council meeting."

The woman bowed again, thanked Kalina and then disappeared out the door. That had decided it then, Kalina reached for her Valdiran leathers.

The council chamber was already full when Kalina arrived. She hated arriving late because it meant every eye was on her and watched as she strode the length of the room to take her place at the head of the table. Leif gave her a brief nod as she sat beside him. She suddenly missed the times when he would reach beneath the table and take her hand. She wished with all her heart that they could turn back time, to before the marriage proposal from Askor, and reclaim their blooming romance. But here she was, feeling distinctly alone at the head of the table.

"Who called this meeting?" she said, sitting down. They had all stood as she had entered and they sat just a moment behind her. As the chamber settled into silence once again, Lord Averil spoke.

"We called this council session today in the hopes of making some sort of plan. Lord Illeron tells us that his spies in Askor report that the King continues to gather his army along the western coast, and he is building even more ships. Despite his letter to the contrary, he seems to be preparing for war."

Kalina looked to her Spymaster, an eyebrow raised.

"Yes, your Majesty. It seems that King Blackbourne is indeed gathering his army. He is also building larger catapults than we have yet to encounter and seems to be sending small army regiments into the foothills of the Great Grey Mountains to set up camp and create strongholds there. My spies tell me they are building towers of stone in the mountains. It seems to me that he is preparing to attack the moment you refuse his offer."

Kalina's stomach twisted. Now she really was stuck. It was

either agree to consider marrying the Askorian princeling or begin yet another war they couldn't possibly win, depleted as they already were.

"What about our new ally, Ablen?" She said, a small hope blooming in her chest.

Lady Renfort spoke up.

"The peace we've begun with Ablen is still too young, your Majesty. They will not agree to send troops onto foreign soil a mere few weeks after agreeing to trade agreements and an exchange of ambassadors. We must wait a few years at least to gain their trust before calling on them to fulfill such a large obligation."

Kalina nodded. She knew the noblewoman was right. Ablen may be interested in a treaty, but it didn't mean they would support a war. Chances were, if Ethea declared war with Askor, Ablen would renege on its support and Ethea would once again be alone against the might of the Askorian army. And Askor had had almost seventeen years to rebuild, while the Etheans had been thrust into another war against the Valdir.

"Lord Averil, has there been any further communication from King Blackbourne?"

"Yes, your Majesty. His Majesty of Askor sent another letter just a day ago." He handed her the sealed letter. She slid her finger beneath the seal, cracking the wax.

My dear Queen Kalina,

I hope you don't mind me being so forward, after all we are practically family. Your mother was my beloved daughter-in-law and I cared for her deeply. I do want to apologize for the way my son behaved. I understand you were almost gravely injured by my son when he attacked you and I want to humbly apologize. I admit he was always a bit brash, possessive, obsessive, and a bit too quick to anger.

In the time since my last missive, I have had time to reconsider the terms of my proposal and they have changed. I now propose you wed my youngest son at midsummer. Once the ceremony has taken place, and we all have feasted and celebrated the union of our two nations, then we can negotiate a peace treaty. I think this marriage would greatly benefit both our nations, and isn't what we both want for our nations' peace?

Come and declare peace with us here in Askor, Queen Kalina, and keep both our nations safe.

Sincerely,
King Remon Blackbourne

Kalina sat back in her chair. He had changed from the formal language of his first letter to a much more personal approach. And many of his words continued to be threats disguised at peace offerings. If she didn't accept the marriage proposal, then he would surely declare war. She only had one real course of action if she wanted to keep her people safe.

"Lords, and Ladies." Kalina took a deep breath and stood to address them all. She flicked a glance in Leif's direction, but despite her heartbreaking in her chest, she couldn't spare him more than a second's thought right then. "I have decided to accept the King of Askor's proposal of marriage to his son. We leave within the week for their capitol, Winterreach."

Then she turned and sped from the chamber, her council's astonished outcries following her down the hall. She turned the corner and bent double, her stomach cramping horribly as she vomited right onto the flagstones. She felt a cool hand at her neck and after she wiped her mouth on the back of her hand, she turned to find Kari standing behind her, holding her braids out of the way.

"That couldn't have been easy," Kari said. Kalina shook her head in response.

"I don't have a choice." She handed over the letter, which Kari skimmed quickly.

"You are right, cousin. You can either declare war and fight, and lose, or marry this whelp and perhaps move on with governing your people."

Kalina nodded, hot tears spilling down her cheeks. Kari took her arm and led her farther down the hall. Hilde followed a few steps behind, giving them privacy.

"Or there is the third option," Kari whispered. Kalina's head came up at that. "We will find a way out of this," Kari's voice was quiet but urgent, strong, her bright blue eyes blazing with some inner fire. It gave Kalina a small measure of strength to hear her cousin say those things. "But for now, we need to play his game."

"Yes, you're right. We can't fight this battle from here. We need to get into their castle, and understand their weaknesses, because they are sure to have them, we just don't know them yet."

Kari bared her teeth in a feral grin.

"That's the right attitude, Kalina. You are a warrior of the Valdir, not some soft, pampered royal. You know what is at stake here, and what is needed to win. And for now, you are doing what you can to survive. Later, we will find a way to strike them where it hurts."

Kalina began to smile back as she let Kari's words fill her up. She stood straighter with every declaration and soon she was standing tall again, all traces of tears gone.

"Begin preparing the Queen's Guard for the journey. I will need everyone I can trust by my side." Kari nodded and strode off, a palace guard taking her place by Kalina's side. "Hilde?" Kalina said, turning to her Queen's Guard. "Take me to your husband."

She followed Hilde down towards the kitchens, passing the dining hall of the scribes where Kalina used to eat. Her thoughts strayed to her days as a scribe in the royal library and for a moment she wished with all her heart that she could be back there among the books, alone, researching some topic. She would gladly take the bullying she got from the other scribes over a marriage proposal to an Askorian prince any day. But that was just a child's daydream and now she had to face reality.

They turned left before the kitchen corridor, the smells of cooking game hen with roasted vegetables wafted to them down the hallway. Suddenly Kalina was looking forward to dinner, her queasiness dissipating. As they walked, the castle around them grew damper, darker, and considerably warmer until they came through a doorway into a large room; the walls were covered in many forges that blazed with light and heat. It rolled in waves over Kalina and she was instantly sweating. She hoped they didn't have to stay long, she now longed for a cool flight in the clouds with Maska over the heat that pounded her from every side.

Skaldrik was a bear of a man, his huge arms and shoulders unmistakable among the other men who labored near the forges. Kalina watched as he withdrew a long piece of glowing red hot metal from the forge and began hammering on it over an anvil. When it had done whatever it was he had wanted, he quenched its flame in a bucket of water, the surface instantly boiling. Then he continued to pound on it until the sides were sharp and the metal cooling. Then he placed it on his workbench and turned to Kalina, Hilde, and her palace guard. He wiped his forehead with a large cloth and came over to them, bowing low before Kalina.

"Your Majesty." His deep voice reverberated through her chest when he spoke.

"Skaldrik. It is good to see you. And it is good to see you doing such good work!" She gestured around at the bustling forge.

"It is only thanks to you that I have such a great forge, great tools, and great helpers." He clapped her on the back in a friendly manner, almost knocking her off her feet. She laughed nervously, before turning the conversation to why she was there.

"I heard you wanted to see me?"

"Yes, I have a present for you. Something I think you will like." He crossed to a workbench along the wall opposite the forges and pulled a package from a shelf. He carefully unwrapped it and beckoned her forward. Kalina joined him at the bench and looked down at the most beautiful things she had ever seen.

Two twin axes sat on a bed of canvas. Their hilts gleamed in the firelight from the forges, their blades covered in Runarks, the Valdir's language, and the same symbols the Valdir tattooed on their bodies to bring them strength, wisdom, or luck. Kalina herself had quite a few tattooed on her face, arms, and spine. The ones on the blades were beautifully wrought, carved into the metal when it was still hot.

"Skaldrik, they are beautiful." Kalina reached out and touched their bone hilts, each one carved from a large bone. Bones that large could only come from one place. She looked up at the man in awe. "Where did you get the bones?"

Skaldrik looked down sheepishly.

"When your father's dragon was dying on the battlefield, she asked me to make weapons from her bones. She told me to use her bones to avenge her death and make the greatest weapons known to the Valdir. I have done that, for you my Queen." He bowed so low his hanging silver braids almost touched the floor.

Kalina was both horrified and extremely touched by the gesture. She hadn't known that Skaldir had been a part of her father's scouting party, but suddenly she was grateful that he was, that he had been there when her father's blue dragon Kaya had died beside her King. Tears leaked out from the corners of her eyes and she wiped them away quickly before touching the large man on the shoulder. He straightened, his sadness evident in his sky blue eyes.

"You honor Kaya, Hakon, and myself, Skaldrik. I would be honored and humbled to carry these with me into battle." Then she did something neither of them expected. She hugged the man around his large waist. She had always been short, small even for her age, and even now she barely came up to his ribs, but he knelt before her and hugged her back, tears leaking from both their eyes now at the loss of her father, at the loss of Kaya, and at the losses her people had suffered at the hands of an Askorian Prince.

She stepped away from him, wiping her eyes and sniffling softly. She picked up the weapons, weighing them in her hands. They were perfectly balanced, small as axes went, but the perfect size and weight not only to be thrown but to be used in close combat on the battlefield. They would serve her nicely.

"Thank you," she said finally, as Skaldrik turned back to his forge and the sword he had been working on. Kalina removed her old axes from their sheaths over her shoulders and put her new ones into the sheaths. They fit snugly, and she knew they had been made for it. The others had just been placeholders since the sheath had come from Skaldrik as well. She smiled as she strode from the chamber, Hilde and the guard on her heels. Askor didn't know what was coming for them.

Part 2

Part 2

Chapter 17

FOR THE SECOND TIME IN HER life and in as many months, Kalina found herself standing on the bow of a ship, the wind off the open ocean before her whipping her battle braids around her head. Even wrapped in a thick cloak with wolf's fur at the collar and around the hood, and her Valdir leathers tightened over thick woolen clothing, she still felt the chill slicing through her. Spring hadn't made it to the open sea it seemed. Normally she would have chosen to fly on Maska but the bitter wind had made her think twice and instead, she watched her dragon frolicking in the waves ahead of the ship's bow.

She envied his thick skin that soaked up and held every ounce of sunlight that allowed him to radiate so much heat. She straightened the crown atop her braids, annoyed that the wind was knocking it sideways, and turned back to the deck of the ship behind her.

The ship was called The Sea Wyvern and Kalina felt the name was appropriate. As they exited the bay at Blackwater and moved out into the Emerald Gulf, heading north towards Winterreach and Askor, she watched as the small armada of ships stretched out behind her. They had traveled on horseback north to Blackwater to meet with her troops before boarding ships bound for Askor. She had asked Lord Tameron and Lord Averil to help secure them ships and crews willing to venture into the icy north.

The ship at the rear was a large, flat decked barge with short masts and rows of oars. It was meant as a floating landing spot for the dragons who circled overhead. Maska was accompanied in the sky by Kari's purple Yurok, Jormungand's red Shania, and Leif's golden Arikara. Hilde had insisted on joining her as her Queen's Guard, as had many of the other Valdir women Kari was training, and their dragons traveled in the rear as a sort of rear-guard. In total there were close to a dozen dragons, and Kalina had made sure that Eira had sent a supply of Emberweed with them, the plant that when chewed, allowed the dragons to breathe fire. It was tucked away in the depths of a ships' hold in case of an emergency.

On the other ships were also a contingent of Talon's men, Ethean soldiers, as well as Leif's Valdiran force. They had left her cousin Rangvald in charge of the remainder of her army. If this show of power didn't make the King of Askor think twice about war, then she didn't know what would.

Kari spent the first two days sick and retching over the side with Delisa beside her rubbing her back. Finally, she had been so fed up that she'd jumped onto Yurok's back and flown off. Kalina had laughed, although the rolling of the deck made her nauseous as well. Her cousin scowled as she and her purple dragon skimmed out over the waves. Kalina wrapped her cloak around herself once again and went back to her cabin to read a book.

She had shown the letter from King Blackbourne to Lord Illeron first, eager for his counsel and insight. He agreed it sounded like veiled threats hidden among what seemed like niceties. And it made her sick to her stomach to think that their trip north was all because she'd been threatened and didn't feel she could refuse. She spent hours alone in her cabin or up on deck staring out to sea, shame and fear churning in her stomach. She was letting her people down, all of her people, Ethean and Valdir alike, by agreeing to this marriage.

All she could do was hope that her cousin could come up with a plan, a way to get her out of this mess. She only wished she could get up the courage to talk to Leif, to make him understand why she was doing this. But he had chosen to stay on another ship, and the few times he was on hers to discuss things with Kari or Jormungand, he had all but ignored her. She knew he must be hurting inside, the same as her. She just wished he'd show it, give her some sign he cared for her. But so far, it seemed he had given up on her altogether.

One afternoon Kalina had become fed up with the four walls of her small cabin and was sick of looking at the same faces so she'd called Maska. He'd come dropping like a stone out of the sky above as if he'd been waiting for her to call him for a ride. She tucked her cloak around her and climbed onto his back. Nodding briefly to Kari and Delisa, who stood on the deck a few paces away, she and Maska launched away from the ship and up into the low hanging clouds above. Early Spring on the open sea was a treacherous time to sail, but they had experienced captains adept at making the trip north and they stayed within sight of the coastline.

Maska frolicked among the rain-heavy clouds for a while, Kalina's stress melting away as she laughed at his antics. Soon his emerald green scales were coated in a layer of raindrops that glistened in the meager light that filtered through the clouds, and her own hair and cloak were damp with lingering drops of water. Maska began to descend, taking them closer and closer to the sea waves below and Kalina felt her heart sink with him. She didn't want to get back on that ship where she felt so alone. She didn't want to go back to being queen and marrying an Askorian prince. She wanted to fly away on Maska, Leif by her side, into the mountains to start a life together. But those were the same thoughts she'd had the previous year when she'd run away with Nash, and she knew how that had turned out.

They weren't in a hurry for her to re-board the ship, so Maska lazily skimmed the tops of the waves a few miles further out to sea, their ship a tiny vessel in the distance, a speck against the horizon of land. Kalina watched it for a while, the salty spray off the sea seeming to cleanse her spirit in a way the rain above hadn't. Finally, she turned her head out to sea, searching the vast dark blue ocean for a sign of life. She would even welcome a dolphin or a shark at this point. Anything to take her mind off her own troubles.

A blue fin broke the water a few feet away and Kalina drew in her breath. Maska snorted seafoam and flapped his wings, taking them a few feet higher. There they stayed, hovering over the waves, watching the dark waters below. A second fin broke the surface and Kalina realized it wasn't a single fin. It was one of many, an entire ridge of fins spanning twenty feet long skimmed just below the surface, the constant undulation of the body and the waves causing the odd fin to clear the surface.

She gasped as a serpentine head, dark blue on top, scales covered in a slimy film, broke the surface and sprayed water all over her. It lifted it's chin slowly as it swam, inspecting her and Maska, the underside of its body a pale blue so light it looked opalescent.

"What are you?" she breathed, one hand reaching out wonderingly towards the beast. It must have been as long as Maska, if not longer, huge fins sticking out at regular intervals along its body, stroking through the water powerfully, propelling it forward. It opened its mouth slightly, baring multiple rows of long dagger-like teeth. Kalina shuddered, withdrawing her hand. She wouldn't want to be swallowed by that creature.

"Sea dragon. They are my kin."

Kalina took her eyes off the beast to stare at Maska.

"I thought they were just a legend!"

"They don't usually reveal themselves to humans. But he figures you must be safe since you are with me."

"He speaks to you?" Kalina looked back at the sea dragon, his mouth still open in what almost looked like a hiss.

"His voice is at a level you cannot hear, but I can hear him just fine. He asks why you ride upon my back like a land dolphin."

It took Kalina a moment to realize he must mean a horse.

"She is my partner, my friend, my companion, my Queen," Maska told the sea dragon. The creature eyed Kalina with eyes as dark as the ocean floor, no light reaching them. Finally, it stuck its head back beneath the waves and together she and Maska watched as it slipped deeper into the sea, until she could no longer make out its sinuous body.

"Wait till I tell Arikara. I don't think she'll believe me!" Maska said, excitement and triumph in his voice. Kalina smiled a bit sadly at her friend, her heart both full and empty all at once. She wanted to go tell Leif, to share with him the amazement at seeing a sea dragon, but she knew he wouldn't want to hear it because their tenuous friendship had been shattered the moment she'd read that first letter from the King of Askor.

That night a storm hit their ships, tossing them like toys afloat on the waves. Kalina lay in her bed, Delisa beside her and Kari dozing fitfully in a chair by the door as the wind howled outside, the rain lashing the small portholes of her cabin. Delisa was cuddling with her, fear as well as the cold that seemed to permeate their bones forcing the contact. Kalina didn't mind though since it helped to drive away the loneliness she was feeling. She hoped fervently that Maska and the other dragons had made for land and were holed up somewhere safe, out of the gale that rocked the ship so violently.

There came a sudden BOOM that shook the cabin and made Kalina and Delisa sit bolt upright in bed. It was loud enough to startle Kari from her sleep, and she could usually sleep through anything. A figure burst through the door, rain-drenched and dripping on the floor. Kalina was out of bed in an instant, a dagger in her hand. Kari was behind the person a split second later, a dagger to his throat.

When the lightning flashed again they all saw the face under the oiled cloak was Jormungand's.

"Kari, it's okay. Put it away," Kalina said, sheathing her own knife.

Kari released Jormungand and stepped away, lowering her knife. Kalina began to pull on her leather vest and cloak. She mostly slept in her clothing these days, never quite sure of how safe she was on a ship full of men Lord Averil had helped pick.

"Your Majesty," Jormungand began, averting his eyes as she dressed and Delisa put on her own bodice beside Kalina. "One of the other ships has capsized in the storm. We don't yet know how many were lost but a rescue effort has started. You are needed on deck to command."

Kalina swallowed, fastening her own thick cloak about her throat. She had to command because Leif was on a different ship and because she was the highest authority on the boat. But that knowledge didn't give her confidence.

"Lead the way, Jormungand."

Kari and Delisa followed them out onto the deck, the wind howling in their ears. Kalina couldn't hear anything above the sounds of the wind, rain, and waves. Booms crashed overhead, followed by bright flashes of lightning and in the intermittent light, Kalina could just make out a partially capsized vessel off their starboard bow. She staggered to the railing while the Sea Wyvern rolled beneath her and clutched at the railing. She felt Jormungand touch her shoulder to get her attention. He placed his mouth close to her ear so she could hear him as he yelled above the roar of the storm.

"What should we do?"

"Send out the skiffs, see if you can gather up any survivors," she yelled back. He nodded, fear and determination on his face as he stepped away from her and towards where the crew was wrestling down the mainsail, tying it down tight. Kari stood at Kalina's side, watching as another nearby ship, the one Kalina hoped that Leif was on, also deployed their smaller skiffs. She prayed to Skaldir, the Valdir's god, and the gracious Mother that there were survivors and that they would find them alive and safe.

It felt like hours passed as the boats deployed and made their laborious way across the ever-shifting seas, the rain lashing down

making it hard to navigate. More than a few men were lost overboard
as the storm raged on around them. The ship beneath her continued
to pitch and sway and it took every ounce of her strength to keep
holding onto the railing. She saw Kari beside her, both hands on the
railing around Delisa as her friend crouched, her eyes squeezed shut.
Kalina opened her mouth to yell at them to go back inside when a
shout rose over the sound of the storm. Kalina turned just in time to
see a huge wave crash over the deck on the opposite side of the ship
and sweep towards them. She barely had enough time to suck in a
breath before her hands were ripped from the railing and she was
pitched overboard with the force of the freezing water.

For a few dizzying seconds she spun under the churning waters
of the storm-tossed sea, and she couldn't tell which was way up. But
another bright flash of lightning showed her the surface and she
kicked out strongly towards it, her lungs burning for air. When she
broke the surface she sucked in a lung full of air only to be plunged
under again and spun around by a second wave crashing over her
head. Once again, just as she was about to give up and suck in a breath
of seawater, she managed to surface and suck in air, coughing and
choking on the salty brine of the ocean. The waves continued to
tumble her until she was utterly spent, her muscles exhausted from
swimming, her lungs aching and screaming for air, her head dizzy,
her eyes burning.

The only thoughts spinning through her head were those of
survival. And regret. She was going to die here, in this ocean. And
what a useless death it would be. She wished she could see Maska
one last time, to tell him she loved him, to fly with him one last time.
She wished she could see Leif one last time, to tell him she loved
him, that she had since the moment she'd first looked into his grey
eyes. She wished for a lot of things. But she was so tired. Too tired
to keep going, keep swimming.

This time when the waves plunged her under she didn't
struggle, she let the ocean take her where it wanted, the burning of
her lungs an almost distant annoyance as she drifted beneath the
surface, staring into the empty inky depths. But they weren't as
empty as she'd originally thought. An undulating, sinuous body was
swimming right for her, something shiny clutched in its massive
jaws. Before she could even let out an underwater scream, she was

swept up, her hands clutching at spiny ridges and soon, the welcome chill of fresh air hit her face and she gulped in deep breaths of the salt-laden air.

But that was all she remembered for a time, her mind slipping in and out of consciousness as the creature beneath her moved through the waves. She didn't fully open her eyes until she was laid gently on soft sand, the feeling of solid land beneath her making her stomach roil. She sat up. Above her was the great head of a massive creature and in the next flash of lightning, Kalina saw that it was the sea dragon, its large-scaled head dripping seawater, seaweed hanging from one large horn.

"Thank you," she croaked out, her throat raw from swallowing so much seawater, from dragging in breaths of cold air, from screaming. The dragon lowered its head, looking at her with those big dark eyes before it slowly slipped back into the crashing surf and into the dark ocean beyond.

Chapter 18

KALINA WATCHED THE SEA DRAGON disappear before rolling onto her side to vomit up what felt like buckets full of salty water, it searing her throat as it exited her body. When she finally felt empty, her lungs and stomach feeling blessedly hollow, she lay back on the sand and closed her eyes, slipping into a deep sleep.

The next morning the sun rose over calm waters and Kalina sat on the beach, awaiting rescue. She had awoken, alone on a small spit of land a few miles out to sea. Something sparkled beside her and she reached out, digging her own silver and blue dragon scale crown out of the sand. She rinsed it off in the ocean and placed it back onto her already tangled and salt-encrusted silver locks. As the sun glinted off the small waves that lapped the sandy spit of land she occupied, a shadow passed overhead. She shielded her eyes and looked up to see sunlight on green scales as Maska descended to land on the sand beside her.

"They thought you were drowned. I told them you were alive and safe somewhere," he said as he approached her, his head lowered so she could collapse against him in a tight embrace. She wrapped her arms as far as they would go around his head, her own resting between his eyes.

"I thought I was drowned, too. But the sea dragon saved me."

"I saw him in the waves as I flew here. He pointed the way."

Kalina's heart was immeasurably full, despite her close call with death. She felt calm inside like the storm had somehow washed her clean. She was eager to see Kari, Delisa, Leif, Talon, and Jormungand again, but she also was happy to spend a few more moments alone on a sun-warmed beach with her dragon.

"I've missed you, Maska," she whispered into his scales. He rumbled a purring growl of agreement. "I wish we could just stay here, not forever, but just for a while." She let out a long sigh before breaking away from him. "But I must get back to reality."

"One day we will go for a flight into the mountains and stay. One day we will have peace," he said, nudging her in empathy.

She smiled and nodded at him before climbing into his saddle. He launched them into the sky, a spray of sand stinging her cheeks as he flew back out to sea and the waiting ships that were small specks on the horizon to the north.

When she slid off of Maska's back onto the Sea Wyvern's deck she was almost bowled over by Delisa as she ran into her, hugging her fiercely.

"I'm alright, Delisa," she said, letting out a small laugh that was choked off when Delisa squeezed tighter.

"I thought you were dead. I thought you were gone." Delisa's voice came out as a small sob. Kalina was taken aback. Growing up, Delisa had been her only friend, and she had certainly missed her when she'd left the abbey behind in search of the Valdir, but she hadn't truly known how much she'd meant to her childhood friend until just now. She squeezed Delisa right back.

"I know. But I didn't. I'm here."

Someone cleared their throat and they broke apart, Delisa and Kalina both wiping tears from their eyes.

"We are happy you are alive and unharmed, your Majesty." Lord Illeron bowed low, and when he straightened, he made eye contact with Kalina. There was relief in his eyes. She could tell he'd been worried for her too. She was surprised how much that meant to her.

"Yes, we are very happy you have returned to us." Lord Averil beamed at her, but his smile didn't reach his eyes. Kalina would have bet money he would have been happy to see her dead.

"Thank you. I am lucky that a sea dragon saw fit to save me."

Murmurs flew around the gathered crowd of crew and nobles. Soon, the gathered Valdir began chanting, their words a quiet susurration of sound that sent a chill down her spine.

"Valdira, Valdira, Valdira."

"Valdira? What does that mean?" Delisa said beside her. Kalina shook her head.

"I have no idea."

Lord Illeron and Lord Averil began dissipating the crowd, sending sailors back to their posts and guards back to their ships. Kalina glanced over at the scattering group of Valdir and saw Leif standing amidst them, his grey eyes intense as he watched her. She turned away from him, unable to hold his gaze. He had gone weeks with barely looking at her, and now he couldn't tear his eyes away? She didn't know what she was supposed to feel anymore.

"I need a bath," she said to Delisa who led her to her cabin. At the door, she turned and looked back once more at Leif. He hadn't moved, his eyes still tracking her.

Kari came into the cabin as Kalina undressed behind a screen while Delisa poured some freshwater into a large bucket. A proper bath would have to wait but at least Kalina could wash and get the salt from her hair. Kari sat in the chair by the door and began digging under her nails with her dagger.

"Kari," Kalina said as she began to wash behind the screen.

"What?"

"What does Valdira mean?" It was a term she had heard before, something she'd read maybe among the scrolls of the Valdir when she'd spent time studying at the mountain with her aunt Eira. But she couldn't quite remember its significance.

"It's just a term of endearment," Kari said offhand. But Kalina knew it was anything but a casual nickname. She stuck her head around the screen and scowled at her cousin.

"Kari," she reprimanded.

"Fine. Valdira is a myth, a legend told by our people. Valdira was a Valdir maiden long ago who caught the attention of our god Skaldir. He thought she was the bravest fighter and the most beautiful woman he'd ever seen. So he came down to seduce her. But Valdira was already betrothed to a young Valdir warrior. She wouldn't be swayed. Skaldir is known for his jealousy and anger, so he turned her betrothed into a sea dragon and banished him to the Emerald Sea. He thought that would keep Valdira from her love, but she refused him again and flew her own dragon to the sea, where she swam among the waves with her love, the sea dragon, forever."

"That's a beautiful story, Kari, but I'm not sure how that makes me like Valdira," Kalina said ruefully as Delisa scrubbed her head with a soap that smelled of lavender. Kari sighed and put her knife down.

"It is said that one day Valdira will come back again and she will tame the sea dragons as well as those of the sky." She paused. "They think you are the second coming of Valdira. That is why they chant the name."

"That is ridiculous. The sea dragon saved me because he liked Maska. We met him earlier while we were out flying."

"Sea dragons are said to be solitary and vicious creatures, Kalina. They don't just save people."

"Clearly, this one did."

They all fell into a charged silence as Kalina wrapped her dripping hair in a soft towel and pulled a robe on. She sat down on the bed and began rubbing her head dry, thinking. Maybe this would be a good thing. The thought of her own people likening her to a legend made her feel strange. She wasn't a fierce warrior, and she had never denied a god. But maybe she could be like Valdira and deny the King of Askor if only to prove to herself she could.

She emerged an hour later, clean and in a long woolen dress, onto the deck as the sun began to set. Hilde had offered to scrub her Valdiran leathers clean, and Kalina had been forced to wear one of the cold weather dresses she'd brought for court. Her wolf fur cloak was pulled up around her neck to keep off the chill wind from the ocean. Although Spring was in full swing in the south, it was slow to reach the northern waters of the Emerald Bay, and even slower to thaw Askor. From what she had read in the library before they'd left, Askor's northernmost parts were always covered in ice, and only the southern half, near the Great Grey Mountains, ever thawed in the late spring and summer.

They were drawing ever closer to Winterreach, Askor's capital and seat of power, but first, they had to cross the deepest stretch of the Emerald Gulf. The Northern Deep stretched from just outside Winterreach, north into the Ice Gulf where enormous shelves of ice floated on the ocean's surface yearlong, making travel impossible and dangerous when the ice crashed into one another.

Kalina was standing by the rail, looking out to sea, when she felt a presence beside her. She turned slightly and found Lord Illeron clad in a stiff grey wool coat, his hands clasped behind his back. He stood near enough to speak, but he never turned towards her. By now she was used to his aloofness, his ability to blend into the crowd. He had been the first to vouch for her as Queen and she would forever be grateful for that. He had also helped her grandfather hide her as a baby. Of all the Ethean nobles, she trusted him the most. And she'd even come to value and respect him as her advisor.

Kalina's thoughts were pulled away from Lord Illeron when something moved beneath the waves a way out to sea. A dark mass, larger than she would have thought possible, moved there, bowing the surface of the water but not actually breaking the surface before disappearing once again into the depths. Her pulse sped up as she watched. Was it the sea dragon? Or something much more sinister?

"There are things in the Northern Deep that we would do best not to disturb," Lord Illeron said softly beside her. That was when Kalina realized the entire ship had gone still. Only the creaking of the rigging and mast and the soft lapping of waves against the hull made any sound. She turned to look, all of the sailors were at their posts, but they stood, as if waiting for something. Even her own people had picked up on the tension and were quiet.

"What is it?" she asked softly, turning back to the dark, churning water.

"A beast. Or many. No one really knows. If it is disturbed, those who are attacked don't live to tell the tale."

Goosebumps rose on her arms and a shiver went down her spine. Suddenly she was very grateful to be aboard the ship and not back in that dark water. She remembered the feeling of the sea closing over her head, the helplessness and fear that had consumed her as she'd waited to drown.

"I'm not sure we'll be any safer once we reach land, your Majesty." Lord Illeron shifted on his feet slightly. Kalina eyed him out of the corner of her eye, one eye still fixed on the dark water. Maybe he was right. Maybe King Blackbourne was just as bad as any deadly sea monster. She would have to be careful.

Chapter 19

WINTERREACH, THE CAPITAL OF ASKOR, loomed before them, consuming the cliffs around its harbor. It was a sprawling, enormous city with imposing granite walls that surrounded its entirety. Kalina had to clamp her mouth shut as she stood in the bow of the ship and watched it approach. The castle rose up on the bluffs behind the city, huge, grey and imposing. It had sloped roofs to keep the snow off and high ramparts of the same grey granite as the city walls. She had a hard time envisioning it in the peak of summer. The city still held a layer of snow, the peaked roofs covered in a soft white blanket.

She shrugged her wolf fur cloak a little higher around her neck to keep the chill off and turned back to the ship. Ever since the night she'd gone missing, Leif had remained on her ship. She wasn't sure whether it was to keep an eye on her out of love or duty. She supposed it no longer mattered. All she felt when she looked at him was a vast emptiness in her chest, a hollow feeling that she couldn't seem to shake. He stood by the starboard rail, watching the other ships behind them enter the harbor. Huge war galleys from Askor were maneuvering alongside each ship, blockading them in, as well as serving as escort. It made Kalina nervous as she watched their escape close.

Leif turned to search the deck and paused as his eyes alighted on her before moving on and calling Kari over to him. He spoke in quick words and Kari nodded before making her way up to Kalina's side. Kalina's heart sank even further. Leif couldn't even bring himself to talk to her directly anymore. That was going to make this entire trip even more difficult.

"I think it's time to mount up and fly above this until we are sure we are welcomed," Kari said as she came to stand beside her queen.

"I agree." Kalina felt a bit like she was running from a fight, but when it came to King Blackbourne she couldn't be too careful. And coming in riding her dragon, as she had with the Askorian delegation, would show that she was powerful, a force to contend with.

Maska and Yurok circled lower at their calls, and Kalina

mounted up, once again grateful for the warm skirt of her dress and the wool-lined leather pants she wore underneath. She decided she'd send Calla a thank-you note for thinking of everything when helping her pack. Her face was immediately numb with cold, however, as Maska launched his bulk into the sky above the ships, hovering out of range of their largest catapults.

She and Kari, along with her Valdiran Queen's Guard, stayed aloft above the harbor for what seemed like hours as their ships docked, then disembarked. She took the time to study the city beneath her, searching the streets, wondering what type of ruler the King was. Were his people starving? Were they well cared for? Was there crime? She searched for and found the main road and then watched as large carriages ferried her people from their ships up to the castle. The carriages were pulled by huge oxen like animals with long shaggy fur that Kalina had never seen before in the south.

When she saw Leif signal the all-clear to her and the dragons that surrounded her, Maska dove for the courtyard of the castle where her people were filing out of the cramped carriages and going about the effort of unloading. A small group of well-dressed nobles stood in the doorway to the castle entrance, their backs stiff as they watched the group arrive. Maska landed with a huge thud, a cloud of ice and snow flying up around them. Kalina slid from his back as soon as the cloud settled, and within moments Leif was by her side. Kalina almost stepped back in surprise but schooled her face as he spoke.

"Their delegation is waiting for us, your Majesty," he said as he approached. Kari landed on his other side and dismounted.

"Where are the dragons supposed to go?" Kari said. She strode to Kalina's side, taking off a pair of fleece-lined gloves like the ones Kalina had and stuffing them into her waistband.

"I'm sure our hosts will let us know shortly," Kalina said, striding forward, her guards dismounting and falling in behind her. Soon her entire party, their small contingent of soldiers as well, were crossing the large courtyard inside the gates of the castle proper. As they approached the steps, the faces of their greeting party became clear.

Kalina recognized Prince Julian, his spare frame still richly clad in velvets, a long coat pulled up against the winter chill that surrounded them. Beside him was an old man, stooped and bent with age, but his eyes were bright and sharp as they assessed Kalina. On his head, he wore an old iron crown with no adornments. Kalina knew immediately this man was King Blackbourne. On his other side was another man, older than Prince Julian by a few years, his dark eyes and dark hair a mirror of his brothers, but his eyes were more cunning, sharp like his father's. He stood taller than all the others as well, his body muscled from heavy sword practice Kalina assumed, based on the long sword he wore strapped to his hip.

A young woman stood a few paces back, a long black dress adorned with jewels and bright silver threads woven through it fell to the ground, spreading out around her in a pool of darkness. She had flaming red hair that fell in curling waves down her back and on her head, she wore a bright silver crown covered in diamonds that glittered despite the overcast sky above them. She couldn't have been much older than Kalina herself, and she wondered if this was the new queen or one of the wives of the princes. She didn't have long to wait.

"Queen Kalina Stanchon," King Blackbourne said giving her a slight bow. Kalina bowed stiffly back, bracing herself for what was to come. "Welcome to Askor. My son Prince Julian will meet with your entourage and help them get settled."

"Thank you, your Majesty."

"This is my son Endre, heir to my throne. And this is my new lady wife, Queen Malin."

Kalina gave each a small bow. When she straightened, Queen Malina's cold blue eyes were on her, appraising her. Kalina tried a small smile but the woman did not return it.

"We have refreshments waiting for you and your guests. You must be hungry after such a long journey," the King said. He began to turn away, but Kalina spoke up.

"Your Majesty, what about our dragons? Where might they go?"

He turned and eyed Maska and the other dragons with no more than a passing glance as if they were a novelty, a pet.

"Ah, yes. Julian, you will find a place for the dragons as well. Clear out a stable or something suitable." He waved a hand dismissively at his son and Kalina saw a muscle tighten in Prince Julian's jaw before he turned to obey his father.

Kalina looked back at her people and caught Delisa and Talon's eyes. Both gave her a nod, letting her know they would take care of things. She looked to Maska, whose dark star-flecked eyes regarded her. She was nervous about leaving him, letting him out of her sight, but unless she wanted to make things more awkward and strange, she'd have to trust that he could take care of himself. Then she began to ascend the steps, her small entourage following behind. The red-haired woman ahead of her was now clutching the old man's arm and talking low and fast into his ear as they walked into the castle.

The other prince, Prince Endre, turned to Kalina and gave her a tight smile before bowing before her and offering her his hand.

"Your Majesty, may I escort you?"

Kalina hesitated for the barest moment before thanking him and taking his arm, letting him lead her inside. She resisted the urge to look back at Leif or Kari. She couldn't imagine what they must be thinking.

The inside of the Winterreach castle was just as bleak and imposing as the outside. Walls of grey granite cut into precise blocks and then carved with symbols as the only adornment lined each hallway and room. The stone was carved with swirls and lines and in some places, like around door mantels, the carvings depicted scenes of war and violent battle. Kalina shivered slightly as Prince Endre led her beneath a huge carving of a battlefield covered in the dead that adorned the throne room entrance. Askor was known for its prowess in battle, she supposed.

Prince Endre looked sideways at her and Kalina smiled.

"Askor is colder than I expected," she said as a way to cover her unease. The prince smiled at her and nodded.

"We are a tough people who have managed to survive and thrive here year-round."

Kalina narrowed her eyes as he led her before the dais.

The elderly King Blackbourne and his young queen ascended the few steps to their stone-wrought thrones and sat down. There was a small crowd of people gathered to the side, a group of well-dressed noblemen and their wives, along with a few men and women Kalina knew instantly were the other princes and princesses of Askor. They all shared the same dark hair and eyes that the king had, that Prince Terric had had.

"Your Majesty, please, join us for refreshments," the King

said, gesturing to the laden tables.

"Thank you, your Majesty."

She nodded to her entourage and the small group began to make their way towards the tables of food. The Askorian nobles and royals watched them, muttering amongst themselves. Kalina straightened her spine. She felt vulnerable, alone, and judged. It wasn't a feeling she relished and she felt like she was back in the abbey where she grew up, the bully Mari making fun of her as she walked by. But Kalina was a queen now, she wouldn't show these people any weakness.

A young dark-haired man who looked a lot like the king approached her. She stiffened as he bowed before her and smiled. Despite his resemblance to his father, this young prince didn't exude the same malice that the other princes seemed to.

"Your Majesty, I am Prince Simen. I believe you and I are to be wed."

Kalina took a small step back, eyeing the young prince. So this was the man she was supposed to marry. He was tall and around her age, his brown eyes more of a dark amber than true brown. He smiled at her tentatively.

"Very nice to meet you, Prince Simen."

"Can I help you fill up a plate?" He gestured towards the food.

"Yes, please." She took his arm now that Prince Endre had released her, joining his father on the dais.

Prince Simen led her to a table filled with strange delicacies laid out prettily on delicate plates. Most of what she saw was unfamiliar and he began by picking up a small plate and asking her what she wanted.

"Whatever you think is best, your Highness. I am new to your country and don't know what foods you have that are good."

"Then I would be happy to show you some," he said giving her a smile. He pointed to a pile of some kind of pinkish food. "This is a type of shaved and dried white fish. It has a mild salty flavor and is best eaten with butter." He put a few pieces of the fish and a small pat of butter on the plate. Kalina watched with interest, aware that all eyes were on her back as she followed the Prince down the buffet line.

"What is that?" she said, pointing to rolled pieces of dough that smelled sweet and looked like they were filled with a dark paste. Prince Simen smiled tentatively.

"Those are my personal favorite. They are pieces of rolled cake dough that are fried and then stuffed with cocoha."

"What is cocoha?" It was something she'd never heard of.

"It is a sweet delicacy that can be melted into liquid form or hardened. We import it from Saldor. My personal favorite is to melt some in hot milk."

Kalina smiled back at the prince then. She had heard of Saldor, read about the country in fact. It was a small country somewhere to the south of Wostrad and she knew it was where much of the sugar crop was grown. She had never heard of cocoha and when she was handed the plate it was the first thing she tried. It melted in her mouth with a creamy and slightly bitter taste but mixed with the buttery cake it was a perfect combination.

"How do you like it?" the prince asked, taking a bite of his own.

"Delicious," Kalina purred around the mouthful. She swallowed and bit into another. Her hungry stomach grumbled happily as she tried the various foods on her plate. Finally, the King cleared his throat and the whole throne room went quiet.

Chapter 20

KALINA PUT THE PIECE OF FISH SHE was nibbling back down on her plate and set it on a nearby table and paused to listen to what the King of Askor had to say. Lord Illeron, who had been sampling his own plate of food, stood chatting with Kari and Leif a few feet away, put his own down and followed behind her. Lord Averil was currently stuffing his face and chatting amiably with Prince Julian and a princess whose name Kalina didn't know. Prince Simen put his own plate aside and watched his father, his face full of a mixture of expressions that Kalina couldn't quite read. Was it fear on his face? Or hatred? Or was it something else?

King Blackbourne raised a hand, silencing the muttering of the small gathered crowd. Everyone fell silent and Kalina briefly caught Kari's and Leif's eyes. They both moved and took up flanking positions behind her. She wasn't about to be caught off-guard in this court. She was surprised when the King began by praising her and her people for their resilience.

"The Valdir are an ancient people. They have endured many centuries of persecution and slavery, and yet, here they stand before us, stronger than ever with Ethea at their back. Queen Kalina, you have accomplished more in the last year than many others who were raised in the court would accomplish in a decade." The King's eyes flashed towards his youngest son, Simen, who's expression darkened at his father's words. Kalina had to fight not to raise an eyebrow. Did the King disapprove of his youngest son? "Now," he continued. "We are delighted that you accepted our proposal of marriage and our invitation to visit our fair capital. And in honor of your presence here, my lady wife insisted on throwing you all a welcome ball."

The new Queen stood, her red hair seeming to glow as she addressed them.

"Esteemed guests. Tomorrow night, after you have all rested, there will be a ball held right here in the throne room. I will have tailors sent to your rooms this evening to check whether anyone needs any clothing made. And we will showcase all our culinary delicacies with a banquet and share in some traditional dances." She smiled graciously, and it transformed her face into something bright and warm instead of cold and beautiful. Kalina would have to wait and see if this woman was an ally or an enemy.

"Thank you, your Majesties. You truly honor us," Kalina said, bowing slightly.

"Now please, enjoy yourselves for as long as you'd like, and tomorrow we will visit some more," The King said and stood to leave. Kalina's eyes narrowed as the Queen took his arm and led him from the throne room. Prince Endre followed his father with his eyes as the older man left the room, but his expression gave away nothing. Kalina turned away from eyeing the crown prince and found Prince Simen still beside her.

"Would you like a tour once you are settled into your rooms?" His face was transformed, seeming eager and open, and Kalina decided that she liked him well enough. She still had no desire to marry him, but perhaps they could at least have a friendship to start with.

"I would like that very much, thank you."

When Kalina opened the doors to the suite of rooms she was staying in, she was greeted by dark mahogany furniture and a few large hangings that hung suspended from the granite walls. The floors were covered in plush carpets in an attempt to warm up the space but it still seemed dark and gloomy.

Delisa was already there, unpacking her trunk and airing the dresses to smooth out the wrinkle. Kalina collapsed onto the bed as Kari and Hilde, her ever-present shadows, searched the rooms. Kari had chosen Runa, Asa, and Gyda, the women Kalina had met when she'd trained with the Queen's Guard a few weeks before, to come on this trip with them. Runa however, didn't have a dragon, and had traveled with the other servants and guards on the other ship with Talon and his second in command, Captain Higgs.

"The Queen's Guard and myself will sleep in your changing chamber. There are already cots in there for servants, and in this place I'd rather be close at hand in case something happens."

Kalina agreed wholeheartedly and right now she was too tired to argue.

"That did seem to go strangely well back there," she said rolling her head back to look at the door. "I expected the King to be like his son, arrogant, rude, manipulative and controlling. But so far he has been nothing but gracious if a bit stand-off-ish."

"Didn't he send you veiled threats in those letters?" Kari asked as she slouched into a nearby chair.

"Yes. So I expected more of the same, but it seems he is either playing the long game, or it was unintentional, which I doubt."

"Did you see his wife?" Kari asked with a small derisive snort. Delisa, who was standing beside the bed near Kalina, shot a glare at Kari who put her hands up in defense. "She is nothing compared to you, Lisa." Delisa smirked and went back to folding Kalina's clothing. Kalina smiled up at the ceiling of the chamber.

"Yes, she seems... odd."

"Odd is an understatement. What woman that age would want to marry an old codger like him?"

"Money, fame, power, love..." Delisa chimed in. Kari and Kalina both looked at her. She shrugged innocently. "What? There are many reasons someone might marry someone of a different age."

Kalina realized Delisa was talking about herself and Kari. Kari was almost ten years Delisa's senior, a fact Delisa was forever bemoaning and Kari was self-conscious of.

"All of the above for her, except maybe love," Kalina muttered.

A knock on the door startled her and she sat bolt upright. She realized it was either one of her own entourage checking on her, or Prince Simen come already to fetch her for a tour. She still wore the same weather-worn cloak she'd walked in with and a salt-stained dress.

Delisa went to answer the door, and after a whispered word, stepped aside to admit Leif into the room. Kalina hastily ran a hand over her wind-whipped braids and stood. Leif stayed awkwardly just inside the door, his hands clasped behind his back. Kalina both loved and hated to see him this way. She missed him terribly, and this strange silence between them was pulling at her heart. But she loved the way his shoulders looked in the Valdiran and Ethean uniform, a style she and Kari had come up with right after her coronation. It was specific to the Valdiran troops who fought in the Ethean army, and Leif, being the Ethean army commander, wore his own officer's uniform. Her own Stanchon coat of arms, two crossed swords on a field of green, was finely wrought in silver thread across his chest, the red leathers of the Valdir on his legs and the uniform itself a deep maroon to match the red leathers.

All Ethean army soldiers wore all green tunics with the crossed swords, but the Valdir soldiers wore maroon. It made them stand apart, just like their silver hair and their dragons made them stand out on a battlefield.

"What can I do for you, Commander?" Kalina asked, the question coming out too formal, too much like she was his queen and not his former sweetheart.

"I came to let you know that myself and Jormungand are staying down the hall and around the corner. Lord Illeron is across the hall from you, and Lord Averil is beside you." He gestured so she would know which direction. "The tailors will arrive after dinner, which will be served in our rooms, or so we've been informed by Prince Julian. Talon and Captain Higgs are staying with the men down in the barracks. The King has graciously cleared out an entire wing for us." He said 'graciously' with no small amount of sarcasm. Kalina knew he didn't trust the King of Askor as far as he could toss him.

"What about the dragons? Where is Maska?"

"There is a large stable that was originally built to house draft horses and their wagons. It has been emptied for the dragons and they say it is quite comfortable."

Kalina let out a small sigh, one of her worries allayed. There was a pause then, pregnant with anticipation, with some unnamed emotion Kalina couldn't name but her eyes met Leif's and for a brief moment, she thought he might open his arms for her to run into them. His shoulders twitched, his fists clenched at his sides. But he didn't reach for her, he just left them hanging, cold and empty. Kalina swallowed and straightened her spine.

"Thank you, Leif. I will see you tomorrow then."

He bowed to her, then to Delisa and Kari before leaving the room. Kalina let out a breath and began unfastening her cloak, handing it to Delisa to wash and hang.

"He loves you, you know," Delisa said as Kalina began unbuttoning her dress. She froze, mid button.

"What? No. He, we, there might have been something once but it's gone. I'm promised to Prince Simen now." She continued unbuttoning and shucked off her travel-stained gown and walked naked towards the bathing room. "I need a bath."

Soon she was soaking in a warm tub, steam curling around her in lazy circles as she lingered. She had already scrubbed herself from head to toe, more dirt than she'd like to admit coming away with the fragrant soaps that an Askorian maidservant provided.

"What's your name?" Kalina asked the woman when she came in to bring fresh towels. She was only a few years older than Kalina and very pretty. She had dark hair and the prettiest green eyes Kalina had ever seen.

"Seri, your Majesty." She curtsied low and Kalina smiled.

"Thank you for the towels, Seri."

The maid blushed as Kalina stood from the bath and reached for one, wrapping it around herself. Delisa bustled in just then carrying a thick robe which she wrapped swiftly around Kalina, steering her back into the bedroom.

"Since Prince Simen is coming to escort you about the castle we need to get you presentable."

Kalina smiled and sat before a golden filigree mirror, letting Delisa braid her hair down her back, letting pieces slip-free in soft waves. Then she dressed Kalina in a comfortable dress of green silk. Underneath Kalina wore warm fleece-lined pants to keep away the cold and a soft purple cloak went over top. Her blue and silver crown finished the ensemble. She looked ethereal in the mirror as she inspected herself.

"Prince Simen won't know what hit him," Delisa said satisfactorily. Kari snorted from the other side of the room.

"What is it, Kari?" Kalina asked, turning, one eyebrow raised at her cousin.

"Nothing. You just look like a trussed up peacock."

There was a beat of silence before all three of them burst out laughing. Kalina bent over, her stomach aching at the image in her mind. Then she removed the purple cloak and reached for a spare wolf-pelt cloak.

"You aren't wrong," she said, throwing it around her shoulders. "I'll stick with something a bit more traditional."

A second knock made them all look to the door in anticipation. Delisa smoothed her dress and went to answer it. When she stepped aside, Prince Simen stood in the doorway, a deep blue cloak over his own shoulders.

"Shall we, your Majesty?" He held out his hand which Kalina gratefully took. Kari stood and knocked on the dressing room door. Runa opened it and joined Kari as they followed the pair out of the room.

Prince Simen led Kalina away as she looked back to give Delisa one final, fleeting look. Delisa gave her a small wave and an encouraging smile.

Chapter 21

KARI AND RUNA TRAILED BEHIND Kalina and Prince Simen as they strode through the imposing granite halls of Winterreach Castle. Kalina was comforted for once by their presence instead of annoyed at being followed everywhere. They were her shadows that kept her safe. She relaxed a bit as Prince Simen tucked her arm under his elbow and led her towards the unknown.

"How much do you know about Winterreach, your Majesty?" he asked, looking at her sideways, his amber eyes open and honest.

"Please, call me Kalina."

He smiled at her.

"That's a very beautiful name. Kalina. I like the way it rolls off your tongue. It suits you."

Kalina bit her lip to stifle the giggle that almost bubbled up and out of her chest. She'd never had anyone say her name was beautiful and somehow it seemed absurd. What was wrong with her? She swallowed hard and smiled up at him in response.

"Thank you, your Highness."

"Simen. Please. If we are going to be informal, then I must insist."

She nodded graciously. He was leading her down a dark hallway now, but ahead was an open space, light pouring down.

"The castle was built five hundred years ago when the Askorians broke from the rest of the empire and reclaimed their homeland. It was built as a bastion against any who came to attack us, and in the last five hundred years, it has never been breached." Simen gave her a history lesson as they entered a large room filled with lights. Chandeliers filled with candles hung from the ceiling, and people milled about. Most were dressed in fancy clothing, expensive fabrics, and jewels, which glinted at her from every corner. A din filled the room as everyone talked and laughed. One person cheered, making Kalina's head whip around curiously. There were tables placed around the room at regular intervals, a small stage lit up one corner, and a long bar occupied another. Kalina frowned, trying to figure out what everyone was doing. Heads turned in their direction as they passed, murmurs following them as they wove through the crowd. But the prince beside her seemed unconcerned.

She looked up at the high vaulted ceiling and saw that there was a balcony overhead, draped in rich curtains and occupied by plush couches that could be curtained off for privacy.

"What is this place?" she asked, looking down at one of the strange tables as they passed. It was curved, with one chair sitting inside the half-moon and seven chairs sitting along the outside of the curve. Six of the seven chairs were occupied by richly dressed nobles, laughing and drinking as they played a game. A man in one chair wore a servant's uniform and Kalina caught the glimpse of playing cards and chips.

"It is our gaming hall. Surely your castle at Ravenhelm has one?"

Kalina shook her head in denial. She'd never seen anything like this place.

"And what do you do in a gaming hall?"

"Why, you play games! Here we play a myriad of card games and games of chance like Devils' Crossing, and Wise Man's Preach. I even enjoy playing Brazen on occasion." He gestured around them at different tables, but she couldn't discern a difference between any of the games being played. And she had never even heard of any of those games. She'd only ever played the one card game, Liar, with her friends.

One nobleman sitting at a nearby table raised his glass to them.

"Good evening, your Highness! Have you come to join us for a game?"

"No, Lord Baymer, not tonight," the prince responded with a smile. They continued walking, weaving between crowded tables.

"Why come to a place like this to play? Why not play in the privacy of one's own rooms with friends?"

"To win money of course!" said Simen.

"What? People actually waste money on this type of thing?" She turned to look at her escort, her eyebrows rising as she saw the grin on his face. "What a waste." She turned back to the room as Simen's face fell beside her. "What are the couches for? The stage?"

"You can also come and watch a comedy play, or dancing, or spend time drinking with friends upstairs in the lounge." He cleared his throat, visibly chastised by Kalina's clear dislike of the room's use. "Some call it the pleasure hall. I thought you'd like it. Most women do."

Kalina decided to let him down easy. She smiled sweetly at him and took his arm again.

"I'm not like most girls, Simen. Show me the library, the stables, the practice yards. Show me where you are keeping my dragon and we'll be fast friends." She led him from the room and back into the hallway, leaving the noise and bustle behind. Once they were out of the crowded space, she felt like she could finally breathe again. Eventually, he smiled at her.

"Then let's go see the library." And he turned their footsteps down a new hallway.

A few gloomy passages and stairways later and they found themselves outside two massive wooden doors ornately carved. They were similar in style to her own Ravenhelm library doors, but the carvings depicted war scenes rather than the delicate carvings of wyverns and dragons that adorned her own. Simen pushed them open and they slid forward on silent hinges. The smell of parchment, ink, leather, and dust hit Kalina and suddenly she felt like she was greeting an old friend, her heart settling inside her. She let go of Simen's arm and walked forward into the silence and welcome darkness of the library.

Like her own beloved one, this library was dimly lit so as to avoid the possibility of fire, and to keep the books from fading or discoloration. Books sat on long shelves that led off into the darkness before her. Since arriving on Askorian soil, she'd felt unsteady, out of place. Now she felt a bit more confident in herself.

"How big is it?"

"It extends for the rest of this entire floor."

Kalina frowned. Her own library extended three floors and had to be at least twice the size of this room on each floor.

"Oh, ours is much bigger," she said, clearly disappointed. Prince Simen quickly stepped forward and took her arm.

"Then let's go visit the practice yards. They are near the dragon eyrie that we built."

That perked up Kalina's interest, but she narrowed her eyes at the prince.

"Eyrie? I thought your father said they would clear out a stable."

She watched carefully as Simen's back stiffened momentarily

before he relaxed and recovered.

"My father was probably just having a laugh, a private joke. As soon as he knew you were coming to visit, he had an eyrie built for the dragons so that they would be comfortable." He smiled at her but Kalina noticed that it didn't quite meet his eyes. Her suspicion grew.

"Strange. Your father doesn't seem like the joking type."

Simen remained quiet as he led her down another set of stone stairs that came out into a small courtyard. He led her through a wooden gate and into a large practice ground made of packed dirt. Large wooden stands surrounded it on either side, filled with currently empty seats. At the far end of the practice field, she could see the entrance to the barracks and stables, where a small group of soldiers in green and maroon were milling about.

"There are your men. Shall we go over and see they are settled?" Simen asked graciously. She nodded and let him lead the way. She cast a meaningful look over her shoulder at Kari who strode a few paces behind and had heard everything they said. She knew her cousin would have things to say about it later.

"Sir Talon!" Kalina called out and let go of Prince Simen's arm to stride ahead of him. Talon was standing by the barracks door, speaking with Captain Higgs and a few of his men. As she approached, the men went inside after giving her a small bow and Kalina was left with Captain Higgs, Talon, and the prince.

"How are the barracks? Are they to your liking?" she inquired of her friend. Talon brushed a stray lock of brown hair from his eyes, the light freckles across his nose and cheeks standing out on his pale face. No matter how much time he spent outside training his men, he never seemed to get darker, but his freckles always seemed to stand out more. And he had started growing a beard, making him look a bit older.

"They are very nice, your Majesty," he said formally, his eyes flicking to Prince Simen. "The King was very generous in giving over an entire barracks for our use." He gave the prince a low bow.

"It was nothing! That barracks was barely used anyways, and honestly, I'm happy to see it filled with smiling faces!" Prince Simen was pouring it on thick, really trying to impress Kalina. She turned back to Talon and rolled her eyes with a small smile.

"It is our honor to be here, your Highness." Talon bowed once more. Kalina fought not to roll her eyes. All this bowing and scraping. It was one thing she missed about being only with the Valdir. They never bowed and scraped. They never tried to impress her with fancy words, nor was deception the language they learned at their mother's breast. They were straightforward, honest, trustworthy people who treated her with respect but not deference.

"I'm glad to hear you are settling in. Glad to see you here, Captain Higgs." She said. Captain Higgs was a tall man, lean and only in his late twenties if Kalina was any judge. His light auburn hair stood out among the dark-haired Askorians like a flame. He smiled warmly at her and bowed.

"Glad to be of service, your Majesty."

Kalina smiled to them both, and said her goodbyes, and then turned away, wandering over to an archery target. Prince Simen followed, turning back once or twice to look at Talon and Captain Higgs who continued their conversation, now joined by Runa and Kari.

"Your men seem very loyal to you."

"Of course they are. I am their Queen." Kalina said as she pulled a beautifully made recurve bow from a display near the target. It was already strung, which struck Kalina as strange since usually you didn't want to leave a bow strung for storage, but she shrugged and grabbed a small quiver of arrows from a nearby table.

"No, I mean, they treat you like a friend."

"How so? All I saw was them being formal." She carefully notched an arrow to the string and brought the bow up to shoulder height, using three fingers to draw back on the string until her thumb was aligned with her jaw bone.

"They were formal because of me, not you."

He didn't seem to miss anything. Perhaps this young prince wasn't an enemy after all. Perhaps he could be used to her advantage. Perhaps they would make a better match than she'd originally thought. That thought stopped her short. Was she actually considering following through with the marriage? She shook her head and looked back to the target. Kari would come up with a solution before it was over. She knew it.

"Talon knew me before I was Queen," she remarked as she notched a second arrow, drew, and then released a breath along with the arrow which found the center of the target. "And I've spent hours training with him and Captain Higgs in the practice yards of Ravenhelm."

The prince's eyebrows shot up. Clearly, he wasn't used to women being fighters, warriors.

"Do all women fight as you do, or your two women guards do?" He asked, coming to stand beside her and eyeing the target. He snagged up his own bow and nocked an arrow, drew and let fly. His arrow thudded into the target a mere hair's breadth from her own. Kalina gave him a rueful smile, which he returned.

"Not all, but many Valdir women fight, and I am encouraging more and more Ethean women to fight. My cousin, Kari," she nodded in her cousin's direction, "started a Queen's Guard made up entirely of women."

Prince Simen ran a hand through his short-cropped dark hair, his head tilted sideways as he appraised her.

"You are perhaps, more interesting than I thought."

"And you are, perhaps, not as dull as I thought."

He smiled broadly at her then.

Chapter 22

THE THRONE ROOM OF THE CASTLE was decorated like a winter wonderland: every inch covered in white. White florals wound around stairway banisters, adorned tables and chair backs, and hung from the ceiling. Long swaths of white and sheer fabric covered the granite walls, hung from the ceiling, and covered tables, making the space feel both warmer and colder at the same time. Crystalline glasses with a sparkling white wine were being served, each dish white and sparkling. Even the delicacies were dusted with white sugar.

Kalina stood with Kari by the buffet table sampling the strange fare that Askor had to offer. She was dressed in a pale blue dress that flowed over her shoulders and spilled out around her on the floor. It was made of a diaphanous material that seemed to both float like a cloud and flow like water. It felt luxurious to wear and she immediately knew she'd be commissioning more dresses like it in the future. It wrapped her body and clung to her hips before flowing to the ground, a deep-v neckline and gathered fabric at the shoulders that spilled over her back made her feel like some sort of fairy queen from legends.

Kari was in an equally flowing pale purple dress. She kept self-consciously tugging at the neckline, trying to cover herself. Kalina hid a smile behind her hand as she watched her cousin awkwardly decline a dance with a young Askorian nobleman who only had eyes for her chest. When the man had retreated with a lecherous grin on his face, Kari scowled over at Kalina who was hard-pressed to hide her laughter.

"You don't know how beautiful you look, do you cousin?" Kalina asked, setting her nearly empty plate aside. Kari crossed her arms over her chest.

"They wouldn't like me so much if I was facing them in battle," she grumbled. Kalina laughed out loud at that, and finally she saw the corner of Kari's mouth twitch in amusement.

"That they wouldn't. You are the fiercest woman I know." Kalina put an arm around her cousin's waist and gave her a small squeeze. Although physical affection was rare for Kalina, after a few drinks of that sparkling wine she was feeling very friendly indeed.

She might even give the King a hug if he didn't watch himself.

"You better be careful too, my Queen. The nobles may be too intimidated to approach you but the royals seem to have eyes only for you."

Kalina followed Kari's look across the ballroom and saw that the royals were clustered by the dais. Prince Simen was watching her, a small smile on his lips. His older brothers and sisters were mostly looking at her with slight scowls and an emotion she had trouble naming. She wasn't sure if it was hatred or hunger, but either way, she felt like a piece of meat on display.

She turned and found Leif a few feet away, a half-filled plate of food in his hands. He was watching her with such intensity that the breath caught in her throat. She looked into his grey eyes and wished that the room would melt away, that they could be alone together once again. But he blinked suddenly and looked away, turning back to the food table. Kalina watched a blush spread up his neck, his ears turning red as he studiously ignored her.

She swallowed hard before turning back to the dance floor. Guests twirled around in a beautiful kaleidoscope of colors. She let her eyes go unfocused for a moment, the colors swirling and smudging together before her. She jumped slightly when a cool hand landed on her shoulder. She looked up into the kind face of Lord Illeron. He gave her a bow and held his hand out.

"May I have this dance, your Majesty?"

Kalina took his hand with a small curtsey, still slightly flustered, and followed him onto the dance floor, looking back apologetically at Kari who scowled alone by the edge of the crowd. As Lord Illeron placed his hand gently on her waist and began pulling her into unfamiliar dance steps, she watched Leif and Jormungand join Kari. She sighed. At least her cousin wasn't standing alone anymore.

The next person to snag her hand was Prince Simen. His easy manner and smile put her instantly at ease. She was surprised that after only a day she had grown to like this young man so much, but found she did. She may not want to marry him, but perhaps he could at least be an ally, a friend. As they spun to the music, they talked of little things. After their archery practice the day before she had taken him to the eyrie to meet Maska. He had been full of genuine awe and joy at meeting a dragon, and began asking Maska many questions. Kalina had sat down on a nearby hay bale and laughed until Prince Simen had stopped his questioning sheepishly. Tonight, he was still full of questions but this time about her.

"How did you find the Valdir? I understand you were raised in an abbey as an orphan and you didn't know who your parents were?"

Kalina sighed before giving him the bare bones of her story. He nodded along eagerly. He was genuinely interested in her.

"What was it like meeting your father?" he inquired.

"It was like coming home. I felt in my bones that it was right, that he was my family. I only wish I'd known him longer-" she trailed off, as memories of her father, Hakon, swam before her eyes. "I learned so much about the Valdir from him."

"What are the Valdir like?"

"Tribal, warriors, fiercely loyal," Kalina said, her eyes drifting back to Kari, Leif, and Jormungand who still stood by the buffet, alone in a sea of strangers. "They are unlike any other people I've ever met. I'm proud to be one of them, to be their Queen."

Prince Simen smiled as he too watched her friends across the room.

"I'm looking forward to getting to know them. You know, there is a story about dragon riders here in Askor as well."

She perked up at his words and turned to look up into his amber eyes.

"What is the story?"

"It is said that in the wilds of northern Askor, near the Snowcap Glacier, north of Icewell and the Riverlands, in the forest, live a race of dragon riders, not unlike your own Valdir. But no one has seen them in centuries. Stories still occasionally float around, about people going missing in the wilderness and claims that they were taken by giant white dragons, or people coming out of the woods raving mad, talking about white-clad people who hunted them. It's all rather silly, but interesting, considering." He smiled down at her, and Kalina's mind began churning.

"I wonder if we are distantly related," she murmured, half to herself. She could imagine a giant white dragon with a white-clad, silver-haired rider atop its back. There were no legends among the Valdir about other dragon riders, but perhaps those stories were lost to time.

"I wouldn't be surprised. But if they ever did exist, they are long gone."

Kalina nodded absently in agreement as the song came to a close and they slowly stopped dancing. Prince Simen stepped back from her and she had to focus back on the moment. She felt a little off-balance as he bowed to her, begging her to save him a dance later in the night. She agreed with a smile and began to wander back to her friends when another hand snagged hers. It was Prince Endre, the eldest prince, and heir to the throne. He bowed over her hand regally and she was forced to give him a small curtsey in response.

"May I have the honor of this dance, your Majesty?"

She nodded her assent and then settled into a stiff rhythm as the music began anew. After a few turns around the dance floor, Kalina's mind was beginning to wander when the Prince spoke.

"I knew your father, you know."

The statement caught Kalina so completely off guard that she tripped over her own feet and stumbled. After she had righted herself with the prince's help, she looked up into the Crown Prince's dark eyes. He and her father would have been the same age, had her father still lived.

"Oh? You knew him?" She tried to feign nonchalance but knew she was failing to keep her emotions from her face and voice.

"Yes, I faced him in battle many times over the years towards the end of the war, including that final battle before he fled with his people."

Kalina's heart clenched in her chest.

"I admired him. He was a fierce fighter. I can tell that you possess that same fire."

"Thank you, your Highness." Kalina barely forced the words out. Feelings swam through her and she wasn't sure what she was supposed to feel. As the song wound down, Prince Endre bent to kiss her hand. When he straightened he said something that turned her veins to ice.

"I hear your baby brother, my nephew, is missing. I do hope he is found soon."

He smiled at her and walked away. She had to resist the urge to run after him and stick one of the knives she had hidden in her bodice into his back. She hadn't forgotten her little brother. In fact, the moment her ships had entered the harbor she'd ordered Lord Illeron to seek out his informants and see if any new information could be gleaned. So far he had reported nothing. Her brother wasn't in the castle or the city of Winterreach. But then where was he? Kalina knew she needed to ask the King himself.

She'd just snagged a new glass of bubbly wine when she felt someone at her back. She turned, her dress swirling around her. The Queen, her fiery red hair a flame among dull candles, stood behind her, her face plastered in a kind smile.

"Your Majesty, I wonder, would you do my husband the honor of a dance? He is old and needs someone to escort him down to the dance floor. Would you be so kind?" She gestured to the dais a few dozen feet away. The King atop his throne was eyeing her as she followed the queen up the steps. She offered her arm to him and he took it.

"I'd be honored to dance with you, your Majesty," Kalina said, giving him a small curtsey before helping him down the stairs. He was old, but by the force of his grip on her arm, she knew he was anything but helpless.

"The pleasure is all mine, your Majesty," he said with a grin. He was missing quite a few teeth and the grin made him seem more than a little mad. He put an arm around her waist, pulling her in tight against him and she had to fight every nerve in her body to keep from pulling away and sticking a knife in his side. Diplomacy had not been a part of her training with the Valdir and it was something she was fast learning since coming to Ravenhelm. She couldn't solve all her problems with violence, and sometimes she had to endure unwanted touches, something she'd never dealt with before.

He spun her around the dance floor, his hand slipping ever lower on her back until he was practically cupping her bottom. She kept moving his hand higher as politely as she could. She supposed she wasn't much younger than his current queen, so clearly he had eyes for younger women, but the way he was acting felt possessive and it made her skin crawl.

"Your Majesty," she said as the song began to wind down. "Have you heard anything more about my brother, Osian?"

The King's dark eyes snapped to hers. His body may have been frail, but his mind was sharp, his eyes clear and black, the iris' nearly indistinguishable from the pupils. He studied her for a moment before responding.

"No. I haven't heard a thing because you are keeping him hidden in that castle of yours. He is as much our prince as he is your brother. I would suggest you consider giving him to us to raise. But we will speak on that tomorrow. For now, enjoy the ball."

He stepped away from her, leaving her more frustrated than ever, her skin feeling dirty where he'd touched her. She wiped her hand on her dress, looking around for Kari. A soft hand on her lower back made her spin but she stopped short when she saw it was Leif. He was watching the retreating back of the King with a mixture of hatred and suspicion. He took her hand and spun her around and into his arms as the music changed.

"I don't trust him," he whispered into her ear.

Kalina's heart leapt. Was Leif back to being her friend? Was he willing to be her confidant again, not just her general? Or was he just strategizing? This hot and cold routine of his was wearing on her. But she tried to calm her racing heart as they danced, doing her best to ignore his nearness and the leather and wind scent of him.

"I don't either. I never have."

He looked down at her, and, for a moment, she saw something else in his eyes. The same thing she'd seen a hundred times before when he'd been someone who'd cared for her. But then his eyes went distant and he looked away, back up into the swirling crowd around them.

"You look beautiful tonight, your Majesty." His voice held no emotion as he spoke. There he went with the formality again. She rolled her eyes in response but didn't deny it.

"Do you really think so?" Her voice held the edge of a blade. She was so tired of tiptoeing around each other. She wanted to get the truth from him. "Did you ever really care for me, Leif?" She asked in a harsh whisper. His grey eyes flicked to hers for an instant, his back stiffening.

"That's not-" he hesitated, "I don't-". He let out a long sigh. "I don't know what that has to do with anything. You are marrying a foreign Prince. What more do I need to know?"

She wanted to scream at him that she wanted to marry him, that she wanted only him. She wanted to tell him she was in love with him. That she had been for months. But she couldn't. Not surrounded by strangers and nobles from Askor. Not with her brother's life and the fate of her kingdom lying in the balance. She let out a long sigh as she dropped her hands and stepped away. The music fading around them.

"Just forget I asked. Thank you for the dance, Leif." Then she turned and walked away, leaving the hall, Kari trailing behind.

Chapter 23

THE COUNCIL CHAMBERS WERE CHILLY and Kalina pulled her cloak higher, snuggling into the wolf fur for warmth. She looked around at the gathered people, a mixture of Etheans, Valdir, and Askorians. King Blackbourne sat in an imposing oak chair, his slightly hunched form brooding over the gathered nobles. Lord Illeron and Lord Averil sat beside her, and Kari stood behind her, her arms crossed over her chest as if she was trying to intimidate anyone that looked at her. Leif sat on the other side of Lord Illeron, studiously ignoring Kalina's glances.

Prince Julian sat rather stiffly to the left of his father, while Prince Endre sat on his father's right-hand side. Prince Endre seemed more at ease, and as Kalina watched the two brothers she realized that Prince Julian hated his elder brother. The younger prince kept throwing scowls at his brother. She didn't doubt that they had been in competition all their lives, and Julian was always second to the crown prince. She wondered what it had been like, growing up with King Blackbourne for a father. No wonder they were all so cold and distant. Prince Simen was a strange outlier among them.

A few other Askorian nobles, many of whom Kalina had been introduced to but had promptly forgotten their names, rounded off the table. It was hard enough keeping her own nobles' names straight, let alone those of another country. Kalina had met more people in the last year than she had in her entire life growing up at the Abbey. She sighed as the last noble finished talking about meager crop yields and bickering farmers until it seemed it was finally her turn. She straightened as the King spoke.

"Thank you, Lord Lithern. I will take your suggestions under advisement." He looked up and met Kalina's eyes. "Now, to the business of Ethea."

"Thank you, your Majesty-" Kalina began but the King cut her off by continuing speaking. She looked sideways at Leif and caught his eye for a moment. She rolled hers and she saw the corner of his mouth twitch.

"While Ethea has a new ruler, and my son was deposed and then killed, it seems they continue to cause trouble for Askor. My grandson, Osian, was being held captive in the Great Grey Mountains by a band of Valdir. And now I've been told that he is missing, perhaps dead." His dark eyes seemed to pin Kalina to the spot. He wasn't telling the truth, at least not all of it. "I assumed that Queen Kalina had been hiding him from me but she assures me, and her council assures me, she is not. She was just trying to keep him safe. But now they have lost him. I offer a reward. Three hundred thousand gold pieces and title to anyone who can find him and bring him home to Askor. I made this same offer this morning to my troops and to the ship captains. They will search high and low for my grandson." Murmuring erupted around the council table at the declaration.

Kalina's blood ran cold. Of course, he would want Osian only for himself. Of course, he would offer an obscene amount of money to recover him. Kalina didn't even think they had that much gold in her own treasury, let alone all of Ethea. How would she manage to get her brother back now? She forced herself to smile at the King.

"Thank you, your Majesty, for being so diligent in searching for my brother." She gave him a sweet smile. No need to let him know how much she wanted to leap across the distance between them and rip his heart out through his chest still beating. For the first time since arriving she missed wearing her twin axes. When she was in her dresses she didn't carry the axes but she still carried multiple daggers on her person at all times, leaving the axes safely tucked under her bed.

"Now, we must discuss the terms of our new alliance with Ethea. When my son was King alongside her mother, he was granted equal power to rule. It was agreed upon with her father when the engagement was brokered. Now, had I known my son was receiving damaged goods, I would have pushed for him to have full control of Ethea, but alas, that part was kept from me." The King gave Kalina a small smirk. All his kindness and accommodation from the last few days was a farce. Just a way to make her and her people feel comfortable. She tried to keep her temper in check, a blush traveling up her scarred and tattooed cheeks.

"My mother had been previously engaged to my father. It was the war with Askor that necessitated a change, and it was not one my mother favored. As a result, I was hidden away and my mother married Terric."

"Yes, she was engaged. To a heathen, a barbarian prince from the Wastes. A prince who abandoned her once he knew the war was over." His sharp eyes bore into her.

"A prince who tried to save his people from destruction." Kalina glared back, her own stare just as harsh. They were sparring without swords, their only weapons their tongues and their goal to see how much they could hurt one another. A soft hand on Kalina's arm had her looking to Lord Illeron beside her. He shook his head slightly. She was letting her emotions dictate the meeting. She took a deep breath and when she let it out she tried to let the anger go with it. "But we're not here for a history lesson. We are here to discuss the future."

"Too right you are, your Majesty," Prince Endre spoke up, giving his father a steadying look. "What my father is trying to say is that my brother Terric had equal say in the running of the country when he was married to your mother. And my brother Simen deserves the same."

"The same rights as our Queen?" Leif sat forward in his chair and Kalina watched his jaw clench and unclench in frustration. The comments about the Valdir had clearly affected him. He had been a small child when he and his family had been forced to flee their homes and head into the Wastes. He remembered the fear and uncertainty. "Prince Simen is not equal to our Queen. She is the Queen of both the Valdir and Ethea. She is a dragon rider. He is just the youngest prince, one of many." Kalina could have kissed him for that. Despite what was or wasn't between them, he still fought for her. He still had pride in her being his queen. She looked back to study the faces around the room. Those were fighting words, words that could spark another war.

"I think what my general is trying to say is that this situation is different. I am not my mother. I was heir to two crowns the moment I was born, and I hold more responsibility on my shoulders."

"All the more reason to share the load with my son." The King said, steepling his fingers before him. He gazed at her over them, as if just by looking at her she would cow, bend and scrape. But she never would. Not to him.

"All the more reason for me to maintain my current position and level of power. I am a new queen. If I suddenly gave up half my power to a foreign prince, even if we were married," she almost couldn't choke out the word, "that might weaken my position. It might destroy what trust I've gained from my people." The King's mouth twitched in a smile. Kalina's heart sank. She'd just proven his point. That she was a young, inexperienced queen who needed help. And he thought he would be the one to give it. "No," she said forcefully. "I won't share power. I'm sorry." She put her foot down. She wasn't going to be bullied by him.

"Your Majesty," Lord Averil finally spoke up. Kalina ground her teeth together at the sound of his voice. Sometimes, she wished she'd just pitched him overboard during that storm. "Perhaps his Majesty has a point. The responsibility of ruling two peoples that are so different is a huge burden. Learning to share power with your husband might ease that load." His tone was placating with a dash of condescension. Kalina's anger rose once again.

"I said no, Lord Averil. I will not give up power to an Askorian prince. Either we find a way to rule together with him as my consort, and a king in title only, or we find another way to make peace."

"I think this conversation may have to be continued tomorrow." Prince Endre said, eyeing his father's and Kalina's faces. "Thank you, Queen Kalina, for your presence in our council chambers today." He bowed his head slightly to her. She couldn't decide whether she was grateful or angrier. Now the Askorians would have more time to plot and find a way to make her give up her entire kingdom into their power. At least she had a better understanding now of what they wanted.

"I agree. Until tomorrow." She stood and gave a small curtsey to King Blackbourne and a nod to Prince Endre before exiting the cold chamber. She wanted to fly with Maska. That would help to clear her head, and then she wanted a warm bath to take away the chill that was settling deep into her bones.

"Your Majesty," Lord Illeron said as she walked down the hall, making her pause. "We need to find a way to make peace with him."

"I know. But I can't figure out what to give him that will appease him."

"Perhaps we give him part of the Great Grey Mountains. That is what the last war was about- mining rights. Maybe if we give him part of it that will satisfy him enough to make a deal."

Kalina thought a moment. She made eye contact with Leif who

stood just a few paces behind Lord Illeron, listening. Kari stood beside Kalina, her face red with pent up rage. If Kalina gave up the Great Grey Mountains, it would not only take away part of the Valdir's territory, their homeland but also it would take away part of the natural barrier between their two countries. It would give them a foothold on her side, making her vulnerable. But it might be their only shot at securing her freedom to rule.

"I'll think about it." She gave the older man a smile. "Thank you, Lord Illeron." As she turned to go, she caught a glimpse of Lord Averil exiting the council chambers talking rather intimately with King Blackbourne. She frowned. Since when had the lord and the King become so familiar? She decided to think about that later, after her flight and a bath.

Chapter 24

THAT EVENING AFTER HER LONG, hot bath, a note arrived. Delisa closed the door to the hallway and brought over a sealed purple envelope.

"I wonder who it's from?" she mused as she handed it off to Kalina and then resumed brushing out Kalina's silver locks. Despite having gotten used to wearing battle braids every day, Kalina was relishing the feeling of having her hair unbound and hanging down her back in long waves to the top of her bottom. She wished she could wear it down when flying with Maska but knew it would only get so tangled from the wind she'd have to shave it off.

"I don't know."

She opened the letter. The dark blob of wax had a fox symbol in it, but it wasn't one she was familiar with. Inside was an elegantly written letter.

Dear Kalina,

I do hope you'll forgive my informality. I really hope we can be friends.

Would you join me for tea at half-past the midday bell tomorrow? I would consider it an honor.

Yours,
Malin

"Who is Malin?" Delisa said, reading the short letter over Kalina's shoulder. Kalina realized she knew who it was.

"The Queen of Askor. She is now Malin Blackbourne but was originally Lady Malin Crevan." The fox symbol made sense now.

"Well, the letter seems nice enough. You should go, and try to be friends. Maybe it will make this whole debacle go more smoothly."

A small squeak sounded from the hearth where the maid Seri was setting the evening's fire. Kalina turned towards her.

"Is there something wrong, Seri?"

The girl's eyes were wide in fear, but she shook her head violently no.

"No, your Majesty," she barely whispered.

Kalina eyed the frightened girl, her mind spinning.

"Was it something we said about the Queen?"

Seri's eyes widened at her words.

"Please, what can you tell us? I don't want to go in blind." She reached out for the girl's hand and Seri joined them, sitting on the couch. "I promise, whatever you say won't leave this room."

Seri looked between her and Delisa, the door and the changing room door where Kari and the other guards slept. Kalina could practically smell the fear on her. Finally, the maid swallowed hard and looked at Kalina.

"You aren't like any royal I've ever met, so I will tell you." Her voice was soft but steady. "The queen is not your friend, your Majesty. She puts on a kind face but then will do everything she can to ruin you. She-" the girl trailed off before clenching her jaw and continuing. "There is a rumor that she killed the last queen, Prince Simen, and Prince Ivan's mother, in order to take her place as the next queen. She is ambitious and cruel."

Kalina sat back at the girl's words. So the Queen was a murderer who would do anything to be in control. It didn't surprise Kalina but she had hoped that the first impression of the young queen had been wrong.

"Thank you very much for telling me, Seri." Kalina said gently, patting the girl's hand. "Are you happy here? Do they treat you alright?"

Seri shook her head slowly.

"You don't know, your Majesty?"

Kalina frowned. "Know what?"

"All of the servants here are indentured. We are here working off a debt, not because we want to be here. But you never pay off the debts." Her voice began to hold an edge of anger as she spoke. And then it seemed as if a dam broke and words came spilling out. "My father was a merchant, high up in the merchant's council and he was working hard towards gaining a lordship. But one day, a few years after the war, a huge storm sank most of his ships, losing him his entire fortune. He begged the King to help him rebuild, to loan him the money so he could rebuild his fleet and begin trading again, paying the King off in a few months. The King agreed but said if my father failed to repay him, then he would take me as an indentured servant. I was to work until my father's debt was paid."

The bitterness was clear in her voice. "My father never rebuilt the ships. He began drinking, gambling, hoping he would win big and he wouldn't have to pay back the debt. His few remaining ships began to lose shipments, and soon he was broke, destitute, and sick. We lost our nice house down on Potter's Row and were forced to live in a hovel by the docks." She sniffed, wiping a tear from her eye. Kalina's chest ached in empathy for the girl. "He never repaid the debt. One night they came for me. I was dragged from my bed with my mother screaming and my father wailing. They told me I would work until the debt was paid, but the debt will never be paid. My mother left my father and is now living in Ablen with her sister. And my father is dying, alone in that hovel." Tears spilled in earnest down her cheeks and she wiped at them fiercely.

Kalina looked to Delisa who had a horror-struck look on her face and gestured for her to hand the maid a handkerchief. Delisa did, dabbing at her own tears. Kalina gently wiped the tears from Seri's face.

"Listen, Seri. Your story is safe with us. We won't tell anyone you told us. When I leave, I promise I will find a way to pay your debt and get you back to your father. But if I can, I'll try to change the King's mind on indentured servitude. No one should be forced to work, especially forced to for someone else's debt. It's too much like imprisonment." Kalina knew what that was like. Trapped in a cage, all your hope and life draining out. She thought suddenly of Nash, trapped in the dungeon back at her own castle. He had tried to kill her, but only because they had killed his dragon. She vowed to do right by him and get him out. Perhaps there was a home where he could stay, or perhaps he could go be with their people in the mountains. At least he'd be free then.

"Thank you, your Majesty." Seri gave her a deep curtsey before kissing Kalina's hand. Kalina's face flushed at the attention and she quickly pulled the girl to her feet.

"No need for that nonsense. Just run along. I don't want you getting into trouble on my account."

As the midday bell rang the next day, Kalina found herself nervously straightening her dress as she stood outside Queen Malin's chambers, waiting to be announced. She had never been alone with another Queen before and that old familiar pit in her stomach was beginning to fill with panic. She fought hard to tamp it down as the door before her opened and a maidservant ushered her inside.

The queen's rooms were even more opulent than her own. Velvet curtains swaged from huge windows that looked out over the harbor. A long balcony sat beyond two double glass doors, boxes filled with now-dormant flowers waiting for spring to finally descend on its railing. Every inch of her sitting-room was covered in lush carpets, every wall covered in beautiful hangings. Her couches were plump and inviting and Kalina's eyes felt like they were going to bulge out of her head as she looked at everything. There were shelves filled with beautiful trinkets, the surfaces inlaid with gold. Kalina's own rooms in her own palace had a sort of comforting nobility to them, but they weren't as ostentatious as this room.

Queen Malina sat on a pretty red settee, her red hair flowing down around her shoulders and spilling over her blue dress in russet waves. She was one of the most beautiful people Kalina had ever met, and that beauty intimidated her slightly. But she wouldn't let it show as she gave the queen a small curtsey. She had to remind herself that she was every bit the equal of this woman, and in fact, she was above her as the sole ruler of Ethea and the Valdir.

Queen Malin flashed a coy smile at Kalina before gesturing to a nearby couch.

"Please, Kalina, sit."

Although Kalina normally preferred for people to call her by her name instead of being formal, she wasn't sure she liked this woman's immediate familiarity. But she decided to play along, at least until she discovered if this woman was an ally or a foe.

"Thank you, Malin. Your rooms are lovely."

"Thank you. I designed them myself. I do love being surrounded by pretty things."

Kalina accepted a cup of tea from a nearby maid and noticed that the maids were not pretty however, they were in fact exceptionally plain. Either the queen was lying, or she only liked pretty things she could control. Malin saw Kalina looking and one corner of her perfect mouth quirked up.

"And you are very pretty, aren't you? Under those tattoos and that scar. A little cosmetics and you'd be stunning." Malin's voice held an edge and Kalina knew they were on treacherous ground. She smiled demurely at the other queen.

"Not nearly as beautiful as you are, Malin. I'm sure the King is completely in love with you."

Malin smiled at that and tossed her hair over her shoulders. A little flattery always went a long way.

"He is. He gives me whatever I want."

Kalina smiled politely at that. Perhaps this woman was the key to ending indentured servitude or even to help her negotiate her marriage to Prince Simen.

"How are you enjoying Askor? Have you and my son-in-law made friends? Are you falling in love yet?"

"Prince Simen has been very gracious and kind to me and I'm looking forward to our many years of friendship." Kalina gave Malin an equally sweet smile. "Askor is very lovely but very cold. I never expected it to still be this cold so close to summer. Ethea has its harsh weather, but nothing compared to this." She gave a little shiver, hoping that it appeased the queen, making her think Kalina was weak, in need of care.

"It is very bleak sometimes. Where I'm from, there are green hills as far as the eye can see. But I traded that in for this dismal view in exchange for, well, power." Her green eyes glittered.

"Where are you from?"

"I'm from Ablen, but my father moved me here when I was just a child. He was the ambassador for Ablen in the Askorian court. I was raised here, among the Askorians."

"That must have been a hard change," Kalina ventured, hoping to pull the conversation back around to the subject of power.

"Ablen is weak, a small island country full of dreamers. Askorians are strong, powerful, and fearless. I aspired to become like them."

"Speaking of power, do you share equal power with the King?" It was a gamble, but one she was willing to risk.

"Not exactly," Malin said slowly, her eyes narrowing. "I am in charge of the castle and it's everyday activities. It is a very large and important task."

Kalina had to bite her lip to hold back a snort. Malin might be cunning, but somehow she had failed to see that the King had relegated her to being no better than a chamberlain or a castle steward. But Malin seemed to think it was equally as important as running the country so Kalina nodded sagely.

"A difficult task. I cannot do it myself, so I have to hire others to do it for me."

"Oh, so do I. But it's the illusion of power that counts."

"You seem to understand how important that is, power. I am being asked to give up half my power to Prince Simen when we wed. But I don't want to give it up. It's too important. Do you think I should keep it?"

"Keep your power as queen? Of course not! Your husband should be running the country, not you. There are more important things you could be focusing on."

Kalina felt a little confused. Malin was either crazy, or stupid and Kalina couldn't quite figure out which one.

"Like what? What could be more important than my power?"

"Well, for starters, parties. Parties keep the nobility satisfied. And frankly, with Prince Simen running things, you will have time to focus on other things." The disdain in her voice was clear as her eyes traveled up and down Kalina. Suddenly, Kalina felt as if she hadn't showered in months. "He brings a certain sophistication to your court that is decidedly lacking. All those animal furs and leather. So barbaric!"

Anger boiled under the surface as Kalina clenched her fists. Had Malin brought her here just to insult her? Clearly, she wasn't going to find support from this venue, so Kalina made herself relax her fists and give the Queen a pleasant smile.

"Of course. You would know more about that than me." She stood and gave the Askorian queen a slight bow of her head, her anger barely in check. "I'm sorry to leave you so suddenly, Queen Malin, but I find that my stomach is quite upset. It's all the rich food and the fish, you see. My barbaric stomach isn't quite used to it yet."

Malin stood to watch her go, a sweet and knowing smile on her face.

"It will get used to it in time. Do be careful on your way out, wouldn't want anything to happen to you on your way back to your rooms."

As soon as the door closed behind Kalina her shoulders slumped. She had walked out stiff-backed, fingernails digging into her palms. All she knew was violence and fighting, not matching wits and battling with tongues, and yet the longer she lingered here in this court, the more she found herself doing it. Was this really where wars were fought when you were king or queen? In the council chamber rather than the battlefield? She didn't like it one bit. She preferred the simplicity of battle, where you knew exactly who your enemy was. But she was above this, above this petty, childish, shallow queen. She was the Queen of the Valdir and Ethea. If anyone could survive in a hostile foreign court, she could.

Chapter 25

AN ARROW THWACKED INTO THE center of the target, sending pieces of hay flying. Kalina stood at the other end of the archery field, a longbow clutched tightly in her fist. She had come here to clear her head before dinner, where she'd have to face the King again, along with all his sons, as her recent meeting with Malin had made her too angry to think straight.

With every arrow she shot, she put some of her anger, frustration, fear, and loneliness into the shot, letting it go as the arrow hit home in the target a few dozen paces away. Finally, her quiver was empty and she trudged to the target to pull the arrows from where they were stuck into the hay. As she returned to her shooting line she noticed a figure standing beneath the eaves of the barracks, watching her. Her heart gave a jolt, thinking it might be Leif. She desperately wanted to see him. But when the figure detached itself from the shadows she realized it was Prince Simen. It felt like a stone had plunked into a pond, sending rippling waves out. Sadness eddied from her but she straightened her spine and plastered a smile on her face as the prince approached.

"Prince Simen, to what do I owe the pleasure of your company?"

The prince smiled back at her and brushed his dark hair from his eyes, turning to squint down at the target.

"Well, I thought I'd come practice with you. If we are to be married, perhaps we should spend more time together, get to know one another."

Kalina smiled at him, genuinely this time. Despite his father, and despite their differences, Simen wasn't all that bad. She put her bow away before turning back to him, her twin axes clutched in her hands.

"I think it's a wonderful idea."

They began slowly, sparring together on the dusty parade ground before the barracks. Kalina saw Captain Higgs and Talon watching them from the barracks door, but she ignored them. She had once entertained the idea of a romance with Talon, but even though it had only been a year ago, it seemed like a lifetime. They had become two very different people since then, and while she still thought of him fondly, those feelings were gone. She hoped they were gone for him as well. She didn't like the thought of him watching her spar with her future husband with jealousy in his heart.

Soon they began picking up speed, the Prince's short sword clanging against the metal of her carved axes ringing out across the arena. She lost herself in the exercise, in the dance that was sparring and fighting. She loved the feeling of her muscles working, blood surging through her veins, her body performing at its highest level. Growing up in the abbey she'd never thought this would be her life. She never thought she'd love fighting, flying on dragons, being a queen. She had worked in a kitchen, and her greatest love beside exploring the nearby woods, had been reading books in a dusty old library. Admittedly it was still one of her favorite things, but her head had been filled with stories of adventures, and now she was living one.

With a final clang, the two royals broke apart, both breathing heavily, sweat pouring down their brows despite the chill air blowing through the parade grounds. Kalina wiped her forehead and turned, only to be brought up short by the small crowd that had gathered to watch. Her Queen's Guard, along with Talon and Higgs, stood watching, smiles on their faces, proud of their strong queen. Even a few Askorian nobles were gathered, whispering behind their hands. No doubt commenting on how unladylike it was for a queen to wield axes and wear leather pants, let alone fight. Kalina stood up, her head held high despite her burning cheeks as she turned back to Prince Simen.

"Would you like to come with me to visit Maska? We can talk in private there, and none of this rabble," she flicked her eyes towards the nobles tittering to each other, "would dare enter the eyrie."

Simen smiled at her, a mischievous glint in his eyes, and nodded.

"Perfect."

He followed her off the parade ground, sheathing his sword, and down a side path. She put her axes in their sheaths on her back, adjusting the straps across her chest as they walked.

"So tell me, Prince Simen. Where is your mother?"

"My mother is dead, actually. She's been gone two years now."

Kalina stopped so abruptly that he ran into her, his hands

grabbing her shoulders to keep them both from falling.

"I'm sorry-" he began but she cut him off, turning to face him.

"No, I'm sorry. I should have remembered." She mentally kicked herself for forgetting what Seri had said that morning.

"It's okay, I promise. I am doing alright. I miss her every day, but I'm coping." He gave her a wan smile and she pressed her lips together, assessing his face. He was lying but she wasn't sure it was sadness she saw in his eyes.

"What happened?"

Simen hesitated for a moment, and a look Kalina couldn't quite identify crossed his face.

"I'd gone fishing with my brothers, Edvard and Ivan. And when we'd returned to shore, there were riders waiting. They told us our mother was dead. We raced to the castle but they already had her body displayed in the throne room, covered in high mountain sage. They said she'd died suddenly, with no explanation. The doctors suspected it was her heart, it just gave out. But I knew my mother. She was strong. She spent every day working in her gardens or tending to the horses. She was no stranger to hard work."

Kalina could see the sadness and hurt on his face and she reached out, unsure why she was touching him, to lace her fingers lightly in his. He smiled at her gratefully, seeming to take strength from her support.

"What do you think really happened?" She whispered.

"I think Malin killed her. But nobody will believe me. Even Ivan believed the doctors. But Malin was one of her ladies' maids, and I'd always seen my father looking at her. That woman is a snake dressed in pretty clothes."

Anger. That was the look in Simen's eyes. He was angry. Kalina understood that. She had felt that same anger at his older brother Terric. She had wanted him dead, and she could see that Simen felt the same about Queen Malin. She squeezed his hand before dropping it.

"I believe you. And I agree."

He raised his eyes to hers, shock and relief mingled there. Kalina smiled at him and led him further down the path and into the dark eyrie where the dragons were housed. Maska had the biggest stall, and it was stacked high with sweet-smelling hay. He was curled within it, his tail laid gently over his nose, the dangerous spikes on the end pointing away from his eyes.

"Maska." Kalina breathed as she slipped inside and stepped over his foreleg to put her hands on the side of his head. He unfurled and stretched like a big cat, yawning to show off all of his teeth, each the size of a man's forearm. Kalina saw Simen withdraw a step and she laughed out loud.

"You remember Prince Simen, Maska."

Maska's green head came up as he eyed the prince.

"Yes. The Princeling. Well met." His deep voice rumbled through the eyrie.

Kalina smiled at her dragon's nickname for the Prince.

"Well met again, Maska." The prince stepped forward and leaned both elbows on the stall's gate. "When are you going to take me flying, Kalina?"

"When Maska is ready. When I'm ready." She grinned over at him wickedly. "Tell me more about your mother."

They spent the rest of the afternoon talking about his childhood growing up in the castle, his relationship with his mother and how she used to make him warm lavender milk before bed, and tell him stories of the Askorian dragon riders of old. Kalina told him about growing up as a ward of the abbey, and her discovery that she wasn't an orphan after all.

"I'm sorry my brother treated you and your mother so terribly." Simen said as they both lay in the hay, propped against Maska's warm side as the dragon snored away. "He never was my favorite. He was the second oldest, and I think he always envied Endre. He was constantly trying to compete with him, prove to Father that he was better. I only ever knew him from his brief visits but it seemed to me he resented Father for sending him to Ethea."

"I only knew his cruelty," Kalina replied. "And my mother suffered the most at his hand." She pointed to the scar that still marred her cheek. She had finally grown used to it; like her Runark tattoos, it was just a part of her face now, but it still brought back horrible memories. "He gave me this to remember him by."

Simen's face hardened for a moment before he reached out and gently traced the scar with a finger. Kalina fought the urge to pull away. But he was so gentle that she relaxed slightly.

"I'm sorry. I promise, Kalina, that I will never hurt you. Ever. And for all I care, you can keep your power. I'm content with doing whatever."

"If only your brother and father felt that way."

They both let out a sigh at the same time and then laughed. The great bell that stood atop the temple in town chimed the hour and Kalina let out a second sigh.

"We must go get ready for dinner." She was surprised at how much she didn't want to leave. But they stood to go and Kalina patted the sleeping Maska gently on the side. She waved to Prince Simen as he left the eyrie and she turned to close the door to Maska's stall.

A movement further down the hall caught her eye and she turned, one hand going to an ax over her shoulder. In the late afternoon light filtering in through the doorway, Kalina saw Leif standing in the stall next to Maska's, one hand on Arikara's golden side. Their eyes met for a moment and her heart skipped a beat. Had he heard everything they'd said? What must he think of her? He nodded to her before turning away, his back to her. Her heart clenched in her chest and her throat felt tight. She had to leave the dragon eyrie or else she knew she'd start to cry.

Chapter 26

A TAPPING SOUND PULLED KALINA'S attention. Beside her, Lord Averil's foot was bouncing up and down, seeming to count down the seconds until the King of Askor answered her. The King sat in his chair, his back hunched, his fingers steepled before his face, his eyes watching her. She did her best not to fidget, but she couldn't help her eyes from sliding sideways to look at Prince Endre who sat beside his father, one hand fisted atop the table. She wondered what they were thinking.

She had just suggested that she take a tour of the country, get to know its people better since she was to marry one of its princes. She wanted to truly assess the might of this country if she was going to be selling herself and her freedom to it. Or if she managed to find a way free, she wanted to know exactly what she was giving up.

"It sounds like a waste of time and a safety risk," Prince Endre said. Kalina could see the knuckles of his clenched fist turning white. For some reason that satisfied her, knowing she was frustrating him that much. She smiled, but not at the prince. Perhaps she was more like her cousin Kari after all: always ready for a fight.

"Yes, your Highness. If I'm going to be giving up half my power to an Askorian prince, then at the very least, I should get to know his country. I will, after all, be the wife to one of their beloved princes." She smiled sweetly at the heir, doing her best to channel every ounce of charm she'd learned from Delisa. Growing up together, Delisa had always been able to charm their way out of any scrape that Kalina inevitably got them into. And when they'd gotten older and the boys, and girls, had taken notice of Delisa's long dark curls, dark eyes, and curves, she'd become a master at flirting and charming them as well. Kalina had always envied her friend's confidence. She had never felt like she quite fit in. And as it turned out, she didn't. She was different, a queen of two very different worlds. "You're asking a great deal of me, a lot of personal sacrifice. The least you can do is give me a few measly things, and then I'm happy to negotiate."

She felt like she was coaxing an unruly baby dragon into her arms. She glanced at Lord Illeron, who was eyeing her, looking impressed. Maybe she was getting better at the political side of things.

"Your Majesty," Lord Averil chimed in. She almost rolled her eyes. Of course, he had an opinion. "Is it wise to expose yourself in such a way? As much as we want this alliance and marriage with Askor, would it not be putting our brand new queen at too much risk to take a tour of the country? With you so newly on the throne of Ethea," he shrugged, his eyes flicking to the King of Askor. "We can't stand to lose you to some mishap on the road." He smiled at her and she smiled graciously back. She knew a threat when she heard one.

"Thank you, Lord Averil, for your concern. But I believe that I can handle myself." She turned back to the King who was now flicking his gaze between her and Lord Averil.

"Your Majesty, I have to agree with Lord Averil," he said. "We wouldn't want to put you at undue risk. Perhaps once you are married to my son, and officially a princess of Askor, then we could arrange a tour. Introduce you as our new princess properly."

Kalina narrowed her eyes. She knew what this was. She would bet a million gold pieces that the moment she married Prince Simen and went on tour, some horrible accident would befall her and Simen would take the Ethean throne.

"Thank you for your concern for my well-being, your Majesty," she said, sitting forward in her chair. "But I will be marrying Prince Simen back in Ethea, with my own family around me. I cannot possibly spend any more time away from my throne than I have to." Indeed, she'd been getting almost daily reports from Valdir runners who were flying over the Great Grey Mountains on their dragons to bring her messages from Eira and Rangvald on the state of her country in her absence. The sooner she got back there, the better.

"That is something we have yet to discuss. A quiet ceremony here in Askor before you leave for Ethea would go a long way towards appeasing Prince Simen's friends and family," began Prince Julian, but Kalina held up a hand. She could see Leif a few seats away from her stiffen at the mention of the ceremony. Kalina's gut clenched. She wished with all her heart she could just talk to him about everything.

"Your Highness, your Majesty. It seems to me that Ethea is

getting the bad end of the deal here. First I'm going to give up half my ruling power to Prince Simen, then I'm supposed to get married here? What's next? What more will you add to the list of demands?"

"Queen Kalina, this is a negotiation." King Blackbourne's eyes were blazing.

"Fine. If we're supposed to be negotiating terms of my marriage, of peace, then one of my terms is that you end indentured servitude."

The entire chamber fell silent at her words. Kalina waited in the stillness, the sound of Lord Averil's jouncing leg growing louder and louder until Prince Endre stood, his fist pressed into the table before him.

"You overstep, your Majesty. It is not for you to say how we run our country," he said. Kalina smirked, standing as well.

"And yet you presume to tell me how to run mine. At every turn, I'm being told you want certain trading rights, passage across our southern lands to Wostrad, that you want to be written into my trade agreement with Ablen. Well, no more. This negotiation is a farce." She stepped away from the table, her small entourage standing to join her at the door. "I will honor our agreement, King Blackbourne, when you and your council can learn to negotiate and treat Ethea fairly." Then she stormed out, leaving stunned faces in her wake.

Kalina found herself walking out of the castle to the parade ground. It seemed like the safest place in the entire castle. There was a wide-open space and a wide-open sky above. She had felt hemmed in, trapped since she'd arrived. And the parade ground felt like the only place where she had weapons at her disposal and space enough to use them.

There she paced, unsure of what to do. Had she just ruined any chance she had at negotiating a true and lasting peace? Was she now in more danger than ever, in a foreign country so far from her home? She continued to pace, her deep red dress dragging in the dirt behind her. Delisa was going to be mad she was ruining it but just then she didn't care.

Talon approached her from the barracks, the sight of his boyish face and brown curls instantly helping to calm her. He reached out as if he was going to hug her but then thought better of it.

"Is everything alright, Kalina?" he asked hesitantly, eyeing her stiffness. She shook out her hands and rolled her shoulders. She needed to calm down, find a way to repair what she might just have broken. She would have to call for another council tomorrow to try to smooth things over. The sun was setting over the western wall of the castle and now all she wanted was to eat dinner quietly in her rooms with her Queen's Guard and Delisa and then go to bed with a good book. She stopped pacing and looked up at her friend.

"No, everything's not alright. But it will be. I'll make it be." She gave him a tight smile, which he returned. "Goodnight, Talon. And thank you." She meant for checking on her, for being her friend in such a lonely place. Somehow she had always known in her heart that Talon would never abandon her.

"Goodnight, my Queen." He bowed and returned to the barracks. Kalina let out a long sigh, before turning her own steps towards the palace.

Just as she turned the last corner to her rooms, Hilde and Runa following slowly behind her as they had all day, she ran smack into Prince Endre. The dark-haired Prince steadied her before stepping back and giving her a small bow.

"I'm sorry I startled you, your Majesty." He was always so polite. It made Kalina sick. Didn't he ever just want to yell and scream? She knew she did. But like a good queen she waited until she was high in the sky on Maska and alone to scream out her frustration and rage at the futility of it all. So she plastered a sweet smile on her face and gave him a small curtsey back.

"It's no bother, your Highness."

"I was actually hoping to run into you."

Ahh, that was why he was lurking in her hallway, a place he had no reason to be.

"And why is that?"

"To give you a warning. You are pushing the boundaries here. We want peace, but not at the disrespect of our country, our traditions, and how we rule our people. It might be best if you take some time to consider what is really important to you before we negotiate further."

Kalina glared at him, her smile dropping away.

"Is that a threat, your Highness?" she asked, her voice deadly.

Her hands were itching to grab the knife she had stashed against her lower back, tucked into her belt, and plunge it into his chest. Prince Endre's eyes flicked over her shoulder at Hilde and Runa before landing back on her own ice blue ones.

"Not at all. Merely a suggestion for how to proceed."

"I will find my own way, without your help," Kalina said coldly. "And I would like to meet with your council tomorrow morning. Consider this my final offer." She pushed passed him, her guards quickly following. "Goodnight, Prince Endre," she said over her shoulder as she opened the door to her rooms and slipped inside, leaving him red-faced in the hallway. She didn't care what threats he threw at her. She wasn't going to smooth things over. She was going to stand up for herself and insist upon a few things tomorrow at the meeting.

"Where's Seri?" she asked as she entered. Delisa was reading quietly by the fire, her feet propped in Kari's lap where Kari was massaging them gently. Delisa looked up and frowned.

"Actually, I haven't seen her all afternoon. I thought she would have shown up to bring more firewood or to ask if we wanted dinner."

Kalina waved a hand and crossed to her table were pieces of paper and writing utensils sat. She scribbled a quick note before handing it to Runa.

"Please take this to Lord Illeron. I need to speak with him. And find out where Seri got to. I'd like to have dinner here with Lord Illeron."

Runa nodded and left quickly. Delisa put down her book and came over to help Kalina change out of the red dress. She complained lightly about the dust and dirt covering the hem but Kalina was too preoccupied to care. When Runa returned not long later she had troubling news.

"Seri's gone. I asked the cook where she'd gone but the woman just said that a pair of guards came for her an hour ago and escorted her out. She hasn't returned. The cook promised to send another girl up with dinner and to run you a bath. I'm sorry, your Majesty."

"Gone?" The color drained from Kalina's face as she realized her mistake. Seri was the only servant she'd had any close contact with since arriving in the castle. When she'd asked for an end to indentured servitude today in council they would have assumed it was Seri who had told her. Had they just reassigned her? Or had they done something worse?

"Oh no." She felt suddenly sick. Once again she was hurting those around her, those she had begun to care about.

"What? What is it?" Delisa said, putting her arm around Kalina's shoulders and steering her to a chair.

"This is all my fault. I'm the reason Seri is gone." She explained what had happened in the council.

"There's nothing you could have done, Kalina. At least you tried. At least you didn't sit by while good people have everything taken away from them," Delisa said.

Kalina didn't believe her, not really. There was so much more she could have done. A knock on the door distracted them and Lord Illeron entered, followed closely by a large tray of dinner food. Kalina pushed aside her guilt and sadness and instead focused on him. They had work to do.

"Lord Illeron, we need to make a plan."

Chapter 27

"THANK YOU FOR MEETING AGAIN with me, your Majesty." Kalina stood before the King and his council, addressing them. Today she had worn her Valdiran leathers both to intimidate and to help her feel strong, connected to her people. It helped her hold her resolve when Prince Endre and the King glared at her with such intensity. "I know that all we are trying to do here is what's best for our countries, our people." Hesitant nods happened around the council table. "And I know that together, we can both be stronger nations."

"Then we should put this matter to rest once and for all," the King said. "You will agree to our terms and marry my son, or go back to your country with your tail between your legs and prepare for war."

Kalina's jaw clenched. He wasn't going to mince words. So neither would she.

"Then you will agree to my terms as well. This is, after all, a negotiation." She locked eyes with the King, her own gaze as intense as his. "You will change your laws on indentured servitude, putting a cap of five years on each persons' service. Those who have already served more will be immediately released. You will be content with your son having only partial power over the Etheans, but the Valdir are mine alone to rule. And we will split the Great Grey Mountains in half down the middle. You will control the northern part of the range, and we the southern. That will give you valuable mines and resources. That is what the original war was about, and now I'm giving you half my mines. Your son and I will get married in my country, witnessed by my people, but you and your family are welcome to attend. And you will return my brother to me safe, and unharmed. He will then spend half the year with me in Ethea, and the other half with you, here in Askor. And when he comes of age, he will be allowed to freely choose where he goes and what he does with his life." She paused, taking a deep breath and letting her words sink in. "Are my demands clear?"

The King's face had grown steadily redder as she'd spoken. Prince Endre was looking at her with a small amount of respect. Prince Julian was looking utterly shocked and disgusted, his lips twisting in a sneer. Kari hadn't figured a way out of the marriage yet, so she had to make the best of a terrible situation. Her own council was just as grim-faced as she was, but Jormungand was eyeing her and she could see a muscle twitching in Leif's strong jaw. She wondered what he was making of all this. He couldn't possibly believe that she wanted to marry Simen, or that she had any say in this. All she could do was fight for some modicum of control and hope for the best.

Finally, the King spoke.

"I will concede to your demands, but you will marry my son here, in Askor, in a week's time. And you will give him equal control in your entire kingdom, including the Valdir." He gave her a partial smile. "Those are my new terms."

Kalina's gut clenched. She might free people like Seri, but she would be putting herself at extreme risk by marrying Simen here. Once they were married and he had control, then if anything happened to her... she couldn't bear the thought of what the King of Askor would do to the Valdir.

"I will have to think-" she began, adopting an uninterested tone.

"No," the King interrupted, his voice rising. "You will decide now or else this means war. There will be no further negotiation." The entire council chamber rang with silence following his words.

Give a counter offer. Give a counter offer.

The words kept running through her mind. She pressed her knuckles into the tabletop and looked sideways for a moment at Lord Illeron. His own eyes were full of worry while his face remained blank and passive. He was the master of spies, after all, and he knew how to hide his emotions. She finally looked at Leif, their eyes locking and remaining so for a few moments for the first time in what felt like months. She wished they had had a few moments to talk, so she could tell him she was doing this to protect him. To protect the Valdir.

"Fine. I'll marry your son here, in one week. But I retain full control over the Valdir."

"It is done then. We will begin planning for the wedding." The King stood to go. "Pleasure doing business with you, Queen Kalina." Then he stood and left the chamber, his sons and nobles filing out behind him. She didn't even get to ask about her brother. Was he alive? Did they have him? When would they return him to her?

Kalina's stomach twisted and she had to swallow hard at the bile rising in her throat. She felt like she'd just sold herself. Suddenly peace didn't seem like a good enough reason to give up half her power, and possibly her safety, to Askor. She slumped back down into her chair and put her head into her hands. She heard her own council file out. She only looked up briefly when Lord Illeron placed a hand softly on her shoulder.

"You did the best you could." He murmured.

"It wasn't enough." She felt like crying, screaming, sobbing. Once she was alone but for her guards she stood and walked from the room. A hand snagged her arm as soon as she left. She spun, pulling a dagger from some hidden place and had it to the throat of her attacker in an instant. But the grey eyes she stared into were no threat, although they did hold anger.

"How could you do that? You've sold our country to a mad man." Leif's voice was urgent and low, pitched so no one but her could hear it, not even her guards. His hand was tight on her upper arm but not enough to hurt her. Even in his anger and fear, he was gentle with her. She shook him off. He didn't understand. And suddenly her own anger and fear was boiling up through the thin sheet of ice she'd tried to build over it.

"And what would you have done? Put our people through another war? How many more people are going to die for me? How many more of our own people are we going to lose to Askor?" It came out fierce and fiery and she saw Leif's eyes change as he stepped back. "Would your father have wanted another war? Would mine?"

"No. I suppose not." He took a second step away.

Kalina watched as he left her standing in the hallway, breathing hard, tears gathering in her eyes. She wiped angrily at them with her sleeve and stormed back to her rooms to grab her wolf trimmed cloak and thermal padded riding gear. She needed to get away, as far away as she could. She needed time to think.

"Where are you going?" Delisa asked, wringing her hands in distress as she watched Kalina change with abandon.

"Flying," was all she said as she left her rooms and practically ran down to the dragon eyrie, her guards barely able to keep up. As she barreled into the eyrie, a second arm snagged her and she tore her arm free, pulling one of her axes from its sheath and brandishing it. Prince Simen stood in the light from the doorway, his hands held up in defense. His handsome face had gone ashen. Her own body pulsed with fury.

"I'm sorry, your Majesty." He took a tentative step forward and Kalina lowered her ax, slowly putting it back into its spot along her back. "I heard about the council and wanted to come see you were alright."

"I'm fine," she lied, turning back to a now agitated and concerned Maska.

"I need to talk to you," Simen persisted.

"Can it wait?" She threw Maska's saddle over the giant spikes along his spine and then climbed up. "I need to go flying."

"It's important. Very important."

Kalina turned and saw fear and worry in Prince Simen's eyes. He really did have something to say. She let out a long sigh.

"Fine. You can come with me."

"Are you sure, Littling?" Maska's deep voice rumbled through the stall.

"Yes, I'm sure. We should probably keep getting to know one another. If we're going to get married," she didn't mean for it to come out so bitterly but it did. Simen noticed and she saw his face blanche. She did her best to push her anger aside as she fastened the large leather buckles on the saddle underneath Maska's belly. She climbed up and then offered a hand down to the prince. "Well, come on then."

A small grin spread across his face and he took her hand.

Chapter 28

WIND ROARED IN HER EARS AS MASKA flew. Behind her, Prince Simen clung to her waist, his face pressed into the leather of her back, his eyes squeezed shut. She should feel sorry for him and ask Maska to slow down, to fly lower and slower. But she needed this speed as he winged south towards the Great Grey Mountains. Below them, the snow-covered plains gave way to verdant green and brown Riverlands, small farms dotted between the bright blue flowing rivers that snaked and wound their way south towards the mountains. Finally, Maska began to descend and she could see a snow-covered peak rising before them, it's top disappearing in the clouds.

"Maska, take us down," she called over the roar of the wind in her ears.

He tucked his wings and dropped like a stone. Behind her Simen let out a choked gasp that was snatched away by the wind, but Kalina let out a long yell, a mixture of joy and frustration. Just a few minutes flying on Maska and she'd felt her anger and fear melt away. She was free, and no one could touch her up here in the sky. Her own guards hadn't been able to follow. Runa and Asa had been on duty, and while Asa had tried to get her own dragon out of the eyrie in time to follow, Runa had run back towards the castle, no doubt to get Kari. But by the time they got their act together, she and Simen were long gone on Maska. Later, Kari would berate her for leaving alone with Simen, but she wasn't alone. She was a better fighter than he was, and she had Maska. If anything, he should be the one concerned for his life.

Maska came to a sudden and jolting stop in mid-air, his enormous wings flapping hard as he slowly lowered them to the top of a green hill at the base of the mountains. In less than an hour, they'd covered leagues of distance, and finally, Kalina felt like she could breathe. When he'd alighted on the grass, Kalina pried Simen's fingers from her waist and slid down off her dragon. A few moments later, Simen's tall, lanky form crashed to the ground unceremoniously beside her.

"Oh, blessed land," he moaned and lay down on the dew-covered grass. Kalina let out a chuckle and sat beside him as Maska's large bulk struck the earth and he rolled onto his side to sun-bathe.

Kalina smiled indulgently at him as she waited for the prince to regain control of himself. When he finally sat up beside her, his thin face was decidedly grey.

"Are you going to puke? Because if you are, please do it far away from me."

A wan smile spread across his lips and he tucked his knees into his chest and rested his chin on them.

"Do you always fly like that?" he asked, eyeing her. She tilted her head back and closed her eyes, soaking in the midday sun like a dragon.

"No. And we'll fly lower and more slowly on the way back. I just needed to get out of there as soon as I could."

He nodded sagely as though he understood. They were quiet for a few moments, and he picked at the grass before speaking.

"There's something I've been wanting to tell you. And with my father rushing things, I think I need to tell you now, or never."

She cracked her eyes open and watched emotions play across his face.

"Go on," she encouraged, giving him a small smile. He drew in a deep breath.

"I don't want to marry you. I can't marry you."

Kalina let out a bark of laughter.

"I don't want to marry you either, Simen, but we're a bit too far gone for that now, aren't we?"

He began shaking his head, frustration, and sadness clear on his face.

"No, you don't understand. I'm already promised to another, and I refuse to break that engagement, regardless of my father's will. I will leave Askor before I'll marry you. I love her," he finished lamely.

The smile died on Kalina's face. He was serious. He was going to throw this all away, put them all at risk, to uphold a previous promise. The whole situation reminded her too much of her own parent's situation, but the ramifications were immense. Her fear came roaring back and she broke out in a cold sweat, but she also felt a strange sense of relief that was so colossal she could not hold it within her. It seemed to spread out in waves around her.

"You'd be plunging us into war, you know," she said, looking out at the Riverlands that stretched north before them. "But if we're being honest, I don't want to marry you either."

He nodded beside her, tearing a leaf into tiny pieces. He cleared his throat.

"I'm sorry, Kalina, for what it's worth."

Kalina turned back to him and took his hand in hers, squeezing.

"Prince Simen, you have become my friend in this last week. And whatever you do, whether you decide to marry me or not, you will always be welcome in Ethea."

He squeezed her hand back gratefully before dropping it. Kalina went back to watching the Riverlands.

"What is she like?" she asked. Out of the corner of her eye, she saw his face light up, and she smiled softly as he began to describe the woman he was going to marry. Fear weighed heavy on her as they flew back north to Winterreach Castle a few hours later. Behind her, Simen seemed more at peace, more himself and she found she truly did like the young man. She was glad he was her friend and on her side, but it didn't help their prospects of winning another war against Askor. She'd have to find a way to appease the King of Askor. When they dismounted she hugged Maska goodnight, making sure he had plenty of food and was comfortable. Prince Simen walked with her back to the palace where he embraced her briefly before bidding her goodnight.

She needed a plan.

Kari paced the room before her, gesticulating to punctuate her angry words. Kalina sat at her small table, arms crossed over her chest. She wasn't budging. Kari could yell and scream all she wanted but Kalina wouldn't change her mind. Delisa sat beside Kalina, stiff and waiting.

"I can't believe that you agreed, that you're going to let Prince Simen just leave! We will be at war in a matter of seconds and stuck in a foreign capital no less. What do you expect us to do, Kalina? We can't protect you, and we can't leave without them noticing." Kari's voice was rising with each word.

"Shh, calm down, Kari. I have a plan, sort of," Kalina said, uncrossing her arms and standing to pace like her cousin. It must run in the family.

"And what is that?" Kari snapped, turning the full might of her glare onto Kalina. Kalina kept pacing.

"We send everyone without a dragon back, claiming they are going to get supplies for the wedding. That they are bringing guests. Then only those of us with dragons remain. Once the game is up, we fly off. We leave them in the dust and go home to prepare for war." It was a weak plan. But she was running out of options.

"We won't survive another war," Kari ground out. "You know that. We need another option." She resumed pacing, the energy coming off her palpable in the room. Kalina let out a long sigh, her mind racing. She followed her cousin across the room and back. They needed a way to avoid war.

"What about Jormungand? Or Rangvald?" Delisa said, tentatively. Both Kari and Kalina stopped pacing.

"What about them?" Kari said.

"Well, aren't they both Valdiran princes? Both the eldest children of your father's siblings? Couldn't they take your place? Marry an Askorian princess instead? I would suggest Kari marry Prince Ivan but...well." Delisa smiled sheepishly over at Kari who blushed slightly in response. "I'm a bit too selfish for that."

Kalina began pacing once again. It was a possibility. It would still ensure that someone was in power, and it might appease the King enough to call off the war. It was worth a shot.

"Rangvald will never agree," Kari said with conviction. She did know her brother better than any of them. "But perhaps Jormungand will agree. You'll have to go talk to him, convince him, Kalina."

"I know. I have to try."

And with that declaration, she left her rooms heading down the corridor and around the corner to knock quietly on Jormungand's and Leif's door.

Chapter 29

SHE HOPED WITH EVERYTHING SHE HAD that Leif wasn't in his room, that instead, her cousin Jormungand would answer. For once, her prayers were answered and the hulking mass of Jormungand filled the doorway. His beard had grown and he'd begun braiding the ends. It was strange, but the look suited him somehow. He eyed her with the same blue eyes she had before bowing low and stepping aside for her to enter.

"To what do I owe the pleasure of your visit, your Majesty?" He had always been formal with her, ever since she'd beaten him in single combat and fought by his side in battle. Ever since he'd stopped trying to depose her and instead became her ally. It both annoyed and comforted her.

"Is that fresh bread I smell?" She said, sniffing her way across the room to a table freshly laden with bread and different types of cheese, along with slabs of roasted meat.

"Have as much as you'd like." Jormungand joined her at the table, smiling as she grabbed a piece of bread and ripped it in half, stuffing it full of meat and cheese. She bit into it hungrily, realizing that it was now past dinner time and she hadn't eaten since that morning.

"I came to talk to you about something," she said around mouthfuls. He raised an eyebrow at her. "First of all, nice beard."

He grimaced at her before bursting into a deep laugh.

"I was wondering when you'd notice."

"I noticed," she lied. "I just haven't had a chance to sit and talk with you much since we arrived."

"Cousin, you haven't ever really sat and talked with me." He gave her a grin. He was right of course. Things had happened at breakneck speed since the day she'd met the Valdir since she'd taken her place among them. And that hadn't changed since she'd met Jormungand. She made a promise to herself to spend more time getting to know him like she had with Rangvald and Kari.

"You're right. I've been a bad friend."

"But a good Queen," he assured her. She rolled her eyes and stuffed the last of the bread into her mouth, wiping her hands on her leather pants. Now, to business.

"I have a proposition of sorts for you."

"Oh?"

"We find ourselves in a bit of a dilemma. Prince Simen came to me today and said he won't marry me. That he's leaving. He knows it will plunge us into war, but he's in love. I can't take that from him." She paused. Jormungand had put down his own food and was frowning at her. She swallowed and continued, suddenly nervous. "I think we might be able to both get what we want: he can marry his lady and I can remain free, unbound by a political marriage. But it means I'd need to propose an alternative to the Askorian council."

"And what is your solution to keep us from war?" His deep voice had gone gravelly.

"Well, you, actually. You are a prince of the Valdir. You hold a place of power in Ethea. I propose that you marry one of King Blackbourne's younger daughters instead. It wouldn't put an Askorian on the throne, but-," he raised a hand, cutting her off.

"It's a nice idea, Kalina, but it would never work."

"Why not?" Fear gripped her heart once more. What little hope she'd been harboring beginning to ebb away at the shake of his head.

"Because I am not interested in marrying a princess. I'm not interested in marrying any woman in fact."

Kalina just stared at him for a moment, dumbfounded.

"Then who do you want to marry?"

"Halvor."

For a moment Kalina had no idea who he meant. But then the image of a round-faced bear of a man with long silver battle braids and kind brown eyes surfaced. She had met him in Windpost, the village he and Jormungand had run together. He had always been at Jormungand's side. She shook her head in confusion.

"But you left him in the mountains."

"And as soon as things settle down, I plan to join him there. I am your cousin and your council Kalina, but I don't plan to live in Ravenhelm forever. I will go home to Halvor."

Kalina dropped her head into her hands, all traces of hope gone. This would mean certain war. A sob broke from her chest before she could stop it, and suddenly she was crying, tears streaming down her cheeks. Jormungand left his chair to kneel before her, taking her in his huge arms and rubbing her back as she cried. The panic that she had spent so many months learning to master, to conquer, came roaring to the surface like some unleashed beast and it was all she could do to keep herself from blowing apart.

"We'll think of something. Hush now," Jormungand murmured in her ear. She began to laugh through her tears. Here she was, a queen, being comforted by a big burly Valdir. She was the one destroying everything once again, not him. She should be the one on her knees, begging him, and all her people, to forgive her. "When is the Prince marrying his lady?"

"I don't know," she choked between sobs. "He said he'd be running away with her, but I don't know when."

"Then we have to prepare. We must get everyone without a dragon out before they find out."

Kalina sat back and looked up at him, a small smile on her tear-stained face.

"That's what I said." She let out a small hiccup and they both smiled. She began to feel a little better, the panic subsiding to a small beast instead of a large one. One that she could begin to tame. "I'll go find Kari. You go find Leif and tell him. We have to move them tonight."

She stood, wiping her face and crossed to the door where she paused. She turned back to her cousin.

"Thank you, Jormungand."

He gave her a bow as the door opened in Kalina's hand, and she turned, startled. Leif stood there, his handsome face drawn, dark shadows beneath his eyes. His grey eyes darted between Kalina and Jormungand and then he saw how upset she was. His eyes narrowed.

"What happened?"

But Kalina couldn't make the words come out. Half of her wanted to throw her arms around him and tell him the news that she wouldn't be marrying the prince after all. That they could finally be together. The other half of her was terrified he would reject her. Terrified he had moved on. Terrified he would be so angry at her for putting her people in danger once again. The beast in her chest gave a roar and she was suddenly overwhelmed. Tears threatened and her throat closed around her words. She pushed past him and down the hall, wanting to get away as quickly as possible.

Just before she turned the corner two figures almost bowled

into her. She steadied herself on Kari's arm, looking between her and Lord Illeron.

"We have a problem," Kari panted, and Kalina realized they'd been running.

"What is it?"

"It seems our young Prince was caught trying to sneak from the castle not long ago. He admitted to his father than he refuses to marry you and is instead marrying someone else." Kalina's blood ran cold at Lord Illeron's words.

"It's already happening then?" She looked to Kari who nodded with a grimace.

"That's not the worst of it though."

Kalina looked back and forth between them, all thoughts of love and marriage gone like the drying tears on her cheeks.

"What is it? Tell me!"

"The dragons. They've been captured."

Kalina began shaking her head, and then tried to push past her cousin but Kari stopped her with a hard hand on her arm. Kalina tried to shake her off, to run to check on Maska, to prove that he was safe, that he couldn't be captured, but Kari only squeezed harder until Kalina was forced to look into her cousin's cool blue eyes.

"They are captured, Kalina. We cannot save them. Not as we are."

"Then what in Skaldir's name are we supposed to do?" Her voice was hoarse with fear.

"I can sneak you out. But only if we do it quickly," Lord Illeron said, his usually calm face hard with worry.

A scream echoed down the hallway from the direction of Kalina's rooms and together the three of them turned the corner only for Lord Illeron to pull them into a shadowed alcove guarded by a suit of armor. Together, the three of them watched in horror as a group of Askorian soldiers dragged Delisa from Kalina's rooms by her hair as she kicked and screamed obscenities at them. Kalina had never seen her friend so furious. Kari was coiled like a snake about to attack but Kalina grabbed her cousin's arms with Lord Illeron's, holding her as they watched a guard punch Delisa in the stomach, quieting her. It took both of them to keep Kari from following after her lover.

"We can do nothing from a jail cell," Kalina whispered furiously in her cousin's ear, her own heart racing in anger and fear. Kari's body seemed to slump in on itself then, along with Delisa's as the guards dragged her away. Kalina looked at Lord Illeron's face in the darkness of the corridor. Even her master of spies was scared now, his eyes wide.

Footsteps sounded from behind them and Leif came running around the corner. Before the guards down the hall caught sight of him, Kalina stepped out into the passage and snagged the front of his leathers, dragging him back into the alcove with her. By now it was a tight fit, and if anyone found them they'd look like sardines packed into too small a jar. She put a finger to her lips, indicating he needed to stay silent.

There they stayed until the sounds of tromping footsteps faded. Then they quickly squeezed out of the hiding space.

"What was that all about?" Leif asked.

"Did Jormungand update you?" Kalina asked. He nodded. "Good. Well, the Prince was caught trying to leave, and now they've captured all our dragons." She watched as his face drained of color and then hardened.

"What's next? Who do I have to kill to get Arikara back?"

"I need to get you four out of here. Where is Jormungand?" Lord Illeron asked. Leif started running back down the hall to his rooms. Lord Illeron turned to her and Kari. "Go and get the barest essentials, and don't forget warm cloaks. Meet us back here in five minutes." He then followed Leif while Kari and Kalina ran to her rooms.

They were a mess, a chair overturned, a vase shattered on the floor, and Kalina's trunks lay open on the bed, already partially packed. She ignored those. She was already wearing her Valdiran leathers, so she grabbed an over-the-shoulder bag and began stuffing things into it: a pouch of money, her gold dragon scale armor that Leif had made her, her double axes which she strapped to her back, and her crown. At that moment she wore her small silver circlet, the same one she wore into battle, but the pretty blue one her father had given her mother she tucked inside her bag. Then she threw her wolf fur cloak around herself and joined Kari by the door.

"Where's Runa, Hilde, Asa, or Gyda?" Kalina asked, referring to her other Queen's Guards.

"I don't know. I hope they weren't captured by the guards We can't worry about them right now. They can handle themselves. And like you said, we can't do anything from the dungeons."

Kalina nodded, her jaw set. Although it felt like she was running from a fight instead of meeting it, she knew that they just didn't have the numbers to fight the Askorians on their home turf. She would have to get out, find allies, and then attack. She would get Maska back.

Chapter 30

THE UNDERGROUND PASSAGE WAS dark and damp, and by now Kalina's clothing was sticking to her sweat-slicked skin. They were all hunched low to avoid banging their heads on the overhead rocks. Lord Illeron had told them that Lord Averil was a traitor and he'd been working with Askor the entire time. Kalina wasn't all that surprised. She had seen the man in close conference with the King after many of the council meetings, after all. And he's always seemed to advocate for whatever the King wanted. It made her sick to her stomach to know he was responsible.

"I'd had my suspicions but could never directly connect him to Askor. But today I happened upon them in a corridor and overheard him discussing your marriage with the King," Illeron said, ducking beneath a low outcropping of rock. The tunnel had been dug from the bedrock below the castle itself.

"He always did agree too quickly with whatever the King of Askor said," Kalina said as she stepped down after him into what felt like ice-cold murky water. She shivered in disgust as a smell assaulted her nose.

"Lord Illeron, do I even want to know what I'm stepping in?"

"No, your Majesty. These tunnels were once used to transport goods as well as waste from the castle to the riverboats. But now they just transport waste."

Kalina began breathing through her mouth to avoid the smells but she knew that it was just coating her tongue. She suppressed a gag and continued after the Spymaster, deeper into the dark. He held a torch ahead of him, and behind them, Leif held a torch as well. Leif and Lord Illeron had arrived at Leif's rooms to find them deserted. Jormungand had already left to warn Talon and Captain Higgs. Kalina could only hope they were safe.

"Lord Averil orchestrated all of this, didn't he? Not just the marriage, but us coming here, the dragons, and now this?" Kalina asked into the dark.

"I'd always thought he was a bit simple," Kari said behind her. "But then again, he was the first to oppose you. And he has continued to oppose you right and left since you took the throne, he just does it in such a way you don't always notice. A man like that wouldn't risk

your disfavor unless he had someone more powerful behind him."
"Before I took the throne he was Prince Terric's staunchest
supporter. I should have been more suspicious of his actions in the
first place." Kalina mentally chastised herself for not kicking him off
the council sooner. But she had been trying not to rock the boat too
much once she'd taken the throne. Leaving him on the council
placated many of the angry nobles. But he had supported the
Askorian King's side since the beginning. And now she was paying
the price.

"Do you think they will hurt the dragons?" she asked, hoping
no one would answer. She wasn't sure she wanted to know.

"I doubt it. They took them captive for one of two reasons: to
control you, or to control them. Perhaps they want a flying force so
that they can contend with your Valdiran forces." Lord Illeron kept
them moving through the dark. Kalina's feet were freezing but sweat
dripped from her forehead and her back was beginning to protest
being hunched over in the passageway. She couldn't imagine how
the other three felt since they each stood at least a head taller than
her.

Finally, faint light peeked through at the end of the tunnel, and
Kalina's heart lifted slightly. They might just get out of this alive.
But the end of the tunnel was blocked by an iron gate. Lord Illeron
pulled and then pushed at it, but it was rusted shut and refused to
move. Leif and Kari pushed past Kalina, Leif handing her his torch
and together, he and Kari shoved and kicked at the gate.

Kalina turned back to the black passage, fear and worry
gnawing at her. That's when she heard the echoed shouts and the dot
of torch-light at the far end of the tunnel. She quickly dumped her
torch into the river of filth beneath her, extinguishing the light.

"Everyone, you might want to hurry up. We are being pursued."

Lord Illeron cursed under his breath and put his own torch out.
Hopefully, they hadn't been seen, but there was no guarantee. Leif
and Kari pushed harder and there was a groan of metal as the gate
finally pushed outwards. The gap was small but they all squeezed
through it out into the night and onto a small stone ledge. Below
them, a river rushed, and farther along the ledge, there was a dock.
Torches flickered around the dock, and a large barge was moored
there.

"Make for the barge," Lord Illeron said, ushering them before him. Kalina followed Leif and Kari along the tight ledge. One slip on the moss-covered rock and they would tumble into the freezing river below. She would bet that they wouldn't survive long in the water. It rushed swiftly over the rocks below, white water undulating and swirling. Kalina was a strong swimmer, but there was no way she could keep her head above water while fighting the extreme cold. She shivered at the thought and focused on her footing.

The barge was wide and shallow and filled with garbage. They could see a crew of dockworkers loading bags and bins full of refuse. All four of them crouched beside a pile of crates on the dock. Kalina kept looking behind them at the iron gate that stood open. Any moment Askorian soldiers would pour from the underground tunnel and they would be caught. Lord Illeron crouched beside them, his thin face grim.

"You'll need to sneak aboard. It's due to leave any minute. Once it's on the water, wait until the river is calm and smooth enough for you to swim to shore. Swim to the northern bank. I will have someone meet you there but it may not be tonight."

"You aren't coming with us?" Leif asked, his eyes narrowing. Lord Illeron shook his head.

"I need to stay in the city, see what else I can learn from my agents, see what can be done to free the dragons. I will report to you as soon as I know anything useful." He turned to look at Kalina then. "You are the bravest person I know, Kalina." Her eyes went wide at his informal address. He had never said her name, except when pairing it with her title. This somehow felt more intimate, personal. "I held you as a baby, delivered you to the abbey and Father Martin. I remember those days. I always got reports from Father Martin about your well-being, your antics." He smiled at the memories. She had always gotten into trouble as a kid. "Reading those letters aloud to your grandfather was a highlight for both of us." He placed a gentle, fatherly hand on her scarred cheek. "Be safe, my Queen." He pulled her into a brief hug, startling her.

Then he was standing and striding along the pier to engage the sailors and workers loading the barge. Kalina's heart tightened in her chest. She worried this would be the last time she'd see the Spymaster.

"We have to move," Leif said, and together the three of them slunk out from behind the crate and down the short dock to the side of the ship. They quickly went up the gangplank and onto the deserted barge. Just as they disappeared over the lip there was a shout.

"We need to hide!" she said desperately. They looked around but the only viable hiding place was in the thick of the garbage where two tall crates sat. As they crouched behind it, their backs to the far side of the barge and the river, Kalina tried not to think about what they stood upon. Her feet sunk into the muck and the smell was so strong it was a struggle to breathe.

"What if someone comes around this side? We'll be seen!" Kari said, her usually smirking face now full of fear. Kalina wished she knew what to say to make it better.

"We'll just have to hope we can make it far enough without being detected that they can't turn back," Kalina said. Kari nodded in understanding as they crouched, waiting. The sky overhead was a dark, cloud-covered void, the only light coming from the lamps aboard the ship and the torches on the dock. They would only be seen if the torchlight fell on them. Kalina sent up a quick prayer to Skaldir, the Valdir's god, that they wouldn't be found. Then she followed it with a quick prayer to the Mother, the Ethean goddess, for good measure. Perhaps they would just get out of this alive.

After what felt like an eternity crouching in the cold, they heard the sailors clamoring back aboard and the sounds of the gangplank being raised. Soon the barge was pushing away from its mooring and sliding out into the rushing river. Kalina stood to peer over the edge of the crate and watched as a small group of soldiers poured from the underground tunnel onshore, their torches barely reaching into the river. She could hear their shouts as they searched for her and her companions, but didn't find them. She hoped Lord Illeron was safe.

Soon the dock and the soldiers were out of sight around a bend, and the heavy darkness of night closed in around them. They had no idea how long it would be until they could slide over the side to safety but Kalina spent the entire time with her stomach in knots. Her feet were freezing and all she could think about was seeing Delisa being dragged away by her hair and the fear that Maska must be feeling, locked up, away from the freedom of the sky. She was already feeling his loss keenly, and the loss of the freedom he gave her. She felt trapped, bound to the land around her, a land that wasn't even her home.

It was hours before the river slowed and widened, but finally, it did and there was no doubt this was where Lord Illeron wanted them to disembark. Kalina's feet were already so frozen from the trek through the underground passage and standing in muck that it was hard to get moving again. She followed Kari and Leif over the side of the ship, dropping into the freezing cold water with as little sound as possible. Together they swam hard towards shore, their breath catching in their chests, their teeth chattering loudly. When Kalina wearily pulled herself onto the northern bank there were no lights from the castle visible, only the dark trees on either bank and the small lanterns bobbing from the ship as it slipped away downstream. All she wanted to do was lie down and sleep, but she forced herself to climb the small rocky outcropping and follow Leif and Kari as they led her into the woods.

The trees here were wide apart, glimpses of the sky above them visible through the towering trees. She slumped against a trunk, her feet so numb she could no longer feel them, her body shivering so violently she thought she'd shake apart.

"We ne-need a f-fire," she chattered. Kari looked as exhausted as she felt but she nodded. Leif looked tired but determined.

"Each of you gather three armloads of the driest wood you can find and meet back here. I'll gather kindling and find a place to build a fire." Leif stalked off deeper into the forest.

Kalina nodded belatedly at his back and forced herself to stand upright, using the tree for balance. She began searching the ground and low hanging branches for dry wood. After about ten minutes she had gathered her first load of firewood. She went back to the tree she'd leaned against, but Leif was nowhere to be found.

"Leif?" she called hesitantly into the deep, dark woods. Every part of her was cold now, her wet clothing stiff with frost. If she didn't get warm soon she was afraid she might keel over and die. "Leif? Wh-where are you?" Her teeth chattered so hard she almost didn't get the words out. Finally, his familiar shape emerged from the trees.

"Over here. I've found a rock to reflect the heat."

Kalina had no idea what he was talking about but she followed him to where he'd made a small pit and had a bundle of kindling waiting nearby. She dumped her armload beside it and turned to get more. By the time she'd returned with her third armload, Leif had a merry little fire glowing, and Kari was sitting beside it, feeding it larger and larger sticks.

"Here, sit here." Leif guided her to sit on the side of the fire with the rock face to her back. Then he went off into the night. Kalina held her hands out to the slowly growing fire, grateful for its warmth.

"Where'd he go?" She was thankful her voice didn't waver as much.

"To get something to help reflect the heat I'd guess." Kari was hunched over her knees, trying to keep her body heat inside while the fire grew. Her face was all hard lines in the firelight and Kalina could only imagine what she was feeling, but she'd bet it was similar to her own fear and grief.

Leif came back a few minutes later with a few dead logs, and Kalina watched as he and Kari began erecting a sort of lean-to, it's inside facing the rock wall but not touching it. Kalina felt a bit useless but she knew she'd only be a hindrance as they used more sticks to create a roof and then cut pine boughs to weave between them, creating a thick roof. Kalina noticed that as they worked, it became steadily warmer around her. She peeled off her soaked wolf fur cloak and slung it up over the rock so that it hung down to dry. Kari and Leif did the same, peeling off their outer layers and hanging them to dry out.

"How do you guys know what to do?" Kalina asked, rubbing her now throbbing toes. The warmth flooding them was lovely but painful. She supposed that the pain meant she wasn't going to lose a toe to frostbite after all.

"We grew up learning how to survive. Even in the high desert of the Wastes, you can still freeze to death at night. We were taught how to build a fire, how to build a shelter, how to stay warm." Kari explained. "Now I just wish we had some food."

Her cousin was right. They wouldn't be able to survive out here for long. She could only hope that whoever Lord Illeron was sending would arrive soon.

"So, what's the plan?" Kari said after a small silence. Kalina's eyes met Leif's for a brief moment before he looked away.

"We wait for Lord Illeron's contact. Then we make a plan," Kalina said, shrugging.

"But Delisa is in there. Yurok is in there. They are suffering. Skaldir only knows what that bastard is doing to them. We need to go back as soon as we can." Kari's voice held such bitterness, such vehemence, that it wrenched at Kalina's already aching heart. How much more pain could they all endure? How much more could she endure? If she lost Maska- no, she couldn't think about that. She had watched Nash go crazy after his dragon's death. She couldn't bear to think of what she might do if she lost hers.

"We will make a plan, Kari. I promise we will get them all back safe and sound."

Leif looked at her again, and for the first time in months, she saw a spark of his old self, their old friendship there. He gave her a small smile of approval, of appreciation. She only hoped she could live up to her own words.

Part 3

Chapter 31

AS DAWN LIGHT FINALLY BROKE through the heavy cloud cover to reach the forest floor, Kalina woke. She was swaddled in her freshly dried cloak, the heat of the fire having dried it quicker than she'd thought, the hood pulled up tight. Both Leif and Kari looked like dark brown lumps beneath a soft layer of freshly fallen snow that had come down in the night. She sat up and shook herself off, stretching and then feeding a few small twigs to the dying embers before her, stirring them to life. Soon she had a merry little fire glowing.

Just as she was about to wake the others up and suggest they try to find some food, a great roar filled the clearing, followed by the unmistakable concussion of giant wing beats. All three of them were on their feet in an instant, weapons drawn. It couldn't be a dragon, it would take at least another day for someone to fly there from the Great Grey Mountains, and from what little Kalina remembered of the geography of Askor, they were far to the north, not far from the base of the Snowcap Glacier.

A huge bulk landed with a mighty thud between the trees a few paces away, and Kalina let out a small gasp. The dragon was unlike any she'd seen so far. The face was craggier, more monstrous and stone-like than her cat-like Maska. He even had a beard of small whiskers that hung down around his chin. But the strangest thing was his scales: he was ice blue in color, and if he had stood still against a snow-covered background, Kalina would be hard-pressed to pick him out. She barely had time to glance at his rider before a second huge dragon settled onto the ground, effectively cutting Kalina and her companions off from escape unless they scaled the rock behind them. This dragon was pure white, except for brown and black splotches all across his scales, giving him the look of a piebald horse. He blended in well with the mottled tree and snow-covered landscape they currently occupied.

Both riders were female as far as Kalina could see, and although they were dragon riders, she didn't release the tight grip she had on her twin axes as the two women dismounted and approached. The one that dismounted the ice blue dragon unwrapped a thick piece of white cloth from her head and face that had been protecting her from the wind and freezing temperatures and Kalina let out a little gasp at the woman beneath.

Her hair was silver and hung in twisted locks that would have reached her waist had they not currently been tied back with a white piece of cloth. Blue, silver and white beads glimmered in the morning light throughout the dreads. Her skin was heavily tanned from sun exposure and her eyes were piercingly blue, like Kalina's, like Kari's.

The other woman had similar hair, and Kalina realized it was a style they wore, much like her, Kari, and Leif's battle-braided hair. Her skin was also deeply tanned but her eyes were a more muted blue. She had kinder features than the ice blue dragon rider. Kalina stepped in front of Leif and Kari who began to protest but she held up her hands and put her axes on the ground before her.

"We wish you no harm, dragon rider," she said, her hands held out before her, empty. The ice blue dragon rider gave her a tight smile.

"We know, Kalina, Queen of the Valdir and Ethea."

Kalina took a step back.

"Did Lord Illeron send you?" she asked hesitantly.

"Yes. I am Sunniva, leader of the Vanir. We have come to take you and your people to our camp." She gestured to her companion. "This is Astrid, my second-in-command. Two of you may ride with her, the Queen with me." She turned to walk back to her dragon. Kalina looked around at Kari and Leif, feeling confused and astonished.

"How did you find us?" she asked.

"Takoda smelled your campfire from a mile away and led us here," the Vanir woman said, adjusting her dragon's saddle. Kari shrugged at Kalina and grabbed her small bag of belongings off the ground. Leif eyed the women before doing the same.

"I will follow wherever you go," he said, his voice low and quiet. She nodded back in acceptance.

"Let's go then." She grabbed her own bag and followed Sunniva to her ice-blue dragon.

"This is Takoda." Sunniva introduced. He snaked his huge head down to get a good look at Kalina.

"Well met, Queen Kalina of the Valdir." His voice was as deep as the ice floes that dominated northern Askor and it resonated through Kalina. She shivered slightly before responding.

"Well met, Takoda. May I ride on your back?" She thought it might be polite to ask since he hadn't offered.

"Yes."

Kalina gave him a small bow and then followed Sunniva up into a double leather saddle. She strapped herself in and then pulled her cloak tightly around herself. That's when she inspected Sunniva's clothing. She wore leather like Kalina's but hers were bleached white, to blend in with their ice-covered surroundings. But over top, she wore a strange woolen cloak with a white fur-trimmed neckline that wrapped around her shoulders and upper torso, clearly keeping in the heat and not flapping away in the wind like Kalina's cloak did. Perhaps she could ask Sunniva to get her one once they arrived wherever they were going.

"Where are we going?" she asked over the roaring of the wind as Takoda beat his enormous wings to gain altitude.

"To my village. There you will be safe."

"Where is your village?" Simen had mentioned the Vanir, but not their name. He had said they hadn't been seen for hundreds of years. Suddenly, a dozen unanswered questions occurred to Kalina but she bit them back. There would be time, she hoped, to have them answered.

"North," Sunniva said, and then they were winging their way north, deep into the snow-covered wilderness.

The Vanir village was nestled between two ice-capped peaks, a dense forest filling the valley between and hiding the village from view. One end of the valley was blocked by the huge ice floes of the Snowcap Glacier, the other by high mountain peaks beyond. These mountains were much taller than her beloved Great Grey Mountains, the tallest peaks she'd ever seen, their sides covered in a thick layer of snow and ice. There was no way in or out except by dragon. The only indication of a village there were the occasional spirals of smoke that drifted up through the thick canopy below. It was no wonder they'd gone undetected for centuries. No one could get up here to bother them.

Sunniva and Astrid landed with their dragons in a clearing a mile or so south of the village and together their little group walked the rest of the way. Underneath the tall trees, the branches had been stripped away for the first twenty or so feet so that the dragons could walk comfortably beneath their spreading branches.

Kalina was introduced to the piebald dragon, named Hinto. He had an easy laugh and he walked beside them, making jokes about them almost freezing to death.

"You are like newborn dragons trying to walk on a frozen lake," he pointed out with a deep chuckle as they slipped and slid on the hard-packed snow beneath the trees. Kalina was exhausted by the time any habitation came into view, her muscles screaming at keeping her upright and her bottom a little sore from slipping and falling a few times. Hinto had used his tail to help her up when she'd fallen.

The village consisted of a few dozen log cabins, sturdily built, their entrances covered over in huge wolf furs, twice the size of any wolf pelts Kalina had ever seen. Leif nodded to them and whispered in her ear.

"We have wolves that big in the Great Grey Mountains, but you rarely see them. Usually, only the dragons will spot them when flying very high and they are notoriously hard to kill." He looked around at the houses that were slowly waking up, their inhabitants coming outside to see the newcomers and cook their breakfast over outdoor firepits. "These people are hearty and strong. I wouldn't be surprised if they've killed this many of the beasts themselves, rather than the dragons."

Kalina saw a fierce respect in Leif's eyes as he surveyed the Vanir. She knew her own people were strong, but the Vanir had successfully avoided detection for so long, and they had eked out an existence in such a harsh and barren landscape. Perhaps they were stronger than the Valdir.

A cry caught Kalina's attention and she looked up, surprised to see a familiar face among the gathering crowd of Vanir. Bri, the girl Eira had set in charge of her little brother Osian back in the Valdir camp, ran forward, her battle braids in disarray, fresh tears streaming down her face. She fell at Kalina's feet and prostrated herself, sobbing. It took a moment for Kalina to parse out what she was saying.

"Your Majesty, I am so s-sorry. I c-couldn't get away, and th-then they had me!" Her sobs and hiccupping obscuring the rest of what she said. Kalina knelt before the girl and pulled her up, smoothing the hair away from the girl's plump, freckled face.

"Bri. There's no need for tears. I am glad to see you alive." She hugged the girl to her, and Bri's arms went around her waist tightly. Kalina held in her questions for a moment, letting the girl relax. It was all she could do not to scream for her little brother, but she knew Bri would tell her what had happened once she'd calmed down. When Bri's crying had lessened, Kalina lifted the girl's face. "Where is Osian, Bri? Where is my brother?"

"He's here."

Kalina's heart leapt in her chest and then she was standing, dragging Bri with her and then following the girl through the crowd, ignoring the curious faces of the Vanir arranged around them. Bri brought her to a warm looking hut with little windows cut into the wooden walls. The Valdir girl pushed back the door flap and Kalina followed her inside, hope raging through her for the first time in months. She had all but given up on her little brother, convinced that King Blackbourne had done something horrible to him. But suddenly, there he was, playing quietly on the floor of the hut, a Vanir woman quietly rocking in a chair nearby, making what looked like was one of those wrapping shawls she'd seen Sunniva and Astrid wearing.

"Osian," Kalina breathed before leaning down to scoop him up in a tight hug. He had grown since she'd last seen him, and he was sitting on his own, babbling baby sounds and learning to play with toys. She saw a little wooden dragon on the ground where he'd been a moment before. She breathed deep the sweet scent of him and felt some of the broken and lost pieces of her heart fall back into place. He was safe.

Chapter 32

"YOU ARE WELCOME HERE, QUEEN KALINA." Sunniva stood in the doorway, watching as Kalina clutched her brother to her. Bri stood to the side, tears spilling down her freckled face. Kalina reached out an arm and Bri leaned into her side.

"Thank you, Sunniva." Kalina kissed her brother's head and handed Osian back to Bri. Bri had carried him this far, she could trust the girl to take care of him a little longer. She turned to the older Vanir woman that sat in a chair, knitting needles in her hand, and gave her a slight bow. "And thank you for taking care of my brother and Bri."

The woman's green eyes crinkled at the corners, her lined face kind. Despite her features, the woman was built like an ox, all broad shoulders and wiry muscles. She stood up and went to Bri, putting a hand on the young Valdir's shoulder.

"It was no trouble. Osian is a fine young man, and Bri is the bravest young lady I've seen in a long time. She says she wants to come to the castle when she grows up and serve under you."

Kalina looked to Bri and smiled.

"I would be honored, Bri."

"I am Torill. The big man standing outside is Gunnar, my husband. This is our house, and you are welcome here."

Kalina glanced out the wolf skin door flap that Sunniva was holding aside and saw a big bear of a man standing beside Kari and Leif. Kari looked coiled, stretched taut as if she might snap at any moment. Leif was stony-faced and grim, his eyes fixed with intensity on her within the hut. She sighed. She couldn't keep them waiting.

"It's a pleasure to meet you Torill. And thank you for letting us stay. But I must go reassure my companions and show them that Osian is alive and well." She ran a hand over Osian's head, ruffling his dark curls. Bri followed her out the door, Sunniva, and Torill in close pursuit.

Astrid stood beside Gunnar, along with a few other Vanir, their hands not far from their weapons as they eyed Kalina and her companions. It seemed they were no more trusting than she trusted them, but here they were. They'd have to find a way to make peace.

Kari rushed to Bri and Osian, kissing both the girl and the boy on their brows and hugging them tight. Leif laid a firm hand on Bri's shoulder and gently touched Osian's back, but his eyes never left Kalina, who turned back to the blue-eyed leader.

"Sunniva, you said this is your village. Am I correct in assuming these are your people, and you're their leader?" Sunniva was only a few years older than Kalina, perhaps in her mid-twenties, but she had an air of authority about her that was unmistakable.

"You are correct."

"Then would you mind telling me how Bri and my brother arrived here, who the Vanir are, and how we've never known about another race of dragon rider before? And how do you know Lord Illeron? Why didn't he tell me of your existence?" Kalina couldn't help herself; the questions just poured from her like a dam breaking. Sunniva gave a small chuckle and put a hand on Kalina's shoulder.

"All in good time, Queen. First, let's get you all a hot bath, clean and dry clothing, and something to eat. Then we will discuss your questions."

Kalina reluctantly agreed. Despite the gnawing questions, a hot bath sounded like the most heavenly thing in the world. She followed Sunniva and Astrid along with Kari to a communal women's bathing house. It was situated over a small hot spring that sprang from a nearby rock formation and filled a small communal pool. A log house with two rooms had been built over the top, the pool split into two by a man-made dam, and the dirty water channeled outside the doors. Kalina slipped gratefully beneath the water and Astrid took away her and Kari's clothing to be washed. The heat was heavenly, and soon Kalina was drifting in and out of consciousness, lulled into a light slumber by the rising steam and heat and the soft murmuring of voices that filled the bathhouse.

"Kalina?" Kari's voice made her sit upright, splashing slightly as she looked around, slightly confused. "You fell asleep and were snoring," Kari said, splashing water at her with her fingertips. Kalina waved her away, yawning hugely and stretching. Despite the luxury of a hot bath and the bliss of dozing off, the weight of all that had happened settled back onto her shoulders and soon she was ruminating on what to do next.

An hour later they were gathered in a large long log-built hall that was clearly used for communal eating, celebrating, and meetings. There were long benches set around huge pinewood tables. Kalina, Kari, Leif, Bri, and Osian sat on one side of one, while Sunniva, Astrid, Torill, and Gunnar sat on the opposite. Kalina couldn't help but marvel at the similarities between the Vanir and the Valdir. Even their names had been drawn from the Runark language, spoken by the gods. And now, with her people dressed in their off-whites, greys, and blues, they looked more alike than different. So many questions filled her head, but she had to pick the right ones. First things first.

"How did Bri and Osian come to be here?" she asked, stroking her brother's soft brown curls as he lay against her breast, sleeping.

"We often fly patrols across the Riverlands to the southern mountains. Usually, we are hunting, sometimes we are searching for supplies. One such patrol a few months ago came across a small party, armed to the teeth, dragging a silver-haired girl and a baby through the snow. We don't abide violence against children, let alone children who look like they could be one of our own. So we rescued her and the baby. She told us her story, told us of the Valdir, and an ancient myth among our people was suddenly confirmed," Sunniva concluded.

"What myth?" Kari asked, picking absently at the scarf that covered her torso. She looked softer somehow. The lighter colors smoothed out Kari's rough edges.

"The myth that we weren't alone. That millennia ago we split from a larger group of dragon riders and came north. The reason for the split is long lost to the snows, but the myth that we are descended from a southern race of dragon riders has been passed down for generations. Bri confirmed that for us."

Kalina frowned. If they knew Lord Illeron, then how could they not know about her? The story wasn't quite adding up.

"But then how do you know Lord Illeron?"

Sunniva shook her head.

"We don't know this Lord Illeron personally. But we do know one trader, whose name is Bron, who knows where we are. He signaled that he was coming yesterday evening and we met him in the woods after midnight. He told us that we would find three strangers by the river and that they would need our help. He told us one of you would be named Queen Kalina. When he told us that, we knew he told the truth for Bri had mentioned you before. So as soon as the light came, we went searching for you."

"How have you never heard of the Valdir before? We were in a war with Askor for over a century, and it only ended a few decades ago. And for the last year, I've been at war with a prince of Askor who had taken the Ethean throne from my mother." Kalina shook her head in disbelief. "How could you not have known?"

Sunniva shrugged noncommittally.

"We never cared to know. For hundreds of years, the King of Askor has hunted us, and whenever we were caught or captured, we were either tortured or sold into slavery. It is a well-kept secret, I imagine. And so in order to avoid that fate, we all fled into the wilderness, only coming out when absolutely necessary. We isolated ourselves from the rest of the world."

"Are there more of you than in this village?" Leif asked, ever the tactician. Kalina let a small smile flit across her lips at him before turning back to Sunniva. This village seemed small in comparison with her own Valdiran camp in the mountains, but she had seen enough to know the small huts and structures sprawled out into the mountains around them. She was sure it was larger than she thought.

"There are seven Vanir clans, each living in villages throughout the Ice Fang Mountains. We often trade with one another but all of us remain hidden from the outside world, beholden to no one."

Kalina understood that all too well. Her people had fled from Ethean rule to escape a war that they were losing. They fled to keep their people safe, much like the Vanir.

"So, the King of Askor knows about you?" She was genuinely surprised that Blackbourne hadn't mentioned it, or used it as a way to control her.

"The current one has been particularly cruel, and only those high up in his court know of our existence. A few years back they attacked one of our villages and killed many, and enslaved a few, mostly Vanir women. The noblemen keep them locked in their private estates, not allowed out, not allowed freedom." Sunniva's voice had grown bitter. "Many of us lost friends and family that day. I lost someone I loved dearly." Her face had fallen, her usual tough exterior cracking for a moment.

"Then I have a proposition for you, Sunniva." Kalina handed the sleepy Osian back to Bri. "The King of Askor captured our dragons and some of our people. They languish within his walls while he amasses his armies to attack our country. Will you help us free our dragons, and fight back against the King of Askor? He has declared war on Ethea for the second time, and especially on the Valdir by capturing our dragons and we will not stand for it." Suddenly, the vague outlines of a plan began taking shape in her mind. "Will you join us?"

Sunniva looked to her companions, who had stayed quiet throughout the exchange. Astrid's face was fierce as she nodded to her leader. Torill and Gunnar nodded as well and Kalina relaxed slightly at their acceptance. Sunniva turned back to Kalina and her companions, looking them in the eyes before resting on Kalina.

"We will call all seven clans for a Gunnlaug and make a plan."

"What is a Gunnlaug?" Kari asked.

"A great gathering of the clans." Sunniva smiled grimly at them all and a spark of hope caught in Kalina's chest. Perhaps they would join her. Perhaps they had a chance. Perhaps, with her own forces rallied and these Vanir fighting by her side, they could take back their dragons and their people from Askor and finally win the war.

"Then let's get started," Kalina said, smiling back.

Chapter 33

KALINA STEPPED OUT OF TORILL'S cabin and headed back to the gathering hall. She'd just put Osian to bed, with Bri falling asleep beside him, and the fires in the small village were growing dim. The only light that penetrated the dense trees was the flickering of campfire light and the occasional star that poked through a break in the canopy overhead.

They had spent the entire afternoon and evening brainstorming ideas for how to attack the castle, how many troops they'd need, and how to free their captive dragons. Kalina had penned letters to both Eira and Rangvald, as well as to the monarchs of Ablen and Wostrad. Despite the chilly departure of Wostrad's delegation a few months ago, she hoped that they might join with her, along perhaps with Ablen, in fighting against Askor. She hoped with all her heart that Ablen answered the call, or they would be sorely outnumbered.

What Askor lacked in resources, they made up for in military might. Most of their young boys attended their prestigious military academy that sat just off the northwestern tip of Askor in a city called Stormbell. Kalina had only read about it in books in Askor's library, but it seemed that their men and boys were trained for military life at a young age. Once they graduated, they were given professions, and then they bided their time. Once war was declared, the men of the country would gather at the capital to receive their orders. Kalina didn't know their exact numbers, but considering how depleted her own army and people were, she knew it would be more than they could defeat in battle. So she would need allies, as many as she could get, and as many aerial troops as could be found.

She was still contemplating their plan when a hand shot out of the dark and grabbed her wrist. Within mere heartbeats, she had drawn a blade and had it poised to slit the throat of her attacker, her body quivering with anticipation of a fight. But the face that loomed out of the velvety darkness was Leif's, his grey eyes wide in astonishment. Kalina let out a breath and lowered her knife.

"Don't scare me like that. I could have gutted you."

"And I would have let you, my Queen." His voice was silky and quiet and seemed to slide over her skin like water. She looked more deeply into his eyes and saw the truth written there. He wouldn't have fought her, he would have let her kill him.

"Why?" she breathed. His hand on her wrist loosened as he stepped back a pace and Kalina felt the distance between them grow by miles.

"Because it is your right, as my Queen."

Anger, bright and vicious, bloomed up within her. She had finally had enough of his distance, his formality, his disinterest. She wanted this settled once and for all.

"You know I had no choice, Leif. It was either marry Simen or plunge us into war." Her voice was harsh but she didn't care as she continued. "But you abandoned me. You left me as soon as the going got tough. As soon as you realized you couldn't have me for yourself, you left."

She watched in satisfaction as his face crumpled. Good. She was finally getting through to him. Finally crumbling that stony exterior.

"What was I supposed to do? Be your man on the side? Pine after you while you went off and married a foreign prince? I couldn't do that. So I ended it."

"We didn't even talk about it. There was no discussion."

"You're right, my Queen," he practically spat. "There was no discussion because you made the decision without me. So I made mine without you."

"Did you ever really love me?" she asked, her anger beginning to fade. He was right, after all, she had put them in this situation in the first place. How could she truly blame him for trying to save himself?

"I did, once."

Leif let go of her wrist then and turned to stalk away into the darkness. Kalina felt deflated, empty. And all she wanted was to call after him, to tell him to stop, that she wanted to be with him. But in the wake of all that had happened, she knew he'd feel like it was a consolation prize. And she didn't want that for him. She swallowed hard against the tears that threatened to flow down her cheeks and turned back towards the long wooden hall and the light that spilled from its door. She had cried over him enough. She had other things to worry about than a jilted lover. They were at war.

The next few days were spent in councils and training sessions with the Vanir. Kalina and Leif avoided one another whenever possible, but she couldn't help but shoot him furtive glances across the village whenever he was in sight.

She spent hours every night playing with Osian and then putting him to bed, grateful for uninterrupted time with her little brother. She had decided he should be raised in the Valdir highland camps, instead of at the castle in Ravenhelm with her in order to keep him safe and to allow him to grow up away from the taint of politics and royalty. But that also meant she'd never really get time to bond with him in the way she wanted. Perhaps that would change once they went home. Perhaps she would keep him at the castle with her instead.

A week after they'd arrived in the Vanir camp, a cry went up, announcing visitors. Kalina stood from where she'd been helping Torill make bread by an outdoor fire and wiped her hands on her white pants. She, Kari and Leif had decided to remain in their Vanir clothing, at least until it was time to go into battle when she knew she would don her Valdir leathers once again. But in the extreme cold of the northern Ice Fangs, it was warmer to wear Vanir clothing.

The concussion of many wing beats met her ears and she ran to the entrance to the village, closely followed by Kari and Leif, Torill and Gunnar, and finally, Astrid and Sunniva, who had been on the opposite side of camp. A scout Kalina had briefly met named Dag and his pale purple dragon landed on the edge of the glacier, behind him a riot of colorful dragons landed, and her heart soared.

She searched for familiar faces and found many. Eira sat atop her burnt orange dragon, Achak, and was at the head of the fleet. But Kalina saw other Valdir she'd known who'd chosen to stay back at the highland camps, including her former council members, Arvid, Asta, and Ingvar. All three had left the capital as soon as they'd realized how cramped and confined it was, and instead, accepted Kalina and Leif's invitation to help her run the highland camp with Eira and Halvor.

As the Valdir filed in among the trees, their dragons following Dag's dragon off to where the Vanir's dragons had dug dens into the mountainside, Kalina caught sight of Halvor among the warriors. His hulking frame was hard to miss. After greeting Eira and her former council members, she went to Halvor, to give him the news about Jormungand.

"I'm sorry, Halvor. I never meant for him to be captured, taken," she concluded after recounting what had happened at the castle. The big man's face had fallen at the news and a single tear had slipped down his cheek. He hastily wiped it away before looking up at his queen.

"You did what you could, your Majesty. And we will get him back."

She appreciated the determination in his voice. She put a hand on his broad shoulder and squeezed.

"That we will, my friend. That we will."

That night there was much feasting, as a second Vanir clan had arrived later that afternoon. The small valley was beginning to feel cramped and Kalina wondered how much longer they would be able to avoid detection with this many people and dragons coming and going. It was good to be surrounded by her own people once again and she spent hours talking with Eira and catching up. Eira had been ecstatic about finding Osian and Bri and had hugged them both tight until they both began to protest. It helped to heal Kalina's bruised and broken heart.

The next evening as they were all settling in around a campfire in front of Torill and Gunnar's house, another shout went up from the border of the camp. Kalina followed Kari and Sunniva to the edge of the camp where a small ring of Vanir guards surrounded a tall cloaked figure.

"Remove your hood, stranger," Sunniva demanded. The stranger reached up and pushed back his hood, revealing a long face. Kalina cried out and rushed forward, throwing her arms around Lord Illeron. The older man hugged her back.

"Lord Illeron! You are alive!" When she stepped back and released the man she turned to Sunniva. "This is my Spymaster, who contacted your trader and asked you to find us. He is the reason we escaped the castle alive."

Sunniva's eyes narrowed in suspicion and she didn't lower her weapon, a short bow with an arrow aimed right at the man's heart.

"How did you find our camp?"

"Your trader friend brought me within walking distance. He told me which direction to take. He said to tell Sunniva that 'the summer holds much promise'. Although I confess, I don't know what that means."

Sunniva relaxed her bow, taking a step back, a small smile playing on her lips.

"In that case, be welcome, Spymaster."

Kalina finally let out a breath, relieved that he hadn't been shot on sight. She turned to him, eyeing him from head to toe.

"You must be cold. We can talk by the fire."

They all trudged back to Torill's fire where Torill served Illeron a bowl of hot bowl elk stew. He dug in gratefully and told Kalina and Kari his story between bites. He had gone back into the city, holing up in a nondescript tavern until the search for Kalina had died down. Then he had used his many contacts and spies within the city to find out what was happening in the capitol. It seemed their dragons were being kept in their eyrie, which had been built with their size, weight, and strength in mind. Kalina had been mistaken, they weren't converted horse stables. King Blackbourne had planned to take the dragons all along and had the stables built just for that purpose. Lord Illeron also said that Kalina's entourage was imprisoned beneath the castle, their ships confiscated, and Prince Simen had been confined to his rooms. The King was amassing an army to strike Ethea and he was using the lands north of Winterreach to do it.

"So they don't know about us, or where we went? They won't come here?" Sudden fear of Askor getting ahold of her brother once again took hold. She also didn't want the Vanir put at risk any more than they already were. There were women and children here, along with the very old who deserved protecting.

"Not that I've been able to find out. I believe we are safe here. But our people have not been treated kindly within the castle, and the fate of the dragons is unknown," Lord Illeron said.

"Then we need a plan. We need to at least try to save our dragons and our friends before the war starts. He will use them against us if we don't." He already was, she thought. She looked around the campfire at new friends and old. "We will sneak in tomorrow as the rest of the Vanir arrive and our army assembles." Heads nodded around the fire in agreement. Kalina's stomach clenched in anticipation.

Chapter 34

THE NIGHT SEEMED TO STAND FROZEN around them as they slunk through the quiet streets of Winterreach towards the towering castle walls. Kalina had originally chosen a small group of fighters to accompany her: Kari, Lord Illeron, and Leif, but then Torill had volunteered. Kalina had asked her to stay behind and help Bri look after Osian. Eira had offered to come as well but Kalina needed her to be her eyes and ears while she was gone. So, she had also chosen Astrid, and Sunniva, who had insisted ongoing, and finally, Dag. Together, the seven of them had donned their weapons and flown as close to the city as possible without being detected. Lord Illeron had led them into the city through secret ways only he knew.

The sun had set as they'd landed and had entered the city under the cover of darkness. Torches lit the high imposing granite walls, and Kalina paused in the cobblestone street for a moment to stare up at their magnitude. She hadn't really considered how hard it might be to break into Winterreach castle. What if they failed? What if she couldn't free Maska, or Delisa or Jormungand? What if they were lost forever? She shook her head and ran to catch up with the others. She couldn't think that way. She glanced sideways at Leif as they ran down the street that bordered the long wall around the castle. He ran with an easy grace, and she couldn't help but admire the lean line of him, his strong jaw and the way his body moved as he ran. But as he looked towards her she quickly focused on the road ahead, refusing to let him see the longing in her eyes.

Lord Illeron led them to a postern gate, a small, ancient wood door set deep into the stone, an iron padlock holding it in place. He produced an equally ancient key from somewhere inside his cloak, fitted it to the lock and turned it. It made an awful screeching sound as it turned, and Kalina found herself instantly on the balls of her feet, looking around in all directions for an attacker, something to fight. But there was nothing, and with a shove, Illeron had the door open, ushering them through.

Kalina looked up at the massive stone archway as she passed through it and she found herself in a vegetable garden, realizing they must be near the kitchens. The cold air smelled faintly of rosemary and thyme as they made their way to a door that led into the castle itself. Illeron knocked three times, paused, and then knocked three more times. Then he motioned for them to hide. Kalina melted into the shadows below the towering castle walls where soldiers patrolled at regular intervals. She pulled her hood still higher, keeping her silver hair covered and hidden beneath its dark folds.

After what felt like a lifetime, the door to the kitchens opened and a maid stepped out onto the small patch of cobblestones that outlined a pathway through the garden. She was wiping her hands on her stained apron and watching the dark. Wonderful smells of baking bread wafted towards Kalina and her stomach gave a small gurgle.

"Ademar?" The woman called into the dark. There was a rustle and Kalina saw Lord Illeron step into the light. She frowned. Had she known Lord Illeron's first name? She must have, but she couldn't recall when it had been told to her. Her cheeks warmed slightly with shame at not knowing her most trusted Ethean council member's first name. She joined him as the rest of their party left their hiding spots.

"This way," Illeron said, ushering them inside the kitchen where the maid let them out into a servant's hall after looking both ways for anyone who would discover them. Then Lord Illeron led the way down the hallway and up a flight of stairs, further into the castle and farther away from safety. Kalina's stomach clenched the deeper inside Winterreach castle they ventured, watching around corners and hiding in alcoves and inside small rooms whenever roaming guards went by. Finally, they paused on a lower floor, slowly snaking their way towards the parade grounds and the dragon eyrie, when Kalina spoke up, whispering to Lord Illeron.

"But what if we can't escape on the dragons? What if we are caught and have to flee?"

He looked back at her, his hood hiding much of his long features. There was grey stubble on his cheeks now, and it made him look more intense than he already seemed.

"Back the way we came. Or the way I took you the first time we escaped."

He started forward, crossing the large hallway to the stairwell that led down and out into the parade grounds and the eyrie beyond. As they crossed the threshold of the stairs and out onto the packed earth of the training grounds, she couldn't help but look over at the barracks where only a week before she'd seen Talon and Captain

Higgs standing. She could only watch and hope that they were safe and well and that the King hadn't taken to torturing any of her people. Yet.

The group paused in the shadow of the farthest barracks, to catch their breath and discuss their attack on the eyrie, crouching to avoid the eyes of the soldiers that were currently marching past on the wall just beyond.

When Illeron outlined the plan, it seemed foolproof, but the hairs on the back of Kalina's neck were standing on end and her stomach was churning in constant knots. All the what-ifs and maybes flowed through her head and she was reminded of the last time she'd broken into a castle. It had been right after her mother's death, so she could claim her throne. This time it was a rescue so she could defend that throne. She sent up a prayer to Skaldir for strength and to the Mother for guidance. Maybe, just maybe, they could get through this.

The doors to the eyrie were large rolling doors on massive iron hinges that were currently chained shut. There were Askorian soldiers patrolling the perimeter in two minutes intervals and the padlock on those doors would prove too much for them to cut or pick in time.

"There is a small side door with a much smaller lock that will be easier to pick," Lord Illeron said. He glanced up at the large clock tower that was just visible over the outer wall. "I have a distraction planned for midnight. It will delay the guard patrols but I don't know how long. We will have to act quickly."

Leif and Sunniva nodded. They each had a set of lock picks that Illeron had given them and they had spent the day practicing using them. Leif looked to the Vanir leader and nodded.

"You'd better try first. You're better with them than I am." He gave a small self-deprecating smile. "I'm all thumbs!" Sunniva smiled back and then looked at Kalina.

"You ready?"

Kalina nodded. Kari reached out and squeezed Kalina's hand, her eyes as hard as her Queen's. Then the clock began to strike midnight. They waited one heartbeat, then two. Kalina's stomach began to drop into her feet, a growing fear that there was no distraction, and they would miss their window of opportunity.

Then they heard a shout echo across the courtyard. All nearby guards turned towards the sound, their weapons raised. This was their opening. Kalina bolted from their shadowed hiding spot and ran to the corner of the eyrie, peering around it. The guards on this side were running off in the direction of the commotion and she could see the smaller iron door that led inside to where the dragons were. Sunniva slipped ahead of her to the door, pulling her picks from the small pouch in her cloak.

The Vanir made quick work of the lock and soon the sound of opening metal hinges shattered the silence. Kalina froze, waiting for someone to cry out, to come running, but there was nothing. She slipped inside behind the Vanir leader, immediately the familiar musty smell of the dragons filling her nostrils. But there was another smell underneath it, the smell of rot, decay, blood, and iron. It made her stomach flip inside her, and fear grow.

The eyrie was lit by a single torch that hung in a bracket by the door. Kalina pulled it down and ventured farther inside, making for the stall she had left Maska in more than a week before. Her heart was in her throat as she turned the corner. She didn't know what she expected to find but a chained and defeated looking Maska was not what she'd wanted to see.

His usually emerald green scales were dull and dusty, the floor of his stall covered in his own feces, his wings held down with weights, his forelegs, back legs, and tail shackled to a metal plate in the floor. Her chest felt squeezed by overwhelming sadness and fear as she stepped closer, pushing her hood back from her face, revealing her silver battle braids, her scarred cheek, her Runark tattoos. She wanted to make sure he knew her, in case the captivity had changed him.

"Maska. Maska, my love," Kalina said softly, handing the torch to Sunniva who began lighting others. Kalina could hear her companions moving around her, Kari and Leif making their way to their own dragons. Sunniva, Astrid, and Dag went to help free the other captive dragons, but all Kalina could see was Maska's sleeping face.

He cracked an eye, his third eyelid slowly retreating until she could see the full black circle, spotted with stars that were his eyes. He lifted his head suddenly, rearing back from her, clearly disoriented and scared. She put both hands out, hushing and murmuring to him as he looked around, took in his surroundings and his rescuers.

"Kalina? Littling, is that you?"

Kalina all but sagged in relief at his deep voice. She stepped to the stall door and pushed it open.

"Yes, sweet Maska, it's me. We've come to get you out of here. To get you free." Every part of her wanted to run to him, to bury her face in his warm scales and feel his hot breath on her neck and forget any of this ever happened. But time was of the essence here and the bell outside had stopped tolling. It was only a matter of minutes before they were discovered. "We need to get you free from these chains."

"There is a master key, but only the King carries a copy," Maska said, his giant head snaking down. He sniffed Kalina thoroughly as she inspected the lock.

"Sunniva, can you pick these locks?" she called, and the woman vaulted over the wall to the next stall, taking out her picks.

"I believe so," She said and got to work. Kalina turned to Lord Illeron who had stayed by the door to the stalls, hovering and watching.

"How are we going to get them out of here without raising alarm? How are we going to get the others from the dungeons?"

"You won't. You'll have to leave them imprisoned for now. It would be impossible to free them without fighting your war here and now, with just the seven of us. And to get out, you'll have to either burn this building down or break down the roof and fly out."

Kalina didn't like the idea of leaving her people to rot in a cell, but she realized that they had no other choice. She had known it might be a long shot, freeing the dragons and her people, but that didn't make it hurt any less. As Sunniva unlocked the first of the manacles, Maska stretched his neck to the ceiling and inspected the huge timbers that stretched overhead. While the floor of each stall was made of solid metal plates, the building was constructed of massive timbers.

"I could perhaps break out of this roof, but a fire would weaken it nicely," he said.

"Fire it is then," Lord Illeron said nodding to Kalina who dug in her cloak for a handful of Emberweed. Each of the Valdir and

Vanir had brought a small handful, just enough for a few minutes of flame.

Sunniva unlocked Maska's last shackle and went to free the next beast. Kalina saw Leif working just as diligently on the other side of the eyrie. This wasn't an eyrie, Kalina realized. This was a prison. She was surprised she hadn't seen it before now. These weren't stalls, they were cells. Nausea rose within her at the thought, and she vividly remembered the days when she'd been stuck in a cell. She turned then and threw her arms around Maska's long neck.

"I missed you so much." She was practically sobbing now, but she swallowed it down as best she could. Maska snaked his head around her, cocooning her momentarily in warmth.

"I missed you too, Littling."

Sudden shouting echoed through the building and Kalina jumped back from Maska as they heard soldiers pouring in through the open door on the other side. Kalina turned panicked eyes to Lord Illeron.

"Everyone mount up! Now!" She shouted, launching herself onto Maska's bareback, clinging to the long spines that protruded from his neck. She stretched down and offered the Emberweed to Maska who swallowed it whole, the rumbling starting in his belly.

"What about Delisa?" Kari screamed at her from a few dragons over, her purple Yurok leaking smoke from his massive jaws.

"I'm sorry," Kalina said, her heart shattering inside her. They wouldn't be able to save Delisa. Not now anyway. Perhaps they could make a second rescue attempt. Kari's faced hardened and she turned away. Kalina turned back to Lord Illeron and reached a hand for him but he looked up at her and then down at the torch in his hand.

"Go. Now. I will delay them."

Before Kalina could scream at him to get on, to not be stupid, that they could burn their own way out, Lord Ademar Illeron turned and disappeared into the hallway, torch held out to the side, igniting the boards around him as he ran headfirst into the oncoming soldiers.

Chapter 35

KALINA SCREAMED AS MASKA, along with his fellow dragons around him, reared up. Maska opened his jaws and flame rocketed out of his mouth onto the wooden beams above. Kalina covered her head from falling debris as he and the other dragons shouldered their way out through the rapidly weakening roof. Kalina was coughing, her lungs full of smoke. Through the haze and fire she could see soldiers pouring into the long room, bows held aloft. But small bows like the ones they carried had no effect on thick dragon scales, and the projectiles bounced harmlessly off as Maska ripped down a massive beam and climbed up through a hole in the eyrie roof.

Kalina held on for dear life, dragging in grateful gulps of clean, cold night air as they sat for a moment atop the building, Maska stretching out cramped wings before launching into the sky. She could see Leif and Arikara a few dozen feet away doing the same, and a bit farther on, Kari and Yurok getting ready to take flight. Sunniva, Astrid, and Dag had mounted Jormungand's red dragon, Asa's light blue one, and Gyda's grey dragon. Together, they all winged into the sky above Winterreach castle. Gaining altitude, Kalina could see the Askorian soldiers below preparing their war machines and catapults for an aerial assault. But they were soaring away east now and would be out of range within moments.

"Stay east until the edge of the forest, and then turn north to the glacier. There is a camp there of Vanir, my ancient ancestors," Kalina explained to Maska as they flew. She told him of all that had happened while she'd been gone and he told her about his capture. On the night she and Simen had returned to the castle, the dragons' evening venison had been drugged with valerian and he and the other dragons had fallen into a deep sleep. When they'd awoken, they'd been chained. He made no mention of torture of any kind, but through the deep magic that ran between them, she could sense his immense sadness, his pain. Anger stirred within her. She would make the King of Askor pay for his crimes against her, her dragon, and her country. She would avenge all those she had lost since she'd first discovered she was Valdir.

"Good. Hold on to that anger, sister. Use it to fight."

A voice broke through Kalina's imaginings of tearing the King limb from limb. She turned to see Sunniva flying beside her on Jormungand's red dragon Shania. The Vanir's own blue eyes ablaze with the same hatred and anger as her own. She nodded to the Vanir leader, before glancing back at the scattered line of dragons flying behind them in the night sky. With an aerial legion at their back, Ethea attacking from the west, and maybe Ablen attacking from the east, they just might have a chance. Kalina stoked the anger inside her and a ferocious smile played across her lips.

It was a happy reunion all around when they landed in the Vanir village just as the sun rose over the horizon. Halvor was waiting for them when they landed and Kalina's heart sank when she saw his eyes roving over their faces hungrily, especially when he saw Shania. Kalina put a hand on his shoulder as he passed, knowing there was nothing she could say to fix the situation. She stayed by Maska's side, leading him further into the camp to where Eira stood with Osian in her arms beside Torill's fire.

"Anyone hurt?" she asked, looking over their shoulders towards the others. "Were you able to free anyone?" Kalina shook her head and sat on the ground heavily, Maska flopping to the cold earth behind her. As Kari approached, Eira gave her daughter a fierce hug.

"We weren't able to free anyone but the dragons. And I don't know what happened to Lord Illeron," Kalina said her voice choking on the words, filling Eira in. Ademar. His name kept echoing in her head. She put her head into her hands and wept, the sudden torrent of emotion brought on by a night of no sleep and too much excitement and stress. She had already lost so many men. Could she stand to lose more in a war?

A gentle arm around her shoulder made her look up through her tears at Eira who crouched beside her. Osian was perched on the older woman's hip, chewing on one of Eira's long braids. Kalina smiled at her aunt's warmth, along with Osian's beloved face. She reached out to take her brother and bounced him on her lap for a moment, before hugging him to her. At least she had him. She was fighting this war for him, and other children like him who wanted to live in a time of peace. She would have to make sure she won.

Kalina paced the long stretch of wood floor between two massive tables in the long hall of the Vanir camp. The last of the

Valdir had arrived, each dragon carrying at least one Ethean soldier on its back across the mountains, adding a small ground force to the one they already had. The final clan of the Vanir arrived not long afterward for the Gunnlaug, filling the small valley to the brim.

The Gunnlaug was a large meeting, usually held at important times when every head of clan was needed to make decisions. It began with a large banquet full of drinking and celebrating, allowing the clans to come back together and catch up with one another. Kalina and the Valdir joined in but she was a little overwhelmed by the noise and boisterous nature of the Gunnlaug. She remembered her own Valdir celebration experiences being a bit tamer in comparison.

The door to the hall banged open and everyone turned to look as a huge Vanir with a long braided silver beard stepped inside. He grinned around at them all before striding purposefully to a seat beside Sunniva.

"Sunniva, how good to see you!" he boomed, clapping her hard on the back. "I see your little clan has been doing well."

Kalina watched as Sunniva stiffened in her seat.

"Greyson. Glad you could join us," she ground out through her teeth. Greyson grinned.

"You know I can never resist a Gunnlaug!" He surveyed the gathered Valdir and Vanir still grinning. "And who are these lovely newcomers?" He winked at Kalina. She scowled slightly. She couldn't decide whether she liked his brusque personality or not.

"This is Queen Kalina of the Valdir and Ethea. These are her entourage." Sunniva then introduced Kari, Leif, and Eira. Greyson nodded all around. Finally, he turned back to Sunniva.

"So, why am I here? Why did you drag me all the way from my mountain home for a Gunnlaug?"

"The Valdir are our brethren, our cousins, our friends. They are going to war against Askor and would like to ask us to join." Sunniva said, standing up to look the large Vanir in the face. "So you will sit, and give them your attention."

Greyson smirked at Sunniva but sat anyway, turning to look at Kalina expectantly. She drew in a breath and began explaining why they needed the Vanir's help. When she finished, she put her hands on the big table before her.

"And so I ask you, will you join us in a war against Askor?"

640

She searched each face around the table in the gathering hall, looking for allies among them.

"Leave us to talk it over," Sunniva said with a polite nod to Kalina. The Queen of the Valdir stood and left the hall with her entourage in tow. While they waited for the Vanir to decide, Kalina leaned against Maska who lay outside the lodge, curled into a small ball in the freezing snow. That was something Kalina had begun to notice. The Vanir's dragons were specially equipped to live in colder climates. They tended to be larger-bodied than her dragons, and somehow were able to regulate their body temperatures better than the Valdir dragons could. So there was Maska, curled up like a cat trying to stay warm. She felt a twinge of sadness for him.

A last the door to the gathering hall opened and Sunniva beckoned them inside. When they'd finally taken their seats, the Valdir waited in anticipation for the Vanir to deliver their answer. Finally, Sunniva spoke.

"The Snowy Owls will join." Her conviction evident in her voice, her beautiful face determined.

"The Black Wolves will join," Greyson said beside her. The Black Wolves were a northern tribe of Vanir from up by Crystalmount and the Ice Gulf to the north.

Soon after, all the other clans joined. The White Bears, the Red Foxes, the Brown Elks, the Blue Dragons, and the Golden Eagles. Each leader spoke up, pledging their fighters to her cause. Kalina had to fight to hold back tears as hope flooded her chest.

There wasn't a place you could go to be alone anymore. In the hall around her, the heads of each clan and her own council members gathered for a war council. Kalina's own army was only days away from making landfall south of Winterreach in Askor's Riverlands. Aerial scouting had revealed that the Askorian army was arrayed north of the city, in a vast sea of white tents. So Kalina had instructed Rangvald to land the army to the south, making their way up the rivers and waterways until they could go no farther, and then march inland where they would meet up with her aerial legion. She had also learned from one of the other Vanir clans that a second army, almost as large as the first was stationed north of Stonewell on the eastern coast of Askor. The plan was set, it was solid. So why was her stomach in knots?

The doors to the hall banged open and a Valdir messenger that she recognized strode in, removing fur-lined gloves from his hands, and unwrapping a cloth from around his face. She had sent him to Ablen on her behalf in the desperate hope that they would help by attacking the eastern coast. He gave her a small bow.

"Report, Kalern," Kalina said, anxiety churning in her gut.

"The King and Queen of Ablen sent their regards and their support. They are happy to have Ethea as an ally, and their ships are now poised to attack the eastern coast of Askor at your command. They will land in Stonewall within a few hours once they've received word."

Kalina's heart lightened. If they could manage to split Askor's forces, then it would stop them from getting bottle-necked and fighting a war on two sides.

"Very well. Once you've rested, please fly back and instruct them to attack with all haste. We must try to keep that half of his army occupied."

The messenger nodded and bowed to her, heading back out the doors. Kalina finally sat down, Eira on one side of her and Kari on the other. Now was the time to make the final decisions.

"We need an advantage. We have the dragons, yes, but they have catapults that can shoot fiery rocks into the air. If we aren't careful, if someone gets distracted, they will die." She remembered all too well Geir's death. He was Leif's father, her second in command, and her own father's best friend. He had been killed by a catapult when he had failed to swerve mid-air. She didn't want the same thing to happen now to more people and dragons. "Back home we have something called Emberweed. My Valdir have brought our entire supply."

"What is Emberweed?" Sunniva asked for the benefit of the other leaders. She had seen it in use during the rescue, but the other chief's had never heard of it.

"It is a weed that once dried and consumed by a dragon, mixes with the acids in their stomach to allow them to breathe fire."

"I thought that was a myth, some silly legend we told our baby dragons?" Astrid said, a small smile on her face. "It can't be real?"

"Would you like me to demonstrate?" Kalina asked, excitement finally beginning to replace the worry and fear in her chest.

"Absolutely." Sunniva stood, the other clan leaders followed, and together they crossed the threshold to the outdoors. Maska and many of the other dragons waited outside in the cold, curled in on themselves like enormous cats. The Valdir's dragons were not quite built for the extreme colds, not like the ice dragons that the Vanir rode, and they sometimes had trouble regulating their body temperature. Kalina wasn't built for this climate either, and she pulled her wolf skin cloak tighter around her as they waited for a young Valdir to fetch a small packet of the Emberweed. Finally, when he returned, Kalina held it up to Maska.

"Want to give them a little show?" She asked, grinning mischievously. Maska opened his mouth in a toothy smile back and took the packet from her hand, swallowing it whole.

Within a few moments, his belly began to glow like the deep center of a forge fire. He rumbled for a moment before belching flame ten feet long into the night sky above them. Sunniva and the other Vanir gasped, stepping back, their faces lit by the Dragonfire. Maska kept the flame going for a few minutes before letting it die, his belly considerably darker when he finished. He let out a few smaller bursts of flames and then there was no more.

"The riders will carry pouches with them, to be fed to their dragons while fighting. If we target their war machines, their command tents, weapons, and supplies, then perhaps we will have a chance. They outnumber us four or five to one, even with Ablen and all of Ethea at our backs. We are few but we are mighty!"

Sunniva grinned at her, the other clan leaders smiling behind her, looks of awe on their faces. Sunniva took her own ax from her belt and held it aloft for all to see.

"To war!" she exclaimed, the Vanir and Valdir cheering in response.

That night they sat around a large bonfire as the Vanir played songs; eerie and melancholic tunes from strange flutes and drums rose into the darkness above, echoing off the branches overhead. Kalina sat back against Maska's warm side, her face to the fire, with Osian asleep on her chest. This was the calm before the storm, and she knew it. So she took every moment she could to savor it. In a week she would be knee-deep in gore on a battlefield instead of warm by a fire with her brother. She pressed a soft kiss to his forehead and looked up to see Leif watching her from across the orange and yellow flames. His eyes were intense, but soft at the same time, and when he noticed her staring back, he nodded to her. It felt as though something had shifted then, but Kalina didn't quite know what.

Chapter 36

THE RIVERLANDS SOUTH OF WINTERREACH were bitterly cold, the wind howling across the open plains, causing tents to flap, banners to snap and campfires hard to keep lit. Kalina paced back and forth in the large command tent, surrounded by her council and the seven Vanir clan chiefs. They all stood around, eating and drinking, and waiting. Five days ago Ablen had attacked the eastern coast, drawing King Blackbourne's eastern forces into battle. Now her own regiments were due to land any moment now, the waiting feeling interminable. Once the full force of her army arrived, they were to march on Winterreach Castle, and hopefully defeat the King, end the war, and rescue her incarcerated people.

A shout went up from the direction of the river. Rangvald's ships had been sighted. Kalina looked to Leif who stood nearby, and together they strode from the tent. The camp around them was sprawling, numbering in the thousands and filled almost entirely with Vanir, dragons, and Valdir. They had left their small Ethean ground force back at the Vanir camp to protect it, while all able-bodied Vanir came to fight. And now there were huge deep-water galley's sailing up the center of the river, where it was deepest and widest. It would be a challenge offloading all the soldiers and supplies.

Kalina organized multiple dragons and riders to start ferrying people over to the northern shore from each ship. She could see at first glance that Rangvald had brought the entire Ethean army. There were dozens of ships, all flying the crossed swords on a green field banner. She hadn't even known that many ships existed in the Ethean armada.

When she spotted Rangvald's silver hair among the disembarking Etheans alongside his burnt orange dragon Una she ran to meet her cousin. She flung herself into his arms, and startled he took a step back, laughing over his shoulder to Leif and Kari who watched.

"I've missed you, cousin," Kalina said in his ear before pulling away to look at his face. His handsome face and blue eyes so like her own were more lined, more careworn than the last time she'd seen him when she'd sent him to get control of her army. Looking around them it seemed he'd done a good job.

"Where'd you get all the ships?" Kari asked, on her tip-toes and looking down the river.

"Well, I called in a favor with Wostrad. They were willing to loan ships, but not military might. So they sent these with minimal crews north where we boarded and made all haste here."

"How many men did you bring?" Leif asked, stepping forward to clasp Rangvald's hand.

Kari came and gave her brother a fierce hug before he could answer. Finally, Rangvald turned and pointed down the shore of the river.

"The big galleys hold about two hundred men. Each smaller one holds between fifty to one hundred fifty men. All told I've brought the entirety of the current standing Ethean army, numbering about four thousand."

Kalina bit her lip, doing mental math. That meant their combined army stood at around six thousand. But all reports from her spies told her that King Blackbourne had an army of well over ten thousand. And that was just here at the castle, not including the force to the east. That was almost a two-to-one odds. And would the dragons along with the Emberweed, what little they had, be enough to tip the scales? She had to hope so.

"Good. Then let's assemble and begin marching north. Load the dragons up with the weapons and gear. I want the soldiers as unburdened as possible."

Kalina went back to the command tent where the others waited and gave the command to move out. Then she went through the back tent flap to her own small tent which was connected to the command tent and began packing. When she stepped outside, her bag thrown over her shoulder, she saw Leif waiting by Arikara and Maska in the morning light.

Things had changed between them since that night around the campfire after the Gunnlaug. He had softened towards her, his iron resolve to put distance between them had wavered and broken, and suddenly she felt like she'd gotten her best friend back once more. Things weren't back to normal, but they were better and Kalina finally had hope for her future.

Two days later the vast armies of Askor came into view on the Riverlands before Winterreach castle. Kalina stopped her army, setting up camp across the vale from the enemy, and within eyesight. She set up sentries and patrols, and the air was constantly filled with wing beats as various airborne patrols flew through the skies.

The council tent was crowded, the gathered people tense as they prepared to attack. Kalina sat fiddling with a cup of wine, watching the Vanir chief's, including Sunniva, argue over the best course of action. Sunniva wanted to send in an aerial attack, going on the offensive. Greyson surprisingly agreed with her, but the leader of the Blue Dragons didn't want to put their dragons at such risk. She suggested that Kalina send in her foot soldiers before the dragons, to help thin and distract the Askorian troops. Others had different ideas about how best to attack. Kalina was a queen but she hadn't been raised to be a tactician. She usually left those things to people like Leif and Rangvald who had been raised during war. Both were sitting to her right, suspiciously quiet. She gently kicked Leif under the table and he looked over at her. Kalina gestured to the arguing chiefs as if to say,

"This is where you come in. Do your job!"

Leif raised one eyebrow with a look that said, "Aren't you the Queen? Isn't this your job too?"

Kalina let out a long sigh and sat up straighter.

"Ladies and Gentlemen," she said. But no one listened. Sunniva was now arguing rather loudly with Greyson, the chief of the Black Wolves. He was a particularly fearsome and stubborn chief and he and Sunniva had continued to butt heads since the Gunnlaug.

"Excuse me!" Kalina yelled, startling many of the gathered people into an awkward silence. Kalina stood up straighter, tugging on her leathers and looking around the large table. "I am no tactician. But I am Queen of The Valdir and Ethea, and you will listen." She looked to Greyson and Sunniva, the latter smirking up at her, while the former scowled into his own cup of wine. "Tomorrow, we are attacking the greatest army on this continent, and for all we know, in the world. We are outnumbered, and out armed, but what we lack in numbers we make up for in spirit and passion. King Blackbourne's army is made up of cowards and those only there as a matter of duty. But we are so much more. The Vanir and the Valdir are cousins, we share the same ancestors. We are family, the ice dragons and our dragons as well. And we have fought with Askor for too long. We have been under the boot of Askor's tyranny for too long. I will leave the specifics to Leif, but for my part, I will be out there fighting to protect my homeland. Fighting to end a war that has stretched on for centuries and decimated my people. Fighting to give the next generation safety. Fighting to finally have peace." She paused to look around the room and gestured to them all. "Why do you argue with one another? What are you fighting for?"

Silence followed her words, and she stood for a few moments, watching the shifting and uncomfortable faces of all those gathered. Finally, she tipped her goblet back and finished her wine, and then slammed the cup on the table, making everyone jump.

"I'm going to bed to rest up for tomorrow. I suggest you all do the same once Leif and Rangvald have outlined the battle plan." Then she turned on her heels and left a stunned room in her wake.

But she didn't rest. Not really. Instead she lay on her bedroll and stared up at the shadowy ceiling of her tent until the talking and fires outside had died down. A single voice rose and fell above the soft sounds of a camp falling asleep. A woman's voice singing a song in a long-forgotten language that Kalina didn't know. She focused on that voice and allowed it to lull her into an uneasy sleep.

A hand shook her awake and she looked up into Kari's concerned face.

"What is it?"

"Intruders in camp. I think you should hurry."

Kari left her and Kalina rushed to get dressed, pulling on her Valdir leathers and her battle crown, leaving the Vanir whites behind. She strapped her twin axes to her back and left the tent. It was still dark outside, the air freezing and she tied her fur-trimmed cloak around her neck as she followed Kari and a torch-wielding Ethean to a tent. Kari held the flap aside for her and Kalina ducked inside, the warm glow of lamplight illuminating the tent walls and lighting the faces of the two prisoners who knelt before her.

Prince Simen and his older brother Prince Ivan both knelt in the center of the tent, their hands tied behind their backs and their faces covered in bruises. Kalina looked to the two men standing guard over them. Leif and Rangvald had their arms crossed over their chests. Leif was giving Prince Simen a particularly deathly stare which almost made Kalina laugh but she held it in and addressed their prisoners instead.

"Prince Simen, Prince Ivan. What brings you to our camp?"

Prince Simen looked up and through swollen eyes gave her a big smile. His brother's face, however, was stoic, his eyes hard as he surveyed Kalina from head to toe.

"Queen Kalina! I was hoping I'd get to speak to you before they killed me!" he said rather cheerfully. Kalina did let out a small bark of laughter then. She had begun to miss Simen's eagerness, his boyish charm, his honesty.

"I'm glad they brought you to me instead of one of the Vanir. They might have killed you on the spot." She watched as Simen's eyes lit up with excitement at the other dragon riders' name.

"The Vanir? Is that what they are called? Are you related to them? How did you find them?" Prince Ivan gave his brother a shove and Simen fell silent, his mouth snapping shut. He looked to Kalina and gave her a small shrug. She smiled even broader but then pressed her lips together. This was no time for fun. She had to be serious. For all she knew they were spies.

"Why are you here?" she repeated.

"Well, we came to fight on your side."

Kalina looked to Prince Ivan and somehow doubted that was true for him.

"And you came to make sure your little brother didn't get himself killed, is that it?" She said to the older prince. Ivan nodded.

"I couldn't let him go alone."

"Admirable, Prince Ivan." Kalina turned back to Prince Simen. "And why, pray tell, would we let you fight for us?"

"Because my father is crazy, absolutely mad. He kept me locked up in my rooms and locked my fiancée, Evelyn, in the dungeons. Her father pleaded that she be released but my father refused. He said that I would marry no one if I wasn't going to further the alliance."

"How did you escape then?" Kalina pulled up a nearby stool and sat at eye level with their prisoners.

"Ivan here convinced Father that fighting would be good for me. That it would get the silly notion of running away with my love out of my head. But Ivan has always supported me. Even now." Simen looked sideways at his older brother who rolled his eyes back.

"I refuse to fight for Askor. And I believe that you will win. That perhaps you have a chance to help me free Evelyn and to live my life the way I choose instead of as just some pawn in my father's plan for domination."

Kalina felt for him. She really did. Just a few weeks ago she'd felt the very same, just some pawn in the King of Askor's sick game to take over Ethea. But here she was, fighting an all-out war that she wasn't sure she could win. But she wasn't about to tell Prince Simen that, especially not with Prince Ivan watching.

"I hope you can understand our predicament here, Simen. I cannot let either of you fight on our side. Not on the battlefield. I might believe you, but do you truly think that the Vanir will believe you? After years of oppression and violence against their people? They would as soon kill you as look at you." She shook her head. "I'm sorry, but you will both remain locked up and away from the fighting." She nodded to Leif and Rangvald. "But I want you to know, Simen, your loyalty and trust has not gone unnoticed. When we win this war, you will leave with your Evelyn wherever you wish to go in peace." She imbued her words with as much confidence as she could muster and then stood and left the tent. Kari followed her outside and Kalina put her hands on her hips.

The night was fading around them, the inky blackness of the sky fading to a deep blue and purple as light slowly returned to the world. Today was the day that would determine their fate. Whether they lived or died. She turned in a circle, taking in the lightening sky and the sleepy army camp just beginning to stir around her as it woke up. And that's when she saw the dark cloud on the horizon to the south.

Chapter 37

"**WHAT IS THAT?**" **KALINA ASKED,** pointing over the tops of the tents and out over the Riverlands to the south, still covered in a layer of snow and ice. The dark cloud was getting closer and she was beginning to panic. What new threat would they have to contend with?

Beside her, Kari squinted into the distance.

"It looks like some huge flock of birds."

But that didn't make any sense. Kalina launched herself into a run, darting between tents and sleeping bodies of men, women, and dragons, making her way back to her own tent behind the command tent. Just outside she found Maska, still dozing. She shouted his name as she got close and he came awake in an instant, his night-dark eyes sparkling with their inner stars. She vaulted onto his back and pointed at the oncoming cloud.

"Take me up there." Within moments they were airborne and he was winging his way swiftly towards the thing, or rather things, in the sky. They began to take individual shape the closer they drew. Kari was right, they did look like birds, but birds of every hue imaginable. And as Kalina drew closer, she began to smile. She knew what they were even before Maska was forced to dive below the huge flock of wyverns that flew straight towards them.

Kalina let out a whoop as the wyverns flew overhead, their own soaring voices joining her own as they began to circle and slowly make their way towards the ground at the southern end of her camp. Kalina and Maska followed them down and were soon met by Kari and her purple Yurok in the air. Kari's eyes were wide as she took in the fleet of wyverns. But Kalina was triumphant as they landed beside a small green wyvern that had been leading the pack.

Kalina dismounted and ran to the wyvern, throwing her arms around its neck and hugging it tightly.

"Savath! Oh, how I've missed you!" Tears came unbidden to her eyes as she held her old friend. When she pulled away, she saw joy and gratitude on the wyvern's snake-like face.

"It is good to see you, Littling." Savath's voice brought back such sweet memories of her first flight for Kalina. It had been such a pure moment, before everything had gotten so complicated, back when she was just an orphaned girl in an abbey looking for adventure.

"What are you doing here?" Kalina looked around at all the wyverns who surrounded her now. "And why are there so many?"

"They have all come for you, Littling. You fight to keep them free. You fight against a King who would capture and enslave us."

Kalina remembered the captive wyverns who had dragged the war machines that killed Leif's Father into the Wastes. She remembered how grateful they'd been when she'd ordered their release. Tears continued to flow freely down her cheeks.

"Thank you, Savath. You may have just turned the tide of this war."

With the added wyvern aerial support, they now numbered hundreds more. And a wyvern could carry a man, or supplies if need be. They were smaller and more agile than dragons and Kalina could think of a dozen ways in which they would be useful on a battlefield. She turned to Maska who stood patiently by.

"Savath, this is Maska, my partner."

Maska bowed his head deeply to the smaller wyvern, their colors complementary in the morning light: Maska emerald and Savath grass green.

"He will be your battle commander, along with Arikara and Yurok. Any questions you have, you can ask them and they will direct you and your forces."

Savath lowered her head in acceptance to both Kalina and Maska before turning to her troops of wyverns, giving them instructions. Kalina turned back to Maska, pressing her forehead against his huge scaled one.

"I have to go prepare."

"Go, Littling." Kalina smiled. Both Savath and Maska had always called her Littling, and it had become somehow precious to her. "I will see you before the battle commences."

Kalina joined Kari and together they flew on Yurok back to the command tent to tell the others the good news.

In her tent, she began strapping on the golden dragon scale armor that Leif had made her from Arikara's shed scales when the tent flap opened without preamble. Kalina drew her knife and turned to see Leif standing in the doorway, his handsome face twisted in an emotion she couldn't quite name. She sheathed her blade and returned to buckling on her armor.

"I almost knifed you," she said matter-of-factly. Leif nodded and stepped forward, helping her fasten the long dragon scale shirt under her arm. She left off struggling and let him help her.

"But you didn't." His voice was soft, making Kalina look up into his eyes. "Kalina, I-" he trailed off as he finished fastening her shirt and she slowly lowered her arm. His fingertips brushed over the exposed skin of her wrist for a moment before he reached for the leather bracers and began putting them on for her.

"What is it, Leif?" She was gentle, not wanting to scare him off, to ruin what small peace they'd found between them. Finally, he let out a long sigh.

"I want to ask you to stay here, to not fight. To flee, to run home and hole up in Ravenhelm and never come back out."

Kalina opened her mouth to reply, to say she'd never do that when he looked into her eyes, his grey ones full of some unnamed feeling.

"But that wouldn't be the woman I fell in love with."

Kalina snapped her mouth shut at his words, all protestations dying on her lips. Love? Did he just say he loved her?

"The woman I fell in love with never gives up, never runs from a fight, would never sit on the sidelines while her people suffered."

"Well, I did run that one time-," she began but he swiftly put a finger to her lips to shush her.

"You ran because you wanted freedom. You ran because you thought it was the right thing to do. But you never gave up. And you came back fighting. And now, you fight for your people's freedom." He put a finger beneath her chin and gently tilted her face to his, their height difference suddenly apparent. "And I love the woman before me."

Kalina's knees felt weak at those words. She opened her mouth to speak but before she could say anything, his mouth was on hers, drowning out any protestation or declaration. He kissed her sweetly at first, but soon there was an urgency to it, a need that only the looming tide of battle and death could instill. She met his urgency with her own desperation, devouring his kisses with a fervor that surprised even herself. She had never wanted anyone as much as she wanted him now. And yet, the only thing that passed through her mind was a vision of him lying dead on the battlefield. She broke away suddenly, panting with the pent-up need and fear.

"We must go," he croaked, his voice hoarse from their sudden passion. "I will see you on the field, my Queen." He gently kissed her hand, his eyes locking with her tear-filled ones before quickly exiting her tent.

Kalina stood there, alone for a few moments, gathering her breath and her fear. The panic and fear she'd learned to master so many months before were always lurking, waiting to catch her off guard, and now they were clawing at her, constant reminders. She swallowed hard, stuffing them down deep, covering them up with fierce determination and hope. For now, she had hope.

Chapter 38

THE ETHEAN FOOT SOLDIERS WERE arrayed across the vale before Winterreach castle, the Askorian army taking up their position across from them. Kalina sat astride Maska on a small rise, looking down into the vale. Leif and Arikara were by her side, her the army stretched before them, and beyond, across a great swath of field, they could see King Blackbourne and his forces arranged on the far hill, watching the fighters assemble. She had changed her mind just an hour before and allowed Prince Simen to fight with them because he was her friend, but she kept him close by her side. He stood by Maska's front left foot, his hand on his long sword, his face set as he watched his father's army across the empty field.

Kalina wasn't going to wait until King Blackbourne attacked, she was bringing the fight to him. She signaled her flying battalion led by Rangvald high in the air. A second aerial battalion led by Sunniva and consisting entirely of Vanir fighters flew in formation behind the Valdir and they swept out over the soon to be battlefield. Dragons in a rainbow of colors swooped overhead, casting great shadows on the ground before them, speeding towards Askor's army, their legs each clutching giant rocks, trees, and even hunks of ice from the glacier to the north.

Kalina's gut clenched in anticipation as she watched them fly in close enough to release their cargo on the waiting army and then turn quickly back to the safety of her lines. Askor's army retaliated as the rocks fell, launching volleys of arrows skyward and great flaming projectiles upward into the afternoon sky. But the dragons had been ready. They easily dodged each projectile and kept flying, as their dropped load thudded into the enemy lines, decimating whole squadrons of Askorian soldiers.

Next came the foot soldiers. Leif signaled to his captains and they began marching forward en mass. Kalina watched, her heart in her throat as each side sent volleys of arrows toward one another, the Askorian catapults doing irrevocable damage to her forces. But she gritted her teeth and sent in the wyverns with a second barrage of stones and projectiles from the sky. She cried out slightly in horror as a few wyverns fell from the skies, victims to the catapults, but the majority, including Savath, were able to drop their rocks and turn

655

back without getting killed.

"Target those catapults!" Leif roared above the din of battle, signaling to the aerial squadrons that flew overhead.

Rangvald motioned once again to Sunniva and together they flew closer, their battalions of dragons behind them, aiming for the catapults. Kalina watched as Sunniva dove, Astrid right behind her towards a catapult on the ground. Together the two women and their dragons tore the launching arm off the structure and carried it high into the sky, dropping it down on the screaming soldiers below. Kalina let out a breath she'd not known she'd been holding. Rangvald and his forces destroyed the other catapults in a matter of minutes, using a combination of large chunks of ice dropped directly from overhead and tearing the mechanisms apart as Sunniva had.

The battle raged on as the sun drew towards the western horizon, Askor's forces never seemed to dim or slacken, their lines ever replenished while Kalina's lines grew weaker, fraying at the edges, her soldiers beginning to flag. She was itching to be down there, fighting alongside her men as she had done with the Valdir in the past. But Leif, as well as many of her council members, had agreed that she was more valuable alive than dead.

She looked to Leif whose grim face confirmed her fears. She nodded to him and he signaled to the dragons to make yet another pass, this time each equipped with Emberweed. Massive gouts of flame erupted all across the battlefield as the dragons flamed great swathes of the enemy. For a moment, it looked like that was the advantage they needed, like they might be turning the tide of the war, and Kalina was just about to launch the rest of her forces forward into a final push to press their advantage, when a horn blew from somewhere behind her.

She turned in her saddle, and Maska snaked his head to peer backward.

"What do you see?" she asked anxiously. Maska's eyes were better than hers; he could see a small mouse running through the grass from a mile in the sky. He let out a snort of anger.

"A second Askorian force, the one from the eastern shore, has snuck up behind us," he said. "We are surrounded."

Kalina's heart sank in her chest. Leif reached across the distance between them and grabbed her hand reassuringly. She squeezed his hand back absently but her mind was racing. What had happened with Ablen attacking the eastern force? Where did this second army come from?

"Direct the wyverns and some of our ground troops to the rear, see if we can keep them back a while longer. Prince Simen, is there any way to break your father's lines? Any weakness you know of?"

"No, your Majesty. He has a huge supply of indentured and enslaved men and women to fight for him. He is not picky. He will throw every man, woman, and child in this country before you in order to win."

Kalina froze in her seat, watching the Prince's face.

"Did you say enslaved? Indentured? Are those people there because they are being forced?" She pointed out to the bloody battlefield where the fighting still raged. The Prince nodded.

"Yes. Part of the reason we are so mighty a nation is because we require military service from every single man born within our country's borders."

"Stop. Stop the fighting," Kalina whispered, suddenly having trouble breathing. They were killing innocent men and women. They were dying for a mad man's war. For her war. Her army was fighting out of loyalty and support and desperation. King Blackbourne's was there because they had no other choice. She couldn't kill them. "Stop. Surrender." She looked up into Leif's grey eyes, fear and immense sorrow filling hers.

Leif looked at her like she was mad for a moment before realization dawned on his face. Then he too became enraged. He bellowed to his captains to withdraw, to sound the surrender. Kalina watched in helpless sadness, fear, and rage as her armies broke away from the fighting and ran. A boom sounded beside her and she looked over to see Sunniva on her ice blue dragon, with Kari landing beside her, both angry and concerned.

"Why are we retreating? We need to keep fighting!" Sunniva said.

"We have them on the run, Kalina. Let us do our jobs!" Kari was obviously frustrated and Kalina could see an echo of their old quarrel in her cousin's eyes. But this time she wasn't being overly cautious. She was trying to save lives. She couldn't burn an entire army of innocents.

"Their army is full of slaves," she ground out, clutching her ribs. Her breath seemed trapped in her chest, panic a rising tide within her. "We cannot keep killing the innocent. Not anymore."

Kari and Sunniva looked to Leif who nodded.

"Tell everyone to retreat, and raise a flag of surrender."

"No." Kalina put out a hand to stop them. "Raise a flag of parlay. I need to speak to Blackbourne."

"Are you sure that's wise?" Leif asked, worry evident in the crease between his brows. Kalina nodded, the pain in her chest subsiding and a plan began to take shape.

"Yes. I need to see the King."

They met in a tent on a hill to the east, away from the city and the vale before it where their soldiers lay dead and dying. Kalina brought Leif, Sunniva, Kari, and Prince Simen with her. She left Rangvald in charge of the army and Eira in charge of setting up a field hospital to care for the injured. She didn't know what to expect but she entered the tent with her head held high and an expectation in her heart.

King Blackbourne was already seated in an oaken chair, his voluminous robes flowing around him, hiding the frail body that lay beneath. His age was certainly showing, his grey wisps of hair thinner still on the sides of his balding pate and his skin was sallower than the last time she'd seen him. But stress and war would do that to a person. There were bags beneath her own eyes that she hadn't had a year ago.

Arrayed behind him stood Prince Endre, Prince Julian, and his Queen, Marin. The redheaded woman smirked at Kalina when she entered, her foxes' eyes inspecting Kalina from head to toe, no doubt thinking that Kalina didn't look a thing like a queen. But Kalina didn't care in that moment. She was on a mission.

"King Blackbourne. Thank you for meeting with me."

"It seemed I didn't have a choice unless I wanted to slaughter your army in their beds." He said cruelly. Kalina gave him a smile anyway.

"You'd never catch us sleeping. But that's not why I'm here. I am here to discuss the terms of a parlay. A way to end this war between Askor and Ethea once and for all."

The King raised an eyebrow at her, obviously intrigued.

"And what, pray tell, is this marvelous proposal? I'd be interested to learn what you think will put an end to this war."

Kalina steeled herself before stepping forward and throwing one of her gauntlets at the King's feet. A gasp went through the tent, for she'd not told her own people her plan.

"I challenge you to one-on-one combat. Winner takes all. You know as well as I that as long as we are both living there will be war. So let us end this. Civilly, humanely, with as little loss of life on both sides as possible."

King Blackbourne eyed the gauntlet and her for a few moments, and Kalina's gut churned in anticipation and fear. But she held his gaze, refusing to show him any signs of weakness.

"Very well. But due to my age, I reserve the right to appoint a champion."

"Agreed. You have that right, but if I win, then you must agree to abide by the terms of the agreement. No more war. Peace between our two lands, and I as Queen upon your throne."

"Agreed. But it is a fight to the death."

Kalina hesitated the barest moment, her eyes flicking to Leif's. In that moment she saw pride as well as fear mixed in his gaze. Her heart lurched. She'd known it might come to this. Was she willing to die for peace? She was.

"Agreed." She looked back to the King. "Who do you appoint?"

"My son, Prince Endre."

Kalina's heart flipped. She had never seen Endre use the long sword he always wore strapped to his side but she would bet he knew how to use it. She nodded to the older man.

"Fine."

"I will agree to this on one condition," the King said quickly.

Kalina could see a greedy gleam in the old man's eye. But she nodded for him to continue.

"I will only agree if, once I win, the ice dragons will submit to my rule."

Kalina looked at Sunniva whose beautiful face was enraged. Sunniva's eyes locked with hers and Kalina gave her a small nod. Sunniva's face fell, fear as well as hope mingled there, and she nodded back.

"Fine. If you win, the Vanir are yours to command."

The King grinned, his crooked yellowed teeth making Kalina's stomach churn. She hoped this was the right gamble.

"Very well. Sunset, on this very hill."

"Done."

Sunset was only two hours away. Just enough time for her to prepare her people to flee should everything go wrong. Just enough time to say goodbye to Leif, just in case. Just enough time to spend one final flight with Maska. Just enough time to prepare to die.

Chapter 39

A CIRCLE HAD BEEN DUG INTO THE dirt and snow atop the hill, creating a small quagmire of freezing mud. Kalina stood on one side, her closest companions arranged around her, watching as King Blackbourne spoke quietly in Prince Endre's ear. Prince Endre had stripped down to his dark leather pants and a thin cotton shirt that blew in the chill breeze that kissed the hilltop. For the first time, Kalina could barely tell that he was as old as her father had been. He seemed just as formidable an opponent as a young, strapping warrior. She shivered as she watched him.

"Keep your leathers on, but let's take off the dragon scales. Too flashy," Kari said. Kalina tore her eyes from the prince to look into her cousin's eyes.

"They are quite light actually. I'd like to leave them on." Her eyes darted to Leif who stood a few feet away. He gave her a small smile. Kari shrugged and helped her strap her axes to her hips for better access. Kalina slipped a knife into her boot as well, just in case. She slid a look toward the prince preparing across the muddy circle and saw he had his sword strapped to one hip and a wicked long dagger strapped to the other. She sucked in a deep breath then let it out. The last time she'd done this, fought someone for a throne, had been against Jormungand, back when he'd challenged her right to rule. This was no different, she told herself. The Valdir were trained to fight from birth, as were the Askorians, and she had beat Jormungand. So she could beat Endre. She hoped.

Kalina looked over her friend's shoulders to where Maska stood at the edge of the gathered crowd. His night eyes watched her solemnly. She had said all she'd needed to say to him. She'd flown with him one last time, just in case this ended badly. And she loved him with a fierceness that gave her strength. He opened his jaw in a dragon smile, exposing teeth as long as her forearm. He would avenge her if she died, she knew. He'd go mad with the loss, the deep magic unraveling within him. Like Nash had. That was the only thing she regretted. She didn't want to leave Maska alone and mad but she had no choice. Not if she wanted to stop the killing. She turned to Leif.

"Promise me when you get back home, you will find some

quiet farm for Nash to live on. No one deserves to spend their life in a cell." She looked up into his grey eyes and saw them soften. He wouldn't kiss her, not here surrounded by the enemy. But he reached out and squeezed her hand tightly, trying to convey all his feelings in that one touch, in that one look.

"I promise, my Queen."

She had said all there needed to be said to him, too. A quiet half-hour spent in her tent, holding one another and speaking softly. He had done his best to take her mind off the very real and looming possibility that she might die by talking about the future, their future. A future so bright and beautiful that Kalina hoped with all her heart that she could see it come true.

"Don't you dare give him that sad smile, my girl." Eira was before her now, pushing Leif aside. "Don't you dare think about dying, you hear me? You are going to fight. Fight with everything you have."

Kalina pulled her aunt close in a tight embrace, tears pricking at her eyelids as she squeezed them shut.

"I promise. I'll fight."

Sunniva was there when she released Eira.

"Use that anger, sister. Use it to win. I will not be a slave to that man."

Kalina nodded and clasped forearms with her long-lost kin.

"I will."

And then it was time.

She stepped into the ring opposite Prince Endre. His stony face was set and she could not read his emotions at all. She did her best to copy him, shoving down her rising panic and fear and settling into the place within her that allowed her to fight, to kill. A calm washed over her as the King of Askor stepped forward.

"This fight is to the death, winner takes both the kingdom of Askor and the kingdom of Ethea. As well as the loyalty of the Vanir and the Valdir. May the best man, oh-," he looked at Kalina and smirked. "Excuse me, or girl- win." Then he stepped back.

Kalina clenched her jaw, ignoring his jabs, and focused all her attention on Prince Endre, to the exclusion of all else around her. The outside world faded away and only the fight and her opponent mattered.

They circled for a moment, drawing ever closer, neither fighter keener to strike the first blow than the other. Finally, Kalina grew frustrated and lunged, her axes swishing through the air a hair's breadth away from Endre's ear. He side-stepped her blow and came in low while she was extended, his short sword biting into her upper left thigh. She hissed as she jumped back and resumed circling. It was a stupid mistake, leaving herself open, but they couldn't circle forever. Endre's face never moved, never even cracked a smile at his hit.

Kalina lunged again, this time ready for his attack, but instead of going low he went high, dancing out of the way of her ax and landing a second blow on her upper right arm. This time the cut was a bit deeper, and blood immediately began to soak her tunic. He was deliberately allowing her to launch and then hitting where her padding and protection were weakest. So Kalina settled back, content to wait for him to attack her next.

He seemed to sense her game and he conceded, stepping inside her guard more quickly than she thought possible and trying to skewer her middle. But the golden dragon scales did their job, turning aside the long sword in a glancing blow that knocked the wind out of her. She managed to swing her ax low and catch the edge of his leg, blood spurting. He stepped away, letting out a sharp breath.

She took his momentary distraction as an opportunity. She drew her second ax and came in with a two-handed approach, axes whistling through the air, one high and one low. He wasn't expecting her to attack and he stumbled back a step, as she stomped forward, lunging with her right ax to sever two fingers on his left hand. They went flying through the air, and for a moment, the world seemed to still and she watched their bloody progress across the sky until they hit the mud below them in a sickening squelch. Time sped back up, adrenaline pumping through her veins.

Endre roared and her eyes snapped back to his face. He came in wildly, blindly, savagely, and it was all she could do not to slip in the mud as she backed up frantically, trying to avoid his blows to her head, belly, and legs.

Suddenly she slipped, her legs going out from underneath her as she landed hard in the mud, a freezing cold mixture splattering up and covering her from head to toe. The outside world came rushing back, the crowd let out a gasp as she lost her grip on her axes and they slid away in the mud, just out of reach. She scrambled to get back up, to reach for her weapons, but a swift kick to her abdomen had her sprawling on her back, the slick feel of mud covering her skin.

Prince Endre stood over her, panting, his left hand dripping gore onto the ground. She could finally see emotion on his face, and it was fear. Fear and rage. Emotions Kalina knew all too well. He raised his sword above his head, and Kalina knew in her bones this was her end.

She had failed.

No one was going to save her. This was on her head alone, and the entire fate of her people, Ethean, Valdir, Vanir, and dragons alike, weighed on her shoulders. She felt that burden like a physical pressure, holding her down, pinning her to the mud. It was her fault. She had failed everyone. Was she really giving up, to die here in the mud like some worm crushed beneath Askor's boot?

"No!" The scream tore out of her throat, raw and animalistic.

The sword came down a split second later and found flesh and blood and mud, but no bone. No vital organs clung to the blade. Only her shorn off battle braids lay in the mud.

Kalina had rolled away just in time, the crown Prince's sword slicing through her scalp and battle braids on her left-hand side, taking a chunk of skin and hair with it. She had left her boot knife embedded in his thigh, too. Screaming as she rolled, she used her momentum and anger to launch herself across the slippery mud and to grasp an ax in her hand, her other discarded.

And then she was on her feet gingerly touching the side of her face, coated with blood and mud, her golden armor stained red and brown. Before her, Prince Endre knelt, his left hand around the knife in his leg, unable to withdraw it due to his missing fingers. Kalina was behind him in an instant, drawing his chin back and placing her ax blade against his throat.

"To the death!" Yelled the crowd, egging her on, inviting her to slice the Prince's throat. Kalina was tempted. She wanted to spill Askorian blood, as she'd wanted to all day. But she also wanted to see the look in King Blackbourne's eyes as she killed his heir and son. She looked up and found his face in the crowd, but she didn't see fear or sadness or even love there. She saw only sneering anger and disgust. It made her feel sorry for the Prince whose life she held in her hands. And suddenly, she knew deep in her gut that the King would never abide by their agreement. He would continue to fight her and slaughter her people.

Prince Endre closed his eyes tight, as if waiting for the end to come. Kalina raised her ax above her head, and released it.

Across the circle from her, King Blackbourne fell a moment later, crumpling to the ground, her ax buried in his chest cavity. Chaos erupted. And Kalina released her grip on Prince Endre's hair.

"Long live the King," she muttered as hands seized her suddenly from both sides. She fought as they dragged her away, as her people began to riot, as fighting broke out. She made eye contact with Leif through the crowd and smiled.

Chapter 40

BEFORE THE ASKORIANS COULD DRAG her off, a shout rang above all the rest.

"Halt! In the name of your King, halt!"

The Askorian soldiers on either side of Kalina paused, the general chaos dying slowly around them as Prince Endre pushed himself to his feet and reached out to a nearby soldier who offered him his shoulder to lean on.

"Halt. I am your King now. And I say, release Queen Kalina."

Murmurs flew around the gathered crowd, faces frowned and there were a few cries of protest. But King Endre put up his injured hand for silence.

"Listen to me, Askorians. From this day forward, we will have peace with Ethea. There will be no more war between our people. No more bloodshed. Askor is no longer interested in conquering its southern neighbor, but instead, embracing them as friends and trade partners. If Ethea accepts our offer of friendship, of course." The King gave her a small bow.

Kalina's heart rose, hope flooding her. She had wondered if her bet would pay off, if she was right in putting her faith into the older prince. But she hadn't expected such a warm welcome. The soldiers on either side of her dropped her arms, and she began limping back to her people, and to Maska who had bellowed and perhaps trampled a few people in his desperation to reach her. She put a hand up to his face and looked into his night-dark eyes. Then she turned to the new Askorian King.

"Ethea accepts. As do the Valdir. But I do not speak for the Vanir in this." She nodded to Sunniva. Sunniva's face was still a mask of anger, but she took a deep breath and stepped forward.

"The Vanir are our own people, ruled neither by the Askorians or the Etheans. We accept your friendship on one condition."

"And what is that?" King Endre asked, wrapping a clean bandage around the missing fingers on his hand as he watched the leader of the Vanir.

"That you cede us our ancestral lands. The Snowcap Glacier and the Ice Fang Mountains. Gift us those, and we would be happy to call you friends."

"Does this make you the Queen of the Vanir then?" The King asked, pulling the knife from his leg with a grunt before wrapping the wound. "Shall I call you Queen?"

Sunniva nodded, her face thoughtful.

"Yes, I believe I am."

"Excellent. I suggest that we all part ways, tend to our wounded and dying, and reconvene on the morrow. I invite you all into my castle to discuss a peace treaty and agree on terms before you depart for home." He looked directly at Kalina and bowed his head in respect to her. "Until tomorrow, your Majesties."

And then he turned and left, using a soldier as a crutch to walk down the sloping hill and back to his waiting army. His people slowly filed away, leaving her standing on the hill, covered in blood and mud, her shocked people beside her.

"That's it then?" Kari said, her voice strange and bemused. "It's just over?"

Kalina turned to her cousin, suddenly feeling woozy from the pain.

"Yes, I think so. That's why I challenged him. I had a hunch that as soon as I killed his father we'd be free." She swayed on her feet then, and Leif was at her side in an instant, holding her up.

"We need to get you patched up." He waved Kari over and together they carried her to Maska's back. Leif flew with her on Maska back to their camp and carried her into the medical tent. Kalina didn't remember much of the short flight, only that her head was swimming now, and every part of her hurt. But she did remember the soft bed he laid her in, Eira's cool hands roaming over her scalp, and then the warm water washing away the mud and gore. After that she slept, her dreams blessedly empty.

The following afternoon she stood in the Askorian throne room with Leif, Kari, Rangvald, Halvor, Prince Simen and Prince Ivan, her head wrapped in a bandage. Maska and the other dragons remained outside in the main courtyard guarded by a host of Valdir. Just because King Endre had declared a peace didn't mean she trusted him entirely.

The new King sat atop his throne, his brother Prince Julian by his side. Queen Marin was nowhere in sight, and Kalina could only hope the vile woman was gone from these halls.

Kalina was practically buzzing with anxiety. They had spent all morning negotiating a peace treaty that benefited all parties involved, but the only mention of her people who had been imprisoned was for the new king to say they had been released and were being tended too. But now she waited with her court, anticipation building.

Across the throne room, Sunniva, Astrid, and Greyson stood with Torill and Gunnar beside them. All five Vanir were talking together, hotly debating something. Finally, Sunniva nodded her head, Astrid stepping away and letting out an exasperated sound and Torill turned to hug her husband. Kalina raised an eyebrow at Sunniva who gave her a small smile.

The Vanir Queen had fashioned a crown out of iron for herself, not unlike Kalina's own battle crown that currently sat askew atop her bandages. Sunniva's crown resembled thorns and brambles rather than the delicate vines of Kalina's. Sunniva was taking to being Queen of the Vanir like a dragon to air. And Kalina supposed, in a way, Sunniva had already been their queen, in all but name.

King Endre stood and descended the steps to join his guests. He took a glass of wine from a nearby servant and raised it high in a toast.

"To peace and friendship."

They all repeated his toast and drank from their own glasses, but Kalina's eyes never stopped roaming the hall, searching for danger.

"I have a gift for you all. Partly to fulfill our recent peace treaty, and partly to abolish an age-old tradition. I have just dispatched a writ for all of Askor that indentured servitude is no longer legal. All currently indentured servants are to be released of their obligations at once, and given enough money to travel wherever they wish. Effective immediately, I will open up a school here in Winterreach to provide job training to those indentured and offer many of them positions here at the palace, as I suspect there will be many vacancies."

Kalina's heart soared at his words, and she couldn't stop herself from speaking up.

"There was a maid here, her name was Seri. Can you find her for me, please? I'd like to offer her a position in Ethea if she'd like it."

Prince Endre gave her a small, gracious smile and turned to instruct a nearby servant.

"Are all these servants free men?" she asked, pointing to the various servants around the hall serving food and drinks to the gathered guests.

"Yes. I released them last night and then offered them well-paying jobs to stay on. I even gave them their month's wages upfront. Many chose to remain."

Perhaps he wasn't faking, perhaps this King was going to be a much better man than his father.

"Ahh, here is your second gift." He motioned towards the side doors that were opening as people began filing through. Kalina's eyes went wide when she recognized familiar faces. Delisa was head of the pack, her skirts held up in her hands, her long dark hair flowing around her as she raced towards them. Behind her was Jormungand, his hulking frame a mite thinner than before, his beard a bit longer, but his eyes no less fierce. The rest of their captured companions followed, including Kalina's Queen's Guards, Asa, Runa, and Gyda and her old friend Talon, Captain Higgs in tow.

Delisa gave Kalina a quick, tight, hug but her eyes were only for Kari who was practically vibrating with anticipation beside her. Kalina released her friend quickly and passed her along into Kari's waiting arms. The two women embraced, Kari burying her head into Delisa's shoulder, and small sobs could be heard as Delisa stroked the woman's head. Kalina's heart swelled further as she watched her best friend and cousin together. Then arms were around her and she turned to find Talon embracing her. When she pulled away, she saw tears standing unshed in his eyes.

"I thought we'd lost you," he said quietly, his hands holding her upper arms tightly. "I thought you were dead."

She smiled up at her friend, his brown hair still flopping into his eyes. She pushed it aside.

"You'll never lose me, Talon. Not ever. I'm stronger than that."

Leif pulled Talon in for a hug as Kalina greeted her Queen's Guard and Captain Higgs, learning from him that their soldiers had been locked in their barracks since the night she'd fled. She finally turned to greet Jormungand, only to see her other cousin in a fierce embrace with his lover, Halvor, the two men openly crying. They leaned back to look at one another before their lips met in a hard kiss and then returned to their hug. Kalina reached over and took Leif's hand in her own. Surrounded by so much love, she couldn't help letting the small moment of public affection seep through.

It was good to have her people back around her, but she realized that one person, whom she missed dearly, was missing. Lord Illeron. She dropped Leif's hand and turned to King Endre who was watching the reunions with a faint smile on his face.

"Thank you, Your Majesty," she said gratefully to King Endre. "What about Lord Illeron? Did he, was he captured?" she asked hopefully. The night they'd rescued their dragons, Kalina hadn't let herself believe he was dead. She had instead tucked that fear away to deal with on a different day, and instead had let a small spark of hope that he had survived fester there. Now that spark died at the look on the new King of Askor's face.

"I am sorry, Kalina. He was killed in the fire that engulfed the eyrie. We pulled his body from the ashes the next morning and my father burned what remained." The King's eyes fell. He was clearly ashamed of his father's actions. Kalina swallowed hard against the hard knot that was in her throat.

"Thank you for telling me." She turned back to her people, tears leaking out the corners of her eyes, and tried to just be grateful that most of them had made it out of this alive. She couldn't say that about so many others.

A hand alighted on her shoulder and she turned to see the face of the King. He had descended from his throne when she'd had her back turned. His eyes were soft and knowing.

"Will you do me the honor of having lunch with me before you leave? I wish to discuss a few things before you go."

Kalina nodded.

"Of course, your Majesty." She gave him a sad smile in return.

"You are also welcome here in this castle, although I'll understand if you don't wish to stay. Your old rooms have been cleaned and prepared, your things returned to you."

"Thank you. I believe we will take you up on your offer." As nice as the Vanir camps were, she wanted to sit in a comfy chair by a roaring fire and doze off while reading a book. She wanted a hot bath and warm, clean sheets. She wanted comfort and safety.

After their afternoon spent in the castle, she and her council moved themselves back into their castle rooms, while Sunniva and her army departed north once again. Kalina had promised the new Queen that she would come to visit before they left south for home. She sent Rangvald home along with the army, watching from the shores of the rivers as they boarded their ships and pushed away from shore. She kept Talon, Captain Higgs, and their small contingent of soldiers with her for protection.

It took a solid week of preparation to leave. All their property, including the ships they'd arrived on, had been seized and it took some time to get them back and get them ready to travel. Kalina took that time to heal, spend time with Maska and Leif, and learn from Delisa her story. She had also learned that while Ablen had attacked the eastern shore, Askor's eastern force had split in two, suspecting a distraction, and instead had sent a force to surprise her army from behind. Kalina was grateful for Ablen's support and planned to tell them so upon her return to Ethea.

Two days before they were set to depart she flew to Sunniva's camp in the mountains and found it was expanding, many from the other seven clans having decided to stay. Kalina had embraced the older woman when she'd landed and entered the village, and together they went once again into Torill and Gunnar's cabin, it's room filled with warmth. Kalina had also come to take Bri and Osian back with her. Torill now sat with Osian asleep against her ample breast, with Bri sitting beside her, letting the older Vanir stroke her hair.

It was such a sweet sight to see that Kalina was loath to break it up. She had also talked with King Endre and agreed that when Osian was old enough, he would come for a visit, to meet the other half of his family. But for now, he was hers.

"Bri," Kalina cleared her throat before continuing. "Do you want to stay here? With Torill and Gunnar?" The girl's eyes brightened as she looked up at the two who flanked her. Bri's parents had been lost in the Long War, before Kalina had ever come to the Valdir throne. And she hadn't had anyone to take care of her except Eira, when Eira could. But Bri's eyes fell on Osian and she shook her head sadly.

"No, your Majesty. As much as I love them, my duty is to you and to Osian. I will come home."

Kalina nodded in understanding, but before she could speak, Torill burst out in excited chatter.

"Sunniva has already approved Gunnar and me to go with you back to Ethea. We can help raise Osian, and we'd like to adopt Bri as our own. Gun and I never could have children-," she stopped speaking abruptly as Kalina smiled. Beside her, Sunniva was also smirking, and Bri was practically bouncing in her seat, looking from Kalina to Torill and back.

"Of course you can, Torill," Kalina said. "On one condition." They all stilled, waiting. "That you and Gunnar become ambassadors for your people. Teach the Valdir about the Vanir. Show them your ways. And be my go-between with Sunniva." She looked to the other Queen who nodded in agreement.

"Of course we will," Gunnar boomed out, his own happiness too much to contain in his huge body.

"It's settled then. Can I trust you to fly Bri and Osian safely back to their village in the Great Grey Mountains?"

"Yes, you can, your Majesty." Torill gave her a bow, as best she could with a sleeping Osian in her arms and Bri ran across the room to throw her arms around Kalina's neck.

"Thank you, oh, thank you!" she squealed. Kalina let out a laugh, hugging the girl back.

She left the Vanir with Maska laden down with gifts for her people, and mixed emotions of sadness and joy. She waved goodbye as Maska winged away south and west to Winterreach Castle, and soon, home.

Chapter 41

KALINA HAD SOMEHOW ALWAYS imagined the King of Askor's rooms to be very dark and gloomy, instead, she found them rather inviting. But perhaps that had nothing to do with the room, and instead, the man who stood there smiling at her as she entered.

King Endre was nothing as she'd expected. He still walked with a limp from her dagger to his leg, and he now wore a leather glove on his left hand to protect his finger stumps, but he seemed to show her no ill will. Her own injuries were healing nicely, but she'd had to shave the left side of her head to let the wound heal properly. She'd still be left with a nasty scar, but she no longer minded scars. Each scar on her body told a story about survival, about pain, about joy. Each scar had helped to shape and mold her into the queen she was. Without them, she'd still be the naive orphan girl living in a remote abbey, oblivious to her destiny.

The King pulled out a chair by a big bay window that looked out onto the harbor below. It was a gorgeous view of the Riverlands and the sea beyond to the south. The meal the King had spread before them was simple: a hot stew filled with chunks of venison and root vegetables. It was savory and Kalina enjoyed dipping a warm roll in it. She watched the new King closely as they sat and ate in silence until she couldn't take it anymore.

"Why are you not like your father? He raised you, and when I first met you, I thought you were just like him." She cut straight to the heart of the matter. It was her last day in the city, their ship due to sail on the morning tide. She didn't come here to mince words.

King Endre paused his eating, a spoonful halfway to his mouth. He put it down slowly and wiped his mouth before answering.

"My father was a cruel man. When I was a boy, I watched him rule with an iron fist, never allowing for one inch of mercy. At first, I idolized him and his power. As did my brothers. But as I grew, I saw the way he treated our mother. I saw the way he treated the servants, even the nobles. I saw how he never showed kindness, mercy, understanding, or caring. I saw his cruelty when Ivan was born, and then Simen. He beat them when he was drunk, which was often. This was at the end of the Long War when things were going badly on both sides. My brother Terric was cunning and power-hungry. He knew he'd never take the Askorian throne from me, so he thought to take yours from your mother." He broke off, looking out the window at the harbor below, seagulls dancing outside the windows on the ocean breeze. "I knew when my mother died I wouldn't be like him. She made me promise. Made me swear on her death bed. So for years, I played his games. I became very good at it. But now," he turned back to look at her. "Now I want to be better. I want to build something my own children will be proud of."

Kalina believed him. She had stopped eating while he'd spoken, but together they resumed, finishing the meal in companionable silence. As the last of the dishes were cleared away, he stood and motioned for her to join him as his doors opened.

"I have two final gifts for you." He motioned to the woman coming towards them.

"Seri!" Kalina gasped, and she stepped forward to take the girls hands. Seri fell to her knees before the royals, her face to the floor.

"Your Majesties!"

"Seri, stand up, please. No need to kneel." Kalina hauled the girl to her feet and then looked sideways at King Endre.

"Seri is a free woman. I believe you have a proposition for her?" He asked, raising an eyebrow at her. Kalina grinned and turned back to Seri.

"I would like to offer you a position in Ethea, in my castle as one of my maids." She saw Seri's eyes widen for a moment, and then fall. She rushed on, concerned. "Or you can be a cook or a stable hand. Or even one of my guards if you'd like!"

"Your Majesty, I would love to, but…" She trailed off.

"But what?"

"My father."

Kalina waved a hand.

"Bring him with you. I will give him a place too if he can get sober. And if he can't, I'll give him a comfortable bed to sleep it off."

Seri's face suddenly lit up in excitement. She bent and kissed Kalina's hands, thanking her for her generosity. Kalina waved her off, dismissing her to go find Delisa and make arrangements. Kalina turned back to the King.

"Thank you. That was very kind of you."

It was his turn to wave her off.

"It was nothing. And now for my final gift." He signaled a servant by the door who bowed slightly before opening it and admitting two soldiers who carried the bedraggled form of Lord Averil between them.

"My Queen!" he cried out when he saw her, falling to his knees, hands and feet shackled. He began to crawl forward towards her, his hands clasped in a plea. "Please, forgive me! I was blackmailed by the late King! I didn't know what I was doing! Please!"

Kalina took a disgusted step back. Bile rose in her throat. Lord Illeron had hinted that he was to blame for Prince Terric's escape at his execution. That he had tried to orchestrate her murder. And he was certainly to blame for this whole debacle in Askor. She couldn't stand to look at him.

"Get him out of my sight." She turned her back on him and looked at King Endre. "He can rot in your dungeons for the rest of his life. I don't ever want to see him again."

The King nodded and motioned for the guards to take him away. Lord Averil began to scream, hysteria clear in his voice as he begged her to forgive him. But Kalina just walked to the window and looked down at the bustling city below and tried to focus on something, anything else.

When the closing door finally muffled his screams, the King put a light hand on her shoulder.

"I'm sorry. My men discovered that he and my father were in collusion. They planned to marry you to my brother and then murder you, giving Ethea and the Valdir into Askor's hands."

Kalina nodded mutely. She had suspected as much. But it was still tough to see the man responsible. A man to whom she had given so many chances. A man she had only kept on her council out of respect for the other members who insisted he be there. She clenched her jaw. There were going to be some changes when she got home. Finally, she turned to Endre and reached out to clasp his forearm.

"Thank you, for all you've done for us, your Majesty. Your kindness and friendship won't be forgotten."

She had convinced her Queen's Guard member Runa to remain in Askor as her ambassador; not long after, Captain Higgs, who was weet on Runa, offered to stay as well. Both were going to be her eyes and ears in this place once she returned home. She felt more content as she left the King's rooms knowing someone would be here to watch their backs.

Just outside the King's door, she ran right into Prince Simen who had been lurking about. She didn't know whether it was her he'd come looking for, or his brother, but she was glad to see him.

"I just wanted to come say goodbye," he said hesitantly after a quick embrace. "And I wanted to say thank you."

"For what?" Kalina asked.

"For risking everything. For risking war. I owe you my happiness, Kalina."

"Are you and your betrothed happy then?"

He beamed at her, and she found herself beaming back, genuinely happy he was happy.

"We got married two days ago in a small ceremony."

"Congratulations!" she said, hugging him.

They spoke of small things, each apologizing and repairing in turn. Finally, it was time for Kalina to go pack and get ready for her departure the next day. They promised to write, and he promised to visit, claiming he wanted to see the famed Ethean Wastes for himself. Kalina promised to have a room waiting for him and his new wife.

The next day dawned cool, but the breeze off the ocean was warm, the sky above bright blue. Perhaps spring was finally descending on this frozen northern world. Kalina stood on the deck of her ship, watching the quay slip away, waving to Captain Higgs and Runa on the dock. She looked up to the sky high above and saw Maska flying there, dancing and playing in the bright blue expanse, a golden shape at his side. A presence behind her made her turn and she saw Leif standing there, his handsome face cracked in a small smile.

"You know what today is?" he said softly. Kalina shook her head.

"It's St. Martin's Day."

One year. Was that all it had been since she'd left her abbey? It felt like a lifetime.

Epilogue

KALINA SAT BEFORE THE ORNATE gold-edged mirror and smiled. The left-hand side of her head was shaved. It was a preference now, rather than because of her scar. She'd tried growing it out after they'd returned from Askor a few months ago, but the scar had always seemed to make the hair stick out at odd angles. So she'd opted to just keep it short. Eira had given her a salve to rub on it and the one on her cheek to help break up the scar tissue and it seemed to be working, making both scars less noticeable and softer. Not that she minded anymore.

There were more Runark tattoos in dark red fresh ink on her face. These were warrior marks. Marks of pride. Marks she had earned. She wasn't ashamed of the way she looked. She thought she looked tough, yes, but she looked strong too. Like a warrior. Not a scared little girl anymore.

Delisa came up behind her and settled the silver and blue dragon scale crown on her head over her freshly done silver battle braids. Kalina's bright blue eyes were smudged with kohl, and her lips tinted red. An intricate necklace made of delicate strands of silver woven together like lace lay upon her breast, and silver bangles jingled on each of her wrists. She reached over and stroked the sleeping grey form of Moose, the tabby cat who was curled on a pillow beside her. She had missed him dearly while she was away.

"You look stunning, Kalina," Delisa said, leaning down to kiss her cheek. Kalina blushed slightly, standing to inspect her reflection in the full-length mirror. She wore a silver gown that clung to her waist before flaring out around her. It had a deep V-neck and tight sleeves that perfectly accentuated her curves and muscles. It was made of a gossamer fabric inlaid with diamonds that sparkled like the night sky. She felt ethereal in it. She felt like a queen.

"Are you ready?" Kari stuck her head around the door, her own silver braids pulled up into an elaborate crown atop her head. She also wore a dress, but one in shades of deep purple to match her Yurok.

"I think so, yes."

"Let's go. Everyone is waiting." Kari was impatient as always and Kalina rolled her eyes at her cousin while Delisa giggled beside her. Delisa followed them out, making sure the train of Kalina's dress didn't catch on the door.

The trio made their way down to a small courtyard in the garden, just a little ways away from the fountain that had been Kalina's favorite when she'd first arrived at Ravenhelm Castle. There they found Calla and Anders. Calla handed baby Issa, who was a year old now and walking, to her husband and came over to fuss about Kalina, straightening the dress that she herself had made.

"It looks lovely, Calla, stop fussing."

Calla stepped back, wiping her eyes gingerly with a handkerchief before accepting Issa back from Anders.

"You just look so lovely."

"It's time," Anders said, holding out his arm for her. Kalina took it gracefully and turned to give one last look to Kari and Delisa. She smiled a radiant, excited smile at them and then walked with Anders through a hedgerow and into the rose garden beyond.

Instrumental music was playing, drifting on the air as they walked down the aisle, surrounded on either side by gathered guests. Across the garden, two reptilian heads in green and gold leaned over the hedge, watching. Kalina saw Father Martin and Father Nic from Hywell Abbey sitting in a nearby row and Father Nic gave Kalina a wink as she walked by. Scholar Alexil with his white hair sticking out sat beside Margy and Mistress Aynne, Margy giving her a small wave.

Talon sat beside a pretty blonde girl and he gave her a tiny wave as well. Her Valdir friends and family sat in the aisle, each giving her huge smiles: Jormungand and Halvor, Eira and Rangvald, Asa and Gyda, Hilde and Skaldrik. Lord Tameron and his wife, and Lady Renfort sat watching her, perhaps even judging her as she walked by but she didn't mind.

Then came the foreign dignitaries. The ambassadors from Ablen and even Wostrad sat beaming at her. And in the front rows sat Bri and Osian in a place of honor, Torill, and Gunnar behind them. Sunniva sat beside them, and on the opposite side of the aisle sat the King of Askor with his pretty new young wife, Prince Simen and his new wife, and Prince Ivan.

But although Kalina gave them each small glances, she really only had eyes for the man that stood at the end of the aisle before the altar, dressed in traditional Valdiran leather armor that gleaned blood-red in the sun. The man she was about to marry.

Leif.

The End.

Turn the page for a bonus scene!

Bonus scene

SNOW WAS FALLING OUTSIDE THE castle windows, the gardens, and harbor beyond the panes of glass covered in a blanket of white. Kalina stood, holding a thick blanket around her naked shoulders, watching the big flakes as they drifted to earth. Tomorrow was the Mid-winter Festival, and she was looking forward to the festivities, the games, and especially the food. But right at that moment, she was enjoying the solitude and peace that snowfall seemed to bring.

Movement stirred behind her and suddenly Leif was there, his muscled chest bare. He shivered slightly and Kalina opened her blanket for him to slide inside, taking up a spot behind her. He gently kissed the top of her head and wrapped his arms around her, watching the outside world.

"We should probably call for breakfast to be brought up," he said softly. Kalina smiled as his voice rumbled through her, reverberating into her bare back.

"In a minute. I'm enjoying this."

Outside, two dragons shot up from one of the courtyards into the grey sky, one green, and one gold. Together, they frolicked through the winter air, diving and spinning. They looked so happy, filled with utter joy at the snowfall. Watched their dragons fly together seemed to overwhelm Kalina with an emotion she couldn't quite name. It was like homesickness, even though she was home, and a euphoria so immense she felt drowned in it. Suddenly there were tears in her eyes.

They fell, splashing onto the blanket and she sniffed, wiping at her cheeks.

"Are you alright, my love?" Leif said, turning her to face him. He cupped her cheeks in his hands and kissed her eyelids gently. She let out a small laugh. She felt a little silly for crying but what else was she supposed to do with so much emotion?

"I have something to tell you," she began, excitement flutter in her stomach. Leif tipped her chin up so she was gazing into his grey eyes.

"Yes?" He kissed her gently on the lips, wrapping an arm

firmly around her waist so she was pressed up against him.

"I'm pregnant."

He smiled.

The End

If you enjoyed this book please share it, review it on Goodreads, Bookbub, and Amazon.

Sign up for her newsletter to be the first to learn about new releases, catch free bonus content/short stories, and random animal photos. Join her Facebook group for exclusive content and giveaways.

About the Author

R.A. Lewis is a sci-fi and fantasy author. She lives in Oregon with her husband, three dogs, four cats, and 247 fish. R.A. Lewis has two degrees from the University of Oregon in Psychology and Sociology and loves to explore mental illness, trauma, and the depths of emotion and passion in the human experience within her writing.

Her favorite ways to recharge (so she doesn't pull her hair out from arguing with her characters) are reading, daydreaming, hiking, spending time with her human and fur family, watching zombie movies/shows, swimming, working out, and napping.

You can visit her on Facebook (R.A.LewisAuthor), Instagram (@author.r.a.lewis), Amazon (ralewis), her website (www.authorralewis.com), Goodreads (@RALewis), or Pinterest (authorralewis). You can also follow her on Bookbub for reviews.